GALÁPAGOS
REGAINED

GALÁPAGOS
REGAINED

JAMES MORROW

ST. MARTIN'S PRESS

NEW YORK

GALÁPAGOS REGAINED. Copyright © 2014 by James Morrow. All rights reserved. Printed in the United States of America. For information, address St. Martin's Press, 175 Fifth Avenue, New York, N.Y. 10010.

www.stmartins.com

The Library of Congress Cataloging-in-Publication Data is available upon request.

ISBN 978-1-250-05401-2 (hardcover)
ISBN 978-1-4668-8092-4 (e-book)

St. Martin's Press books may be purchased for educational, business, or promotional use. For information on bulk purchases, please contact the Macmillan Corporate and Premium Sales Department at 1-800-221-7945, extension 5442, or write to specialmarkets@macmillan.com.

First Edition: January 2015

10   9   8   7   6   5   4   3   2   1

FOR PETER G. HAYES,
who builds knowledge,
cultivates wisdom, and makes an art of friendship

If we accept the scholarly consensus, then the Percy Bysshe Shelley Prize, with its peculiar aim of proving, or disproving, the existence of a Supreme Being, was a fundamentally frivolous affair, barely worth a footnote in any but the most exhaustive history of Victorian Britain. The present author disagrees. For many years I have believed that the Great God Contest—and the consequent expedition that the intrepid Chloe Bathurst undertook to the Galápagos Islands—might be fruitfully reimagined as a novel, and here is the result.

CONTENTS

Book Two
THE WHITE RADIANCE OF ETERNITY

Book Three
A PREFERENCE FOR THE APE

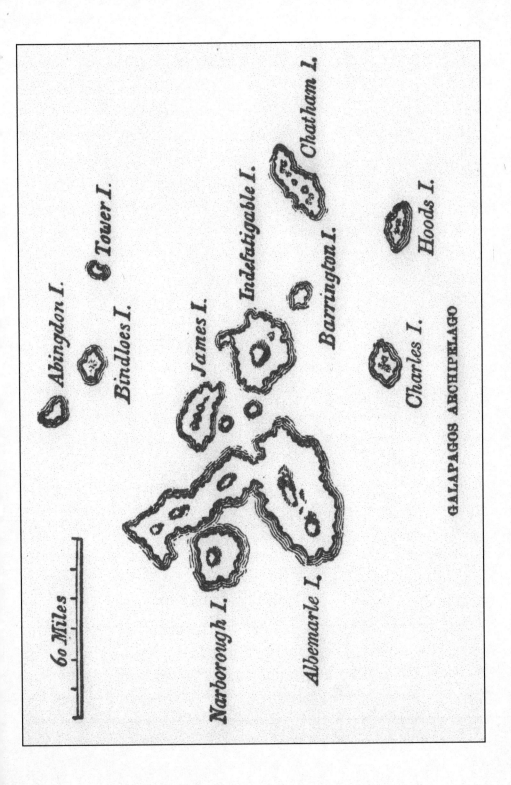
GALAPAGOS ARCHIPELAGO

Life, like a dome of many-coloured glass,

Stains the white radiance of Eternity.

—PERCY BYSSHE SHELLEY

The Pigeon Priest of County Kent

That Sunday morning the Reverend Granville Heathway delivered "The Testament of the Trees," the most ambitious sermon of his career. For nearly an hour he preached about the totality of Creation, from mushrooms to thrushes, lilies to alligators, wasps to lobsters, kangaroos to Christians, including the very parishioners who'd so graciously accorded him their attention. Granville's sermons were normally more modest in scope—"homey little homilies" his wife, Evelyn, affectionately called them—but after reading William Paley's remarkable tome, *Natural Theology,* he'd been moved to declaim its argument from the pulpit.

Of all the religious puzzles that periodically troubled Granville's flock, none vexed them more than the Almighty's seeming acquiescence to human and animal suffering, a paradox to which Mr. Paley had provided an astute solution. Superfluity was the way of the world. By producing an overabundance of progeny, every bonded pair of earthly creatures was making a payment in kind on the survival of its species. Inevitably this reproductive redundancy brought starvation, sickness, and misadventure to many an individual, but such pain was a logical necessity. God could not have designed the laws of Nature otherwise.

Whenever he allowed himself a respite from his clerical responsibilities,

Granville pursued activities as unassuming as his average sermon. He cultivated his vegetable garden, reread Mrs. Radcliffe's novels, and played cribbage with his son, Bertram, surely the brightest lad in County Kent. But Granville's foremost passion was pigeon breeding. A decade earlier, upon his promotion to parson of St. Mary's Church, Down Parish, Granville had purchased three female rock doves and their mates, and before long he and his dear Evelyn were presiding over a large family of birds, all gifted with an uncanny instinct to return to their native cote.

In time it became Granville's custom, following Sunday services, to provide each departing churchgoer with a copy of the sermon and, if the parishioner so desired, a live pigeon in a wicker cage. The parishioner would go home, write out a brief question or remark keyed to the homily, affix the scrip to the bird's leg, and send it winging back to the parsonage. On Sunday morning, before mounting the pulpit, Granville would distribute detailed and individualized letters of reply. Thus did he maintain a private correspondence with his congregation's more inquisitive members, thoughtfully addressing their confusion about good and evil, salvation and sin, Heaven and Hell.

Upon finishing his *Natural Theology* sermon, Granville realized that, given the topic's complexity, the demand for caged pigeons would be high. What he hadn't anticipated was the behavior of his parishioner Emma Darwin, mistress of Down House and wife of a renowned naturalist and geologist. No sooner had Mrs. Darwin accepted from Bertram a pigeon called Ajax than she summoned her six-year-old son and his younger sister. The children carried their own wicker birdcage—Willy grasping one side, Annie the other—which they straightaway presented to Granville. The cooing, bobbing occupant was a rock dove with an elegant scarlet crest.

"Like yourself, my husband breeds homing pigeons," Mrs. Darwin explained, resting a gloved hand against her most recent contribution to reproductive redundancy, a conspicuous pregnancy swathed in a flowered muslin gown.

"An activity he prefers to hearing my sermons," noted Granville.

"As usual, Mr. Darwin went sauntering about the village instead of following me to church."

Mrs. Darwin had made no secret of her preferred denomination: she would much rather belong to the Unitarian congregation in Bromley—but St. Mary's was, as she put it, "ever so much more convenient for a woman in a delicate condition." Whenever Granville's parishioners turned towards the altar to recite the triune-inflected Nicene Creed, she and Willy and Annie faced the other way. And yet despite their theological differences a bond of friendship had formed between Granville and Mrs. Darwin. Many were the anguished conversations in which he and the distraught woman had engaged concerning her husband's nonconformist (some might say nonexistent) religious beliefs. She feared that, come the Kingdom, she and her beloved Charles would be marked for eternal separation—though she seemed to take solace in Granville's insistence that Christ's infinite love would triumph over Mr. Darwin's transient folly.

"Last night I fell upon a clever idea," Mrs. Darwin continued. "Were you to write my husband a personal message, and were your words to reach him via the pigeon medium, he might take it seriously."

"What should my message say?" asked Granville.

"Merely invite him to attend next Sunday's services."

"Does this bird have a name?" asked Granville.

"Annie has christened her 'Cherub.'"

"How appropriate that it was your Annie who named her, for tradition tells of a connection between birds and Saint Anne," said Granville. "Whilst contemplating a lark feeding its young, Saint Anne suddenly desired children of her own. Eventually she bore a daughter, the very Mary destined to carry our Savior. I suspect there's a homily in there somewhere."

"I don't believe my husband would be moved by that topic," said Mrs. Darwin. "Were you to continue preaching on William Paley, however—"

"Then Paley it will be!"

Returning to the parsonage that afternoon, Granville lost no time finding a scrip and, aided by his quizzing-glass, filling it edge to edge with words calculated to pique Mr. Darwin's interest: ACCOMPANY YOUR WIFE ON SUNDAY, AND I SHALL ADDRESS THE MYSTERY OF THIS BIRD'S CREATOR, WHO GAVE US THE WORLD AND ITS LAWS. YRS., REV'D. HEATHWAY. He coiled up the paper—the smallest of scrolls, he mused, like a

Torah for mice—then deposited it in Cherub's capsule and released her to find the Down House dovecote.

By Tuesday morning a majority of pigeons had made their way back to St. Mary's, the sole exception being Ajax. Much to Granville's satisfaction, many parishioners had profited from his *Natural Theology* sermon, their responses blending *cris de coeur* with shouts of affirmation. I SEE NOW THAT LIFE IS A VALE OF BOTH TEARS AND MIRACLES, noted Mrs. Rashbrook. NATURE'S HARSH IMPERATIVES ARE AT ONCE BEWILDERING AND SUBLIME, wrote Miss Hawkins. I HAVE RESOLVED TO JOIN WITH THE PHILOSOPHERS IN DECLARING, "WHATEVER IS, IS GOOD," averred Professor Tandy. EVERMORE SHALL I GRIEVE FOR MY SON, BUT NOW THE SADNESS IS LESS, proclaimed Captain Maxwell.

Ajax arrived late on Thursday afternoon, gliding onto the parsonage grounds as the sun kissed the bracken. With quivering fingers Granville unstrapped the capsule and retrieved Mr. Darwin's reply: THOUGH I ADMIRE THE AUTHOR OF ALL BIRDS AND BEASTS, I DO NOT BELIEVE HIM A CHURCHGOING SORT OF DEITY. YRS., CHAS. DARWIN.

"True, we've lost this initial skirmish, but I'm not prepared to quit the campaign," Granville told Mrs. Darwin at the start of Sunday's services. "For today's homily, I had indeed contrived a sequel to my thoughts on *Natural Theology*. Instead I shall preach on Joseph and his brethren, saving 'The Revelation of the Rocks' for your husband's eventual appearance."

"Alas, Reverend, the situation is worse than we imagined," said Mrs. Darwin. "Charles tells me he intends to write a treatise directly refuting Mr. Paley. He will assert that the Earth's primal life-forms underwent a kind of self-development, changing mechanistically into the species we see around us today. At least he has promised to delay its publication until after his death."

"Take heart, Mrs. Darwin," said Granville, making a cylinder of his intended sermon and slipping it into his pocket. "My pen is not yet dry. Next week you and the children must arrive here toting a Down House pigeon—Cherub or one of her kin—and the following Sunday as well, and the Sunday after that." He offered the good woman the warmest smile in his repertoire. "We shall bring your geologist to Jesus yet."

BOOK ONE

A DOME OF MANY-COLOURED GLASS

*Treating of Our Heroine's Stage
Career, Including Accounts of Her Momentary
Madness and Ignominious Dismissal*

W hen Chloe Bathurst was seven years old, living in Wapping with her widowed father and tiresome twin brother, she decided that her future prosperity would be best secured by the arrival, sooner rather than later, of a wicked stepmother. The evidence was beyond dispute. Cinderella the ash-maiden, Snow White the dwarf-keeper, Gretel the hag-killer—in each such case a young woman had found happiness only after her father had wooed and wed a malign second wife.

By her ninth birthday Chloe had come to recognize the naiveté of her wish, and she felt just as glad Papa had neglected to marry a bad person. (Indeed, she felt just as glad he'd not remarried at all.) As it happened, this oversight was not the only accidental boon Phineas Bathurst bestowed upon his daughter, for he also inadvertently guided her towards a glamorous profession. Whereas some men are congenital blacksmiths and others constitutionally sailors, Phineas was a natural-born puppeteer, given to seizing upon whatever inert object might lie to hand—clock, kettle, mallet, lantern, fish head—and blessing it with the gift of mobility and the power of speech. Illusion mongering, Chloe concluded, was in her blood. She must become an actress.

Amongst Papa's many *pièces bien faites,* she had particularly fond memories of a dialogue between a wine bottle and a flagon of ale, each arguing that its ancestors had done the better job of making human beings the oafish and dullard race they were. She likewise cherished an encounter between a hammer and an apple, the former blaming the latter for the Fall of Man, the latter vilifying the former for its collaboration in the Crucifixion—a dispute neatly resolved when the hammer turned the apple to mash, declaiming, "And so Popish power once again has its way with Jewish lore."

Several years into Chloe's quest for theatrical fame, an irony presented itself. Whatever role she was playing at the moment, her personal circumstances would soon come to reflect the fate of the character in question: not in faithful facsimile—and here was where the irony emerged—but in mirror opposite. If Mr. Charles Kean, manager of the Adelphi Theatre and director of its shamelessly melodramatic offerings, had entrusted to Chloe the blind flower-seller Nydia in *The Last Days of Pompeii,* the tragic Queen Cleopatra in *Siren of the Nile,* or any other doomed and desperate heroine, she knew that ere long her life beyond the boards would be filled with suitors and champagne. But if she'd been tapped to portray a woman for whom all came right in the end—the brave French castaway Françoise Gauvin in *The Raft of the Medusa,* the Southern belle Pansy Winslow in *Lanterns on the Levee*—she could safely assume Dame Fortune was preparing some unpleasant surprises. So compelling did Chloe find this phenomenon that in time she became a connoisseur of irony per se, to a point where no instance of vivid incongruity, from gaunt glutton to tippling vicar, blushing trollop to fastidious tramp, escaped her notice or failed to amuse her.

It was therefore with joyous anticipation that, two days after her twenty-fifth birthday, Chloe contracted to essay the lead in *The Beauteous Buccaneer,* Mr. Jerrold's violent narrative of the historical female pirate Anne Bonney, who'd fought and plundered side by side with her friend, Mary Read, and her lover, Captain Jack Rackham, prince of freebooters. As staged by Mr. Kean, *The Beauteous Buccaneer* was a dark divertissement, replete with long shadows, choruses of wailing nereids, and *misterioso* trills boiling up from the orchestra pit. In one particularly poignant episode Pirate Anne deposited her newborn infant (whom Jack had refused to acknowledge as his own) at the gates of an orphanage, bidding the baby a tearful farewell, then melting into the fog. The final scene found Anne being hauled onto a gallows, outfitted with a noose, and hanged.

Chloe's future, in short, looked rosy. She could practically taste the oysters and the sparkling wine. And yet, strangely enough, in the case of *The Beauteous Buccaneer* the usual disjuncture between her life and her art did not obtain. No sooner had she finished cleaning her face following her fifteenth Saturday matinee performance (so that her painted brow changed from white to rose, and her cherry lips turned pink) than a visitor entered her dressing-room—her very own wayward father, who at last report had been working as a dustman in St. Albans. His arrival occasioned in Chloe sharp and sudden pangs of remorse, for he wore a pauper's uniform, complete with brown hempen tunic and matching skullcap, and his hands displayed the scars and scabs of one who'd been condemned to relentless toil.

"Yes, child, your eyes do not deceive you," said Phineas. "I'm living at Her Majesty's expense in Holborn Workhouse—a place no sane person would enter of his own free will. Thus does our nation hold down the high cost of poverty."

"Papa, you should have *told* me," Chloe moaned.

"I should have told *myself*," said Phineas with a shiver of chagrin. "Instead I kept pretending the world was about to provide me with a living."

She slipped behind her fan-folded Chinese screen and began shedding her pirate costume—leather corset, crimson-striped pantaloons, gleaming black boots—in favor of street clothes. "When last we dined together, you had hopes of becoming a hackney coachman," she remarked from her makeshift boudoir.

"A vocation at which I would have succeeded had my passengers not expected me to possess a promiscuous familiarity with London geography," said Phineas. "Shortly thereafter I became a carpenter's assistant, a calling I abandoned upon realizing that my maul bore a grudge against my thumb. Next I apprenticed myself to a locksmith, leaving his service after he told me that burglars would one day drink my health."

Chloe stepped free of the screen, brushing her taffeta skirt into place, her chestnut hair now secured with mother-of-pearl combs, a gift from a former swain. Briefly she contemplated herself in the looking-glass. Her features were inarguably attractive: large eyes, straight nose, high cheek-bones—a face for launching, if not a thousand ships, then certainly a fleet of robust fishing smacks.

"You must be famished, Papa."

"Not so much for food, dear child, as for your charming presence. Offer me a bite of cheese, though, and I shan't refuse."

Sensing that her father's hunger was rather greater than he allowed, she suggested they repair to the Cloven Hoof for some supper and a pint of ale. At first he demurred, saying, "Surely my daughter would be ashamed to appear in public with a man dressed in a pauper's uniform."

"No more than her father would be ashamed to appear in public with the most notorious lady buccaneer ever to stain the pages of English history," said Chloe, tying on her green velvet bonnet. "Take my arm, Papa, and I'll procure for you the fattest pie in Covent Garden."

It was for Chloe a measure of her father's despondency that, as they sat in the noisy and smoke-filled tavern awaiting their respective orders of mutton stew and kidney pie, he declined to bestow life on any inanimate object. In the past he would have introduced the candles to one another, exhorting them to seize the day ere their paraffin flesh melted away. Or he would have transformed the napkins into shrouds worn by spectral rats, encouraging the phantom rodents to haunt the dog who'd murdered them.

The food arrived promptly. Fervently devouring his pie, washing it down with tidal gulps of ale, Phineas explained that he was obliged to eat quickly, for his furlough ended at sundown.

"They've got you doing hard labor like some Hebrew slave in Egypt," said Chloe, indicating her father's ravaged hands.

"Breaking stones, grinding bones, picking oakum."

"Oakum? Is that a crop?"

"Now that I think about it, aye, 'tis a kind of crop, sown with malice and harvested in misery. From dawn to dusk we stoop over masses of discarded rope, untwisting the fibers for shipbuilder's caulk. The overseer's not satisfied unless our fingers bleed."

"We must liberate you from that abhorrent place." A tear exited Chloe's left eye, tickling her cheek as it fell.

"I came not to unload my troubles but to offer my accolades." Phineas removed his pauper's cap and kneaded his brow with the ball of his thumb.

"You saw my performance?"

"From a secret vantage on the catwalk. You make a splendid blackguard, darling. I loved how you stabbed the bosun in the gizzard when he discovered your true sex. The audience got its money's worth in blood."

"In beetroot juice, actually."

Chloe leaned back in her seat, her roving gaze confirming her worst fears. Half the customers were staring at the moist-eyed actress. Her irony bone began to sing. Normally when dining at the Hoof, she hoped that the patrons, having just seen her onstage, would accord her admiring glances—but now that she had their attention she wished them all gone.

"Watching you drink Jack Rackham under the table was equally enthralling," said Papa, daubing her tears with his napkin. "I assume that wasn't rum in your glass."

"Weak tea."

If Phineas Bathurst had ever entertained a sensible idea in his life, Chloe was unaware of it. Even his decision to marry the beautiful Florence Willingham had been fundamentally barmy, for she had evidently possessed the disposition of a gorgon conjoined to the ethics of a snake. In the opinion of the neighborhood gossips, Phineas's wife was determined to put him in an early grave, and it was only her own death (minutes after the respective births of Chloe and her brother) that thwarted this ambition.

"Listen, Father, I am lodged in Tavistock Street with the woman who played Pirate Mary." Chloe slurped down a spoonful of broth. "You are welcome to sleep on the floor each night till you find employment. We'll steal a mattress for you from the properties department."

"Your generosity touches me, but my situation's more complicated than you imagine," said Phineas. "For all my fifty years, I still own a stout arm and a strong back, and so the workhouse authorities count me a great asset. Give old Bathurst an extra helping of gruel, and he'll pick oakum with a frenzy to shame Hercules sweeping the stables. But should I ever leave the place, those same authorities will hunt me down and toss me into debtors' prison."

"You're in arrears, Papa?"

"For the past two years, I've availed myself of England's peerless network of moneylenders. I'm proud to say that, thanks to my continuous expectations of solvency, I donated most of this income to people even needier than I. In time my creditors' patience ran short, and I saw no choice but to don a pauper's uniform and flee to a workhouse."

"What is the total of your debts?"

"Let me tell you about my favorite scene, Pirate Anne leaving her baby at the orphanage. It brought a lump to my throat."

"Father, please, I must know the sum."

"If you insist on dragging arithmetic into our conversation, the figure may be obtained by adding four hundred pounds to five hundred pounds."

"That's nine hundred pounds!"

"Such a mathematical prodigy you are, Chloe, a regular Isaac Newton. And now, to calculate the absolute and final total, we must reckon with six hundred additional pounds."

"Good Lord! You owe fifteen hundred?"

"Yes. Correct. Plus interest."

"How *much* interest?"

"Five hundred, more or less."

"Sweet Jesus! Two thousand pounds?"

"I know it sounds like a king's ransom, but I've researched the matter, and for two thousand pounds you could barely redeem the bastard son of a pretender to the Scottish throne."

Chloe stared at the remainder of her stew, for which she presently enjoyed no appetite. "I have but four pounds to my name."

Not surprisingly, Phineas now inquired after the third member of the family, doubtless hopeful that Algernon had found some profitable occupation, and it became Chloe's duty to report that, to the best of her knowledge, her twin brother was still the incorrigible gamester and jack-of-no-trades he'd always been.

"The dear boy, so utterly his father's son," said Phineas. "The rotten apple never falls far from the crooked tree." He rose and attempted without success to assume a military bearing. "Thankee for the pie and ale, child, which for several glorious minutes made me forget the frightful workhouse porridge."

"When shall I see you again?"

"I am promised a second furlough in eighteen months' time."

"During which interval I'll move Heaven and Earth to free you."

Bending low, Phineas kissed Chloe's cheek. "No, child. Don't do it. Keep treading the boards, acting your heart out, making Anne Bonney live and breathe and suffer for her sins."

"Truth to tell, I find Anne so implausible a character I cannot rise to the occasion of her portrayal. Surely I was born to play better roles than those Mr. Kean gives me—and in better venues than the Adelphi."

"Including the role of a wife?" said Phineas in a tone of affectionate reproach. "I needn't tell you, darling, there comes a time in every actress's life when she's no longer suited to beauteous buccaneers, beguiling French castaways, or even the Queen of Egypt."

"'Tis a cruel profession I've picked," Chloe agreed, solemnly pondering the fact that, whereas twenty-five did not sound like a terribly advanced age, the same could not be said of a quarter-century. "You'll be pleased to hear that not long ago Mr. Throckmorton, who portrayed Jack Rackham this afternoon, proposed to me—and displeased to learn I rejected him." She squeezed her father's bristly hand. "Hear my vow, Papa. One morning whilst you're sitting down to unravel the day's hemp, I shall appear at your side. In a trice we'll gather up a barrel of plucked oakum and bear it by hired coach to St. Katherine Docks. On the River

Thames lies a pirate sloop, which I've fashioned with my own hands, and once we've caulked her timbers with the oakum, we'll climb on board."

"And sail away," said Phineas, screwing his skullcap into place.

"On the morning tide. In time we'll reach an uncharted isle where the bananas taste like roast beef and the coconuts are bursting with ale."

"And the natives are all lyric poets as handsome as Lord Byron and witty as Mr. Pope." Phineas made a jaunty pirouette, as if to tell the on-lookers that, though bent, he was not yet broken. "If my daughter doesn't get a lyric poet out of this adventure," he said, sauntering away, "I want naught to do with it."

In a universe rife with ambiguity and riddled with whim, Chloe Bathurst knew one thing for certain. No matter how great her popu-larity with aficionados of tasteless spectacles, any actress in the employ of the Adelphi Theatre would never accumulate two thousand pounds. Even before learning of her father's predicament, she'd endeavored to join a more prosperous troupe. Over the years she'd secured auditions with the great patent houses—the Drury Lane, the Haymarket, the Covent Garden—all three still trading on the fact that, prior to the The-atre Regulation Act, they'd been the only venues in London licensed to mount respectable fare. The directors offered her not a word of encour-agement. Her voice, they insisted, was ill-suited to substantive plays. She could never do right by Goneril, Ophelia, Rosalind, or even Juliet.

When Mr. Kean assumed management of the company, Chloe had hoped she might enjoy a corresponding increase in salary, for that con-ceited actor regularly insisted he was not in the business of directing mere melodramas. He preferred the term "tragical romances," which sounded to Chloe like the sort of challenge a dedicated thespian could meet only with the aid of monetary incentives. She'd first learned of Mr. Kean's affectation when, eight days before the show was to open, they got around to rehearsing *The Murders in the Rue Morgue*, Mr. Buckstone's adaptation of a mystery story by the American writer Mr. Poe.

"What a marvelous potboiler we have here," remarked Chloe's

colleague and rooming-companion, Fanny Mendrick, after the company had read the script aloud. A pocket Venus whose ringing voice seemed transplanted from an actress twice her size, Fanny had been cast as Mademoiselle Camille L'Espanaye, fated to die at the hands of an Indonesian orang-utang. "But I'm not looking forward to getting rammed up a chimney by an ape."

"I do not direct potboilers," Mr. Kean informed Fanny. "I direct tragical romances."

"Show me a maiden being ravished by an orang-utang, and I'll show you a potboiler," said Chloe.

For all his vanity, she admired Charles Kean, who was touchingly devoted to his actress wife, the protean Ellen Tree, cast as the mother of the orang-utang's victim. Chloe also pitied him. As Dame Fortune had arranged the matter, Charles Kean was born the son of Edmund Kean, England's most celebrated actor, now fifteen years deceased. Though gifted in his own right, Kean the younger seemed destined to spend the rest of his life boxing with his father's shadow.

"I beg your pardon, Mr. Kean, but I must agree with Miss Bathurst," said the dashing Mr. Throckmorton, who'd lost Chloe's hand but secured the role of Inspector Dupin. "Here at the Adelphi we do last-minute rescues, ridiculous coincidences, volcanic eruptions in lieu of plot resolutions, and apes stuffing young women up chimneys. It was ever thus."

"They do potboilers at the Lyceum," retorted Mr. Kean. "They do potboilers at the Trochaic and Sadler's Wells. Perhaps you'd be happier working for *those* tawdry houses."

"A question, Mr. Kean," said Chloe, who'd been assigned the part of Dupin's mistress, a character not found in the original tale. "Since we're all tragical romancers these days, might we be paid a tragical romancer's salary?"

Mr. Kean confined his reply to a sneer.

In subsequent months the Adelphi Company labored to do right by *The Murders in the Rue Morgue,* and the next season found them investing considerable time and energy in *Siren of the Nile,* a triumph followed by their especially tragical and singularly romantic presentation of *The*

Beauteous Buccaneer. Although the role was abominably written, Chloe had taken substantial pleasure in portraying Anne Bonney—but then came the luncheon with Papa, after which she could barely drag herself on stage, his plight having soured her on the world and all its institutions, not excluding the theatre. And then one Wednesday evening, as she stood beneath the noose prior to her execution, something snapped within her soul.

The scene had begun in normal fashion, with Pirate Anne's eleven-year-old urchin daughter, named Bronwyn by the orphanage authorities, arriving at the gallows seconds before the hangman would deliver her mother to the Almighty's mercy. Overwhelmed by this first and final reunion, Anne delivered a mawkish speech imploring her child to rise above whatever proclivity for iniquity she'd inherited from her buccaneer parents.

"Let me be a lesson to thee," said Anne. "Cleave to the straight and narrow, lest thou, too, be hanged for a pirate."

Bronwyn stumbled forward and kissed the scaffold, whereupon the hangman dropped the noose over Anne's head. A priest mounted the platform and, approaching the prisoner, made the incontrovertible point that repentance was superior to roasting in the flames of Hell.

"Ne'er hath God heard the prayers of so remorseful a miscreant!" declared Anne to the imaginary offstage mob. "Ne'er hath Heaven attended the words of a more sorrowful sinner!"

"Dear Lord, receive the shriven soul of this fallen woman," cried the priest, "who hath seen the error of her ways!"

Now the gas lamps arrayed along the proscenium went dim, leaving the stage lit only by a shimmering shaft of limelight trained on Chloe's face, at which juncture the fount of her despair (constrained till this moment by decorum and Mr. Jerrold's script) flowed forth, alien words filling her throat like rising gorge.

"A famous writer insists that nothing so wonderfully concentrates a person's mind as knowing he's to be hanged at dawn," she told the offstage mob, a departure from the text so radical that it shocked her as much as it doubtless bewildered those playing daughter, priest, and executioner. "But he neglected to mention that such mental clarity persists until the moment of death. Aye, my friends, 'twould seem I've been vouch-safed a vision of the future. Mine eyes behold a great English Queen pre-siding o'er an empire more mighty than ancient Rome. But all is not well in Victoria's realm. Whilst merchants get rich and nobles grow fat, the people suffer."

Chloe slipped out of the noose and, like a little girl playing hop-scotch, jumped over the trapdoor.

"I see workhouses built to imprison the destitute, as if poverty were a crime and not a tragedy. I see broken men, sickly women, and, aye, help-less orphans forced to live on green meat and rancid gruel. I see these wretches spending day after day breaking stones and untwisting rope till their fingers bleed and blisters bloom on their palms. And so I implore ye, tell your children to tell their children to tell *their* children that such conditions must never come to pass on Albion's shores. I know that in the name of Christian charity our descendants will petition Her Maj-esty, appeal to Parliament, shame the aristocracy, remind the Church of its duties—whatever it takes to close the workhouses and give our low-born brethren their due in love and bread!"

Suddenly an Adelphi patron shot from his seat and began screaming like a lunatic. "Hear! Hear! Listen to the pirate!" Half-blinded by the limelight, Chloe could barely see her votary, but he appeared to be a wild-eyed youth with a feral beard. "She speaks the truth!" he persisted, wav-ing a stack of papers about as an arsonist might wield a firebrand. "Last month a brilliant pamphlet rolled off the presses—*Manifest der Kommu-nistischen Partei* by Karl Marx and Friedrich Engels, which I've just trans-lated into English! It tells how the bourgeoisie will cease exploiting the proletariat only when workers control the instruments of production!"

Hisses, boos, jeers, and catcalls greeted the agitator's outburst.

"Shut up, you anarchist snake!"

"One more word, and I'll ram your nihilist teeth down your atheist throat!"

"Give us that lady Barabbas, and send the Jacobin to the gallows!"

"Tar his Chartist hide!"

"Feather his Socialist skin!"

No sooner had the agitator's antagonists stopped shouting than a smattering of stentorian voices came to his defense.

"Property is theft!"

"All power to the proletariat!"

"Crush the bourgeoisie!"

"Redistribution now!"

"Votes for workers!"

"God bless Tiny Tim!"

"God bless us, every one!"

Fearful that a riot was in the offing, Chloe stepped onto the trapdoor, placed the noose about her neck, and spoke the last lines of Mr. Jerrold's script: "Merciful Jesus, I pray that thou wilt lead my dear sweet Bronwyn along the path of righteousness! Send me to Perdition if such be thy will"—as always, the executioner now wrapped his gloved hands about the lever—"for I've just glimpsed Paradise in my daughter's smile!"

" *'Ein Gespenst geht um in Europa'*!" cried the agitator, reading from his manuscript. "'A ghost is haunting Europe'! 'The ghost of Communism'!"

And then, as always, the limelight faded to black, an interval sufficient for Chloe to sneak away whilst the property master climbed the scaffold stairs and suspended an effigy from the gallows crossbeam.

" 'The poor have but their chains to lose'!" the agitator continued. " 'They have a world to gain'!"

The limelight flared to life, illuminating the dangling corpse of Pirate Anne.

" 'Laborers of all nations, come together'!"

The dazzling ray died, the curtain descended, and the playgoers charged pell-mell towards the exits, eager to distance themselves from this foul and heady thing called Communism.

Beyond her impatience with Mr. Jerrold's simpleminded conception of Anne Bonney, Chloe would admit that the lady pirate's life and her own were not entirely discontinuous. Just as Anne and Jack had indulged in activities almost certain of procreative consequences, so had

Chloe allowed her first great love—Adam Parminter, the dapper son of a Brighton family grown rich by trade—to thrice seduce her at age seventeen without benefit of linen condom or other prophylactic measure, the ensuing catastrophe sparking in Mr. Parminter the same degree of callousness with which Jack had greeted the prospect of fatherhood. Whereas the prince of freebooters had persuaded Anne to leave their baby at an orphanage, the Brighton bounder had recommended that, in lieu of a marriage between Chloe and himself, she take hold of the infant when it arrived, carry the creature down to the Thames, and set it adrift, "rather like the newborn Moses, though without the seaworthy bassinett."

"I shall do no such thing," Chloe informed him.

"It's a more common practice than you imagine," Mr. Parminter insisted.

"And I'm a less ordinary person than you suppose," said Chloe, gasping from the hideousness of her paramour's scheme and the nausea of her sixth week. "You may have stolen my innocence, but my conscience is yet my own, and it requires me to nurture this child, even as I banish you from my life."

In the dreadful days that followed, Chloe repeatedly asked herself whether she believed the noble words with which she'd greeted Mr. Parminter's idea, never arriving at a fixed answer. Fortunately, she had in Fanny Mendrick not only a shoulder on which to cry but also a friend in whom to confide. The two stage-struck young women were on the point of making their first appearances before a London audience, having been cast as novice nuns in the Olympic Theatre's production of *The Haunted Priory*. Set in medieval England, this supernatural melodrama, newly penned by Mr. Buckstone, gave Chloe, as Sister Margaret, ten whole lines to speak and Fanny, as Sister Angelica, eight. Were Chloe not so miserable, the situation would have appealed to her sense of irony—for what incongruity could be greater than a ruined ingénue portraying a chaste fiancée of Christ?

"Oh, Fanny, am I mad to imagine I might bring up a child whilst pursuing a career on the stage?"

"As long as your ne'er-do-well father and prodigal brother remain ne'er-do-well and prodigal, then 'mad' is the proper word," replied Fanny. "For all its contempt of convention, I fear the theatrical world will not accommodate your indiscretion."

"By my calculation the creature arrives in seven months' time," said Chloe. "I have but two hundred days to find employment more consonant with motherhood." She endured yet another twinge of procreative nausea. "You're a churchgoer, Fanny. Will I burn in perpetual flames for conceiving a bastard child?"

"Though not a theologian, I am given to understand that the whole idea of Christ is to keep Hell's population to a minimum." Fanny rested a soothing hand on Chloe's cheek. "No, friend, you will not burn, and—if I can help it—neither will you starve."

Two nights later, both actresses stepped on stage in the premiere performance of *The Haunted Priory*. Their one and only scene had taken Sister Margaret and Sister Angelica to the subterranean crypt wherein lay the remains of former abbesses, for the novices wished to investigate the legend that the ghost of Abbess Hildegard stalked the place—a ghost with a secret: the location of a buried treasure. Hugging each other to quell their fears, the novices waited in the musty darkness, and then, at the stroke of midnight, the revenant appeared, covered in a moldering shroud and speaking in a voice like a corroded penny whistle—the estimable Ellen Tree in an artfully restrained performance.

"Yea, verily, a chest of doubloons is hidden on these grounds," said the ghost of Abbess Hildegard in response to Sister Margaret's query.

"Being poised to take the vow of poverty, Sister Angelica and I shan't spend the gold on ourselves," Chloe assured the ghost. "Rather, we would use it to renovate the priory."

"Giving the surplus to the poor," added Fanny.

"The treasure has lain in the earth these past two hundred years," said the ghost, "and there it will remain till the end of time."

"I am sore perplexed," said Fanny. "With the hoard in question, we could found an orphanage."

"And save the soul of many a harlot," added Chloe, suddenly aware of a viscous fluid migrating down her leg, warming her skin as it sought the floor. My baby weeps, she thought. The wretched thing sheds tears.

"Our Lord preached that wealth is the worst of Lucifer's many venoms," said the ghost, "poisoning the souls of all who seek it."

The sticky dribble became a flood. Chloe's bowels constricted. Panic clogged her windpipe. Glancing at the boards, she saw the blood pooling beneath the hem of her habit. The last line of the scene—*Of all the women of my acquaintance, living or dead, you are quite the wisest, Abbess Hildegard, for you've given me to understand that this treasure, unearthed, would prove a bane worse than the Black Death*—belonged to Sister Margaret, but Chloe could not speak it, being about to faint.

Having noticed the rushing red gobbets, Fanny straightaway swooped to the rescue, saying, "You are quite the wisest woman I know, Abbess Hildegard, dead or alive, for you have taught me how this treasure would prove a burden as dire as death—and now we must away, for Sister Margaret is enduring an onslaught of the vapors."

Fanny curled an arm about Chloe's shoulder, and together they staggered out of the crypt, at which juncture the set, the theatre, and the world went black.

Upon returning to consciousness Chloe found herself backstage, sprawled across the four-poster that had served as Abbess Hildegard's deathbed in act one. Fanny knelt beside her, cooling her brow with a damp kerchief, whilst Ellen Tree sponged away the sanguine remnants of the frightening event. Props from Olympic Theatre productions gone by loomed out of the shadows—a ball gown, a suit of armor, a siege cannon, Macbeth's head on a pike.

"Am I dying?" asked Chloe.

"Not in the least," said Fanny. "Be still. Tomorrow we feed you beef for breakfast—"

"At my expense," said Ellen Tree.

"By way of restoring the blood you've lost," Fanny explained.

"Blood—and everything," said Chloe as relief and exultation washed through her, borne on a tide of qualified remorse.

"Don't worry about tomorrow night's performance," said Fanny. "I shall collapse Margaret and Angelica into a single character."

"I myself once endured the very trial that befell you tonight," added Ellen Tree. "You are likely to recover in full."

"For reasons known but to Himself, God decrees that certain creatures must not come into the world," said Fanny, an observation on which Chloe was willing to let the whole cataclysmic matter rest.

But for the fact that the audience who'd witnessed Chloe's improvisation during the Wednesday evening performance of *The Beauteous Buccaneer* included a journalist in the employ of the *Times*, the affair might never have come to the public's attention. Owing to the efforts of that anonymous scribbler, however, half the city spent the following Friday gossiping about Miss Bathurst's gallows speech. DISTURBANCE AT ADELPHI THEATRE, shouted the page-two headline for the 17th of March, 1848. ACTRESS HARANGUES AUDIENCE WITH POLITICAL RANT, ran the first subheading. MOB VIOLENCE NARROWLY AVERTED. Amongst the consumers of this narrative was Chloe herself, who, upon reading of her recklessness, felt as if she were back on the gallows, the trapdoor opening beneath her feet. Seeking to distract herself, she fixed on an adjacent article summarizing the arguments of Marx and Engels's *Communist Manifesto,* including their colorful conclusion that "the bourgeoisie produces its own gravediggers," the victory of the proletariat over the propertied classes having been ordained by a Wheel of History impossible to roll back—an idea she found genuinely diverting, though not sufficiently so to alleviate the misery caused by her emergent notoriety.

Later that afternoon, upon arriving at the theatre, Chloe discovered a note from Mr. Kean attached with sealing wax to her dressing-room mirror. *Report to me immediately,* it read.

Nervous and fretful, she approached the manager's office, her palms so damp she could barely turn the doorknob. Mr. Kean stood behind his desk, mallet in hand, tapping a nail into the plaster. Upon completing the task, he decorated the wall with a framed certificate indicating that Her Majesty had appointed him Master of Revels.

Seated on plush chairs, Fanny, Mrs. Kean, and Mr. Throckmorton greeted Chloe with tepid smiles. The presence of her disappointed swain prompted Chloe briefly to consider—and reaffirm—her commitment to chastity, the best available approximation of the virginity she'd surrendered long ago. Not only was Adam Parminter the first man to seduce her, he'd also been the last. Although a slap on the cheek normally sufficed to deter a suitor's untoward advances, occasionally she'd been obliged to introduce her favorite family heirloom, Grandpapa's bayonet, into the relationship.

Mr. Kean offered Chloe a chair, but she declined, explaining that she prided herself on receiving bad news without swooning.

"Naturally I should like to overlook Wednesday night's rabble-rousing," the manager began, gesturing towards a copy of the *Times* splayed open on his desk. Even at this distance Chloe could read DISTURBANCE AT ADELPHI THEATRE. "But I fear we have a crisis on our hands. Either play-goers will boycott us to protest your tirade, or a Chartist mob will show up one night hoping to witness a repetition of your outburst. Ergo, I took the liberty of printing up an addendum to be pasted onto each patron's playbill. 'For this evening's performance'"—he flashed his wife a smile—"'Anne Bonney will be played by Ellen Tree.'"

Mrs. Kean *née* Ellen Tree shifted uncomfortably in her chair.

A queasiness spread through Chloe. "Am I banished for tonight only, or have you permanently cast me as woebegone Abigail in *The Streetwalker and the Scalawag*?"

"Spare us your self-pity," said Mr. Kean. "Mrs. Kean and I intend to award you three pounds in severance pay, a sum sufficient to cover your needs till some other company employs you."

"If I choose to remain a woman of the theatre, it will be as a dramatist, not an actress," said Chloe. "Amongst the plays I intend to write is the saga of a second-rate highwayman doomed to compete with the reputation of his late uncle, the greatest thief of his day—rather the way the son of a famous actor might end up living in his father's shadow."

A frown contracted Mr. Kean's brow. Saying nothing, he used his handkerchief to polish the glass protecting his Master of Revels certificate.

"Mightn't we give Chloe another chance?" asked Fanny.

"She doesn't know what came over her on Wednesday," added Mr. Throckmorton.

"I know *precisely* what came over me," said Chloe. "My father has been condemned to die of hard labor through no fault of his own—or, rather, through several faults of his own, none grave enough to merit such a fate." Extending her index finger, she tapped the article concerning *The Communist Manifesto*. "I've already got a plot. Our second-rate highwayman takes his troubles out on his fellow robbers, dismissing them from the gang one by one. Desperate, the thieves hire a sorcerer to conjure up an avenging phantom. And so it happens that, just as Ebenezer Scrooge was visited by the ghosts of Christmas Past, Present, and Future, so is our hero haunted by the spectre of Communism. Frightened out of his wits, he re-employs his former colleagues, and they straightaway stage a series of benefit robberies, using the proceeds to feed the residents of the nearest workhouse."

"Lurid, but I like it," said Mr. Throckmorton.

"Overwrought, but oddly gripping," said Fanny.

"What you've described sounds like a melodrama," said Ellen Tree, gazing at her husband, "but with some effort it might become a tragical romance—am I right, dear?"

"I think not," said Mr. Kean.

"I'm going to call it *The Bourgeois Bandito versus the Wheel of History*," said Chloe.

"It's time you cleaned out your dressing-room," said Mr. Kean.

"You'll have to find another dagger for Pirate Anne," said Chloe. "The one I use each night is no prop but a bayonet bequeathed to me by my paternal grandfather, who fought at Waterloo."

"On which side?" said Mr. Kean.

"That's enough, dear," said Ellen Tree.

"Whether the dagger is a prop or not, I don't doubt you'll take it with you," said Mr. Kean, "along with everything else that isn't screwed to the floor."

"With all due respect, madam, I don't write tragical romances," Chloe told Ellen Tree. "I write chillers about escaped lunatics," she added, fixing on her former employer as she swirled out of his office, "melodramas about gentlemen infected with lycanthropy, and sweeping sagas of intrepid lady explorers who take jungle gorillas for their lovers. If ever you need a potboiler, Mr. Kean, don't hesitate to look me up."

2

Chloe Finds Employment on the Estate
of Charles Darwin, to the Benefit of Certain Giant
Tortoises, Exotic Iguanas, and Rare Birds

Needless to say, she did not intend to write a play about a second-rate highwayman, or any such spectacle for that matter, no melodrama seething with ghosts and ghouls, no plum pudding spiced with virgins imperiled by mad monks—and yet Chloe fervently hoped the theatre would remain her primary means of support. Although she disagreed with Mr. Shakespeare's conclusion that all the world was a stage, in truth the stage was all she knew of the world. Aided by the faithful Fanny, she compiled an exhaustive list of London houses, then called upon each manager in turn, presenting herself as Mademoiselle Jeanne Feuillard, newly arrived from the Comédie-Française. In every instance she was rebuffed—such was the imprecision of her French accent, the notoriety of her final performance as Anne Bonney, and the transparency of her claim that, although she resembled the actress whose image graced the posters in the Adelphi Theatre lobby, she and that deranged young woman were two different people.

"Mademoiselle Feuillard—*c'est-à-dire*, Miss Bathurst—you are not without talent, but neither are you without reputation," said the manager of the Majestic with an extravagant sneer.

"The next time I wish for my theatre to break out in a riot, you are the very mischief maker I shall call upon," said the proprietor of the Trochaic.

"I share your compassion for the downtrodden, Miss Bathurst, but this is a commercial enterprise, not Sherwood Forest," said the owner of the Odeon.

Sixteen houses, sixteen rejections: it was time to try something else—but what? Adrift in the great city, friendless save for Fanny, penniless save for Fanny's patronage, Chloe had reached the frayed end of her ragged rope. Hunger became her daily fare, cold her nightly portion, conditions that might well have advanced to malnutrition and *la grippe* were her rooming-companion not possessed of so charitable a nature.

"A gift of bread on a pauper's table, a donation of coal to a friend's warming-pan—these are the measures by which Christ assays our souls," Fanny explained.

"Then you'll not be wanting for a berth in eternity," said Chloe.

"Promise me you'll avoid that degraded sorority to which our profession is oft-times compared."

"No, dear friend, never that—you have my word."

"Have you considered the milliner's trade?" asked Fanny.

"I was not born to make a lady's bonnet, but to have a gentleman's hat land at my feet as the curtain falls," said Chloe.

"Perhaps you should become a flower-seller like Nydia in *The Last Days of Pompeii*."

"Nydia's business prospered only because she was blind. The condition is easy enough to feign, but I would rather be despised than pitied."

"A seamstress? A laundress? A draper's assistant?"

"I have a better idea."

And indeed she did. An aficionado of Miss Austen's novels, Chloe had long ago assimilated the universally acknowledged truth that a single man in possession of a good fortune must be in want of a wife, and of late she'd deduced the logical corollary, that a wife married to a prosperous man yet burdened with a slew of children must be in want of a governess.

To wit, she would tutor the progeny of the well-to-do, a vocation at which, though she had no particular fondness for either children or gentlefolk, she could imagine herself succeeding.

Shortly after sunrise each morning, Chloe slipped out of bed and purchased the *Times,* scrutinizing the tiny print under SITUATIONS AVAILABLE: TUTORS AND GOVERNESSES until her eyes crossed and the typography floated free of the page like a leaf fallen on still water. She responded by post to thirty such advertisements and subsequently secured a score of private interviews. Beaming a soft smile and assuming an equally dulcet voice, she began each such audience by informing the lady of the house that, owing to her theatrical experience, she was competent to teach not only elocution, singing, and French but also history, geography, and ethics, for the loftier dramas in which she'd appeared (or at least seen performed) had treated extensively of these subjects, most conspicuously Monsieur Crébillon's *Rhadamistus and Zenobia,* Herr Hebbel's *Maria Magdalena,* and Voltaire's *Alzire.*

"Ethics, you say?" snorted the prickly Lady Routledge. "Do you truly believe there's a moral lesson to be gleaned from a piece of thundering nonsense like *Rhadamistus and Zenobia?*"

"By populating his play with bestial kings, Crébillon shows us that authority knows nothing of virtue," said Chloe. "The playwright assails the arrogance of those who imagine their blood is purer than that of the masses."

Lady Routledge seemed to be experiencing an unpleasant odor. "A worthy theme, I'm sure, though not one to which His Lordship and I would expose our sons."

"Then we have poor, trusting Clara in *Maria Magdalena,* seduced by her boorish fiancé, who deserts her for the mayor's daughter," said Chloe (enduring a pang provoked by the memory of her liaisons with Mr. Parminter). "Ere the curtain falls, the unfortunate girl has drowned herself and Herr Hebbel has laid bare the foibles of bourgeois society."

"My sons do not need anything laid bare for them, Miss Bathurst, and certainly not by you. As for the infamous Voltaire, I've heard he was a sworn enemy of God."

"Not so much of God, My Lady, as of organized churches. In *Alzire* Voltaire reveals how the Christian army that destroyed the Inca Empire left little of value in its place."

"Alas, Miss Bathurst, this interview should have ended before it began."

Sad to say, Chloe's encounter with Lady Routledge was typical of the *pièces mal faites* in which she appeared that spring: an auspicious beginning, a wobbly second act, and a calamitous climax. Perhaps Fanny was right. Perhaps she should become a milliner or a seamstress.

When Chloe first clamped eyes on an advertisement indicating that on Sunday afternoon (between the hours of noon and four) a Mrs. Charles Darwin would be interviewing prospective governesses at her husband's estate in Down, County Kent, she decided to ignore it, having no reason to imagine the meeting should go better than its predecessors. But then she noticed the final line, SYMPATHY WITH EDUCATIONAL THEORIES OF M. ROUSSEAU DESIRABLE, and her hopes soared, for she'd once seen Ellen Tree portray Sophie in an adaptation of the philosopher's most acclaimed novel.

On the evidence of *Émile*, Jean-Jacques Rousseau believed that amongst every child's instincts were compassion, curiosity, and a love of adventure. The tutor's job was to nurture these virtues, forswearing all forms of coercion and restraint. Very well, thought Chloe, if it's amity Mrs. Darwin wants, I'll become the most genial governess ever to draw breath in Britain. If freedom is the order of the day, I'll let her offspring run wild as South Seas savages.

Although her liquidity was at low tide—shake her purse, and you would hear naught but a single farthing clink against a bereaved ha'penny—Chloe straightaway secured the steam-train fare in the form of yet another loan from Fanny. Upon arriving at Bromley Station (so ran her scheme) she would spare herself the hackney-coach fee by donning her calfskin boots, hoisting her parasol against the afternoon sun, and walking all five miles to Down Village, where she would change into her best clogs prior to the interview. A well-laid plan, to be sure, which proceeded to go spectacularly awry. Detraining, Chloe was thrown off balance by her portmanteau, accidentally wedging her foot between the last step and the station platform, thereby wrenching her ankle. The pain was implacable—knife-sharp when she moved at a normal pace, spasmodic when she shuffled—and, worse yet, a storm now arose, so she was obliged to trek through a downpour against which her little *parapluie* proved useless. At five o'clock she presented herself at the estate in the sorriest of conditions: cold, wet, muddy, exhausted—and one hour late.

Mrs. Darwin behaved with exemplary graciousness. Ignoring the raindrops cascading from Chloe's bonnet and sleeves, she ushered her into the drawing-room, a commodious space boasting a bay window offering a panorama of sodden pastureland punctuated by mulberry trees and a Spanish chestnut. Mrs. Darwin proposed to serve her visitor a cup of chamomile. Given her half-frozen state, this offer delighted Chloe, though she accepted it with a studied restraint that she imagined bespoke refinement.

"I apologize for my tardiness," she said. "Alas, at some point during my railway journey, my purse fell prey to a pickpocket," she added (knowing that the truth might suggest an inveterate clumsiness), "and so I couldn't hire a fly. If you and Mr. Darwin are about to have supper, I shall gladly wait here."

"A pickpocket, Miss Bathurst?" said Mrs. Darwin. "Oh, dear." She was a sweet-faced woman whose notable aspects included extravagant brown curls, pink cheeks, a pouty lower lip, and a pregnancy of perhaps six months' duration. "Mr. Darwin and I should be pleased to put you up and provide for your return to London."

"Am I to infer the other candidates have come and gone?"

"One stayed behind, a Miss Catherine Thorley, to whom I awarded the situation ninety minutes ere you arrived."

So often had Chloe's profession required her to sob on cue, she'd forgotten how it felt to weep spontaneously, but now such an episode was upon her, muffled cries breaking from her throat, fat tears welling in her eyes. Mrs. Darwin relieved Chloe of her cup and saucer, then placed a tender hand on her shoulder.

"I shall write to you the instant I learn that one of my relations requires a governess," said Mrs. Darwin.

As if summoned by the din of Chloe's despair, a tall gentleman strode into the room bearing a terra-cotta flowerpot covered with a pie plate, his confident carriage marking him as master of the house. Beetle-browed and side-whiskered, with a nose suggesting a small but assertive potato, he was far from handsome, though Chloe found him attractive nonetheless—physically magnetic and also, by the evidence of his kind eyes and warm smile, a person of abiding benevolence.

"There, there, my dear," he said, observing her tears, "it can't be as bad as all that," a banality last spoken to Chloe by her gladiator lover in *The Last Days of Pompeii*. As articulated by Mr. Darwin, the platitude acquired a certain profundity—and he was right, she decided: it wasn't as bad as all that. "If you like," he continued, setting the flowerpot on the piano stool, "I shall lend you a pound or two till you find employment elsewhere."

"I fear I've run short of elsewheres, sir," said Chloe. "My peers in the theatre have spurned me, and yours is the twenty-first household where I shan't become governess."

"Miss Bathurst, meet Mr. Darwin, the county's most celebrated naturalist and geologist," said the mistress of Down House. "Charles, this is Miss Bathurst."

"Charmed," said Mr. Darwin, then snapped his fingers so emphatically that Chloe half expected to see a spark. "I have an idea. Tonight, Miss Bathurst, you will sleep in the guest room."

"The servants' quarters," Mrs. Darwin corrected him.

"The servants' quarters," he agreed. "After you awaken, exit by way of the veranda, then proceed to the vegetable garden and thence to the rear gate. You will find me up and about, rambling through the thicket and pondering some scientific problem or other. Before our stroll is done I shall have made my proposal, and you will have given me your answer."

"Good heavens, Charles," said Mrs. Darwin, pursing her lips in mock exasperation, "it sounds as if you mean to ask for our visitor's hand in marriage."

"When a man has so marvelous a creature as you for a wife," said Mr. Darwin, "he requires no additional brides. You are a harem unto yourself."

Mrs. Darwin blushed and lowered her head. Her husband issued an affectionate laugh. These people, Chloe surmised, took every imaginable pleasure in each other. Happiness was a hobby that she, too, hoped to pursue one day, but for now she must attend to more practical matters.

Mr. Darwin removed the pie plate from the flowerpot and pointed into the cavity. "*Annelids,*" he announced.

"Earthworms, Mr. Darwin?" muttered his wife in a world-weary tone, as if crawlers on the piano stool were but one amongst many oddities that accrued to her husband's profession.

Saying nothing, he flipped back the piano lid. Gaze fixed intently on his worms, he struck the keys with both fists, filling the room with a distressing discordance. "Once again, they make no response." He assaulted the keys a second time. "Not a wriggle, not a tremor, not a twitch. Yesterday they ignored Master Willy's flute, the day before that Miss Annie's tin whistle."

"Our firstborn son and elder daughter," Mrs. Darwin explained.

"I daresay, I've all but proved that earthworms are deaf."

"My goodness, that finding must be as significant as Mr. Newton's universal gravitation—am I right, dear?" said Mrs. Darwin, her lips assuming a wry curve.

"How blithely we underestimate the humble earthworm," Mr. Darwin persisted. "Were it not for this species's contributions to soil formation, agriculture would be at a standstill throughout the Empire and the rest of the world."

Mrs. Darwin now summoned a willowy domestic named Mary, instructing her to find accommodation for Miss Bathurst. The servant bobbed her head deferentially, then guided her charge along a candlelit hall hung with pastoral landscapes, Chloe limping as inconspicuously as her ankle permitted. Suddenly a rambunctious band of children came spilling down the stairs. They brushed past Chloe and marched towards the drawing-room with its earthworms and its doting parents. The tall, serious boy was surely Master William (studiously ignoring his little brother), whilst the taller, giggling girl was certainly Miss Annie (casting a protective eye on a toddling sister). Near the end of the parade marched a young woman cradling a babe to her bosom, a nursemaid, no doubt, followed by a second lass holding a chalkboard on which she'd written, "In Adam's fall, we sinned all," the capital letter *A* in "Adam" rendered in boldface, the lowercase *a* in "all" likewise enhanced.

For a fleeting instant Chloe endeavored to despise Miss Catherine Thorley, this person to whom she'd lost the coveted post. Her nemesis had at best eighteen years, exuded an air of rusticity, and evinced no obvious competence to cultivate Rousseauian curiosity in young minds. But then a sudden generosity took hold of Chloe, and she bestowed a smile on Miss Thorley, who smiled back. Blighted by workhouses, crippled by Parliamentary inertia, torn by Chartist unrest, the British nation in 1848 was not exactly Heaven on Earth—and yet by Chloe's lights Mother Albion always had certain perennial virtues on display, not the least of which was governesses for whom even Adam's lapse from grace could be turned to pedagogical advantage.

Hopes aloft, senses alive to the melodious larks and sun-soaked sky, Chloe stepped off the veranda and entered the grassy, clover-dotted back lawn of Down House, hobbling past an oval flower bed bursting with lilies and larkspur. Her ankle felt better, and she moved at a sprightly pace to the brick-walled vegetable garden. Gimping quickly through the arched entrance, she sauntered amidst patches of turnips, rhubarb, and runner beans, then lifted the rear-gate latch and crossed into the wild environs beyond.

True to his prediction, Mr. Darwin had reached the thicket ahead of her. "Welcome to my sandwalk," he said, indicating a path of pulverized flint mottled along its entire course with medallions of sunlight, flanked on one side by a tangled woodland and on the other by a vacant field. "I laid it out myself, an ellipse fit for every sort of rumination."

She drew abreast of the scientist, and they proceeded towards a cottage located at the far swerve of the path, Mr. Darwin smoking a cigarette whilst propelling himself forward with his walking-stick. "Down to business," he said. "Beyond the invertebrates whose deafness I demonstrated yesterday, other species occupy these premises, and they all require care and feeding."

Chloe cringed. A sour curd congealed in her stomach. She could imagine cultivating Mr. Darwin's roses or whitewashing the walls of his villa, but she had no desire to become his goose girl, milkmaid, or resident shepherdess. "I grew up in the streets of Wapping. I am ignorant of farm animals."

"The creatures to whom I allude know nothing of farms."

He guided her off the sandwalk, past a copse of birch and alder, and from there to a meadow dominated by a fantastical building suggesting an immense hoop-skirt frame. The thing was easily as large as the dome of St. Paul's Cathedral, its circular windows arrayed like portholes on a ship, whilst an exoskeleton of iron girders arced heavenward to support a gleaming glass vault.

"My zoological garden," Mr. Darwin explained, directing Chloe towards a riveted bronze door, evidently the only entrance.

Stepping into the strange edifice, she heard a chorus of tweets and chirps, even as she beheld a tableau of golden sunflowers and blossoming vines. Her nose, meanwhile, admitted fragrances so numerous and heady—cloying, piquant, tart, lemony, rank—she seemed to be inhaling the olfactory essence of Creation itself. "An aviary, is that what you call it?" she asked, noting the little birds perching on the vines, pecking at the sunflowers, and swooping across the crystalline ceiling.

"A more accurate term would be 'vivarium.' This dome is an aviary, herpetorium, and arboretum, all in one."

"Herpetorium?"

"Here be dragons." Mr. Darwin drew her attention to a sector jammed with granite boulders. A troop of large hideous lizards—some bright yellow, others a sallow gray, all sporting spines, scales, and surly faces—lay on a far rock, absorbing the sun. "Land iguanas from *Las Encantadas*, an archipelago six hundred miles off the coast of Ecuador." He rapped his knuckles on a firebox surmounted by a cylindrical boiler. Affixed to the curving walls, the attendant iron pipes pursued a loop apparently meant to supply the vivarium with steam heat. "Thanks to our furnace, these lizards suffer our English winters without complaint."

"*Las Encantadas.*" Chloe hummed the musical syllables. "So it's an enchanted place?"

Mr. Darwin nodded and said, "Sailors of long ago thought the islands went drifting magically about the Pacific Ocean when no one was looking."

He next led Chloe past a palisade of bamboo towards six colossal tortoises: primeval beasts with serpentine necks and plated shells, shambling amidst cactus plants so tall they bid fair to be called trees. The tortoises, too, traced to the Encantadas, he explained. In fact, these animals had given the islands their Spanish name, *Galápagos*.

"I didn't know a tortoise could grow so large," said Chloe.

"Until human beings appeared in the Encantadas, these creatures had no natural enemies, and so they were free to become as big and blatant as they wished."

"How did you acquire such a menagerie?"

"In my youth I joined the company of H.M.S. *Beagle* on its mission to chart the South American coastline. My duty was to provide the skipper with intellectual companionship, though I was nominally the brig's naturalist—a position that, as you see, I took rather seriously. Our mockingbirds descend from bonded pairs I brought back from Galápagos, likewise our finches and vermillion flycatchers. The tortoises and iguanas are the very beasts I persuaded Captain Fitzroy to take on board. His officers were forever insisting we cook a specimen or two, but to the man's credit he wouldn't hear of it."

"How did you snare so many birds?"

"Most Galápagos creatures, including those with wings, are tame as lapdogs." Mr. Darwin guided Chloe to a pond the size of the Adelphi stage. Several varieties of lizard, equal in ugliness to their terrestrial brethren, occupied the limpid depths and surrounding sandstone pylons. "Behold our marine iguanas. Initially I assumed their pond should be topped up with brine, but it happens they also thrive in fresh water. The job will find you helping my gardener, Mr. Kurland, in feeding the reptiles, cultivating the vegetation, providing nesting material for the birds, mucking out the place, and, come winter, supplying the firebox with coal—though your duties will extend to an intangible domain as well. I shall call it 'affection.' Mr. Kurland finds little to admire about my zoo. Mrs. Darwin is similarly unmoved. She thinks the tortoises stupid, the lizards grotesque."

"I shall treat your menagerie most tenderly," said Chloe.

"It's the only point on which Mrs. Darwin and I disagree—well, that, and the immortality of the soul."

"Your wife is a freethinker?"

"Quite the contrary."

"I see."

"She keeps exhorting me to join her and Master Willy and Miss Annie for Sunday services at St. Mary's in the village," said Mr. Darwin. "Alas, I cannot attend in good conscience. At one point my wife convinced the Reverend Mr. Heathway to send me personal invitations via rock dove—the parson and I are both pigeon fanciers—but he gave up after my fifth expression of regret." He rapped his walking-stick against a pylon, prompting its scaled occupant to dive into the pond with a great splash. "It's settled, then—you shall be my assistant zookeeper!"

"May I assume the position comes with a salary?"

"Forgive my forgetfulness," said Mr. Darwin, chiding himself with a smile. "Don't tell Mrs. Darwin, but I mean to pay you what Miss Thorley will receive for tutoring the children, forty pounds every year."

Forty pounds, mused Chloe. Not enough to redeem Papa, and well below the sixty per annum she'd netted during the Adelphi Company's halcyon days, but sufficient for staying alive whilst she devised a strategy for growing rich. "At a yearly rate of forty pounds, I shall give your birds and beasts the best Rousseauian education within my competence."

Mr. Darwin laughed melodically. "Rousseauian, you say? Splendid. We mustn't corrupt these noble animals with civilization."

"Rest assured, I shall never equip an iguana with a pocket watch or send him off to work in a textile mill."

"As for my tortoises—promise me you'll give them no cigars to smoke, spirits to drink, or waistcoats to wear."

"You have my solemn word."

"Miss Bathurst, you are obviously the right woman for the job."

Later that afternoon she took the steam train back to London and retrieved from 15 Tavistock Street her most precious belongings, including her mother-of-pearl combs, her grandfather's bayonet, and the gown of burgundy velvet she'd worn as the dauntless Françoise Gauvin in *The Raft of the Medusa* (she fully intended to return it one day), plus two items that would make splendid gifts for the eldest Darwin children—an Italian snow globe for Master Willy and a French doll representing *Le Petit Chaperon Rouge*, Little Red Riding Hood, for Miss Annie (both tokens from suitors whose names she'd forgotten). The rooms were deserted, Fanny being at the theatre playing Pirate Mary, so Chloe left a note telling of her new situation as an assistant zookeeper and promising to send ten shillings each month. The irony did not escape her. For the past fourteen weeks Fanny had been meeting the landlord's bill *in toto*, and only now, having moved elsewhere, would Chloe be paying her fair share of the rent.

Even after a fortnight of caring for the Down House menagerie, she couldn't say whether she was indeed the right woman for the job, but one fact was clear—Mr. Kurland, a gnarly wight of acerbic disposition, was ill-suited to zookeeping. In his opinion maintaining the vivarium was demeaning work, the brute iguanas and loutish tortoises being ignoble substitutes for the cows and swine he thought he'd been hired to tend, whilst the birds were but "fiendish little devices through which the Devil contrives to squirt shite upon our heads," and so he was happy to let Chloe make the vivarium her exclusive domain.

Naturally Kurland never bothered learning the names Mr. Darwin had given his tortoises—but Chloe soon did: Boswell and Johnson from James Isle, Tristan and Isolde from Charles Isle, Perseus and Androm-eda from Indefatigable. As for the lizards, they had yet to be christened, and so she set about bestowing biblical names on the aquatic iguanas and literary appellations on their terrestrial brethren, a task she performed with all the joy of Adam bringing taxonomy to Paradise.

The economy of the zoological dome, Chloe soon realized, turned on its elaborate network of passionflower vines, as well as its soaring stands of prickly-pear cacti. To nurture the vines, she routinely irrigated the soil with well water, thereby underwriting the survival of the tree-dwelling finches and arboreal mockingbirds, who feasted on the fruits and seeds. The cactus plants required little moisture, but she was obliged to spend many hours protecting the roots from moles—an essential task, for the low-hanging fruits were a favorite food of the tortoises, mocking-birds, and ground-dwelling finches. The land iguanas, meanwhile, pre-ferred a menu of sunflowers, bluebells, and daisies, which she dutifully cultivated throughout the southwest sector.

Although the marine iguanas eagerly consumed the kelp that thrived in the vivarium's pond, under Chloe's administration they learned to ap-preciate whatever produce the Down House cook, Mrs. Davis, whom everyone called Daydy, had deemed unfit owing to spoilage. To augment the tortoises' diet, Chloe again turned to the detritus of Daydy's kitchen. The carapaced reptiles would eat almost anything, from rotting apples to fish eyes, sausage casings to poultry viscera, though they utterly lacked a predatory instinct, cheerfully ignoring the vermillion flycatchers who perched so trustingly on their heads and shells.

Beyond the Sisyphean task of keeping the zoo free of animal waste, the most unsavory of Chloe's duties required her to scour the meadows for the remains of whatever hare, hedgehog, or badger the dogs had run to earth that week. Upon locating a carcass, she would put on canvas gloves, then use a tin pail to bear the foul thing and its attendant load of fly eggs to the vivarium. About half of the emergent maggots were consumed by the ground-dwelling birds, whilst the other half survived to become adult insects, which the flycatchers, true to their name, would snatch on the wing.

And what of Chloe's promise to form emotional bonds with the zoo's denizens? In the case of the birds, affection came easily, for she never tired of watching them hopping amongst the passionflower vines and cactus pads like bejeweled machines wrought by a meticulous wizard. The tortoises likewise charmed her, for they'd become in her imagination a kind of deputation advocating on behalf of all the world's ungainly and misbegotten creatures. For a full two months she regarded the iguanas with distaste, but then they, too, won her over. Unapologetic in their homeliness, unrepentant in their self-absorption, these dragons seemed to be saying, "Love us for what we are, for we shall never be anything else"—and so she did.

Whilst Chloe looked to the welfare of Mr. Darwin's reptiles and birds, Miss Thorley did the same for his offspring. Each morning beginning after breakfast, nine-year-old Willy and seven-year-old Annie learned about the world from their industrious governess. At one o'clock Miss Thorley would deliver Willy and Annie to the kitchen employees for a midday meal, after which the youngsters were free to play with their four siblings in the nursery or (if they so chose) assist Miss Bathurst in the vivarium. For Chloe the advantages of having a private staff were many. The arrangement not only reduced her work load, it also provided the reptiles and birds with a surfeit of nurturance—to say nothing of the fact that Willy and Annie were learning valuable lessons in animal husbandry and waste management.

"I've always been partial to the name 'Annie,'" Chloe told Mr. Darwin's eldest daughter. "In my days as an Adelphi player, I received favorable notices for my interpretation of a pirate called Anne Bonney."

"You were an *actress*, Miss Bathurst?" gushed Annie, a child of sunny disposition and luminous intelligence. (She would never be so foolish as to wish for a wicked stepmother.) "How exciting!"

"I trod the boards for nearly nine years, beginning when I was sixteen." Chloe and Annie were crouched beside the vivarium's furnace, watching Willy use a garden trowel to remove the ashes from the firebox preparatory to supplying it with fresh coal.

"You played a *pirate*?" said the boy with uncharacteristic fervor. (He was normally as gloomy as his sister was effervescent.) "I *like* pirates. Did you ever disembowel anyone?"

"Willy, that's a horrid question," said Annie.

"On the stage I've skewered many a blackguard, but rarely in real life," said Chloe, opening the knapsack containing the children's gifts. "We shall now address a happier topic." From the sack she produced the snow globe and passed it to Willy. Inside the sphere a comical scarlet Satan lounged on a golden throne. "This is for you, Master William."

"Is that the Devil himself?" asked Willy, cleaning his sooty hands by rubbing them on a passionflower leaf. "I love it!" He shook the globe, causing porcelain chips to swirl through the trapped water—the proverbial snowstorm in Hell. "Begone, Lucifer! Willy Darwin has brought you a blizzard!"

"And this is for you, Miss Annie," said Chloe, retrieving the Red Riding Hood doll and pressing it into the child's grasp. The doll's ceramic face—a confluence of ruby lips, apple cheeks, and merry eyes—uncannily mirrored the features of the person in whose possession it now lay.

"How lovely!"

"She comes all the way from France," said Chloe. "*Le Petit Chaperon Rouge.*"

Annie threw her spindly arms about Chloe and kissed her fleetingly on the lips. "Oh, Miss Bathurst, I shall treasure it always. Now if I only had a wolf."

"Tell Father to whittle you one," grumbled Willy. "He does whatever you ask of him."

At this juncture Chloe was tempted to spellbind the children with the lurid and sardonic tale Willy's snow globe inevitably called to mind, Mr. Poe's "Never Bet the Devil Your Head." But then she thought better of the idea, sensing that Mrs. Darwin would not approve, likewise the ghost of Monsieur Rousseau, so instead she simply asked her charges to assist her in dismantling the furnace pipes and purging them of soot.

In time Chloe noted that an irony flourished within the noisy estate she now called home. The Charles Darwin who took such an inordinate interest in earthworms was condemned by certain infirmities to assume the posture of his beloved *annelids*. Although this horizontality doubtless served well for producing children, it surely frustrated his scientific endeavors (the botany projects he pursued in the potting sheds, the pigeon-breeding experiments he conducted in the backyard cote, the barnacle dissections he performed in his study). On his worst days he was up and about for only two or three hours, after which, beset by a wracking headache and a high fever, he took to his couch, not far from the basin that, owing to his spells of vomiting, he was obliged to keep at hand, occluded by a Chinese screen.

Not surprisingly, he rarely left the villa. Only once that autumn did he go to London, where he bought a cameo brooch for Mrs. Darwin and attended a meeting of the Geological Society. He much preferred that his colleagues come to him—and come they did. Amongst the illustrious visitors to Down House were the virile young botanist Mr. Joseph Hooker, recently returned from an expedition to the Antarctic, the affable Mr. John Gould, England's greatest ornithologist, and the crusty Professor Charles Lyell, celebrated throughout Her Majesty's realm for his *Principles of Geology* (a book that, as Mr. Darwin remarked to Chloe, "will be favorably impressing its readers even after the mountains for which it so eloquently accounts have turned to dust"). Occasionally the scientific triumvirate of Hooker, Gould, and Lyell spent the night, but usually they made a day trip of it, staying only long enough to partake of an afternoon meal. Because these luncheons normally occurred in the vivarium, Chloe oft-times found herself eavesdropping on the sages' conversation (understanding but a fraction of what she heard), meanwhile pursuing her zookeeping tasks and supervising the children as they rode about the dome astride the tortoises like sheiks on camels.

Gradually it dawned on her that the master of Down House was no less renowned than Professor Lyell, thanks largely to his book chronicling his journey around the world. When Chloe asked Mr. Darwin if she might peruse *The Voyage of the Beagle*, he lent her a copy of the third edition. Every night, upon retiring to her little room, she read another chapter. Having scant interest in coral reefs, barrier beaches, silicified trees, sea slugs, cuttlefish, or fossil quadrupeds, she skipped the sections treating of these subjects, savoring instead the scenes in which Mr. Darwin held center stage. In his youth he'd been quite the adventurer, galloping with gauchos across the Pampas, hacking his way through a Patagonian jungle seething with hostile Indians, and traversing the Andes on a mule. He'd survived a volcano in Chile, an earthquake in Concepción, and the mountainous seas off Cape Horn, which had nearly capsized his ship.

But the most striking passages in *The Voyage of the Beagle* were the author's fiery denunciations of chattel slavery, an institution Chloe herself had come to detest whilst appearing as the Southern belle Pansy Winslow in *Lanterns on the Levee*. "On the 19th of August we finally left the shores of Brazil," Mr. Darwin wrote in the final chapter. "I thank God I shall never again visit a slave-country. To this day, if I hear a distant scream, it recalls with painful vividness my feelings when, passing a house near Pernambuco, I heard the most pitiable moans, and could not but suspect that some poor slave was being tortured." And then, a paragraph later, "These deeds are done by men who profess to love their neighbors as themselves, who believe in God, and pray that His will be done on Earth! It makes one's blood boil, yet heart tremble, to think that we Englishmen and our American descendants, with their boastful cry of liberty, have been and are so guilty."

The sacred imperatives of the Sermon on the Mount versus the sordid institution of the Christian slave trade: so it appeared that Chloe's employer, like she herself, was attuned to irony—a coincidence she planned to exploit to her father's advantage. Here we are, sir, the most civilized nation on Earth, sending innocent folk to abominable workhouses, as if they'd deliberately arranged to be poor. One might as well imprison a malaria victim for having the audacity to run a fever. Do you not agree?

She wondered what sum Mr. Darwin might be persuaded to donate to Papa's deliverance. Certainly not the whole two thousand pounds. (A man will spend that much in acquiring a house but not on assuaging his indignation.) Perhaps she could convince him to part with two hundred. It is beyond your powers to liberate the Brazilian slaves, she would argue, and the American slaves as well, but you *can* help to save one blameless wretch from death by toil. Contribute to my fund, sir, and God will reward you with your first good night's sleep in years.

On the twentieth day in April, 1849, Mr. Darwin sponsored at Down House a luncheon of particular import, for this would be his last opportunity to see Mr. Hooker prior to the swashbuckling botanist's departure on yet another plant collecting adventure. Chloe spent the morning mucking out the zoological dome, whilst Daydy passed the same interval preparing roasted joints of lamb, plus puréed turnips, stewed spinach, and broiled mushrooms.

Upon their arrival, Mr. Darwin conducted the scientific triumvirate towards the vivarium. Parslow the butler followed with a salver holding ginger biscuits and three bottles of sherry wine. Entering the contrived jungle, Mr. Gould and Professor Lyell acknowledged the children with friendly waves—Master Willy was riding Johnson the tortoise, and Miss Annie had just mounted Isolde—whilst Mr. Hooker, as prepossessing as ever behind his spectacles, favored Chloe with an amiable wink.

Shortly after the guests assumed their places at the linen-draped table, Mr. Gould and Mr. Hooker began conversing about a noxious phenomenon on which the *Evening Standard* had been reporting for the past four months. It concerned the Percy Bysshe Shelley Society: a band of young, wealthy, sybaritic Oxford graduates who'd recently acquired for their debauches a private manse in the heart of town. Under the guidance of Lord Rupert Woolfenden, the twenty Byssheans were staging at Alastor Hall a competition whereby they would award an immense cash prize of £10,000 to the first scholar, scientist, or theologian who could prove, or disprove, the existence of God.

"What a scandalous project," said the dour Professor Lyell, who'd evidently not heard of the prize despite its being, in Mr. Hooker's words, "the talk of all London."

"I quite agree," said the roly-poly Mr. Gould, pouring a glass of oloroso. "Though the problem is not without a certain, shall we say, philosophical interest?"

"From my own perusal of the late Mr. Shelley, I infer that he possessed a first-rate mind." Mr. Hooker availed himself of the amontillado. "True, it was reckless of him to write 'On the Necessity of Atheism,' though I feel that, in sending Shelley down for it, the University College officials displayed a decided want of imagination."

Chloe's first instinct was to hustle Willy and Annie out of the zoo, lest they learn prematurely there was such a thing as atheism, but she elected to stay, partly because the children seemed oblivious to the scientists' chatter but mostly because the phrase "ten thousand pounds" held an intrinsic allure. After settling down beside the iguana pond, she distributed her attention amongst five activities: minding her charges, sipping tea, eating hard-boiled eggs, pretending to read a pamphlet titled *The Fruit Farmer's Guide to Mole Management,* and listening furtively to the gentlemen's conversation.

"You know what this damnable prize amounts to?" said Lyell, filling his glass with Manzanilla. "It's a ten-thousand-pound bounty on the head of God."

"Judas got but thirty pieces of silver," said Hooker in a tone Chloe thought oddly jocular given the seriousness of the subject.

"One might assume that on first principles these Oxford rakehells would skew the competition towards the atheist view," said Gould, "and yet by the *Standard*'s account they happily entertain arguments on the Almighty's behalf."

"But how do they sort the robust proofs of God from the feeble?" asked Lyell.

"The same way they sort the substantive refutations from the trivial," said Gould, sipping his wine. "Each contestant makes his case before a panel comprising three Anglican and three freethinking judges. The whole sorry circus convenes every fortnight, with a preselected theist and a corresponding unbeliever traveling to Oxford and presenting their arguments." The ornithologist clamped a friendly hand on Mr. Darwin's knee. "Charles, you've been strangely silent concerning the Great God Contest. Are you not outraged that these *flâneurs* would turn theology into a game?"

"Nowadays I make a point of abstaining from outrage," Mr. Darwin replied. "It's bad for the digestion. That said, I feel bound to reveal that, were I to conduct the judges about my little zoo, I might very well collect the prize, provided they understood my commentary."

"I'll wager I could understand it," said Hooker, savoring his sherry. "Pray tell, sir, what manner of God proof lurks within your menagerie?"

"Charles has in mind the Argument from Design," said Lyell. "William Paley's *Natural Theology* and all that. No watch without a watchmaker."

"You misunderstand me, gentlemen," said Mr. Darwin, biting into a ginger biscuit. "I would win the contest by *negating* the Deity."

Somehow Chloe prevented a mouthful of tea from reversing direction and spouting out her nose.

"Piffle," said Lyell.

"Needless to say, I have no intention of *entering* the competition," Mr. Darwin declared. "For one thing, my wife would never hear of it."

"And for another, you'd be violating your own religious convictions," said Lyell.

"Up to a point," said Mr. Darwin with a raffish smile.

"Charles, you hold us on tenterhooks," said Gould. "Please explain yourself."

"I cannot explain myself—only God, wherever He may be, can do that—but I shall attempt to explain my theory." Mr. Darwin brushed biscuit crumbs from his lower lip. "Look about you, gentlemen, and you'll see the Encantadas replicated on a small scale. A question springs to mind. Why did God treat each Galápagos island as if it were—almost, but not quite—a biologically sovereign realm? Why did He install slim-beaked warbler finches on Albemarle Isle but large-beaked ground finches on Chatham? Why do the tortoises on the northern islands have shells suggesting igloos, whilst the specimens on the southern islands have shells resembling saddles, and the centrally located creatures wear simple sloping shells? What's more, when we travel to other equatorial archipelagos, why do we meet no reptiles or birds that mirror the Galápagos types?"

"Scintillating questions," said Gould.

"As an analogy," said Hooker, "I've often wondered why the Kerguelan cabbage, quite the most ridiculous of vegetables, flourishes in the Indian Ocean but nowhere else."

"Simply because God initially laid down a template for every species, that doesn't preclude the emergence of variations, even ridiculous variations," said Lyell. "When I consider how the Almighty built a benign plasticity into the scheme of things, my faith is renewed, not shaken."

"Spend a moment contemplating three marine iguanas from different Galápagos islands," Mr. Darwin persisted, "and a conundrum presents itself. So utterly distinctive, these creatures, and yet so fundamentally similar. Miss Bathurst, will you please show us some living illustrations of this mystery?"

Startled to be drawn into the conversation, Chloe dropped the hard-boiled egg she was about to peel. "Certainly, sir," she said as the egg wobbled away. Gaining her feet, she stretched her arms over the iguana pond like a heathen priestess blessing its waters. "That red aquatic lizard is Jezebel from Hood's Isle. Note also black Melchior from Tower. Our big multicolored fellow is Shadrack from Narborough."

"Three separate addresses, three kinds of coloration, utterly distinctive, fundamentally similar," said Mr. Darwin. "And then one day, following the orbit of my sandwalk, I fell upon an answer. Like every other lizard known to science, the first iguanas to live in Galápagos were strictly terrestrial—but over the ages some colonies found it expedient to inhabit the archipelago's coastlines, drawing sustenance from the sea. This natural transmutation process continued even after these iguanas became full-blown aquatic creatures, hence our red, black, and multicolored species. A similar story might be told of the three varieties of Galápagos giant tortoise. For example, Miss Bathurst?"

Though once again caught off guard, she rose to the occasion, indicating the nearest tortoise with her index finger. "Domeshelled Boswell from James Isle"—she pivoted and pointed—"saddle-backed Tristan from Charles Isle"—again she pointed—"slope-backed Perseus from Indefatigable."

"Boswell, Tristan, and Perseus: all reasonably good swimmers and thus arguably sharing an ancestor that, once upon a time, inhabited South America," said Mr. Darwin. "By riding the Humboldt Current westward from the mainland, one or two small but seaworthy tortoises could have reached the Encantadas, where in time their descendants became huge, for if no other animal regards you as prey, it matters not how conspicuous you appear. I would further hypothesize that our bright yellow, flat-spined terrestrial iguanas, found on a majority of islands, share a South American heritage with our sallow gray, high-spined iguanas, exclusive to Barrington."

"So your terrestrial iguanas can *also* swim?" asked Hooker.

"Not very well, but that doesn't tell against my theory. The ancestors of our land lizards could have traveled from the continent to Galápagos on uprooted trees or floating mats of vegetation." Mr. Darwin moved his flattened hand up and down as would a raft adrift on ocean waves, then fluttered the fingers of the opposite hand in a pantomime of flight. "Now what of our birds? The anatomical evidence suggests that all four Galápagos mockingbird species sprang from a long-tailed type that flew over from Ecuador or Peru. In the case of our vermillion flycatchers, I believe that during my round-the-world journey I spotted the parent kind on the South American mainland, broader of wing than its Encantadas posterity and gifted with a heartier song. As for my finches, they're probably all descended from a continental species called the blue-black grass-quit."

"I could provide the judges with stuffed specimens of that very creature," said Gould, draining his glass. "Not that I would ever make a bid for the Shelley Prize," he added, so vehemently that Chloe thought perhaps he meant the opposite.

"I'm hearing Buffon's idea of allied species sharing a pedigree," said Lyell. "I'm hearing Lamarck's notion of evolution through the inheritance of acquired characteristics. But neither hypothesis constitutes a disproof of the God of Abraham."

"Not only do our two species of terrestrial iguana boast an ancestor in common with our aquatic iguanas," Mr. Darwin continued in a tone of constrained exasperation, "but were you to travel back far enough in time, you would encounter an extinct creature that prefigured *every* variety of iguana to be found *anywhere* in the world. These primal lizards shared the Earth with primal turtles, primal snakes, and primal *Crocodylia*, all of them in turn sprung from a species of cold-blooded, egg-laying, scaly-skinned animal."

Mr. Gould switched allegiances, oloroso to Manzanilla. "An archetypal reptile? How intriguing."

"Not *archetypal*, John, nothing so poetic and Platonic as all that," said Mr. Darwin. "For it happens that our originary reptile in turn traces to a mutable stock of proto-reptiles."

"So where does it all end?" asked Hooker.

"You mean, 'Where does it all begin?' By my lights the natural history of our planet is like a fantastically complex shrub or tree. Follow the twigs, and you'll come to the branches, that is, to the first types of mammal, reptile, amphibian, and fish. But why stop there? Why not scurry along the branches until we reach the trunk, where we'll meet the most primitive lineages yet, ancestral insects, crustaceans, mollusks, amoebas, and algae. The journey continues, ever downward, until finally, at the base of the trunk, we come upon a single, seminal form. Need I point out that we've long since parted company with Genesis chapter one? And there's the rub, gentlemen. If God played no role in the cavalcade of life on Earth, from protozoans to primates, it behooves us to wonder why He goes to all the bother of existing."

"Good heavens, Charles, you really *do* have a shot at the Shelley Prize," said Hooker. "If I were an Alastor Hall rakehell, I'd be impressed."

"My desire to impress those *poseurs* is nil. Ah, but here comes Parslow. Let us forget my eccentric speculations and enjoy Daydy's culinary arts."

The butler entered the vivarium pushing a tea cart laden with the feast. Speaking not a word, he deposited generous portions of lamb and vegetables on each guest's plate.

"Come, come, Charles, is your Tree of Life really so outlandish an idea?" said Hooker. "Did not your illustrious grandfather Erasmus posit that all warm-blooded creatures arose from a single filament?"

"That estimable savant could describe no *mechanism* of transmutation," Mr. Darwin asserted, then added, clucking his tongue, "but I can."

"So can the Church of England," said Lyell.

"Tell us about your mechanism," said Hooker.

"I'd rather not. It's like confessing a murder."

"You're amongst friends," said Gould. "We'll help you bury the body."

"First lunch, then deicide," said Mr. Darwin.

By Chloe's reckoning it took the sages a mere thirty minutes to consume a meal that the staff had spent four hours preparing. Whilst the gentlemen ate, the children dutifully amused themselves, Willy ensnaring a cactus plant with the *bola* his father had brought back from Patagonia, Annie enacting a conversation between her Red Riding Hood doll and its lupine nemesis. (Mr. Darwin had indeed whittled a wolf for his eldest daughter, cloaking it in the dry and scraped pelt of a Derbyshire hare.) No sooner had the sages cleaned their plates than Parslow appeared, carrying a tray of puddings and a bottle of port.

"I'm eager to hear about your momentous crime," Hooker told the master of Down House, whereupon the butler blanched and hastily withdrew.

"I'll begin by making a naïve observation," said Mr. Darwin. "Within any sexually reproducing population, the offspring vary, yes? My Annie, my Henrietta, and my Betty are not duplicates of Mrs. Darwin, nor do they mirror one another. In this phenomenon lies the success of those who seek to improve domestic livestock. Chance provides the breeder with unsolicited novelties that he proceeds to exploit, selecting who shall mate with whom—and thus perpetuating desirable characteristics. And so we get horses faster and stronger than their ancestors, sheep with thicker fleece, and cows of greater fecundity. I contend that, just as a man might produce a superior pig by design, so might Nature craft a better boar by accident."

"But how, Charles—*how?*" asked Gould, eating a forkful of apple tart.

"Our planet is forever in flux. Even as we speak, the Earth's face is changing through natural processes of erosion, sedimentation, and vulcanism. If that canny geologist Lyell were here, he would corroborate me."

"Pass the cherry tart," said Lyell with a pained smile.

"From an individual animal's perspective, every alteration in its environment must be greeted with grave suspicion," said Mr. Darwin. "Ofttimes the creature finds itself standing by helplessly as temperatures plunge, food supplies diminish, plagues appear, and enemies flourish. But occasionally Nature favors an endangered population, gifting a few offspring with characteristics not only fortuitous but fortunate—a luxuriant pelt, equal to the harshest winter; a mighty jaw, stronger than the toughest nut; a hearty constitution, able to survive epidemics; elongated limbs, crucial for outpacing predators. Compared to their cousins, these lucky juveniles are more likely to survive into adulthood, find mates—"

"And pass along the felicitous trait!" interrupted Hooker. "What a pretty hypothesis!"

"Eventually the modification spreads through the population, giving rise to a new variety, type, race, or species," said Mr. Darwin. "Whilst conducting the judges about my zoo, I would bid them notice the broad, flat tail of Shadrack the marine iguana, essential for propelling him towards his underwater kelp dinner. Did Shadrack's parents have such an appendage? Most probably, which is why they lived long enough to make Shadrack. His distant round-tailed relations, however, lacked this advantage, and so they lost what the Reverend Thomas Malthus famously called 'the struggle for existence.'"

"I must say, sir—your argument enjoys the merit of logic," said Gould.

"As did Satan's presentation to our Savior," said Lyell. "Forgive me, Charles. I didn't mean to compare you to the Devil."

"Nor yourself to Christ, I trust," said Mr. Darwin.

The geologist scowled, licking cherry juice from his lips.

"What other adaptations would you commend to the judges' attention?" asked Gould.

"The sturdy beaks of our ground-dwelling finches," Mr. Darwin replied, "ideal for penetrating the fruits on which they feed. The slim beaks of our warbler finches, perfect for extracting insects from trees. The long bills of our Hood's Isle mockingbirds, useful for cracking open nutritious booby eggs in their native habitat. The short bills of our Chatham mockingbirds, suited to consuming the *palo santo* seeds that sustained them back home. Finally, the arched shells of our saddleback tortoises, a modification that enabled them to reach the higher fruits on their beloved Charles Isle cactus plants."

"Have you committed your theory to paper?" asked Hooker.

Mr. Darwin snapped his fingers in the same emphatic fashion that had heralded his decision to offer Chloe a situation at Down House. "Miss Bathurst, would you please go to my study and rummage about in the desk, left side, lower drawer? You'll find a sketch of thirty-five pages titled 'An Essay Concerning Descent with Modification.'"

"I'll fetch it straightaway, sir," said Chloe, setting down her tea.

"No, I don't want the sketch. Retrieve what lies beneath—a manuscript called *Towards a Theory of Natural Selection*. In your absence I shall mind the children."

"As you might imagine, I have mounds of questions," said Hooker. "The problem of blending, for example. If a male marine iguana boasting a powerful tail mates with a female of more feeble extension, wouldn't their offspring inherit mediocre tails?"

"Not to mention the problem of time," said Lyell. "The drama you're describing would have taken many millions of years to unfold. Can our planet truly be so ancient? I'm delighted that my book made buttered eggs of Bishop Ussher's six-thousand-year-old Earth, but really, sir, you're talking about a considerable slice of eternity."

"Then there's the problem of Man," said Gould. "Are you impish enough to apply this theory to *our* origins? Yes, Charles, you wily son of a monkey, I believe you are."

"Excellent questions, all three, and quite possibly fatal to the theory of natural selection," said Mr. Darwin. "Let me offer my provisional answers."

Chloe left the zoological dome in a state of frothing frustration, for she greatly desired to know how Mr. Darwin would address the objections raised by the scientific triumvirate. Anyone wishing to claim the Shelley Prize with a disproof of God—herself, for example—must be prepared to speak of blending, time, and Man. This hypothetical contestant could not allow a pious judge to wreck her case by appealing to regressive lizard-tails, a young planet, or a Supreme Being's decision to bless His favorite creatures with rational intellects.

Of course, she had no intention of simply stealing her employer's theory. That would be wrong. Also, it might not work. After all, she'd comprehended barely half of what Mr. Darwin had told his guests, so it was likely that, unless she received instruction from the master transmutationist himself, the Anglican judges at Alastor Hall would succeed in befuddling her. No, the ideal scheme would find her traveling to Oxford only after Mr. Darwin had endorsed her project and tutored her in the nuances of his disproof.

Entering the study, she found the manuscript in the specified location, nestled beneath the crumpled, tea-stained, thirty-five-page sketch from which it had descended. She snatched up *Towards a Theory of Natural Selection* and scurried away, leaving "An Essay Concerning Descent with Modification" in place. By the time she was back in the vivarium, Mr. Darwin had dispensed with blending, time, and Man. Now he was talking about crustaceans.

"That's right, Joseph. The male of the Chonos Isles barnacle has two organs of procreation."

"Two?" said Mr. Hooker. "I find it difficult enough maintaining one."

Catching sight of Chloe, Mr. Darwin cut the conversation short with an embarrassed laugh. "Ah, Miss Bathurst, *there* you are. Kindly deliver my theory to our botanist."

She quirked Mr. Hooker a smile and placed the pages in his grasp.

"Impressive," he said, leafing through the manuscript. "But I shan't have time to read it ere I embark for India."

"Take it with you, Joseph," said Mr. Darwin. "Last month I paid a scrivener to transcribe a fair copy, which I keep under lock and key. I've instructed Emma to publish it upon my death. Were you to mislay these pages, I shouldn't count the loss a tragedy."

"Nevertheless, I shall endeavor to protect them," said Hooker.

"Charles, you've found a convert," said Gould.

"I'm scarcely converted," said Hooker. "Merely curious."

"Miss Bathurst, I suspect you found our scientific chatter impossibly tedious," said Mr. Darwin.

"*Au contraire,* I thought the conversation entrancing," she said.

"Such a sweet girl you've hired, Charles," said Lyell in a treacly tone. "I'll wager she's intelligent, too. I pray you, Miss Bathurst, give us your opinion of this Tree of Life business."

"May I speak freely, sir?"

"Of course," said Lyell.

"I think Mr. Darwin's idea makes a ripping good yarn," said Chloe, acting the part of a person who understood transmutationism. "As to its truth or falsity, I am not competent to venture a conclusion—but I must say I shan't ever look at a finch's beak, a mockingbird's bill, a tortoise's shell, or a lizard's tail in quite the same way again."

And with that the four gentlemen issued merry guffaws and returned to their pudding, though Professor Lyell laughed last and ate least.

3

We Meet the Reverend Malcolm Chadwick, a Man of Limber Frame and Nimble Mind, Before Whom Atheists Quake and Skeptics Grow Dyspeptic

In the weeks that followed her accidental encounter with the theory of natural selection, Chloe performed her Down House duties with particular diligence, scrupulously nourishing, nurturing, and mucking up after Mr. Darwin's menagerie—but she worked even harder on her days off. Every Tuesday afternoon she slipped into the village, entered the Queens Head Inn, and culled through discarded copies of the *Evening Standard*, eager to learn the latest exploits of the Percy Bysshe Shelley Society. According to Jasper Popplewell, the journalist who regularly reported on the Great God Contest, "the Almighty has been neither vanquished nor validated at Alastor Hall," and the £10,000 remained unclaimed.

Equally encouraging to Chloe was her discovery that, although the London-based administrator of the Shelley Prize refused to allow the common run of applicant to take his proof or disproof to Oxford (lest the Byssheans be subjected to the rants of fanatics and the ravings of cranks), that same worthy normally blessed any argument that turned on tangible artifacts—and what could be more tangible than a broad-tailed marine iguana or a slim-beaked warbler finch? In one especially arresting presentation, a version of the Argument from Miracles, a Northumberland bishop had paraded "a collection of discarded crutches and abandoned Bath chairs before the judges, graphic testaments to the Creator's healing hand." The petitioner did not prosper, the freethinking judges noting that the vast majority of prayers on behalf of the halt and the lame went unanswered. But what most struck Chloe was the hopeful bishop's employment of physical props. A crutch was a truly vivid thing, though hardly more vivid than the egg-cracking bill of a Hood's Isle mockingbird.

In another notable albeit unsuccessful submission, an attempted "refutation of the Jehovah hypothesis," a Chelmsford apothecary had taken Saint Anselm's Ontological Proof—because one can conceive of a Perfect Being, such an entity necessarily exists, actualities being *ipso facto* superior to ideas—and turned it on its head. The apothecary had prepared a diagram, dense with mathematical formulae, allegedly demonstrating that "the only thing more astonishing than a universe created by a *bona fide* supernatural being would be a universe created by a nonexistent supernatural being." Surely this chart, reasoned Chloe, though rendered in the boldest strokes and brightest colors, had not been more compelling than the arched carapace of a Charles Isle saddleback tortoise.

Two days after Mr. Darwin acquired a new microscope for his barnacle studies, built especially for him from a French prototype, Chloe resolved to confront him with her plan, figuring that the instrument had put him in a good humor. She found him in his study, alternately smoking a cigarette and enlarging the latest object of his curiosity. "A freshwater clam," he explained, pointing to the microscope stage. "It arrived this morning from a Greenwich naturalist who shares my fascination with the means by which aquatic invertebrates are dispersed from their birth sites. He mailed me the clam along with a diving beetle to whose leg it was attached. Thanks to the offices of that insect, this clam may have traveled a full three miles from home, eventually reaching the bend in the creek from which my friend retrieved both vehicle and rider."

"And they survived the ordeal of postal delivery?" asked Chloe.

"The clam is doing splendidly. The beetle, alas, arrived suffering from terminal dehydration." Mr. Darwin clutched his stomach, doubtless to palliate his nausea, then indicated a jar on his desk. "I sealed the creature therein, then added a dram of hydrogen cyanide, that he might know a quick death. Aren't you supposed to be in the vivarium, Miss Bathurst?"

"Please, sir, if you could spare me a moment of your time."

"Heaven forbid I should accord greater consideration to a beetle than to my assistant zookeeper."

She began by reporting on a misadventure recently endured by Perseus of Indefatigable (her Trojan tortoise, she decided, the ploy by which she would redirect Mr. Darwin's attention from invertebrates to herself), explaining that on the previous evening the creature had slipped off a boulder and injured his leg—though with Master Willy's assistance she'd successfully bandaged the limb. When Mr. Darwin issued an approving *hmmmm*, she asked him whether, "transmutationally speaking," Perseus with his intermediate carapace was more closely related to Boswell the domeshell or Isolde the saddleback. The ruse worked. Her employer forgot his clam, stepped away from his microscope, and proffered a warm smile. "Marvelous question, Miss Bathurst. Alas, my theory is not yet so refined as to provide a definite answer."

"Even in its present state, your idea is quite the most exciting I've ever encountered. If it were a novel, it would be *The Mysteries of Udolpho*."

"Really now?" Mr. Darwin lifted an eyebrow, evidently uncertain whether her aim was praise or flattery.

"It's so excellent a conjecture, in fact, that with your permission I shall submit it to the Shelley Society."

He scowled and said, "I think not."

"Naturally I intend to credit you in full and turn over the greater part of the prize, seven thousand pounds, keeping but three thousand for my troubles."

"And what troubles might those be?"

"Mastering your species theory, rehearsing my presentation, transporting the illustrative birds and beasts to Oxford."

"Am I to infer you're an atheist, Miss Bathurst?"

She leaned towards the microscope and surveyed its amorphous occupant, which the device had enlarged to the size of a tuppence. "You should infer merely that I'm prepared to *portray* an atheist, if I might thereby keep my father out of debtors' prison. The Jehovah hypothesis holds no interest for me one way or the other."

Grasping his tweezers, Mr. Darwin transferred the clam from the microscope stage to a dish of water. "What you're suggesting is out of the question."

"I take your point, sir. Permit me to offer you *eight* thousand pounds, retaining for myself a mere two, the sum I need to save Papa from his creditors."

"No, Miss Bathurst, my *point* has eluded you. The theory of natural selection is not for sale." Mr. Darwin pulled a handkerchief from his waistcoat, wiping his fevered brow like a barman mopping up a splash of ale. "Let me add that I'm sympathetic to your father's plight. Is he really two thousand pounds in arrears? That's only twenty more than I paid for this estate. How does a man squander so much money?"

"Phineas Bathurst is forever accomplishing feats that would daunt the average mortal. You may be sure the bulk of his debt traces to philanthropy, not prodigality."

"I shall contribute two hundred pounds to whatever fund you've dedicated to his salvation," Mr. Darwin promised.

Chloe sucked filaments of air through her clenched teeth. Two hundred pounds—the precise figure that, after pondering the tender abolitionist soul who'd written *The Voyage of the Beagle*, she'd imagined him donating. "May I make a suggestion? Allow me to become fluent in transmutationism. I shall carry the argument to Alastor Hall, ascribing it to an English naturalist who wishes to remain anonymous. Mr. Popplewell will duly report on my performance. If your theory proves palatable to a majority of *Evening Standard* subscribers and furthermore elicits the admiration of those readers who consider themselves scientists—"

"And also wins the prize."

"And also wins the prize, you'll be free to step forward and claim authorship of the most important idea in the history of biology. As for myself, I would expect no more than twenty percent compensation."

"Miss Bathurst, I am out of patience with you."

"I had no wish to give offense, sir."

Taking hold of the beetle jar, Mr. Darwin held it up to the bay window and contemplated the doomed inhabitant. "Let there be no ambiguity in this matter. My mockingbirds, finches, reptiles, and brain are not now, nor will they ever be, at your disposal. Export them beyond Down House, and you'll have made an enemy of a person who would be your benefactor."

"I understand, sir."

"Might I offer some advice, Miss Bathurst?" Pivoting towards his desk, Mr. Darwin set down the jar, apparently satisfied that the beetle had passed away. "Forget this blasted competition, embrace the Jehovah hypothesis, and pray that your father lives to see his creditors dead and buried. And now you will return to your duties."

What other choice did she have? None, by her own reckoning. How many better paths lay before her? Zero, she ruefully concluded. Just as Pirate Anne was forced to abandon her baby on the steps of a monastery, so was Chloe now obliged to appropriate the transmutation sketch under cover of night and spirit it back to her room, there to transcribe all thirty-five pages ere they were missed.

She laid the groundwork of her scheme with excruciating care, clearing the clutter from her writing-desk and equipping it with certain essentials she'd acquired by milking her purse dry at Creigar & Sons, Stationers—a stack of blank paper, a fountain pen, two nibs, three pots of ink—plus four candles obtained from Parslow on the pretext that she intended to stay up late reading *The Count of Monte Cristo*. She wriggled into her burgundy-velvet *Raft of the Medusa* gown, the better to blend with the darkness, then put on slippers, the better to mute her tread, and irrigated her throat with barley water, lest she betray herself with a cough.

By midnight the household was deathly still, Mr. Darwin and his wife having retired to their bed-chambers, the children sleeping soundly, the servants snoring noisily, the dogs whimpering in their dreams. Step by silent step Chloe crept down the hall and, at one with the night, slithered into the study. A batten of moonlight streamed through the bay window, bright enough to illuminate her deed without betraying it. The lower-left desk drawer protested her knavery, squeaking more loudly than when she'd obtained the full-blown treatise for Mr. Hooker, but at last "An Essay Concerning Descent with Modification" glided into view. Holding her breath, she removed the pages with the dexterity of a pickpocket. She exhaled, swallowed hard, and eased the drawer back into place.

Above the throbbing of her heart and the chugging of her lungs a second noise arose, the creak of human footfalls. She dropped to her knees and, crawling like an iguana, hid behind the couch. Cautiously she peered into the gloom. A flame floated across the study, followed by the extended arm of Mr. Darwin, dressed in a silk robe and holding a candle, its radiance enhanced by a globe. With the aid of his walking-stick he shuffled towards his bookcase and, setting his lamp on the reading table, slid a thick novel from the shelf. Only after he was ensconced in his overstuffed chair, poring over Mr. Thackeray's *The Luck of Barry Lyndon*, did Chloe play the lizard again and, manuscript in hand, exit softly on all fours.

Once back in the servants' quarters, she lit the candles, then enacted her plan with the ticking efficiency of a trainman's watch. The pen nib skittered across the page, neatly replicating Mr. Darwin's sentences, each character crisply formed. No bleary-eyed medieval monk transcribing Scripture had ever accorded a text greater fealty. She never wrote "maladoptive" when the word was "maladaptive," never "evaluation" instead of "evolution."

To Chloe's immense satisfaction, the essay addressed the thorny questions raised by the luncheon guests. Why were random but felicitous advantages—and random but pathological disadvantages—not diluted through blending? Because if inheritance worked that way, then familial diseases such as hemophilia would have long since disappeared. Why should we think our planet old enough for natural selection to have worked such wonders? Because the more closely geologists pondered mountains, valleys, deserts, and seabeds, the more testaments they saw to a vast antiquity. Was the theory of transmutation so all-inclusive as to embrace Man himself? On this point, the author was adamant. Consider our vestigial anatomical features. Consider our resemblance to apes. There was never an Eden, a talking serpent, a fall from grace. Eve was a fiction. Adam be damned.

At long last, her second ink-pot almost drained and her energies all but depleted, she copied out the final paragraph.

There is grandeur in this view of life, with its powers of growth, assimilation, and reproduction having been originally breathed into one or a few kinds, and that whilst this our planet has gone circling according to fixed laws, and whilst land and water, in a cycle of change, have gone on replacing each other, that from so simple an origin, through processes of gradual selection and infinitesimal modifications, endless forms most beautiful and most wonderful have been evolved.

She had merely won a battle, of course. There remained the matter of the war. Victory would be hers only after she'd gathered up palpable proofs of transmutation—secure in their adaptive shells, proud of their strong tails, pleased with their useful beaks—and displayed them before the judges. Whence would come this evidence? A momentous question, but not one her weary brain was required to answer this night.

She blew out the candles, then huddled protectively over the essay's moist, newborn twin. For reasons not readily apparent, her favorite speech from Mr. Jerrold's *Wicked Ichor* popped into her mind. "We live in the shadows, cast out of Christendom, fleeing the cross," said Carmine the vampire, as interpreted by Chloe, to her fellow undead brides. "And yet we ask no man's pity, for 'tis not mere blood we seek but the thrill of mocking the cosmos. Will you look yourselves in the eye, dear sisters, and deny that this be true?"

When at last the pages were dry, she wrapped them in her woolen scarf and hid the bundle beneath her pillow. Let us be honest, she told herself. Not mere blood but the thrill. Not just the purse but the praise. Will you look yourself in the eye, dear Chloe, and deny that this be true?

Moving stealthily towards the study, sketch in hand, Chloe apprehended a pleasing sound, the cadence of Mr. Darwin's snores. She approached the desk on tiptoe, grasping the handle of the lower-left drawer. The sleeper stirred but did not awaken. His lamp, nearly spent, emitted the aura of a sickly glow-worm. She gave the drawer a tug, then immediately wished she hadn't, for the compartment squealed like a frightened pig.

"Who's there?" demanded Mr. Darwin.

She froze—a futile gesture, immobility being a poor approximation of invisibility. The essay rattled in her fingers. Blood thundered in her ears. Involuntarily she relaxed her grasp. The thirty-five pages cascaded to the desktop and lay still, shimmering silently in the moonlight, exhibit number one in her forthcoming trial for intellectual larceny.

"Remain silent," said Mr. Darwin firmly. "You're a clever girl with your tongue, and I want no commerce with that organ right now. Nod if you understand."

She nodded.

"Mere words could never mitigate this act."

Again she nodded.

Suddenly he was by her side, leaning on his walking-stick as he gathered up the scattered sheets. "Your offense could not be clearer. Against my explicit instructions you slipped in here and appropriated my essay. Your intention, no doubt, was to take these pages back to your room and copy them ere they were missed."

Chloe nodded a third time—not a mendacious reply, she decided: prior to copying the pages, she had indeed intended to do so.

"My responsibility to this household is self-evident," Mr. Darwin continued. "I cannot abide so reckless a schemer beneath my roof. Tomorrow you must delegate your zookeeping duties to Mr. Kurland, as you will be leaving Down House the following day." He secured the essay beneath the beetle jar. "Until the hour of your departure, I shall hide my sketch in a place you would never dream of looking—and the same goes for the scrivener's copy of the longer treatise. Do you understand why I'm compelled to banish you? You may talk now."

"I understand," she rasped, a tear trickling down her cheek.

"I am sorry, Miss Bathurst. Truly."

She swallowed audibly. "I shall miss Master Willy and Miss Annie."

"I know. They speak highly of you."

"Now that I think on it, I shall also miss our lizards and tortoises."

Mr. Darwin caressed the beetle jar. "I realize this was not a common burglary, nor are you a common burglar. Should you find another situation involving either reptiles or children, I shall say nothing of this incident to your new employer. Moreover, I intend to place two months' pay in your pocket ere you depart."

"I don't deserve your generosity, but I shall accept it."

From his robe Mr. Darwin produced a packet of cigarettes, then removed one stick and inserted it between his lips. "Attend my every syllable," he said, his voice grown cold again. "Beginning on Sunday, this estate and its grounds are forbidden to you." The unlit cigarette bobbed up and down like a semaphore. "I shall instruct Mr. Kurland to keep an eye peeled for enterprising actresses seeking to abduct my animals."

"Were our situations reversed, I would take the same precautions," said Chloe, wiping her tears with the sleeve of her gown. "Upon returning to my room I shall pray to God that my former employer might one day forgive me."

"No need to entreat Heaven, Miss Bathurst—your former employer stands before you, and he grants his forgiveness." He extended his arm and splayed his fingers. "I hope we might part as friends."

"I am humbled by your graciousness," she said, shaking Mr. Darwin's hand. And by the way, she declared silently, I mean to win the Great God Contest. I have your essay, and I shall win. Though I must take

Bluebeard as my husband, hire Satan as my solicitor, and dance a fandango with the Angel of Death, the prize will be mine.

A s he strode through the leathern splendor of the Alastor Hall library, that arena in which he'd spent so many hours defending both the honor and the actuality of his Creator, the Reverend Malcolm Chadwick, Vicar of Wroxton, brooded on the paradoxical fact that he actually admired the Percy Bysshe Shelley Society. Their banquets partook of a primordial gluttony, their clothing of a quintessential vanity, their comportment of transcendent sloth. The Devil himself might profit from a visit to Alastor Hall, where he would likely learn a thing or two about genuine aristocratic dissolution, as opposed to the predictable drunkenness and tiresome fornication pursued in less professional dens of iniquity.

Tonight, as always, the rites had begun in the drawing-room, Lord Woolfenden officiating alongside his present mistress, the buxom Lady Isadora, the rakehells smoking their opiates, declaiming their execrable sonnets, and listening to a recitation honoring their late, lamented idol. Although the revelers normally preferred to hear a scene from *Prometheus Bound* or a passage from "On the Necessity of Atheism" or "A Refutation of Deism," this evening they'd experienced Lord Clatterbaugh reading from Shelley's favorite philosophical work, *De Rerum Natura* by the Roman poet Lucretius, its six chapters celebrating the irreligious teachings of the ancient Greek sage Epicurus. Clatterbaugh had selected Lucretius's account of the fate of Iphigenia, sacrificed by her own father, Agamemnon, so that the gods might grant the Achaean war fleet fair winds during their voyage to Troy.

> *Dumb with dread, her knees giving way, she fell sinking to the earth.*
> *In that dark hour it availed the hapless daughter nothing*
> *That it was she who'd first bestowed the name of father on the King.*
> *Uplifted by royal attendants, she was straightaway borne to the altar*
> *Though not to play her part in joyful marriage rites*

Or hear the happy sound of nuptial songs.
Instead the stainless maiden, at the very age of wedlock, was taken
To the holy stone to die beneath her father's knife,
Lest his ships endure a perilous crossing to Ilium.
Such are the monstrous deeds inspired by faith's fell promptings!

Next everyone had repaired to the banquet hall, there to consume suckling pig, roast pheasant, and gallons of champagne, whilst Lord Woolfenden's brace of peacocks strutted freely about, their gaudy plumage spreading behind them like the flags of a fabulous Oriental empire. At eight o'clock, goblets in hand and lovers in train, the Byssheans had adjourned to the library, sprawling across the velvet divans surrounding the arena in which would be waged this evening's war of wits.

"I am stuffed with pork and famished for gossip," said Malcolm as he mounted the steps to the dais, seating himself on the Anglican side of the judges' bench between the Reverend William Symonds and Professor Richard Owen. "What argument will our Christian petitioner submit tonight?"

"At dinner Lady Isadora told me we are to witness the most rational of all God proofs," replied Mr. Symonds, the geologist whose magisterial *Old Stones* contended that volcanoes attested to a loving Creator, for without a divine hand modifying their eruptions would not human civilization have been long ago smothered in lava?

"The most rational?" said Professor Owen, the scowling anatomist who'd put a name, *Dinosauria*, to the immense lizards who, if the fossil evidence spoke truly, had once inhabited Sussex. "Ah, then it's to be the Cosmological Proof, splendid! Of course, my loyalties will always lie with the Teleological Proof. What a piece of work is a man—and a marigold as well." During the past year the judges had heard dozens of contestants argue that, given its innumerable instances of meaningless and even absurd design, from flightless birds to soft-shelled crabs, the world hardly bespoke the purposeful aims of an omnicompetent Deity. Owen had in every instance flummoxed the petitioner with teleology, adducing hundreds of creatures so perfectly fitted to their habitats that one could almost see the Almighty's fingerprints on their feathers, pelts, hides, and scales.

"And what dish might our Godless petitioner be serving?" asked Malcolm.

"When I put the question to Woolfenden, he told me it would be the most powerful of all such arguments," piped up Harriet Martineau as she joined Henry Atkinson and George Holyoake on the atheist side of the bench. From her ear bloomed an enormous brass trumpet, which she steadied with one hand whilst the other clutched a copy of her book, *Letters on the Laws of Man's Nature,* with its brazen insistence that *Homo sapiens* was not necessarily God's favorite creature. "We all know what *that* means."

Of the freethinking judges, only Miss Martineau exhibited by Malcolm's lights a subtle mind, hence his resolve to befriend her once the prize was awarded. At a previous Shelley Society gathering, when the Christian contestant had offered up a bundle of cast-off crutches and other evidence of medical miracles, she had flustered him with a question to which Malcolm had yet to form a riposte. If God was so eager to dispense supernatural remedies, Miss Martineau had wanted to know, why were there no recorded instances of His healing an amputee?

"And what *does* it mean?" Owen inquired.

"Cancers and cataclysms," replied the squirrelly Mr. Atkinson—Miss Martineau's co-author—laying a hand on her sleeve. Try as he might, Malcolm could not fathom what virtues Miss Martineau saw in Atkinson, whose contributions to their collaboration must have been perfunctory at best. "Plagues and poxes. Toothaches and earthquakes."

A shudder traveled through Malcolm's frame. Of all the classic disproofs of God, the problem of unmerited pain was the one he most feared. Merciful Father in Heaven, deliver us from the Argument from Evil.

"Mumps and mosquitoes," said Mr. Holyoake, editor of *The Oracle of Reason,* genially joining the game. "Ticks and rickets. Tubercles and tumors."

It was obvious why the Byssheans had been drawn to Mr. Holyoake. Two years earlier, during one of his Socialist lectures, he'd noted that

Her Majesty's religious institutions were costing the Government £20,000,000 annually, even as the national debt hung like a millstone about the people's collective neck. England, Holyoake suggested, was "too poor to have a God," and it might be prudent "to put the Deity on half-pay until our finances are in order." In Malcolm's view the free-thinker's subsequent fate—six months in gaol for blasphemy—was un-just, for his remarks could hardly have offended God Almighty, who was after all not some prickly parson from Swindon but the Creator of the universe.

The judges' conversation was interrupted by the simultaneous arrivals of Popplewell of the *Evening Standard*, who took his customary seat in the ancient-history alcove, and Lippert, majordomo of Alastor Hall, who handed his master a slip of paper. Holding his goblet aloft like a torch, Lord Woolfenden rose from his divan—no simple operation, given his girth. (Everything about the man was excessive, his great stomach, froggish eyes, booming voice, prolix poems.) He tossed his mauve silk scarf insouciantly over his shoulder, glanced at Lippert's note, and faced his fellow sybarites. "Taking the field on God's behalf, we have the Rev-erend Terrance Sethington of Berkshire, who will attempt to sway the bench with a version of the Cosmological Proof."

The cleric in question, a towering figure with eyebrows so bushy they suggested caterpillars inching towards the ark, swaggered into the li-brary pulling a child's wagon whose cargo lay beneath a gauze veil. Self-confidence radiated from Mr. Sethington like warmth from a winter hearth, and Malcolm speculated that tonight, at long last, the entire bench might come to agree that God had been substantiated.

Reaching under the veil, the petitioner drew forth a croquet mallet and a wooden sphere. "The Cosmological Proof is the soul of simplicity," he began, setting the sphere on the floor. "As Thomas Aquinas reminds us, nothing moves of its own accord. We can stare night and day at this croquet ball, waiting for it to change position, and it won't budge by a cricket's whisker." Mr. Sethington applied his mallet with a force con-siderably short of the supernatural but sufficient to send the sphere rico-cheting off the dais. "None would doubt that my mallet moved the ball, that I moved the mallet, or that my impulses moved me. Ah, but what moved my impulses? And what moved that which moved my impulses? Learned judges, we have fallen into an infinite regress, an abyss from which we can escape only by assuming the existence of a divine agency. Saint Thomas reasoned that this Unmoved Mover is perforce the Creator-God of Christian revelation."

"Even when that Creator-God resembles a Berkshire parson playing croquet?" inquired Miss Martineau, eliciting from the Byssheans a peal of contemptuous laughter.

"Saint Thomas pondered not only the problem of movement but also the riddle of causality," said Sethington, undaunted. He returned to his wagon and yanked the veil away, revealing a wire cage in which a ruffled hen sat atop a clutch of eggs. "A hen can never cause herself, but only her eggs. These eggs can never cause themselves, but only those creatures we call chickens." The contestant seized the cage and paraded it before the judges. "Once again we find ourselves in the valley of the shadow of infinite regress."

"Which came first, the chicken or the croquet ball?" said Holyoake.

"To circumvent that void," Sethington persisted, his voice rising to a crescendo, "we must posit a First Cause—God—the nonphysical being from whom all physical things sprang! *Quod erat demonstrandum!*"

As the petitioner sat down on the dais, Lady Isadora quaffed champagne and addressed the bench. "Our Christians will now render their verdicts."

"Bravo, Mr. Sethington," said Owen. "You have my vote."

"*Quod erat* indeed," said Symonds.

"Although the Cosmological Proof has a venerable history," said Malcolm, "I cannot believe Saint Thomas would wish to see it illustrated with either poultry or sporting implements, and so I shan't endorse this presentation."

"Mr. Sethington, you have favorably impressed two of our Anglican judges," said Lady Isadora. "If two of our freethinkers are similarly moved, the prize is yours."

"The Cosmological Proof is famously lucid but notoriously flawed," said Miss Martineau. "Those who embrace this argument imagine that God Himself is somehow exempt from the infinite regress. But why should that be the case?"

How lamentable, thought Malcolm, that this brilliant woman would ally herself with unbelievers. He wondered if their incompatible theological views would preclude future intellectual congress. Equine of face, stumpish of form, and hard of hearing, Miss Martineau was less than alluring, but never had a person of her sex so fascinated him.

"I fail to follow your reasoning," said Sethington.

"I shall put it as simply as I can," said Miss Martineau. "If God created the universe, then who created God?"

"God is by definition uncreated," Sethington replied.

"Then we might as well say the universe is by definition uncreated and subtract God from the equation," noted Atkinson. "Aquinas possessed a keen intellect, but his proof proves precisely nothing."

"Shall I tell you of another crack in your cosmological egg?" said Holyoake to Sethington. "Even if we decide that our infinite regress must terminate in a supernatural being, why assume we're talking about the God of Christian revelation? The entity in question might be the Hindoo's Brahma, the Northman's Odin, the Grecian's Apollo, or a mystic elephant who defecates planets instead of turds."

The *flâneurs* laughed appreciatively.

"We are sorry, Mr. Sethington," said Lady Isadora, "but it appears you will leave our meeting no wealthier than you arrived."

The petitioner rose, packed up his Cosmological Proof, and, grasping the handle of the wagon, trundled wordlessly away.

"We shall now indulge in a short intermission," declared Lord Woolfenden.

Goblets were filled, cigars ignited, witticisms traded, trysts scheduled, and bodices fondled, after which the master of Alastor Hall clapped his hands and called for silence. Receiving his cue, the evening's second petitioner—a popinjay in a flowered silk waistcoat—entered the library accompanied by a squat hireling bearing an ancient traveling-chest, the unwieldy burden riding on his back like Quasimodo's hump.

"Visiting us tonight on behalf of disbelief is Sir Basil Wanderly of Blackthorn Hall," said Woolfenden, "who means to undermine the consensus concerning God's goodness."

As the fop approached the judges, the hireling opened the trunk, revealing a score of wide-mouthed bottles, each packed in straw and filled with a liquid preservative. The receptacles, Malcolm observed, contained all manner of ugly, prickly, slimy, and otherwise untoward things.

"God's reputation precedes Him," Sir Basil began. "Omnipotent, omniscient, and, most pertinent to my presentation, omnibenevolent. But if compassion is the Almighty's *sine qua non*, then His Creation will necessarily be free of gratuitous cruelty. In my observations, however, something like the *opposite* is the case. Behold the type of Australian jellyfish known as the sea-wasp."

Receiving his cue, the hireling produced a bottle containing the pickled remains of a creature resembling a diaphanous parasol outfitted with tentacles. "A sea-wasp's every limb sports venomous syringes," noted Sir Basil, "which means an entangled swimmer may anticipate a slow and agonizing death. I cannot but wonder what sort of God would fashion such a beast."

"A nasty God," said Atkinson.

"A nonexistent God," said Miss Martineau.

"Now behold my guinea-worm," said Sir Basil, "whose *modus operandi* makes the sea-wasp seem like a saint."

The hireling set the jellyfish on the dais. Returning to the trunk, he brought forth a specimen suggesting a segment from a child's kite string, though there was nothing remotely frolicsome about the creature.

"Drink from a river in India or Africa, and you risk ingesting the immature larvae of this worm," said Sir Basil. "Although the male measures but a few inches, the female grows to the three-foot monster you see before you. Day after day she burrows through her host's tissues, a migration that normally terminates in the leg but sometimes in the breast, scalp, tongue, or generative organs. When the worm's head meets the inside surface of the skin, an excruciating blister forms. By immersing the lesion in a cold stream, the victim can gain some relief, as this induces the creature to emerge into daylight and burst, releasing her immature larvae into the water. There now comes the problem of removing the worm's impacted corpse, more painful than a malignant tumor. The usual method is to wind the thing about a stick."

"What a ghastly beast," said Miss Martineau.

"Small wonder Jehovah declines to show His face in public," said Atkinson.

Next the contestant submitted specimens of the warble fly, "a creature that God in His mercy has instructed to breed in the nasal passages of horses and cattle, so that the maggots will have plenty of cartilage to devour upon hatching." The subsequent exhibit was a moth called *Lobocraspis griseifusa*, "which on the counsel of our loving Creator uses its proboscis to irritate the eyes of water buffalo and other defenseless livestock, thus provoking a supply of nourishing tears." Then came a collection of male bedbugs, "an insect that Heaven has favored with a procreative member so long that he rarely bothers about the female's genital opening, preferring to stab her and release his seed into her bloodstream." And so it went, bottle after bottle, invertebrate after invertebrate, until all twenty indictments decorated the dais. "I could offer additional specimens, but I've no wish to cause the Supreme Being further embarrassment. Stendhal put it well: God's only excuse is that He does not exist."

Lord Woolfenden rolled off his divan, picked his way amongst the horizontal hedonists, and bowed before his freethinking guest. "Our atheists are impressed by your circus of horrors, but I wonder if you've rattled those amongst us of a Christian persuasion."

"Your Lordship, the mere existence of vermin does not give a believer pause," said Mr. Symonds. "With Adam's fall came Nature's corruption. We should not be surprised to find vestiges of that catastrophe in far-flung corners of the globe."

Malcolm said, "In confronting the phenomenon of evil, we must remember Herr Leibniz's insight that ours is the best of all possible worlds—emphasis on the *possible*. The physical stuff that constitutes the universe is *ipso facto* flawed," he continued, striving mightily to believe himself, "for if external reality were entirely good, it would not be God's *handi-work*—it would be *God*, full stop. In short, Sir Basil's worms are the price we pay for tangible existence. Without such blemishes on the face of Creation, we should not have a world at all."

"I was once privileged to hear John Henry Newman speak to the problem of seemingly pointless suffering," said Owen. "The great cleric averred that ostensibly unjust tribulations harbor a secret benevolence."

"Having devoted many hours to pickling God's sins, and finding not a single hidden harmony therein," said Sir Basil, "I remain far less impressed by Father Newman than by Abbess Ich-Newman."

"Abbess who?" asked Lady Isadora.

"The remorseless ichneumon wasp," said Sir Basil, "who lays her eggs inside a caterpillar's living body. When the larvae hatch, they eat the caterpillar alive."

"How unseemly," said Lady Isadora.

"Alas, Sir Basil, I fear you've not persuaded our believers," said Lord Woolfenden, "but I must thank you for an engaging presentation."

As the hireling began packing up the exhibits, cushioning each bottle in straw, Malcolm released a moan of trepidation. Although Sir Basil's monsters had failed to carry the day, sooner or later the Argument from Evil would descend upon the contest in an impossibly potent form—and Malcolm did not want to be there when that disaster occurred.

The guinea-worm was last to enter the trunk. For Malcolm the awful creature evoked an episode from the Book of Numbers: Jehovah punishing the backsliding Israelites by sending fiery serpents to bite and burn them—a plague He lifted only after they'd confessed their sins to Moses. What most intrigued Malcolm was the manner of the Israelites' cure. Just as a guinea-worm victim could find relief by wrapping the parasite's corpse around a stick, so were the Children of Israel saved when Moses set a brass serpent atop a pole for everyone to see.

Worm and stick, serpent and pole—was it all mere coincidence? Or was Numbers in fact a catalog of diseases and their treatments, allegorized as a series of encounters between the Israelites and their irascible

God? Malcolm imagined that he might one day explore this notion in depth, writing an exegesis to which he would be pleased to put his name, assuming he could keep his pride from devolving into pridefulness.

K indly as always and solicitous to the end, Mr. Darwin saw to it that no breath of scandal or whiff of disgrace attended Chloe's departure from Down House. He told the assembled staff that, having grown weary of "the mute universe of lizards and tortoises," Miss Bathurst had decided to direct her nurturing instincts "towards a more appreciative audience, notably a brood of human children." Owing to her charm and intelligence, he added, she would "doubtless soon obtain a new situation." Indeed, were his own progeny not already under excellent tutelage, he would hire her himself.

With a tremor in her voice and a stricture in her throat, Chloe said good-bye to Master Willy and Miss Annie. The children listened uncomprehendingly as she praised their natural Rousseauian goodness. Later that morning Chloe visited her feathered charges, bidding *au revoir* to the mockingbirds, flycatchers, and finches. Next she addressed the lizards, telling them that she'd greatly enjoyed their taciturn and unpretentious company.

The giant tortoises occasioned the most difficult farewells. Chloe felt embarrassed to be rubbing their shells and insisting she would never forget them. After all, the ancestors of these creatures had walked the Earth long before the advent of the sympathetic emotions, and when sorrow had at last appeared on the scene, tortoises had doubtless recognized it for the softheaded and useless sentiment it was. In their antique wisdom Boswell of James Isle, Isolde of Charles Isle, and Perseus of Indefatigable (whose injured leg was healing splendidly) knew better than to trouble themselves with yearning—but Chloe did not, and so she wept.

As the shadows of evening drew nigh, she climbed aboard the steam train for London. Settling into her seat, she thought of those times in her life when, having fallen into the Slough of Despond, she'd managed to escape. In each case she'd begun by cataloging her present advantages—and so she now made a list. Asset number one: the six pounds from Mr. Darwin. Asset number two: her copy of the transmutation essay, secured in her portmanteau. Asset number three: her incipient scheme, precise as an arrow and simple as a stitch. It called for her to use her severance pay in renting illustrative specimens from England's zoos. Equipped with these scaled, beaked, and feathered testaments, she would travel to Alastor Hall, present her disproof of God, and set the ghost of Shelley to grinning.

Detraining at Charing Cross Station, she headed towards the Adelphi Theatre in quest of Fanny Mendrick, with whom she hoped to share lodgings once again. For Chloe, such a bargain would hold clear advantages—she could employ 15 Tavistock Street as her base of operations whilst assembling her menagerie—though she feared the arrangement might prove unpalatable to her rooming-companion. No, dear Fanny, during my days at Down House I did not learn to sew, so I shan't mend your dresses, nor to launder, so I shan't clean your sheets, nor to cook in the French manner, so you mustn't expect meals laden with luscious sauces. I can offer you only my camaraderie and, for the immediate future, my half of the rent.

Midway through her trek across the nocturnal city, Chloe came upon a ragamuffin selling Tuesday's *Evening Standard*. Without asking permission, she seized the topmost copy and turned to page three, which indeed featured Popplewell's account of Saturday night's goings-on at Alastor Hall. Heart astir, she scanned the headline, COSMOLOGICAL PROOF FAILS TO AUTHENTICATE JEHOVAH, then the subhead, ANGLICAN JUDGES REJECT ARGUMENT FROM EVIL, and finally the illustration: a snake emerging from an African native's chest, labeled *Guinea-Worm Victim*. Despite the disturbing image, she laughed out loud, unnerving the ragamuffin. The purse remained intact. The race went on.

Upon reaching the Strand, she surveyed the Adelphi Theatre billboards and saw that *The Beauteous Buccaneer* had ended its run: hardly a surprise—without Miss Chloe Bathurst in the principal role, who would patronize that overripe melon? The new offering was *Via Dolorosa*, Mr. Bulwer-Lytton's iambic-pentameter dramatization of the further adventures of Veronica, the woman who'd swabbed Jesus' brow as he'd limped towards Golgotha (thereby imprinting his face on her veil in a kind of first-century daguerreotype). Three years earlier, when the South-wark Company was poised to mount the world premiere of *Via Dolorosa*, Chloe had auditioned for the part of Veronica, having read the entire play by way of preparation. The venture came to naught. Not only did the director decline to cast her, but Chloe had nearly drowned in Bulwer-Lytton's cataract of verse, in which treacherous tides of forced rhymes concealed perilous shoals of distressed metaphors. The present produc-tion featured Fanny as Veronica—the perfect role for an actress of such radiant faith.

By the testimony of her smile, Fanny was delighted to find her former rooming-companion waiting at the stage door, and she refrained from any show of skepticism when Chloe insisted that her departure from Mr. Darwin's employ had been voluntary, "driven only by a longing for the cosmopolitan life I'd left behind."

"How bold of you to follow your heart's desire and walk away from a secure situation," said Fanny.

"Somewhat bold, yes, but largely foolhardy. At the moment I lack for a roof over my head."

Fanny kissed Chloe's cheek and said, "Allow me to cast you once again in the unfolding drama that is my life."

"There's an even greater boon you can perform for me. Were you to drop by Mr. Kean's office tomorrow and acquire a dozen sheets of statio-nery bearing an engraved image of this theatre, I should be evermore in your debt."

"I love you, Chloe, but I shan't commit a robbery on your behalf," said Fanny.

"Think of it as undeclared borrowing. If my scheme comes to frui-tion, I'll supply Mr. Kean with foolscap enough to paper over Hyde Park."

"And what scheme might that be?" asked Fanny.

"As Pirate Anne says to Jack Rackham when he first visits her boudoir, 'All in good time.'"

The following day, upon receiving from Fanny a goodly quantity of Adelphi stationery, Chloe inked her Tavistock Street address onto every sheet, forthwith drafting and posting the letters by which she hoped to acquire the illustrative specimens. Mindful of Fanny's fondness for God, Chloe declined to tell her why she sought these creatures. Instead she beguiled her friend with the same falsehoods that, Dame Fortune willing, would bring the exhibits her way.

"Perhaps you recall how, in leaving the Adelphi, I told Mr. Kean of my desire to write plays," said Chloe. "It happens that during my sojourn at Down House I fell upon a worthy subject, and I straightaway composed the first two acts. I call it *The Ashes of Eden,* spun from Mr. Darwin's pulse-pounding adventures in the Galápagos archipelago."

"What sorts of pulse-pounding adventures?" asked Fanny.

"The usual. A hair's-breadth escape from headhunters, a battle with a gigantic iguana, a flight from an erupting volcano. But primarily my play concerns Mr. Darwin's insights into the method by which God tenanted the islands with their distinctive varieties of bird and beast."

"It sounds perfect for the Adelphi, thrilling and edifying all at once."

"Here's the rub, Fanny. My artistic vision can be realized only by bringing live animals on stage. Towards that end I've written to various zoological institutions. If they will lease us the necessary creatures, I shall be inspired to finish the third act posthaste."

Within a fortnight Chloe received—from the associate director of the Royal Zoo—the first response to her campaign: an altogether maddening and abysmal missive.

7 June 1849

Dear Miss Bathurst,

    We are in receipt of your letter concerning your theatre company's forthcoming production. Alas, although we have in captivity several large lizards from Indonesia, we are deficient in the Galápagos types your spectacle requires.

As for the fabled giant tortoises, over the past decade we've made numerous attempts to procure live specimens. Unfortunately, every sea captain we commissioned swindled us, claiming that the creatures had become sickly en route *back to England and needed to be cooked on the spot.*

I regret that we cannot be of service. Her Majesty's Zoo is ever eager to raise the cultural horizons of the London citizenry, and we were genuinely intrigued by the possibility of a cooperative venture with the Adelphi.

> Yours, etc.,
> Mordecai Bramble

Later that week two more such dispiriting letters arrived. Although the Pimlico Natural History Park owned a terrestrial iguana from Indefatigable Isle and another from Chatham Isle, their keeper insisted that he was "loath to put them on stage night after night, a trauma certain of shortening their lives." The undersecretary of Her Majesty's Tropical Arboretum in Regent's Park wrote, "*The Ashes of Eden* sounds like a worthy endeavor, and yet we would never populate our cosmopolitan paradise with creatures hailing from a place so desolate as Galápagos. Relocate your play to the jungles of Malaysia, and we shall happily assist you."

Undaunted, Chloe cast her net wider, contacting zoos in Paris, Brussels, and Amsterdam, but she failed to snare a single serviceable vertebrate. Refusing to admit defeat, she attempted to obtain preserved specimens. The strategy proved bootless. A Trinity College herpetologist replied that, although he curated several mummified reptiles from the South American continent, "Alas, our collection stops short of the Encantadas." A King's College ornithologist declared that the Adelphi Theatre was in his opinion "a bawdy-house by another name," and he would not rent Chloe a stuffed Galápagos mockingbird even if he had one.

Her salvation took the unlikely form of the *Evening Standard* for Tuesday the 24th of July. Habitually she turned to page three. The headline proved gratifying. SUPREME BEING SURVIVES BIBLICAL CONTRADICTIONS. It was the subhead, however, that truly enthralled her. DILUVIAN LEAGUE TO RECOVER GENESIS ARK FROM ARARAT. The adjacent engraving depicted the prophet Noah urging pairs of zebras, elephants, and giraffes to board his famous vessel. What on earth? Could it be? Did some wily theist intend to win the prize with the ultimate version of the Argument from Relics?

ALASTOR HALL, OXFORD. On Saturday evening the judges of the Great God Contest heard the Argument from Biblical Errors. Mr. Enoch Brattlebone, an amateur philologist, exhibited a stack of pasteboard sheets onto which he'd transcribed dozens of alleged scriptural mistakes.

In the inaugural chapter of Genesis, God first creates every sort of animal, with Man serving as the climax of the process, whereas in chapter two the Almighty, having apparently started the whole business over again, brings Adam on stage in advance of the beasts. In Leviticus, bats are categorized as birds, rabbits as cud-chewers, and insects as four-legged. In Matthew, Judas casts down his silver pieces and then hangs himself, whereupon the chief priests use the money to purchase a field, but in Acts it's Judas who purchases the field, a tract on which he dies when his abdomen bursts open.

With lucidity and passion the Anglican judges explained why such anomalies should not trouble believers. The Reverend Mr. Symonds speculated that at the time of Moses bats were birds, rabbits chewed their cud, and insects had four legs. Professor Owen proposed a version of Judas's death in which the priests unstrung his corpse with the intention of interring it, a plan they abandoned when the villain's remains exploded on the burial ground, which they'd purchased in his name. The Reverend Mr. Chadwick simply stated, "Let us not discount God's glorious forest for a few aberrant leaves on solitary twigs."

Visiting Alastor Hall on Jehovah's behalf was the Reverend Mr. Dalrymple, president of the Mayfair Diluvian League, who submitted various images of Noah's ark ensconced in its final resting place, Mount Ararat in Anatolia. None of this evidence—neither the pen-and-ink sketches nor the watercolors nor the daguerreotypes—impressed the freethinking judges, who declared them fraudulent.

"My colleagues and I anticipated such a reaction," said Mr. Dalrymple, "which is why we intend to undertake an unprecedented archeological expedition. After securing the necessary funds, we shall sail the good ship Paragon *through the Bosporus to the Black Sea. Disembarking at Trebizond, our party will proceed overland to Ararat, scale the slopes, excavate the ark, and tow it to England."*

At this point Lord Woolfenden waxed enthusiastic, saying, "We salute your ambition, Reverend. What's more, we're prepared to invest three hundred pounds in your adventure."

Although moved by the Shelley Society's generosity, Mr. Dalrymple noted that the project would cost in excess of £2,000. With a trenchant smile Lord Woolfenden averred that an organization as Godly as the Diluvian League should have no problem raising the difference.

"But let us make your task even easier. We shall be pleased to grant you an official commission—provided that a majority of our judges concurs."

An interval of high drama ensued. Polled by Lord Woolfenden, the Anglicans on the bench agreed that Mr. Dalrymple should be permitted to raise ark-hunting capital in the Society's name. The atheists then cast their ballots. Mr. Atkinson voted nay, saying, "Your Lordship, I believe it behooves you to grant commissions neither to churchgoers nor to freethinkers." Miss Martineau abstained, saying, "I can see both sides of the question, and I am fond of neither." All eyes now turned to Mr. Holyoake. "An atheist, I would argue, is a person who has naught to fear from the facts," he declared. "If the Genesis ark is real, I should like to know it, and so I vote aye."

Chloe accorded the remainder of Popplewell's piece (quotations from the Reverend Mr. Dalrymple praising the judges and the Byssheans) but a cursory glance, for her mind was aglow with an incandescent idea. If the Oxford rakehells were willing to endorse the Mayfair Diluvian League, then surely they would authorize her to collect biological evidence for a Godless universe. Fairness demanded that the Shelley Society patronize a journey to Galápagos by the—by the what? The Natural Selection League? The Tree of Life Society? The Transmutationist Club? Yes, that sounded right. The Byssheans must underwrite the Albion Transmutationist Club, England's newest scientific organization.

So jubilant was Chloe at the prospect of outmaneuvering the Diluvians, she decided to celebrate, treating herself to grouse and beer at the Cloven Hoof, then attending a performance of *Via Dolorosa*. As mounted by the Adelphi Company the play proved strangely engaging, and Chloe realized she'd been wrong to scorn the text on the basis of a single reading.

She was especially touched by the climax of act one—Veronica wiping blood and sweat from Christ's face. Act two came to a thrilling conclusion when a band of Zealots, having enchanted their swords by cleaning them with Veronica's veil, defeated Caligula's soldiers in a skirmish. Act three found the heroine assuming the mantle of evangelist, healing the sick and spreading the news that love had superseded the Law. Angered by this perceived critique of their religion, a Pharisee mob carted Veronica down to the Mediterranean Sea and set her adrift in a fishing boat, along with Lazarus, Mary Magdalene, Mary the mother of James, and Mary the mother of John. The outcasts suffered hunger, pirates, sharks, and whirlpools, and yet they persisted, reaching France and inaugurating the Provençal legend of *les Trois Maries*.

As Chloe strode through the foyer of the Adelphi and entered the churning metropolis beyond, her buoyant mood evaporated, yielding to reflections concerning not only her imminent voyage (which promised to be as perilous as Veronica's) but also the emergent rivalry between the Mayfair Diluvian League and the Albion Transmutationist Club. From the loftiest aristocrat to the lowliest commoner, all Christendom would want the Ararat mission to succeed and the Galápagos quest to fail. The

King of the Universe was on surely the Diluvians' side, and so was the Queen of England. And Miss Chloe Bathurst? All she had was her finch beaks and her mockingbird bills, her iguana tails and her tortoise shells: beautiful things, to be sure, beautiful and subtle and true—and yet so easily ground to dust by the colossal keel of Noah's ark.

4

*The Pigeon Priest Moves from His Parsonage
to a Madhouse, Even as Our Heroine
Arranges to Circumnavigate a Continent*

A woman adept at creating illusions but in thrall to only a few, Chloe knew that she could not simply march into a Shelley Society meeting and charm the rakehells into sanctioning her expedition. Not, at least, until she'd digested Mr. Darwin's theory in all its clawed and carapaced particulars. Thus did she take to haunting the Jubilee Market coffee-houses, inundating her intellect with chocolate and caffeine whilst perusing her illicit manuscript.

Each time she read "An Essay Concerning Descent with Modification," she grew even more appreciative of Mr. Darwin's talent for shoring up his argument with anatomy and embryology. "The wing of a bat," he'd written, "the paddle of a porpoise, the hoof of a horse, and the hand of a man all exhibit a unity of type," hence the near impossibility of distinguishing these structures from each other "in the early stages through which the corresponding foetuses pass." One might also infer transmutation from "abortive organs," structures for which a plant or animal had no need, "the teeth of the narwhale being a famous instance, likewise the nipples of male mammals, also the tailbone—the coccyx—of the species called *Homo sapiens.*"

Varied and ingenious were the ways Mr. Darwin had found to push

God farther and farther off the stage of natural history. These days no physicist was obliged to "spurn Newton's laws and insist instead that the planets cleave to their orbits in direct obeisance to the Creator's will"—so why shouldn't biologists, *mutatis mutandis*, enjoy the same privilege? In the next paragraph Mr. Darwin bemoaned the scriptural literalism whereby the flat-spined species of Galápagos land iguana and the high-spined type "must have been separately created from the dust of Albemarle Isle and Barrington respectively." Equally untenable was the biblical implication that "all four species of Encantadas mockingbird reflect four different divine initiatives."

After a fortnight of industry fueled by enough coffee to refloat Noah's ark, Chloe decided she'd achieved an almost connubial relationship with the Tree of Life. Unless she missed her guess, she would take Alastor Hall by storm, bearing away either Jehovah's head on a silver salver or (the next best thing) an official commission to arrange His ruin somewhere east of Eden and west of Ecuador.

On Friday the 10th of August, in the shank of the wet afternoon, after fastening her hair beneath her green velvet bonnet, hiding her purse in her bodice, and prudently removing all jewelry from her person, Chloe belted her grandfather's bayonet about her waist and set off for Seven Dials, the district where her little brother—having come into the world a half-hour ahead of Algernon, she'd always thought of herself as the elder sibling—had at last report established himself as a flamboyant faro player who could normally be counted upon to lose. Amongst his many unsavory acquaintances Algernon surely numbered a few disgraced sea captains, at least one of whom should be willing, for a cut of the profits, to assist the Albion Transmutationist Club. If she appeared in Oxford having already procured a ship, she reasoned, the Shelley Society would smile all the more broadly on her quest.

Arriving in the wretched rookery, she decided that although Seven Dials had a logical enough name (the streets converged on a pillar encrusted with sundials), an equally appropriate appellation would be Seven Sins. At every turn yet another reprobate activity met her gaze, from opium smoking to gin swilling, cockfighting to whoremongering. Each time Satan invented a new vice, she mused, he tested it out in the Dials ere inflicting it on the world at large.

She pestered landladies, importuned beggars, and distributed pennies with the alacrity of a child tossing bread crumbs to ducks, until at last a busker with a violin told her that the wastrel Bathurst frequented a gaming establishment called the Butcher's Hook in Earlham Street. The thoroughfare in question, she soon learned, was a gathering place for trollops. Moving amongst these pocked and syphilitic women (painted like harlots, not actresses, she decided), she pondered her present embargo on carnal pleasure, promising herself that, in the name of eluding the diseases of Venus, she would remain chaste until her wedding night.

Cautiously she entered the Butcher's Hook. It was like stepping into an enormous hearth whose fire had died with the coming of dawn: stale, cold, murky, ashen. She spotted Algernon almost immediately, slumped in a nearby booth and contemplating an empty tumbler whilst shuffling a pack of cards. He did not look up but merely grinned and said, "Sweetest sister, how marvelous to see you."

"How did you know 'twas I, little brother?"

"Through a gin glass darkly," he replied, indicating the tumbler. His skin was sallow as candle wax, his hair tangled as a thrush's nest. "Allow me to buy you a libation."

"Ginger beer, if you please."

Spreading his cards faceup across the knife-nicked table, Algernon rose and kissed Chloe's cheek. Stubble covered his chin like gnats mired in flypaper. As she slid into the booth, her twin repaired to the bar, returning apace with a glass of faux beer and a tankard of stout, both crested with foam. "I hope you don't mean to engage me in a *tête-à-tête*"—from the fanned deck he selected the knave of clubs—"for I'm needed at the faro table. Tell me, sister, is this the card I should play against the dealer?"

"I pray you, grant me an hour of your time."

"I've never trusted the knave of clubs"—he retrieved the knave of hearts—"nor his lovelorn cousin, either. I shall exile 'em both from this afternoon's tournament. Let me guess. You're here concerning our ne'er-do-well father's plight, which you imagine his ne'er-do-well son might remedy."

"Listen, dear brother, and you'll learn the solution to all our problems—yours, mine, and Papa's. It involves a game so bold as to put your precious faro in the shadows."

She took a long swallow of ginger beer, then told Algernon of the great prize and how she'd become privy to a scientific theory that bid fair to claim it. Any persuasive presentation of this argument required live, exotic creatures that she intended to procure by traveling to the Galápagos archipelago. The rakehells had already underwritten one such expedition, a hunt for Noah's ark, so it seemed reasonable to suppose they would sponsor another.

With each successive revelation Algernon's eyes increased in diameter. She couldn't tell which aspect of her tale had most beguiled him—the size of the purse, her plan to sail around Cape Horn to the equator and then back to England, or her intention to pass off Mr. Darwin's idea as her own—but in any event she felt emboldened to set forth the hypothesis itself, and so she offered up her narrative of bat wings and baby tails, horse hooves and porpoise paddles, whale teeth and Welshmen's nipples.

"Being possessed of a hazy belief in a nebulous God, I'm not eager to cast my lot with atheism," Algernon admitted. "That said, I shan't reject your theory out of hand. The problem is simply this—I cannot make any sense of it."

"We shall begin anew," said Chloe, at once exasperated and galvanized. Leaning over the array of faceup cards, she extracted the knave, queen, king, and ace of diamonds, plus the deuce of spades. "Imagine that everyone in this den has become enamored of that great American bluffing game, poker. Let us further assume that, according to the house rules, a sequential run of royalty can turn the corner to embrace a deuce. Ergo, I'm holding a desirable hand—"

"A straight."

"A straight, exactly: knave, queen, king, ace, deuce, likely to prosper once the final bet is called. Now suppose my environment changes, and I find myself in a different gaming establishment, such as—"

"The Tinker's Damn!" cried Algernon.

"The Tinker's Damn, where the rules forbid a leap to the deuce. Owing to its altered habitat, my hand has been enfeebled, a mere ace high. Destined for a quick death, it will leave no progeny behind."

"Nothing would please me more than to say I follow your reasoning."

"Now consider a different set of circumstances. I'm back in the Hook, pondering my round-the-corner straight, when I'm suddenly whisked away to—"

"The Drunken Lord!"

"The Drunken Lord, an establishment where aces aren't allowed to leap but—*voilà!*—deuces are always wild, so that my two of spades has become—"

"A ten of diamonds, for a—"

"A royal flush, brimming with adaptive traits and thus certain to propagate those advantages through subsequent generations. *Now* do you follow my reasoning?"

"I know that royal flushes generally reign supreme, but does that mean I understand Mr. Darwin's idea? If I had to make a wager, I'd say no."

"You disappoint me, Algernon."

"Chloe, *ma chère*, listen to your one and only twin brother. Whoever God might be, His divine self surely does not play at cards. I, on the other hand, do little else, and so I must take leave of you and attempt to turn my fifty quid into a hundred."

"First you must agree to help me reach Galápagos."

"I think not," said Algernon, quaffing the dregs of his stout.

"Would you rather Papa dropped dead from breaking stones in a workhouse?"

Algernon rolled his eyes, pursed his lips, and, gathering up his playing cards, marched towards a corner of the room shrouded in a fug of cigar smoke and oil-lamp vapor. Chloe remained in the booth and sipped her ginger beer, her mind abuzz with her favorite passage from Mr. Darwin's essay. "Amongst wild creatures," he'd written, "the choice of a mate oft-times resides with the female." In other words, a savannah was arguably more civilized than a city, for how could one improve upon an arrangement whereby a female bird or beast pondered a pool of suitors, weighed their respective merits, and selected the one who most struck her transmutational fancy?

Algernon returned sooner than Chloe expected, grim, stooped, and crestfallen. "Might I finish your drink?" he mumbled in the voice of a man noticing he'd forgotten to put on his trousers that morning. "My brain's now so befuddled it can't tell ginger beer from ale."

She seized her glass and plunked it down before Algernon. "Having just lost fifty quid, the thought of winning ten thousand now appeals to you—am I correct?"

"I have a friend and fellow gambler," he said, nodding, "one Merridew Runciter, a criminal of considerable accomplishment." He drained the ginger beer in a single gulp. "Upon inheriting the brigantine *Equinox* from his late uncle, old Merry abandoned his scandalous vocation as a highwayman to pursue a respectable career in smuggling. I'm confident I can inveigle him into lending us his ship and assuming command."

"That's the spirit, brother," said Chloe, assembling a fragile house from his playing cards. "You've caught the fever."

"I suggest we offer the old rascal a five percent interest in the Shelley Prize, plus a second five percent to divide amongst his crew, which leaves us with a sum sufficient to free our father and feather our nests." Algernon licked a lacy veil of foam from his mustache. "This is a bad business, sister—I hope you know that. As our Savior once remarked, there's no profit in gaining the world only to lose one's soul."

"We're not talking about the *world*, Algernon, merely ten thousand pounds." She poked the house of cards, causing it to wobble and then collapse. "Let us gather our tortoises whilst we may, and let the Devil take the difference."

True to Algernon's prediction, Merridew Runciter proved eager to donate both his ship and his avarice to the lucrative cause of God's demise. He drafted a statement explaining "to the Right Honorable Lord Woolfenden" that, as master of the brigantine *Equinox*, he would "lease said vessel to the Albion Transmutationist Club for the purpose of bearing biological specimens from the Galápagos archipelago to England." Although attracting a crew would not be difficult—he need merely promise them pieces of the Shelley Prize—he hoped the Society would grant the expedition £300, so he might "provision the ship, repair the hull, and retain competent officers."

On the ides of August, Chloe and Algernon visited the administrator of the Great God Contest, Mr. Gillivray, in whose Kensington offices all petitioners were required to audition. When he'd met with the Diluvian League, she speculated, Mr. Gillivray must have been particularly struck by their daguerreotypes of Noah's ark, and so she'd resolved to impress him with an equally vivid prop. After introducing herself as a zookeeper and her brother as an importer of gaming supplies, she flourished a two-foot-high piece of shrubbery she'd pilfered from the Adelphi, all wire twigs and silk leaves, explaining that the world's every bird and beast had come into being without divine assistance, as branches on a majestic but entirely natural Tree of Life. Mr. Gillivray listened carefully, frowned thoughtfully, and proclaimed that her presentation was certain to amuse his employers. Come Saturday the 22nd of September, she and her brother should betake themselves to 4 Mansfield Road, Oxford, arriving punctually at eight o'clock in the evening.

When the fateful day arrived, Chloe and Algernon boarded a crowded steam train out of Paddington Station, passing the two-hour journey to Oxford wedged into a compartment with four rowdy students, the wire tree sitting on her knees like a lap dog. Upon reaching their destination, she and her brother purchased meat pies from a street vendor and gobbled them down, forgoing the final bite to keep their fingers clean. They proceeded on foot along High Street, pausing to admire the spired splendor of University College, the institution from which Percy Shelley had been expelled for his essay celebrating atheism. Although darkness was coming on fast, Chloe could still make out the entablature above the door—a priest blessing a student, the surmounting caption reading *Domimina Nustio Illumea*, "The Lord Is My Light."

They bid the stone scholar farewell, then followed the crenellated town wall to Alastor Hall, a three-storied, Corinthian-capitaled monstrosity dwarfing the adjacent structures, bowing only to honey-colored Mansfield College across the way. Chloe checked her brooch-watch: 7:30 p.m. A liveried footman answered Algernon's knock, then admitted the contestants to the vestibule, a rotunda ringed by portrait heads of wrinkled Romans, each set on a pedestal. Outfitted in a white peruke and a peach cutaway coat, an ancient gentleman tottered into view, identifying himself as Lippert, the majordomo. After determining that the woman and her brother were the expected atheists, Lippert led them into an antechamber and bade them wait until Lord Woolfenden introduced the evening's disproof of God. Whilst Algernon lounged on the *méridienne,* Chloe opened the library doors a crack and stared through the chink like Pyramus seeking a glimpse of Thisbe.

Her first impression of the Byssheans was that they cultivated so towering a caliber of fakery as to make Bulwer-Lytton's ridiculous historical melodramas seem like eyewitness chronicles. Whereas Algernon had acquired his reputation as a lotus-eating sybarite by following his natural inclinations, these overdressed toffs (with their chalked faces, perfumed neckcloths, pomaded hair, and mistresses in dishabille) were merely playing roles, like actors strutting across the boards. Only one audience member aspired to respectability, being modestly attired and neatly coiffed—most likely the *Evening Standard* journalist, Mr. Popplewell.

A person of Falstaffian figure and Mephistophelean smile, Lord Woolfenden introduced the night's first contestant as "Mr. Venables, instructor in entomology at Eton College."

The petitioner, a squat dumpling of a man with a surfeit of chins, strode confidently towards the judges' bench. From his valise he extracted three objects and set them on the dais: a big glass jar, a ceramic Star of David, and a globe the size of a Galápagos tortoise egg, mounted on a stand and painted to represent Earth's moon.

Shifting her constricted gaze, Chloe surveyed the Anglican judges. Thanks to her familiarity with Mr. Darwin's book collection, she quickly identified Professor Owen (whose choleric countenance decorated the title page of *Report on British Fossil Reptiles*) and also the Reverend Mr. Symonds (whose engraved portrait served as the frontispiece of *Old Stones*). It followed that the remaining Anglican, a somber and gangly young man, must be the Reverend Mr. Chadwick.

"The Argument from Cosmic Correlations turns on the improbably large number of symmetries in the universe," Mr. Venables began, "all of them best understood as evidence planted by our Creator, that we might feel confident of His existence." The contestant picked up the lunar globe, showing it to the judges. "Consider how, viewed from Earth, the diameter of the moon appears the same as that of the sun. Owing to this congruence, the human race is periodically awed by solar eclipses, those grand displays of indomitable sunbeams fringing our planet's satellite. 'God is real,' the corona tells us. 'God is love and light, eternally shining behind whatever lumps of woe might briefly block a person's way in life.'"

Next Venables presented the bench with his Star of David. "Now consider this familiar image, sacred to God's Chosen People. Not only does the Mogen David decorate many a synagogue, it also adorns the heavens. For as every schoolboy knows, our planet revolves about the sun accompanied by six other such bodies: Mercury, Venus, Mars, Jupiter, Saturn, and Uranus—that's right, six, the number of vertices that define a Star of David. 'God is near,' the configuration tells us. 'Even before the Creator revealed Himself to the Hebrews, He had announced Himself to all Mankind.'"

The petitioner removed a brass bell from his vest pocket and rang it vigorously. An instant later Lippert and the footman appeared, straightaway making a circuit of the library, snuffing candles and stanching gas lamps. The resulting darkness drew everyone's attention to the glass jar, which—*mirabile dictu*—was filled with tiny twinkling lights.

"Behold those creatures called fireflies," said Venables, displaying the luminous receptacle to the judges. "After my uncle in Pennsylvania shipped me the necessary chrysalises, I raised seven generations at Eton.

Of a summer night nothing delights me more than to release a colony of fireflies in my orchard and watch them flashing against the vault of Heaven until they become indistinguishable from the stars. The message could scarcely be clearer. Just as God made every fire that burns in the sky, so did He fashion every beast that crawls upon the Earth."

Whilst Lippert and the footman reignited the candles and turned on the gas lamps, a plump woman—the notorious Lady Isadora, no doubt—invited the judges to evaluate Mr. Venables's efforts.

"This is perhaps the most persuasive demonstration we've encountered thus far," insisted Professor Owen. "I'm quite prepared to reward our visiting entomologist."

"Aquinas argued that a doubter might find his way to God through reason alone," said Mr. Symonds. "Our contestant's fiery insects illuminate that very path."

"Though I appreciate the cleverness of Mr. Venables's correlations," said Mr. Chadwick, "I cannot give this presentation my assent, for his examples seem to me arbitrary in the extreme."

The first freethinker to speak was Mr. Holyoake, whose bulbous nose and profuse side-whiskers Chloe recalled from an engraving accompanying a newspaper account of his trial. "The Correlative Proof has always suffered from a fatal statistical naiveté," the convicted blasphemer began. "A one-in-a-million event cannot be thought supernatural if there are a million opportunities for it to occur. Because our planet is home to a vast insect population comprising hundreds of thousands of species, it would be surprising *not* to find one or more kinds endowed with the trait of phosphorescence."

Next to speak was a hatchet-faced woman—this had to be Miss Martineau—holding an ear trumpet and dressed in black crêpe, as if in mourning for the Deity in whom she did not believe. "Here's another fact Mr. Venables won't find soothing: the Earth's celestial brethren no longer number six, the planet Neptune having been observed and named three years ago. Let me suggest that, if our guest wishes to corroborate God through astronomy, he should keep abreast of the field."

Last to hold forth was a nondescript gentleman whom, by process of elimination, Chloe identified as Mr. Atkinson. "The philosopher David Hume put it well. The human ego is predisposed to, quote, 'spread itself on the world,' projecting private prejudices onto public domains. Mr. Venables's globe, star, and fireflies are no more theologically significant than those *other* phenomena in which we see meanings that aren't there, such as clouds, crystals, tea leaves, and ink stains."

For a prolonged and poignant moment Mr. Venables stared blankly into space, fuming silently. Lord Woolfenden thanked the contestant for diverting the Byssheans with his "lambent though fallacious God proof," then abruptly dismissed him.

An intermission ensued, during which the rakehells indulged in a majority of the sins on view in Seven Dials.

"Tonight's atheist presentation will come from Miss Chloe Bathurst, formerly of the Adelphi Theatre Company," said Lord Woolfenden upon reconvening the contest. "Since leaving the stage, she has pursued a career as a naturalist and currently presides over the Albion Transmutationist Club. Assisted by her brother, Mr. Algernon Bathurst, a dealer in gaming implements, she will enlighten us with a theory drawn from her zoological ruminations."

Affecting a confident air, and doing so with such skill as to feel appreciably imperturbable, Chloe swooped into the library, leafy prop in hand, Algernon at her side. "Behold the Tree of Life!" she exclaimed, setting the little bush on the dais. "No, I do not show you a sacred shrub from Eden, for this specimen is of a quite different order. Gourmands agree that, although its fruits may at first burn the tongue like gall, in time they come to taste sweet as honey!"

Having delivered her carefully rehearsed prologue, she proceeded to improvise a tissue of lies, declaring that, as the keeper of a large private menagerie, she had oft-times found herself in conversation with "scientists who roam the world collecting biological specimens." Over the years her curiosity had been aroused by travelers' accounts of "creatures that belong to different species yet retain membership in one grand family or another—the finches, thrushes, turtles, vipers, toads, and so forth."

Inevitably she'd found herself wondering "why God would make so many kinds to so little purpose." The more she thought about the problem, the more convinced she'd become that, by appealing to natural processes of selection and transmutation, "we can trace each particular type of plant and animal back through countless generations and innumerable varieties to one primordial creature, just as each leaf on this shrub leads to a branch that then takes us to the trunk, which in turn brings us to the taproot, from which we may infer an original seed."

Every eye in the library, she sensed, was fixed on her face and form. Each ear was attuned to her voice. Even the surrounding ramparts of books seemed alive to her words.

"I ask you, ladies and gentlemen, where and when in this grand spectacle of unsupervised speciation must God appear? Where and when do we need the flashy theatrics of Genesis chapter one? I answer as follows: nowhere and never."

Miss Martineau said, "So it's your contention that all living things owe their existence to a single germ cell?"

"Correct."

"Not excluding Man himself?"

"That's right."

"What an exhilarating idea!" exclaimed Miss Martineau.

"'Not excluding Man himself,'" echoed Mr. Holyoake. "I'm glad you warned me, Miss Bathurst, lest I betray an unseemly surprise when a baboon shows up at the next Holyoake family reunion."

"My theory does not count baboons, chimpanzees, gorillas, or orangutangs amongst your progenitors," Chloe explained. "It suggests, rather, that today's humans and modern apes boast an extinct common ancestor."

"Fiddlesticks," said Professor Owen. "For my money, your shrub is no more a disproof of God than an elf is an elephant."

"I shall make one point in the petitioner's favor," said Mr. Chadwick. "To wit, I do not understand her argument and therefore scruple to call it worthless."

"I confess to sharing the vicar's perplexity," said Woolfenden, whereupon the other rakehells murmured in agreement.

"Might I lay a proposition before this august body?" asked Chloe. "Sponsor an expedition to the faraway Galápagos archipelago, for it happens that those volcanic islands harbor vivid illustrations of my theory. I speak now of certain rare giant tortoises, bizarre marine iguanas, and strange terrestrial lizards—plus uncommon finches, flycatchers, and mockingbirds. To see such specimens in the flesh is to know that transmutation has occurred on our planet time and again."

"We have already secured a ship and a captain," noted Algernon, handing Runciter's letter to Lord Woolfenden. "Were you to grant us three hundred pounds with which to engage officers, lay in supplies, and caulk the *Equinox*'s hull, we could set sail within a month, returning to Oxford in less than a year."

"In summary, just as the Diluvian League asked the Shelley Society to finance a hunt for Noah's ark," said Chloe, "so do we now beseech you to patronize our quest for the Tree of Life. Give us the funds, plus a written commission whereby we might attract a crew, and we shall settle this pesky God question once and for all."

"We're prepared to endorse your project and seed it with cash, Miss Bathurst, provided that a majority of our judges is sympathetic," said Woolfenden. "I assume that our freethinkers are keen to have you fetch these wondrous reptiles and birds."

"Bring 'em on," said Atkinson.

"I yearn to ride about town astride a giant tortoise," said Miss Martineau.

"By its fruits ye shall know the Tree of Life," declared Holyoake.

"Whereas our Anglicans are probably less eager to see you sail away on the *Equinox*," said Woolfenden.

"The proposed expedition would be a waste of everyone's time," said Symonds.

A nay vote—and yet Chloe heard in his voice a whiff of equivocation.

"The object of Miss Bathurst's quest is not a tree but a weed of corrupt pedigree," said Owen.

Another nay vote—but again she detected a note of doubt.

Before delivering his verdict, Mr. Chadwick rose from the bench and stood at full height. Despite a certain gawkiness, the man cut an impressive figure. Chloe suspected that half the ewes in his flock accepted the Jehovah hypothesis largely in consequence of their infatuation with this bony Quixote of a cleric.

"I've already noted that Miss Bathurst's argument eludes me in the main, and what I *do* comprehend of it strikes me as dubious at best."

Chloe's palms grew moist. Her bowels contracted into a knot of dread.

"Now permit me to fence with myself," Mr. Chadwick continued. "I cannot but recall Mr. Holyoake's response when asked to sanction the Diluvian League's mission. An atheist, he insisted, has naught to fear from the facts. Surely the same holds true for a Christian. And so I say, 'Send Miss Bathurst to Galápagos!'"

A mellifluous warmth rushed through Chloe's veins. With a single sentence the Reverend Mr. Chadwick had crystallized the conditions whereby she might rescue Papa from the jaws of privation, pluck Algernon from the clutches of dissolution, and be awarded the plummiest part an actress could ever hope to play. Strutting towards the judges' bench, she ascended the dais and pointed to the illustrative shrub.

"Until I come back from Galápagos, bearing the Tree of Life, you will have to make do with this facsimile," she said. "I know you will supply it with the best imitation water and the finest artificial sunlight." She turned and, humming the bawdy ballad through which Jack Rackham had wooed Anne Bonney, followed her little brother out of the library.

Although the Reverend Granville Heathway did not particularly mind his incarceration in Wormleighton Sanitarium, the food being palatable, his keepers agreeable, the appointments generous—he even had an escritoire—and the view from his barred window a pastoral panorama complete with shepherd, flock, and meadow, he worried that his residency in a lunatic asylum might prompt some people to suppose he'd gone mad. In Granville's opinion his recent change of address, from his Down Village parsonage to this Warwickshire barmy bin, did not bespeak a permanent loss of reason. He'd simply mislaid that faculty for the moment, the better to travel unimpeded through his mind's many *terrae incognitae.*

True, prior to his internment, Granville had exhibited behaviors that arguably indicated lunacy. His project of eating the Book of Revelation, for example. Just as the medieval Rabbi Löew had nourished his clay golem by feeding it written prayers, so had Granville sustained his soul by attempting to devour the Apocalypse. He'd gotten as far as the Whore of Babylon, whereupon his beloved Evelyn, flesh of his flesh and bone of his bone, declared that she would walk out the parsonage door and never return if he consumed even one more vision of Saint John the Divine.

But it was not until Granville had begun scouring the countryside for scarecrows and setting them on fire that Evelyn arranged for his residency at Wormleighton. The failure of his fellow Englishmen to appreciate the scarecrow menace was for Granville a continual source of frustration. By day these effigies were benign, keeping the nation's crops from harm, but at night they transmogrified into agents of Satan, suffocating innocent citizens in their beds by cramming straw down their throats.

His promise to enter Wormleighton quietly had turned on two conditions. First, he must be allowed to bring along a dovecote, some unhatched pigeon eggs, and a hot-water bottle to serve as an incubator. Second, if the Mayfair Diluvian League, of which he was a charter member, ever mounted its search for Noah's ark, the explorers must send him regular reports via the first generation of pigeons he raised in the asylum. Initially the leader of the hunt, the Reverend Mr. Dalrymple, dismissed this request as "the quintessence of impracticality." But then Granville's son, Bertram, having absented himself from his teaching duties at St. Giles Grammar School and joined the company of H.M.S. *Paragon,* agreed to collect all eight pigeons from his father's cell, secure them aboard the ship, and dispatch them sequentially as the expedition progressed.

Right before they'd bid each other good-bye, Granville had received Bertram's promise that the first pigeon he released would be Cassandra (the most intelligent of the birds and the one most likely to find her way back to the asylum). Day after day, Granville sat in his white-walled room, his gaze alternating between the window and the empty dovecote. Where was Cassandra? Had she fallen prey to a hawk? Gotten waylaid by a storm? Blasted from the sky by a scarecrow wielding a fowling piece?

And then one morning, shortly after Granville had consumed his breakfast of kippers and buttered oatmeal (not as nourishing as the Apocalypse but still savory), Cassandra came winging through the window bars, warbling triumphantly. O glorious dove! O blessed bird! O angel with a tawny beak! For a full minute she circled the cell, at last settling atop the cote. Deftly Granville unstrapped the capsule from her leg, then extracted and unfurled the scrip, only to be astonished by the minuscule hand in which Bertram had written his message.

Fortunately, amongst the personal effects permitted to Granville was a brass-framed quizzing-glass for reading Holy Writ (his keepers having allowed him a Bible after he'd sworn not to eat it). The device proved equal to the infinitesimal, recovering Bertram's words from the microscopic realm and displaying them before Granville's incredulous gaze.

Dearest Father,

Greetings from the Orient! I hope that this, the first of my dispatches, finds you in better spirits than when we sat in the asylum garden discussing my imminent adventure and your recent internment. How infuriating that your keepers have failed to understand that your present mental state is in fact an extravagant form of sanity.

The month of August found us navigating the Mediterranean Sea, dropping anchor off the fabled isle of Crete. After reprovisioning in Ierápetra, we negotiated the Dardanelles, then crossed the Marmara and set our course for the Bosporus, until at last we reached the capital of the Ottoman Empire.

Constantinople! Has ever a city been blessed with a more euphonic name? Speak the word slowly. Con-stan-ti-no-ple. Do you hear the enchantment in those syllables, Father? I'm sure you do, for this is the most mysterious, beautiful, and—if one believes the stories about a local hookah-den—magical metropolis on Earth.

Thirteen of Sultan Abdülmecid's courtiers awaited us on the docks, a delegation headed by the Grand Vizier, Mustafa Reshid Pasha, an urbane person with a remarkable beard, long and curved like a scimitar. I soon inferred that, prior to our departure, the Reverend Mr. Dalrymple had corresponded in French with Mustafa Reshid, who'd mastered that tongue during his diplomatic missions to Paris. And now these two worldly gentlemen were finally meeting face-to-face.

Mustafa Reshid and the courtiers directed our party into a coach drawn by four Arabian horses. Our first stop was the Hippodrome, built by the Romans as a chariot-racing arena and presently employed by the Turks for their own equestrian spectacles. Then came Hagia Sophia, formerly a Byzantine church, now a mosque ringed by soaring minarets. Next we saw the forum of Constantine, featuring an immense Roman column believed to contain, in the Grand Vizier's words, "evidence that we are indeed in the land of Noah, including the adz with which he built the ark and the skull of the first African lion to come on board."

The most curious item on our itinerary was the Hookah-Den of Yusuf ibn Ziayüddin. Given the lateness of the hour, Mustafa Reshid declined to take us inside, but he assured us we weren't missing much. He called it "a rank and shoddy establishment" that stayed in business only in consequence of "a legend more fabulous than anything Scheherazade ever told the Persian King."

"Let me guess," said Captain Deardon. "The ghost of Sinbad the Sailor is in there right now, puffing on a water-pipe and recounting his escape from a cyclops."

"You are close to the mark," said the Grand Vizier. "Our more credulous citizens will tell you that the den is frozen in the Christian year A.D. 1000, at the height of the Byzantine Empire, drawing its cus-

tomers not only from distant towns and faraway lands but also from epochs yet to come."

"That makes no sense," I observed.

"You are correct, Effendi. The claim strains credulity. My body-guards patronize Yusuf ibn Ziayüddin, and they have yet to meet a pilgrim from the future. Still, there is a certain logic to the legend. Constantinople has always been an intellectual crossroads, a place where a mad philosopher, visionary poet, or wandering soothsayer might find a sympathetic audience—and so in His beneficence Allah exempted one tiny patch of Byzantium from the laws of time and chance."

As dusk shrouded the city, the Grand Vizier escorted our party to the Topkapi Palace with its spectacular view of the harbor. After assigning each of us a private suite, Reshid Pasha's majordomo explained that we would next descend to the southwest courtyard, shed our clothing, and avail ourselves of "that most civilized of amenities, a haman," *by which he meant a Turkish steam bath. Striving mightily to avoid giving insult, Mr. Dalrymple explained that we English do not have nakedness in our culture, then hastened to add that he had no objection to public bathing* per se, *especially not the sort practiced in Constantinople.*

The following morning, as we all sat in an elegant salon eating bread, cheese, honey, and fruit whilst drinking preternaturally strong coffee, I came to understand that the bond between Reshid Pasha and Mr. Dalrymple is more in the nature of a treaty than a friendship. It seems that several months ago they struck an accord whereby the Grand Vizier would assist the Diluvian League in excavating Noah's ark, reprovisioning the Paragon, *and granting both vessels safe passage through the Bosporus. For his part, Dalrymple will intercede with the Archbishop of Canterbury, who will in turn urge Her Majesty to form an alliance with the Ottoman Empire prior to Turkey's coming clash with Russia (an inevitable conflict, Reshid Pasha believes, given the Tsar's desire to drive the Moslem infidel out of Europe).*

For the remainder of our repast, we discussed what lay ahead for the Diluvian League—a 700-mile voyage to Trebizond, followed by a

180-mile overland passage. Reshid Pasha proposed not only to equip the expedition with victuals, sweet water, sailcloth, rope, and sledges but also to lend it the talents of Ahmed Silahdar, commander of his bodyguards, who has considerable experience negotiating the harsh terrain of Anatolia. Most auspiciously, Captain Silahdar will bring along his twenty best men.

Ere the conversation ended, I learned to my astonishment that Reshid Pasha endorses the Diluvian League's mission (which he sees as "a quest to glorify Almighty Allah and by extension the Prophet, peace and blessings be upon him"). Nevertheless, he has misgivings, which he did not forbear to share with Mr. Dalrymple—to wit, he is reluctant to commit soldiers and supplies to an Ararat adventure when, according to the Holy Koran, the ark resides on Mount Al-Judi. By our third bowl of coffee a compromise was reached. Initially the party will search the location suggested by Genesis 8:4, but should that venture fail, everyone will proceed to the place specified in Sura 11:44. I hope Mr. Dalrymple performs a meticulous survey of Ararat. How scandalous it would be if the League left the true Judaic ark sitting where Noah abandoned it and instead brought back a false Moslem ark from Al-Judi.

When the Paragon sails again, I shan't be amongst her passengers. True, I could accompany the expedition as far as Trebizond—but then I would have to stay on board, tending the birds, for Captain Deardon has told me he cannot allow his crew or Silahdar's men to "waste their energy bearing the dovecote south to Ararat." So it appears that the next three months will find me in residence at the palace. One day soon I may revisit Hagia Sophia, the better to appreciate its splendor. I may even slip into Yusuf ibn Ziayüddin's establishment, though I doubt that I'll encounter any travelers from the future.

Your loving son,
Bertram

Upon reading his son's message, Granville knitted his brow and furled the scrip, as momentous in its own way as the paper prayers that had nourished Rabbi Löew's golem. He deposited the pigeon missive in the drawer of his nightstand. Although the news from Constantinople was heartening—how marvelous that the Grand Vizier had decided to help facilitate the ark hunt—Granville was troubled by Bertram's dismissal of the Hookah-Den of Yusuf ibn Ziayüddin. Once again the dear boy was being unreasonably chary of the irrational. To paraphrase Saint Anselm's Ontological Proof, the only thing more perfect than an imaginary way station for time travelers would be an actual way station for time travelers, and because a person can conceive of such a place it must ipso facto exist.

Certainly Granville, if given the opportunity, would gladly enter Yusuf Effendi's establishment and sit down amongst the water-pipe users. The chances were excellent that the hookah-den would one day be honored with a visit from Jesus himself—not the Galilean carpenter of the Gospels, of course, but rather the Lord of the Parousia, eager for some peace and quiet amidst the hurly-burly of the Second Coming. Granville would happily buy Christ a bag of hashish and listen to his troubles. It was the least he owed the Word made flesh.

Although Chloe Bathurst's acting career officially began with *The Haunted Priory*, her stage debut had in fact occurred in a school pageant written and directed by her parish priest. Chloe had portrayed Little Aggie Teal, whose parents had neglected to baptize her, a lapse that assumed cosmic proportions when, after being run down by a horse, she arrived unshriven at the gates of Perdition. Before Satan could take the child under his membranous wing, the Redeemer himself materialized in the Bottomless Pit bearing a christening font (a development that, even at age ten, Chloe thought inane). Aggie begged to be sprinkled, Jesus complied, and she was whisked heavenward like smoke up a flue.

Fifteen years later, as Chloe and Algernon approached their father's place of imprisonment, her irony bone began to sing. Whereas the fake Hell that had nearly claimed Aggie Teal announced itself as Lucifer's domain, all leaping flames and prancing imps, the real Hell of Holborn Workhouse presented to the world a soothing and fastidious aspect. Its stone façade was whitewashed, the path neatly raked, the hedges meticulously trimmed.

The inner reaches told, or rather exuded, a different story—a narrative of fumigants locked in a losing battle with proliferating vermin and unemptied chamber pots. After wandering the facility for several minutes, Chloe and Algernon found their way to a courtyard where the cottage of the superintendent, Mr. Wadhams, stood in isolation from the stench. Upon learning that the intruders were Phineas Bathurst's offspring, Wadhams, a pompous autocrat who seemed to be concealing turnips beneath his waistcoat, insisted that, contrary to whatever rumors their father might have circulated during his furlough, he was neither underfed nor overworked. As for the proposed visit, Wadhams would allow it provided Mr. Bathurst continued picking oakum throughout and received from his children no gift of food or spirits.

The superintendent now summoned a cudgel-carrying overseer, one Squibble, who led Chloe and her brother down a spiral staircase to a subterranean chamber lit only by ensconced candles. As her eyes adjusted to the gloom, a grid of refectory tables materialized, each piled high with rigging and towlines. Dressed in paupers' uniforms and supervised by two sentinels armed with truncheons, the inmates took no notice of the newly arrived party but instead pursued their bloody-fingered toil, tearing apart the ropes and shoving the wads of fiber into bushel baskets. Squibble cleared his throat, then thrice banged his cudgel on the stone floor, the harsh reports echoing off the moist walls. Seated at the nearest table, flanked by a pockmarked man and a snaggle-toothed woman, Phineas Bathurst looked up, squinted through the murk, and, recognizing his daughter, smiled like a child eating Christmas pudding.

"Chloe!" he cried, rising to receive her embrace.

"Papa!"

"Keep plucking, Bathurst!" snarled Squibble. "This is a workhouse, not a mineral spring!"

"I see you've brought my prodigal son," said Phineas.

"Good morning, Father," said Algernon.

"He might be prodigal, but at least he visits," said the pockmarked man.

"Perhaps *my* children will show up someday," said the snaggle-toothed woman, "though the odds are better that Wadhams will install an oakum-picking machine down 'ere and pay us two quid a day to drink gin and watch it run."

"When last we talked, you were supporting yourself primarily through vicissitudes," said Phineas, fixing his son with a reproving stare.

"That is still the case," said Algernon. "Vicissitudes have always done right by me, and they continue to claim my allegiance."

"If you're determined to waste your life at basset and faro, you should at least waste it in style," said Phineas. "I pray you, become the Robin Hood of cardsharpers, cheating wealthy gamesters and giving half your profits to the poor."

"Time is short," said Chloe, "but our message is simple." Bending low, she whispered in her father's ear. "Your children are soon to undertake a long—and profitable—sea voyage."

"It's all true, sir," rasped Algernon. "Our scheme enjoys the endorsement of twenty Oxford dandies, three renowned blasphemers, and the Vicar of Wroxton. Your deliverance is at hand."

The news of his children's proximity to wealth had an immediate effect on Phineas. Whistling a sprightly air, he rooted through the jumble of rope and selected two equal segments, one of hemp, the other of jute. With his torn but nimble fingers he sculpted the cords into hangman's nooses, then brought both creations to life.

"Ere my retirement to this establishment," the hemp noose declared, "I cleansed the world of nearly three hundred murderers, includin' nine Bombay thuggees, two regicides, and a Lambeth maniac specializin' in streetwalkers."

"An impressive record," the jute noose conceded, "but mine's more remarkable yet, for in my day I strangled sixty men sent to the gallows on false testimony."

"How can you boast of such a thing?" asked the hemp noose.

"When a government executes its citizens willy-nilly," replied the jute noose, "the people grow fearful, accordin' their rulers the blindest sort of obedience. I'm proud to have made my small contribution to England's social stability."

The pockmarked man bobbed his head approvingly. "'Tis common knowledge that half the hangings at Newgate send blameless souls to oblivion."

"This visit has ended," declared Squibble. "Phineas Bathurst, you will speak no more treasonous bilge within these walls, lest you yourself become a candidate for the scaffold."

"Executin' treason-mongers a speciality," bragged the jute noose.

"Upon my return to England, I shall systematically employ this country's gambling dens in redistributing the Empire's wealth," Algernon promised his father.

"We love you, Papa," said Chloe as Squibble ushered her towards the stairs. "Even as we seek our fortune in the New World, you will never be far from our thoughts."

"Be thee well," said Phineas.

"Good luck," said the hemp noose.

"Godspeed," said the jute noose.

Whereas Miss Bathurst's dubious baboon theory of human origins was, as far as Malcolm Chadwick could determine, a monolithic hypothesis, not yet fractured into competing varieties, Samuel Wilberforce's nickname—"Soapy Sam"—enjoyed no such scholarly unanimity. One theory traced the epithet to the bubble-light quality of the bishop's sermons. Another explanation referenced his habit of punctuating his speeches with a florid hand-washing gesture. The least sympathetic conjecture turned on Wilberforce's slick and slippery practice of passing off a parody of an opponent's position as an accurate paraphrase, a skill through which he routinely won philosophical arguments without resorting to reasoned discourse.

Summoned to the bishop's elegant Oxford abode four days after Miss

Bathurst's presentation, Malcolm knew he was about to encounter neither Sam of the frothy homilies nor Sam of the spotless hands but the
third Wilberforce, the crafty polemicist. The bishop intended to scold
him, as he often did in the wake of a Shelley Society meeting. Malcolm
was still smarting from Wilberforce's reproach following the most recent
appearance at Alastor Hall of the Argument from Evil. "According to
the *Evening Standard,* you unhorsed the contestant through Leibniz's
observation that ours is the best of all possible worlds," said the bishop.
"I especially appreciated your coda, 'emphasis on the *possible.*' Splendid.
Of course, you might have given an *example* of God deferring to necessity. I myself would have adduced the case of bone. The Creator had no
choice but to make our skeletons vulnerable to breakage, for otherwise
we'd be unable to move."

Upon answering Malcolm's knock, Wilberforce's grouchy and officious
butler guided him into the oak-paneled privacy of the library, where the
reading table held a splayed copy of the *Evening Standard.* ATHEIST
JUDGES UNIMPRESSED BY COSMIC CORRELATIONS, shouted the page three
headline, but it was the subheading that had probably caught Wilberforce's attention: FREETHINKING FEMALE NATURALIST TO SEEK PROFANE
"TREE OF LIFE." The paragraphs concerning Miss Bathurst featured quotations from prominent Oxonians, including barrister Andrew Peach,
don Wilfred Glenister, physician Amos Crichlow, and rector Simon
Hallowborn, who'd called her, respectively, "a deluded fool," "an obstreperous wench," "a conceited troublemaker," and "the Covent Garden
Antichrist."

Though hardly an antichrist, Miss Bathurst was surely amongst the
most unappetizing persons Malcolm had ever met. Unlike other contestants of scientific bent, this flighty zookeeper seemed not to care particularly whether God existed, just so long as she pocketed the £10,000.
Should he ever become inspired to write an ode to womanly intellect, he
would select as his subject not the unprincipled Chloe Bathurst but the
formidable Harriet Martineau. Despite her ungainly ear trumpet and
intractable atheism, Miss Martineau remained for Malcolm the paragon
of her sex.

"By rights I should be furious with you," boomed Wilberforce, rushing into the library like a diminutive but implacable tornado. "You could have nipped Miss Bathurst's preposterous argument in the bud, but instead you handed her a ticket to Ecuador."

"If her argument is preposterous, we have naught to fear from it," said Malcolm.

"Don't waggle your Aristotle at me, sir," said Wilberforce. "On the face of it you've bungled this whole affair—yet I believe you may have dealt the Devil a deuce."

"How so?"

Wilberforce sidled towards the shelves devoted to printed sermons, including his own collection, *Sabbath Orations for All Occasions*, a volume thick with (in Malcolm's view) feeble theodicies and anemic exegesis. "By ratifying Miss Bathurst's quest, you have guaranteed that the judges will hear no more of transmutation for at least a year."

"Which gives us time to detect the flaws in her idea," noted Malcolm.

"Better yet, it gives us time to learn where she got it in the first place," said Wilberforce.

"You don't believe the hypothesis is original with her?" asked Malcolm, entering an alcove reserved to Martin Luther and John Calvin, twenty tattered volumes, their bindings now gutters for dust. Evidently Wilberforce hadn't visited the Reformation in years.

"Recall that Miss Bathurst is by training an actress, once employed by such sordid emporia as the Adelphi Theatre," said the bishop. "Are we really to believe that a scatterbrained thespian devised this Tree of Life persiflage on her own? Mark my words, she stole the theory from some *real* scientist. We must locate the man and alert him to the theft."

"And once he realizes what mischief is afoot, he'll come to Alastor Hall and explain why his conjectures don't constitute a disproof of God—is that what you have in mind?"

"Precisely," said Wilberforce, lathering his hands, "which is why I'm giving you a new assignment. Miss Bathurst surely appreciates your recent patronage, so you should have no trouble gaining her trust and learning the origin of her species theory. Indeed, I suspect you'll have coaxed the cat from the bag long before the *Equinox* rounds the Horn."

"Good Lord, Sam, are you suggesting I accompany her on the voyage?"

"No, Malcolm, I'm *insisting* you accompany her."

"An order from my bishop?"

Wilberforce nodded emphatically. "It's all been arranged. For the humbling sum of two hundred pounds, Captain Runciter will engage you as ship's chaplain."

"Two hundred pounds is not *humbling*. It's twice what I make in a year of sermonizing on dry land."

"Runciter is not paying *you*," Wilberforce explained. "The Diocese is paying *him* to take you on. An unsavory arrangement, but the best we could manage on short notice."

"I'm entirely the wrong man for the job," protested Malcolm. "From the moment I clamped eyes on her, I found in Miss Bathurst a person of unbridled arrogance and unmitigated egotism."

"Quite possibly she has a different opinion of herself. The two of you will have much to talk about. If you're wondering who might replace you on the judges' bench, fear not. Owen and Symonds have welcomed me into their fellowship."

Taking Malcolm's arm, Wilberforce propelled him through a set of French doors into the sun-dappled conservatory beyond. The room contained three trilling nightingales in a wicker cage plus two somber men in recumbent postures, one lounging on a divan, the other sprawled across a couch, the first dressed in the blue uniform of a naval commander, the second wearing the immaculate cassock and clean white bib of a cleric who could afford either a laundress or a wife. The bishop made the introductions, presenting Captain Adrian Garrity, "master of the *Antares,* leaving Bristol three weeks hence for the Galápagos archipelago," and Mr. Simon Hallowborn, "servant of the Lord and passenger on that same brig," to Malcolm Chadwick, "the canniest advocate God ever had," then poured everyone sherry from a crystal decanter.

"The Encantadas have become a popular destination," Malcolm observed.

The pallid and sinewy Simon Hallowborn rose and took a swallow of wine, setting his glass atop the piano lid. "Every fortnight I read the *Standard,* eager to learn of your latest adventure amongst the rakehells."

"And I've seen *your* name in that same paper," said Malcolm. "I suspect the epithet you contrived for Miss Bathurst, 'Covent Garden Antichrist,' is going to stick."

"Allow me to state the obvious," said the rector. "The Church owes you a debt of gratitude for defeating every supposed disproof to cross your path, thus exposing this contest as the ludicrous national distraction it has become."

"A distraction, exactly," said Wilberforce. "And yet I worry that even if Miss Bathurst's Tree of Life dies a dog's death at Alastor Hall, it may eventually flourish elsewhere in Britain. I'm pleased to report that at last month's General Synod we took steps to preclude that possibility."

"It's a devilishly dexterous scheme," said Captain Garrity, a lantern-jawed giant who looked capable of severing a towline with his teeth.

"Dexterous, to be sure," said Wilberforce, "but the Devil had naught to do with it."

Fearing that he was about to hear something ignoble, Malcolm drifted into the vicinity of the caged nightingales and attempted to calm himself with their song. Bequeath to transmutationism the world's finest lathe, he mused, give it a flawless loom, a perfect kiln, and still it could never fashion such creatures without divine assistance.

"When the rector and I set sail for Galápagos, our passengers will include scores of criminals from Dartmoor Prison, all slated to reinvigorate an Ecuadorian penal colony on Charles Isle," said Garrity. "The overseers in Quito call the place Ciudad del Diablo, the Devil's City—'Mephistropolis' on all the Royal Navy's maps."

"To understand Her Majesty's unusual interest in Mephistropolis," said Hallowborn, "we must go back nineteen years to the moment when a young American frontiersman, one Orrin Eggwort, took title to Charles Isle. Evidently Eggwort had fought with great valor during Ecuador's war of independence, and so President Flores awarded him his own private island. Eggwort lost no time turning his portion of Galápagos into some sort of Christian utopia and appointing himself emperor—that's right, emperor—as well as *de facto* administrator of the penal colony."

"With the coming of the *Antares*," said Wilberforce, "the population of Mephistropolis will increase by ninety-two English-born convicts—four times the number of Ecuadorian inmates—a figure sufficient to make Charles Isle of a piece with Her Majesty's global penal system. The present Galápagos governor, one Jonathan Stopsack, should then have no difficulty breaking Eggwort to the rank of figurehead and assuming jurisdiction over the whole archipelago, per the 1832 agreement between London and Quito making the Encantadas at once a British protectorate and an Ecuadorian possession."

A disconcerting grin claimed Hallowborn's face. "Beyond their political utility, our ninety-two prisoners will have a spiritual mission as well. Upon disembarking, they will perform a boon on God's behalf."

Malcolm winced and took a long sip of sherry.

"The General Synod, as it happens, was gifted with a twofold revelation concerning the reptiles and birds with which Miss Bathurst intends to demonstrate her theory," said Wilberforce. "First revelation: these creatures are so unloved by Providence that we should regard them as the very spawn of Satan."

"When the Bishop of Panama stumbled upon Galápagos in 1535," added Hallowborn in a tone of corroboration, "he thought he'd found the Devil's *pied-à-terre*."

"Second revelation: nothing would please God more than the elimination of these demonic beasts," said Wilberforce.

"Elimination?" said Malcolm, dumbfounded.

Garrity replied, "My sailors will get rid of the birds: you may be sure we're not about to give fowling pieces to criminals—they'll receive only machetes for the lizards and wire garrotes for the tortoises. If the convicts do their jobs properly, Governor Stopsack will reduce their sentences accordingly."

"We call it the Great Winnowing," added Hallowborn.

The sherry suddenly turned against Malcolm, causing his brain to reel and waves of nausea to roll through his stomach. "What an appalling idea."

"A deadly poison demands a strong emetic," said Wilberforce, clasping Malcolm's shoulder. "Do you remember how John the Baptist called for every unwholesome tree to be cut down and thrown into the fire? For John alone knew that Christ had come, 'whose winnowing-fan is in his hand, and he will purge his threshing-floor.' So shall we scrape Galápagos clean of its wicked finches, depraved mockingbirds, fallen tortoises, and sinful lizards."

"If there's a biblical precedent for your scheme," asserted Malcolm, cringing internally, "it would be the massacre by which Herod sought to murder our Savior in his crib."

"Do not confuse a slaughter of the innocents with a cleansing of the corrupt," said Hallowborn.

"I want no part of this horrid plot," said Malcolm.

"Nor do we ask you to take one," said Wilberforce. "We merely request that throughout your passage to Galápagos you refrain from speaking of the Great Winnowing. And, of course, once it becomes known aboard the *Equinox* that the Encantadas have been harrowed, you must not reveal that the Anglican Communion lent Heaven a hand."

Seeking to settle his stomach, Malcolm entered into what he imagined was a Saint Francis of Assisi sort of rapport with the nightingales. The birds bestowed their healing gifts upon him, even as he took refuge in a comforting thought. At the moment Stopsack and Eggwort might be acquiescing to the proposed mischief, but surely when it came down to it the Governor would never allow his archipelago to become an abattoir, nor would this so-called emperor stand by whilst intruders butchered the reptiles whose meat sustained his community.

"Very well, Sam—I shall remain silent," Malcolm said. For the nonce, he thought.

"Do we have your solemn word?" asked Wilberforce.

"Another order from my bishop?" Malcolm replied, straightaway receiving a nod.

"Remember, sir, to swear before the mortal likes of Sam and myself is perforce to swear before God," said Hallowborn. "Our Creator occupies all places at all times."

"A theological point in which I require no instruction from you," Malcolm told the rector, offering the nightingales a sweet Franciscan smile. "I daresay that, even as He sheds His grace on Oxford, God has betaken Himself to Galápagos, that He might minister to its fallen tortoises and sinful lizards. Yes, Sam. Yes, Simon. You have my word."

Throughout the week preceding the *Equinox*'s scheduled departure, Chloe's energies were consumed largely in evading Mr. Popplewell, who insisted that she submit to an *Evening Standard* interview, "so that thousands of Englishmen might satisfy their curiosity concerning the woman who would put God in His grave." Ever since he'd published his article about the "freethinking female naturalist," with its scurrilous quotation from the Reverend Mr. Hallowborn—"I am moved to call Miss Bathurst the Covent Garden Antichrist"—she'd wanted no truck with Popplewell, his wretched newspaper, or his salivating readership. She could only hope that when she finally gave her prize-winning performance at Alastor Hall, amongst the journalists present would be a sober and appreciative *Times* reporter, perhaps even the one who'd written with such verve about her final gallows speech at the Adelphi.

Beyond the unease Chloe felt at being branded an antichrist (a discomfort leavened somewhat by the satisfaction she took in the epithet), the most troublesome consequence of Popplewell's piece was Fanny Mendrick's discovery that her rooming-companion harbored atheist sympathies. So bitter was the subsequent altercation between Chloe and Fanny that the wreckage of their friendship was surely but one more such quarrel away.

"I don't know which fact gives me greater pain," said Fanny. "That you would murder your Creator or that, having done so, you would collect ten thousand pounds in blood money."

"It's my Christian duty to help my father pay his debts," said Chloe.

"And is it your Christian duty to spit on Christianity?"

"Oh, Fanny, how it grieves me to cause you unhappiness."

"Then burn your ticket to Galápagos."

A particularly exasperating aspect of his "freethinking female naturalist" article was Popplewell's penchant for making a philosophical debate sound like a penny dreadful. In his estimation the interconnected voyages of the *Paragon* and the *Equinox* constituted a "cosmic regatta" between irreconcilable worldviews.

On the one hand, allied with the Church of England and the dictates of tradition, we have Captain Deardon and his company of Anglicans, coursing towards Ararat. On the other, braving the wrath of the faithful and the ire of the angels, we have Captain Runciter's band of unbelievers, heading for Galápagos. Make no mistake, O my readers—the real prize in this race is not £10,000. Whichever company brings back the better evidence will be giving us to know whether we descend from the loving hands of Providence or the hairy loins of primates. Is it any wonder Miss Chloe Bathurst is amongst our nation's most talked-about figures, her praises sung in every hellfire club from Lowestoft to Liverpool, even as her damnation is recommended from thousands of pulpits throughout Great Britain?

On Monday morning Popplewell tracked Chloe to a Bond Street milliner's shop, hovering in the shadows as she opened her purse (newly fattened with Shelley Society funds) to procure an extravagant white Panama hat, perfect for keeping the equatorial sun from ravaging her skin. Upon completing the transaction, she informed the journalist that if he did not absent himself she would seek out a constable and complain that she'd been "subjected to the advances of the lecherous scribbler Pop-plewell." Her nemesis departed straightaway.

The following afternoon she sat down with Mr. Abernathy of Maritime Enterprises, the corporation charged with equipping the voyage, receiving his assurances that the *Equinox* would put to sea with an abundance of animal pens and birdcages. Returning to the street, she again encountered Popplewell. Before he could speak, she told him that unless he disappeared instantly she would visit the nearest magistrate and "swear out a complaint against the unscrupulous penny-a-liner Pop-plewell." Again the scoundrel fled.

Wednesday morning found Chloe and Algernon at the British Museum, where they spent three damp and frigid hours poring over hand-colored maps of the Encantadas, an experience redeemed for her by the delight she took in seeing the positions and shapes of the islands whence came Mr. Darwin's reptiles and birds. (Charles Isle resembled a walnut shell, Indefatigable a fried egg, Narborough a mushroom cap, Albemarle a gouty foot.) Exiting the map room, she and her brother were importuned by Popplewell. This time around, she deferred to Algernon, who brandished his furled umbrella and waved it about whilst feigning derangement. The journalist vanished.

Chloe would admit that the "freethinking female naturalist" article had brought one blessing into her life. Thanks to Popplewell's pen, the management of the Adelphi Theatre now perceived her not as a nuisance with anarchist sensibilities but as a resourceful bluestocking capable of wheedling £300 from the Shelley Society, which meant that her dealings with the playhouse need no longer take the form of theft. Instead she could walk through the front door of a Wednesday afternoon, seek out Mr. Kean, and propose to buy, for two pounds sterling, the female pirate regalia that had figured so prominently in *The Beauteous Buccaneer*. Like most aspiring transmutationists, Chloe was not superstitious, and yet she could not but impute certain arcane powers to these costumes: by outfitting herself as Pirate Anne or Pirate Mary she would *become* Pirate Anne or Pirate Mary—women who, owing to their many years of sinking ships and accumulating doubloons, were far better suited to the imminent voyage than was Chloe Bathurst, who'd never even seen the Atlantic Ocean, much less sailed upon it.

Mr. Kean cheerily accepted her offer, dispatching his wife to the wardrobe racks. Ellen Tree returned promptly, costumes in hand. Chloe left the manager's office in good spirits, clutching a muslin sack stuffed with the talismanic garments.

No sooner had she stepped into the foyer, now overrun with playgoers leaving the matinee performance of *Via Dolorosa*, than a tall figure with a walking-stick planted himself in her path.

"Good afternoon, Miss Bathurst."

She could scarcely credit her senses, which disclosed not only the haggard features of Mr. Darwin's face but also the rasp of his cough and the acrid aroma of his tobacco. "Hello, sir," she replied, her throat constricting as if she'd fallen prey to one of her father's talkative nooses.

"How felicitous to find you here." Mr. Darwin puffed on his cigarette, exhaling a pungent zephyr. "I've been searching for my erstwhile zookeeper all day." Elaborating, he revealed that after arriving on the morning train he'd made inquiries at the Adelphi. Eventually Fanny Mendrick had stepped forward to explain that she and Miss Bathurst were "friends and fellow lodgers whose affection has been compromised by the Shelley Prize." On apprehending that she was speaking with Chloe's former employer, Miss Mendrick had offered him directions to their rooms, noting that Miss Bathurst was usually "out and about until sundown, making preparations for her awful sea voyage," and so he'd resolved to spend the afternoon on the premises, watching Miss Mendrick portray the saintly Veronica.

"Have you been well, Miss Bathurst?" asked Mr. Darwin, flourishing the "freethinking female naturalist" edition of the *Evening Standard*.

"I must confess to considerable fatigue. Pondering the arguments I overheard in our vivarium"—it would be best, she decided, not to mention her stolen copy of the essay—"is a wearying vocation. May I assume you are furious with me?"

"I have my usual complaints," said Mr. Darwin, vaulting past her question whilst massaging his temples. "Headaches. Nausea. Insomnia. Each month I go to Malvern for Dr. Gully's cold-water treatments. They seem to help. Yes, Miss Bathurst, I am furious with you, though my feelings are tempered by a certain begrudging wonder that you have come so far so fast."

Sensing that he needed to get off his feet, she guided Mr. Darwin into an alcove decorated with posters for Adelphi productions gone by: *The Beauteous Buccaneer, Wicked Ichor, The Raft of the Medusa, The Rime of the Ancient Mariner, The Murders in the Rue Morgue.* He eased himself onto a velvet-upholstered bench, so that a lithographic hodgepodge of pirates, vampires, castaways, wraiths, and orang-utangs swirled above his head like the *dramatis personae* of a nightmare.

"If you're planning to expose me as a fraud, I can hardly blame you," she said.

"Tomorrow, Miss Bathurst, yes, *tomorrow* I might inform the *Standard* that you've contrived to pass my species theory off as your own." He secured his walking-stick upright between his knees in a tableau suggesting a Hindoo cobra emerging from a basket. "But *today* I wish only to praise my zookeeper. One might even say I've come to offer her a benediction."

"A benediction?" she said, astonished.

"Don't overestimate my sympathy. Had I two thousand surplus pounds, I would cover your father's debts, then arrange for you to tell the world you no longer believe in transmutationism. That said, I must allow as how a part of me wants you to claim the prize, for it happens that my relationship with God—"

"Assuming He exists."

"Assuming He exists, our relationship is in such disarray that I should be glad to see Him thrown down."

"'For 'tis not mere blood we seek but the thrill of mocking the cosmos.'"

"How's that?"

"A line from this confection by Mr. Jerrold," said Chloe, pointing to the *Wicked Ichor* poster. "If you want me to win the contest, why not give me that scrivener's copy of the full treatise? Whilst you're about it, why not lend me your menagerie, thus sparing me a journey to the New World?"

"Why not, Miss Bathurst?" said Mr. Darwin indignantly. "Why not? Because a greater part of me is horrified that my idea has been dragooned into so tawdry an enterprise."

"In your shoes, I would feel the same way."

"Furthermore, though personally prepared to forsake theism, I question whether anyone has the right to deprive his fellow humans of its comforts."

"Were I to give the issue more thought, I would surely agree with you," she said. "Tell me of your difficulties with the Almighty."

Mr. Darwin rose and strode up to the *Raft of the Medusa* poster, an image that, though intended to evoke the famous painting, took as many liberties with Géricault's masterpiece as had Bulwer-Lytton's play with the historical facts. "Before finding my true calling, I intended to become a physician. Oft-times my training required me to visit private homes, attending to patients whose illnesses were so contagious that no hospital would admit them. I saw many an innocent child suffer and die."

"And you wondered why a loving God would permit such a state of affairs?"

"No, back then I never doubted His goodness."

Mr. Darwin fell silent. A tear coursed down his cheek, followed by another. At last he spoke two syllables.

"Annie."

"Annie?"

"The signs are unmistakable. Night and day she lies a-bed, clutching that doll you gave her, vomiting, spitting blood, burning with fever, her little heart racing. She has consumption—I know it." Mr. Darwin jabbed the floor with his walking-stick, as if to wound the world that had sickened his child. "Consumption. There—you see? I found the courage to speak the word. My dear sweet Annie has pulmonary consumption."

Now Chloe, too, began to weep, soon sobbing with all the ferocious hopelessness of Cleopatra cradling her dying Antony. "That child is a gift from the angels."

"There are no angels, Miss Bathurst. As His earthly avatars God appoints only vengeful demons."

From her reticule Chloe withdrew a handkerchief, using it to daub first Mr. Darwin's tears and then her own. "Vengeful demons," she echoed, blowing her nose. *"C'est vrai."*

In an apparent bid to change an intolerable subject, Mr. Darwin gestured towards the central figure in the *Raft of the Medusa* poster, Françoise Gauvin, standing in the prow of the improvised vessel and frantically signaling the *Argus*—though ultimately the frigate had sailed into the sunset, heedless of the surviving *Medusa* passengers (fifteen out of an original hundred and fifty, the others having succumbed to thirst, duels, murder plots, and suicide). "Is that supposed to be you?"

"I portrayed a fictitious female survivor," Chloe replied, absorbing the last of her tears. "Throughout the play she struggles to forestall her shipmates' descent into cannibalism. Her best speech finds her scrambling atop a pile of corpses and screaming, 'He who would eat his fellow man must answer to his God!' One night, just to be clever, I added, 'And he who would eat his God must answer to his fellow man!'"

"Should I assume the piece is allegorical? Is the raft a metaphor for the world?"

"The playwright, Mr. Bulwer-Lytton, has proven himself a stranger to symbolism and other literary felicities. I believe he was drawn primarily to the luridness of the tale. When next you see Miss Annie, give her a kiss from me."

Mr. Darwin pivoted on his heel and fixed Chloe with a marine iguana's implacable stare. "Get thee to South America, Miss Bathurst. Find your inverse Eden. Who am I to judge your overweening ambition? We're a damned and desperate species, the lot of us, adrift on a wretched raft, scanning the horizon with bloodshot eyes and hollow expectations. Go to the Encantadas. Go with my blessing."

Having made his parting remark, Mr. Darwin firmed his grip on his walking-stick and, wreathed in cigarette smoke, shambled into the Strand, doubtless seeking to distract himself with the sights, sounds, and fragrances of London, a desire that the indifferent city would surely fulfill straightaway, with myriad sensations to spare—and yet it seemed he was also looking for a ship, the frigate of his most fervent desire, the *Argus* that would never come.

5

Chloe Explores St. Paul's Rocks, Home to Brown Boobies, Black Noddies, Belligerent Crabs, and Her Greatest Admirer

B y a regrettable turn of the cards and a woeful rotation of Dame Fortune's wheel, the date on which Chloe and Algernon undertook the final leg of their journey from London to the moored *Equinox* coincided with the moment that the leaders of the Chartist movement had elected to stage political demonstrations throughout England. The 20th of October, 1849, began innocuously enough, Chloe awakening in a Haslemere inn, slipping into her Pirate Anne costume (indubitably the proper ensemble for the first day of her grand adventure), and collecting her luggage, including the sandalwood box in which she now stored the transmutation essay. She proceeded to the courtyard, joining her waistcoated, beaver-hatted brother and their fellow travelers: a solicitor on holiday with his wife and their two daughters. Everyone scrambled into the Great Southern Transit Company coach, which promptly set off for the seacoast, and by ten o'clock the passengers were breaking their fast in Brighton.

The trouble began in Portsmouth, its public square so clogged with Chartist protestors that the coachman had to maneuver through a treacherous labyrinth of back streets, a strategy likewise required by conditions in Bournemouth and Weymouth. Although Chloe imagined that these delays might necessitate a full day's postponement of the voyage (a dreadful possibility, the ark hunters having left two weeks earlier), that was certainly preferable to being waylaid by the protestors, who brandished not only placards but also pitchforks, cudgels, and, in a few alarming cases, firearms.

Overlooking the dissidents' uncouth appearances, she decided their desires were not unreasonable. VOTES FOR ALL MALE CITIZENS ran the most common sentiment. Other signs insisted SECRET BALLOTS ARE A SACRED RIGHT, whilst others promoted A COTTAGE FOR EVERY HONEST WORKER. But Algernon (as prescient in political matters as he was inept at faro) declared the movement moribund. The Chartists' demands, he told Chloe, would not be seriously addressed until a generation of plebeians presently in embryo got themselves born, came of age, took note of their lamentable condition, and laid their case before a newly minted Parliament.

"Once we've collected the prize," said Chloe, "we must donate a portion to the cause of economic justice."

"Sweetest sister, don't count your chickens ere they've transmuted," said Algernon.

Surveying the angry placards, Chloe speculated that human beings might do well to petition God in this fashion, as opposed to the more modest medium of prayer. She wondered what demands she might herself post on Heaven's gates. NO PULMONARY CONSUMPTION IN PERSONS UNDER FORTY. Yes, that had the proper ring. LAZARUS GOT A SECOND CHANCE, HOW ABOUT ANNIE DARWIN? A fair question, she decided.

Despite her fears, the coach reached Plymouth by early afternoon, well before the turning of the tide. Upon shedding the solicitor and his family in the town center, the driver proceeded to the harbor, with its soaring groves of masts and bristling hedges of bowsprits. The docks swarmed with protestors, including not only the expected Chartists but also a faction of religionists enraged by Chloe's project, plus a deputation of freethinkers. This third group, predictably, was in the minority, their placards correspondingly tepid: HAIL AND FAREWELL, TRANSMUTATIONISTS . . . A FAVORING WIND FOR THE GREAT QUEST . . . CHLOE BATHURST, AVATAR

OF REASON. God's defenders, by contrast, brought bravado to their epigrams: NO SUCCOR FOR THE BRIDE OF BEELZEBUB . . . DOWN WITH THE SLUT OF SCIENCE . . . AS JESUS CURSED THE FIG TREE, SO HE REVILETH THE BATHURST TREE.

"Their vehemence frightens me," she told her brother. "On the other hand, I rarely stirred such passions at the Adelphi."

"Enjoy this moment in full," Algernon advised her, "for all infamy is fleeting."

The coachman halted alongside the gangway, then hopped free of his box and opened the door as a party of four *Equinox* crewmen scurried into view and began unstrapping the trunks, duffels, portmanteaus, and valises from the roof.

"In my capacity as leader of this expedition," Chloe told her brother, "I shall now issue my first order."

"As opposed to the ten thousand you've given me in your capacity as my elder sister," said Algernon.

"Get thee to the hold and ascertain that our animal pens and birdcages have been competently secured."

"Your wish is my command."

"No, little brother. My command is your command."

As Algernon instructed the crewmen to stow the luggage in the cabins reserved to himself and his sister, the religionists shifted tactics, from verbal abuse to vegetable aggression. Putrid onions flew at Chloe from all directions, glancing off her shoulders and skidding along her back. Moldering potatoes followed, and then came decaying cabbages, arcing through the air like so many guillotined heads being tossed about the Place de la Révolution at the height of the Terror. Although the onslaught greatly distressed her, she took solace in having worn a buccaneer costume instead of her burgundy-velvet Françoise Gauvin gown.

The religionists made ready to launch a second assault, retrieving more missiles from a pony cart jammed with the slimy arsenal, but before they could strike again an elegant and well-favored man in a brass-buttoned frock coat appeared on the quarter-deck, wielding a pistol and commanding a dozen sailors armed with muskets.

"Trim their beards!" shouted the first officer, for surely that was the man's rank. "Rattle their wigs! Fire!"

The sailors raised their muskets and unleashed a fusillade over the heads of the throng.

"Stand down!" the first officer ordered the protestors. "Drop your weapons!"

The religionists scanned one another's faces, quickly reaching an unspoken consensus, then spilled their missiles onto the wharf in a mad circus of tumbling bulbs and rolling tubers.

Algernon guided Chloe up the ramp and into the vicinity of their benefactor, who at close range proved more handsome still, a maritime Adonis with cobalt eyes and a cleft chin. "Mr. Bathurst, I presume?" he said, prompting a nod from Algernon. "Ralph Dartworthy, captain's mate, at your service."

"Allow me to present my sister," said Algernon.

"*Enchantée, Mademoiselle Bathurst.*" Mr. Dartworthy lifted Chloe's hand to his lips and kissed the back of her pirate glove.

"I must thank you for delivering us from the rabble," she said.

"And I must thank *you* for chasing after this great prize," said Mr. Dartworthy. "My piece of it, I'm told, comes to two hundred pounds. Captain Runciter hopes that you and your brother might join him for supper at eight o'clock."

"Tell the old rogue we accept his invitation," said Algernon.

"And will *you* be at the captain's table, Mr. Dartworthy?" asked Chloe.

"'Tis not every day a man gets to dine with an antichrist," he replied with a sly smile. "I've never before seen a person change wine into venom or bread into stones. I wouldn't miss it for the world."

Amongst the useful bits of information Chloe had acquired during her theatrical career was a formula for removing stains from cloth. The secret lay in a confluence of soap, water, lemon juice, and doggedness. Although citrus fruits were understandably at a premium aboard the *Equinox* (their efficacy against the scurvy being a proven scientific fact), she nevertheless persuaded the sea-cook to peel two lemons, keep the pulp for his tea, and present her with the rinds. Laboring strenuously in her cramped poop-deck cabin, she successfully scrubbed the foul-smelling smears and blotches from her buccaneer ensemble.

Upon removing the last spot, she changed into her burgundy-velvet gown and returned to the open air, just in time to observe the crew unbinding the brig from the wharf. The arrival of a woman on the weather deck did not go unnoticed by the sailors, who variously inspected her with slack-jawed amazement, wide-eyed salaciousness, and a cringing discomfort that she interpreted (given her reputation as the enemy of all things holy) as the fear of God. Mr. Dartworthy was everywhere at once, consigning some men to the sheets and braces, sending others up the shrouds, so that the foresail, headsails, topgallants, and royals were soon loosed into the press of the wind, each great block of canvas falling into place like a curtain demarking the end of an Adelphi Company melodrama.

As the westering sun inflamed her wake, the *Equinox* sailed free of the harbor and scudded into the channel, so that Chloe in time found herself surrounded by vast tracts of water. Her skin prickled, alive to the salt air and the impending quest, even as her mind reeled with the humbling geometry of the sea. Here on the mighty North Atlantic, the normally wide gap between the intimate and the infinite did not obtain. Her cabin was absurdly small, and yet just beyond its confines lay the unbounded main, endless in all directions.

Although Chloe's accommodations suggested a sarcophagus, the captain's quarters were as capacious as a bishop's tomb. As she approached the linen-draped table, her velvet gown glowing in the candlelight, four gentlemen set down their goblets, rose from their chairs, and bowed. Clamping eyes on Captain Runciter, a bulky man with a silver beard, she pictured him perched on the Tree of Life, the branch cracking beneath his weight and returning him to his apish ancestors. He introduced himself in a booming voice, averring that, although he disapproved of deicide on first principles, he intended to get everyone to Galápagos and back without misadventure.

"I'm pleased to see you looking so well, Miss Bathurst, after your encounter with the mob," said Mr. Dartworthy, pulling out a chair and guiding her onto the plush cushion.

"But for your gallantry, sir, my buccaneer ensemble would have been irretrievably tarnished," she said.

"By the by, your animal pens and birdcages are all safely on board." Algernon took hold of a green bottle and filled her glass with a honey-colored fluid. "Have some wine, sweetest sister."

"A commendable Tokay," noted a third personage, a gangly man in a parson's collar.

"What would we ever do without our pirate costumes?" Algernon replenished his own glass. "Oft-times I've said to myself, 'I can't imagine what I'll wear to Her Majesty's next ball.' And suddenly the answer dawns on me."

"Speaking of the theatre, I was recently privileged to observe one of your performances," said the unidentified cleric to Chloe.

"As the Beauteous Buccaneer?" she asked.

"As a Shelley Prize contestant," replied the stranger with a furtive smile—and suddenly she recalled him: the vicar who'd cast the deciding vote in favor of the quest. "We've not been formally introduced." He extended his arm, nearly knocking over his Tokay glass. "Malcolm Chadwick, your brother's cabinmate."

"Forgive me for not recognizing you," she said, shaking the vicar's hand. "The low light deceived me, as did my assumption you were still in Oxford."

"Needless to say, Mr. Chadwick has no interest in whatever financial rewards this expedition might yield," Captain Runciter explained. "The Oxford Diocese has appointed him ship's chaplain. Mark my words, ere this voyage is done our crew will have need of spiritual solace. Thanks to that scribbler Popplewell, word has been flying up and down the Channel that anyone who signs aboard the *Equinox* is risking his immortal soul."

"Which doubtless made finding men difficult," said Algernon.

"In fact, we had to turn applicants away," said Mr. Dartworthy. "For a British sailor, evidently, killing God does not feel as bad as owning a piece of the Shelley Prize feels good."

Now the food arrived, a cornucopia of roast beef, baked ham, and fresh mackerel, served on china plates by the captain's steward. The vicar offered a laconic grace, and then everyone set upon the feast.

"Miss Bathurst, I want you to know that, for all my loyalty to the Church of England, I am intrigued by your species theory," said Mr. Chadwick, indicating her with his fork, its tines holding a nugget of beef. "I look forward to discussing its sources and implications with you in the weeks to come."

"We may talk about my idea whenever you wish," she said, feigning nonchalance. "It's the least I owe the man who persuaded Woolfenden to patronize us. But please satisfy my curiosity. Who's taking your place on the judges' bench?"

"None other than Bishop Wilberforce. Let me add that I've permanently recused myself from the contest, as my association with this expedition cannot but compromise my objectivity concerning your alleged disproof."

"Well, sister, there's a piece of luck," said Algernon. "With the impossibly pious Soapy Sam on the bench, no upstart atheist will bag the prize in our absence."

Chloe chewed a morsel of ham and nodded in assent. Algernon was right—at the moment both Bishop Wilberforce and Mr. Chadwick were precisely where she wanted them. And yet the vicar's presence seemed as contrived as anything in a Bulwer-Lytton melodrama. Ship's chaplain indeed. Something exceedingly odd was afoot.

"Forgive my suspicions, Reverend, but would we not be within our rights to consider you a Jonah?" asked Mr. Dartworthy, as if he'd read her mind. "After all, you want our mission to fail. You hope we'll return to England with nary an illustrative specimen."

"On my view, the Galápagos creatures pose no threat to God's credibility," said Mr. Chadwick. "As I asserted back at Alastor Hall, a Christian has nothing to fear from the facts."

"Though when I consider the fate of the great library of Antioch," said Mr. Dartworthy, "I would say the facts may have much to fear from a Christian."

"Good heavens, Ralph, you sound like one of those blasted freethinkers yourself," said Runciter. "I don't care if you're a secret Chartist, a closet Jacobin, or a procurer for a Persian seraglio—but I won't have you gainsaying Her Majesty's Church at my table!"

"Sir, you've smoked me out," said Mr. Dartworthy. "Your first officer is one of those blasted freethinkers, answering on occasion to the name of atheist."

Chloe reddened with pleasurable dismay. It was one thing to *pose* as an atheist (by way of acquiring a small fortune and overdue adulation) and quite another actually to *be* an atheist. To what depths did Mr. Dartworthy's disaffection run? Would he feel at home amongst the Byssheans of Alastor Hall, writing lewd poetry with one hand whilst groping a paramour with the other?

"So we have two unbelievers amongst us," said Mr. Chadwick, "and two men of faith—am I correct in labeling you a Christian, Captain?"

"A very bad Christian," said Runciter, "a Christian who has violated all ten commandments and several bylaws as well, but a Christian nevertheless."

"We shall leave it to Mr. Bathurst to break the tie," said Mr. Chadwick to Algernon. "Given your efforts in support of Miss Bathurst's cause, should I take my cabinmate for a religious skeptic?"

"Although the Almighty and I aren't on speaking terms, I would never presume to doubt His existence," said Algernon. "How, then, to explain my membership in the Transmutationist Club? Let's just say I am my sister's keeper."

"The sea is a dangerous place for a woman," said Mr. Chadwick, nodding.

"So is dry land," said Chloe.

"Tell me, Reverend," said Mr. Dartworthy. "Do you and your fellow vicars ever get together for wine-tasting parties, using the residue of Eucharists gone by? 'Here, Father Lambert, try Father Frickert's Château

Absolution from Easter Sunday of 1832, an excellent vintage with a lingering bouquet.' 'I quite agree, Friar Alcott, but have you appraised Father Marbury's Vin d'Infini from Ascension Sunday of 1798? It has a *je ne sais quoi* not attained since Thomas à Becket himself was performing the magic at the altar.'"

"That will be all, Ralph," said Runciter. "Mr. Chadwick is not amused."

"But neither am I offended," said the vicar. "Irreverence is always an embarrassment to itself, especially when mouthed by village atheists like Mr. Dartworthy. God is not so easily mocked."

"I'll drink to that," said Runciter, raising his glass.

"To what?" asked Algernon.

"To the unmockability of God."

"Hear, hear," said Algernon.

"God is not mocked," said Mr. Chadwick, elevating his wine.

"But village atheists are always fair game," said Mr. Dartworthy.

"To the unmockability of God," said Chloe. As opposed to the cosmos, she thought. "And to the necessity of village atheists," she added, assuming her most provocative Carmine the vampire smile—the trick was to keep the lower lip immobile—and bestowing it on Mr. Dartworthy.

Like compass needles in thrall to a lodestone, each goblet sought out its companions, all five connecting with crystalline clinks.

"It's going to be a long voyage," said Mr. Dartworthy, offering Chloe an admiring glance. "And owing to the presence of the lovely Miss Bathurst, it promises to be an enchanting voyage as well."

A long voyage: quite so. In fact, the most monotonous odyssey imaginable, Chloe soon realized, a one-way ticket to tedium and beyond. Day after day, week upon week, the *Equinox* cleaved to her course, south by southwest, ever onward, bound for the great port city of Fortaleza on the Brazilian coast, where Captain Runciter intended to reprovision ere beginning the protracted journey to Cape Horn. Having laden the brig with plenty of victuals, sailcloth, and potable water, he was loath to stop anywhere between the fiftieth parallel and the equator. The *Equinox* pursued a negative itinerary, a succession of ports not called, from La Coruña to Lisbon to Tenerife to St. Jago. An aura of disgruntlement hung over the decks, the inevitable mood of a crew that needed, as Mr. Dartworthy told Chloe with a hasty grin, "wine, women, and song of the sort found in harbor towns, as opposed to the grog, onanism, and chanteys available on the *Equinox*."

Although Chloe could appreciate the crew's desire to stretch their legs and engage in other acts of elongation, the need to outdistance the ark hunters trumped all other considerations, and she thanked Dame Fortune that the crossing to Brazil would occur without any hiatuses beyond those occasioned by doldrums, storms, and what Mr. Dartworthy called "Captain Runciter's peculiar notions of how to plot a course." Nevertheless, there were times when she yearned for the marvels of the terrestrial world (dogs romping through Hampstead Heath, children sailing toy boats on the Serpentine, street musicians playing their squeezeboxes in Piccadilly). Deep and awesome as the Atlantic might be, it lacked for variety and drama. The sea was impressive, but it did not have a plot.

True, the present adventure featured intriguing fauna—flocks of greedy gulls, schools of rambunctious porpoises, herds of playful right whales, not to mention Second Officer Hugh Pritchard's noisy monkey, a capuchin named Bartholomew, forever clapping his paws and shrieking *chee-chee-chee*—but she took little joy in these creatures and their antics. With their opaque pedigrees and obscure lineages, each such bird and beast reminded her that she was not so much impersonating a naturalist as living a lie. How close together on the Tree of Life would Mr. Darwin place a storm petrel and a goshawk? What common progenitor did a Cape Verde dolphin share with a Thames River water vole? At what point did Bartholomew's ancestry become synonymous with that of his human owner? Here and now, on the sunbaked decks of the *Equinox*, her ignorance seemed as vast as the omnipresent ocean.

Beginning each evening at eight o'clock Chloe was obliged, as a regular guest at the captain's table, to witness Mr. Dartworthy and Mr. Chadwick debating the mystery of First Causes. Spirited and erudite though they were, these exchanges did nothing to relieve her languors, for in fact she'd grown sick of the whole God question, even when it touched directly on the Shelley Prize. Were it not for her fascination with the brig's first officer, she would have declined Merridew Runciter's dinner invitations—an option embraced by her brother, who preferred to play at dice and cards with the able-bodied seamen amidst their dank, odiferous hammocks.

Although Mr. Dartworthy's understanding of transmutationism seemed patchy at best, he clearly reveled in the prospect of having his atheism corroborated by the Galápagos fauna, even as Mr. Chadwick accused that same atheism of being little more than its own variety of faith. "And a poorly reasoned faith withal," said the vicar shortly after the *Equinox* crossed the Tropic of Cancer, "lacking the sort of robust evidence on which my own convictions are founded. I speak of Holy Writ and the testament of visible Creation."

"May I assume you do not believe in trolls, Reverend?" Mr. Dartworthy inquired by way of retort.

Mr. Chadwick answered with a glower.

"Would you assert that such skepticism constitutes an act of faith?" Mr. Dartworthy continued. "Must you have a religious revelation ere entertaining doubts about trolls? Do you need a heavenly choir to appear before you, singing, 'Hear us now, Vicar of Wroxton, and know cave monsters for a delusion'?"

"If I thought as you do, I should never get out of bed in the morning, for fear of finding the world had lost all coherence," said Mr. Chadwick. "Face it, sir, even *you* don't think as you do. An atheist cannot begin to tell us why the trees bud every spring, or why a drover might lose his heart to a goose girl, yet when did you last spurn a piece of fruit or a maiden's smile because apples and desire must be taken on faith?" From his coat pocket he produced a small Bible, slapping it onto the table like a gamester playing the ace of trumps. "Read the Book of Job, and you'll see that we can account for the ways of birds, beasts, and heavenly bodies only by evoking a supernatural agency. 'Where wast thou when I laid the foundations of the Earth? Who laid the cornerstone thereof, when the morning stars sang together, and all the sons of God shouted for joy?'"

"The next time you compare God to a troll," Captain Runciter told Mr. Dartworthy, "our friendship will emerge the worse for it."

"Freethinkers have their books, too," Mr. Dartworthy replied, then revealed that his favorite such text was *The Rubáiyát of Omar Khayyám*, which he'd first learned about from a fellow mariner, a dervish who'd stopped whirling long enough to translate the poems into English. "I keep the manuscript in my bunk. When we get to Fortaleza, I shall betake myself to the nearest cantina, there to sip Madeira"—he leaned towards Chloe and brushed her hand—"whilst our resident player whispers irreverent verses in my ear: 'Allah, perchance, the secret word might spell. If Allah be, he keeps his secret well.'"

"I should be happy to amuse you in such a manner," she said, blushing.

Occasionally Mr. Chadwick tried to lure Chloe into these symposia, particularly when the talk touched on biological matters. Having promised to answer the vicar's questions about her species theory, she normally acquiesced to his invitations, though they seemed motivated less by curiosity than by rancor.

"I don't doubt that the Almighty built a certain flexibility into the natural world," said Mr. Chadwick as the brig blew across the tenth parallel, "but a mutable Creation hardly negates Genesis."

"Once we reach Galápagos and I begin collecting specimens," said Chloe, hoping the subject would change sooner rather than later, "you may find yourself possessed of a different opinion."

"Truth to tell, I don't care if First Causes are ever discussed at this table again," said Captain Runciter. "I insist that for the rest of the evening we address political matters exclusively."

"Excuse me, Miss Bathurst," said Mr. Chadwick, ignoring the captain's plea, "but it appears you can explicate your idea only in reference to a few particular Galápagos reptiles and birds. A theory without universal application is not a theory at all."

So unnerved was Chloe by the vicar's challenge that her stomach suspended its efforts to digest her dinner. "Were we to sail to the South Seas after visiting the Encantadas," she replied, "we would find scores of islands overrun with exemplars of transmutation, but I hesitate to pro-long our voyage by a year."

"In a week or so we sail past a minor archipelago, St. Paul's Rocks, do we not?" said Mr. Chadwick, turning to the captain. "Might we drop anchor for an hour, so that Miss Bathurst can show me some living, breathing arguments for her hypothesis?"

"I shall honor your request," said Runciter, "on the understanding that the subsequent night's conversation will concern not only tropical fauna but also the revolts on the Continent and the famine in Ireland."

"I doubt that St. Paul's Rocks offers compelling evidence for descent with modification," said Chloe, calling to mind Mr. Darwin's opinion, as expressed in his travel journal, that the place was of far greater interest to geologists than to biologists.

The vicar faced Mr. Dartworthy and said, "Such a brittle theory our zookeeper means to foist upon the world."

Chloe grimaced discreetly, her teeth clenching behind sealed lips. How insulting of Mr. Chadwick to call her a zookeeper instead of a naturalist when she'd put far more energy into masquerading as the lat-ter than the former. The vicar had thrown down the gauntlet—and now she was obliged to pick it up. Perhaps during his visit to St. Paul's Rocks Mr. Darwin had overlooked a telling species or two.

"Very well, Mr. Chadwick, I shall escort you about the islands in question."

"Might you include *me* in your adventure?" asked Mr. Dartworthy.

"I should greatly value your companionship," Chloe replied, imagin-ing that he would make not only a credible Antony in *Siren of the Nile* but also a splendid groom in *Miss Bathurst's Nuptials*.

"You see, my fair philosopher, the impending archipelago is danger-ous, home to wild beasts and savage aborigines." Mr. Dartworthy lifted his lips in a wide white topgallant of a grin. "You'll be glad I'm there, for I never met a jaguar I couldn't tame or a cannibal I couldn't trick into his own pot."

"What about sea serpents?" asked Chloe, displaying a smile that, she'd been told, carried all the way to the last row of the Adelphi Theatre.

"I've heard that the waters around St. Paul's Rocks are teeming with 'em."

"Sea serpents are my speciality."

"Don't forget your harpoon," said Runciter, chuckling.

"Good idea, sir, but I won't need one," said Mr. Dartworthy. "I'll simply inform the monsters that they're descended from maggots, whereupon they'll shrivel up and die of shame."

The longer the Reverend Granville Heathway occupied Wormleighton Sanitarium, the more he wondered why Dante had not included boredom amongst the punishments he'd inflicted on his damned souls. True, tedium did not equate precisely to fiery rain, burning tombs, or suffocating feces, but it was excruciating all the same. Day in, day out, Granville sat in his cell, alternately bemoaning his circumstances and reading the single pigeon missive from Bertram. Once each fortnight his dear Evelyn paid him a visit, and together they would stroll about the grounds of the asylum—but she kept these encounters barbarously brief, departing the instant he began discoursing upon the scarecrow menace.

Every time Granville secured an interview with Dr. Earwicker, chief administrator of Wormleighton, he begged permission to pursue some hobby or other, lest his incarceration in the madhouse cause him to go insane. Dr. Earwicker's response never varied: the medical director, Dr. Quelp, had permanently banned all frivolous pastimes. Provided with painting supplies (quoth Quelp), the typical Wormleighton resident would devour the pigments as if they were sweets. Presented with a whittling knife or knitting needle, that same lunatic would in the first instance slit his wrists and in the second poke out an orderly's eyes.

But then one ebullient spring morning Granville became the beneficiary of a miracle. Summoned to Dr. Earwicker's office, he learned that in his case (and in his case alone) Dr. Quelp had rescinded the ban on hobbies. Before the week was out, Granville would receive camel's-hair brushes, blank canvases, and tubes of pigment.

Upon returning to his cell, he beheld a familiar presence, his Muse, a golden-eyed, honey-haired creature called Mireille. She told him to imagine that, after arriving on Crete, Bertram had explored the island's famous labyrinth. Wandering through the corridors and culs-de-sac, torch in hand, Granville's son had in time encountered the chimera whose creation Daedalus had supervised and whose fate Theseus had sealed. Bertram and the man-bull had then engaged in a titanic struggle—a wrestling match that, Mireille insisted, must become the subject of the priest's first painting.

The instant Tobias the orderly brought the materials, Granville set to work on *Bertram versus the Minotaur*, growing so absorbed in the chiaroscuro battle that he failed to notice the arrival of the pigeon Theodora. Only after he'd rendered the figures in full and begun adding details (the red veins flashing in the Minotaur's eyes, the blood flowing from Bertram's wounds) did Granville glance up to behold the messenger strutting atop the dovecote. Hastily he unstrapped the capsule, unraveled the scroll, and seized his quizzing-glass, straightaway determining that Bertram had written in even smaller characters, and at even greater length, than before.

Dearest Father,

Two days ago the Grand Vizier and I stood on the pier and watched as the Mayfair Diluvian League climbed aboard the Paragon, *followed by Captain Deardon and his crew. Next to embark was Captain Silahdar, an athletic man who might claim kinship with Hercules, and then came the twenty promised soldiers. As the sails grew gravid with Bosporus wind, I decided that, if so stalwart a party fails to recover Noah's ark, it won't be found in this century or even in this millennium.*

Later that afternoon, I stole into the Hookah-Den of Yusuf ibn Zi-ayüddin, curious to learn more about the legend that the place attracts time travelers. At the risk of defaming Yusuf Effendi's establishment, I shall report that it recalls Christian representations of Perdition, the air vibrating with a burbling noise suggestive of boiling pitch, the ceiling obscured by a dense mantle of hashish smoke evocative of sulphur fumes. Sensing intuitively why I'd brought my custom here, Yusuf Effendi (an elderly gentleman, half-blind from cataracts) asked about my vocation. No sooner had I described myself as a grammar-school geology instructor than he indicated a fleshy man dressed in a friar's robes, seated before a dormant double-hosed hookah.

"Behold a person who will profit by your companionship," said Yusuf Effendi. "Do not allow appearances to deceive you. He is not so much a monk as a pilgrim in search of Nature's secrets."

After purchasing a bag of hashish, I approached the friar and introduced myself as a schoolman, an Anglican minister's son, and a straggler from a British archeological expedition en route *to Trebizond. When I offered to share my euphorigenic hemp, a smile brightened his owlish, bespectacled face.*

"Being well educated in botany, I can tell you that hashish derives from the female parts of Cannabis sativa," *he said. "My speciality, however, is* Pisum savitum, *the pea plant. You see before you Gregor Mendel of the Augustinian monastery of St. Thomas in Brünn. I walked here in a mere six weeks."*

"You covered the distance from Moravia to Turkey on foot?" I asked, astonished, then shook our hashish into the hookah bowl.

"And I'm glad I did, Herr Heathway," Friar Mendel replied. "Since turning thirty I've suffered from an excess of avoirdupois. *Thanks to my recent trek, I shed a dozen pounds, even as I traveled backwards as many years. Did I perform the computation correctly? You and your fellow Englishmen are living in 1849, ja?"*

Nodding, I ignited the hemp. "Yusuf Effendi tells me you desire to know Nature's secrets."

In defiance of the gloom Friar Mendel's eyes twinkled. "To put it in a nutshell—or, in this instance, a peapod—I am gradually lifting the veil from the mystery of heredity."

"Tell me more." I sucked on my hose, drawing the cooled smoke into my lungs.

From his robe Mendel produced a wooden box, flipping back the lid. Dry, rumpled, spherical seeds filled the compartment. "I selected the humble pea plant because its traits sort readily into contrasting pairs:

inflated pods versus pinched, tall stalks versus short, et cetera. The mon-
astery afforded me ample space for my garden, one sector dedicated to the
study of albumen color, another to jacket tone, the rest to bud position,
pod hue, pod texture, stalk height, and—the trait on which I first
concentrated—seed shape."

"Hmmaaahhh," I said, speaking on behalf of the hashish. Evidently
I'd become a kind of puppet, the Cannabis *my ventriloquist. "I have an*
inkling of what you're talking about. My father breeds carrier pigeons.
Hmmaaahhh."

Mendel sucked on his hookah hose, raising a noisy chain of bubbles in
the water jar. "In shape a Pisum *pea will be either wrinkled, oblate, and*
ugly like a scrotum, or round, smooth, and lovely like a breast." Sensing
my shock, he added, "Why should Augustine be the only Augustinian
who's privileged to wrestle with concupiscence?"

The hashish not only agreed with me, it also validated Mendel's
sentiment. "Good question!"

"It took me forever to establish a true-breeding line of plants yield-
ing only round seeds and a second line yielding only wrinkleds. Left to
their private passions, these creatures would have fertilized themselves, the
anthers swelling with the thrill of procreation until"—the monk thrust his
arms outward—"they burst *within the capsule and sprayed their bounty*
on the female organs."

"I shall never look at a pea in quite the same way again."

"Being bent on hybridization, however, I emasculated each plant of
*the wrinkled-pea type—*snip, snip *went my scissors, and the anthers*
fell away. Next I borrowed a basting brush from the scullery and began
transferring pollen from the stamens of my round-pea plants to the stig-
mas of their wrinkled-pea relations—two hundred and eighty-seven
such acts of artificial fertilization in all. Then came the waiting game.
God's sunshine caressed my plants. His rains nourished their roots. In
time my pregnant buds turned into pods. I opened them up, and what
do you think I found?"

"Peas?"

"Of course peas, Dummkopf*"—Mendel slapped the table—"but*

every one was round, even though wrinkling had characterized half *the parents!"*

"You must have been amazed."

"Not in the least, for I already had my theory in hand. I'm sorry I called you Dummkopf.*"*

"It's quite all right," I said *(though it wasn't).*

"Every Pisum *fancier knows that roundness is a pea's expected shape, but I am the first to ask whether the occasional wrinkles appear capriciously or lawfully. Pondering the problem day after day, I grew convinced that every reproductive cell, whether a male seed or a female egg, carries a constellation of heredity units. Whereas the dominant type of unit determines one category of traits, the deferential type governs another category. Such a recessive characteristic—wrinkling in peas, for example—will find expression only if two corresponding hereditary units show up during the mating process."*

Mendel *flourished a fountain pen, which he subsequently employed to illustrate his conjectures, drawing capital* R's *to mean "Round" and lowercase* w's *to mean "wrinkled" on the back of a hashish menu.*

"Consider the erotic experience I arranged for my true-breeding parent plants. Pollen from round-pea vines entered the bridal bower bearing their dominant R *units, where they paid court to wrinkled-pea ova bearing deferential* w *units. Throughout their wedding night, the* R's *and* w's *mingled to determine not only the outward aspect of the next generation but also—pay close attention—the composition of the sex cells of those future plants. As the buds turned into pods, they had only* Rw *or* wR *combinations to work with, so naturally all the peas looked round, given the subservience of* w *to* R.*"*

"I believe I follow your logic," I said.

Mendel *suckled his hookah hose, inhaling an extravagant cloud of* Cannabis. *"This is great shit."*

"I quite agree."

"When I examined my other hybridization plots, I discovered that in every case the dominant trait had prevailed—yellow albumen over green, gray jackets over white, inflated pods over pinched, green pods

over yellow." The monk contemplated the nozzle of his hose. "I've heard that indulging in Cannabis *creates a desire to munch on something."*

"Now that you mention it—"

With his palm Mendel scooped a cluster of dried peas from his seed box, jamming them into his mouth. "Have some," he said, chewing. "I've got thousands more back in Brünn."

I accepted the invitation, acquiring and consuming a crunchy handful of Pisum *seeds.*

"So there I was," my water-pipe companion continued, "staring at my jars of round first-generation seeds and theorizing that these hybrid Rw's and wR's could bring forth plants bearing both sorts of pea. There was but one way to prove it."

"Wait for next spring, sow the seeds, and observes what happens."

"Precisely! I passed the winter thinking more about Pisum *than did God on the sixth day of Creation. I realized that once I'd planted my round peas and permitted Nature to bless the buds with male and female organs, four kinds of self-fertilization would occur, Rw, wR, RR, and ww. What's more, given that R always trumps w, the ratio of round peas to wrinkled in the pod-children of my hybrids should be three-to-one."*

"I'm on the edge of my seat," I said (though my precarious posture probably owed more to the hashish than to Mendel's narrative).

"Spring came. The peas went into their pots. Sun and rain made their respective contributions. The plants emerged, matured, indulged their reproductive appetites. The buds turned into pods. I snapped one off, opened it up. Within lay both sorts of pea, round and wrinkled! I opened another pod. Round and wrinkled, side by side! And so it went, pod after pod. The chief characteristic of the wrinkled hybrids had re-emerged as if by magic. No, that's wrong—by mathematics: for when I brought in the whole crop, it happened that 5,474 peas were round and 1,850 were wrinkled, the very three-to-one ratio I'd predicted!"

"You are the Nostradamus of biology."

"Not the Nostradamus, the Newton. I can now say with confidence that every generation of plant, bird, and beast is endowed with discrete and segregated packets containing numerous hereditary units, one packet

from the mother, one from the father, each unit keyed to a particular trait. No matter how long their association with one another throughout a species's natural history, these factors do not interact. They are the inviolate molecules of God's modus operandi. *Standing there in my hot garden, surrounded by grids of potted plants, I grasped the law whereby suppressed characteristics reappear in grandchildren, grandnephews, grandnieces, great-grandchildren, and so on. I've done it, Bertram! You're sucking weed with the man who solved the supreme biological riddle!"*

"I assume you lost no time publishing."

The monk set aside his hookah hose, stood up, and put on his skullcap. "I'm a scientist, not a dilettante. More work lies ahead of me, which is why I must begin the long trek back to my monastery. Suppose I were to mate round-yellow hybrids with wrinkled-green ones? In what ratio will their progeny appear? I would predict nine-to-three-to-three-to-one, wouldn't you?"

"Excepting my father, you are quite the cleverest cleric I've ever met."

"When I return to Constantinople, you and I shall do this again. Who knows—perhaps I'll be a famous botanist by then instead of an impoverished deacon. If such is the case, I'll pay for our hashish."

And with that heartfelt vow, perhaps the first of its kind ever uttered by an Augustinian monk, Gregor Mendel left Yusuf Effendi's establishment. I lingered for another hour, smoking and ruminating, then returned to the palace for a nap. My dreams were rapturous, a vision of pea plants sprouting outside the tomb wherein was laid our Lord's body.

Your loving son,
Bertram

As he secured the message in the drawer of his nightstand, Granville's heart swelled with a parental pride so prodigious that he imagined the organ bursting like one of Mendel's anthers. Somehow Bertram had transcended his suspicion of all things metaphysical to embrace Yusuf Effendi's hookah-den. Confronted with a friar living ten years in the future, Bertram had accepted the paradox without complaint.

Granville passed the rest of the day adding final touches to the Minotaur painting, pondering the monster's scientific impossibility. Even the world's brightest monk could never crossbreed a bull with a human female. And yet Granville found himself believing not only in the Minotaur portrayed on the canvas but also in the one that each night wreaked such loud havoc in the cellar of the asylum. Might a person celebrate the laws of Nature without violating the imperatives of enchantment? If not, then Granville would remain loyal to his chimeras, leaving Gregor Mendel's pea plants to fend for themselves.

They look like God's teeth," noted Mr. Dartworthy, gesturing towards the gleaming white peaks of St. Paul's Rocks. "The Almighty has lost His molars, and they've fallen into the sea."

"One day Mr. Dartworthy is going to say something witty," said Mr. Chadwick. "Miss Bathurst, I pray you, inform me the instant that event occurs, even if you must awaken me from a sound sleep."

The three companions were standing on the foredeck, passing Mr. Dartworthy's spyglass back and forth as the *Equinox* tacked around St. Paul's Rocks. Squat, bald, and glazed with dung, the dwarf archipelago comprised five distinct islets, the largest perhaps a mile in circumference, plus a scattering of lesser outcroppings. In *The Voyage of the Beagle,* Chloe recalled, Mr. Darwin had recorded the peculiar fact that these formations were neither volcanic upwellings nor coral atolls but instead reflected the fluctuating contours of the seabed.

"How do we account for their whiteness?" asked Mr. Chadwick, relaying the glass to Chloe.

"Bird droppings," she replied confidently.

"Those are gannets, are they not?" asked the vicar, indicating the nearest flock.

"To be exact, the kind of gannet called a brown booby." Scanning the largest formation, the notched and serrated Southwest Isle, Chloe failed to discern a single creature that might give credence to the species theory—not one transmuted lizard, tortoise, finch, or mockingbird. "As opposed to the blue-footed boobies we shall meet in the Encantadas."

A half-hour later, Mr. Dartworthy having spotted an anchorage site, ordered the hook dropped, and arranged for the bosun to row them ashore, Chloe and her fellow adventurers stepped onto dry land for the first time in seven weeks. The tropical terrain appeared *firma* but not *fecunda*. True, beyond the ubiquitous gannets, whose females apparently declined to build nests (instead laying their eggs directly on the rocks), she noted two varieties of noddy—the brown and the black—which made their nests from seaweed, plus an aggressive species of crab, waiting to steal whatever fish the male noddies might bring home for their mates. But on the whole Southwest Isle was no more an evolutionary showcase than *The Beauteous Buccaneer* was *King Lear*.

"As I feared, there are very few illustrations to hand," said Chloe, fanning herself with her Panama hat. "I shall merely aver that the brown noddy and its black cousin share a common ancestor, now extinct, a bird that in turn traces to a proto-noddy."

"We are not impressed," said Mr. Chadwick.

With its nasty crags, stinking kelp, and abundant excrement, Southwest Isle fell considerably short of an equatorial Eden, and yet the birds exhibited the same primordial innocence as their distant relations back in the Down House zoological dome, making no fuss when the explorers approached. The nearest avian community comprised a half-dozen black noddy nests, two holding vacant shells, two containing female birds incubating their eggs, and two sheltering a mother and her newly hatched chicks. No sooner had Chloe taken this census than a crab appeared, seized a squawking chick, and—before the mother could intervene—dragged the victim back to its lair.

"Behold the struggle for existence." She pointed towards the crab's abode. "Just as wind, rain, ice, and vulcanism sculpt our planet's face, so do predation, disease, famine, and extinction transmute its creatures."

"Not the least of the reasons a healthy-minded person must prefer Genesis to your baboon theory," said Mr. Chadwick.

"Suffering is but part of the story," Chloe hastened to add. "I have posited not a web of death but a Tree of Life, a phenomenon in whose

branches roost countless female birds and beasts, forever selecting partners and bearing offspring."

"Reverend, what do you think of the mechanism to which Miss
Bathurst alludes?" asked Mr. Dartworthy. "Is mating merely the most
efficient way God could devise for human beings to perpetuate themselves, or did He also have our carnal pleasure in mind?"

The vicar scowled and said, "A lady being present, I suggest we have
this conversation at another time and place."

"A lady and two dozen female noddies," noted Chloe.

As the remorseless sun dipped towards the distant coast of Brazil,
Chloe and her fellow explorers returned to the longboat, whereupon the
bosun ferried them to the opposite shore. Alas, beyond the expected
seabirds and crustaceans, Southeast Isle proved as biologically barren as
its sister formation.

Given her certainty that the present archipelago supported no vertebrate more interesting than a noddy, Chloe was shocked when, guiding
her companions along a shelf of silicate carpeted in lichen, she heard
sounds of a sort only the highest ape produced. Yes, no question, this
island had a female human tenant—though perhaps, judging from the
frantic timbre of her voice, a person of addled wits.

"Praised be the sibyls of coincidence!"

Chloe fixed on the speaker, a castaway standing atop a balding knoll.
Suddenly the agitated woman charged down the slope and across the
beach, a rucksack riding on her shoulders, one hand gripping a spyglass
not unlike Mr. Dartworthy's. Her gown was woven of dried kelp, her
bonnet of grass, so that she seemed to belong as much to the plant kingdom as to the animal.

"What interesting specimens one finds in the tropics," said Mr. Dartworthy.

"All hail the sylphs of serendipity!" Moving with a singleness of
mind, if a mind was indeed what lay beneath that weedy brow, the castaway set her glass on a mossy boulder, rushed up to Chloe, and grabbed
the puffy sleeve of her pirate blouse. "Solange Kirsop at your service."

She pointed towards the anchored brig. "And if that's the *Equinox*, then you must be Miss Bathurst."

"Indeed," said Chloe, fascinated and perplexed.

"Also known as the Covent Garden Antichrist and the She-Devil from Dis," said Solange Kirsop, caressing Chloe's cheek. A pendant swayed from the castaway's neck, the pewter setting sculpted to resemble a lion's paw, a fat red gem fixed in the claws. "Before embarking on the *Lorelei*, I read the *Evening Standard* every day. Mr. Popplewell's reports on your expedition enthralled me."

"She-Devil from Dis?" said Chloe.

"As in Dante's *Inferno*. I may be a trollop's child, but I spend more money on books and less on beer than an Oxford don."

"As it happens, I am a connoisseur of such ironies," said Chloe.

From her rucksack Solange Kirsop drew forth a wine bottle, then yanked out the stopper and downed a mouthful. "You have the look of a ship's officer," she told Mr. Dartworthy. Receiving his nod, she added, "I pray you, sir, take a draught of claret"—she waved the bottle in his face—"a gift from the Queen of St. Paul's Rocks to her handsome vassal."

"I never drink in the morning," he said.

"Neither do I, but here on the equator it's always noon," said Solange. "Since my marooning forty days ago, the most amazing jetsam has washed up here, including a case of claret, a brass spyglass, and my ruby pendant. It's really glass, I know, but it makes me feel like a duchess." She took a second swallow, then offered the bottle to the vicar. "You, on the other hand, seem not a nautical person at all."

"I am a man of the cloth," said Mr. Chadwick, gesturing the wine away.

"As I am a woman of the sheets," said Solange.

"My faith is Church of England, so I shan't purport to forgive your sins, but neither shall I presume to judge them."

"Attend my tale," said Solange.

The castaway proceeded to reveal that she'd never known her father, a knave who'd thought nothing of deserting his harlot lover, Gwyneth

Kirsop, *in extremis* and their child, Solange, *in utero*. Owing to her mother's ingenuity and devotion, Solange had been spared a life of street-walking. Instead she'd become first the consort of a Stepney barrister, then the doxy of a Finsbury perfumer, and finally the ardent companion of the brilliant Dr. Lucian Humberdross.

"Lucian called me his courtesan. That word did me proud. Last year he got himself appointed physician to the governor of Barbados, right before Mama died of the typhus. On the day after she was laid to rest, Lucian and I sailed for Bridgetown."

The courtesan took a sip of claret, then resumed her story, telling how the master of the *Lorelei* had proved to be a superstitious man. After the brig suffered three consecutive days and nights of heavy weather, Captain Balch decided that Solange must be a sea-witch. And so, despite Dr. Humberdross's tearful pleading, she was stripped down to her chemise and put ashore on Southeast Isle to die.

"Not long into my ordeal, I told myself, 'Solange, you sorry child of circumstance, if you wish to survive, you'll need a religion to sustain you.' Now Her Majesty's Church has never appealed to me, nor the Popish sort of eternity either, and so I rummaged about in my soul, seized hold of my personal demons, and flung them into the sky. The constellations that shine above this archipelago are in truth the little bits of Lucifer that once burned within me." The courtesan pointed heavenward. "When the stars come out tonight, you'll see a succubus who stays eternally youthful by bathing in her lovers' blood."

"We must get this demented woman aboard the *Equinox* without delay," said Mr. Chadwick.

"For once you and I agree on something," said Mr. Dartworthy.

Solange fixed Chloe with a voracious gaze, her glass pendant flashing in the sun. "It's time I expanded my spiritual horizons," said the courtesan. "From this moment on, I'm not just the disciple of my demons—I'm also a follower of the incomparable Miss Bathurst."

Despite the equatorial heat, a chill passed through Chloe's frame. True, her self-appointed apostle had lost her moorings. Yes, the castaway was a candidate for Bedlam. And yet it seemed that this same Solange

Kirsop could peer into a person's soul as easily as Mr. Darwin observing barnacles through his microscope. Perhaps she really was a sea-witch.

"I imagined God's *bête noire* would be taller, with flaming eyes and crimson hair," the courtesan continued. "No matter, darling. Were my she-devil a dwarf, I would still serve her. The gold is there for the getting, and you and I and your lovely friends will pocket it as planned. No doubt you mean to put your share to a benevolent use."

"My father is but one degree of remove from debtors' prison," said Chloe, growing dizzy beneath Solange's incandescent stare.

"And yet becoming rich is the least of your ambitions—am I right? You've been granted a peach of a part, and you mean to play it to the hilt."

"True," said Chloe.

"Look west of the moon tonight," said Solange, "and you'll see a demon who delights in dousing coastal beacons, sending ships to their doom."

"Rubbish," said Mr. Chadwick.

"My disciple is distraught," said Chloe, taking Solange's hand. "Miss Kirsop has been too long without human companionship," she added, touching the castaway's muddy brow. "And once we're back on the *Equinox*, I should like her to share my cabin."

An assortment of torments plagued Malcolm Chadwick as he staggered across the weather deck towards the improvised theatre—not only the clerical collar scratching his neck but also the sunburn gnawing his shoulders and the *mal de mer* roiling his stomach. Wincing and gasping, he appropriated an empty chair between Third Officer Colin Flaherty, a taciturn Irishman with a fondness for rum, and Second Officer Hugh Pritchard, a freckled Welshman whose pet monkey sat on his hip like a miniature Siamese twin. As the capuchin shrieked in his ear, *chee-chee-chee*, Malcolm looked towards the pageant that Miss Bathurst had prepared to celebrate the brig's imminent crossing of the equator. Evidently such rituals were the norm on mercantile and survey ships, but rarely did they enjoy the supervision of a professional thespian.

Although impossible to ignore, the commotion in Malcolm's guts was as nothing compared to the turmoil in his soul. Two aspects of St. Paul's Rocks had particularly troubled him: the unhinged Miss Kirsop—that pitiable harlot who'd made a religion of her own depravity—and the resident animals. The castaway was indubitably the lesser evil. True, Miss Kirsop was delusional, and yet Malcolm believed that through God's grace she might escape the dark heathen wood in which her mind now wandered. By contrast, the archipelago's seabirds and crustaceans had caused him unutterable distress, each such creature a reminder of the Oxford Diocese's designs on the supposedly maleficent fauna of the Encantadas.

Dressed in a burlap shift, Miss Kirsop emerged from the forecastle and proclaimed that she was Amphitrite, "a nubile nereid who in my naïve youth allowed an oafish sea-god to take me as his bride." Malcolm would admit that she'd scrubbed up well, her bronzed skin glowing in the tropical sun, her lustrous raven hair flourishing on a scalp no longer infiltrated by weeds. On hearing Amphitrite's epithet, the sailors in the audience applauded. (It seemed probable that none could define "nubile nereid," but apparently the term sounded gratifyingly lewd.) Miss Kirsop then explained that the pageant concerned "the eternal battle between my glorious companion, Athena, mistress of wisdom, and my doltish husband, Poseidon, master of maelstroms."

An instant later Miss Bathurst, cast as Athena, came on stage dragging a canvas sack. She wore a *peplos* of bedsheets and a helmet improvised from a bailing bucket. Next to appear was Ralph Dartworthy as Poseidon, gripping a trident and dressed in a sailcloth robe, an oakum beard swaying from his jaw. After sticking her tongue out at Dartworthy, a gesture that set the audience to chortling, Miss Kirsop invited them to travel with her through time and space to Cecropia, an ancient Greek city. "Behold King Cecrops," she said, whereupon Algernon Bathurst stepped forward wearing a cape that was once a Union Jack, "who has brought prosperity to his people by refusing to propitiate Zeus with the blood of birds and beasts."

Malcolm grimaced, pained by an irony of the sort Miss Bathurst relished. Although the pagan ruler Cecrops disdained animal sacrifice, the

Anglican clerics Wilberforce and Hallowborn embraced it—for what term other than "animal sacrifice" adequately described the Great Winnowing? Ever since his visit to St. Paul's Rocks, Malcolm had grown increasingly miserable over the vow of silence he'd made in the bishop's conservatory. By acquiescing to the Oxford Diocese's scheme, had he struck an accord with the very same Satan whose progeny allegedly infested Galápagos?

"The rivalry between Athena and Poseidon came to a head when the King announced that whoever offered his city the best gift would become its patron deity," narrated Miss Kirsop as Mr. Bathurst assumed his throne, which strongly resembled a cook's stool. "Poseidon straightaway appeared in the palace yard and drove his trident into the ground."

Dartworthy approached a bloated wineskin that lay on the deck like a basking seal, spearing it abruptly and releasing a dozen gallons of seawater.

"A majestic fountain gushed from the Earth," Miss Kirsop continued, "but when the King drank thereof, he found it salty."

Mr. Bathurst soaked a sponge in the puddle, brought it to his lips, and feigned to suck up brine. An expression of disgust contracted his features.

"And so the King rejected the gift," said Miss Kirsop.

Bathurst hurled the sponge at Dartworthy.

At first Malcolm wondered why Poseidon was faring so badly in the equatorial pageant. How peculiar that the ship's company took pleasure in the humiliation of the greatest maritime deity. But then he apprehended the obvious. A sailor did not love the sea. A sailor loved a dry bed, fresh meat, painted women, and full measures of grog. For the crew of the *Equinox,* mocking Poseidon was a splendid sport—their way of avenging themselves for soggy hammocks, rancid food, carnal privations, and relentless drudgery.

"Now Athena presented her gift, a sapling bursting with olives," said Miss Kirsop.

Miss Bathurst opened her canvas sack and removed a miniature tree (not unlike the prop she'd brought to Alastor Hall) complete with belaying pins for branches and rum corks for fruits. Her brother plucked an olive and pretended to consume it.

"King Cecrops understood not only that Athena's gift supplied delicious food," said Miss Kirsop, "but also that the pits would germinate more such trees. And so he accepted it, making Athena the city's patron deity and changing its name to Athens. My enraged husband then attempted to slay the King, an ambition that, I am happy to report, Athena stood ready to thwart."

No sooner had Miss Kirsop completed her speech than Dartworthy rushed at Miss Bathurst's brother with his trident. The intended victim stepped aside. Before Dartworthy could attempt a second thrust, Miss Bathurst removed her helmet and aligned it with Poseidon's weapon. Dartworthy lunged, skewering the helmet, just as Miss Bathurst had doubtless intended—for she instantly wrested the encumbered trident away. Freeing the trident from her headgear, she hurled it across the stage, driving the prongs deep into the larboard gunwale. The wooden shaft vibrated like a tuning fork. The crew whooped and clapped, reveling in Poseidon's disgrace.

As the cheering faded and the phantom curtain fell, an urgent breeze wafted across the weather deck. Captain Runciter, rising, ordered the crew to provide the yardarms with maximum canvas. Assuming that the wind held true, Malcolm calculated, the *Equinox* would gain Fortaleza within four days. He wondered what sorts of currents, zephyrous and aquatic, had thus far accompanied the Reverend Simon Hallowborn and Captain Adrian Garrity. Most likely the *Antares* was already coursing southward along the coast of Brazil, her crew practicing daily with their fowling pieces, rehearsing the Great Winnowing by blasting seabirds from the sky.

A crude and un-Christian hope took form in Malcolm's imagination. He pictured the *Antares* coming apart in the churning seas off Cape Horn. The brig's company survived unscathed, including Simon Hallowborn, as did all ninety-two Mephistropolis convicts, everyone washing ashore on Tierra del Fuego. Mindful that their rescue probably lay many months in the future, the castaways founded a self-sustaining colony—and then one glorious day Mr. Hallowborn experienced a change of heart, the scheme to slaughter the Galápagos creatures now striking him as woefully misguided. The redeemed rector fell to his knees, clasped his hands in prayer, and thanked the Almighty for sinking his ship.

The days that followed the presentation of her equatorial pageant were the most satisfactory Chloe had yet known aboard the *Equinox*. Although she'd relished the sailors' applause, her happiness had less to do with the pageant's reception than with the adulation her acolyte was lavishing upon her.

"Your forthcoming performance in Oxford will rank with the achievements of Catherine Clive and Sarah Siddons," said Solange, kissing Chloe's cheek. "My she-devil navigates by the brightest light in the heavens, a star called aesthetics."

"Exactly," said Chloe, squeezing the courtesan's hand.

"The aesthetics of theatre and the aesthetics of deicide," said Solange. "I needn't tell *you*, of course, I needn't tell the Covent Garden Antichrist, but a world without God will prove more pleasing to our eyes and more nourishing to our minds. We must love the butterfly for its own sake, not as a testament to some nonexistent deity's tedious omnipotence."

"And the dung beetle, too, and my ugly iguanas back in County Kent," said Chloe. "Oh, Solange, do I really have fortitude enough to win the day? My Cleopatra could win it, and my French castaway, and Pirate Anne, and perhaps even Carmine the vampire, but I am none of those people."

"Darling, I think you are all four," said Solange. "But should you feel your courage falter, remember the boon you're bringing to humankind. If there exists a species of ignorance certain to keep increasing the premiums on the bliss it buys, then a belief in God is surely that creature."

"My dear Solange, let me invite you to stand by my side when I address the Alastor Hall judges."

"You do me a great honor."

Chloe decided that she'd never been in so gratifying a *tête-à-tête*—an exchange made all the more marvelous for taking place on the 24th of December. It was as if Solange were making a Christmas gift to Chloe of her sea-witch's wit. If this conversation could somehow continue forever, she would count herself the happiest of women.

But the idyll did not endure. Indeed, it ended abruptly. For the very next morning a hurricane descended on the *Equinox,* a celestial maelstrom that in turn whipped the equatorial Atlantic to an unimaginable fury, as if the ocean were a soup set a-boil in Lucifer's own kitchen.

Hour by hour, the tempest increased in violence, its thunderclaps rattling the air like Judgment Day trumps. Believing that by imagining herself as Pirate Anne she would get the better of her fear, Chloe traded her chemise for her buccaneer ensemble, then ventured into the gale. Although she'd endured numerous stage-bound aquatic catastrophes, most memorably the tidal wave that had drowned blind Nydia in *The Last Days of Pompeii,* nothing had prepared her for the present spectacle. Towering fountains of rain blew across the *Equinox* from gunwale to gunwale. The torrents saturated her clothes and drenched her skin, then penetrated more deeply still, diluting her blood, turning her marrow to paste.

Peering through the cataract, she saw that the weather deck was deserted, as if the crew had been swept overboard. She looked heavenward. Like monkeys clambering about in treetops, dozens of sailors labored amidst the yardarms, reefing the canvas. She steeled herself, vowing to remain steadfast before Nature's wrath. Defiantly she opened her mouth, admitting the squalls, for she-devils must traffic in audacity—they grew strong by kissing volcanoes, eating fire, taking suck from storms.

Algernon and Mr. Chadwick stood near the mainmast, gripping a ratline to keep from toppling over, evidently awaiting orders, though to Chloe it seemed obvious that they could best serve the ship by staying out of the way. "We've already been dragged north of Fortaleza!" her brother informed her, yelling above the screaming wind. "Runciter's hoping to make landfall at Parnaíba or São Luís!"

In a spasm of anger Chloe pulled her grandfather's bayonet from its scabbard and plunged it into the mainmast. Damn this hurricane! Damn each lightning bolt and thunderclap! Owing to this unthinkable cataclysm, the Mayfair Diluvian League would beguile the judges with their confounded ark long before the *Equinox* returned from Galápagos.

"We've learned our lesson, haven't we?" she shouted, her words borne by a bitter laugh. "Never offend Poseidon with a pageant!"

"It's God we've offended!" cried the vicar.

She returned to her cabin, shed her sodden costume, and climbed into her bunk. Soon her disciple joined her, so that they became proximate as newborn twins. The sea continued to roll and pitch, as if to rid itself of the *Equinox* as would a bull determined to throw its rider. Stuck fast by terror, Chloe and Solange embraced more tightly yet, but then a half-dozen raps on the cabin door disturbed their wretched privacy.

"Miss Bathurst!"

"Yes?" replied Chloe, recognizing Mr. Dartworthy's voice.

"We're sinking!"

"Impossible!"

"I agree! We're sinking anyway! There's a place for you and Miss Kirsop in the launch! Hurry!"

Hurry, *bien sûr*—no other course made sense. Chloe quit the bunk, secured her Panama hat with a piece of twine, and once again costumed herself as Pirate Anne, the wet fabric raising goose bumps on her arms and legs. From her trunk she retrieved the boxed transmutation sketch and the Pirate Mary costume, passing the garments to Solange.

"Meet me on the weather deck!"

Fleeing her cabin, Chloe entered a scene of utter pandemonium, dozens of frightened sailors scurrying every which way, combers of foaming white water spilling across the planks. Atop the forecastle, several midshipmen attempted to lower the quartet of jolly boats. Was the *Equinox* truly sinking? The dreadful fact could not be doubted, for the weather deck now listed so radically that a chaotic mass of ropes, buckets, barrels, and sea chests lay jammed against the starboard gunwale.

Suddenly Solange appeared, and together the women climbed to the poop deck, great waves rising on both sides like Red Sea ramparts in thrall to Moses's magic. Mr. Dartworthy emerged from behind a swirling spout of rain and, taking Chloe's hand, guided her aft. She looked over the rail, beholding the longboat that had conveyed them to St. Paul's Rocks, now crammed with mariners and nearly swamped. Descending the rope ladder, Solange and Mr. Dartworthy in train, Chloe bemoaned her situation, as bereft of aesthetics and devoid of justice as any she'd ever known. She was supposed to be moving horizontally just then, off to the Encantadas, not vertically towards some pathetic launch.

The women clambered over the keelson and assumed their seats, whereupon Mr. Dartworthy presented them with tin buckets and told them to start bailing. Chloe surveyed her fellow evacuees, the cream of the ship's company. Captain Runciter sat in the bow, arm curled about the tiller. Mr. Dartworthy held the mooring tethering the longboat to the *Equinox*. Whilst Mr. Pritchard and Mr. Flaherty deftly nocked the forward oars and slipped them into the sea, Algernon and Mr. Chadwick struggled to likewise position the aft oars.

"Cast off!" shouted the captain over the din of the gale.

Mr. Dartworthy untied the rope. The doomed *Equinox* lurched drastically to larboard, as if the longboat had been supporting the brig and not the other way around. Chloe and Solange bailed furiously, laboring to rid the launch of rain from the heavens and brine from the swells.

"Pull!" cried Runciter. "Put your backs into it! Pull, or we're all dead!"

Gasping and grunting, the four rowers worked their oars, stroke upon stroke, and within twenty minutes the longboat was a hundred yards clear of the wreck.

"My fair philosopher, I fear you've lost the contest!" exclaimed Mr. Dartworthy.

"Not until somebody else has won it!" screamed Chloe.

Frantically she removed another bucket of water—and another, and still another. Pausing, she endured a fit of coughing, then fixed on the foundering brig. Like some fissured and forsaken Atlantis, abandoned by her every patron deity, the *Equinox* made a clockwise revolution, then spun a second time, a third, a fourth, until finally she shuddered stem to stern, shivered plank to plank, admitted the sea to her bowels, and vanished.

But the Shelley Prize did not go down with the ship, or so Chloe now required herself to believe. The animal pens and birdcages were headed for the bottom of the ocean, but the treasure still lay in Oxford, waiting to be borne away on the backs of ancient tortoises and venerable iguanas. The Transmutationist Club would triumph yet. She would win the world's applause. It was a simple matter of being shrewder than King Cecrops, more resourceful than Lord Poseidon, and as wise as Lady Athena.

BOOK TWO

THE WHITE
RADIANCE OF
ETERNITY

6

*Recounting a Journey up the Amazon River,
Featuring Lush Panoramas, Voracious
Piranhas, and a Sun That Rises Even As It Sets*

Throughout that interminable first night in the storm-tossed long-boat, the *Equinox* castaways suffered largely in silence, mutely enduring their multiple tribulations, from soggy biscuits to salt-caked clothing, aching muscles to sickening waves, squalls of rain to spasms of dread. Whenever a castaway spoke, it was only to speculate about the fate of the men they'd left behind on the foundering brig. Presumably all forty-two sailors had escaped in the jolly boats, but when the rain finally subsided and the sun rose, disclosing a smooth and benevolent sea, the expected flotilla was nowhere to be seen.

Exchanging not a word, Mr. Dartworthy and Mr. Pritchard erected the mast and hoisted the sail, thus setting the launch on a rapid westerly course and making the oarsmen's task less burdensome. In time the collective mood shifted, and everyone began to chatter. Reminiscing promiscuously, the castaways talked of cozy taverns, convivial brothels, sainted mothers, favorite uncles, lost loves, found dogs, and Christmases past (excluding the 25th of December, 1849, the date on which the hurricane struck), even as they pointedly avoided the subject of death by thirst and exposure. Fearful that this wanton nostalgia would ultimately prove destructive of morale, Chloe introduced a new subject, remarking on how at the last minute everyone had salvaged an item of personal significance. Mr. Pritchard, not surprisingly, had rescued his pet monkey. Mr. Flaherty had secured three bottles of rum in his breeches. Captain Runciter had seized his sextant, Mr. Chadwick his Bible, Algernon his playing cards, Solange her glass pendant. But the choice that most impressed Chloe was Mr. Dartworthy's decision to retain his translation of *The Rubáiyát of Omar Khayyám*.

"I've not forgotten our appointment with your poet," she said to the first officer, setting her palm atop the manuscript. "You're going to sit in a Brazilian cantina drinking Madeira whilst I declaim his verses."

"It was our planned afternoon in Fortaleza that inspired me to select these quatrains over my cigars," Mr. Dartworthy replied.

"Might I ask what *you* salvaged, Miss Bathurst?" inquired Mr. Chadwick. "Besides your Panama hat, I mean."

Chloe flourished the sandalwood box. "I grabbed my latest effort to put my species theory into words"—she fingered the twine that bound the hat to her head, determining that the knot held firm—"including nuances that occurred to me during the voyage. Thirty-five pages worth ten thousand pounds."

The conversation now veered towards a more urgent topic: how to keep the longboat from becoming their collective coffin. Algernon proposed turning around and sailing to St. Paul's Rocks, where they could survive on gannets and crabs till a rescue ship appeared. (Were not the known virtues of that archipelago preferable to the hostile Indians and horrendous insects of the Brazilian coast? Had not Miss Kirsop survived on St. Paul's Rocks for over a month, and had she not been saved?) Although Chloe found merit in Algernon's argument, Mr. Dartworthy was quick to reject it, insisting that they would "do far better running from heathen cannibals than fighting over the last edible crab on Miss Kirsop's little islands."

Mr. Pritchard suggested that whatever their destination they should dismantle the mast, bisect it with Miss Bathurst's bayonet, and convert each half into an oar, "thereby increasing our rowing power by one-third." Mr. Dartworthy called the idea "ingenious in its own way" but declared that the launch would reach its goal more efficiently if they left the rigging in place.

Mr. Flaherty spoke up next, recommending that they exploit the happy fact of a priest in their midst. If the Reverend Mr. Chadwick were now to hear an honest confession from everyone, God might elect to blow them to Fortaleza. The vicar replied that the Almighty was not to be petitioned in so crude a fashion, "though it is appropriate for us to turn our hearts towards Heaven," then led the castaways in the Lord's Prayer, a recitation to which Chloe willingly lent her voice, whilst Mr. Dartworthy and Solange maintained a conspicuous silence, as befitted a village atheist and a she-devil's disciple.

"Having talked to God, ye will now listen to me," said Runciter. "Just as I was master of the *Equinox,* so am I now lord of this launch. What manner of man is your captain? Well, he's evidently incompetent, having steered his ship directly into a hurricane. He's likewise something of a coward, having abandoned that same ship when honor demanded he go down with it. He must furthermore answer to the charge of greed, as he has not forsaken our original mission. For all this, know ye that in the weeks to come my every word will be taken for a law and my every caprice for a canon, and any man who mutinies will wish he'd drowned in the gale."

"Begging your pardon, sir," said Mr. Flaherty, "but am I to understand we're still chasing after the prize?"

"That is my meaning," said Runciter.

"Spoken like the competent, brave, and philanthropic leader you are," said Chloe.

"Whoever opposes this plan risks the wrath of the Covent Garden Antichrist," Solange added.

"You speak out of turn, strumpet," said Flaherty.

"I'm a *courtesan.*"

"I don't mean to dampen our hopes," said Pritchard, "but according to the Admiralty's maps, the fattest part of the South American continent lies between here and Galápagos."

"Then we shall cross the fattest part of the South American continent," Chloe insisted.

"The Amazon River will get us most of the way there," added Runciter.

"It flows in the wrong direction," noted Mr. Dartworthy.

"Then we shall paddle against the current," said Chloe.

"And after the Amazon come the Andes," said Pritchard.

"If a man can climb a mast, he can climb a mountain, and so can a woman," said Chloe.

"And after we reach the Encantadas, how do we get the menagerie back to England?" asked Mr. Dartworthy.

"We'll think of something," said Chloe.

"My she-devil always thinks of something," said Solange.

"With all due respect, Captain, do you not grasp the meaning of our misfortunes?" asked an exasperated Mr. Chadwick, tapping his foot against a bailing bucket. "Will you not allow that God sent the storm to warn us off this impertinent quest?"

"We appreciate your knowledge of the Almighty's motives, but today we shall confine the conversation to matters of naked avarice," Runciter replied. "By my reckoning our company has been reduced by three-quarters, which means everyone's share in the treasure has increased. Mr. Pritchard, for example, now stands to gain five hundred pounds."

"My captain practices an amiable arithmetic," said the second officer. "Do you hear that, Bartholomew?" he told his monkey. "We're rich!"

"Whereas Mr. Flaherty will walk away with four hundred," said Runciter.

"Let us toast our wise leader," said the third officer, brandishing one of his rum bottles. With the sole and unsurprising exception of the vicar, the company retrieved their various water receptacles. A half-dozen arms reached towards Flaherty, who awarded each *Equinox* survivor a splash of spirits. "To Captain Runciter!"

"Captain Runciter!" echoed Chloe.

"Captain Runciter!" chorused Solange, Algernon, Pritchard, and Mr. Dartworthy.

"To myself!" cackled the former master of the lost *Equinox*.

Seven tin cups connected beneath the equatorial sun, a cadence so spirited it suggested a telegrapher clicking out jubilant news, though by Chloe's lights the toast's true recipient was she herself. On numerous occasions throughout history, men had sworn fealty to unruly women—to Boadicea and Jeanne d'Arc and even Pirate Anne Bonney. Whether they knew it or not, the longboat's company was now pledged to escort her up the Amazon, over the mountains, and across the sea to Galápagos. They had vowed to help her uproot the Tree of Life and bear it back to Oxford. They had even promised to follow her as she marched through the gates of Perdition, strode into the Devil's palace, and inquired of His Satanic Majesty whether Hell had need of a queen.

When at long last their ordeal ended, five days after the *Equinox* went down, the hungry, thirsty, and exhausted castaways having blown into the Baía de Marajó and received succor from a passing band of priests *en route* to their mission outside Curuçá, Chloe was quick to appreciate the incongruity of her situation. Her irony bone sang like a glass chalice. A half-dozen black-robed Jesuits had bestowed the finest quality of Catholic charity on a bedraggled bunch of English adventurers— and yet those same castaways sought to humble the whole of Christianity, including its famous Papist form. Over the course of her career Chloe had enacted many roles, some sympathetic, others villainous, but this was the first time she'd played a wolf in sheep's clothing.

"I eat their bread, I drink their wine, and I feel like a hypocrite," she said, sipping red crianza.

She was sitting between her devoted disciple and prodigal brother in a mosquito-netted cloister adjacent to a crumbling sandstone church with twin bell towers, the three explorers having retreated to the sheltered arcade to escape the burning eye of the tropical sun and the avid mouths of sand-flies and fire-ants. It was the tenth day of their sojourn amongst the Jesuits. Compared with the blind malice of the sea, the Missão do Sagrado Coração seemed to Chloe a paradise on Earth, and with each tolling of the bells she thanked Solange's sibyls of coincidence for bringing her to so serene a sanctuary. True, the wine was sour, the heat stifling, and the insects voracious, but these hardships were as milk and honey compared to the grueling labor and intolerable privations of life in a longboat.

"And yet, for whatever reasons, I don't *mind* feeling like a hypocrite," she added.

"An irony within an irony," said Algernon, lifting a goblet to his lips.

"The Covent Garden Antichrist does not trouble herself with mundane regrets," said Solange.

Now Mr. Chadwick appeared in the cloister, straightaway adding a sardonic note to the conversation. "How impressive that Miss Kirsop knows more about our antichrist than does our antichrist herself."

"Poker, anyone?" inquired Algernon, shuffling his cards.

A flurry of frowns greeted this suggestion. Chloe suspected that her brother would have better luck convening a game amongst the nautical members of their fellowship, but earlier in the week Captain Runciter and his officers had gone by mule cart to Belém-do-Pará, their aim being to scour the beaches for *Equinox* refugees and, no less importantly, persuade some packet-steamer skipper that, instead of hiring unreliable aborigines or disgruntled half-breed *caboclos* frontiersmen to serve on his next voyage upriver, he should instead engage a company of English shipwreck survivors. Before his departure, Runciter had told Chloe and Solange that he intended to represent them as "Claude Bathurst" and "Solomon Kirsop," eight able-bodied seamen being a more marketable commodity than six plus two women. Given her loosely fitting pirate blouse, Chloe reasoned, not to mention her talent for affecting a tenor voice (two assets her disciple likewise possessed), the deception should prove simple to sustain.

"May I speak frankly, Miss Bathurst?" asked Mr. Chadwick.

"When have you ever employed any other idiom?"

The vicar gestured past the gauzy mosquito curtain towards a flagstone plaza bustling with Indians, all of them belonging to the Tupinambá tribe, a sturdy people with tawny skin and cropped black hair suggesting scholar's caps. Whether these aborigines had sequestered themselves in Sagrado Coração voluntarily or through clerical coercion Chloe could not say, but they certainly seemed happy enough. Dressed in cinnamon-colored shifts, they laughed and sang as they rethatched the roof of the church, repaired the priests' fleet of canopied *tolda* canoes, and tended the goats and peccaries in the livestock pens. Even as the mission Indians labored beneath the relentless sun, their children sported on the plaza, trundling hoops, bouncing balls off the walls (rubber was apparently as abundant in Amazonia as vermin), and firing toy arrows at straw targets, all the while sucking on skewered fruits as if they were lollipops.

When not maintaining the mission or receiving instruction in the Roman catechism, the Tupinambás evidently spent their days outside the walls, tending the priests' pallid plots of manioc and cacao, the latter crop sown in deference to the European passion for chocolate. According to Mr. Pritchard (who'd once tried his hand at farming), the plantation's sorry state was not exceptional. Given the region's poor soil, torrential rains, and ravenous leaf-cutter ants, agricultural prosperity was unlikely ever to visit the Amazon basin.

"How can you pursue your campaign against God," Mr. Chadwick asked Chloe in a reproving tone, "when you behold the blessings these padres have brought to the heathens? Can you not see that your project is a petty vendetta at best?"

A queasiness spread through her, not unlike the emotion she endured whenever, standing on the stage, she suddenly forgot her lines. In her eagerness to win the Shelley Prize, had she ventured upon waters no mere mortal should dare to navigate? In her determination to triumph at Alastor Hall, had she bitten off so large a portion of presumption that even Jonah's whale would not attempt to chew it? The Sagrado Coração priests were obviously uplifting the Tupinambás. By what rights would anyone put so benevolent an enterprise out of business?

She set her goblet on the table, having lost her taste for wine, exploration, and deicide. "Your questions give me much food for thought," she told Mr. Chadwick.

"Much meat for muddlement," Solange corrected her.

Chloe made no reply but simply scratched a sand-fly bite on her ankle.

The following Sunday, as billows of afternoon heat blanketed Curuçá, a troupe of mission children staged a pageant for their English visitors. Whilst the young players emoted in the plaza, Chloe and her companions sat on the church steps and watched, luxuriating in the shade of palm fronds held by the children's parents. The pageant unfolded in Tupi, the *lingua franca* of the eastern basin, and yet she had no trouble following the action, for the players had selected as their subject the story of Noah and the Flood. To form their ark, the children had joined two dugout canoes into a catamaran, one hull holding the patriarch and his family, the other filled with little balsawood tapirs, jaguars, anacondas, sloths, and caimans (an indigenous variety of alligator). Although the children portraying Noah and his clan took obvious delight in their roles, the inundated sinners had even more fun, gleefully flailing and screaming as the remorseless waves sucked them down.

Inevitably the pageant put Chloe in mind of the Reverend Mr. Dalrymple and his ark hunters. Quite possibly they'd already reached Constantinople and were now sailing along the Turkish coast towards Trebizond. Until recently, the thought of Dalrymple making substantial progress would have greatly distressed her, but today she felt indifferent towards her God-fearing rival, for she'd yet to formulate a riposte to Mr. Chadwick's accusation that her own quest was "a petty vendetta at best."

When at last the children's ark came to rest on Ararat, a stately priest named Cristóvão Pinheiro stepped into the plaza, a sun-struck silver cross glinting above his heart. Speaking first in Tupi, then in Latin, next in Portuguese, and finally in English, he placed the pageant in an appropriately Christian context. "After the waters subsided," Padre Pinheiro explained, "God remained true to His word. In keeping with the rainbow covenant, He refrained from additional worldwide floods. Instead He challenged Mankind with a different sort of deluge, the blood of our Lord and Savior Jesus Christ, for only through that crimson cataract, flowing down the slopes of Calvary and thence into the whole of Creation, might the world be washed clean of Adam's sin."

With the coming of dusk the Jesuits recited their evening prayers, the Latin syllables soughing across the plaza like consecrated surf, after which Padre Pinheiro invited the adventurers to the refectory for a light supper of steamed clams and broiled caiman. Presiding over the meal was the head of the mission, Rapôso Sampaio, a seraphic man with a belly of equatorial contours, his presence occasioning in Chloe more convulsions of uncertainty. Like the other Sagrado Coração priests, Padre Sampaio radiated a quintessential kindness, and any renegade actress who presumed to shut down his mission had better be prepared to justify her decision. Was God's nonexistence a sufficient reason for calling His authority into question? Here and now, at this particular juncture in her fortunes, she simply did not know.

"This afternoon you missed an entrancing pageant," said Mr. Chadwick to Padre Sampaio.

"So I'm told."

Padre Pinheiro rapped his knuckles on his forehead, as if to shake his brain in its cradle, forcing the organ to locate bits and pieces of English amidst the welter of Portuguese, Latin, and Tupi. "I hope you found sufficient scriptural integrity in the children's interpretation. We know how protective you Protestants feel towards the Bible"—he accorded the vicar a merry wink—"in contrast to us Papists, who can scarcely be bothered to read the thing."

"I'm not a man to make an idol of Holy Writ," said Mr. Chadwick. "Recall that the Church of England began as Roman Catholicism by other means. We became Protestants only *en passant*."

"Ah, the wonders of transmutation," said Solange.

"I agree with Mr. Chadwick—today we saw a magnificent production," Algernon declared. *"Um espetáculo maravilhoso,"* he added in the strained voice of a man who doesn't speak Portuguese speaking Portuguese.

"Alas, a shadow hung over the children's efforts," said Padre Pinheiro. "Before the week is out, those adorable little *crianças* will be gone, nevermore to roll their hoops across the plaza or snuggle with us in our beds, and their parents must also leave. We're permitted to catechize a given clan for only a month, after which everyone goes to Ilha de Marajó and joins the Corpos de Trabalhadores, which are little more than forced-labor gangs. At least we get to save the Tupinambás' souls before the overseers break their backs."

"Some people would say we've made a Devil's bargain," said Padre Sampaio, parking his palms on his considerable stomach. "However, if we advocate too vociferously for the Indians, the bosses in Belém will protest to the provincial governor, who will in turn speak to the Emperor, who will send a complaint to the Holy Father in Rome."

"But surely the Pope would take your side," said Mr. Chadwick.

"Relations between our order and the Vatican are strained at best," Padre Pinheiro explained. "In the middle of the last century, the Society of Jesus was booted out of the Church altogether, remaining an *entity non grata* for fifty-six years. Our humble mission survived the expulsion of 1759—we survived the Brazilian war of independence and the bloody Cabanagem rebellion that followed—but we would never survive the renewed hostility of the Holy See."

"We've prattled quite enough about *our* problems," said Padre Sampaio. "Mr. Chadwick tells me you intrepid naturalists hope to reach faraway Galápagos."

"We seek the primordial Tree of Life," said Chloe.

"Miss Bathurst exaggerates," said Mr. Chadwick, grimacing. "Our desire is to study the islands' exotic reptiles and birds."

"No, I'm telling the truth," said Chloe, struggling to recover her freethinking side as an inverted turtle might strive to aright itself. "We shall prove the material unity of all plants and animals or die in the attempt."

"If the Tree of Life yet flourishes, the place wherein it grows has been evermore denied to mortals," said Padre Sampaio. "You certainly won't find it off the coast of Ecuador."

"The creature we hunt is biological, not biblical." Even as she spoke, Chloe's foundering faith in the quest grew more buoyant. "Scriptural trees hold little interest for us—though they may be more accessible than you suppose. If birds ate of Eden's fruits, they would have scattered the seeds far and wide. A descendant of the Tree of Life or the Tree of Knowledge might very well grow today in Persia, another in Egypt, another in Anatolia, another right here in Amazonia."

"Such is the utility of excrement," said Solange.

"Miss Kirsop has been too long at sea," said Mr. Chadwick in a voice somewhere between speech and expectoration.

"Perhaps you would like to stay here, Reverend," said Padre Sampaio. "You could help us in our work amongst the Tupinambás, while your coarse companions reach the Encantadas on their own."

"An appealing proposition," Mr. Chadwick replied. "But just as you must save heathen souls, so must I tend to my vulgar flock."

"What we need now is a friendly game of poker," said Algernon abruptly, producing his pack of cards. *"Vamos bater um pôquer?"*

Against Chloe's expectations, her brother succeeded in convening a game that night, a protracted seven-card-stud tournament that lasted until matins. Instead of poker chips the players used stale discs of unconsecrated communion bread, a choice so scandalous by Mr. Chadwick's lights that he refused to participate, though the Jesuit players—Padre Sampaio and Padre Pinheiro—decided that such a profane employment of the Host underscored the radical discontinuity between its natural and post-sacramental forms. The big winner was Algernon (evidently poker suited his talents better than faro), who walked away with sixty wafers. But the priests held their own, each making a seven-wafer profit, whilst Chloe and Solange lost their stacks *in toto.*

As it happened, the poker game had the effect of restoring in full Chloe's belief in the Albion Transmutationist Club. Even as she blundered away her wafers, invariably failing to discern whether a fellow player was bluffing or not, she recalled the lesson in natural selection she'd taught Algernon back in Seven Dials (the same poker hand becoming, depending on its environment, either a straight, a mere ace-high, or a royal flush). What a piece of work was the Tree of Life! How sublime the notion that had blossomed in Mr. Darwin's brain! Yes, she decided, yes, God's nonexistence *was* a sufficient reason for calling His authority into question, whatever quantity of benevolence the Jesuits might be lavishing on herself, her friends, and the benighted Tupinambás.

Two weeks later Mr. Pritchard and his monkey returned to the mission, the former bearing glad tidings. Thanks to Captain Runciter's bargaining skills, the wayward company of the lost *Equinox* had secured employment aboard the packet-steamer *Rainha da Selva,* the Queen of the Jungle. Her skipper, one Hélio Gonçalves, had contracted to transport a ton of goods and sundries a thousand miles up the Rio Amazonas to the Rio Negro, then northwest along that tributary to the burgeoning provincial capital, Manáos. Barring unforeseen circumstances, Capitão Gonçalves's vessel would steam out of Belém-do-Pará ten days hence—which meant that Miss Bathurst and her companions must leave the mission at first light. As for the forty-two *Equinox* castaways who'd escaped in the jolly boats, they'd evidently made their way to the Baía de Marajó and joined the crew of a French merchant vessel bound for Marseille.

Upon hearing Mr. Pritchard's report, Padre Sampaio told the English adventurers they would find Belém to be "a beautiful city patterned on the incomparable Lisbon," as opposed to Manáos, "a hodgepodge modeled on nothing at all." Until recently, he added, Manáos had been called Barra, after its monumental sandbar. In renaming the settlement, the district governor had sought to honor the heritage of the region's vanished Manaó Indians—though Chloe suspected that, given a choice between not being exterminated by the Portuguese and having a city named after them, the natives would have selected the first alternative.

The journey to Belém, two days and fifty miles by mule cart southward from Curuçá, proved dreadful, a trial in which the remorseless sun and the omnipresent invertebrates conspired to maximize the travelers' misery. Seated in the load bed along with Solange, the vicar, and her brother, Chloe lurched to and fro as Mr. Pritchard, in the driver's seat, guided the reluctant mules along the crumbling and rutted Estrada dos Jacarés. Throughout the trip she clutched both the boxed transmutation essay and a Tupinambá reed basket containing dried fish and manioc bread from Padre Sampaio, all the while suffering the appetites of sandflies, chigoes, sauba ants, and bête-rouge ticks (roaring evolutionary successes every one, she mused, grand-prize winners in the Malthusian struggle for existence). But at long last the travelers were rewarded with Cidade das Magnas, the City of the Mangos: fair Belém, whose more attractive features—its baroque churches, pristine houses, sumptuous governor's palace, streets shaded by Asian fruit trees, and great central cathedral—fully affirmed Padre Sampaio's admiration for the place.

It was only after everyone had moved into the Hotel da Antonio José Landi, however, the bill having been paid by Capitão Gonçalves in anticipation of their employment aboard the *Rainha da Selva*, that the mule-cart ordeal finally evaporated from Chloe's mind. All during the long and languorous afternoon, she and her disciple washed each other in a porcelain tub (fingertips rippling along soapy skin, palms kneading sore muscles): a venerable Brazilian tradition, she decided, pondering the ancient warrior-women whence the Amazon River had taken its name—for doubtless those daughters of Bellatrix had derived as much satisfaction from pleasuring one another's flesh as from breaking their enemies' bones.

Cured of weariness but not of hunger, Chloe and Solange descended to the hotel saloon, where they proceeded to share a seafood supper with their fellow adventurers. Though pleased to be once again in the vicinity of the alluring Mr. Dartworthy, Chloe was disappointed by the vacuous conversation he and Captain Runciter elected to impose upon the gathering. Back at the Jesuit mission, the talk had variously encompassed the Catholic view of the rainbow covenant, the need to avoid antagonizing the Holy See, and the joy of walking in the light of God. Here in Cidade das Magnas, by contrast, there was evidently only one subject worth discussing: rubber—raw *hevé*, that is, liquid latex, the thick, milky fluid that surged through the countless stands of *cau-chu* trees that flourished everywhere in the basin, a vein of white gold stretching from Belém to distant Manáos to faraway Iquitos in Peru.

A boom was in the making, Mr. Dartworthy averred, popping an oyster into his mouth. The past decade had found hundreds of industrious Indian *seringueiros*—rubber tappers—systematically harvesting latex, curing it over wood fires, and selling the resulting spheres, the fat and unwieldy *peles*, to predatory middlemen, the *aviadors*. Last year alone,

Mr. Dartworthy noted, Manáos had sent two thousand tons of rubber down the river for exportation to northern centers of commerce, and the *aviadors* would probably ship twice that much next year. Even as the English adventurers sat chattering about the *seringueiros* and their vaguely romantic, largely wretched lives, scores of would-be rubber barons were descending on Manáos, determined to turn that scrofulous city into a cosmopolitan metropolis commensurate with the great capitals of Europe.

Captain Runciter now distributed the pasteboard passports that Capitão Gonçalves had forged on his new crew's behalf, then flourished an additional document, a crumpled sheet of yellow paper. "If you doubt that the barons would have Manáos become the Paris of Amazonia, consider our bill of lading," he said, devouring a cuttlefish tentacle. "We'll be hauling six crystal chandeliers, eleven gilt-framed mirrors, seventy-five satin cushions, nine brass spittoons, six rolls of velvet, fourteen Chinese screens, one upright piano—"

"Excuse me, sir," said Solange, savoring a morsel of eel, "but whoever compiled that list is less interested in creating the Paris of Amazonia than a Nineveh on the Rio Negro. Each of those goods is destined for either a saloon or a bordello. I'll wager the bill also includes mercury powder, the medicine by which harlots treat the diseases that accrue to their profession."

Runciter cast his eye down the page. He clucked his tongue, exhibited a grin, and informed Solange she was correct.

"Show me a jungle saloon, and I'll show you a slew of gaming tables littered with poker chips and playing cards," said Algernon gleefully. "When we reach Manáos, I'll do my part to swell the coffers of the Transmutationist Club."

"Obviously a man needn't go all the way to the Encantadas to make a fortune in the tropics." Mr. Flaherty used his jackknife to prise meat from the tail of a bright blue lobster. "Perhaps I'll stay behind in Manáos and become a gambler like Algernon, or maybe I'll start a rubber empire of my own."

"If you aspire to the status of *baron da borracha*, you've selected a promising career." Mr. Dartworthy took up his crab mallet and cracked open his supper with, as Chloe judged the gesture, supreme savoir faire. "Hardly a week goes by without someone finding a new use for latex." He forthwith reeled off so impressive a catalog of *hevé* products, from boots to garters, gaskets to fire hoses, railway bumpers to bicycle tires (to say nothing of Mr. Macintosh's rainproof coats), that an eavesdropper might have mistaken him for a stockjobber selling shares in a rubber plantation.

"You've forgotten the most useful device of all," said Solange. "Check the bill again, and you'll see that a large quantity of Amazon rubber routinely returns to Brazil in the form of those remarkable sheaths invented by Colonel Quondam."

"Miss Kirsop is right again," said Runciter.

"When patronizing the brothels of Manáos, please do my sister courtesans a favor and wear a quondam on your pizzle," said Solange. "This applies even to you, Mr. Chadwick."

"Miss Kirsop, I would be within my rights to leave you behind in Belém," Runciter noted.

"That won't be necessary, sir," said Mr. Chadwick.

"Personally, I like having her along," said Mr. Pritchard, feeding a slice of melon to his monkey. "She makes me laugh."

Chee-chee-chee! shrieked Bartholomew.

It occurred to Chloe that if you wanted to redeem a tedious dinner conversation, you could do worse than hire Solange Kirsop. True, this sea-witch might one day choke on her own prodigal tongue. Yes, she was probably riding for a fall. Ah, but what a fine figure she cut in the saddle, a crazed woman astride a wild horse, vaulting hill and hummock, leaving the rest of humanity behind in the stables to mend harness and muck the stalls.

Shortly after dawn on the morning of their scheduled embarkation, the women slipped into their buccaneer ensembles, then secreted their valuables in their newly purchased valises (Chloe's essay, Solange's glass pendant), concealed their hair (Chloe employing her Panama hat,

Solange her Pirate Mary bandana), and descended to the hotel lobby, all the while practicing their tenor voices, the better to deceive Capitão Gonçalves. They straightaway engaged two Tupinambás, muscular boys who owned a dual-seated litter and proposed to transport them to the waterfront for a mere fifteen *réis*. Soon the women were flying along the Rua dos Mercadores with its neat rows of whitewashed shops, their red-tiled roofs glowing in the morning light, and then came a public square hemmed by orange groves, its flagstones thronging with portly Brazilian citizens, tanned American businessmen, befuddled European emigrants, lithe Indians, and morose West African slaves. Arrayed in natural liveries of violet and amber, tiny lizards skittered along the branches of the mango trees, oblivious to the ancestors they held in common with the formidable iguanas thriving on a Pacific archipelago.

A half-hour later Chloe and Solange stood on the quay and looked across the Rio Pará towards Ilha de Marajó, beyond which lay the mouth of the mighty Amazonas. Even at this early hour the harbor swarmed with Indian workers and migrant *cabanos,* half of them employed in removing *peles* from the ketches and barques moored to the docks, the other half bearing the harvest to the central pier and loading it onto ocean-going ships doubtless bound for London, Marseilles, Bremerhaven, and other European ports. Mounds of rubber rose everywhere in configurations suggesting Egyptian pyramids. Should Halley's Comet fall on Belém that morning, Chloe decided, it would bounce right back into the sky.

She had no difficulty locating the *Rainha da Selva*, partly because the adjacent dock was piled high with mirrors, spittoons, a piano, and other items specified in the bill of lading—but mostly because the man on the foredeck of the ramshackle side-wheeler seemed precisely the sort of rogue who'd do business with a scoundrel like Runciter.

"Ahoy there," said Chloe, pitching her voice to a masculine register. "Have I the pleasure of addressing Capitão Gonçalves?"

The skipper dipped his glossy, balding head. He was a blockish man with bristled cheeks and skin as coarse as *cau-chu* bark. "Are you with Runciter's gang?"

"Able Seaman Claude Bathurst at your service," rasped Chloe, nodding.

"Able Seaman Solomon Kirsop," said Solange in her imitation tenor.

"If you're able seamen," asked Capitão Gonçalves, "why do you come sauntering down the dock with the gait one normally attributes to the female sex?"

"An astute observation," said Chloe, stalling for time and bartering for *deus ex machina*. "In point of fact we're refugees from the commedia dell'arte, adept at female impersonation."

Capitão Gonçalves glowered.

"By which Claude means we're escaped *castrati* in flight from indenture to a Milano opera company," said Solange.

The skipper sneered.

"Though an honest answer to your question would touch on the fact that we're women," said Chloe, pulling off her Panama hat and releasing a cascade of chestnut hair.

Before she could learn whether the master of the *Rainha* was incensed or merely confused by their masquerade, a cabriolet clattered into view and disgorged the rest of their party. Captain Runciter, alighting, saluted Capitão Gonçalves, then listened patiently whilst the skipper accused him of "delivering twenty-five percent fewer men than you promised."

"It's worse than you think," Runciter replied with disarming candor. "Not only is Chloe Bathurst an actress and Solange Kirsop a harlot, a distinction in which you will find what difference you may, but Miss Bathurst's brother is a gambler who, before embarking on the *Equinox*, had never been to sea. Moreover, our companion Mr. Chadwick is a priest whose previous nautical experience was limited to immersing infants in baptismal fonts."

Gonçalves snorted like a boar in high dudgeon and vanished into his cabin, returning promptly with a large paper scroll, tattered and torn but carefully secured in a leather pouch, as a pirate might preserve a treasure map. He unfurled the poster, which featured a young woman dressed in the glittering regalia of Queen Cleopatra, the caption declaring, THE

ADELPHI COMPANY HAS THE HONOR OF PRESENTING MISS CHLOE
BATHURST IN *SIREN OF THE NILE.*

"My sister married a London barrister," Gonçalves explained. "Three years ago, visiting my relations, I not only savored Miss Bathurst's performance, I also stole the poster. I shall be honored to escort her up the Amazon, much as Antony accompanied her down the Nile—provided she and her trollop friend are willing to work their fingers to the bone."

"Beyond the bone," said Chloe, torn between gratitude for this sudden piece of luck and dismay over Gonçalves's fancying himself a latter-day Antony.

"I'm a *courtesan*," said Solange.

Chloe and her companions spent the rest of the morning loading the packet-steamer with saloon appointments, brothel paraphernalia, and the two essentials of survival on the Rio Amazonas—mosquito paste and potable water—plus ample stores of provender: cassava bread, plantains, bananas, *caxirí* beer, Brazil nuts the size of cannonballs. As the sweaty British subjects labored in the suffocating heat, Capitão Gonçalves held forth concerning life aboard the *Rainha*. Captain Runciter, he explained, would be demoted to first officer, whilst Mr. Dartworthy assumed the position of chief engineer, assisted by Mr. Bathurst. Mr. Pritchard would serve as helmsman, Mr. Flaherty as stoker, and the vicar as primary *homem da proa*, forward lookout. As for Miss Bathurst and Miss Kirsop, they would become *bichos da seda*, silkworms, charged with maintaining the gossamer netting that surrounded the packet's weather deck, lest her crew be tormented by insects.

"I shall now tell you our most important rule," said Gonçalves. "*Vocês tem que ficar no barco*—stay on the boat. We'll stop for boiler wood in Monte Alegre and Villa Nova, but otherwise we belong to the *Rainha*. The Oyampis are waiting out there to catch and eat us, likewise the Tapajós, Bonaris, and Hixkaryánas. If Indians don't get you, a jaguar might, to say nothing of our scorpions, electric eels, anacondas, coral snakes, vampire bats, stingrays, and candiru: worm-like fish that will enter your—I believe the English word is 'orifices'—and must be cut out. As for our piranhas, though they're not quite the killing machines of

Amazonian lore, you won't see me wading or swimming, especially if there's blood in the water. Did I mention our diseases? Malaria, dysentery, cholera, typhus, yellow fever? The *Rainha* is our citadel. We shall not want. Avoid the jungle. Stay out of the water. Understood?"

"Understood," chorused the chastened crew.

"You will now satisfy my curiosity," Gonçalves continued. "What brings you vagabonds to Brazil? You call yourselves naturalists, but I don't believe that any more than you do."

"We seek a faraway archipelago," Runciter explained.

"According to rumor, a person might employ the Galápagos reptiles and birds in disproving the existence of God," said Chloe. "Oddly enough, certain sybarites in England will pay handsomely for such an argument."

"So in truth you're a greedy gang of bounty hunters," said Gonçalves.

"Well, yes," Mr. Dartworthy admitted.

"Myself excluded," Mr. Chadwick insisted.

"I had no idea philosophy could turn a profit," said Gonçalves. "Tell me, what's the going price these days for God's scalp in a cigar box?"

"We would prefer not to disclose the sum in question," said Chloe

"Larger than you might imagine," said Runciter. "Several thousand pounds."

"You may be sure that on my return trip our hold will be jammed with *peles*," said Gonçalves. "By all means, senhors and senhoras, run our Creator to earth. I've never had much use for Him, nor He for me. If you want my opinion, though, there's more money to be made in rubber."

The Reverand Granville Heathway stepped back from *Gregor Mendel Pollinates His Pea Plants* and contemplated the emergent painting. Although Bertram's second pigeon missive had provided but a minimal description (chubby, bespectacled, owlish), Granville believed he'd wrought an adequate representation, capturing not only the monk's outward appearance but also the intellectual fires blazing within. Mendel, he decided, was much like his experimental peas, whose exteriors offered misleading clues to their essential nature.

But what of the drama itself? Did this painting convey the fertiliza-tion act with sufficient sensual intensity? There he stood, Moravia's bright-est monk, basting implement in hand, bent over a nubile specimen of *Pisum savitum*, dusting pollen onto the stigma. Granville decided that he'd given the moment its due. All that remained was for him to provide the sky above Brünn with a dazzling sun, and the scene would be complete.

He loaded his brush with orange pigment, but before he could touch bristles to canvas Ezekiel came swooping in from Constantinople. The cou-rier had encountered inclement weather, as evinced by his soggy tail and dripping wings. What remarkable creatures were homing pigeons, brave, noble, and faithful. If only madhouse proprietors boasted such virtues.

Dearest Father,

In the interval since my last letter we have heard nothing from the ark hunters. Mustapha Reshid Pasha estimates that by now the Para-gon *must be in Sinop Bornu. Once she reaches Trebizond, nexus of a semaphore system, Captain Silahdar will send the Grand Vizier a mes-sage apprising him of the expedition's progress.*

Yesterday Gregor Mendel returned to the Bosporus and dispatched a message to my suite, proposing that we meet in Yusuf ibn Ziayüddin's establishment. Upon my arrival in the hookah-den, the monk gave me to know he still suffered from impecunious circumstances, and so I agreed to pay for the hashish.

"Well, Friar Mendel, how have you and Nature's secrets been get-ting on?" I asked as we sucked on our hoses.

"It's Abbot *Mendel now. Back home everybody is living in 1868, and I've just become head of the monastery." The monk cracked his knuckles. "Do I lament the loss of time for my research? Not really. Sci-ence and I are no longer companionable."*

"When last we spoke, you were planning to cross a round-yellow line of pea plant with a wrinkled-green generation," I said, perplexed by Mendel's abdication of his destiny. "What went wrong?"

"Actually, the experiment was successful. Allow me to explain. I'm not at odds with science per se *but with a particular scientist."*

As before, Mendel pulled out a fountain pen and decorated the back of a hashish menu with alphabet letters. He wrote R's and Y's for dominant "Round" and "Yellow" traits, w's and g's for recessive "wrinkled" and "green" traits—all the while lecturing me on his adventures in hybridization.

"With feverish fingers I opened the pods. I quickly realized that a majority of the peas were both round and yellow, the possible dominant-dominant permutations being nine in number, RRYY, RwYY, wRYY, RRYg, RRgY, RwYg, wRYg, wRgY, and RwgY. I also saw many round-green peas, tracing to the three dominant-recessive combinations, RRgg, Rwgg, and wRgg, and quite a few wrinkled yellows, children of the recessive-dominant possibilities, wwYY, wwYg, and wwgY. The smallest subset, of course, was the solitary recessive-recessive group, the wrinkled greens, my wwgg's. I began counting, eventually determining that my double-hybrid plants had yielded 315 round yellows, 108 round greens, 101 wrinkled yellows, and thirty-two wrinkled greens— the very nine-to-three-to-three-to-one ratio I predicted when last we smoked Cannabis!"

"Congratulations!"

"Next I shuffled three traits. Can you imagine how nerve-wracking it is to cross a round-yellow-gray-jacket line with a wrinkled-green-white-jacket strain? I nearly went out of my gourd. And yet somehow I made my garden grow, obtaining the varieties my calculations predicted."

"You are indeed the Newton of biology."

The monk offered me a jack-o'-lantern grin. "Collectively my double-crosses and triple-crosses make the strongest case imaginable for the segregation of heredity units. The factors governing a given trait—pea shape, for example, or jacket tone—operate independently of those controlling any other characteristic you care to name: albumen color, bud position, pod texture, pod hue, stalk length. Generation upon generation, the sovereign atoms of descent retain their integrity. They do not blend. They cannot dilute one another. Quod erat demonstrandum."

"At this point the average scientist would have been tempted to publish. But doubtless you designed further experiments."

"Do you think I'm crazy? I rushed my monograph into print before you could say 'Till Eulenspiegel.' Early in 1866 it graced the pages of the Transactions of the Brünn Natural Science Society *under the modest title 'Experiments in Plant Hybridization.'"*

"Whereupon you became famous."

"Whereupon I became despondent. Nothing happened, Bertram. No letters from fellow researchers. No invitations to scientific congresses. I mailed my article to the renowned Karl von Nägeli in Munich, accompanied by a long letter. Weeks went by. And still more weeks. Finally, three months after receiving the secret of life in his mailbox, the great botanist deigned to write back, and you know what he said? He said my work was 'only beginning.' Seven years of meticulous experiments, thirteen thousand recorded observations—thirteen thousand—and my work was 'only beginning'!"

"How exasperating."

Mendel removed his spectacles, cleaning the lenses with his handkerchief. "My reply, as you might imagine, was extensive, twelve pages covered in my smallest hand. More months of silence. Finally Professor Nägeli answered. Of my self-defense he said nothing. He merely noted that he was sending me some Hieracium *seeds, hawkweed, and suggested I use them in future investigations." The monk inhaled a goodly measure of hashish. "My career is over, Bertram—I realize that now. At sunrise tomorrow I begin the long trek home, where I shall strive to become the best abbot our monastery has ever known."*

"May God go with you."

"Never again shall I gaze upon a Pisum *or a* Hieracium *without feeling sick. In fact, the only plant that finds favor in my eyes these days"—he pointed towards the water pipe—"is our friend* Cannabis. *Give me a large enough garden and a few more years, and I'll breed a generation of hashish so powerful it will melt your melancholy in a single puff."*

"So perhaps you'll become famous after all."

"I think not."

Rising in perfect synchronicity, Mendel and I floated towards each other. We embraced. He told me I'd been an apt pupil and a comforting

presence in his life. Naturally I wanted to thank him for enlightening
me, but before I could voice that sentiment the wizard of heredity slipped
away, trailing behind him a cloud of smoke and a fug of broken dreams.

Your devoted son,

Bertram

Upon placing the message in his nightstand drawer, Granville seized his loaded paintbrush and approached *Gregor Mendel Pollinates His Pea Plants,* blessing the abbot with an orange sun, so that his experiments might prosper. He heaped the sky with clouds, populated the trees with finches, and scattered a dozen bumblebees amongst the vines.

As darkness descended, Granville stretched across his pallet, but sleep eluded him. If only he could walk free of the sanitarium, Bertram's bulletins secured in his satchel, the painting of Mendel tucked under his arm. He would travel to Munich and track down Karl von Nägeli.

"Hear me, Herr Professor," he would say, flourishing the canvas. "Fifteen years from now this Moldavian monk will send you a monograph. Study it carefully, lest you do its author, yourself, and the scientific world a disservice. If you think me mad"—here he would hand Nägeli the pigeon missives—"then read these messages from the future."

Already Granville could hear Dr. Earwicker's voice chirping in protest. "I'm sorry, Reverend, but we cannot allow you such an outing. Your plan is more irrational, even, than your project of eating the Apocalypse."

Amongst the many disadvantages of being thought insane, Granville concluded ere falling asleep, was that nobody believed a word you said.

Shortly before the *Rainha da Selva* steamed free of Belém, Malcolm Chadwick had wisely told himself that a difficult and protracted voyage lay ahead. He knew to expect an ordeal. And yet, despite these mental precautions, he was not prepared for what actually befell him, that most primeval of Christian trials, a long dark night of the soul.

The farther Malcolm traveled up the sinuous ochre Amazon, contemplating the world as reflected in the great equatorial basin, the more dreadful that world became, forsaken by the Hebrews' Yahweh, the Mussulmans' Allah, and Her Majesty's God. He could barely bring himself to eat. The faculty of prayer deserted him. Celebrating the Eucharist, he decided, would be as pointless as serving a banana to a cat.

The first five days elapsed without incident, the packet-steamer chugging effortlessly past a northern piedmont of thicketed hills and a southern plain planted with sugarcane and tobacco, both shores punctuated by the occasional Indian cottage, trading post catering to *caboclos* frontiersmen, or fishing village populated by mestizo river-folk, the flamboyant *ribeirinhos*. Screeching and squawking, gulls, noddies, and other seabirds wheeled overhead, reminding travelers that for many miles the lower Amazon was synonymous with the Atlantic Ocean. Throughout this phase of the journey Malcolm took genuine pride in his job as *homem da proa*, shouting warnings to Mr. Pritchard at the helm whenever the *Rainha* appeared headed for a canoe, ketch, rock, grass island, or *barco da borracha* coursing towards Belém under full sail.

By the sixth day the jungle was upon them, ranks of twisted trunks forming living ramparts along both banks, their branches festooned with tangled vines and gobbets of hanging moss. Sanctuary to multitudes of visible predators and hidden contagions, the trees cast thick and malignant shadows on the river, so that its waters now seemed a kind of weeping wound scored in the flesh of a black-blooded demon. It was as if the *Rainha* had steamed into the heart of the Argument from Evil, and with each passing mile Malcolm felt yet another stone drop from the mosaic of his faith.

As endured by Saint John of the Cross, the long dark night of a believer's soul signaled eventual redemption. Such despair foretold an ecstatic union with Christ. But Malcolm could imagine no such light shining at the headwaters of the Amazon—only more mosquitoes, scorpions, and predatory candiru fish, only more malaria, typhus, and yellow fever, only more Jesuits acquiescing to a forced-labor economy. He saw at best the Divine Clockmaker of eighteenth-century Deism, though the inert and indifferent gods of Epicurean philosophy seemed a more plausible hypothesis, as did the nonexistent God of Miss Bathurst's ambitions.

Curiously enough, his one reliable source of solace was that same exasperating actress. He and Miss Bathurst had of late enjoyed several stimulating conversations (despite the wretched heat, infinitude of mosquitoes, and endless throbbing of the *Rainha*'s engine) concerning the mystery of art and the enigma of personhood. If Miss Bathurst could be believed, then her she-devil side, so appealing to the fawning Miss Kirsop, was naught but an affectation—a costume to be put on and taken off as readily as her pirate regalia.

"I shall remain the Covent Garden Antichrist for as long as the role suits my purposes," she insisted, "not one minute more."

"Let me suggest that the role has *never* suited your purposes," said Malcolm. "Renounce your mystique whilst ye may, Miss Bathurst, ere you start believing it."

"You forget I'm a professional player." Her eyes narrowed with scorn. "I know the difference between beguiling an audience and fooling myself."

"Whether actors, actresses, vicars, harlots, gamblers, or sailors, we're all members of our own audiences and thus vulnerable to self-deception," said Malcolm. "I fear you take too much pleasure in this antichrist affectation. Beware, Miss Bathurst, lest you carry the game too far."

It did not help Malcolm's disposition when, in the middle of their second week on the river, Mr. Flaherty was eaten alive by piranhas. The catastrophe was of the drunkard's own making. Shortly after they'd put to shore for the evening, anchoring in an inlet two miles east of the Rio Tapajós, Flaherty declared that he was going for a swim, the torrid climate having become unbearable. Despite his companions' protestations, he swallowed some grog, stripped down to his linen, and dove off the transom. Unfortunately, the crew of a passing *barco da borracha* had selected that moment to throw overboard the bloody residue of their roasted peccary dinner, and by the time Malcolm, Dartworthy, and Gonçalves realized the implications of this action, it was too late.

For several minutes the famished fish were content to fillet the peccary's remains, but then they turned on the swimmer, and the banks of the Amazon reverberated with screams so ghastly they seemed to shred the veil of dusk. Gonçalves raised the amidships lantern high, casting its beams across the water. Pritchard threw out a lifeline. Dartworthy launched the dinghy and paddled it into the darkness, returning in time with a version of Flaherty in the stern, an abridgement so pitiable that Malcolm took to muttering, again and again, "There is no God."

In the soft glow of the lantern Flaherty appeared to be dressed in a sailor's white trousers, but then Malcolm realized that the brilliant stalks extending from the man's pelvis were not breeches but bones, their flesh shucked away. Astonishingly, he still lived, and after they lifted him onto the afterdeck he groped towards his naked femurs, as if seeking to move them in the absence of tendons. Somehow he put words to his predicament, alternately begging God to have pity on him and cursing that same deity for a monster. At length his body ran short of blood, and he gained admittance to the hospice of Heaven.

Within twenty-four hours of Flaherty's death, Malcolm attempted to disown his earlier convulsions of doubt. "I truly love Thee, Lord," he muttered repeatedly, until he believed it, or believed that he believed it—though he no longer imagined that the institutions of religion, especially the Church of England, enjoyed any prestige in the Almighty's eyes. To wit, he must forswear the chicanery he'd been sustaining on the Oxford Diocese's behalf. He was not ready to tell Miss Bathurst about the plot against the Encantadas fauna (she would surely vilify him for not informing her sooner, so he might as well inform her later), but he would certainly confess that he'd boarded the *Equinox* under false pretenses, at the behest of Bishop Wilberforce, on a mission to identify the person who'd actually devised the species theory.

"I implore your forgiveness," he pleaded after apprising her of the ruse.

"I am less offended by your masquerade than by your assumption that I'd failed to penetrate it." Miss Bathurst's lips hovered between a smile and a smirk. "As for the originality of my idea—you are correct: it did not spring from my brain alone. But I shan't name my collaborator, lest you convey the information to Wilberforce, who would proceed to harry the scientist in question."

"You should know that since leaving Belém I've come to see your irreverence in a new light," said Malcolm. "I keep thinking of Percy Shelley's 'Mont Blanc.' 'The wilderness has a mysterious tongue which teaches awful doubt.'"

"The loss of Mr. Flaherty weighs on us all. I understand how his wretched death might lower your opinion of Providence."

Much to his dismay, Malcolm realized that his curiosity concerning transmutation had become so intense that he wanted to read the thirty-five pages Miss Bathurst had composed several days before the *Equinox* went down. "If I'm doomed to lose my faith, I should like to get it over and done with," he told her. "Might you grant me a few hours alone with your essay?"

"Though continually seeking converts to the Church of Awful Doubt, I fear you wish to scan my sketch for errors, the better to gainsay my presentation to the Oxford judges."

"When I said I had recused myself, I meant it," said Malcolm. "Never again shall I darken the door of Alastor Hall. Consider your situation as follows. To transfix the judges, you must practice your presentation on another intellect, and yet none aboard the *Rainha,* including that dilettante Dartworthy, is capable of sustaining such a conversation—with the possible exception of myself."

This reasoning evidently struck a chord in Miss Bathurst, for the following morning, shortly after Malcolm had assumed his post in the prow, she appeared beside him and silently deposited the sandalwood box in his hands. He dared not study the pages just then, lest the price of his enlightenment be the *Rainha*'s collision with a sandbar, but once his watch had ended he disappeared into his cabin and pored over "An Essay Concerning Descent with Modification." Risking the annoyance of Dartworthy, Pritchard, and Miss Bathurst's cardsharp brother, he read many sentences aloud, the better to grasp their import, including the author's final ringing insistence that there was "grandeur in this view of life," according to which perspective "endless forms most beautiful and most wonderful have been evolved."

As an account of the origin of species, Miss Bathurst's transmutation sketch was lamentably bereft of implausibility. As an alternative to the

Book of Genesis, it was woefully lacking in contrivance. True, an enemy of the theory might point to mankind's presumably divine attributes (speech, reason, the moral sense), but the essay insisted that those faculties were all prolifically prefigured in Nature. Too, there was the dilution problem—the question of why a desirable trait bequeathed to a creature by its mother was not canceled by a contrary trait from the father— though the author noted that the persistence of hemophilia from generation to generation argued against "treating simple blending as the essential mechanism of heredity."

With a leaden heart Malcolm returned the essay to the sandalwood box, which now seemed to him a coffin, or more precisely a royal sarcophagus, the sweet-smelling cavity holding not only an apparent disproof of God but also His heavenly remains. For a full minute he contemplated the receptacle, then climbed into his hammock and blew out the candle. The sudden darkness startled Pritchard's capuchin, who issued a piercing *chee-chee-chee*.

Hush, jesting Bartholomew, thought Malcolm. Softly now, thou foolish monkey. Good night, my clownish little cousin.

As her journey aboard the *Rainha da Selva* progressed, Chloe found herself comparing her present environment with the only other river of her acquaintance. Whereas the Thames was simply another London thoroughfare (wetter than most but easily negotiated by bridge or skiff), the Rio Amazonas was a world unto itself, at times exhibiting the quietude of a sepulcher, at other times unleashing so loud a cacophony—bird squawks, monkey howls, the roars of jaguars and ocelots, the percussive glunks of Surinam toads—as to become a vast concert hall, inhabited by creatures of such rapturous beauty, from golden pierid butterflies to rainbow-colored macaws, scarlet hibiscus to purple orchids, they seemed émigrés from Eden. And always there was the awesome scale of the thing, three thousand miles from genesis to gulf, its tidal depths drawn (or so Gonçalves averred) from the snowy mountains and rushing rivers of six great nations—Ecuador, Peru,

Colombia, Venezuela, Bolivia, Brazil—their waters spilling ever downward, ever eastward, to form a phenomenon larger than the continent of Europe.

Indifferent though the Amazon basin might be to the prosperity of mortals, for the *Rainha*'s company the place soon proved nutritious beyond measure, a vast tureen filled with an inexhaustible soup. As the unofficial cook aboard the side-wheeler, Mr. Pritchard was forever supplementing their food stores with the river's bounty, using the galley's corroded iron stove to prepare clams, eels, snails, and a succulent sort of manatee called a cowfish. If the Albion Transmutationist Club was ultimately bested by the Mayfair Diluvian League, it would not be because the freethinkers were less well fed than the ark hunters—though sometimes Chloe longed for a lump of butter on her clams or a dollop of jam on her cassava bread.

As she pursued her new vocation as a *bicho da seda,* she occasionally pondered Fanny Mendrick's suggestion that, having been dismissed from her theatrical employment, she should consider the vocation of seamstress. At the time this notion had seemed ridiculous, and yet a seamstress was what she'd become. Just as Homer's Penelope had wrought and unraveled a perpetual tapestry, so did Chloe and Solange regularly mend the fragile curtains using silk filaments threaded through steel needles, thus securing the weather deck against marauding vermin. Each invader favored a particular time of day, the wasps sallying forth in the morning, the sand-flies and piums in the afternoon, the mosquitoes in the evening, the vampire bats at night. Chloe took satisfaction in knowing that, beyond their affection for hideous lizards, she and the master of Down House now shared a connection to the vermicular world: Darwin the student of earthworms, intrigued by their sensoria (or lack thereof), she the aficionado of silkworms, grateful to them for saving herself and her companions from innumerable stingers, fangs, and proboscises.

At first Mr. Flaherty's grisly demise occasioned in Chloe sharp pangs of remorse: were it not for her quest, he would still be alive—but then Mr. Chadwick reminded her that the drunkard had joined the adventure of his own free and greedy will, "knowing that a journey to Galápagos might entail lethal hazards." Even so, she could not fully extricate her conscience from the situation, and she resolved that if her club claimed the prize in the end, she would give part of her share to the wretch's surviving relations.

As the listless days slogged by, Chloe came to feel she'd made a mistake in lending the transmutation sketch to Mr. Chadwick. At the time her decision had felt like a rational response to his argument that, once he'd internalized the pages, his brain might become a whetstone on which to hone her forthcoming Oxford presentation. But now she imagined the vicar recapitulating her own mischievous act, secretly copying the essay word for word. Upon reaching Manáos, he would post the transcription to Wilberforce, so that when she finally appeared before the judges, lizards and tortoises in train, a cabal of scientifically inclined clerics would be lying in wait, ready to put the ax to the Tree of Life. Thus, her first words when Mr. Chadwick materialized in her quarters, sandalwood box in hand, were not "Has transmutationism acquired a convert?" but rather "May I assume that, as an honorable Christian, you forbore to pen a duplicate?"

"Your suspicions, I shall admit, are not groundless," he replied. "A man who would pose as a ship's chaplain, when in fact he's an agent of the Oxford Diocese, is scarcely the soul of probity. And yet I swear that, whilst in possession of your essay, I was not led into temptation."

"Then I must ask what sense, if any, you made of it," said Chloe.

"You will be gratified to learn that I now consider myself a votary of the theory of natural selection."

"Gratified indeed, and enchanted by the irony. Until this moment, I'd admired your decision to recuse yourself from the contest. 'There's a man of integrity,' I said. But now that you accept my theory, I must ask you to accompany me as I return to Belém and book passage to England. Upon taking Wilberforce's place at Alastor Hall, you will cast your vote with the freethinking judges."

"Impossible," said the vicar.

"Oh?"

"To begin with, by now Wilberforce regards himself as a fixture on the bench. He will not relinquish his seat to anyone—certainly not to my befuddled self. What's more, when I said I was a votary, I did not mean that I find in natural selection a disproof of God. Your Tree of Life allows for, and perhaps even demands, the Divine Clockmaker of Mr. Locke's Deism."

"An entity that lies about as far from the God of Christendom as does Ganymede from Gravesend."

"I disagree," said Mr. Chadwick, weakly: trapped in his own Deistic thicket, Chloe decided—though she would admit that her knowledge of Locke's philosophy was limited to her understanding (following upon a footnote in the transmutation sketch) that Shelley thought it an untenable alternative to atheism.

Carefully she secured the sandalwood box beneath her mattress, then imagined a question that would prove pleasurable in the asking, for it incorporated the name of the person she most fancied. "By the by, Reverend, as our *homem da proa,* aren't you supposed to be relieving Ralph Dartworthy right now?"

"How well apprised you are of our village atheist's schedule."

"Mr. Dartworthy's exact location is always of great interest to me."

As Chloe and the vicar left her stifling quarters and ascended the companionway to the weather deck, Mr. Chadwick resumed his disquisition. "Mr. Locke's clockmaker may not be the God of Christendom, but we're still speaking of a divine agency. When you and your collaborator imagine life 'being originally breathed into one or a few forms,' you are postulating an Unmoved Mover and placing that entity at the beginning of time."

"I wasn't present at the beginning of time, and neither were you," she replied, inhaling the mucilaginous air. "I only know that if Genesis is a fable, if Adam was an ape, and if new species may appear *sans* a supernatural mechanism, then we have fatally wounded theism in all its flavors."

"I think not," said Mr. Chadwick.

Chloe and the vicar parted the curtains and proceeded to the foredeck. Mr. Dartworthy sat on a cask of salted fish, alternately surveying the treacherous river and inspecting himself in a small, round mirror. "Tell me your opinion, Miss Bathurst," he said, rising. "I'm inclined to let my beard come in, thus sparing myself the chore of shaving each morning, but I'm loath to acquire too shaggy a mien."

"A jaw so handsome as yours should be exposed to the world," said Chloe.

"It's settled then. I shall live by the razor, taking care not to die by it."

Now Mr. Chadwick officially assumed the four o'clock watch, and for an indeterminate interval Chloe and her companions leaned on the rail as the *Rainha* plowed through the onrushing current, chasing the westering sun. At length the vault of Heaven turned the bright vermilion of a Chatham Isle flycatcher, whilst the clouds became the luscious purple of ripe plums.

"We have breached the bourne of a marvelous realm," said Chloe, taking the mirror from Mr. Dartworthy and holding it up to catch the celestial spectacle. "Here in enchanted Amazonia the sun sets"—she gestured towards the reflection—"even as it rises."

"I am reminded of that splendid May morning when Voltaire, having awakened before dawn, climbed a hill near Ferney accompanied by a visitor," said Mr. Dartworthy. "Reaching the summit, the great philosopher was overcome by the beauty of the sunrise. He removed his hat, knelt down, and cried, 'I believe in you, powerful God—I believe!' And then, scrambling to his feet, he told his visitor, 'As for Monsieur the Son and Madame his mother, that is a different story.'"

"An amusing anecdote, *n'est-ce pas*, Mr. Chadwick?" said Chloe.

"Amusing," the vicar replied phlegmatically. "Obviously you and Mr. Dartworthy are determined to receive me into the Church of Awful Doubt. But even if the entire British Empire ends up subscribing to your irreverent religion, I shouldn't be surprised if God has the last laugh."

"But first He must acquire a sense of humor, a faculty on display in neither the Old Testament nor the New," noted Mr. Dartworthy.

The vicar responded not as Chloe had expected, by sneering at the village atheist, but rather with a self-deprecating sigh. "Even as we speak," he said, "Voltaire stands before God's throne, cajoling Him into cracking a smile."

"Voltaire as Heaven's jester—what a delicious idea," said Mr. Dartworthy.

"As to whether Monsieur the Son and Madame his mother are also present in the palace," said Mr. Chadwick in a doleful voice, "I cannot begin to say."

7

Addressing a Vexing Question: Is Malaria Best Viewed as a Punishment for Improvidence or a Portal to Infinity?

The instant he saw the albatross snared in the rigging of the *Antares*, the Reverend Simon Hallowborn knew that he must be the one to free the bird, not Bosun McGowry, Midshipman Moffet, or Quartermaster Foyle, all of whom had volunteered for the task. Fearing for Simon's life, Captain Garrity had tried to dissuade him from climbing the mizzenmast, even though everyone on board agreed that this albatross, like all albatrosses, was a favorable omen—a reputation tracing to the species's utility as both a harbinger of dry land and an index of strong winds—and thus required immediate rescue. To allow an albatross to die was to invite a curse upon your ship.

A theologically sophisticated man, Simon wanted no truck with maritime superstition. The trapped bird, he knew, was neither a portent nor an augury but rather a Heaven-sent test. God had placed this albatross in harm's way for the sake of Simon's soul. Come spring, when he arrived in Galápagos and started eliminating its satanic fauna, scores of innocent reptiles and birds (recent emigrants whose ancestors had not been designed by the Devil) might accidentally perish. By saving the albatross, Simon would be performing an act of anticipatory contrition.

"I forbid it," said Captain Garrity.

"I am pleased to render unto Garrity what is Garrity's," Simon replied, "insofar as I may also render unto God what is God's."

At this juncture Mr. Moffet and Mr. McGowry appeared on the quarter-deck, the former ostensibly training the latter in how to use a sextant but both men clearly hoping to witness a quarrel between their captain and an Anglican priest.

"You mean to defy me," said Captain Garrity in a prosecutorial tone.

"Only that I might obey my Creator," Simon replied, pulling on leather gloves.

"If you fall and crack your skull, you won't be able to cleanse the Encantadas."

"Adam fell, but I shan't."

Fixing his lips in an insouciant smile, Simon passed his hat to Mr. Moffet, climbed onto the starboard gunwale, and set his boot against the lowest ratline.

"Good luck, Reverend!" called Mr. Moffet.

"There goes a brave man!" shouted Mr. McGowry.

And so it happened that as the *Antares* pursued her southerly course, circumnavigating the bleak and lunar Falkland Islands, Simon ascended, slowly but deliberately, like a pilgrim mounting Jacob's ladder. The winds of the fiftieth parallel chewed his ears and gnawed his cheeks, yet he pressed ever upward. The glazed shrouds frustrated his grasp, and his feet slipped on the frozen ratlines, but still he cleaved to his purpose.

There was much to be said for martyrdom, and none had said it better than the Church Fathers when interpreting Jacob's dream. For the true Christian ascetic, the journey to eternity entailed two sorts of ladders: the scaffolding of penitential acts he erected during his lifetime, and the numinous spiral staircase his soul pursued after death (each turn bringing him nearer to God). The more brutally the weather treated Simon, the happier he became, realizing that he'd contrived for himself a genuine ordeal.

Gaining the mizzentop, he scrambled onto the slick and frigid platform, then turned from the billowing sail and scanned the horizon. By Captain Garrity's calculation, the *Antares* was winning the race, running at least six days ahead of the *Equinox*, but Simon was still gratified to note that the South Atlantic disclosed no sign of another ship. He gritted his teeth, steeled his nerves, and scaled the uppermost shroud. Only after finding himself staring into the massive bird's bright red eye did he recall that his familiarity with albatrosses extended to a dramatization of *The Rime of the Ancient Mariner* he'd seen at the Adelphi Theatre. By a strange coincidence, the principal female part, a wraith called Life-in-Death, had been essayed by none other than Miss Chloe Bathurst—though the *title* role might have better suited her, he now decided, for just as the Ancient Mariner had shot a profane arrow into a holy bird, so did this reckless actress mean to prick the heart of Christendom with her poisonous tree.

Caught in a sudden updraft, the albatross had become wedged between the topsail and its spar. Gripping a shroud-line with one hand, Simon reached towards the bird and seized its tail. He shoved. The albatross, startled, lurched free of the trap and with a shrill cry pressed its webbed feet against Simon's face, the claws digging into his brow. He screamed. Having secured a serviceable perch, the bird spread its enormous wings and took off, soaring over the main topgallant and disappearing from view. As rivulets of blood rushed from Simon's punctured flesh, the spectators on the quarter-deck cheered.

Step by treacherous step, rung by icy rung, Simon descended, all the while drawing comfort from the throbbing holes in his forehead. How gracious of God to stamp him with the same wounds that the crown of thorns had inflicted on Christ.

"'Ah, well a-day, what evil looks had I from old and young,'" said Simon, reciting Mr. Coleridge as he stepped onto the quarter-deck. "'Instead of the cross, the albatross about my neck was hung.'"

"You saved our ship," said Captain Garrity.

"I did my duty," said Simon, though his thoughts were still on the albatross—not the one he'd just rescued, but the bird the Ancient Mariner had worn, its splayed wings locked by *rigor mortis* in a grotesque parody of a crucifix. What a foul thing that corpse must have become, plucked like a Christmas goose, infested with worms, exuding noisome stenches: a foretaste of Hell, in fact, and thus essential to the mariner's epiphany—that glorious moment when, having blessed the beautiful, flashing, multicolored water-snakes sinuating about the ship, he could at long last pray.

As the harsh Brazilian sun bloodied the skies over Manáos, Chloe strolled through the open-air market, a bazaar so bright and gaudy it seemed like a jewel embedded in the navel of the world. Making her way across the sodden, unpaved plaza, her Panama hat shielding her from the blazing rays, she fancied she was leading a parade of her personae: Caribbean pirate, Egyptian queen, Romanian vampire, French castaway, Southern belle, Pompeian flower seller, Mr. Coleridge's spectral Life-in-Death. At the head of the cavalcade marched her present preferred self, the Covent Garden Antichrist. Each time Chloe paused to caress a potter's vase or price a milliner's wares, England's most notorious freethinker did the same. Whenever she inhaled the market's mingled fragrances—the sharp odor of fresh fish, the dulcet savor of perfume, the ambrosial bouquet of bananas—the probable winner of the Shelley Prize likewise inhaled.

Whether Chloe's antichrist persona bespoke some deep and unnamable malaise, as she occasionally feared, or whether it was merely an affectation, as she kept telling Mr. Chadwick, its ascendancy obviously traced to her role in the vicar's rotation from devout Christian to bewildered Deist. Although his crisis of faith was not due entirely to their conversations aboard the *Rainha da Selva* (Mr. Flaherty's death had also played a part), she'd surely helped to enroll him in the Church of Awful Doubt, an accomplishment of which her antichrist side felt proud, though the pirate, the queen, the vampire, the castaway, the belle, the seller, and the wraith were not wholly at peace with the situation.

A sudden breeze cooled the plaza, the sky above the market darkened, and the chickens clucked nervously in their rattan cages, portents that caused Chloe no alarm. She and the rest of the *Rainha's* company had reached Manáos at the height of the wet season, and every afternoon without fail a furious downpour had drenched the city. As the vendors moved to protect their wares with scraps of sailcloth, She tightened her grip on her burlap sack—the day's purchases included a paisley shawl, a white muslin shift, and a bottle of Madeira—and scurried along the scattered, mud-borne mahogany planks known euphemistically as the Bulevar das Palmeiras. An instant later the clouds cracked open. With practiced steps she outmaneuvered the deluge, scurrying from tree to tree and awning to awning, reaching the Hotel da Borboleta Azul before the rain could drench the floral-patterned gown she'd acquired shortly after her brother's first profitable night of poker.

Thanks to Algernon's skill in enticing rubber barons to the gaming tables of the Dragão Verde and relieving them of their ready cash, the treasury of the Albion Transmutationist Club was filled to bursting, each member enjoying in consequence not only a new wardrobe but also private accommodations at the hotel, where every fourth-floor suite came with a feather mattress, a cherrywood dresser, and a large copper washtub. Chloe would not soon forget her first bath in Manáos, the three Arauaki women scrubbing her with a sponge dipped in scented soap, sluicing away the silt, grime, sand, sweat, engine oil, and mosquito paste of her three-week, thousand-mile journey. She had paid the Indians ten réis each, twice what they would have received for ministering to a rubber baron's mistress or an *aviador* middleman's wife.

Amongst the *Rainha's* newly arrived passengers, the person most grateful for the hotel's amenities was not Chloe but her acolyte. Although Solange had thus far managed to cling to the rank of courtesan, she feared that sooner or later she would become (as she confided to Chloe) "a common prostitute, that miserable caste of the supremely touchable." Throughout the final day of their journey—ten miles up the Rio Amazonas to the mouth of the dark Rio Negro and thence another thirty-five miles northwest to Manáos—visions of brothels had haunted Solange, but then came that magical moment when, not long after the company had disembarked, Algernon offered her a share of his poker earnings, and it was obvious that, for the present at least, she would not be obliged to enter her mother's profession.

"Oh, how I wish she could see me now," said Solange. "It was never given to Mama to awaken in a rented room without some libertine snoring beside her."

The women had settled into wicker chairs on Solange's private terrace, their recently bathed bodies swathed in white linen robes, pursuing a conversation that soon came to embrace amorous matters.

"I believe Mr. Pritchard has set his cap for you," said Chloe. "Throughout the voyage he sent many a lascivious wink in your direction."

"I am likewise favorably disposed towards Mr. Pritchard, and I shall come to love his monkey as well"—Solange flashed a prurient grin—"and his other monkey, too."

"Meanwhile, the head I should most like to turn houses the brain of Ralph Dartworthy," said Chloe.

"You've already turned it, darling. I would wager my ruby pendant that the brain in question spends the better part of every day thinking about Chloe Bathurst."

Of late, however, neither woman's imagined paramour had been around to intercept coquettish glances or sly smiles, for both sailors were spending their waking hours with Captain Runciter as he prowled the docks seeking some means of continuing the westward journey (Capitão Gonçalves having already delivered the bordello supplies, acquired a *ribeirinho* crew, filled the *Rainha*'s hold with rubber, and started back to Belém-do-Pará). Runciter's plan was to offer his company's services to any engine-boat skipper who needed to get a cargo upriver to Iquitos, the great freshwater port that the Peruvian government had established on the last navigable stretch of the Amazon. The problem, as Mr. Dartworthy had explained to Chloe, was that the harbor authorities invariably greeted any Brazilian merchant vessel with suspicion, hostility, and occasionally gunfire, for the owner's only purpose could be to harvest latex rightfully belonging to a Peruvian corporation. In consequence, the vast majority of boats leaving Manáos pursued a course that, from the perspective of a Shelley Prize contestant, went in the wrong direction.

Given the prevailing pessimism, Chloe was surprised when, the instant she entered the hotel following her expedition to the market, Mr. Dartworthy rushed towards her wearing a lavish smile and declaring that their troubles were over. Captain Runciter had finally secured posts for everyone aboard an engine-boat called the *Pulga Feliz,* the Happy Flea.

The skipper was a Venezuelan soldier of fortune, one Alfonso Torresblanco, who'd commanded a regiment of Manáos rebels in the disastrous Cabanagem uprising. Capitán Torresblanco wished to hire Runciter's company not only for their nautical skills but also as guardians of an unspecified shipment he intended to take to the headwaters of the Amazon.

"Unspecified shipment?" said Chloe. "That sounds like smuggling."

"Yes, it does," said Mr. Dartworthy evenly.

"Give me a moment to consider the morality of the situation."

"You would murder your Creator, my fair philosopher, yet you hesitate to deal in contraband?"

"The moment has elapsed," said Chloe in a sweetly scolding tone. "Very well, Mr. Dartworthy, we shall assist your new acquaintance in breaking the law."

"The *Pulga Feliz* steams out of Manáos five weeks hence."

"Five weeks? *Five weeks?!*"

"Naturally you are loath to cede such an interval to the Diluvian League, and so am I—though I strongly suspect the ark hunters are enduring delays of their own."

"How might we persuade your Capitán Torresblanco to leave sooner?"

"Alas, he needs a month to collect his cargo, forge our Spanish passports, and fabricate letters of transit."

"Alas indeed."

"Don't tell your friend the vicar we're about to become smugglers."

Chloe responded in her most sensual Carmine the vampire whisper. "It's true that I've formed an amicable association with Mr. Chadwick, but my good opinion of him is not nearly so prodigious as my admiration for you."

And so it begins, she thought, Aphrodite's ebullient tennis match, a whacking good serve if she did say so, and now the ball was speeding towards Mr. Dartworthy's court. He heaved a sigh and said, "Miss Bathurst, it has long been understood within our company that your charms have ensnared this sailor."

Instinctively she sidled towards a quiet corner of the lobby, a miniature arboretum crowded with potted ferns, Mr. Dartworthy following.

"My dear gallant," she said, "your words have brought me such joy that, despite the premise of our quest, I must imagine that a benign Providence governs the world."

"Henceforth I shall consider myself your champion, pledged to bearing you safely to the Encantadas, even if I must carry you over the Andes in my arms."

The thought of assuming a recumbent posture vis-à-vis Mr. Dartworthy had an immediate and incandescent effect on Chloe. She recalled a speech from *Siren of the Nile*, Cleopatra telling Antony that he'd become "a proximate moon, tugging at my blood, raising tides of desire in my veins."

"Since we now both have time on our hands," Mr. Dartworthy continued, "may I suggest that we visit a cantina and keep our appointment with the great Omar Khayyám?"

During the voyage to Manáos, Chloe had learned much about Mr. Dartworthy's life—his decision to abandon the family's sedate trade for the sea (his father and grandfather were both drapers), his South Pacific adventures with the American author Mr. Melville (whose recently published novels *Typee* and *Omoo* included characters inspired by Ralph Dartworthy), the ten months he and Runciter had spent in gaol for "an escapade that, viewed with a magistrate's squint, might be termed piracy"—but little of the inner man, though she hypothesized he had not a caddish bone or loutish ligament in his body: a theory that, she suspected, was about to be put to the test.

"No doubt this proposition will sound rather forward," she said, "but I am inclined to savor Mr. Khayyám's verses in the privacy of my hotel suite."

"Miss Bathurst, you shock me."

"I'm sorry."

"Apology accepted. Shock me again."

"*Voilà!*" said Chloe, pulling the Madeira from her sack. I am the Covent Garden Antichrist, she mused, the She-Devil from Dis, beyond good and evil and everything in between. "We no longer have need of a cantina. Come to my room in a half-hour's time."

A noise like the croak of a Surinam toad escaped Mr. Dartworthy's throat.

"My Lord Poseidon, having lost your trident to me in the great equatorial pageant, you are now required to do whatever I say."

"I am yours to command, my Lady Athena."

"Tap softly on my door. Bring your Persian poetry. Adieu."

As the storm thrashed the city, the raindrops clattering madly against the sealed shutters, Chloe sat in her front parlor, dressed in her white linen robe and sharing a divan with Mr. Dartworthy. After pouring them each a glass of Madeira, he perused his *Rubáiyát* manuscript, employing a fountain pen to number the poems with the aim of producing what he called "a dramatically satisfying effect."

"Are you not thereby violating the poet's aesthetic scheme?" she asked.

"It matters not in what sequence a person reads Omar Khayyám, for there is little continuity from one quatrain to the next." Mr. Dartworthy passed the pages to Chloe. "I decided we should alternate the poet's sensualism with his blasphemy."

"Beginning with—?"

"The sensualism, unless you would prefer—"

"I would not." She leafed through the manuscript and, finding a Roman numeral one, read the designated poem aloud.

> *My love, whence came your smiling eyes so keen?*
> *You must have stolen them from some dead queen,*
> *O little, fragile, laughing soul that sings*
> *And dances, tell me—what do your eyes mean?*

Mr. Dartworthy applauded, then imbibed a mouthful of Madeira. "A magnificent performance, my fair philosopher."

"Second only to the one I shall give at Alastor Hall."

"Were I to learn the meaning of thine eyes, I should die a happy man."

"We turn now to Khayyám the unbeliever," Chloe said, demurely removing her left slipper. Receiving Mr. Dartworthy's nod, she committed her talents to the poet's meditation on the silence of God.

> There are no answers written in the air,
> Pray not, for no one listens to your prayer,
> Great Allah does not see the world below,
> So turn your eyes from Heaven if you dare.

"You did it justice," he said.

"Throughout my theatrical career, I heard only one actress, a Miss Templeton, claim she'd gotten her fill of flattery, and she was lying." Chloe continued to molt, dropping her second slipper and loosening her sash, thus making her thighs accessible to Mr. Dartworthy's discernment. "Let us now revisit Khayyám the sensualist."

> Touch not your flesh of myrrh, your golden hair,
> Except to bring them tender love and care,
> Know your own wonder, worship it with me,
> See how I fall before you deep in prayer.

"Another splendid recitation," said the mariner. "Tell me, my fair philosopher—Chloe—do you know your own wonder?"

"Not my own, perhaps, but surely the wonder of these verses." She availed herself of the Madeira, then leaned towards Mr. Dartworthy and rotated the top button of his silk day-shirt as if winding a clock. "Did I mention that my dressing-table holds such paraphernalia as women use to exempt themselves from procreation?"

"Please know I am not in the business of deflowering virgins."

"Nor am I bent on maintaining my chastity under all circumstances. Like Eve, I long ago surrendered my innocence to a cad named Adam."

The Madeira was performing its intended function, allowing her she-devil dimension to emerge in full. "Your flesh is decorated, Mr. Dartworthy—of this I am certain. Pray tell, what manner of tattoo adorns your chest? A mermaid? A sinking ship? A skull and crossbones?"

"An octopus, actually. I could afford to pay the artist for six tentacles only, as opposed to Nature's eight."

"We need another infusion of blasphemy," Chloe said, straightaway enacting Khayyám's musings on the pointlessness of piety.

> *Alas, for all my knowledge and my skill,*
> *The world's mysterious meaning mocks me still,*
> *And yet I shan't persuade myself that I*
> *Must bow before a supernatural will.*

"A reading to remember," said Mr. Dartworthy.

"I cannot decide which sort of poem moves me more, the paeans to Eros or the odes to doubt. Now comes our third and final hedonistic quatrain."

> *Were I a sultan, say what greater bliss*
> *Were mine to summon to my side than this,*
> *Thy gleaming face, far brighter than the moon,*
> *My love—and thy immortalizing kiss!*

"Might I suggest a brief intermission?" said Mr. Dartworthy, his words alternating with staccato breaths.

"No, Ralph, but you may advocate for a protracted one." It seemed to Chloe that her heart and his were beating synchronously—no, not just those two hearts: at that moment every organic pump in Amazonia was pounding out the same cadence, so that the room thundered with the blood of anacondas, macaws, ocelots, sloths, and stiletto-toothed caimans.

"The poet got it right, my fair philosopher. One kiss, and I shall live forever!"

"Immortality is not a thing to postpone," said Chloe, whereupon she and her mariner rose from the divan and headed towards her bed-chamber, there being no other place in Amazonia that might accommodate their ardor.

Although the Albion Transmutationist Club had never been amongst Malcolm Chadwick's favorite organizations (even the Shelley Society seemed less vainglorious), he admired the *esprit de corps* its members had exhibited throughout their tedious weeks on the river. But now that the quest was on hiatus, with everyone living at the Hotel da Borboleta Azul, it seemed that Miss Bathurst's band had fallen prey to a kind of moral cirrhosis. The city had gotten into their blood, infecting them with a profligacy such as Malcolm had rarely observed outside of Alastor Hall.

Having determined how his company would get to Iquitos, Captain Runciter now spent most of his time swilling *caxaça* rum in the Dragão Verde. Algernon Bathurst, meanwhile, had become a fixture in that same saloon, and although he was finding estimable uses for his gam-bling profits (such as paying Malcolm's hotel bill and buying him a sturdy cotton jacket), all that cardsharping was surely warping what re-mained of his character. As for Miss Kirsop, while she'd not quite re-lapsed into strumpetry, she was nevertheless sinning on a daily basis, or so Malcolm inferred from her frequent visits to Mr. Pritchard's rooms. Worst of all, Miss Bathurst had entered into an equally unsavory ar-rangement with Dartworthy (their assignations were obviously not con-fined to recitations of Persian poetry), and it grieved Malcolm to see so intelligent a woman succumbing to the snares of a roué.

And what of the Reverend Mr. Chadwick? Had the rot of Manáos seeped into his soul as well? Was he censuring others when he ought to be judging himself? Before his conversion to the Church of Awful Doubt, he would have solicited God's assistance in addressing this ques-tion. Instead he paradoxically sought the company of Miss Bathurst, in-viting her to the Parque dos Pássaros de Guarda-Chuva for a picnic complete with bread, cheese, and wine.

"I feel compelled to raise a delicate matter," he told her after they'd settled onto the bench. "I am rarely comfortable discussing the domain Saint Augustine called 'concupiscence,' and so, to reverse a common locution, I shall mince words."

"You may begin by mincing 'concupiscence,' for I'd never heard that mouthful before," said Miss Bathurst, adjusting her Panama hat.

"It has not escaped my notice that Miss Kirsop and Mr. Pritchard are indulging in liaisons."

"Had you moved more quickly, you might have won Solange for yourself," said Miss Bathurst, taking a bite of cheese.

"Do not make light of my distress."

"*Désolé*," the actress replied in a tone partaking equally of chagrin and derision. "You've assembled a splendid picnic," she added, enjoying a sip of claret. "So splendid as to merit a recitation from Mr. Khayyám. 'A book of poems underneath a tree, a loaf of bread, a flask of wine, and thee—couched here beside me—make for such bliss that to Paradise I shan't ever need to flee.'"

"I am likewise alarmed by—"

"By my dalliances with Mr. Dartworthy?"

"I shall happily accompany you to the nearest church"—he pointed towards the Catedral de Nossa Senhora da Imaculada Conceição—"and listen as you confess your indiscretions to Heaven."

"Heaven would hear only that my love for Ralph Dartworthy is the most exquisite thing I've ever known, though his octopus has but six tentacles."

"What?"

"A local idiom."

"I am likewise troubled by your brother's obsession with poker."

"Speak of the Devil!" exclaimed Miss Bathurst.

Malcolm glanced upwards, his gaze coming to rest on the approaching figure of Algernon Bathurst, hugging a canvas sea-bag as a shipwrecked sailor might cling to a floating spar.

"Good afternoon, Reverend," he said in a merry voice. "Hello, sweetest sister."

"Your mood becomes you, Algernon," said Miss Bathurst. "You should traffic in cheerfulness more often."

"Last night all the gods of gaming were with me!" her brother exclaimed. "The contest was seven-card stud. Senhor Nogueiro, the wealthiest baron in Manáos, spreads his four queens and reaches for the pot—but then I tip my hand: the seven, eight, nine, ten, and knave of diamonds! This bag contains over three hundred *contos de réis*, easily worth four thousand English pounds!"

Malcolm expected Miss Bathurst to whoop for joy, but her response was rather more complex—a start of surprise followed by a thoughtful frown and cool words delivered in a sardonic tone. "I'd always known you were a genius at cards, little brother. Your decision to announce your good fortune in public likewise bespeaks great intelligence, for only by being robbed at knifepoint will you elude the guilt that accrues to undeserved wealth."

With a tilted smile Algernon Bathurst acknowledged the merit in his sister's sarcasm. He sat down and said, quietly, "Tell me, Reverend, will it rain today?"

"As it did yesterday, and as it will tomorrow," said Malcolm. "Might I offer you some claret?"

"My luck is intoxicant enough." Algernon clasped his sister's hand and brought it to his chest. "The arithmetic is thrilling. My winnings will cover Papa's debts *in toto*, with enough remaining to pay Runciter a dividend of five hundred pounds. Dartworthy and Pritchard will divide another five hundred, which leaves more than a thousand for our own needs. In short, dear Chloe, we can all go home. Arriving in England, you and I shall appease our father's creditors, rescue him from the workhouse, and live in genteel poverty ever after."

To Malcolm's consternation, and to Algernon's apparent bewilderment as well, Miss Bathurst neither smiled, laughed, nor praised the gods of gaming. Instead she lapsed into a brown study, speaking not a word.

"Sweetest sister, are you not delighted by this turn of events?"

"Naturally I'm pleased by the thought of breaking Papa's chains. I pray you, reward Captain Runciter and Mr. Pritchard as you propose, then join them on the next packet-steamer headed east. Exchange your *contos de réis* for pounds in Belém, hop aboard a brig to Plymouth, and secure our father's deliverance. Mr. Chadwick will want a berth on both of those vessels. As for myself, I intend to press on. I cannot answer for Ralph or Solange, but I suspect they will come with me."

"Do you not grasp what has happened, Chloe? We needn't win that preposterous prize after all!"

"You needn't win it, but I must," Miss Bathurst retorted. "'For 'tis not mere blood we seek but the thrill of mocking the cosmos.' Quite the best of Carmine the vampire's lines, do you not agree?"

"How much wine did you drink before I got here?" asked Algernon.

"Beyond aesthetic matters, I am persuaded that a finding against the Almighty at Alastor Hall will ultimately benefit our human race," said Miss Bathurst. "Solange put it better than I ever could. 'If there exists a species of ignorance certain to keep increasing the premiums on the bliss it buys, then a belief in God is surely that creature.'"

"Chloe Bathurst, I've never been more exasperated with you," her brother seethed, "and I've not forgotten the time you put snails in my bed!"

As he sipped his claret, Malcolm realized that the actress's decision had elicited his qualified admiration. She might be a reckless dreamer, a foe of decorum, and the despair of Heaven, but her refusal to abandon the hunt boasted a perverse élan.

"I've changed my mind about the wine," Algernon told Malcolm. "Pour me enough to make me forget my sister's obstinacy."

"Please recall that at present we occupy not the Garden of Eden but a swamp of iniquity—Nineveh on the Rio Negro, as Solange once put it," Miss Bathurst told her brother. "There are thieves everywhere. I advise you to forego the claret, proceed to the hotel, and hide your money in your mattress."

"Allow me to attempt some wise counsel as well," said Malcolm to Miss Bathurst. "When we make our way across the Andes, you must take care not to drive yourself too hard, lest you ruin your health. You are neither Carmine the vampire, Mr. Coleridge's wraith, nor any other immortal in your repertoire."

"You said 'we,'" she noted.

"If you would have me by your side during the journey, that is where I shall be."

"That you might supervise my friendship with Ralph?"

"That I might help your mission to succeed. Yes, Miss Bathurst, surprising as it sounds, you may henceforth regard me as a member of your club."

"I am deeply moved."

And I am deeply perplexed, thought Malcolm—perplexed and melancholic and in mourning for my Maker.

For all his present religious skepticism, and despite his apparent assent to Solange's aphorism about blissful ignorance and rising premiums, Chloe could make little sense of Mr. Chadwick's decision to join the quest. If he sought to confirm his doubts about God, there were easier means to that end than continuing the treacherous journey to Galápagos. He could simply spend a quiet evening at home, reading Omar Khayyám or Percy Bysshe Shelley or, for that matter, "An Essay Concerning Descent with Modification."

Not surprisingly, Ralph and Solange also chose to remain with the expedition: such was their devotion to atheism, free thought, and Chloe Bathurst (or so she surmised). Mr. Pritchard, meanwhile, after searching his soul and consulting his self-interest, decided to favor an immediate £250 payout over a hypothetical £600 share in the prize. Of course, this meant that he and Solange must go their separate ways, a situation that was causing the courtesan but little regret, "the fire having gone out of our fornication" (quoth Solange). As for Captain Runciter, he sat down, performed the computation, and realized that, with Flaherty eaten and Pritchard also out of the picture, his own share now topped £2,000, enough to retire from smuggling and "live like the king of an impoverished country." So he, too, would be going to the Encantadas.

When not sporting with Ralph or fretting over the time they were involuntarily squandering in Manáos, Chloe assuaged her anxiety by strolling along the wharves of the foggy Rio Negro, contemplating the Indian work teams as they loaded nets filled with latex *peles* onto Belém-bound schooners and brigs. Accompanying Chloe on her fifth such excursion was Ralph, whom she'd invited along, and Mr. Chadwick, who'd invited himself. As the three travelers reached the end of the central pier, the mists parted to reveal a peculiar tableau.

A slender young man—sunburnt, side-whiskered, bespectacled—sat on his haunches inside a ring of dead birds, twelve in all, each with a blazing crimson body, black wings, and a disc-shaped crest. Beyond this strange circle, two Arauaki servants deposited other avian specimens in a crate bearing a London address. At first Chloe imagined that the white man was practicing a religious rite, but then she decided he must be a collector, aiming to sell his birds to European connoisseurs—no, not simply a collector: a scientist, too, for he scrutinized the specimens with an intensity that partook more of curiosity than of avarice.

"Excuse me, sir," said Chloe. "Am I correct to infer you are a naturalist?"

The young man replied in a cheery English accent. "Hunting specimens is the love of my life, or so I persist in telling myself—for why else would a man keep paddling up the infernal Negro and the wretched Uaupés? Thus far I've suffered three bouts of malaria and two snakebites."

"Such hardships are not unknown to me," said Chloe, "for I, too, am a naturalist."

"A profession not typically associated with the female gender," said the collector, rising.

"My sex is evermore evolving. I am Miss Bathurst of Covent Garden, and this is my friend Mr. Dartworthy, intrepid mariner, and my other friend Mr. Chadwick, reluctant Deist."

"Wallace," said the young man. "Alfred Wallace of Hertfordshire. Because you are yourself a naturalist, Miss Bathurst, you will appreciate my thoughts concerning these particular specimens of *galo da serra*, the cock-of-the-rock, genus *Rupicola*."

"Ah, yes, the fabulous *galo da serra*," said Chloe, feigning expertise as deftly as Algernon might bluff a flush.

"What most interests me is the problem of intraspecies variation," said Mr. Wallace.

"A mystery I have pondered as well."

"As you can see, not every *galo da serra* is a luminous red—four of my exemplars tend towards orange. Observe, too, how the width of the tail-band fluctuates from specimen to specimen, as does the diameter of the crest. At what point, I ask myself, do such differences become so pronounced as to demark two separate kinds of bird? Might there exist some physical law, analogous to Mr. Newton's universal gravitation, that governs the progression from variant to variety to species?"

Good Lord, thought Chloe—another transmutationist! Though apparently not in possession of a full-blown theory of natural selection, he was clearly on the scent. She clutched her distressed stomach and then, recovering, undertook to learn whether Mr. Wallace was the sort of scientist who might carry his conjectures to Oxford.

"Believe it or not, the origin of the animal races is my passion as well," said Chloe. "Summer will find me in Galápagos, an archipelago reportedly tenanted with species that boast distinct identities even as they evoke the fauna of Ecuador and Peru."

"Miss Bathurst, you are a woman after my own heart—or I should say, head, for we have trained our intellects on the same conundrum. Were I more solvent, I would now invite you and your companions to lunch. My London agent fetches a good price for my treasures, but after he deducts his percentage my profits are meager."

"Good sir, you must allow us to entertain you instead," said Chloe.

Twenty minutes later, Mr. Wallace's Indians having nailed the crate shut and begun filling a second such container with specimens, everyone sat down to cowfish stew, roasted plantains, sweetmeats, and sangria in the Jacaré Vermelho, a dockside café crowded with cigar-smoking *caboclos* playing dominoes and robust *ribeirinhos* engaged in arm-wrestling tournaments. The subsequent conversation found Mr. Wallace struggling with incompatible oral needs—eating and talking—so that most of his excited sentences entered the air accompanied by flying morsels of manatee.

"From my observations here in Amazonia, I would argue that every species has come into being coincident in time and space with a pre-existing, closely allied type," said the naturalist. "Ah, but does each such advent represent a separate divine initiative, or might we posit *another* explanation?"

"Excellent question," said Chloe.

"When apes do battle with angels, I always put my money on the jungle," said Ralph.

"You're a materialist, then, Mr. Dartworthy?" asked Mr. Wallace.

"In most circumstances, yes. After nine years before the mast, I've learned not to quarrel with typhoons."

"Ralph is too modest," said Chloe. "Though the world's worst hurricane might befuddle him, he handily outmaneuvers the average gale."

"Speaking of apes," said Mr. Wallace, "might we consider the primate family in general? Traveling up and down the Amazonas tributaries, I've studied twenty-one species of monkey. Without exception, the types found on a given shore—the marmosets, for example—diverge markedly from their cousins on the opposite side. Why would God deploy this genus so capriciously? Why does one distinct species inhabit the western bank of the Negro whilst another colonizes the eastern, even though the climate and flora are identical on both sides?"

Chloe forced a smile of scientific camaraderie, even as she grimaced inwardly, for this man's views seemed fully capable of winning the honors at Alastor Hall. "Tell me, Mr. Wallace, will you be returning to England soon?"

"September will find me in the East Indies, collecting and exploring for at least a year—but doubtless I shall in time grow homesick. Indeed, I already have."

"Perchance you've heard of a theological competition in Oxford. Settle the God question to the judges' satisfaction—for example, by presenting a convincing materialist theory of speciation—and you'll walk away with ten thousand pounds."

"Do you believe a person might actually construct a convincing materialist theory of speciation?" asked Mr. Wallace.

"The idea offends me beyond all telling," replied Chloe, prompting Ralph to expel a sweetmeat and Mr. Chadwick to sneeze. "God is the author of all things."

"I quite agree," said Mr. Wallace. "It's true that I seek the law of transmutation, but even if I succeed, I would never soil my discovery by turning it against the Almighty. Whatever principles underlie evolution, they indubitably bespeak God's will."

"Indubitably," echoed Chloe as Ralph gulped audibly and Mr. Chadwick sneezed again.

"Then there's the problem of Man himself," said Mr. Wallace. "Our moral sense, rational intellect, and faculty of speech are manifestly gifts from on high. I've never seen the divine spark in a marmoset, but I observe it daily in *Homo sapiens*."

"I am relieved to hear that opinion from so learned a person as yourself," said Chloe.

"Miss Bathurst cannot begin to tell you how relieved she is," said Ralph, grinning.

As it happened, however, Chloe failed to take pleasure in knowing Wallace was out of the race, for a sudden coldness now gripped her bones, accompanied by a hammering in her skull. She imagined she might be experiencing an overture to malaria—or yellow fever or typhus or perhaps even Annie Darwin's nemesis, consumption: four possibilities she resolved to exile from her thoughts.

"You will excuse me, for I must make certain the Indians loaded my treasures on the proper boat," said Mr. Wallace. "Let me express my gratitude for so memorable a conversation. The three of you have nourished me in body, mind, and soul."

And with that benediction the naturalist slipped away.

"It's over," said Mr. Chadwick wistfully. "At long last, it's over." He closed his eyes and gritted his teeth. "Owing to our Mr. Wallace, Jehovah's coffin has received its final nail. This vicar's faith is extinct."

"I don't follow your reasoning," said Ralph. "The man believes in God."

"When Mr. Wallace insists that a supernatural power undergirds Nature's laws, I hear a poignant yearning but no real argument," said

Mr. Chadwick. "Our friend is merely averring that the universe exists, something I already knew. You have won the day, Miss Bathurst. For me, God is dead in all His aspects, including Aristotle's Unmoved Mover and Mr. Locke's Divine Clockmaker."

"I'm sorry," said Chloe, enduring a spell of terrestrial *mal de mer*.

"No, you're not," said Mr. Chadwick.

"No, I'm not," she admitted, then took a big gulp of wine: a medicinal measure, she told herself—and the draught indeed settled her stomach, simultaneously restoring the warmth to her frame.

"You must be very sad," said Ralph.

"Sad, but not despondent." Mr. Chadwick consumed a final spoonful of stew. "For all I know, I shall soon find my situation tolerable, perhaps even convivial." He popped a sweetmeat into his mouth. "O brave new world, that has such tortoises in it."

Godspeed, little brother."

"Fare thee well, sweetest sister."

Standing together on the thronging and boisterous central pier, not far from where she'd happened upon Mr. Wallace two days earlier, Chloe and Algernon engaged in a protracted embrace. Behind them stood Mr. Pritchard, Bartholomew the capuchin balanced on his shoulder, the monkey tugging on the man's brimless cap, the sailor brooding silently, both mammals apparently impatient to return to England and start spending their £250. Scowling clouds crowded the sky, making ready to spill their daily quota of rain, and yet the sun burned brightly, undaunted by local meteorological conditions on any of its eight planets.

Her spontaneous choice of locution, *Godspeed,* piqued Chloe's sense of irony, a transmutationist soliciting heavenly favors on behalf of a departing voyager being so prodigious an incongruity. "And may you find no occasion to seek the aid of a nonexistent Providence," she hastened to add. At that moment, however, the notion of divine assistance greatly appealed to her, for the throbbing temples and swirling nausea she'd suffered whilst lunching with Mr. Wallace were upon her once again.

"I pray you, reconsider your decision," said Algernon, firming his grip on his sea-bag. "Sail with me to Belém and thence to Plymouth. Converting my *contos de réis* to pounds, finding Father's creditors, settling his debts—these are feats a charming actress can perform far more efficiently than a dissolute gamester. I understand your desire to reach Galápagos, but by going east instead you'll be serving a greater good."

"There are no greater goods," Chloe insisted. "Only incompatible necessities."

"Well said, darling!" exclaimed Solange, arriving on the scene shielded by her pink tasseled parasol, a frippery she'd purchased with her most recent stipend from Algernon. Collapsing the *guarda-chuva,* she sketched a curtsey before her benefactor. "You mustn't lure my she-devil back to England. Her destiny lies in the Encantadas."

"I learned long ago that attempting to dissuade Chloe from her assorted destinies is as pointless as drawing to an inside straight," said Algernon. He pivoted abruptly and headed towards the *Sereia,* the Mermaid, a ponderous stern-wheeler with twin smokestacks and a double deck, her ranks of windows gleaming like silver coins on a gaucho's belt. "*Bonne chance*, sweetest sister!" he called over his shoulder.

Solange turned her attentions to Mr. Pritchard and his capuchin, patting the monkey on the head. "I bid thee a heartfelt good-bye, my cunning Bartholomew. And I wish you a happy life, my excellent Hugh."

Chee-chee-chee! squealed the monkey.

"Bartholomew is sorry you aren't coming with us," said Pritchard. "So am I."

"My place is with Chloe," said Solange.

"This will prove a mortal loyalty, mark my words," said Pritchard. "You're but halfway to the Pacific Ocean. Lethal hazards await you on the upper Amazon."

"Then please accept this invitation to my funeral," said Solange.

Pritchard sighed expansively and, feeding Bartholomew a bit of manioc, followed Algernon up the gangway, the monkey waving his paw in a sprightly *adieu.*

Much to Chloe's satisfaction, her brother had booked passage on a

Corporaçõ de Borracha Brasileiro vessel, its hold jammed bulwark to bulwark with *peles*. Throughout the trip downriver Algernon would presumably enjoy the protection of an honorable captain: no scalawag of the genus *Gonçalves* would steal his purse and throw him overboard. (Indeed, the journey might even increase her brother's wealth, should he decide to visit the *Sereia*'s gaming tables.) But, alas, she could not enjoy these soothing thoughts, for her head vibrated like a citadel absorbing a cannonade, even as chills raced along her limbs like centipedes and her stomach played host to a maelstrom. Waving to Algernon as he stepped onto the stern-wheeler's foredeck, she marveled at the frigid condition of her flesh. The sun was broiling everyone on the lower Negro, herself included, and yet she couldn't stop shivering.

"Solange, I shall require your assistance in getting back to the hotel," said Chloe.

"Are you ill, darling?"

"I fear I'm sickening for malaria. At least I hope I am, because otherwise I've contracted something even worse."

"My dearest she-devil . . ."

It seemed to Chloe that the docks of Manáos had transmuted into a magic-lantern show staged by a demented sorcerer. One by one the luminous glass paintings flashed before her: the *Sereia* leaving the pier—a swaying palm tree—a scrawny yellow dog—a stack of *peles*—a cartload of plantains—an eddy in the river—the choleric clouds. And then, at the glowing core of the enchanted lamp, the candle guttered and died, leaving only a wisp of smoke to mark its passing, frail as a silkworm's thread.

A match flared to life. Whilst the clouds above Manáos burst open, inundating the city, the magic-lantern sorcerer touched flame to wick, presenting Chloe with a second show. *Flash*—Ralph and Mr. Chadwick, easing her onto the hotel bed. *Flash*—her paisley shawl, draped over a chair. *Flash*—Solange, applying a wet cloth to her brow. *Flash*—the ceiling, so fissured it suggested a map of the Amazon basin. *Flash*—the lace curtains, transmuted into wraiths by the screaming wind.

Hour after hour she lay on her mattress, soaking the sheets with her sweat as the sickness filled her fibers and veins. Her teeth chattered like a metronome pacing a tarantella. Towards evening an elderly physician with a limp appeared and offered his verdict.

"The English senhora has malaria, preferable to yellow fever or typhus but still a grave malady," said Doutor Furtado. "The question is whether she has contracted the severe form or the moderate."

Although prepared in her mind for this diagnosis, Chloe was not ready in her bones. The word "malaria" sent tremors of dread coursing through her frame.

"How might we know which type has struck her?" asked Captain Runciter.

She wasn't sure why her brother's dubious friend had joined the vigil. He probably viewed her condition as a threat to his £2,000 share, so he'd come in hopes of somehow aiding her recuperation.

"If the senhora dies," said Doutor Furtado, "we may safely conclude she suffered from the severe form. If she recovers—"

"She *will* recover," insisted Solange, wrapping Chloe in a woolen blanket.

"My fair philosopher, you are about to play your greatest role." Ralph pressed a steaming mug of chocolate to her lips. "Lazarus's stricken sister, who defeated malaria and defied death."

"The truth has set many a person free," added Mr. Chadwick, "but soon Miss Bathurst will go to the Encantadas, there to set the truth free."

Despite her friends' encouragement, Chloe feared that the gods of pathology had not yet done their worst. Her premonition soon came true with a vengeance. For five days she lay within the prison of her ague, alternately enduring gusts of wind from a frigid abyss and gouts of hot ash spewed by a fire-breathing caiman. During her rare periods of lucidity, Doutor Furtado coaxed her into consuming draughts of quinine, "a venerable preparation," as he put it, "from the bark of the cinchona tree." It tasted like mosquito paste spread on offal. Even as the medicine entered her simmering blood, a storm arose within her skull, as ferocious as the cataclysm that had doomed the *Equinox*. Aware of the irony, she prayed for the strength not to pray, but her entreaties went unanswered, and so against her better judgment she opened her heart to Heaven, whereupon Heaven, in its majesty, reciprocated—or so it seemed.

At first she did battle with her revelation. A self-respecting transmutationist will always take the field against a sickbed epiphany. But in time the implacable fact of infinity wore her down, and a putative truth shone forth.

A divine, benign, provisionally knowable Presence lay behind the multifarious façades of the universe. A numinous, luminous, unimaginably magnificent *something*. Call it the flesh of infinity. The light of eternity. The essence of the all. The song of morning stars. Call it God.

Within her reeling brain a *basso profundo* voice arose, intoning, "Chloe, Chloe, why persecutest thou me?" Why indeed? Why mock the cosmos when she could meld with it?

"Infinity!" cried the lapsed transmutationist, forcing the word through the rattling portcullis of her jaw. "Eternity!" shrieked the erstwhile antichrist, lurching into an upright posture before toppling back into the salty fen of her bedclothes.

An indeterminate interval passed. She slept fitfully. Her blood cooled. Her fever broke. She was vaguely aware of her friends speaking in exultant whispers, praising whatever profane force (luck? coincidence? cinchona bark?) they imagined had occasioned her recovery. When at length she surfaced into consciousness, she understood herself to be a transmogrified creature, racked yet redeemed. She had become an apostle of the Presence, its radiance now soothing her soul and easing the ache in her brain. To preserve this exceeding peace she would do whatever the universe might ask of her, even unto the cancellation of her quest.

Throughout the fortnight that followed Miss Bathurst's deliverance from the ague and collision with infinity, Malcolm made a daily habit of walking to the Catedral de Nossa Senhora da Imaculada Conceição, where she could reliably be found of an afternoon, lighting candles, kneeling before sandstone saints, and struggling to translate the captions on the dozen jars filled with martyrs' bones. Accosting her within the holy edifice (which was not really a cathedral but a tumble-down church, as shabby as every other building in Manáos), he would repeat the latest declarations of dismay from Dartworthy, Runciter, and Miss Kirsop. Not surprisingly, Miss Bathurst proved less interested in hearing about the English adventurers' low opinion of her epiphany than in talking about "the glue of the universe," "the flesh of infinity," and "the essence of the all," which to Malcolm's ear sounded like a free-thinker's euphemisms for God.

"How wrong I was to have mocked the cosmos," she declared at the start of their fifth meeting.

"Allow me to suggest that this religious conversion, or whatever you call it, has more to do with malaria than with the workings of eternity."

"And allow *me* to suggest that, concerning the factuality of the numi-nous, Reverend, you had it right the first time," said Miss Bathurst. "Do you remember your recitation from the Book of Job aboard the *Equinox*? Whilst on my sickbed, I heard the morning stars sing together." She si-dled towards the donation box, evidently intending to purchase votive candles. "You will be pleased to learn I'm renewing my allegiance to chastity. My feelings for Ralph now occupy a wholly incorporeal plane."

"Lo, the poor sailor, doomed to suffer the pangs of unrequited concu-piscence," said Malcolm, indulging in an uncustomary sarcasm (and finding the idiom to his liking). He pointed to a statue of the Blessed Virgin. "Your newfound faith has a curiously Romish cast."

"When in Manáos, do as the Manáos-folk do."

With a sinking heart he surveyed the recovering malaria patient. At one time her cheeks had glowed a natural crimson, but now, drained by the disease, they were as wan as uncured *hevé*. Offended by her own locks, those glorious chestnut tresses, she'd chopped them level with her chin.

Upon feeding a 200-*réis* silver coin to the donation box, enough to reify three prayers in wax, Miss Bathurst approached an altar from which rose a painted plaster crucifix surrounded by a grid of tapers flick-ering in glass tubes. Taking the mother flame in hand, she ignited three candles. "This night I shall pray that a consumptive child named Annie might live. I shall also ask the Presence to watch over Ralph and Solange."

"Miss Kirsop will not appreciate your prayer. This morning she said, 'Make every effort to reacquaint Chloe with her senses, so she can lead us to victory at Alastor Hall.' Dartworthy and Runciter expressed similar sentiments."

"Kindly tell them I've been given to know that the Shelley Prize is no longer worthy of our efforts. We are perforce abandoning the hunt for the Tree of Life."

The thought of making this announcement in the vicinity of Miss Kirsop filled Malcolm with foreboding, and he was equally loath to share the news with Dartworthy and Runciter—but he did as Miss Bathurst requested. All three former members of the moribund Transmutationist Club reacted in a predictably physiological fashion, their tirades mixing bile, venom, spleen, and spittle.

"Runciter expects you to write him a promissory note for two thousand pounds, just as though you'd won the prize," Malcolm reported to Miss Bathurst at the start of their Thursday afternoon rendezvous. "Dartworthy insists that, having dragged us to the core of a hostile continent, you're now obliged to bring us the rest of the way to the Encantadas. Miss Kirsop says you've betrayed your most devoted disciple."

"Inform my colleagues that I regret whatever inconveniences I may have caused them. Once well enough to travel, I shall return to England and follow the Presence wherever it might lead me. As for the immediate future, in my prayers tonight I mean to remember my father, my brother, and you yourself, Mr. Chadwick."

For Malcolm one truth was now excruciatingly clear. He must tell Miss Bathurst about the Great Winnowing. By way of rehearsing his presentation, he apprised Dartworthy, Runciter, and Miss Kirsop of the Oxford Diocese's designs on the Galápagos fauna, eliciting from each a torrential indignation. Not until the following Monday, however, standing in the church before the twinkling galaxy of votive candles, as she made ready to light another 200-*réis* investment, did he find the courage to broach the subject with Miss Bathurst herself.

"I owe you a full accounting of Bishop Wilberforce's reaction to your bid for the Shelley Prize," he said. Miss Bathurst lifted her pale, pinched face. Their gazes locked. "Even as we speak, an English brig, the *Antares*, courses towards Galápagos, Captain Adrian Garrity in command. Her passengers include the Reverend Simon Hallowborn—yes, the very Hallowborn who maligned you in the *Evening Standard*—plus ninety-two convicted criminals, all of them condemned to a Charles Isle penal colony overseen by a Christian utopianist who styles himself Emperor Orrin Eggwort."

"You speak of Mephistropolis," said Miss Bathurst knowingly. "Prior to our departure Algernon and I visited the map room of the British Museum. What has a penal colony to do with the Shelley Prize?"

"Upon reaching the archipelago, Mr. Hallowborn will present himself to Governor Stopsack on Indefatigable, after which the ninety-two convicts will take up machetes and garrotes, and then . . ."

"Yes?"

"There is no delicate way to put this. They will massacre—"

"Massacre?"

"All of your illustrative specimens, the rector having convinced the prisoners, and perhaps himself as well, that the ancestors of those birds and reptiles were created by Satan. Needless to say, I'm persuaded that Bishop Wilberforce and Mr. Hallowborn care only about preventing the animals from ever appearing at Alastor Hall."

Miss Bathurst's complexion changed from a marbled pale to a morbid white. Her breathing devolved into gulps and gasps, as if her malaria had abruptly returned. "I have difficulty believing my opponents would go to such monstrous lengths."

"Dartworthy was likewise flabbergasted, also Runciter and Miss Kirsop."

"You should have told me of this ghastly plot many weeks ago." Her eyes burned with the same implacable fury as when her Athena had bested Dartworthy's Poseidon in the equatorial pageant.

"Back in Oxford, Wilberforce extracted a vow of silence from me," said Malcolm, sensing that his excuse sounded as inadequate to Miss

Bathurst as it did to himself. "Even after trading my Anglicanism for Deism, I hesitated to speak to you of the Great Winnowing." He approached the plaster crucifix and casually brushed the Nazarene's bleeding feet. "I hope you won't judge my inertia too harshly."

"Infinity's angels are tolerant of human foibles. My own forgiveness will take longer."

For a protracted minute Miss Bathurst spoke not a word. Slowly, methodically, eyes fixed on the helices of sanctified smoke rising from the altar, she grasped the mother flame and lit a candle. "Tonight I shall pray for Captain Runciter," she explained. "I would also ask the Presence to bless Bishop Wilberforce and Mr. Hallowborn, but I doubt that I can summon the requisite charity." She lit a second candle. "Instead I shall pray for Mr. Wallace, whose mechanistic theory of life may prevent his ever seeing the light of eternity. I shall likewise beseech the universe on behalf of . . . I cannot decide."

"Why not pray for the scientist who burdened *you* with a mechanistic theory of life?"

"A felicitous thought."

"An Englishman, I assume. Yes, Miss Bathurst, I'm trying to trick you into revealing his identity."

"No need for trickery, Reverend, now that you've turned against Wilberforce. My teacher was Mr. Charles Darwin of County Kent, an honorable man—and the father of the child for whom I prayed on Wednesday. He never had the slightest ambition to enter the contest. Indeed, he will not allow the definitive version of his argument, a tome called *Towards a Theory of Natural Selection,* to be published until after his death. I copied the original sketch without his knowledge."

"The Charles Darwin who wrote *The Voyage of the Beagle?*"

Miss Bathurst nodded and, firming her grip on the mother flame, touched her blanched cheek with her free hand. A pensive expression stole across her alabaster face. "Tell me, where do you place the *Antares* at present? Could Hallowborn have reached Galápagos by now?"

"Unless the storms around Cape Horn have been unusually tame this year, I suspect he's not yet free of Tierra del Fuego."

"I must ask a favor, Reverend. On leaving here, please go to the docks and find Alfonso Torresblanco of the *Pulga Feliz*. Inform the capitán that although my brother and Mr. Pritchard have absconded, the rest of us will guard his cargo with our lives. Tomorrow you will gather up Ralph, Solange, and Runciter and bring them to the Jacaré Vermelho at noon. In thwarting Simon Hallowborn, I shall need all the help I can get."

Malcolm doffed his straw hat, then rubbed his brine-soaked brow with his palm. "Miss Bathurst the connoisseur of the cosmos is an impressive woman, but suddenly I see glimmerings of her prior self, the natural-born schemer. Truth to tell, she's the one I prefer."

"Though the conniving Chloe had certain virtues, she was in every way inferior to the person I have become."

And with that remark Miss Bathurst fingered her ruined hair, pursed her pallid lips, and lit a candle for Charles Darwin.

Apprehensively Chloe entered the smoky Jacaré Vermelho, wending her way amidst the domino players and arm wrestlers. Joining her erstwhile shipmates in the far corner, she soon realized that this reunion was unlikely to prove convivial. Apparently her companions had arranged to arrive ahead of her and imbibe large quantities of alcohol, the better to sustain their hostility towards their former guiding light. By the evidence littering the table, Ralph and Captain Runciter had already consumed half a bottle of *caxaça* rum, whilst Solange and Mr. Chadwick had nearly drained a flagon of *caxirí* beer.

"Tell me this infinity folderol is a joke," said Solange, refilling her mug with *caxirí*. "Tell me you're still determined to deliver God's funeral oration."

Chloe hummed softly to herself, serenity spreading through her flesh. "A sacred entity rescued me from death and blessed me with exceeding peace. Thenceforth I became its apostle."

"And prisoner," said Solange.

Runciter sucked down a large measure of *caxaça*. "Religion is a wonderful thing, Miss Bathurst," he said, sounding as though he had a clothes-peg on his tongue, "but rather less wonderful when it compromises your friends' financial security."

"You were cured by quinine, not the cosmos," said Ralph succinctly.

Ignoring the mariner's flippancy, she squeezed Mr. Chadwick's wrist and asked, "Will Capitán Torresblanco still accept our services?"

"He was unhappy to learn that your brother and Mr. Pritchard have quit the crew of the *Pulga Feliz*," said the vicar, nodding, "but then I repaired his mood with a *mil réis* note from our treasury."

"God and the cosmos aside," said Runciter, "the raw fact is that you signed a contract with Ralph and myself, an agreement making us partners in a potentially lucrative business venture, and suddenly you're trying to weasel out of it. That's hardly the behavior of a Christian or whatever it is you've become."

"Owing to my epiphany, I now understand the worthlessness of wealth," said Chloe.

"Piffle," said Solange.

"Hear me, dear friends," said Chloe. "I am going to Galápagos. With any luck, I shall get there ahead of the *Antares*. When the convicts disembark, they'll find me waiting for them, ready to foil the Great Winnowing."

"By what means?" asked Mr. Chadwick, sipping his coppery beer.

"In time a plan will be revealed to me."

"Heralded by a flock of cherubs blowing gold trumpets," said Solange, slurring her words, "and a gaggle of seraphs fluttering silver wings."

Appropriating a stray beer mug, Chloe filled it with the dregs of the *caxirí* flagon. "If Mr. Hallowborn intended merely to kill a great many reptiles and birds, I might allow him his disgraceful conspiracy. But he means to engineer the massacre of a dozen species at least. Extinction is God's prerogative alone. And so I must put a question to you. Are we all still kindred spirits?"

"Meaning what?" said Solange, clucking her tongue.

"Will you become charter members of the Encantadas Salvation Brigade? On Wednesday morning, might we gather aboard the *Pulga Feliz*

as planned, having agreed that there are higher causes than sneering at
God and growing rich?"

For a full minute no one spoke, so that Chloe's skull reverberated
with the mournful thrum of a solitary guitar, the clacking of the *caboclos'*
dominoes, and the shouts of drunken *ribeirinhos* encouraging the arm
wrestlers.

At last Ralph gulped a draught of rum and cast his vote. "Very well,
my fair philosopher, I shall join your latest mad endeavor, but only because I believe that, by the time we reach the Encantadas, you'll again be
wanting to claim the gold."

"I, too, shall enlist, darling Chloe, and for the same reasons as Ralph,"
said Solange. "At your core you remain my she-devil."

"All right, Miss Bathurst, I shall continue to go upriver with you, and
over the mountains, and beyond," said Runciter. "Evidently Ralph and
Miss Kirsop expect you to recover your wits, and who am I to argue with
their prognosis?"

"On to Galápagos!" shouted Mr. Chadwick, lifting his beer mug.

"On to Galápagos!" echoed Chloe, raising her own *caxirí*.

The beverages of Ralph, Solange, and Runciter remained fastened to
the table.

"I care not a fig whether you lift a glass with me today," said Chloe.
"What matters is that you made the right decision, and for that I ap-
plaud you, as would a child named Miss Annie, who loved the tortoises
once in my charge—creatures who would likewise appreciate our resolve
to save their brethren: Tristan and Isolde of Charles Isle, Boswell and
Johnson of James Isle, Perseus and Androm—"

"I shan't celebrate your high-mindedness," interrupted Solange, "but
I'm not above drinking to a tortoise." She raised her beer and cried, "To
Isolde!"

"To Boswell!" shouted Runciter, committing his *caxaça* to the ritual.

"To Perseus!" proclaimed Ralph, waving his rum glass about like a
baton.

Chloe glanced at the adjacent table, where a grinning *aviador* dealer engaged two ancient Brazilians, impoverished *pirahíba* fishermen most likely, in a game of faro. The players studied their pasteboard proxies—a knave of hearts and a queen of diamonds—with a yearning so desperate it was obvious they'd made foolish bets on the next turn of the cards: perhaps they'd wagered the following month's catch, or maybe their cottages, or perhaps even their fishing boats.

Placing the beer mug to her lips, Chloe silently entreated the Presence to keep both innocent old men from harm, then drained her *caxirí* and, turning, surveyed the dazed faces of her fellowship, in whom she was well pleased.

8

Recruited into an Unlikely Army, Our Heroine
Ponders the Doctrine of Just War and Savors
the Virtues of Hallucinogenic Snuff

Like prudence, reticence, and a fondness for fools, maternal instincts did not figure prominently in Chloe Bathurst's psyche. At no point during her pregnancy ordeal at age seventeen had she taken pleasure in the thought of a babe at her breast, and despite her affection for Mr. Darwin's brood she could easily imagine getting through life without once giving birth. For all this, her epiphany in Manáos had arguably partaken of procreation. She had left her sickbed carrying a foetal faith, and she dearly hoped that in the months to come she could keep the gestating creature from harm.

Amongst its enemies, sad to say, were her own traveling companions. Shortly after the *Pulga Feliz* began steaming west along the Solimões (the name by which skippers and traders knew the upper Amazon), Solange tormented her with the vicar's Bible, splayed open to the eleventh chapter of Matthew. "Look here, darling," sneered the courtesan. "The offspring of your sacred entity thinks nothing of consigning whole cities to a fiery furnace—men, women, children, and lizards." As the engine-boat cruised past Codajás, Mr. Chadwick persuaded Chloe to once again lend him the transmutation essay, and that evening he came to her and said, "I hear in these pages not only the ring of truth but the death rattle of a delusion." Two days later, the *Pulga Feliz* having dropped anchor in Tefé to take on boiler wood, Ralph taunted her with a lewd wink and said, "Would you care to join Dr. Quondam and myself for a glass of crianza in a private room in the Hotel da Golfinho?"—the infuriating implication being that in embracing the Presence she was indulging a transient whim and remained a sensualist at heart.

"So squalid a proposition would have beguiled the Covent Garden Antichrist," she replied, "but Miss Bathurst is unmoved."

"Two arms and six tentacles, my fair philosopher."

"You are not a cad, Mr. Dartworthy. I shall thank you to stop talking like one."

Although getting her friends to appreciate her revelation was clearly a doomed enterprise, she remained hopeful of achieving an equally formidable goal: beating Simon Hallowborn to the Encantadas. Alas, while the *Pulga Feliz* eclipsed Capitão Gonçalves's packet-steamer in size and bulk, her boiler and sidewheels were much smaller, making her amongst the slowest vessels on the Solimões. Seeking to counter the *Pulga*'s inefficiency, Chloe implored the Presence to increase the boat's speed, even as she asked the same of Capitán Torresblanco, a tall, ox-eyed, Caracasborn *bravado* who recalled the gruff but noble gladiator Milius in *The Last Days of Pompeii*. After apprising Torresblanco of the plot against Galápagos, she urged him to keep the throttle open, shorten the provisioning stops, and jettison such weighty inessentials as the supplemental anchor and the replacement sidewheel. He replied that although he also wanted to reach Iquitos quickly, her ideas were without merit, and he would entertain no more such suggestions whilst yet master of the vessel she was privileged to serve.

Rebuffed by both her capitán and (as far as she could tell) the cosmos, Chloe decided to give herself completely to her *bicho da seda* duties. As with her employment aboard the *Rainha da Selva*, she took an aesthetic satisfaction in thwarting one sort of insect, the mosquito, with threads created by the larvae of another, the silkmoth. But no such pleasures accrued to her second daily obligation. According to Torresblanco, at any moment brigands might attack the *Pulga* with the aim of stealing their cargo, which meant that, come the noon hour, Chloe was required to slather herself with a particularly foul-smelling variety of mosquito paste, take a rifled musket in hand, and occupy the afterdeck until four o'clock, guarding the ziggurat of crates whilst imagining herself killing—or being killed by—river pirates or renegade Indians.

For nearly two weeks the contents of the crates remained a mystery. Not until the *Pulga* was within a hundred miles of the Peruvian border, cruising past São Paulo de Olivença, did the capitán deign to discuss their cargo. Whereas the smaller boxes held artillery shells, gunpowder, revolvers, and Lepage carbines, the central crate contained a brass cannon that Torresblanco and several *amigos* had recently dredged up from the bottom of the Rio Negro, a relic from their days commanding troops of rebellious mestizo migrant workers—the *cabanos*—in the 1835 uprising. Once it was clear that the gruesome Cabanagem revolt would end in defeat for the workers, Torresblanco had dumped his army's largest cannon into the river, lest the Brazilian government use it to massacre the remaining insurgents.

"Am I given to understand we're headed into a war zone?" asked Solange in a tone of alarm.

"Correct," said Torresblanco, feeding a cashew to his pet parrot, Miguel, a macaw fluent in profanity.

"What *sort* of war zone?"

"The sort in which a cannon would prove useful."

"*Mierda!*" squawked the parrot.

"Are we to assume that hostile forces might start shooting at us?" asked Ralph.

"In a war zone, an exchange of bullets is not an uncommon event," said Torresblanco.

"Confound it, sir, must you be so frugal with the particulars?" demanded Runciter.

"For the moment, *sí*, including those particulars that account for my frugality."

"Capitán, I am deeply offended by your news," said Runciter. "How dare you imperil my company in this fashion?"

"If you mad English explorers wish to avoid danger," said Torres-blanco, "I suggest you stay within the borders of your own belligerent country."

"*La puta madre que te parió!*" cried Miguel.

As it turned out, Merridew Runciter's petulant question was the last utterance Chloe would ever hear him make. The following morning, whilst standing watch by the crated cannon, the luckless master of the lost *Equinox* found himself in the path of an equally luckless anaconda when, heralded by the report of a snapping branch, the serpent plummeted thirty feet towards the afterdeck. Striking Runciter's shoulders, the startled creature coiled about his neck like a demonic scarf. For a fleeting instant Chloe simply stood and stared, shocked by the awesome proportions of the thing, a beast as long and thick as the *Pulga*'s anchor chain. The captain's face grew purple. His eyeballs expanded like hot bubbles. By the time Torresblanco arrived on the scene, machete in hand, and hacked the serpent into four equal segments, Runciter was dead of suffocation.

"The Lord works in mysterious ways," said Solange, inflicting a grin on Chloe.

"Miss Kirsop, I pray you, be quiet," said Mr. Chadwick as, like butchers packing a sausage, he and Torresblanco inserted the corpse into a canvas sack.

"Satan, by contrast, works in obvious ways," said Ralph. "Every time God turns His back on humanity, a frequent occurrence these days, the Devil performs a transparently devilish act."

"Leave her alone!" snapped Mr. Chadwick.

"No, *don't* leave me alone," said Chloe, sobbing. "I killed this man. I lured him to South America, and I killed him."

"His avarice killed him," said Mr. Chadwick. "He never stopped coveting the Byssheans' gold, even after you dedicated our expedition to a higher purpose."

"Let's bury the poor *híbrido*," said Torresblanco.

Because Chloe was the only person on board of a religious sensibility, it fell to her to perform the funeral service. Standing before the sheathed corpse, she offered up a selection from the Book of Common Prayer, a version of the "Order for the Burial of the Dead" that Mr. Chadwick had cobbled together from memory. "'Man that is born of a woman hath but a short time to live,'" she recited. "'He cometh up and is cut down like a flower. He fleeth as it were a shadow and never continueth in one stay. In the midst of life we are in death. Of whom may we seek for succor but of thee, O Lord, who for our sins art justly displeased?'"

Sorrowfully she watched the vicar and the capitán consign her brother's friend to the engine-boat's wake. Weighted with stones, the canvas shroud sank beneath the shimmering emerald face of the Solimões. With a mixture of puzzlement and gratitude Chloe decided that, despite the meaningless brutality of Runciter's death, she still loved the God of her epiphany. The Presence was yet her shepherd, the morning stars still sang together, and she felt confident that, by alloying infinity with ingenuity, she could keep the Encantadas birds and beasts from harm.

At first light on the fourth day in May, 1850, the engine-boat left Tabatinga and crossed the phantom seam demarking the sprawling empire of Brazil from the mountainous republic of Peru. Later that morning, Torresblanco anchored the *Pulga Feliz* in a secluded inlet and assembled his crew on the veiled foredeck. As Miguel squawked out curses, the capitán paced back and forth within the silken refuge, telling Chloe and her friends how, on reaching the Bahía de Iquitos, the *Pulga* would not put to port, lest the Peruvian government seize the cannon. Instead the company would slip furtively onto the main Solimões tributary, the Marañón, then steam two hundred miles to the southwest, about as far as a vessel of the *Pulga*'s draught could proceed without running aground.

"We are soon to enter the region of the Great Rubber War," said Torresblanco, "where the air reverberates day and night with two talismanic names. I speak now of the odious General Zumaeta and the saintly Padre Valverde."

General Zumaeta, the capitán hastened to add, was not a military officer but the bastard son of a Barranca harlot and her *seringueiro* lover. After a brief career overseeing several tin mines near Puerto Etén, an interval during which he notoriously mistreated his Huancabamba Indian workers, Zumaeta had contrived to make himself indispensable to one Rómolo Salazar, a Lima businessman bent on turning the entire Marañón valley into a rubber plantation. It did not take Zumaeta long to realize that Don Rómolo had staked out so many hectares of *caucho* plants along the river that the crop could be profitably harvested only by means of slave labor.

"At first Zumaeta tries recruiting the Marañón tribes to tap the rubber," Torresblanco continued, "but they prove so ferocious even Don Rómolo's mercenary army cannot subdue them. Zumaeta then considers the example set by tobacco and cotton planters of the American states to the north. He decides to import thousands of West African Negroes, a scheme he abandons when the Peruvian government declares chattel slavery illegal. Zumaeta then looks to the coastal Indians he put to work years earlier in the tin mines." The capitán fed his parrot a slice of mango. "Knowing that in the case of aborigines Lima will never enforce the abolition, he takes command of Don Rómolo's mercenaries, launches a slaving expedition to Puerto Etén, rounds up four hundred Huancabamba families, and drags them in chains over the Andes."

Now Torresblanco brought on stage "the second player in the Great Rubber War, the young Dominican priest Hernando de Valverde." Shortly after assuming his duties at the Misión del Misterio Bendecido, Padre Valverde had concluded that God did not want him simply to catechize the local tribes. No, he must also liberate the slaves imprisoned on Don Rómolo's plantation. Towards this end Valverde had raised an indigenous force of Indian volunteers, plus a paid militia of *ribeirinhos*, "skilled with firearms but at present having no arms to fire." Day after day, this ragged army was reinforced by rubber tappers who'd escaped from the plantation, including, as it happened, the three grown children of the Huancabamba chief.

Thus far Padre Valverde had confined the war to skirmishes in the curing depots, but once in possession of the cannon he would attack Zumaeta's main camp, Castillo Bracamoros, which was not really a castle but a fortress of wood and adobe. Here lived most of the mercenary army, plus a half-dozen deputies charged with assaying the Indians' weekly rubber deliveries, as well as two hundred Huancabamba *seringueiros* for whom the stockade had become a fixed abode, Don Rómolo having decided to build no more slave settlements than necessary.

"I must say, Padre Valverde's willingness to take up the sword bewilders me," Mr. Chadwick told Torresblanco. "I think of the Jesuit mission near Curuçá. Padre Sampaio would never start a war, not even against a malefactor like Zumaeta. He has found better ways to help Amazonia's natives."

"If you're suggesting one should not confuse Portuguese Jesuits with Spanish Dominicans, I quite agree," Torresblanco replied. "The Society of Jesus has always fancied itself Christ's earthly army, but when it comes to actual warfare, it's the Dominicans you want on your side. Before the Cabanagem horrors shattered my faith in God, I'd considered pursuing a Dominican vocation myself. Though incompetent at both Latin and compassion, I stood ready to serve the order by fracturing jaws and cracking skulls."

"The shedding of human blood," Mr. Chadwick asserted, "even when it flows through mercenaries defending an ignoble cause, is widely regarded as contrary to Christ's message."

Torresblanco heaved a sigh. "No doubt you're right, Padre. But despite that incongruity, or perhaps because of it, I am devoted to my warrior-priest."

"I believe I speak for my fellow crewmen when I say that Valverde's fight, exalted as it may be, is not our own," said Ralph. "And so we request that, as the boat approaches Iquitos, you put us ashore, so we can enter the city and convince the local police to help us save thousands of Catholic birds and reptiles from a dire Protestant threat."

"No!" shrieked Torresblanco, punching the air with a clenched fist. "I forbid it! Without a crew I could never get the *Pulga* up the Marañón!"

"As the founder of the Encantadas Salvation Brigade, I should like to say a few words," declared Chloe, fixing on a fearsome herd of caimans keeping watch over the lagoon in which the *Pulga* lay. "Dear friends, permit me to suggest that we join forces with Valverde." Although the Presence was surely chary of warfare, that same entity doubtless wanted her to try rescuing the animals—and with a scheme more robust than Ralph's muzzy notion of raising an anti-Hallowborn brigade in Iquitos. "If we help to liberate the Huancabambas, they'll feel obligated to take us along when they march back over the Andes, and then the whole tribe will help us find a way to get from the Peruvian coast to Galápagos."

"No, my fair philosopher," said Ralph. "I followed you into a hurricane. I followed you up a piranha-infested river. But I shan't have you leading me into a storm of bullets on behalf of savages I've never met."

"If you get killed in this dubious war," Mr. Chadwick added, "you won't be able to protect your precious lizards."

"And if you get *me* killed," said Solange, "you'll antagonize your favorite deity, in whose eyes even courtesans deserve redemption."

"We are going to the Misión del Misterio Bendecido," Chloe informed her friends. "After we get there, if you decide against enlisting in Valverde's army, then that is your prerogative."

"A prerogative I intend to exercise," said Ralph.

"Myself as well," said Mr. Chadwick.

"I didn't escape the London streets only to die on a Marañón beach," said Solange.

At this juncture Torresblanco, having evidently decided that reaching the Marañón eclipsed all other considerations, ordered his company back to their posts. As Chloe turned towards the pilothouse, musket in hand, she felt a sudden compulsion to leap off the boat, wade through the lagoon, and disappear into the jungle. Just as other apostles of the Presence had tested their mettle in brutal places—deserts, tundra, mountaintops—so might she profit from pitting herself against the rain forest. Her imagination displayed the ordeal as a kind of magic-lantern show, not unlike the staccato flashes that had accompanied her sickbed tribulations: Miss Chloe Bathurst, alone in the wilderness, charming the caimans—taming the anacondas—beguiling the jaguars—transfixing the fire-ants—mesmerizing the scorpions.

But no, she decided. Just then a distant community of finches needed her, as did a faraway population of tortoises. When she was ready to temper her soul in the jungle, its thorns and scourges would still be there. Firming her grip on her musket, she pushed back the veil, marched past the pilothouse, and began once again to guard the ziggurat.

Whether their good luck traced to the whims of Dame Fortune, the winds of circumstance, or the intentions of some power beyond the nonexistent Supreme Being, Malcolm could not say. Whichever the case, the crew of the *Pulga Feliz*, aided by a caul of morning mist, successfully smuggled the brass cannon from one end of the Bahía de Iquitos to the other. Throughout the uneasy passage, Alfonso Torresblanco counted up the gunboats: thirteen in all—a tally that, the capitán told Malcolm, would enable Comandante Cuarón, Valverde's chief of military operations, to infer whether the Peruvian navy had dispatched any vessels towards the fortress in anticipation of a major Indian offensive in the Great Rubber War.

As the sun climbed towards its apex, the *Pulga* pursued her southwesterly course, reaching Tamshiyaco by late afternoon. Here the mighty Solimões transmogrified into a rather different sort of body, the Marañón, shallower, frothier, swifter. For the next four days the vessel's beleaguered engine fought a squealing, screeching battle with the onrushing river, even as Malcolm observed scores of cargo boats sailing effortlessly downstream with their loads of *bolas,* cocoa, tamarinds, and bananas.

Shortly after dawn on the eighth day of their Marañón voyage, the *Pulga* reached a sector of the jungle from which rose torrents of black smoke, each twisted ribbon indicating a rubber depot. In his mind's eye Malcolm beheld a *seringueiro*: a skinny brown wretch seated before a brazier amidst a haze of creosote fumes, methodically turning the paddle on which the cured *caucho* lay spitted like a roasting boar, the Indian pausing only to pour on more latex to fatten the *bola*. No act of imagination was required to apprehend the stench of the curing process. It penetrated the entire plantation, a toxic pall that, by forcing the birds to flee, had brought to the valley a funereal silence broken only by the *Pulga*'s throbbing engine.

Malcolm now grew preoccupied with a mystery. At no point since lending him the transmutation sketch in Codajás had Miss Bathurst solicited its return. Did she not trust herself to keep the manuscript safe? Left alone with those thirty-five pages, might she set them on fire or pitch them over the stern? Unpalatable as Mr. Darwin's theory might be to an apostle of the Presence, the thing deserved better, and she surely knew as much.

"You've neglected to reclaim your essay," Malcolm reminded her.

"Giving it to me would be like handing pistol and ball to a melancholic," Miss Bathurst replied, thus corroborating his conjecture. "Might I appoint you guardian of the Tree of Life for the duration of our travels?"

Much to Malcolm's satisfaction, her hair had grown back sufficiently to halo her face with soft chestnut curls. "You may—but allow me to offer you something of arguably comparable value," he said, pressing his Bible into her grasp.

"A gift gratefully received," she said.

No sooner had twilight descended than an island appeared, dense with vegetation: Isla de los Loros, according to the chart. They navigated the wider channel without mishap. The gloom thickened. Torresblanco ordered turtle-oil lanterns deployed in the prow. The boat chugged onward, clattering past the Rio Huallaga tributary, until finally, shortly before ten o'clock, the bell tower of the Misión del Misterio Bendecido emerged against the spangled expanse of the moonlit sky.

Limned by a palisade of torches, the wharf held four steam launches and a flotilla of canopied *tolda* canoes. Whilst Torresblanco moored the *Pulga*, a party of *ribeirinho* militia dressed in mud-flecked green uniforms appeared on deck, equipped with crowbars and claw hammers. Swarming towards the contraband, the soldiers uncrated the cannon, revolvers, and Lepage carbines. Briefly Malcolm contemplated the exposed artillery piece, its barrel carved with laurels and blossoms. Such a paradoxical thing, designed to assuage men's appetite for carnage yet decorated to gratify their love of beauty.

Torresblanco strode across the pier, his parrot perched on his shoulder like an outsized epaulet. Malcolm and the other *Pulga* sailors followed, toting their duffels. Counterpointing the militia's frenzy was the stillness of three Indians huddled together on the dock, their gracile frames wrapped in white muslin robes turned to silver cocoons by the lunar light, their black hair glowing like inverted obsidian bowls.

"Prince Gitika?" inquired Torresblanco, approaching the frozen figures. Each Indian was modestly adorned with a toucan-feather headband and a quartz amulet suspended from a leather thong.

"*A su disposición, señor*," said the male Indian, evidently one of the fugitive royal children of whom Torresblanco had spoken, "and here are Akawo and Ibanua, my sisters."

"What do you call your parrot?" asked Princess Akawo. Although their tribe was reputedly of a pacific disposition, the stately demeanor of Prince Gitika's sisters evoked for Malcolm the warrior-women from whom the Rio Amazonas had taken its name.

"Miguel," said Torresblanco.

"*Puta madre!*" cried the macaw.

"Are there more volunteers on your boat, Capitán," inquired Prince Gitika, "or is this the whole of your army?"

"At Olivença we lost a man to an anaconda," Torresblanco replied. "The rest of my company stands before you—our first mate, Señor Dartworthy, our chaplain, Señor Chadwick, and our *bichos da seda*: Señorita Bathurst and Señorita Kirsop."

"We hope to make ourselves useful to you," said Malcolm, "but only Capitán Torresblanco intends to take up arms."

"*No es verdad*," said Miss Bathurst. "I, too, am prepared to join Padre Valverde's army."

"You have *already* made yourselves useful," said Princess Ibanua to Malcolm.

"Because of the Cabanagem cannon," added Princess Akawo, "the tide of the war will now turn in our favor."

"That's the finest artillery piece I've ever seen," said a wild-eyed *ribeirinho*, stepping off the *Pulga*. He flourished his newly acquired carbine. "And this is the finest rifle."

"*Mierda!*" squawked the parrot.

Prince Gitika introduced the soldier as Sargento Jiménez, then presented him to Torresblanco and the *Pulga*'s company, whom the prince insisted on calling "our brave volunteers from Manáos."

Malcolm lost no time apprising Jiménez of his ambivalence towards the Marañón valley campaign, prompting the sargento to reply, "I understand your doubts, Padre, but I can promise that you will never fight in a war more holy than this one."

"Christ blessed the peacemakers, not the avenging angels," said Malcolm.

"Whatever our Savior's present opinion of avenging angels," said Jiménez, "I feel certain he holds them in higher regard than he does the slave masters of the Pacopampa Rubber Plantation."

Fixing on Torresblanco, Gitika proposed to escort him to the Centro de Mando, Comandante Cuarón being anxious to learn how many gunboats the capitán had counted in Iquitos. "When we meet again, Padre," said the prince, turning towards Malcolm, "may it be at the public execution of General Zumaeta!"

Jiménez snapped his fingers, inspiring an aide-de-camp to hand him a turtle-oil lantern. Holding the luminous globe aloft, the sargento marched Malcolm and his friends along an ascending path through the forest, its dark reaches concealing multitudes of insects serenading one another with chirrs and chitters. After negotiating a succession of clay dykes, the party passed through the main gate, beyond which stretched a flagstone plaza where the *ribeirinho* militia and the Indian volunteers were bivouacked in huts and shanties. Campfires blazed everywhere, each ringed by soldiers enacting a curious rite involving a latex syringe. When a given fighter's turn came, he would insert the nipple in his nostril and squeeze the bulb. Instantly the communicant winced and gasped, but his pain soon subsided, leaving him with a countenance as serene as that worn by Miss Bathurst during her Manáos revelation.

"They appear to be taking snuff," Malcolm observed.

"A resinous euphoriant from the *virola* tree," said Jiménez, nodding. "The campfires keep the mosquitoes away, and *epená* keeps the rest of the world away."

It had been a night of vague and sinister shapes, of bizarre tableaux caught by flickering torches and guttering lanterns, but now Malcolm beheld the strangest scene of all. In the center of the courtyard sat a closed wicker carriage the size of a railway coach, its shafts harnessed not to horses but to an oblong pool of silk spread across the ground like a vast *bicho da seda* canopy. Painted on the surface of the deflated bladder was a grinning face embedded in a lunar sphere—the legendary Man in the Moon—accompanied by the words *Jean-Baptiste Lamarck*: a good French name for a Montgolfier hot-air balloon, Malcolm decided, for that was surely the species to which the contraption belonged.

"Do I correctly infer you plan to attack Zumaeta from the sky as well as the ground?" asked Dartworthy, pointing towards the balloon.

Jiménez nodded and said, "By means of his extraordinary flying-machine, Capitaine Léourier will assault the enemy with Cuzco death-eggs."

The sargento guided his party along a columned arcade to a sacristy that now functioned as a barracks, its dirt floor checked with mattresses set on wood frames. Probed by the light of Jiménez's lantern, the niches disclosed stores of thuribles, chalices, ciboria, and vestments. Tonight, mused Malcolm, he and his companions would sleep under circumstances befitting Miss Bathurst's arguably sacred ambition—her campaign to rescue a precious sector of Creation from the ravages of theology.

"Cuzco death-eggs," said Miss Bathurst to the sargento. "Are they a kind of weapon?"

"*Sí*," replied Jiménez, entrusting the lantern to Dartworthy. "Between our aeronaut's bombs and Torresblanco's cannonballs, we are certain of victory."

Having spent the past thirty-eight nights in a damp and filthy hammock aboard a vibrating engine-boat, Malcolm was pleased to find himself staring at a grid of dry and stable mattresses. If the others wished to stay awake and chatter, so be it, but he would discard his consciousness without delay. Stretching his grateful bones across the nearest pallet, he soon found himself aloft, dream-borne, navigating a scarlet sky aboard Capitaine Léourier's fabulous flying-machine. At length he landed back home in Wroxton, a man without a parsonage, a flock, a faith, or an income, yet deliriously happy to be so far away from the bedeviling ambiguities of the Great Rubber War.

Shortly after daybreak, a *ribeirinho* corporal with a walrus mustache and skin the ochre of the lower Amazon strode into the sacristy and informed the *Pulga*'s company that at 7:00 p.m. they should betake themselves to the refectory, where Hernando de Valverde would serve them a meal and offer his gratitude. One hour later, the same soldier appeared and announced that their audience with Padre Valverde had been postponed by forty-eight hours. This change of schedule hardly surprised Chloe. Obviously the warrior-priest must attend to matters more pressing than thanking a disheveled band of English explorers for inadvertently supplying his army with a cannon.

On the morning of her fellowship's scheduled dinner with the priest, Chloe donned her Pirate Anne regalia and explored the mission grounds, observing Prince Gitika and the polyglot Indian army preparing to bring down the fortress. The prince divided his energies amongst three Marañón valley tribes, offering advice and encouragement as, minimally dressed in tree-bark vests and painted *tangas* aprons, they readied their weapons. Decorated head to toe with spirals of red and purple dye, the Bawuni incendiaries applied pitch to the barbs of their arrows and spears. Proudly flaunting their elongated ears, an enhancement they'd accomplished by implanting cassava discs in the lobes, the Ucharu blow-gunners cleaned their preferred implements of war—hollow palm-wood tubes outfitted with conical mouthpieces—and anointed the darts with curare. Distinguished by the braided queues running down their backs, the Yamuna archers methodically strung their six-foot bows, then filled their wicker quivers with arrows, each tipped with the serrated spine of a ray-fish.

Flying firebrands, poison darts, deadly arrows: to Chloe's untutored eye this exotic arsenal seemed fully capable of creating whatever quota of dead mercenaries Comandante Cuarón's strategy demanded. No less industrious than Prince Gitika was Sargento Jiménez, presently drill-ing the *ribeirinho* militia and its attached Huancabamba irregulars, the soldiers and refugees taking up the recently arrived carbines and practic-ing their aim on life-size figures sculpted from straw and mud. Torres-blanco, meanwhile, having seconded himself to the artillery squad, taught his soldiers how to load, prime, aim, and fire the cannon. As the mission walls shook with the percussive thunder of discharging ord-nance, Chloe realized she was witnessing a kind of theatrical rehearsal, a run-through for what would surely be the bloodiest melodrama ever staged in Peru.

Eventually her wanderings brought her to the Man in the Moon air-ship, the *Jean-Baptiste Lamarck,* as fabulous in its own way as Mr. Dar-win's steam-heated zoological dome. Two Frenchmen presided over the deflated silk bladder, one dressed in the black-and-white striped shirt of a Breton sailor, the other wearing the gold-braided blue jacket of an aero-nautical commander, both balloonists scanning the fabric whilst talking at breakneck Gallic speed. Finding a tear in the silk, the sky-sailor dropped to his knees and sutured the gap with needle and thread, whereupon his superior, an elegant man sporting a mustache suggesting an *accent grave* and its *accent aigu* complement, approached Chloe and introduced him-self as Philippe Léourier, master of the flying-machine, and his assistant as André Hervouet, helmsman.

"I am Miss Chloe Bathurst, a well-traveled British naturalist who found it expedient to join the crew of the *Pulga Feliz.*"

"You are a long way from England, mademoiselle," noted Capitaine Léourier.

"As are you from France," Chloe replied. "By this time next month I hope to have placed another thousand miles between myself and London, landing in the Galápagos archipelago."

"Why do you seek the Encantadas?" asked Léourier.

"Originally I'd intended to collect specimens of scientific import, but now I wish only to protect these same reptiles and birds from a fanatical gang of poachers."

"My own quest has likewise been a journey from the sublime to the political," said the capitaine. "André and I have lived in Amazonia for two years now, seeking the fabulous lost city of El Dorado. Day after day, week upon week, we have peered down into the jungle, hoping to glimpse golden spires piercing the mist. *Hélas,* despite excellent resources— the maps I commissioned, the rumors I purchased—we have found nothing, so I decided to lend the *Lamarck* to the cause of defeating Zumaeta."

"I've been watching the Indians prepare their weapons," said Chloe. "They make a formidable army."

"The attack, I am told, will occur tomorrow morning," said Léourier. "Our Marañón valley warriors are indeed stalwart and brave"—his tone turned mordant—"but they are not quite the noble savages of Monsieur Rousseau's philosophy. Did you know that, as a puberty rite for their young women, the Bawunis whip them ferociously? If an Ucharu female accidentally sees her tribe's sacred flutes, she is put to death. When a pregnant Yamuna wife is caught eating meat, her husband beats her, for by this transgression she has rendered his dogs incapable of hunting." The capitaine closed his eyes and winced. "That said, for the moment I am pleased to call these inscrutable aborigines my allies."

"Is this airship of your own design?" asked Chloe.

Léourier nodded and indicated two little windmills secured to opposite sides of the wicker carriage. Rubber drive belts connected both devices to a common power source: a steam engine mounted on the roof, its boiler rigged to supply the pistons with water vapor whilst delivering heated air to the envelope. "I'm especially proud of *this* innovation," said the capitaine. "The earliest hot-air balloons were at the mercy of Heaven's fickle winds. Owing to my propellers and the accompanying rudder, I can chart and follow a course as precisely as any sea captain."

"These bombs called Cuzco death-eggs—whence their peculiar name?" asked Chloe.

"Believe me, mademoiselle, I doubt you are a spy for Zumaeta—and yet I cannot answer your question until we are better acquainted. *Triste de dire,* at the moment our strategy is in jeopardy, for my navigator, the estimable Monsieur Grenier, who was to have been our bombardier, languishes in the infirmary, stricken with yellow fever."

"*Une petite question,*" said Chloe, her thoughts running only slightly ahead of her words. "Does the post of bombardier require any rarefied skills?"

"Only steady nerves and a willingness to follow orders."

"And must this person be of the male sex?"

"*Mon Dieu!*" Léourier placed two fingers against his lower lip, then attracted Monsieur Hervouet's attention with a sharp toot. "Mademoiselle Bathurst has volunteered to be our bombardier. What is your opinion, André?"

"If you ask whether I would prefer to cast my lot with a beautiful adventuress who dresses like a pirate," said the helmsman, "as opposed to a drunken *ribeirinho* who smells like a dead eel, I shall reply as follows. *Pourquoi me posez-vous une telle question?*"

"I sense you are a courageous woman," the capitaine told Chloe.

"Not so much courageous as calculating. My scheme for reaching Galápagos turns on the Huancabambas incurring an obligation to me."

"Beyond her comeliness and her élan, my new bombardier is also conniving—a trait I find *très charmante,*" said Léourier. "And yet I must ask you to excuse me, so that André and I might inflate the balloon for tomorrow's battle. These days a single speech by Louis Bonaparte creates enough hot air to accomplish the job in two minutes, but he is currently in Paris, and so we must use kerosene."

A ssuming the aeronaut was correct about the imminence of the attack on Zumaeta's stronghold, then Padre Valverde's forces, Chloe reasoned, would already be on the move. Curious about the army's present location, she made her way south through the ever-darkening forest until she reached the river. Stepping onto the torchlit wharf, she observed several detachments of incendiaries, blowgunners, and archers climb into their *tolda* canoes and paddle away, apparently headed for whatever island Comandante Cuarón had selected for a staging area. As darkness consumed the flotilla, the artillery squad loaded the cannon back onto the *Pulga Feliz,* then started upstream, Capitán Torresblanco in command, his plainspoken macaw balanced on his shoulder.

Upon her return to the mission, Chloe observed the Huancabamba female fugitives, including the regal Princess Akawo and her equally imposing sister, as they collaborated with a haggard Peruvian physician, Dr. Ruanova, in converting the nave of the church into a hospital. Beholding the bandages meant for stanching wounds, the buckets deployed to catch the gush of severed arteries, and the unequivocal bone saw, its teeth grinning in the lantern light, Chloe began to suspect that in becoming Léourier's bombardier she'd made a dreadful mistake. She shut her eyes, silently inquiring of the Presence whether she would leave the battlefield unharmed. But the God of her epiphany was mute just then. The air held no celestial voices, only the jagged fumes released by Dr. Ruanova as he unstoppered his chloroform bottles one by one, determining the potency of each with a quick sniff.

She fled the hospital and, collecting her fellowship, led them to the refectory, an adobe hacienda whose portals admitted and released streams of priests, novitiates, militia, and aboriginal volunteers. Importuning a sullen *ribeirinho* private, Chloe asked him to lead her to Padre Valverde. The soldier guided the English adventurers into the east dining hall, its frescoed walls featuring biblical episodes of food consumption, including the Manna from Heaven, the Wedding at Cana, and a curious interpretation of the Last Supper (everyone seated outdoors amongst olive trees like Mr. Darwin and his colleagues eating lunch in the zoological dome). A burble of voices drew Chloe's attention to the far corner, where Prince Gitika conversed earnestly with a young man dressed in a white robe cinched by a frayed liana rope.

Rangy, gaunt, and bearded, Padre Valverde so strikingly resembled Chloe's mental picture of Jesus Christ that she briefly imagined the Second Coming had occurred—and perhaps a second resurrection as well, for the priest exuded the sickly air of a man recently returned from the tomb. Gitika acknowledged the adventurers with a quiet smile, then slipped out of the room. Shuffling uncertainly towards his guests, Padre Valverde pointed to Chloe, Ralph, Solange, and Mr. Chadwick in turn, saying, "The actress, the mariner, the courtesan, and the vicar—am I correct? Torresblanco assembled a motley crew indeed."

As the adventurers took their places at the mahogany table, the priest told them the cause of his debilitation. For ten days now he'd been in the throes of malaria, "a case so severe it will preclude my participation in tomorrow's battle." Silently Chloe prayed that Valverde's recovery would be as complete as her own, though by the evidence of his tremulous flesh he'd contracted the disease in its virulent form.

A serving staff of Indians wearing coffee-colored shifts appeared, bearing platters of grilled fish, fried manioc, and roasted plantains, the enchanting fragrances mingling in a culinary rebuke to the stinking rubber depots polluting the valley. Chloe and her companions loaded their plates to the point of avalanche, their wine goblets to the brink of deluge. Valverde assumed his place at the head of the table, serving himself no food but only a splash of Madeira.

"A question naturally arises," he said. "How do I reconcile my vocation with my prosecution of the Great Rubber War? I can address this problem only in reference to the Catholic principle of *jus ad bellum*, the 'just war' theory. But even if our struggle is less virtuous than I imagine, please know that by delivering the cannon you have earned my eternal gratitude."

"My contribution to your just war continues," said Chloe. "I am now Capitaine Léourier's bombardier, Monsieur Grenier being laid up with yellow fever."

"His bombardier?" said Mr. Chadwick in a tone of alarm.

"Terrible idea," said Ralph.

"Don't do it, darling," said Solange.

"Señorita Bathurst, I welcome you to this good fight," said Valverde. "The *Lamarck* will prove crucial to our victory. Capitaine Léourier and I do not see eye-to-eye on all matters, he the French Huguenot, myself the Spanish Catholic, but we are both determined to strike a blow against Don Rómolo's criminal enterprise."

"It's always inspiring when Christians refuse to let theological differences interfere with killing people," said Solange.

Valverde downed his wine and poured himself a second measure. "I believe a certain militancy may be in my blood. My great-great-great-uncle, Fray Vincente de Valverde, was Dominican chaplain to the army of Francisco Pizarro. When the Spanish soldiers conquered this land and murdered the supreme Inca—the god-man Atahuallpa—Fray Vincente fought on the wrong side. His distant relation is fighting on the right side."

Reaching into his frock, the priest produced a tattered pamphlet and displayed it to his guests: *Manifest der Kommunistischen Partei*—a ghost that seemed to be haunting not only Europe per se, Chloe mused, but also one British subject, herself, in particular.

"The authors are atheist materialists," said Valverde, "but for me their manifesto exudes a Christian ethos—unless my German is so feeble that I've misunderstood their argument. Just as the Jewish evangelist Saint Paul revealed the meaning of our Savior's ministry, so have the Jewish thinkers Marx and Engels exposed the mechanism of economic exploitation." Licking his finger, he leafed through the pamphlet until he found a desired passage. "'The modern worker has become an appendage of the machine,'" he read, translating aloud, "'and only the simplest, most monotonous, and most easily obtained skill is required of him.' A perfect description of a rubber tapper's lot in life, do you not agree?"

"As the *Pulga Feliz* steamed through the plantation, my heart went out to the *seringueiros*," said Mr. Chadwick.

Valverde's hollow eyes traveled from the vicar to Ralph to Solange and back again. "How pleased I would be to receive you three into our Bawuni incendiary force, charged with burning down the fortress block-houses."

Mr. Chadwick said, "Although I am in sympathy with your aims—"

"Torresblanco counted thirteen gunboats," interrupted Valverde, "the entire Peruvian river-navy, so we can safely surmise the *marina de guerra* will not reinforce the enemy. Assuming we retain the advantage of surprise and the sponsorship of Heaven, the battle will be over in an hour." He offered Chloe an oblique smile. "The last steam launch for the staging area, Isla del Jaguar, leaves at midnight. Your friends will be amongst the passengers, *no es así*?"

Mr. Chadwick said, "As a man of God—well, an erstwhile man of God, but that's another story—I cannot go to war, even on behalf of the enslaved Huancabambas."

"Nor can I, as a rapscallion with fewer ideals than an oyster has ribs," said Ralph.

"Nor can I, yours being a Christian cause and myself a she-devil's disciple," said Solange.

Padre Valverde sighed and, as if hoping God might provide him with a riposte, glanced heavenwards. The ceiling fresco depicted the Miracle of the Loaves and Fishes.

He lowered his gaze, seized a spoon, and tapped his wine goblet, producing a series of glassy reports. Seven crimson-robed Huancabamba fugitives entered the dining hall, arraying themselves before the English adventurers. At a nod from Valverde, the Indians stripped down to their underclothes, whereupon a pounding nausea took possession of Chloe, her worst such episode since the malaria attack.

Three of the men were missing their left arms, the fearsome amputations having occurred midway between shoulder and elbow. Their chests and backs were engraved with scars variously wrought by whips, knives, and firebrands. The fourth man had a wooden post attached to his right knee instead of a lower leg.

Valverde said, "Behold the balance sheet of the Pacopampa Rubber Plantation, a reckoning etched in defenseless flesh."

Zumaeta's henchmen had attacked the women with equal ferocity. A machete-wielding fiend had deprived one victim of her left breast. The second female lacked for a right hand and the corresponding foot. A smaller tool, a jackknife perhaps, or a corkscrew, had been used to remove the third woman's eyes.

"It all comes down to quotas," said Valverde. "Throughout each and every week a plantation family must tap and cure enough latex to make an eight-kilo *bola*. On Saturday the husband will bear it to the fortress by canoe or donkey cart. If he is infirm, his wife delivers the rubber. God help any Indian who shows up with an insufficiently fat offering."

"Outrageous," sputtered Mr. Chadwick.

"If ever an army boasted *jus ad bellum*," Ralph told the priest, "then such a force is bivouacked within your mission."

Solange turned to Chloe and said, "I wonder why your favorite deity allows such things."

As infuriated by Solange's remark as she was sickened by Zumaeta's cruelty, Chloe sat silently and wept.

Again Valverde nodded. The fugitives reclothed themselves. From a Huancabamba's perspective, the priest explained, the most important object in the fortress was a large weighing machine of Swiss manufacture. Should his *bola* fall even one gram below expectations, the offending *seringueiro* was consigned to a pillory. In most instances he was whipped until tassels of flesh hung from his body, then left on the rack for days as his wounds became infested with maggots. But if the overseer were in a particularly malicious mood, he would flay the victim to death, or turn him into a human torch, or remove his eyes, or hack off some member with a machete.

Valverde rose and embraced the Indians one by one, kissing each on the cheek, and then, pivoting towards his dinner guests, he implored Ralph, Solange, and Mr. Chadwick to consider that making war on Zumaeta was "manifestly the lesser of two evils." He next bid his English visitors *adios*, explaining that he must confer with Comandante Cuarón. Defying his illness, the priest turned briskly, his white robe billowing like the foresail of the lost *Equinox*, and vanished through the rear doorway.

Still weeping, Chloe contemplated the ceiling fresco, the crowd gasping as five loaves and two fish became sustenance enough for an entire congregation. Her tears blurred the panorama, but its meaning shone through the mist. She believed that had she been in the audience that day, she would have stayed to hear the rabbi's sermon even if no lunch was served and everyone else went home to eat. It was better to receive wisdom on an empty stomach than sophistry at a banquet.

As a bloated moon rose over the mission, Chloe led her friends back across the plaza, even as she pondered a possible—and distressing—connection between the maimed Huancabambas and Mr. Darwin's species theory. If an eternal "struggle for existence" was the *sine qua non* of biological and political events on planet Earth, did it not follow that Don Rómolo and General Zumaeta were simply enacting foreordained roles in a predetermined drama of savagery and violence?

When she shared this thought with Mr. Chadwick, he proved entirely unsympathetic. "Though lacking your familiarity with *The Voyage of the Beagle*, I remember its denunciations of chattel slavery. Your Mr. Darwin would be horrified by what occurs at Castillo Bracamoros."

"I don't demean the man," Chloe insisted. "I love the man. But his theory now repels me, for I apprehend it will authorize the masters of the world to further exploit the downtrodden. 'Don't feed the starving multitudes,' the Darwinists will say, 'for such misguided charity encourages them to produce descendants doomed to compete for increasingly scarce resources.'"

"You have taken the words out of the Reverend Thomas Malthus's mouth—a man who, as far as we know, never broke into Charles Darwin's study and stole his transmutation essay."

"And yet I now believe we must trace our origins not to antiquity's apes but to eternity's intentions. Surely you grasp my reasoning."

"I grasp only that, back in Manáos, you experienced a fever dream of the divine," said Mr. Chadwick, "and I'm not convinced it was for the best."

It occurred to Chloe that *epená* might prove a remedy for her exasperation, and so she guided the vicar, the mariner, and the courtesan towards a solitary campfire burning near the base of the bell tower. Seated in a circle, a detachment of Indians enjoyed a final interlude with their euphoriant snuff before embarking on the midnight ferry to the staging area. Catching sight of the English adventurers, Prince Gitika rose, the flickering flames enveloping him in an angelic aura. He gestured Chloe and her friends into his vicinity, then invited them to share his *epená* with himself and his companions: a dozen Bawuni incendiaries, plus the *caboclos* frontiersman from whose torch they would ignite their arrows and spears during the attack, as well as an elderly Dominican priest so reminiscent of Phineas Bathurst that for a moment Chloe imagined Papa had been mysteriously transported to Peru.

When her turn came, she cautiously inserted the syringe in her nostril and squeezed the bulb. A burning sensation filled her nasal cavity, as though her sinuses had been colonized by fire ants. Soon the pain passed, and she found herself walking through a luminous orchard, each fruit and flower aglow with the light of eternity, the collateral shadows obscuring her dread of dying in battle.

To the prince she said, "I have enlisted as a bombardier in Capitaine Léourier's aerial corps."

"For generations to come, the Huancabambas will sing the praises of Señorita Bathurst," said Gitika.

Solange inhaled a full measure of resin, endured the shock, and brushed her fingertips along Chloe's jaw. "Having seen the evidence of

Zumaeta's depravity"—she handed the syringe to Ralph—"I have resolved to spend tomorrow morning setting fire to blockhouses."

"The incendiaries are pleased to welcome the intrepid Señorita Kirsop to their ranks," said the *caboclos* frontiersman.

"I have always regarded soldiers as the dupes of unscrupulous men." Ralph applied some *epená* to his brain, then passed the syringe to Mr. Chadwick. "And yet if I do nothing, Zumaeta's victims will haunt me forever—so I, too, am eager to raze the fortress."

"The stalwart Señor Dartworthy has placed all Marañón valley peoples in his debt," said the old priest.

"Though opposed to violence on general principles," said Mr. Chadwick, "I believe that by joining the Bawuni bowmen"—he absorbed a blast of resin—"I shall be serving a provisionally noble cause."

"I cannot imagine how to repay the dauntless Señor Chadwick and his fellows," said Gitika.

"I can," said Chloe, "but we'll go into that another day."

During the next half-hour everyone consumed additional jolts of *epená* whilst sustaining, by unspoken consensus, a pointed silence regarding the impending fight. Not surprisingly, it was Solange who violated the tacit agreement. "There's something I must tell you, darling," she said, addressing Chloe from whichever precinct of El Dorado the resin had made the courtesan's destination. "Should any harm befall you tomorrow, it would tear my soul in two."

"Glorious goddess," said Ralph, kissing Chloe's hand, "surely you know that my affection for you is deeper than the sea wherein the *Equinox* lies."

Mr. Chadwick availed himself of some *virola* snuff, then joined the chorus. "Despite your impulsive ways, Miss Bathurst, I have come to admire you above all others of your sex."

"My dear friends," said Chloe. "My beloved—my very beloved—my infinitely beloved . . ."

"Numberless are the virtues of *epená*," said Gitika. "It permits a person to speak his most secret thoughts."

"And should the day arrive when the lovely sentiments you feel towards one another wither and die, *epená* will serve you then as well," the old priest declared. "Padre Valverde will tell you otherwise"—he inserted the syringe in his nostril and squeezed the bulb—"but Christ's wounds stopped flowing long ago. His blood no longer irrigates the world. Today we must mend ourselves with resin, or we shan't be healed at all."

9

Venomous Snakes Fall from the Sky,
Fortress Walls Come Tumbling Down, and
a New Plan Hatches in Chloe's Brain

On maps the region was called Tierra del Fuego, but after an eternity of captivity by the violent weather the Reverend Simon Hallowborn thought of it as Terror del Fuego instead. The howling winds, frigid vistas, and subzero temperatures recalled for Simon an indelible tableau from Dante: Lucifer embedded up to his chest in the solid River Cocytus, his wings sending forth blasts so cold they kept the waters forever frozen. With his ship engulfed by icebergs and mountainous waves, Captain Garrity was now measuring her progress not in leagues but in yards, not in days but in weeks. After a full month of applying his nautical skills to the problem, the master of the *Antares* had failed to move her more than halfway along the Strait of Magellan. Ahead lay only more treacherous floes, more quixotic currents, and the point of no return.

As the battle against Cape Horn entered its second month, Simon decided the time had come for him to minister to the wretches in the hold. Buffeted by the turbulent seas, chafed by their manacles and fetters, the convicts would need their spirits lifted—and in fact he was prepared to offer them bracing news: a radically reduced prison sentence awaited anyone who participated in the Great Winnowing!

Heart in hand, Bible at the ready, he broached the Stygian depths of the ship, where ninety-two unbathed and probably unbaptized men lay shackled in their hammocks. Setting down his musket, Mr. Moffet deferentially doffed his cap (doubtless recalling how Simon had saved the *Antares* by rescuing the snared albatross). "Good afternoon, Reverend," said the midshipman, his words turning to spectral vapor. "What brings you to our icy dungeon?"

Simon explained that he wished to address the prisoners, and so Mr. Moffet ordered his charges to fall in before their visitor. As the men climbed free of their hammocks, arranging themselves in irregular ranks and files, their chains clanking discordantly, Simon assayed the atmosphere, which evidently comprised equal parts vomitus, urine, rotten cabbages, and dead fish. "Future inmates of Mephistropolis, may the blessings of our Lord and Savior Jesus Christ be upon you," he said, sinuses aflame with the ambient stench. "As you've doubtless inferred, the *Antares* is trapped in heavy seas—but know that God means to preserve you, for you've been selected to perform a holy task."

A rheumy-eyed prisoner raised his hand as far as the manacle would allow. "The name's Ben Colby, the worst kind of horse thief—the sort what gets caught." Cackles and guffaws reverberated through the hold. "Here's my question, Reverend. If God needs the lot of us, does that mean He'll be raisin' up poor Billy Windham, who expired of the flux on Sunday? Will He be restorin' old Tom Tattle, dead last month of a fever?"

"I come to you not as a prophet, revealing God's mind, but as a simple priest, extolling His mercy," Simon replied. "Devote yourselves to Heaven's agenda when we reach Galápagos, and our Divine Creator—acting through Governor Stopsack and the Oxford Diocese—will diminish your sentences by one-quarter."

"I'd say that calls for a hurrah," said Mr. Moffat.

No one cheered. Instead a dusky prisoner stumbled forward, tripped in consequence of his fetters, and fell across the keelson. "Jake Peach 'ere," he said, regaining his feet, "convicted comforter of wives whose 'usbands can no longer perform the marriage act. 'Eve's what I'm thinkin'.

I'm thinkin' that, before we get unduly grateful for shorter sojourns in 'Ell, we should 'ear what's expected of us."

"Travel with me back through time," said Simon, "to Sunday, the twenty-eighth of October, 4004 B.C.—the seventh day of Creation by Bishop Ussher's calculation. All is in stasis. God is resting. But then comes the fateful eighth day, and with it a terrible event. No, not the Fall of Man, which lies a full week in the future. On Monday the Devil goes wandering to and fro in the newly made world, reaching Galápagos at dusk. As darkness steals across the equator, he plants Perdition's flag on Indefatigable Isle, then seeds the archipelago with hundreds of scaled and clawed monstrosities, much like himself in aspect and temperament."

"Maybe that's what 'appened," said Jake Peach, "but I can tell you this: we don't read of it in Scripture."

"The Bible necessarily omits supplemental narratives and ancillary doctrines," Simon explained. "That's why God gave us the Church of England, that we might enjoy its guidance in reading between the lines of Holy Writ."

A squat convict shuffled forward, his face so dotted with freckles it suggested a cowbird egg. "Harry Trimble 'ere, former flesh merchant. You want us to destroy these spawn of Satan, is that your meanin', Reverend?"

"Upon our arrival in the Encantadas, you will be issued . . . implements," said Simon, nodding, his imagination conjuring up the *Antares*'s armory. After presenting themselves to the Governor on Indefatigable, the ship's company would sail to the largest island, Albemarle, and begin the procedure. Sweeping north from the Sierra Negra, the garroters would strangle the giant tortoises, even as the machete brigade decapitated the lizards, whilst the brig's crew took up the fowling pieces and cleansed the skies of the island's infernal mockingbirds, flycatchers, and finches. "Perform an efficient slaughter, and your freedom will come sooner rather than later."

"Hip hip!" shouted Mr. Moffet.

"Hoorah!" chorused the prisoners.

"Hip hip!" yelled Mr. Moffet.

"Hoorah!"

"Cursed be the giant tortoises, for they are the Devil's children!" shouted Simon.

"Death to the tortoises!" screamed the prisoners.

"Cursed be the land lizards, for their every breath brings a plague!" cried Simon.

"Death to the lizards!" shrieked the prisoners.

"Cursed be the marine iguanas, for they are odious in Heaven's eyes!"

"Death to the iguanas!"

Unable to endure the reek of the floating penal colony another minute, Simon rushed towards the companionway and began his ascent. With every step the angels of mercy pulled him closer to their collective bosom, telling him to be of good cheer, for the *Antares* would not founder off Tierra del Fuego but rather bear to Galápagos ninety, formerly ninety-two, of God's most eager servants. And so it was that, when he settled into his berth that night, Simon pictured himself as newly born, his nativity attended by a retinue of sheep, cattle, swine, and goats, with not a single satanic tortoise or demonic iguana in the lot.

Although perhaps tracing more to *epená* than to honesty, the impassioned sentiments expressed by Ralph on the eve of battle lifted Chloe's spirits, even as those same sentiments stirred within her yearnings not easily reconciled to her newfound appetite for eternity. Returning to the sacristy, alone, her friends having left on the midnight ferry to the staging area, she burned with longing for an embrace from her former paramour. She wanted to feel the press of his arms and savor the scent of his neck. Did it all come down to Mr. Chadwick's curious word, "concupiscence"? Was carnal desire in fact the engine that set the world to spinning, a force more powerful even than the Presence?

Distressed by these profane musings, she shed her clothes and pitched a mosquito tent above her pallet. As she reached towards the turtle-oil lantern, intending to douse the flame, her fingers chanced to brush Ralph's

Omar Khayyám manuscript. The text beckoned. For the next half-hour she lay on her mattress, reading by the primal reptilian light. A particular quatrain commended itself to her attention.

> *What the pen writes for you, it can never*
> *Unwrite, so there's no use being clever,*
> *Don't weep overmuch; let your heart not rage,*
> *Your fate is your fate, now and forever.*

Whether one believed in Allah, Jehovah, Brahma, the Buddha, the Presence, or mere brute circumstance, the sage was telling her, the past was irredeemable. By this time tomorrow, the Battle of Castillo Bracamoros would be a fixed point in history, recorded in impervious ink on a sheet of immortal parchment, each pen stroke immune to human will. An unnerving thought, and yet she soon drifted off to sleep.

The Earth kept turning, the pen kept writing, and a wan light seeped into the sacristy. Chloe awoke and, gaining her feet, slipped into her pirate costume, pleased to note that her brain now seemed free of *epená*. Presently André Hervouet appeared, bearing a steaming mug of coffee and two ripe bananas. She consumed her breakfast standing upright, then followed the helmsman across the plaza through the chilly predawn mist towards the *Jean-Baptiste Lamarck*, where a one-armed Huancabamba refugee stood ready to assist in the launch.

The flying-machine rocked in the wind, its mooring line held fast by an anchor hooked about a sandstone statue of Santo Domingo. The kerosene burner snorted and growled, filling the sausage-shaped balloon with heated air and giving the decorative Man in the Moon the broadest of smiles. Just then the *Lamarck* seemed to Chloe almost a living thing: a belligerent Spanish bull, anxious and expectant, waiting in his chute for the matador to enter the ring.

André guided her onto a stepping stool and thence through the larboard hatch into the wicker carriage. The rear compartment, surprisingly commodious, housed the anchor windlass, a compass binnacle, and a table at which Philippe Léourier sat inspecting a map of the valley, whilst the forward section served as the bridge, complete with helm, throttle, and a circular glass observation port. Glancing up from his chart, the capitaine welcomed Chloe aboard, then pointed to a loosely woven sack slung beneath the open aft window. At least twenty ceramic globes, peppered with tiny holes, lay snared in the webbing like sea urchins caught in a fishnet. Upon closer inspection she saw that each ball consisted of two hemispheres glued together with yet another miraculous Amazonian resin.

"Time did not permit the Yamunas to prepare more death-eggs, but we shall make do," said Léourier. "An ingenious weapon. The shell is formed of fired clay and packed with grass. Dropped from a sufficient height, the egg splits open on hitting the ground."

"*Cependant,* owing to the grass cushion, the two poisonous snakes remain unharmed," said André, assuming his place at the helm.

"Poisonous snakes?" said Chloe, bewildered. "*Pardonez-moi,* but that's absurd."

"Quite so," said Léourier, rising. "And thanks to their absurdity, Cuzco death-eggs are amongst the most terrible weapons ever devised. Confronted with a sudden plague of fer-de-lances, bushmasters, and coral snakes, a soldier will freeze in his tracks and tell himself he's hallucinating, thereby losing time much better spent running away."

Chloe said, "Dropping snakes on people, even ghastly people like Don Rómolo's mercenaries—I must confess, the thought distresses me."

"All's fair in love and dialectical materialism, or so Père Valverde informs us." Léourier abandoned the chart table, approached the open starboard window, and cried, "Cast off!"

Outside the gondola, the one-armed Huancabamba detached the anchor from Santo Domingo's ankles. Burner roaring, the *Lamarck* began a slow ascent, seeking the sky like a bubble rising through a glass of champagne. André worked the windlass, drawing the anchor into its berth beneath the gondola. Once the airship had attained an elevation of perhaps fifty feet, Léourier instructed his helmsman to shut off the burner. André turned the valve. Silence suffused the carriage, palpable as the acrid and ubiquitous fragrance of kerosene. The balloon climbed another twenty feet, then melded with the wind, an event that for all its balletic grace did nothing to calm the tumult in Chloe's stomach.

On orders from the capitaine, André reignited the burner and channeled the steam to the pistons. As the propellers spun frantically, the helmsman piloted the *Lamarck* along the muddy and meandering course of the river. From Chloe's lofty vantage the rain forest appeared forlorn and haunted, the vines like nooses fashioned to hang innocent souls, the palm trees suggesting the splayed hands of a green ogre—though she allowed that her revulsion traced largely to fear: on another day, under different circumstances, the jungle might have seemed paradisaical, and she would have exalted in soaring across it as if borne by infinity's angels.

Approaching the observation port, Léourier ordered a course correction of ten degrees. André turned the wheel, whereupon the capitaine clasped Chloe's hand and explained the key strategic maneuver. First the dangling anchor would "rip open the thatched roof of the enemy barracks." Then the mademoiselle would lean out the aft window and hurl the capsules towards the mercenaries' cots: a simple offensive action—though in handling each egg she must "take care not to drop it on the carriage floor and prematurely release its tenants."

Within an hour the *Lamarck* reached a thickly forested mass bisecting the frothy river: Isla del Jaguar, Léourier revealed—the staging area. At the capitaine's command, André dampened the burner. The propellers spun to a halt. The airship glided soundlessly over the island. Despite a camouflage of vegetation, Chloe glimpsed the brass cannon, its barrel glinting in the sun like a seam of gold flashing through El Dorado's soil. On the far side of the channel rose the fortress, its spiked walls guarded by weary sentries in blue uniforms, their eyes fixed straight ahead, oblivious to the cannon, oblivious to the *ribeirinho* militia crouching behind the banyan trees—and to the Bawuni incendiaries hunkered down amidst the mangroves (reinforced by Ralph, Solange, and Mr. Chadwick)—and to the archers and blowgunners hiding in the reeds, each aborigine adorned with lurid smears of black and yellow war paint.

"Hard right rudder!" shouted Léourier.

André turned the wheel, and the *Lamarck* glided over the ramparts, its palisades so sharp and fearsome as to make Castillo Bracamoros seem not so much a stockade as some fantastical catapult poised to release a thousand spears.

"Activate boiler!" cried Léourier, and André fired up the burner.

Upon spotting the flying-machine, the sentries simply stood and gaped, apparently uncertain whether this contraption belonged to the Peruvian navy or to one of Zumaeta's enemies. An instant later the *Lamarck* reached the barracks, the balloon's shadow gliding across the ground like the incarnation of some dread disease.

"Fix bomb one!" ordered Léourier.

Chloe drew an egg from the sack, transferring it from one perspiring hand to the other and back again. "One fixed!"

Léourier grasped the windlass crank and deftly lowered the anchor towards the barracks, until the ventral prong pierced one corner of the reed canopy covering the sleeping mercenaries. Caught by the wind, the flying-machine pursued a diagonal course, its anchor slitting the thatched roof like a plow turning soft earth.

"Drop one!"

Drop one. So simple a request, though surely repugnant to the Presence. Leaning into the rushing air, she closed her eyes and pictured the tortured Huancabambas back at the mission. She blinked, released the egg, and watched with intermingled revulsion and satisfaction as it disappeared into the chasm.

"One away!" she shouted.

"Bomb two!" ordered Léourier.

She seized a second egg. "Two away!" she cried, surrendering the serpents to gravity.

"Bomb three!"

"Three away!"

"Bomb four!"

"Four away!"

Thus it went, the uncanny mission of the *Lamarck*, egg after egg, until Chloe had sown the ragged furrow with forty serpents.

"Withdraw!" ordered Léourier.

The helmsman engaged the propellers and pushed the throttle lever. The vanes spun furiously, and soon the airship was outrunning the wind.

"Hard a-starboard!"

André obeyed. The retreating *Lamarck* swerved around a cluster of gaol houses, their grounds planted with pillories holding the twitching, moaning, and—in some cases—dead bodies of Huancabamba rubber tappers. Continuing on its ever curving course, the ship scudded over a range of five latex pyramids, each formed of several hundred *bolas,* soon reaching the plaza on which stood the breached barracks.

At first it seemed that the bombing raid had failed to produce the intended pandemonium, but then the doors burst open and the mercenaries poured forth, a cataract of terrified soldiers, only half of whom had thought to grab their rifles. Although some of the newly hatched snakes remained inaccessible to Chloe's gaze—doubtless they'd been dispatched by machetes and bayonets—many appeared in the courtyard, their fangs embedded in ankles, thighs, calves, wrists, and forearms. Each variety of venom had its own characteristic effect. Wracked by pain so great that death seemed a preferable condition, the coral snakes' prey placed revolvers to their heads and pulled the triggers. Driven mad by the toxins in their blood, the bushmasters' victims threw themselves to the ground and implored the Blessed Virgin to save them. The fer-de-lances' quarry endured massive gastronomical disruptions, vomiting copiously and defecating prolifically.

Within the ranks of the panicked army a principle of rational self-interest finally emerged, inducing the more enterprising soldiers to use their rifle butts in pulping the snakes until they resembled externalized entrails. Shortly thereafter an enraged lieutenant came forth and, assuming charge of the chaos, gestured skyward, thus inspiring several infantrymen to raise their weapons and take aim at the hovering *Lamarck.*

"Full speed ahead!" cried Léourier.

André opened the throttle. Now the bullets arrived, effortlessly finding the flying-machine's ovoid bladder, probably the easiest target these troops had ever marked, each strike accompanied by a hiss of escaping air.

"Left full rudder!"

True, the *Lamarck* might have managed a safe retreat without assistance from the ground forces, and yet Chloe was greatly relieved when Capitán Torresblanco's artillery squad fired the cannon. As the reassuring boom echoed up and down the valley, the ball traced a precise trajectory from Isla del Jaguar to the fortress, blowing the left gate off its hinges and distracting the mercenaries from their efforts to bring down the flying-machine. Torresblanco's men loaded and launched a second ball, thus destroying the right gate, whilst the Bawuni incendiaries facilitated the *Lamarck*'s escape with a salvo of flaming arrows and spears, so that in a matter of minutes the blockhouses became indistinguishable from funeral pyres.

"Mademoiselle, I salute you for so skillfully executing your orders," said Léourier as the *ribeirinho* militia stormed into the ruptured stockade, followed by the blowgunners and archers.

"*Merci,*" rasped Chloe.

Despite the leaking bladder, Léourier successfully piloted the *Lamarck* back over the river, then set the ship on a course for the Misión del Misterio Bendecido. A throng of snakebitten soldiers filled the theatre of Chloe's mind. Briefly she thought of Lady Athena, protagonist of her equatorial pageant, for that indomitable goddess had famously sent serpents on a mission to kill the impious priest Laocoön and his sons. "But I am not a goddess," she muttered to herself. She was not even a worthy apostle of the Presence. The sooner she exited Amazonia—the sooner she left behind these sickly winds and demented birds and *fleurs du mal*—the sooner she reached Galápagos—the more fully her sanity would be served.

Just as Alexander had kept the *Iliad* close to hand whilst conquering the known world, so did Malcolm Chadwick carry Charles Darwin's transmutation essay into battle, its sandalwood box strapped over his heart like a breastplate. Though under no illusion that the receptacle would protect him from the mercenaries' bullets, he believed the sketch's proximity might help him to think clearly about certain philosophical matters—questions of justice, mercy, and honor—as the clash of arms played out. The previous night's frustrating conversation with Miss Bathurst continued to plague him, most especially her failure to understand her mentor's preoccupation with the Malthusian struggle for existence. How could she imagine that Charles Darwin sought to celebrate predation, when he so obviously meant to elucidate the material conditions to which all flesh was heir? No matter how horrible the imminent battle proved to be, its justification would have to come from elsewhere than "An Essay Concerning Descent with Modification."

A man whose military education was heretofore limited to Tacitus and other classical sources, Malcolm had not anticipated this wrenching spectacle of mercenaries crying for their mothers, losing sovereignty over their bowels, and shooting bullets through their own arms so that they might be evacuated from the field as casualties. Neither Thucydides nor Livy had prepared him for the Indian archer who, his belly ripped open by a mercenary's bayonet, his viscera spilling out like grain from a torn sack, begged a fellow archer to murder him. Malcolm was equally dismayed to see *ribeirinhos* aim their carbines then lose their nerve (firing impotently at the sky), blowgunners accidentally kill their fellow tribesmen with badly aimed curare darts, and Zumaeta's men accept an incendiary's surrender only to think better of the idea and slit the Indian's throat, the blood rushing down his chest like latex from a *caucho* tree. This was not a just war after all—it was just a war: yet another exercise in consecrated barbarity and sanctified slaughter.

Having resolved to get through the fight without harming anyone, Malcolm practiced the most innocuous arson imaginable. Thrice he nocked an arrow along the string of his Bawuni bow, ignited the pitch-coated head with the torchbearer's flame, and fired at the northeast blockhouse, knowing the place was empty (the guards having joined the mêlée in the courtyard). In the case of his fourth shot, however, he felt compelled to plant a flaming arrow in the abdomen of a mercenary who'd taken aim at Prince Gitika. The failed assassin died shrieking amidst the stench of his own immolation. An instant later Malcolm thwarted an attempt on Sargento Jiménez's life—another screaming death, again the odor of charred flesh. The blood on his hands, he realized, was of the very worst sort, being both anonymous and easily absolved. These nameless burning mercenaries had taken milk from their mothers, caught fish in the Marañón, sported with their dogs, and kissed their children, but now none of that mattered, because they'd all chosen to become foot soldiers, a career that put a premium on being no one in particular.

The enemy infantry had formed three concentric circles between the barracks and the workers' compound. At the hub stood a towering figure with a scar running from his temple to his cheek like the hands of a clock at five minutes past seven—General Zumaeta himself, no doubt, employing the mercenaries as his personal citadel. To Malcolm the soldiers seemed a single organism, an evolutionary error possessing two thousand arms and as many eyes. The blowgunners attacked first, their darts peeling away the front line like a *caboclos* skinning an anaconda. Next the archers joined the fray, gutting the freakish creature. Finally a majestic officer appeared, his ribbon-bedecked uniform announcing him as Comandante Cuarón, and exhorted the militia to fire their carbines—an order that, obeyed, shattered the heart of the beast.

And suddenly it was over, the still vertical remnant of Zumaeta's ruined army lifting their hands aloft and waving white kerchiefs, the general reaching highest of all, even as the northeast blockhouse collapsed in a fiery sphere as large as Léourier's balloon. Though less coordinated than their surrendering comrades, the horizontal mercenaries were almost as active, their damaged bodies twitching amidst the heaps of corpses, some casualties screaming, others moaning, still others simply waiting to die, having arrived at a place beyond pain.

Presently the heroes of the day marched forth—the artillery squad and their stalwart leader, Alfonso Torresblanco, his parrot sitting triumphantly on his shoulder—followed by the incendiaries, including a dazed Dartworthy and an equally stupefied Miss Kirsop, gripping their Bawuni bows, and then came the medical unit, bearing stretchers, bandages, splints, and chloroform. Much as Padre Valverde sought to pursue a just war, so did Dr. Ruanova and his nurses now strive for an egalitarian peace, making few distinctions between allies and enemies as they extracted bullets, plucked out arrows, salved burns, and dressed wounds.

A scriptural tableau took form within the fortress—the war-painted Prince Gitika as Moses, the decorated Comandante Cuarón as Aaron, together freeing the Huancabamba *seringueiros* from their hard bondage to white gold. On orders from Cuarón, a detachment of militia blasted the padlocks from the gaol-house doors. Scores of workers shuffled into the sunlight, rubbing their eyes and surveying the carrion-covered plaza. Despite the din of battle and the smell of gunpowder, these slaves had thus far enjoyed no inkling of emancipation, or so Malcolm surmised from their puzzled faces. Not until Gitika strode into the compound, proclaiming the fall of Castillo Bracamoros in the Quechua language, did the rubber tappers dare believe in their deliverance, subsequently laughing and weeping as they bowed before the prince.

Gitika next turned his attention to the forest of pillories, half of them holding either a recently flogged worker or a dead body. He told the *ribeirinhos* to scour the stockade for hammers, chisels, and axes. The required implements materialized promptly, and the militia set about their task, separating the living Indians from the torture racks. The Huancabamba nurses applied balm to the victims' lacerations, then encouraged them to drink from calabashes filled with an effervescent infusion of *uzao* bark, a medication that (as Jiménez explained to Malcolm) would exterminate the worms inhabiting their wounds.

Taking leave of his grateful subjects, Prince Gitika approached the prisoners of war, still huddled in the courtyard. He grabbed Zumaeta's arm, then pushed and shoved him along a much deserved *via dolorosa*. An instant later, the general stood chained to a bloodstained pillory.

"*Tráigame la balanza!*" cried Gitika, addressing a liberated *seringueiro*.

The rubber tapper disappeared into a bamboo shed, then returned pushing a cart on which rested a machine resembling a discus fixed horizontally atop a clock. Gitika smiled approvingly at the scales, then drew a machete from his belt, approached Zumaeta, and with a few deft strokes cut the beard from his chin. The prince set the whiskers on the weighing pan. The needle trembled, deviating from zero by barely a gram.

"For the past two years," Gitika told Zumaeta in Spanish (whilst Jiménez translated for Malcolm), "you have required every plantation family to deliver eight kilos of rubber each week. Know that we Huancabambas are a fair-minded people. As compensation for our suffering, we shall subtract from your body a mere eight kilos of hair, muscle, flesh, and bone. Those whiskers are not an impressive start, but from small beginnings come great things."

A queasiness spread through Malcolm like venom from one of Miss Bathurst's snakes.

"No es necessario!" cried Dr. Ruanova.

"Gitika, no!" screamed Princess Akawo.

"Stop!" yelled Princess Ibanua.

"For God's sake, listen to your sisters!" shouted Malcolm.

"Let me think—what do we cut away next?" Whistling a discordant tune, Gitika touched the machete to the side of his prisoner's head. "The ears?" The blade hovered before Zumaeta's face. "The eyes? Nose? Lips?" The prince glanced towards the general's manhood. *"Cojones?"*

"Tenga misericordia!" wailed Zumaeta.

"Prince Gitika, enough!" cried Dartworthy.

"Eight kilos, General!" Gitika raised the machete high, slashing the air to ribbons, then brought the blade to within inches of Zumaeta's belly. "By the time you meet the quota, your arms and legs will be sitting on the weighing pan."

The rubber tappers, blowgunners, archers, incendiaries, and *ribeirinhos* cheered in unison.

"Para amor a Dios!" shrieked Zumaeta.

"Extract the quota, but kill him first!" pleaded Miss Kirsop.

Gitika spun on his heel and, sliding the machete back into his belt, sauntered up to Malcolm. "Surely you know I would not have tortured him," he said in English, unleashing a smile in which all thirty-two of his teeth participated fully. "Not the way the executioner spent four hours dismembering the failed assassin of Louis Quinze, or so Léourier tells us. We primitive Huancabambas could never behave in so civilized a fashion."

Now Comandante Cuarón joined the conversation. "My opinion of civilization is no higher than yours, Gitika. That said, we are obliged to hand this monster over to the authorities in Iquitos."

"If we spare Zumaeta, Don Rómolo will have him out of gaol in a day," Gitika replied. "We must put him on trial now. I shall ask our good friend Capitán Torresblanco to act as judge, jury, and executioner."

"As judge, I urge the jury to recall that Zumaeta has committed a thousand heinous crimes," said Torresblanco, stepping away from the *ribeirinho* artillery squad, the parrot still riding on his shoulder. "As jury, I have reached with myself a unanimous verdict of guilty. As executioner, I shall now do my duty."

"*Puta madre!*" squawked Miguel.

With an impressive economy of motion Torresblanco unholstered his pistol, strode up to Zumaeta, and with four closely spaced shots transferred a large quantity of his brain matter from his skull to the ground, where it lay in the dust like a spurt of sentient lava. Clearly no stranger to gunfire, the parrot remained perched on Torresblanco's shoulder, even as dozens of startled jungle birds—red macaws, topaz parakeets, golden tanagers, and flaming cocks-of-the-rock—took wing, so that for a fleeting instant the sky over the Marañón valley acquired a flying rainbow.

Never before had the Reverend Granville Heathway faced so vexing a dilemma. During the night a considerable spider—fat, brown, and oblate, like a walnut with legs—had built her web amidst his painting supplies, binding his palette knife to his best brush, so that he could remove neither implement without destroying the delicate construction. The idea for his next painting had already taken root in his imagination: *The Nativity of Gregor Mendel,* featuring the shades of Aristotle and Isaac Newton attending the monk's birth, laying gifts before his cradle. But he did not dare pick up his brush, lest he deprive the spider of her livelihood.

Within the hour the situation was resolved (though not to the spider's advantage) when Guinevere fluttered into the cell and, perceiving in the arachnid a ready meal, devoured her on the spot. Tears collecting in his eyes, Granville muttered a prayer for his departed cellmate, then unfastened the capsule from the pigeon's leg and rummaged through his nightstand drawer in search of his quizzing-glass.

Dearest Father,

At long last I have news of the Diluvian League. Earlier this week the Paragon *dropped anchor in Trebizond, from which port Mr. Dalrymple dispatched a semaphore message to the Grand Vizier. Captain Silahdar has hired two guides, expert climbers who will escort the expedition across the Coru River, then over the Doğu Karadeniz Range as far as Oltu, a mere 150 miles northwest of Mount Ararat.*

I continue to pass my afternoons in the hookah-den. Most of my conversations with the habitués are too tedious to bear repeating (how sad that so sane a person as yourself gets locked away whilst deluded egoists remain at large), but yesterday Yusuf ibn Ziayüddin commended to my attention Father Pierre Teilhard de Chardin, and I lost no time striking up a conversation with this brilliant Jesuit priest.

To reach the hookah-den, Père Teilhard informed me, he was obliged to journey all the way from the Lyon of 1937, which means he covered an even greater distance than did Gregor Mendel. True, Teilhard came here via railway and hired coach, whereas the monk traveled on foot, though I suspect the Jesuit could have walked if necessary, for at fifty-six he seems as vigorous as a man half his age. Like Mendel, Teilhard is pledged not only to chastity and obedience but also to poverty, and yet he had enough coins in his pocket—"some detritus from our Rockefeller Foundation grant"—to purchase a bag of Cannabis sativa.

"Yusuf Effendi believes that, as a schoolman of scientific bent, I would appreciate your story," I told him. "My personal faith is Anglican rather than Roman—my father oversaw a village parish ere becoming ill—but I intend to be a sympathetic listener."

Père Teilhard filtered a puff of hashish through his thin lips. He cuts a figure at once romantic and cerebral, like a privateer captain commissioned not to plunder enemy ships but to sink inferior ideas. "On the surface my life is enviable, Bertram, un grand cirque *of loving friends and gratifying scientific investigations. And yet, when I return to my proper time-stream, I shall again find myself at odds with my precious bane, the Society of Jesus."*

"What science do you pursue?"

"Paleontology."

"You're a disciple of Mr. Paley? Natural Theology *is my father's favorite book!"*

"A paleontologist studies fossils," Père Teilhard noted, then placed a canvas sack on the table, drawing out five skulls, each markedly different from its fellows. He arrayed the death's-heads in a semicircle about the hookah. A passing stranger might have taken us for heathens celebrating a barbarous rite. "Behold the stations of the human ascent, from ape to man-ape to our own sapient kind. They're plaster casts, of course— the original fossils reside in laboratories and museums. These bones testify to the phenomenon of biological evolution, Bertram, a process whose mechanism will be revealed a decade from now, when the English scientist Charles Darwin publishes his theory of natural selection."

"Which is the skull of Adam?" I inquired.

"In my time-stream only the most hidebound persons regard the narrative of Adam, Eve, and the serpent as an actual historical event."

I scowled and said, "Now see here, Père Teilhard. On my view it's churlish to call a water-pipe companion hidebound."

The priest glowered. "Were I desirous of reproach, I could have stayed in Lyon. My provincial is forever scolding me as you have done."

Glowering back, I said, "If you will ignore my discourteous remark, then I shall ignore yours."

Père Teilhard closed his eyes, savoring his Cannabis *reverie. He blinked and gave my hand an affirming squeeze. "Absolument."*

"For purposes of this conversation, there was never an Adam," I said. "Hereafter our motto shall be 'Let him amongst you who can refute the fossil evidence cast the first bone.'"

My new friend laughed and said, "For the past thirteen years the Holy Office has forbidden me to publish a single word on human evolution, all because of my unfinished paper questioning the doctrine of original sin, which a Vatican minion stole from my drawer."

I sucked on my pipe. Today's featured blend was especially stimulating, making me desirous of further communion with Père Teilhard's supple mind. "Do you accord the Genesis flood the same skepticism you bring to the Garden of Eden?"

The priest puffed and said, "Oui."

I was tempted not only to tell him about the Diluvian League but to inquire whether, in light of his ex post facto *knowledge of nineteenth-century history, the ark hunt had succeeded, but Yusuf ibn Ziayüddin forbids his patrons to seek such information. Instead I asked Père Teilhard how he reconciled his Catholic faith with his insistence that the world's first man was not an unruly Adam but an unlettered ape.*

The priest offered a seraphic smile. "There is no contradiction in ascribing to our species both a divine origin and a simian descent, for the universe is itself an all-encompassing and ever-changing organism. It is le Tout, *the All. In fulfilling our need to come closer to God, paleontology often serves better than prayer." He grasped the smallest skull. Had he claimed that it belonged to an infant chimpanzee, I would not have disagreed. "The Taung baby of South Africa was found and named in 1924 by the anatomist Raymond Dart, who recognized that she was neither human nor ape but something in between. My colleagues believe* Australopithecus africanus *flourished about three million years ago. Three million. Shortly after Dr. Dart published his startling conclusions, the paleontologist Robert Broom burst into his laboratory and knelt before the Taung baby, 'in adoration of our ancestor,' as he put it."*

"An idolatrous response, by my lights."

"The Holy Office would agree with you. But in Broom's place I would have done the same." Père Teilhard pointed to the second fossil, which to my untutored eye suggested the skull of an orang-utang. "Pithecanthropus erectus, the famous Java Man unearthed in 1891. Another missing link, at least a half-million years old, perhaps a million,

manifestly much closer to our own species than to Australopithecus. *These fossils all have voices, Bertram. Their oratorios resound in my soul. I hear cantatas of an evolving cosmos."*

"If a skull ever sang to me, I should begin to doubt my sanity."

"I spent most of the decade following the Great War—"

"Great War?"

"We must not speak of it. I spent that decade as an exile, banished by Rome to the Jesuit school in Tientsin. But I had the last laugh, for I soon joined my fellow paleontologists in looking for fossil primates in the Choukoutien caves. Late in the winter of 1829 we came across this fellow"—Teilhard seized a skull evocative of Java Man— "Sinanthropus pekinensis, *Peking Man, who roamed Asia perhaps thirty thousand years ago. I believe* Sinanthropus *and* Pithecanthropus *are different races of the same species, but that controversy won't be settled soon."*

"I wish you could meet another Romish acquaintance of mine, Gregor Mendel, but he's presently indisposed, residing in the Moravia of 1868. When he and I shared the pipe, he told me of his struggle to solve the riddle of heredity. Does your own era know of him?"

Père Teilhard's smile rivaled that of his Sinanthropus *skull. "No biologist would dispute that our modern understanding of genetics rests on Mendel's work. Two months ago, after lecturing in Philadelphia at a symposium on early man, I was awarded Villanova University's Gregor Mendel Medal." The priest's smile collapsed. "Of course, Mendel himself never received a Mendel Medal—or any such recognition. He died in obscurity, his great paper ignored until the turn of the century."*

"Your news saddens but does not surprise me. An aura of loss clung to the man."

"Mendel's breakthrough was so dramatic it prompted many scientists to declare that mutation is the essential engine of evolution," *said Père Teilhard. "Anti-Darwinists argued that profound alterations in germ cells could lead to correspondingly radical changes in a species's genotype, though now we know that sweeping benevolent mutations are rare.*

Modern evolutionary theory is headed towards a synthesis of natural selection and Mendelian genetics, with the result that Darwin once again occupies the center of the biological universe."

"When the monk and I last talked, he told me he'd given up on impressing his colleagues, but he did hope to hybridize a superior strain of hashish."

"As far as I know, he never achieved that laudable goal." Père Teilhard took a puff, then indicated the next fossil in line, not unlike the skull of a gorilla. "The sacred wheel turns, until at last a true man appears. In 1856 the Neander Valley near Düsseldorf yields a skull fragment from Homo neanderthalensis, *who lived in Europe three hundred thousand years ago." He pointed to the last skull and stared into its eye sockets. "The epic continues, bringing forth a mighty hunter, named for a Cro-Magnon or 'great big' cave in the Dordogne, where the first such skeletons were found. Some fifteen thousand years ago the Cro-Magnons painted astonishing images of bison, mammoths, and bears on the walls of their caves." The priest pitched his voice to a poetic timbre. "Of course, the phenomenon of Man does not terminate in our own species.* Le Tout *remains in flux, and our descendants' descendants' descendants will know a quality of consciousness we cannot begin to imagine. Since first placing my hand on the brow of Peking Man I have understood that* Homo sapiens *is being pulled forward as if by a preternatural magnet, bound for a nexus outside time and space, an ineluctable Omega Point where now and forever God brazes the nodes of infinity to the axis of eternity!"*

Spellbound, I said, "What an enthralling idea."

"You think so? You aren't simply appeasing my ego?"

"Never, Father. Flattery is a sin."

"My dear Anglican, your praise is balm to my aching soul. This past year has been a tribulation. The newspaper accounts of my Philadelphia lectures were très stupides, *a travesty from which thousands got the impression I believe humans emerged from modern monkeys. Monkeys! Sapristi! When I traveled to Boston College, I learned that I would not receive a* Doctor Honoris Causa *after all, thanks to the machinations of the city's Darwin-hating archbishop. And then, once back in France,*

I was reprimanded by my provincial for allegedly calling too much at-
tention to myself." The priest inhaled a dose of Cannabis. *"But now you*
have healed me, Bertram. Tomorrow I begin my return trip to Lyon,
there to write my magnum opus. *If I can explicate my philosophy with*
sufficient lucidity, the superior general will realize I'm more orthodox
than he imagines."

"A splendid plan, Père Teilhard—so splendid that it calls for more
Cannabis. *This time you must allow me, not the Rockefeller Founda-*
tion, to fund our euphoria."

The following morning my friend packed up his skulls and left for
France. After his magnum opus *is published, he will again visit Con-*
stantinople and present me with a copy. I wish him luck. I have never
before met anyone like this cosmically inclined curé. *We don't have mys-*
tics in the Church of England, do we, Father? More's the pity.

Your admiring son,
Bertram

Antique skulls, future Omega Points, the eternal majesty of *le Tout*:
this latest pigeon missive, thought Granville, was the most enthralling
yet. No less compelling were Father Teilhard's references to "the English
scientist Charles Darwin," almost certainly the same Darwin with whom
Granville had once corresponded via carrier pigeon. Apparently the universe was as rife with coincidence as with ancient bones.

After placing his son's fourth letter in the nightstand, Granville enjoyed an unexpected visitation from his Muse. "This latest vision of
yours, this *Nativity of Gregor Mendel,* is sublime, and in time you will
paint it," the golden-haired Mireille informed him. "For your present
project, however, you must illustrate Teilhardian philosophy."

As his patron goddess hovered near the dovecote, Granville stared
(and stared and stared) at the blank canvas, until at last the solution
flashed through his brain. He freed his brush from the spiderweb, loaded
the bristles with white pigment, and touched the tip to the canvas. And
so it was that his third painting came into being, *The Eye of God:* a white
dot on a white background—invisible to ordinary human perception but

available to Granville, for whom the Omega Point had become as real as
the wart on his thumb.

I t was all most ironic. Having spent the morning dispatching snakes
in a manner guaranteed to cause their slaughter, Chloe now renewed
her preoccupation with the salvation of other reptiles: the Galápagos
tortoises and iguanas. All during the airship journey from the fallen fortress to the Dominican mission, she wondered precisely what moves on
her part might checkmate the Reverend Mr. Hallowborn. When no
strategy came to mind, she set about helping Philippe Léourier and André Hervouet deflate the silk envelope and mend the bullet holes. But
her heart remained with the jeopardized animals, whose dire situation
she continued to ponder long after the balloon was healed and the moon
had risen.

Her somber musings occurred in an incongruously joyful atmosphere, the *carnaval de la victoria* that the local aborigines, the *ribeirinho*
militia, and the rescued rubber tappers were staging that night within
the mission walls. At the core of the celebration a bonfire crackled and
roared, throwing quivering shadows on the statue of Santo Domingo,
Padre Valverde's fighters swaying in joyous circles around the flames
whilst inhaling draughts of *epená* and eating prodigal quantities of fish
and caiman, the bellow of the burning logs counterpointing the thunder
of Bawuni drums, the squeal of Yamuna panpipes, and the wailing of
Ucharu flutes. Chloe guessed that perhaps two-thirds of the fighters had
joined the *carnaval,* the others having absented themselves either voluntarily (being in mourning for fallen friends and relations) or pursuant to
a command: guard these prisoners, secure that coffin, dig this grave, go
to the hospital and do as Dr. Ruanova tells you. Sadly but predictably,
Padre Valverde was amongst those missing from the festivity, his malaria having grown so acute that on the physician's orders he'd retired to
a private sickroom.

It occurred to Chloe that the *carnaval* might be a trifle premature, as the final fate of the Huancabambas was not yet decided. The present plan called for Princess Akawo and Princess Ibanua to guide the liberated *seringueiros* through the mountains and thence home to the Rio Jequetepeque valley near Puerto Etén, an arduous but feasible exodus (assuming the fugitives encountered no federal troops authorized to shoot Indians on sight). At the same time Comandante Cuarón would march the Marañón valley tribes and the *ribeirinho* militia into the plantation settlements, freeing the workers and imprisoning the district governors, after which Prince Gitika would lead the remaining Huancabambas home to the sea. Presumably this campaign would be little more than a mop-up operation, accomplished with minimal fighting and light casualties, but Chloe could not but recall Antony's most sardonic line in *Siren of the Nile*, "If you want to make the gods laugh, tell them your plan for winning a war."

Sitting in a circle of *epená* aficionados, whilst amber sparks shot from the bonfire, and the faces of her English and French friends shone like the golden calf of the Israelite apostasy, she alternated her gaze between the frenzied dancers and the quiescent airship. The *Jean-Baptiste Lamarck* lay moored beside the church, the newly inflated envelope looming above the wicker carriage like a gigantic *bola* being cured on an immense spit. Contemplating the Man in the Moon emblem, she suddenly realized that her best hope for getting her fellowship to the sea consisted not in joining the princesses on their trek through the Andes passes (a journey certain to entail hunger, cold, exhaustion, and maddening delays) but rather in chartering the *Lamarck*.

"I once heard a rumor that El Dorado lies near a Peruvian coastal town—Puerto Etén, as I recall," she told Léourier. "Perhaps you should look *there* for your fabled city."

"I am not acquainted with that theory," the Frenchman replied.

"Neither is Miss Bathurst," said Ralph.

Léourier grasped the syringe and inhaled a puff of virola resin. "Mademoiselle, if you wish to avail yourself of my ship and its crew," he admonished her, "simply say so."

"I wish to avail myself of your ship and its crew."

"Granted!" cried Léourier. "How to explain my courtesy? Call it chivalry—a French word, as it happens, *chevalrie* from *cheval,* horse. My *cheval du ciel* is at your disposal."

"*Monsieur le Capitaine,* you are my aeronaut in shining armor!" exclaimed Chloe. "The sooner my company reaches the Pacific Ocean, the sooner we can hire ourselves out to a brigantine headed west along the equator."

"And if you fail to secure such a passage, I shall consider transporting you to Galápagos myself," said Léourier. "You see, mademoiselle, your desire to save the Encantadas creatures touches me deeply. Like yourself, I am a lover of the natural world—for why else would a man christen his airship the *Jean-Baptiste Lamarck?*"

"The lizards of Albemarle will sing your praises," said Chloe absently, suddenly aware that she'd never before heard anyone speak the balloon's full name. Jean-Baptiste—that is, John the Baptist, four syllables that now set the machinery of her mind to whirring. Reaching for the *epená* syringe, she eased the nipple into her nostril and squeezed the bulb. Her brain became a hive of incandescent bees. John the Baptist, crying in the wilderness, wielding his ax against the forest of the petrified past. But what if, two millennia later, God had started sending prophets of John's quality to certain far-flung Hebrew communities, amongst them a clan of Jewish *ribeirinhos* living on the Rio Jequetepeque—a people who were in fact descended from the Lost Thirteenth Tribe of Israel? And what if this messenger to the Huancabambas one day collected some of her followers together and traveled to the Encantadas, straightaway tracking down Simon Hallowborn and telling him of the Almighty's disdain for the Great Winnowing?

"Hallelujah!" shouted Chloe, passing the syringe to Solange.

The courtesan delivered a blast of snuff to her psyche. "Was that an *epená* hallelujah, an antichrist hallelujah, or a light-of-eternity hallelujah?"

"I see how we'll outfox Mr. Hallowborn! I promise you a role in the masquerade, Solange, and you as well, Ralph"—Chloe lurched towards Mr. Chadwick—"and you, too, Reverend."

"Thereby making amends for neglecting to cast me in your equatorial pageant," said the vicar in a jocular tone.

So potent was *virola* resin, Chloe noted, it could elicit whimsy from even so straitlaced a person as Mr. Chadwick. "Before he can raise a hand against the reptiles and birds, Mr. Hallowborn will find himself standing before a mysterious Englishwoman—call her Lady Omega, dispatched by God to enlighten the Lost Thirteenth Tribe of Israel. This prophet will have in train her most stalwart disciples, to be portrayed by six or seven particularly clever Huancabambas."

"I can't imagine who'll be playing Lady Omega," said Solange with a hyperbolic smile.

"By combining charm with theology," Chloe persisted, "I shall persuade Mr. Hallowborn that God abhors his intention to harrow the archipelago."

Léourier relieved Solange of the syringe, partook of its pleasures, and pressed the implement into Ralph's grasp. "You're going to have Peruvian Indians represent themselves as *Jews*, mademoiselle? *Merveilleux!*"

"*Incroyable!*" said André. "*Formidable!*"

"The sooner we take to the air, the better, *oui?*" said Léourier. "*S'il vous plaît*, give André and myself the whole of tomorrow to repair and provision the *Lamarck*. Our party will leave for the Jequetepeque valley the following day."

"Owing to this preposterous scheme, this *scenario* as the Italians would say, I feel as if my darling Chloe has been restored to me," said Solange. "If I can't have my she-devil, I'll settle for an English mystic."

"You will essay the role of Miss Bianca Quinn, a cripple made whole by the healing hand of Lady Omega," Chloe told Solange, then winked at Ralph. "I'm casting you as Professor Edward Cabot, the anthropologist who discovered the Hebrew river-folk and their prophet." She faced Mr. Chadwick. "In time Mr. Hallowborn may question my claim to the mantle of divine messenger, at which juncture *you* will appear and beguile him with your talent for distinguishing true prophets from false."

"Miss Kirsop is right—this scheme is preposterous," said Mr. Chadwick.

"I quite agree," said Chloe.

"By sunrise tomorrow, you'll be embarrassed by the whole thing."

"Embarrassed," echoed Chloe. "Of course," she said. "Syringe!" she cried, whereupon the *epená* went around once more, graciously depriving the Castillo Bracamoros veterans of their immediate recollections—for there was nothing in the day's mélange of blood, fire, serpents, entrails, pain, and death that a person would do well to remember.

Against the odds and in defiance of Mr. Chadwick's prediction, the dew of early morning did not dampen Chloe's enthusiasm for the Lost Thirteenth Tribe masquerade. Quite the contrary. Awakening in the sacristy, her friends snoring beside her, she concluded that only by playing a character so unearthly as Lady Omega might she thwart a plot so depraved as the Great Winnowing.

Within the hour she visited the Huancabamba encampment and outlined the *scenario* (as Solange called it) for Prince Gitika. Not surprisingly, he could make little sense of her desire to protect the Encantadas fauna when thousands of South American animals were slaughtered each year by hunters and trappers. She responded with the arguments she'd made in the Manáos café whilst organizing her friends into the Encantadas Salvation Brigade—even the Oxford Diocese had no right to exterminate whole species; back in England she'd formed bonds of affection with the blood kin of the endangered creatures; a child named Miss Annie would want her to save the birds and beasts. Gitika replied that her reasoning *still* eluded him, but if this Hebrew river-folk chicanery was the best way for his people to repay the English adventurers, then so be it.

"Did Señor Chadwick tell you the scope of my debt?" he asked. "During the battle he saved my life, shooting a flaming arrow into one of Zumaeta's soldiers, and he also rescued Sargento Jiménez."

Chloe heaved a sigh, absorbing Gitika's revelation with mixed emotions. Though delighted to learn that the Huancabambas were even more beholden to her fellowship than she'd realized, she was saddened by the probability that Mr. Chadwick would never forgive himself for acting so valiantly. "If I know the vicar's troubled soul," she said, "he has taken the blood of those mercenaries on his head."

Before their conversation ended, Chloe and Gitika agreed that, rather then accompanying her sister on the overland trek, Akawo must join the balloon expedition. Thus would the Jequetepeque valley natives learn of the victory in a timely manner, and from the princess's credible lips— even as she persuaded her father that the fall of Castillo Bracamoros traced in no small measure to their European guests, and he must therefore fulfill Señorita Bathurst's peculiar desire to borrow six tribesmen and take them to the Encantadas.

Knowing that Chloe intended to spend the rest of the day helping Capitaine Léourier prepare the *Lamarck* for its Andes crossing, Gitika suggested that before searching out the aeronaut she should first visit Padre Valverde. "Mr. Chadwick told me of your own malaria ordeal," the prince explained. "An encouraging word from someone who survived the disease may lift our warrior-priest's spirits."

Thus did the noon hour find Chloe headed towards the infirmary, Gitika at her side. Their route took them through the church that was now a hospital. Attired in gore-spattered smocks, like a community of artists whose preferred medium was blood, Dr. Ruanova and his Huancabamba nurses subjected their patients to the cruelest compassion imaginable, dutifully sawing off shattered limbs, realigning fractured bones, and probing perforated flesh for bullets. Akawo and Ibanua acknowledged their brother with fleeting glances, then returned to the desperate business of saving lives and palliating deaths.

Padre Valverde's private sickroom was a crepuscular place, the walls covered with spasming shadows cast by turtle-oil lanterns. Teeth chattering, flesh quivering, he occupied a straw mattress at the nexus of a death watch whose members included Mr. Chadwick, Capitán Torresblanco,

Comandante Cuarón, and a half-dozen Dominican clerics. Quinine fumes suffused the thick tropical air to create a miasmal vapor laced with the drone of mosquitoes and the screams from Ruanova's clinic. As Chloe and Gitika joined the vigil, Valverde, propped on his elbows, addressed the gathering in the faraway voice of a man recently embarked on the good ship *Epená*.

"Did we destroy Zumaeta's army and free a thousand slaves?" said the priest, sweat rolling down his brow like blood from a crown of thorns. "Yes! Does our victory spell the doom of Don Rómolo and his wicked ambitions? No! Do a hundred Cuzco death-eggs lie beneath my bed? Yes!"

"Drink this," said a weeping novitiate, offering Valverde a draught of quinine.

"*Crack*, go the eggs!" cried the priest, spurning the medicine. "*Crack, crack, crack,* and the snakes burst forth, *hisssss,* wriggling into a world ruled by rubber barons, *hisssss,* rubber earls, *hisssss,* rubber kings! Is that Señorita Bathurst over there?"

Chloe glided soundlessly to Valverde's side. "You will not die," she told him. "Ten weeks ago I was myself stricken with malaria. Look at me, Padre. I am recovered in full."

"A spectre is haunting South America—the spectre of capitalism!" wailed Valverde. "*Hisssss,* and the snakes become *capitalissssmo,* writing each *ess* with their bodies, *capitalissssmo, capitalissssmo!*"

"There are no snakes in the room," noted Torresblanco.

"You *must* take some quinine, Padre," the novitiate pleaded.

"I can see it all!" cried Valverde. "Europeans living in rubber houses, drinking rubber wine, eating rubber food, laying their dead in rubber tombs! And what do the masters of *la técnica* make next? A man with latex skin, latex tendons, latex bones—a latex brain! He is coming, I promise you!"

"Lie still, Padre," said the novitiate.

"Try to sleep," said Mr. Chadwick.

"In thrall to *el hombre de caucho,* the vampires of commerce will suck from Amazonia every last kilo of white gold!" the priest shouted. "They will flay from our Indians every last pound of flesh!" he predicted. "*Aplasssstado*, write the snakes, *aplasssstado*, squashed, *aplasssstado*, squashed, *aplasssstado*!" declared Hernando de Valverde, and then with a strangely mechanistic cry, like a shriek from the engine of the *Jean-Baptiste Lamarck*, he crashed back into the mass of pillows, released a final breath, and surrendered his soul to his Creator.

10

Touching upon an Ancient Theological Riddle: After Resting on the Seventh Day, Did God Appropriate Adam's Foreskin on the Eighth?

Aeolus blew from the east, in soft yet ceaseless gusts, and so the crowded company of the *Jean-Baptist Lamarck* simply drifted, borne by the aether, the better to conserve their fuel. During the flight to Castillo Bracamoros, Chloe had been too frightened to perceive the paradox of flotation in a hot-air balloon: at one with the wind, the voyager has no sensation of forward movement—but now she savored it. Seeking to experience the illusion in full, she peered downward through the larboard window, then invited Princess Akawo to do the same. Below the seemingly immobile gondola, the jungle was sliding west to east. Indeed, the whole planet appeared to be in motion, just as Galileo Galilei had insisted before the custodians of Christian physics, waving their torture instruments in his face, suggested that he might prefer to believe otherwise.

"Now I know how it feels to be an eagle," said Akawo.

"Or an angel," said Chloe.

Doubtless there were differences between life aboard a flying-machine and imprisonment in Mephistropolis, but just then Chloe could not imagine what they might be. In these congested quarters lifting one's arms was a challenge, stretching one's legs a tribulation, appeasing one's bladder a precarious matter of negotiating a chamber pot occluded by a Chinese screen. At least their company numbered only six instead of the expected eight. (Although Monsieur Grenier had survived the attack of yellow fever, he was not yet on his feet, and André had remained behind to nurse him.) But this was cold comfort under colder circumstances, the mountain breezes having already found the *Lamarck* and penetrated the carriage.

Darkness brought a brilliant gibbous moon, shining with such intensity that Léourier declined to drop anchor. Instead he decreed that the *Lamarck* would sail through the night, thus increasing the company's chances of reaching Puerto Etén within three days. From their perch beside the larboard window Chloe and Akawo surveyed the nocturnal forest, which by moonlight suggested the bottom of the sea, the gleaming palm trees and shining vines arrayed across the terrain like luminous starfish living intimately with electric eels.

The following day the *Lamarck* passed through a succession of rainstorms spawned by, as Léourier explained the phenomenon, the collision between hot jungle vapors and frigid mountain air. As the wet winds swirled about the gondola, Chloe, seeking to embroider the Lost Thirteenth Tribe *scenario*, studied the Bible she'd received from Mr. Chadwick on the Marañón. Negotiating Genesis, she happened upon the name "Serug," son of Reu and father of Nahor. Yes, that sounded right. She would call her Huancabamba followers "Serugites." In her imagination the complete saga of the Hebrew river-folk unfolded, beginning with a heretofore unknown procreative act by Jacob—the fathering of a son beyond the dozen fated to sire the Twelve Tribes. (A full third of those progenitors had issued from the concubines Bilhah and Zilpah, either of whom might have easily conceived an extra patriarch.) After coming of age, Serug declined to follow his brothers to Egypt. Instead he took a wife, built a barge, and embarked on a perilous voyage, convinced that a New Canaan lay across the sea. His quest terminated in the Jequetepeque valley, where his children's children's children adopted the Quechua language of their Indian neighbors, even as their skin darkened under the rays of the tropical sun. And then, generations later, just as John the

Baptist had arrived amongst the Old World Israelites, so was the Lost Thirteenth Tribe blessed with Lady Omega, their own private prophet.

When Chloe announced these flourishes, her companions were quick to praise them, including Princess Akawo, who'd evidently grasped the strategy behind the masquerade. "Six of our tribe will set off for the Encantadas with Professor Cabot, who is really Señor Dartworthy, and Lady Omega, who is really Señorita Bathurst," she said, fingering the crucifix Hernando de Valverde had given her the day before he died: a wondrous silver artifact, complete with a sculpted Christ the size of a dragonfly. "After reaching the islands, Señor Dartworthy will tell the English shaman Señor Hallowborn that these Huancabambas are Hebrew *ribeirinhos*. Because Señorita Bathurst knows the mind of the One True God, Señor Hallowborn must listen when she tells him not to harm the animals." Akawo squeezed Chloe's palm. "This Lady Omega, she is rather like the Galilean rabbi of whom poor Padre Valverde so often spoke—am I correct? I hope your enemies do not nail you to a tree."

"Crucifixion is not in the present draft," said Chloe drily, "nor will it appear in the next."

Shortly before noon on the *Lamarck*'s third day aloft, the wind lost its vitality. Undaunted, Léourier engaged the propellers. Like some immense aerial puffer-fish, the flying-machine swam above the Andean foothills, formations so massive that back in England they would have been called mountains. As the *Lamarck* ascended, the temperature plunged, the bitter air sowing a ragged crop of icicles along the engine struts and carriage ropes. In their quest for warmth the passengers embraced one another, stomped their feet, and reached through the roof vents to thaw their hands in the heat of the kerosene burner.

Chloe did not so much fall asleep that night as allow the cold to stun her brain and numb her flesh. At dawn she roused herself. Climbing over the oblivious bodies of Akawo, Solange, and Mr. Chadwick, she stood before the glass observation port. An epic panorama met her gaze: the ice-capped Andes, a thousand times more wondrous than the grandest set ever erected at the Adelphi Theatre. The helmsman of the moment was Ralph, singing a ribald chantey as he steered the ship amongst the crags. Seated at the chart table, Léourier looked up from his map of Peru and cautioned Ralph not to let the *Lamarck* climb above the summits, for at that altitude the air became so thin that "whoever attempts to breathe it will soon grow faint, lose consciousness, and die."

Hour by hour, mile by mile, the balloon negotiated the misty cliffs and snowy slopes, propellers churning, engine grinding. On all sides the Peruvian peaks rose like gigantic teeth, so that Chloe imagined herself as Jonah peering down the gullet of the whale. This notion so beguiled her that she revisited the original biblical narrative, finding herself deeply moved by the hymn Jonah had sung from his fishy prison.

"'I cried by reason of mine affliction unto the Lord, and He heard me'!" Chloe recited aloud. "'Out of the belly of Sheol cried I, and Thou heardest my voice'!"

"Being willing to rescue somebody whom you yourself rammed down the throat of a sea monster does not strike me as the quintessence of compassion," said Solange.

"In France these days, God is practically illegal," noted Léourier. "I cannot decide whether we're better off without Him, or worse."

"We Huancabambas tell ourselves no such stories," said Akawo, pointing to Chloe's Bible. "When we wish to be with our gods, we walk along the river."

"I must ask you a question," said Ralph to Akawo. "If you opened the door and stepped into the clouds, would your gods protect you?"

"Probably not. Our gods are—what is English word?—capricious."

"Then what good are they?" asked Ralph.

"In truth, no good at all," said Akawo. "Ah, but you see, they know themselves to be useless, which makes them so very grateful for our songs and sacrifices."

"I think the God of Abraham might profitably take instruction from Akawo's pantheon," said Mr. Chadwick. "Hear me, O King of the Universe. Stop making covenants you don't intend to keep. Promise nothing, and expect nothing in return."

"A perfectly sensible arrangement," said Solange.

"*Nihil pro quo,*" said Ralph.

Chloe kept her thoughts to herself. Fond though she was of her friends, she wished she might occasionally render them mute—much as Papa, having placed a talkative kettle, loquacious candle, or voluble clock at the center of a puppet play, could on a whim banish it to the country of the dumb, where the creature would remain in splendid silence until he once again gifted it with a tongue.

Hand on the helm, face pressed against the observation port, Malcolm surveyed the valley, the lambent shafts of noonday sun piercing the Rio Jequetepeque like the javelins wielded by the indigenous fishermen. On all sides the dwarf hills and shallow gorges testified to a gratifying fact: the *Lamarck* had traversed the Andes. If the company's luck held, they would reach Akawo's village ere the day was out.

Even as he contemplated the equatorial vistas, Malcolm pondered the equally mottled terrain of his soul, not only the marks left by the murder of the mercenaries but also the stain caused by his newfound and gnawing desire to win the Great God Contest. Now that he'd defrocked himself, he dreaded his eventual return to Wroxton: no parsonage, no larder, no income—problems that the Byssheans' gold promised to dissolve like sugar in hot tea. True, netting the Shelley Prize would entail difficulties he could barely begin to imagine, but for a cut of the £10,000 Dartworthy and Miss Kirsop would doubtless be happy to help him collect illustrative specimens and somehow get them to England.

Malcolm winced strenuously. He gritted his teeth, thinking, *Get thee behind me, Mammon*. If he were an honorable man, he would not try to acquire that tainted purse, lest he thenceforth prefer supping with swine to living with himself.

No sooner had he won this duel with his cupidity than a more immediate threat arose. Directly ahead, a squadron of four condors rode the lofty currents, bound for the *Lamarck*. Even at this distance, Malcolm believed he could infer the flock's collective opinion of the balloon. From a condor's perspective the thing was a rival creature in the struggle for existence.

"*Mon Capitaine,* I think we're under attack!" cried Malcolm.

Elbowing his way to the helm, Léourier shouted, "Hard right rudder!"

Malcolm spun the wheel, thus inadvertently steering the *Lamarck* into a second, larger condor flock. Caws and squawks filled the gondola, followed by a ghastly ripping noise, as if some heavenly tailor, having made a botch of God's trousers, were tearing them apart at the seams. The observation port displayed the whole catastrophe, the hideous bald birds sinking their talons into the marauder, shredding the silk bladder, and releasing its heated vapors into the cool coastal air.

"Christ!" wailed Miss Kirsop.

"Damn!" yelled Dartworthy.

Léourier seized the burner control and shut off the flame—a sensible tactic, Malcolm decided: if they were destined to meet the ground, the collision would be terrible enough without the *Lamarck* becoming a pillar of fire. For a brief instant the wounded balloon buoyed the gondola, but then gravity prevailed, and the flying-machine plummeted towards the valley floor. The passengers loosed a choral scream, discharging blasts of hot breath into the carriage, though not in quantities sufficient to arrest the ship's fall.

Malcolm was surprised to discover that contrary to conventional wisdom his life did not flash before him, no mother weeding her vegetable patch, no father selling nostrums in the family apothecary, no boyhood spaniel chasing rabbits into the bracken. He was aware only of the sickening descent and the *thump-thump-thump* of the gondola scudding along the crests of the trees. An instant later the *Lamarck* made calamitous contact with the nation of Peru, the shock-wave tearing open the larboard hatch and hurtling Malcolm backwards through the portal, so that before blacking out he judged himself a loser in the great evolutionary lottery, bested by some fitter cleric.

Shortly after The Reverend Granville Heathway finished painting *The Eye of God,* his austere rendering of Father Teilhard's Omega Point, he realized he'd not exhausted the subject. The dot in question was the very wink of infinity, worthy of multiple interpretations. Taking up his brush, he dipped it in white pigment and once again jabbed a blank canvas with a quick darting motion, thus bringing *The Second Eye of God* into being.

Other such devotions followed. *The Third Eye of God* begat *The Fourth Eye of God*, which led to *The Fifth Eye of God,* which occasioned *The Sixth Eye of God,* and there would have been a seventh had Granville not run short of canvas. For a full hour he brooded on the deficit, but then Catullus swooped into the cell, landing atop the dovecote. Granville banished the canvas crisis from his mind. What mattered at the moment was the fate of the man his son had called "this cosmically inclined *curé*."

> *Dearest Father,*
>
> *Yesterday morning Mustafa Reshid Pasha invited me to his private suite in the Topkapi Palace, where we shared strong coffee and an even stronger camaraderie. I told him that I had thus far met two alleged time travelers in Yusuf Effendi's establishment: Abbot Mendel and Père Teilhard. The Grand Vizier admitted that, as a devotee of reason and mathematics, he was inclined to explain these encounters in reference to the hashish.*
>
> *"Being a practical man, untutored in metaphysics, I would say that those two worthies were probably—you will forgive my little joke— hookahlucinations. On the other hand, they might have been angels sent by Allah to impart a few minor cosmic secrets to a deserving infidel. Pay close attention to your water-pipe companions, Bertram Effendi. You may learn something of value."*
>
> *Now Reshid Pasha bent closer and in a whispered confidence told me of his exasperation with the Sultan. Two weeks earlier, Abdülmecid had signed a treaty with Louis Bonaparte whereby the Vatican would become the protector of all Christian pilgrims in the Holy Land, whether Catholic, Protestant, or—an inclusion certain of antagonizing the Tsar—Eastern Orthodox. Naturally I asked Reshid Pasha if these developments portended difficulties for the Ararat expedition. Assuming that the Diluvian League recovered the Relic of Relics, could we*

still count on the Turkish government to reprovision the Paragon *and grant both Deardon's brig and Noah's ark safe passage through the Bosporus?*

"*Were Russia to attack us tomorrow, destroy our army, and force the Sultan to sue for peace, then the answer is no," the Grand Vizier replied with frigid candor. "Such a disaster would render moot our scheme to have your Reverend Dalrymple petition the Archbishop of Canterbury on our nation's behalf. But I am guardedly optimistic. Last week Prince Menshikov arrived in Constantinople to persuade the Sultan to renounce this preposterous treaty. I believe he will succeed, thereby delaying the war by a year at least."*

I decided to celebrate Reshid Pasha's prediction by patronizing the hookah-den. No sooner had I filled the hashish bowl than Père Teilhard approached, explaining that he'd traveled by coach all the way from the Rome of 1950. We embraced. He slumped onto a divan, then retrieved from his valise a fat and battered manuscript called Le Phénomène Humain.

When last we sat down to share a pipe, Teilhard had seemed to bear the weight of the world on his shoulders, the Holy See having forbidden him to publish any speculations concerning Adam's fall or Peking Man's rise. Today he looked even sadder, as if sustaining the infinite mass of the Omega Point itself.

Seeking to cheer him up, I indicated the manuscript and exclaimed, "Hoorah—you finished your book!"

"Vraiment, *despite malaria, heart troubles, and Rome's insistence on exiling me to China again," said the priest, inhaling* Cannabis. *"In these pages I have articulated my theory of orthogenesis. Evolution is purposeful, Bertram. Higher consciousness is the human destiny."*

As my friend continued to summarize his book, he grew sublimely animated, his fingers fluttering as if to make a marionette dance. The Gospel according to Teilhard, I soon learned, begins in the domain of prelife, the lithosphere, our planet's inert shell. Over the aeons, the lithosphere becomes surmounted by the miracle of self-replicating molecules, the biosphere, with primitive "viruses" ascending towards bacterial "prokaryotes" that in time evolve into nucleated "eukaryotes," a process that culminates in mammals, including our own simian ancestors. Eventually the biosphere is itself encapsulated by a uniquely human realm, the noosphere, the mantle of thought that enshrouds the world. But the process does not end there. Beyond the noosphere lies the Cosmic Christ, that divine crucible in which all minds will one day meld to form the supreme consciousness towards which le Tout was heading from the moment God declared, "Let there be light!"

"What are the prospects of your thesis seeing print?" I asked.

"Like a sinner standing before Hell's portal, I have abandoned hope," said Père Teilhard, grimacing. "Last year I met with the superior general. He told me if I published Le Phénomène Humaine in any form whatsoever, it would automatically appear on the Index of Forbidden Books. I was not entirely surprised, given the order's reflexive hostility to Monsieur Darwin. The general also explained that if I didn't leave Europe posthaste, the Vatican would again be obliged to exile me. So here I am on a trip to Africa, where Louis Leakey has invited me to inspect his excavations at Olduvai Gorge."

"If it were my decision, Père Teilhard, I would see your book distributed far and wide. Which is not to say I understand your orthogenesis in full."

A husky female voice intruded on our conversation. "It's doubtful whether Pierre himself understands his orthogenesis in full."

The paleontologist and I glanced up to behold a handsome woman of mature years looming over us, dressed in a safari jacket and jodhpurs. She exuded a capacious intelligence, as if her mind encompassed a particularly large sector of the noosphere.

"Lucile!" cried Père Teilhard.

"Mon cher!" exclaimed the woman. "At last I've tracked you down."

The paleontologist made the introductions, presenting me as "my faithful water-pipe companion" and his friend as "Lucile Swan, the sculptress who fashioned the first bust of Peking Man. She is also my best friend in the world."

"*Pierre claims to know all about evolution, yet he scorns its erotic essence,*" *said Miss Swan, inserting an empty chair between Père Teilhard and myself.* "*He knows nothing of concupiscence.*"

I felt my face turn scarlet with mortification, though in this murky place the change was probably imperceptible.

"*I'm no stranger to concupiscence, Lucile, merely to its conventional culmination,*" *said Père Teilhard pointedly.*

Settling into her chair, Miss Swan fixed me with a gaze so luminous it cut through the smoky grotto like a beam from a lighthouse. "*If Pierre's biographers are honest men, they will call me the love of his life.*"

"*When I committed myself to poverty, obedience, and chastity, I intended to honor all three vows,*" *Père Teilhard admonished his friend.*

"*On paper you may be poor, Pierre,*" *Miss Swan replied,* "*but I've noticed that priests who travel with the scientific elite enjoy a posh sort of privation. As for obedience, your Holy Office dossier has grown so thick that Rome now holds you a borderline heretic. Evidently chastity is the only pledge you take seriously.*"

"*Lucile . . .*"

"*This man lives atop a mountain the rest of us can only dream of scaling,*" *said Miss Swan, caressing my hand. She took a puff of hashish, slid the nozzle from her lips, and pointed the tip at Père Teilhard.* "*Once again, my love, I must implore you to descend to my level. Perhaps our species is destined to fuse with a Cosmic Christ. I cannot speak of such matters, and I'm not persuaded you can, either. What we* do *know is that* Homo sapiens *is here because once upon a time a population of celibate algae transformed themselves into lusty eukaryotes. There's no noosphere without ten trillion acts of physical love, Pierre, no transmutation without plenary copulation!*"

"*But one day we shall be past all that,*" *Père Teilhard insisted.* "*The universe is moving forward, Lucile! We cannot return to the* Urschliem!"

"*Listen, Pierre, the instant I finished telling Yusuf Effendi my story, he looked me in the eye and said, 'I am moved by your plight, madam.*

For the rest of the afternoon, my humble cellar rooms belong to you and your holy man.' He gave me a tour of his salle de lit. The sheets are clean. The pillows are soft."

"Please, Lucile. This is madness."

"Hear my logic. Your vows apply only to the life you're living on planet Earth in 1950, whereas at present we occupy a fantastical netherworld emanating from the vanished Byzantine Empire. We may be a far cry from the Omega Point, but we're equally distant from Rome."

"My dearest, loveliest, sweetest Lucile . . ."

Seeing an opportunity to make a judicious exit, I feigned a headache, speculating aloud that it might be eased by a steam bath back at the palace.

"During our hashish intervals, I came to treasure your tolerance for my convoluted Weltanschauung," said Père Teilhard as we embraced for the last time. "If only the Society of Jesus boasted your caliber of patience."

And so it happens, Father, that I cannot tell you the upshot of Miss Swan's designs. Sometimes I feel certain that she and her priest descended to the cellar. At other times I feel skeptical. Would you like to know my preferred outcome? Heaven forgive me, but I hope that the afternoon found Miss Swan and Père Teilhard acting the part of Homo concupiscentus.

> With boundless affection,
> Bertram

Granville felt like dancing. Apart from his son's obtuse failure to grasp Teilhard de Chardin's exhilarating philosophy, the new message overflowed with good news. The quest remained on schedule. Once Noah's ark reached Constantinople, local politics would not prevent its delivery to England, the Russo-Turkish War having been postponed. What's more, Miss Swan had surely found herself in the arms of her beloved. So momentous was this last occurrence that Granville decided to suspend his Omega Point cycle and instead celebrate Father Teilhard's initiation into Eros.

The longer he thought about his subject, the more possibilities it revealed. Owing to the pioneering efforts of Adam and Eve, humans had become adept at perpetuating themselves, and now the union of Pierre and Lucile promised to carry the species to a plane beyond the procreative, the empirical, or even the metaphysical. Having experienced seminal ecstasy, Father Teilhard would be inspired to revise his *Phénomène Humain* over and over until at long last Rome allowed him to share his vision with the world (thousands of readers subsequently coming to perceive themselves not only as living souls redeemed by Christ's blood but also as vibrant cells in an evolving megabrain). True, Granville still lacked for a canvas, but he would make a virtue of privation, imposing his newest painting atop *The Sixth Eye of God*.

He labored all afternoon and well past dusk, until *No Transmutation without Plenary Copulation* had emerged in all its corporeal grandeur. Even in the anemic gaslight seeping into his cell, he could see that he'd done justice to his theme. Being ignorant of Yusuf ibn Ziayüddin's rooms, he'd taken artistic liberties, appointing the *salle de lit* with a gilt-framed mirror and a Persian cat, though the spectator's attention remained focused on the bodies sprawled across the bed. Granville was particularly pleased with his treatment of Miss Swan: Teilhard's pulchritudinous muse, with an emphatic bosom, inviting thighs, and a navel that was the Omega Point. The longer he stared at that holy omphalos, the happier he became, and as he climbed onto his mattress that night, he thanked his Creator for that felicitous innovation called flesh.

Assuming that a person's hot-air balloon must be attacked by panicked condors in the first place, then the wreck of the *Lamarck*—its fitful cruise through a palm-tree grove and thence into the soft sands of the riverbank—could hardly be counted a disaster. Certainly

Chloe would never rank this event with the sinking of the *Equinox*, Mr. Flaherty's consumption by piranhas, or Captain Runciter's suffocation by an anaconda. True, Mr. Chadwick had lost consciousness, but he'd come to his senses almost immediately, and the passengers' appreciable injuries were confined to Solange's sprained wrist, Ralph's twisted ankle, and the vicar's cracked rib, beyond which the company had sustained only lumps, bumps, bruises, scratches, and scrapes. As for the airship itself, Léourier believed that the ruptured envelope and fractured gondola could be repaired using silk from the supply locker and wood from the Peruvian savannah. He even insisted that he could replace the shattered glass in the observation port with transparent sheets fashioned from—of all things—the cured swim-bladders of Rio Jequetepeque fish.

"Swim-bladders?" said a skeptical Chloe. "How *many* swim-bladders?"

"Perhaps a hundred."

"And how long must we allow for the *Lamarck*'s resurrection?"

"If we can enlist the aid of at least twenty Indians, I would estimate three weeks," said Léourier.

"Three weeks?" wailed Chloe, enduring her most virulent attack of frustration since Torresblanco had rejected her various schemes for shortening their voyage up the Solimões. "That is entirely unacceptable, *Monsieur le Capitaine!*"

"Then I fear you will have to reach the Encantadas through the benevolence of a sea captain putting out of Puerto Etén."

"And lo, the clouds parted," said Solange, "and Chloe's favorite deity dropped a thousand swim-bladders at her feet."

"To quote my favorite line from *Siren of the Nile*," said Chloe, "'Sarcasm is but the piety of cynics.'"

Under Léourier's direction the company collected the scattered pieces of the flying-machine and wrapped them up securely in the silk envelope, whereupon Akawo pointed towards the river, declaring that it would take the company directly to the Huancabamba village.

As the journey progressed—the fogbound Jequetepeque on one side, glossy black rocks on the other—Mr. Chadwick cupped his hand about

his cracked rib, Ralph palliated his injured ankle with a crutch improvised from a eucalyptus branch, and Solange soothed her hurt wrist by
complaining about it. The farther Chloe and her companions traveled,
the more signs they saw of the imminent Indian community. Whereas
the river displayed a succession of weirs (walls of woven palm stems affixed to upright posts, forming labyrinths from which no *pirarucú* or
tambaqui fish could hope to escape), the banks featured maize fields,
cassava plots, and sarsaparilla arbors. Beyond these agricultural enterprises spread a savannah scored by arroyos and dotted with trident-
shaped plants bearing fruits not unlike the cactus pads so beloved of Mr.
Darwin's tortoises.

At last the village emerged from the mist, a sprawling settlement
in the form of a wheel, its hub a plaza of crushed stone, each spoke a
row of adobe dwellings. Akawo's unheralded appearance amongst her
people prompted the sort of incredulous laughter and joyful weeping
that might attend a person's return from the dead, which was in fact how
the Indians perceived her arrival, enslavement on the Pacopampa Rubber Plantation being equivalent (as the princess explained to the adventurers) to captivity by Bora-Chi, god of the underworld. No one
laughed louder or wept more copiously than Akawo's parents—the
portly tribal leader, Nenkiwi, and his fine-boned wife, Andoa—who
managed to retain a certain regal bearing despite their intoxication
by bliss.

Solemnly Akawo recited the names of the thirty-two Indians who'd
died from either battle wounds or the late General Zumaeta's malevo-
lence. As the victims' relations slipped into the shadows to grieve, Akawo
announced that if all went well some three hundred liberated *seringueiros*
in Princess Ibanua's keeping would soon return to the Jequetepeque valley,
followed shortly thereafter by another five hundred under Prince Gitika's protection. Not surprisingly, this news sent cheers resounding
through the village, but then the atmosphere turned somber again, as
Akawo reported that amongst these survivors was a score of rubber tappers blinded or maimed on orders from the devil Zumaeta.

With the coming of dusk the Indians began feasting and dancing, a celebration that rivaled in frenzy the *carnaval de la victoria* back at the Dominican mission. There was much *epená* sniffing, of course, especially by Mr. Chadwick, who found in the resin a balm for his cracked rib, and the revelers also consumed many calabashes of *masato*, a beverage fermented from cassava roots soaked in human spittle. In time Akawo bid the Europeans good night, explaining that she wished to tell her father about the Lost Thirteenth Tribe *scenario*. Chloe elected to remain near the bonfire—an ill-considered decision, as it happened, for the flames conjured up the fall of Castillo Bracamoros, including the sobering truth that, for all the distress she'd endured whilst dropping death-eggs on the mercenaries, the whole business had also been rather thrilling.

According to the vicar's pocket watch, the celebration ended shortly before 2:00 a.m. As the Huancabambas retired to their homes, so that the god of sleep, Cona-Caina, might cure them of exhaustion and cleanse them of *epená*, Mr. Chadwick explained to his fellow adventurers that they were permitted to occupy the empty huts on the rim of the village (or so he'd inferred from his fractured conversation with the princess's cousins). Thus did Chloe and her friends fall asleep that night in separate quarters, each such dwelling guarded by a doll-sized image of a local god. She could not identify the stout wooden figure poised at the foot of her pallet, but from his carnal smile she fancied he might be the Huancabamba equivalent of Dionysius—call him Suisynoid: lord of misrule, author of illusions, director of masquerades so persuasive as to deceive even the Reverend Simon Hallowborn.

A t first light Ralph appeared outside Chloe's hut and announced that, having borrowed a donkey cart from the Huancabambas, he was on the point of departing for Puerto Etén, where he would attempt to persuade a whaling master or survey-ship captain to ferry the troupe from Peru to Galápagos. When Chloe praised Ralph for his loyalty to the Encantadas Salvation Brigade, he told her that saving the jeopardized species was the noblest of endeavors, "or so my tattooed octopus believes, despite the gulf separating cephalopods from vertebrates."

Chloe passed the remainder of the day immersing herself in Old Testament narratives—Genesis, Exodus, Leviticus, Numbers, Deuteronomy, and onward—the better to instruct her disciples in their Israelite heritage. She quickly decided that the Book of Judges must not figure in these lessons, for the thing was a horror story from first to last, featuring such gruesome episodes as Jael pounding a tent stake through Sisera's head, Gideon tearing the elders of Succoth apart with briars, and Samson tying three hundred foxes together by their tails prior to setting them on fire.

Ralph returned at dusk, shrouded in gloom. As far as he could determine, Puerto Etén was little more than a fishing village, never visited by ocean-going brigs of the sort that might take them to the Encantadas.

"Our best hope, my fair philosopher, would be to repair the *Lamarck* with all deliberate speed, praying that Mr. Hallowborn does not make landfall in the meantime."

"Chloe will do more than pray," said Solange, joining the conversation. "She will arrange for the universe to intervene on her behalf."

"My dear Solange, here's a conundrum for your irreverent mind to ponder," said Chloe. "Take Yahweh's most famous line from Exodus, 'I am what I am,' translate it into French, and it becomes, *'Je suis celui qui suis.'* Remove the egotistical 'I' from *'Je suis,'* and the result is Jesus."

"You may remove your egotistical 'I' if you wish," said Solange. "As for myself, I believe I'll go catch some fish. I'm told that Monsieur Léourier can use the swim-bladders."

The following morning Akawo collected the Europeans together and announced that Chief Nenkiwi would receive them at noon. When the appointed hour arrived, the princess led the explorers to an adobe structure shaped like a plum pudding: the council lodge, she explained—the place where her father "listens thoughtfully to his advisors before doing as he pleases."

Chief Nenkiwi sat on a fan-back wicker chair that put Chloe in mind of the throne she'd occupied in *Siren of the Nile.* He was a large and bulky man, like a golem wrought from a hillock of Rio Jequetepeque clay, his teeth as bright and uniform as the white keys on Emma Darwin's piano. A half-dozen courtiers milled about in the shadows, along with the village shaman—"our *pagé*," the princess noted—wearing a caiman-tooth necklace and grasping a scepter capped with a peccary skull.

The audience proceeded apace, Akawo rendering the Quechua speeches into their English equivalents and likewise interpreting the adventurers' words. Evidently the princess had explained the *scenario* lucidly to her father, for he began by declaring that he'd already cast the six roles reserved to Huancabambas. Hearing this boast in translation, Chloe realized that the Indians she'd taken for courtiers were actually the chief's choices to portray Lady Omega's followers.

"It happens I know about Israelite tribes," said Nenkiwi. "Back when Chief Caquinte ruled this village—I speak now of my father's father's father—a band of black-robed Jesuits appeared one day, having sailed here from a place called Panama. Their desire was to tell my ancestors about the sky god Jehovah, the Hebrew patriarchs, and the Savior from Nazareth. Those priests are still with us. Would you like to meet them?"

At a nod from Nenkiwi, the shaman stepped forward bearing a reed basket. He removed the lid. Four diminutive human heads lay on a rubber mat like a clutch of Encantadas tortoise eggs. The mouths were sutured shut, as if to prevent the martyred Jesuits from crying out to their Creator as had Jonah from the belly of the whale.

"Good Lord!" moaned Mr. Chadwick.

"*Étonnant!*" gasped Capitaine Léourier.

"So Chief Caquinte killed them?" asked Chloe.

"He gave the command, yes," said Nenkiwi.

"And then he shrank their heads?" asked Ralph.

"Not personally. We have specialists."

"In my former profession," said Solange, "I often dealt with men whose heads I would have liked to cut off and shrink, also their pizzles," a sentence that Akawo declined to translate.

"I understand why Chief Caquinte did it," said Nenkiwi. "He believed the Jesuits wanted to destroy our gods."

Like a father putting his quadruplets to bed, the shaman patted each little head, then solemnly closed the basket.

"Am I to infer that the Huancabambas *still* shrink their enemies' heads?" asked Mr. Chadwick, pressing rigid fingers against his cracked rib.

"On occasion, yes, and then we burn their bodies and mix the cinders into our nightly calabashes of *masato*," said Nenkiwi. "Did the four priests end up in Chief Caquinte's kiln? The historians are silent on this question—but this I know: Jesuit teachings entered our lore only in bits and pieces. I can tell you just three or four stories. The plagues of Eden, Samson and Goliath, the resurrection of Adam—"

"Eve, actually," said Solange.

"Señorita Kirsop makes a joke," Akawo told her father. "The messiah-man Jesus is the one who came back."

"The Deluge story especially fascinated my ancestors," said Nenkiwi. "Some even built a replica of Noah's ark in which to enact secret rites. They believed that if a man spent enough time inside the hull chanting hymns and inhaling *epená*, he would enter the realm of the gods. When the Jesuits found out about the cataclysm sect, they forced it to disband—but the temple remains intact, moored in a swamp near the river."

The chief assured Chloe that, even though his forebears' encounter with the Jesuits had left few contemporary traces, the actors he'd chosen would make excellent Israelites. As Nenkiwi introduced them to Chloe—wise Cuniche, wily Nitopari, honest Pirohua, brave Ascumiche, stalwart Yitogua, steadfast Rapra—she found herself pondering the cataclysm sect. If the ark replica had once functioned as a temple, it would be considerably larger than the catamaran that the children had made for their Noah pageant back at the Jesuit mission. She imagined loading the thing onto a raft and hauling it to the archipelago via a towline leading from the bow to the *Lamarck*. On reaching the archipelago, the Serugites would explain how, long before the coming of Lady Omega, they had constructed a model ark in homage to their primordial ancestor, Noah's son Shem, whose descendants included Jacob, progenitor of the Thirteen Tribes.

"I should like to see your ancestors' temple," Chloe told Nenkiwi. "If it's a credible facsimile of Noah's vessel, we'll want to bring it with us."

"The replica is *very* believable. The cataclysm sect built it to dimensions specified in the Hebrew Bible."

"The *precise* dimensions?" Mr. Chadwick inquired. "You mean three hundred cubits long?"

"Oh, yes," said the chief.

"Fifty cubits wide?" asked Chloe. "Thirty cubits high?"

"Quite so," said Nenkiwi.

Chloe's pulse quickened. Her muscles tensed. Bit by bit, a new version of the *scenario* took shape in her brain. This time around, the Serugites were no longer simply itinerant Hebrews who'd found their New Canaan in Peru—no, now they were the appointed keepers and anointed guardians of the vessel that had saved the world.

"Was your ancestors' temple seaworthy?" she asked.

"To best of my knowledge," said Nenkiwi.

"And is it still seaworthy?"

"I imagine so."

"Might it cross six hundred miles of open water to Galápagos?"

"Most probably."

"Mademoiselle Bathurst, I know what you're thinking, and I salute you," said Léourier brightly.

"You have made our improvident plan more improvident than ever," said Mr. Chadwick approvingly. "Well done."

"Our English mystic is a clever creature indeed," said Solange, kissing Chloe's cheek. "In that regard she is rather like a fox, or a freethinker, or the Covent Garden Antichrist."

As magnificent as its Bronze Age counterpart, the Huancabamba ark rose before Chloe and her fellow adventurers in all its epic splendor. Afloat in a secluded fen, the reed-wrapped hull suggested an immense basket—swollen descendant, perhaps, of the bassinet in which the infant Moses had drifted down to Thebes. Although Chloe regarded the Genesis flood as mythical (the Old Testament had not figured in her Manáos epiphany), this aquatic cathedral was certain to provide the masquerade with an extra measure of credibility. She christened it the *Covenant.*

After subjecting the ark to his professional scrutiny, Ralph declared that only a madman or a deity would attempt to pilot the thing to the Encantadas ere equipping it with masts, spars, sails, helm, and rudder.

"And how much time must we devote to refurbishing the *Covenant*?" Chloe asked.

"I shall defer to the genius who built the flying-machine," said Ralph.

"I would estimate three weeks," said Léourier. "Obviously we must create two teams of aboriginal laborers *immédiatement*. Even as Ralph's men add rigging to the *Covenant*, mine will make the *Lamarck* rise from the ashes."

"A worthy plan, *Monsieur le Capitaine*," said Chloe. "If your team completes its mission first, then we shall go to Galápagos aboard the *Lamarck*. Otherwise, the next vessel to figure in our adventures will be this wooden behemoth." She gestured towards the *Covenant*, then added, in a sportive voice, "Thus spake the leader of the Encantadas Salvation Brigade."

Under Akawo's guidance, Chloe and her friends climbed through the hull portal and into the yawning hollow beyond. Raising their torches high, the adventurers saw that the ark's builders had followed God's instructions precisely, creating three interior decks subdivided into scores of stalls, corrals, and coops. Never before had Chloe found herself in so cavernous a space. If Mr. Darwin had sailed around the world not in a ninety-foot brig but rather in the present vessel, and if he'd discovered on his journey a lost continent teeming with Professor Owen's dinosaurs, he'd have experienced no difficulty bringing back a hundred such dragons.

Because the new fittings would increase the ark's weight and unwieldiness, the transformation could not begin until the Indians had dragged it seven miles west through the Jequetepeque gorge to the sea. Thanks to Ralph's knowledge of ropes and pulleys, Léourier's expertise with rollers and winches, and Chief Nenkiwi's requirement that every able-bodied male Huancabamba volunteer for the job, the thing proved surprisingly mobile. From dawn until midnight the Indians cleaved to their task, hauling the ark through shallows, over sandbars, around boulders, and finally into Pacasmayo Harbor, until at last it lay moored to the main pier, aglow in the moonlight like an albino sperm whale.

The vessel's renovation began on a morally equivocal note, with several score aborigines making an unauthorized journey to Puerto Etén and returning the next morning bearing improbable quantities of timber, canvas, and nails—plus two launches: a longboat and a cutter. The Indians insisted that all these materials had come from a graveyard of sunken fishing boats, a tale to which Ralph did not so much assent as acquiesce. If the project must be accomplished with stolen goods, then so be it.

The gods of ambiguity likewise attended the *Lamarck*'s rehabilitation. It turned out that Léourier had woefully underestimated the number of fish that must be trapped before his team could repair the observation port with cured swim-bladders. The aeronaut's men would have to sacrifice no fewer than three hundred *pirarucús* and *tambaquis* if the airship were to live again.

"At least our Huancabambas will be banqueting on the gutted fish," Mr. Chadwick told Chloe. "I'm quite certain Mr. Hallowborn has no intention of feeding anybody with the creatures that die in the Great Winnowing."

"There will be no Great Winnowing," she said.

Whilst the ark and the flying-machine underwent their respective transmutations, Chloe, Akawo, and Mr. Chadwick herded Lady Omega's six disciples into the council lodge. Before the tutorials began, Akawo unfurled a white cotton robe, elegant as the gown Chloe had worn as the Southern belle in *Lanterns on the Levee*. "Our *pagé* has soaked these fibers in his magic," the princess explained, presenting the garment to Chloe, "so that you will not be nailed to a tree."

"I have never received a finer gift," said Chloe, hoping that, just as her pirate regalia had made her feel like an adventurer, so might this robe turn her into a prophet.

She elected to begin the aborigines' Hebraicization with some of the biblical narratives she'd studied whilst Ralph had undertaken his fruitless expedition to Puerto Etén. The day did not go well. With its odd stories of gods inciting fratricide by preferring mutton to bread—of prideful towers reaching into the clouds, brothers swindling brothers out of birthrights, and fathers binding sons to sacrificial altars—the Book of Genesis mystified the Indians. On the second day they became belligerent, and Chloe found herself substituting Nenkiwi's flattering epithets for sardonic designations, so that her roster of students now comprised stubborn Cuniche, sneering Nitopari, pigheaded Pirohua, quarrelsome Ascumiche, haughty Yitogua, and fickle Rapra.

Compounding the nascent Jews' theological confusion was Mr. Chadwick's belief that they should understand Lady Omega's advent in the context of the Fall of Man. Christ had come to free the Hebrews of Palestine and the Gentiles of the East from bondage to Adam's disobedience, and now the English mystic was performing that same service for the Lost Thirteenth Tribe—or so the Huancabambas must feign to believe.

"Here is what you are telling us," complained Cuniche as translated by Akawo. "One day the universe decides, 'I, Jehovah-Jesus, shall become a Creator, making a planet called Earth and a first man called Adam, fated to disobey me and thus infect himself and his children and his children's children with a sickness called sin.'"

"'Then I shall cause a human version of myself to grow inside a woman,'" Nitopari continued, "'so that, thirty years later, my Creator side can murder my human side and offer up the corpse as a gift to the fallen angel Lucifer, thereby ransoming Adam's descendants from that same demon.'"

"We cannot figure Jehovah-Jesus out," said Cuniche.

"He must be one of those crazy gods the Jivaros worship," Nitopari suggested.

Throughout the Indians' Hebraicization, Solange periodically visited the council lodge, bearing bulletins from Ralph and Léourier. Although the *Lamarck*'s newly installed swim-bladder observation port worked splendidly, the engine was proving more difficult to revive than Léourier had imagined. He feared his airship would not become sky-worthy before the month was out.

"Then Dame Fortune has decided the matter for us," said Chloe. "Noah's ark will take us to the Encantadas—an adventure certain to be simpler and shorter than the forty-day voyage we read about in Genesis."

"Dame Fortune?" said Solange. "Pray tell, mademoiselle, what about your favorite deity? Is it no longer in charge of the universe?"

"Miss Kirsop, I think perhaps we should modify your role in the masquerade," said Mr. Chadwick. "Bianca Quinn was not only palsied in her fall, she also lost the use of her vocal cords—an injury that Lady Omega had failed to heal. I suggest you start practicing your aphasia now."

Solange sneered and stalked out of the lodge.

Shortly after the courtesan's departure, Chloe and Mr. Chadwick returned to the theological matter at hand. They realized that if the Huancabambas were to make sense of the masquerade, Lady Omega must be extracted from the Garden of Eden. In the revised *scenario,* God did not send the English mystic to purge the Serugites of congenital wickedness. Instead she'd come to warn them that shrinking their enemies' heads and eating their enemies' ashes would jeopardize their admission to Heaven.

Beyond their bewilderment over the doctrine of original sin, Chloe's followers could not fathom her insistence that, should Señor Hallowborn express curiosity about the private portions of their anatomies, they must respond by saying, "Eight days after my birth, my foreskin was sliced from my male member."

"What is a foreskin?" asked Nitopari.

"Señor Chadwick, please enlighten our players," said Chloe.

Haltingly the vicar offered an explanation.

"But my jolly rod *does* have a foreskin," said Rapra, placing a hand over his *tangas* apron.

"Mine as well," said Pirohua, guarding his manhood.

"And mine," said Yitogua, shielding himself.

"Nevertheless, you must tell Señor Hallowborn you are circumcised," said Mr. Chadwick.

"Why does Jehovah-Jesus collect His favorite people's foreskins?" asked Cuniche. "Does He put them in His *masato?* Does He make jewelry with them?"

"Ready, everyone?" said the vicar, ignoring Cuniche's questions. "Repeat after me. 'Eight days after my birth, my foreskin was sliced from my male member.'"

"'Eight-days-after-my-birth-my-foreskin-was-sliced-from-my-male-member,'" chanted the Huancabambas.

For the final phase of the Indians' education, Chloe required them to memorize sentences that would presumably increase the masquerade's plausibility in Mr. Hallowborn's eyes. Some of these lines concerned the English mystic's relationship to the Serugites, including "Lady Omega has forbidden us to eat our enemies' ashes" and "How fortunate that Lady Omega need not be crucified." Other lines established the Serugites' connection to Noah and the Deluge, including "With God's guidance, we sailed the holy ark across the sea" and "Century after century, we have guarded the sacred vessel." The majority of speeches, however, revealed the Lost Thirteenth Tribe's familiarity with Hebrew lore, amongst them "God rained fire and brimstone on Sodom and Gomorrah" and "Before Abraham could sacrifice Isaac, a ram appeared in the thicket" and "As punishment for the Tower of Babel, Jehovah confounded the tongues of men."

After Chloe and Mr. Chadwick had spent two weeks instructing the aborigines in a mélange of arrant mendacity and Holy Writ, Solange brought word that the ark was nearly ready to sail, adding that the six disciples must now learn from Ralph how to man the jury-rigged barge. And so it was that, after putting on the white robe she'd received from Akawo, Chloe led her newly minted Jews along the shores of the Jequetepeque towards the sea. When at last the parade reached the moored *Covenant*, she cast a satisfied eye on the three soaring masts with their byzantine configurations of sails, yardarms, lines, and shrouds. Waving her Bible about like a semaphore flag, she exhorted her followers to mount the pier, climb the rope ladder, and join Señor Dartworthy on the weather deck.

"That white robe becomes you, my fair philosopher!" Ralph called down from the gunwale. "'Tis as splendid as the raiment you wear whilst declaiming Omar Khayyám! Thou art surely the canniest prophet in Peru!"

"Think not of *my* role in the masquerade!" Chloe shouted back. "You are tasked with eating, sleeping, and drinking the part of Edward Cabot!"

"'Touch not your flesh of myrrh, your golden hair'!" Ralph recited.

"I'm not that person anymore!"

"'Except to bring them tender love and care'!"

As Ascumiche, the last of the Indians, attained the weather deck, Chloe turned her gaze from the *Covenant,* staring at a range of banyans and mangroves thriving along the tide line. Affixed to the branches like webs spun by an immense spider, a dozen nets belonging to local mestizo fishermen lay drying in the sun.

"'Know your own wonder, worship it with me'!" shouted Ralph. "'See how I fall before you deep in prayer'!"

Determined to place herself beyond the reach of her erstwhile paramour's histrionics, Chloe hurried along the labyrinth of docks, past dories and smacks tied to bollards, their hulls painted in bright yellows, blues, and reds. She paused before a wrecked brigantine, its hull completely submerged. Shorn of canvas, the mainmast and the foremast rose from the water like crosses on Golgotha, their spars holding the largest fishing net in the harbor.

The mass of cords transfixed her. Such an enigmatic thing, that net, partaking less of form than of void, its holes more immanent than its stuff. Was the God of her epiphany an equally paradoxical entity? Did the Presence in fact have a doppelgänger, a profane absence, determined to prevent her from ever again knowing the serenity she'd felt on her Manáos sickbed?

Suspended between the absolute and the abyss, and not very happy about it, she firmed her grip on her Bible, climbed down to the beach, and marched towards the salty savannah.

BOOK THREE

A PREFERENCE
FOR THE APE

11

*Arriving in the Encantadas, Chloe Discovers
the Empire of Duntopia, Where Maximum
Mediocrity Yields Minimum Disappointment*

Blessed by clear skies and buoyed by a following sea, the *Covenant* blew across Pacasmayo Harbor, bound for the Humboldt Current, her Huancabamba crew energized by the honor of serving a ship their ancestors had assembled and held sacred. Either Ralph was a consummate teacher or the Indians were natural-born sailors, but in any event it seemed to Chloe that they performed their tasks—casting off the lines, hoisting the sails, working the helm—with supreme aplomb. Overhead, the gannets squawked with an urgency verging on panic, as if pleading for berths on the ark (a second Deluge being imminent), even as a community of mestizo fishermen waved amiably from their dories and smacks. Evidently these toilers of the sea believed that the *Covenant* posed no threat to their industry, for what sane person would build so elaborate a boat for the mere purpose of catching fish?

Thanks to Capitaine Léourier's generosity, all signs pointed to a safe crossing. Not only had he given Ralph the *Lamarck*'s primary collection of Pacific charts, he'd handed over his best spyglass and sextant, his reserve implements being adequate for the Encantadas journey he would himself be making ere long. According to this newest *scenario*, the instant that repairs were completed, Léourier and Mr. Chadwick would refuel the flying-machine with kerosene from Puerto Etén, take to the air, and land on Indefatigable Isle several days after the *Covenant*. Seeking out Governor Stopsack and Lady Omega, Mr. Chadwick would feign to corroborate the female prophet's exalted status in Heaven's eyes. The vicar would then go straight to Simon Hallowborn and report that this English mystic was truly a divine messenger, privy to God's unfavorable opinion of the proposed massacre.

Chloe spent the first day of the voyage stationed beside Cuniche at the helm, helping him to cut a straight wake. Inevitably she imagined Noah standing on the weather deck of the primal ark, his ears throbbing with the screams of terrified sinners and the howls of drowning beasts. As the patriarch stared at the death-choked waters, his wife and daughters-in-law fidgeted anxiously by his side, whilst Shem, Japheth, and Ham, keeping watch in the prow, praised God for modifying, in the case of *Homo sapiens*, His quota of only two representatives per species.

Shortly before noon on the *Covenant*'s tenth day at sea, an amorphous mass materialized dead ahead, breaking the silvery horizon like an onyx pendant on a pearl necklace. Consulting Léourier's map, Ralph concluded that they were approaching Charles Isle, home of the Christian utopianist who styled himself Emperor Eggwort.

The advent of Galápagos occasioned a dispute aboard the ark. Ralph wanted the troupe to spend the day getting to Indefatigable, so they could perform the masquerade for Governor Stopsack the following morning (assuming the slaughter had not yet occurred), thereby enlisting his allegiance in the struggle against Hallowborn. But Chloe argued that the company should make immediate landfall on Charles Isle, find Orrin Eggwort, and rehearse the show in his presence, so they might learn which parts were persuasive (to a Christian utopianist at least) and which demanded revision.

"My instincts tell me Eggwort will prove a vital ally," she said.

"My instincts tell me he will prove a woeful distraction," said Solange.

"In either case, our leader obviously wishes to clamp eyes on a healthy lizard or tortoise as soon as possible," said Ralph, "and so our goal, Solange, must be Charles Isle, whether you and I like it or not."

As the sun dipped towards its illusory rendezvous with Borneo, Ralph piloted the ark around the island's western shore and dropped anchor in Post Office Bay. Casting her mind back to Mr. Darwin's travel journal, Chloe recalled that the inlet owed its name to the mail delivery system devised in the previous century by a whaling master, Captain Colnett. The linchpin of this institution was a wooden barrel into which outbound European sailors deposited their private correspondence. Philanthropic mariners would then retrieve the letters with the aim of posting them once back on English or Continental soil.

Clad in her white cotton robe, Chloe descended the rope ladder to the longboat, Solange, Cuniche, and Nitopari following, the plan being for Ralph and the remaining Indians to reef the sails, then come ashore in the cutter. Like the devout imitation disciples they were, the Indians fervently rowed their sham prophet across the bay. Terns, storm petrels, and blue-footed boobies rode the thermals and updrafts: scores of birds, alive and well—an avian extravaganza in which Chloe took no delight, for Hallowborn's death list would have included none of those species.

As the longboat drew near shore, she fixed on the breakers, wave after wave smashing against a bifurcated beach, one side covered in green silicates, the other strewn with tuff and pumice rising to cliffs of shining black lava. Swathed in crimson lichens, the volcanic chunks atop the promontories were quite the most beautiful objects she'd ever seen, not only in their outward aspect but also in their talent for locomotion: yes, no question, these rocks were wriggling and twitching—being not rocks at all but, wonderful to tell and still more wonderful to behold, the fabled red marine iguanas of the southern Encantadas!

"Do you see that, Solange?" The arrival of the dove, olive branch in beak, could not have given Noah greater joy than these lizards brought Chloe. "The rocks are moving! We've outrun Hallowborn!"

The Indians labored heroically, stroke upon stroke, until the longboat reached the beach. A dilapidated wharf jutted into the cove. Like teeth protruding from a jawbone, a series of docks extended from the pier to form a half-dozen berths, five empty, the sixth holding a shallop called the *Cumorah*. Hitching up her robe, Chloe vaulted over the gunwale and sprinted through the surf, soon attaining the glassy shore. Arrayed in spikes and spines, their red hides flecked with turquoise, the lizards took no notice of the intruder but simply huddled on their sooty pedestals, soaking up the westering sun and snorting like disaffected basilisks. Each time an iguana exhaled, a filament of seawater streamed from its nostrils, even as the booming rollers showered the colony with spindrift. Occasionally a lizard would slither off its perch, dive into the swirling foam, and vanish, returning with a mass of seaweed clamped in its maw.

Chloe cast an eye inland. The Colnett mail barrel and its adjacent notice board stood at a safe distance from the incoming tide, the fat drum shielded from sun and rain by a peaked roof, beyond which lay a range of volcanic cones perhaps fifteen feet high. She steeled her nerves and scrambled up the nearest slope, the sharp pumice abrading her palms and ankles. Gaining the summit, she set off along the ridge, taking care lest she tumble into a crater, then paused and faced the sea, her robe billowing in the wind. Fastened to the center of the bay, the *Covenant* rode on her hawser, bathed in the coppery afternoon light, her reefed sails hanging from the spars like sloths clinging to jungle branches.

Descending the cinder mountain, she proceeded across a plain broken at intervals by bare trees and leafless thickets, plus stands of pricklypear cacti, the very variety she'd tended at Down House. The stark terrain culminated in a dormant volcano, its slopes covered by a shawl of formerly molten rock, the static waves rolling across the vale like a sea of frozen pitch. To the west the rigid lava yielded to a tranquil pool, domain of ten saddleback tortoises, some lumbering along the shore, others wallowing in the mud. The thirsty ones waded into the shallows and, submerging their heads completely, imbibed prodigal quantities of mossy water.

"It's a miracle!" cried Solange, dashing to Chloe's side.

"Since when do you believe in miracles?"

"I didn't say I believed in miracles," said Solange. "I merely noted that a miracle had occurred."

Acting with unspoken but complete accord, each woman selected a tortoise, then collapsed prone across its carapace. Chloe's creature smelled of ashes, tuff, algae, and muck: a not unpleasant fragrance—in truth quite exhilarating. Briefly she wondered why she felt rather more inclined to embrace this beast than to make a joyful noise unto the Presence. But then she recalled a reflection Mr. Darwin had offered during the fateful Down House luncheon: "I cannot explain myself—only God, wherever He may be, can do that—but I shall attempt to explain my theory." If a great scientist could be a stranger to himself, then she must be permitted the same foible. Tomorrow she might attempt to decipher the riddle of Chloe Bathurst, but for now it was sufficient to hug a tortoise.

For some while Chloe and Solange lay athwart their respective reptiles, watched over by Cuniche and Nitopari, and they would have continued their devotions had the other masquerade troupers not arrived. Ralph was delighted to find Charles Isle so fecund—"Evidently we've gained Galápagos with time to spare!"—but before he could expand on this sentiment six women came striding across the lava field. Clothed in the sorts of calico gowns favored by the wives of North American pioneers, they were presumably citizens of Orrin Eggwort's experimental community, their sunburnt faces evoking the indigenous marine iguanas, each complexion tinted a different shade of red.

"The Supreme Emperor sends you his howdy-do," said the maroon pioneer, addressing Ralph. "An hour ago, Orrin and the rest of us watched you drop your anchor in the bay."

"Lovely ladies, allow me to introduce our company," said Ralph. "I am Professor Edward Cabot, instructor in anthropology at King's College and master of the good ship *Covenant*, out of Puerto Etén. My fellow British citizens include the aerialist Bianca Quinn, palsied last year in a fall but now fully recovered, and Lady Omega, an English mystic who healed Miss Quinn's broken back. Our Peruvian natives count themselves amongst Lady Omega's followers."

"Rebecca Eggwort at your service," said the maroon pioneer, then indicated her five companions and gave their names, the burgundy woman being Sarah, the scarlet Ruth, the strawberry Naomi, the rose Hagar, and the coral Miriam. "Orrin's other wives are back in Minor Zion"—she gestured towards the volcano—"over yonder, behind Mount Pajas."

"His other wives?" said Solange. "You mean, you're all married to Mr. Eggwort?"

"Happily," said Sarah.

"On balance," said the pregnant Ruth.

"Truly happily," said Naomi, likewise in a gravid state.

"I thought Mr. Eggwort was a Christian, not a Persian," said Solange.

"You're darn tootin' he's a Christian," Rebecca replied, "but like many a Latter-Day Saint, Orrin practices the venerable Bible custom of plural marriage. 'If it was good enough fer David and Solomon,' he says, 'it's good enough fer me.' At the moment he's on top with nine wives, whereas our Associate Emperor and our Assistant Emperor ain't got but six."

"Six all together?" asked Solange.

"Apiece," answered Rebecca.

"If Mr. Eggwort proposes marriage to me, I shall refuse," said Solange. "I would never share my husband with another woman, much less a harem."

"We ain't no harem," said Rebecca indignantly.

"Ah, then you're a seraglio," said Solange.

"That's right," said Miriam emphatically. "A seraglio."

"Which would make you all sultanas," noted Chloe.

"Exactly," said Rebecca.

Chloe told herself it didn't matter how many wives the local emperors possessed, so long as they helped her foil the rector.

Ralph said, "Good ladies, we seek word of H.M.S. *Antares* and her illustrious passenger, the Reverend Mr. Hallowborn, who has untoward designs on this archipelago."

"We know all about the Great Winnowin'," said Rebecca. "The way Orrin heard it from the Governor, last year a couple of parsons over in

England took to doin' some serious theologizin' and decided these islands was once the Devil's playground."

"Mrs. Eggwort, do you think it possible Mr. Hallowborn has arrived and the slaughter already begun?" asked Chloe.

"Heck, no, they wouldn't do no harrowin' without Orrin's say-so. He's the only Supreme Emperor in these here parts."

An immense serenity spread through Chloe, a happiness such as she'd not known since her epiphany in Manáos. No slaughter. Not yet.

"We should like to meet your husband."

"Then it will come to pass," said Rebecca.

For the next half-hour the maroon pioneer and her cohorts guided the *Covenant*'s company through the foothills of Mount Pajas, then around the volcano to a three-story stone keep encircled by a brick wall. Armed with a carbine, a uniformed sentry manned the blockhouse, its wooden tower rising from the grounds like a candle set atop a casket. A gallows occupied the center of the exercise yard, its crosspiece devoid of nooses: the naïve observer might have thought it a device for drying clothes—but Chloe, hanged one hundred and six times as Pirate Anne, knew otherwise.

"Mephistropolis, I presume," she said.

"Orrin don't take much interest in our penal colony," said Rebecca, nodding, "exceptin' when Kommandant Hengstenberg stages an execution—then we all turn out to watch. Well, not ever'body. We leave the young 'uns at home. I reckon Hengstenberg's got about two dozen convicts in there, human sludge from the Guayaquil *barrios*. An odd duck, Hengstenberg—odd and old: he deserted from the Prussian army at Waterloo and ain't stopped runnin' since."

Waterloo, mused Chloe—the battle in which her grandfather had wielded his bayonet before it became Pirate Anne's dagger. "I'm glad you don't bring children to the executions."

"The other wives and me, all us *sultanas*—I do like that word of yours—we used to think a boy should be at least eight afore he sees a hangin' and a girl at least ten. Orrin, though, he went and had hisself a revelation on the matter, and it turns out Heaven's amenable to startin' boys off at six and girls at seven. You ask me, the Lord God Jehovah is full of peculiar views, but it ain't my place to judge."

A s the tropical breeze wafted across Charles Isle, raising clouds of ash that rode the sticky air like phantom wasps, Chloe, her companions, and Orrin Eggwort's wives continued their march, entering a fissured basin littered with pumice and broken by patches of anemic pumpkins, weary turnips, and feeble sweet potatoes. Men in flaxen shirts and women in cotton bonnets ambled amongst the crops, tending them with rakes and watering cans. Beyond the gardens lay Minor Zion, and minor it was indeed, a cluster of forlorn shacks with thatched roofs and clinker walls, facing a plaza that, being planted with orchids and lilies, was apparently intended to be mistaken for a village green (although the flowers did no more to mitigate the general bleakness than would a nosegay tossed upon a slag heap). Everywhere Chloe glanced, children cavorted, trundling hoops, kicking balls, skipping rope. Scrawny goats and underfed hogs roamed the settlement at will. The only substantial building was a squat clapboard affair, its front yard displaying a sign reading WHITE HORSE PROPHECY TABERNACLE, its terra-cotta roof boasting a bell tower surmounted by a wooden cross.

Rebecca directed her charges into the vicinity of Emperor Orrin Eggwort, a bony and angular man wearing a straw hat and red homespun shirt, a braided black beard swaying from his jaw. He lay socketed in a hammock suspended from the porch roof of the nearest hovel, sipping water from a silver goblet whilst reveling in the breeze generated by a triad of palm-leaf fans, the motive power being, in each case, a wife. After introducing this second set of sultanas—Constance, Charity, and the pregnant Martha—Rebecca presented the troupers as "Perfessor Cabot, anthropologist, Lady Omega, faith healer, and Miss Quinn, her beneficiary, all of 'em interestin' and harmless English folk newly arrived from Peru on that big boat anchored in the bay."

"Welcome to Duntopia." Orrin Eggwort swept a spindly arm east to west in a gesture encompassing the whole island. "I am master of all I survey." A bright smile broke through his beard. "Thou hast comely wives, Perfessor."

"They aren't my wives," said Ralph. "Did I hear you correctly? Duntopia, not Utopia?"

"Dun—the dullest of all possible colors," said Eggwort, nodding. "Shall I tell you what's wrong with most communities built from scratch? They strive fer perfection, that's what. They go a-whorin' after excellence. Therein lies a recipe fer frustration, wouldn't you agree?"

"I believe I follow your logic," said Ralph.

"Here in Minor Zion, we don't eschew ambition—we fight it tooth 'n' nail. We don't avoid mediocrity—we practice it. I daresay that during the past ten years we've achieved the by-Jiminy pinnacle of diminished expectations." Eggwort clapped his hands. "Cleavewife Rebecca, our visitors look parched."

The maroon pioneer disappeared into the hovel, returning with an earthenware jug and four tin cups.

"Shortly after I decided to let like-minded folks settle on my island," the Emperor continued, "I started castin' round fer a religion that harmonized with my personal philosophy. Unless your experimental community's got the Lord on its side, chaos 'n' anarchy will soon come a-callin'." He flourished a leather-bound volume titled the Book of Mormon. "And then one day I stumbled on the Church of Jesus Christ of Latter-Day Saints, cooked up a quarter-century ago by a confidence man with the auspiciously lackluster name of Joseph Smith."

Rebecca decanted the water, providing each of her English guests with a full tin cup, then passed the fourth cup to Ascumiche, instructing him to share it with his fellow Peruvians.

"After Joseph Smith died, the Latter-Day Saints started splinterin'," said Eggwort. "The Prairie Saints stayed in the Midwest. The Rocky Mountain Saints followed Brigham Young into Utah Territory. And the Galápagos Saints—that is, myself, the lesser emperors, and our wives—we come here. Ever read the Book of Mormon?"

"My tastes run more to Omar Khayyám," said Ralph.

At a nod from her husband, Rebecca refilled Eggwort's goblet, whereupon he began describing how the Latter-Day Saints' sacred text had been set down centuries earlier by Mormon, "a semi-divine personage who spent his life a-listenin' to ghostly prophets and spectral historians," their preoccupation being the immigrant Jews of the New World. Eventually Mormon etched these sundry revelations onto gold plates in a language "long since chewed to oblivion by the teeth of time." Then came the momentous autumn of 1823, when the angel Moroni led Smith to a New York mountain, Cumorah, where all fifteen plates lay buried. Though not a literate man, Smith had little trouble deciphering the Reformed Egyptian hieroglyphics, and his friends were happy to act as scribes while he translated the plates aloud.

"And what a wonderfully benumbin' story they tell," said Eggwort, "page after page of transplanted Hebrews spoutin' Jeremiads, encounterin' Jesus, and fightin' epic battles. Show me a more violent book on the face of the Earth, and I'll by-God eat it."

Chloe winced internally, disoriented by the resemblance between the Latter-Day Saints' sacred text and her Lost Thirteenth Tribe *scenario*. The question, of course, was whether this coincidence would give the lie to her masquerade or provide it with additional credence.

Eggwort deposited the Book of Mormon in Ralph's hands. "I promise you, Perfessor, exceptin' fer some lines swiped from the Gospels, there ain't a single verse herein a man might call galvanizin', upliftin', or edifyin'. Go ahead—take the test."

Opening the volume at random, Ralph read, "'And it came to pass that a long time passed away, and the lord of the vineyard said unto his servant: Come, let us go down into the vineyard, that we may labor in the vineyard. And it came to pass that the lord of the vineyard, and also the servant, went down into the vineyard to labor. And it came to pass that the servant said unto his master: Behold, look here. Behold the tree.' Jacob chapter five, verses fifteen through sixteen."

"Mormon ain't let me down yet," said Eggwort breathlessly.

Ralph passed the Book of Mormon to Solange, who cracked the spine, shut her eyes, and set her finger on a verse. "'Wherefore, all things which are good cometh of God,'" she read, "'and that which is evil cometh of the Devil; for the Devil is an enemy unto God, and fighteth against him continually, and inviteth and enticeth to sin, and to do that which is evil continually.' Moroni chapter six, verse twelve."

"See what I mean?" said Eggwort. "It's as if Mormon done writ the whole thing with Duntopia in mind."

Solange returned the volume to the Emperor. "How clever of Smith to realizeth that Reformed Egyptian should be renderedeth in the English of King James the First."

"I'm confused," said Ralph. "You hold Smith's cult insipid, yet you've brought it to these shores *in toto*."

"The Church of Jesus Christ of Latter-Day Saints ain't no *cult*, Perfessor," said Eggwort in a reproving tone. "We're the most accurate edition of Christianity yet vouchsafed the human race. Just because a revelation is tedious and tiresome, that don't make it false. The more I read these stultifyin' stories, the more convinced I become that the author enjoyed intimate spiritual relations with the Lord God Jehovah Hisself. It would've been easy as pie fer Smith to hire some fancy poet to fix up his book, tossin' in glittery words and highfalutin phrases, but our prophet done kept the sentences just the way they come a-gushin' from his mouth, which fer my money proves their authenticity. Now, I assume you didn't sail all the way from Peru out of any special hankerin' to join our church—but you're welcome to do so anyway, likewise your wives and brownie slaves, providin' ever'body's willin' to swear an oath to me."

"These women aren't my wives," Ralph reminded their host. "The Indians aren't my slaves," he added.

"When we spotted your vessel this afternoon," said Eggwort, "Rebecca and Naomi took to speculatin' it might be the Reverend Mr. Hallowborn's brig, but then I realized that couldn't be true, not such a queer-lookin' thing. If I didn't know better, I'd say that fat boat of yours was the ark of Noah, rigged fer ocean travel. So what sort of ship is the *Covenant*?"

"The ark of Noah," said Ralph.

"Rigged for ocean travel," added Solange.

"Here in Duntopia, we don't make jokes at the Supreme Emperor's expense," said Eggwort.

"These brownies, as you call them, hail from a race living on the Rio Jequetepeque, direct descendants of Jacob's forgotten son Serug," said Ralph. "Two millennia ago the Serugites boarded Noah's ark and journeyed from the Near East to South America, hoping to find a New Canaan. In other words, Your Excellency, you are hosting a delegation from the Lost Thirteenth Tribe of Israel!"

"You just said a mouthful," Eggwort noted.

"I'm aware of that."

"If this Serugite exodus really happened, it would be in the Book of Mormon."

"Evidently Smith lost track of a gold plate or two," said Ralph, a retort Chloe thought rather resourceful.

The Emperor frowned, apparently wondering whether to reject Professor Cabot's narrative as a hoax or embrace it as a missing chapter from Smith's epiphany. "These Indians are *Jewish*?" he said at last. "I've always appreciated Jews. In that regard, I'm rather like God."

"After putting down roots near Puerto Etén," Ralph continued, "the Serugites set about guarding the *Covenant*, performing their task so faithfully that God gifted them with a prophet, the woman in white who stands before you."

Languidly Eggwort extricated himself from his hammock and, hooking his thumbs under his latex braces, swaggered up to Chloe. "You fancy yourself a prophet?"

"In the crucible of my bones all truths are fused," she said, using the voice she'd devised for the wraith in *The Rime of the Ancient Mariner,* "dust becoming clay, clay becoming flesh, flesh becoming spirit. Myriad orbs of vision lie embedded in my being. I am Lady Omega of the ten thousand eyes."

"Here in Duntopia," said Eggwort, "we don't take kindly to visitors holdin' themselves superior to the Supreme Emperor."

"Before the Almighty all creatures stand as equals, be they emperors or indigents, prophets or pariahs, caliphs or outcasts," said Chloe. "Rest assured, Your Excellency, I did not come to imperil your earthly kingdom."

Eggwort issued a hum of satisfaction leavened with skepticism, then strutted up to Solange. "If you're not the Perfessor's wife, then who are you?"

"Bianca Quinn, aerialist, born in Tunbridge Wells but raised in the West Indies," Solange replied using her weirdest sea-witch voice (not an ideal choice, Chloe felt). "Eventually I ended up working for a circus in Lima. During my last performance I fell thirty feet to the ground. I feared I would never walk again, much less on a tightrope, but then my friends bore me by donkey cart to Lady Omega, who laid a hand on my splintered spine, and I was healed."

The Emperor clucked his tongue, then marched back and forth before the Indians like a Turkish general reviewing his janissaries. "Lost Thirteenth Tribe, you say? Keepers of the ark?"

"With God's guidance, we sailed the holy ark across the sea," recited Cuniche, casting a beatific smile on Chloe.

"Century after century, we have guarded the sacred vessel," said Yitogua, according his teacher a loving glance.

"Lady Omega has forbidden us to eat our enemies' ashes," said Pirohua.

"Lady Omega taught us not to shrink our enemies' heads," said Rapra.

"Cain asked his Creator, 'Am I my brother's coat of many colors?'" said Ascumiche.

As Chloe grimaced, Ralph declared, "He intended to say—"

"I *know* what he intended to say," interrupted Eggwort. "I prefer the brownie's version."

"Because his wife disobeyed, God changed Lot's jolly rod into a pillar of salt," said Nitopari.

Ralph hastened to add, "By which he meant—"

"I *know* what he meant," Eggwort insisted.

Cuniche began, "As punishment for the Towel of Babel, God rained foreskins on Sodom—" But before he could finish, Chloe pressed her hand against his lips, then turned to Eggwort, offering him the same smile a *Times* critic had once called the most luminous object on the London stage, not excluding limelight.

"One stormy night I was walking along the banks of the Jequetepeque when of a sudden my ten thousand eyes began to spin," she said.

"From each orb fell scores of tiny tear-shaped lanterns, streaming to Earth and showing me numberless lizards and countless tortoises, and lo, I beheld ninety and two shackled men, and lo, they drew forth their swords and fell upon the reptiles, and in the glow of the lightning and the gleam of the lanterns I beheld the blood of the beasts, that it was blameless!"

"No, those creatures are all hellspawn," Eggwort protested. "Governor Stopsack showed me a letter from Bishop Wilberforce. The Great Winnowin' will be a kick in the teeth to the Devil hisself."

"Wilberforce has slandered the Encantadas fauna," said Chloe. "His theology offendeth our Creator. You must join me in thwarting the slaughter."

Eggwort scratched his head vigorously, as if to recruit every brain cell into interpreting the prophet's words. "Know what I gotta do? I gotta see the brownies' boat up close. If I judge it to be the true Genesis ark, I'm a-thinkin' that my thoughts will become the clearer."

"You may visit the *Covenant* at your earliest convenience."

With one hand Eggwort brought the Book of Mormon to his chest, as if applying a poultice, using his free hand to brush Chloe's sleeve. "Art thou truly a Heaven-sent messenger?"

She laughed and said, "I am what I am."

With the coming of darkness Chloe, Ralph, and Solange climbed into the longboat, whereupon Cuniche and Nitopari rowed them across the bay, the other Huancabambas following in the cutter. The Indians pulled mightily against the current, the watery path illuminated by a full moon shining through a winding-sheet of cirrus clouds. Speaking over the boom of the surf and the splash of the oars, the English adventurers soon reached a consensus: the rehearsal had gone swimmingly. True, Lady Omega's followers had garbled their lines, but the Emperor hadn't seemed to mind. The Serugites were a storytelling people, after all, not bookish like their Israelite forebears, so naturally their recollections of Holy Writ would have degenerated over the centuries.

The following morning, shortly after dawn, Eggwort appeared on the weather deck, having been ferried to the *Covenant* in a dinghy rowed by Rebecca and Hagar. Solemnly he marched from fore to aft and back again, caressing the sacred sails, fingering the holy shrouds, turning the consecrated helm. His tour complete, he sank to his knees, prostrating himself before the mainmast like a pagan worshiping an oaken idol. He pressed his lips to the planks, bringing to this devotion the same ardor he might have invested in kissing the feet of Joseph Smith.

"Orrin's mighty impressed," Rebecca told Chloe.

"This here ark's as genuine as the gold plates of Cumorah," added Hagar.

Hauling himself erect, Eggwort sought out the Huancabambas and, one after the other, caressed the shining black hair of God's chosen brownies.

"This vessel puts a body in mind of Alma chapter ten, verse twenty-two, don't it, Cleavewife Rebecca?" said the Emperor in a hortatory voice.

"'If it were not for the prayers of the righteous, ye would even now be visited with utter destruction,'" Rebecca recited, rising to the challenge, "'yet it would not be by flood, as were the people in the days of Noah, but by famine and by pestilence and the sword.'"

"Well done!" Eggwort cast a minatory eye on Hagar. "And, of course, this holy boat recalls Third Nephi chapter twenty-two, verse nine."

"'As I have sworn that the waters of Noah should no more go over the Earth,' quoted Hagar, "'so have I sworn that I would not be wroth with thee.'"

"Splendid!" Eggwort declared, then sauntered up to Ralph. "Truth to tell, Perfessor, I'm bowled over like a bunch of skittles. I can't say whether it was Moroni or Joseph Smith who mislaid the gold plate in question, but either way your brownies are the by-God Lost Thirteenth Tribe, and Noah hisself surely walked this deck."

"Thou art perspicacity personified," said Ralph.

"Which ain't to say I accept *all* of your anthropoidal notions, Perfessor. Last night our prophet appeared to me as in a dream."

"Nothing good has ever followed the sentence, 'Last night our prophet appeared to me as in a dream,'" muttered Solange.

"Smith's angelic form warned me that the one called Lady Omega was not sent by Jehovah as a messenger to the Serugites," said the Emperor. "The woman is a charlatan."

"I shan't conceal my bewilderment, Your Excellency," said Ralph, indicating Chloe with his spyglass. "Thou art bearing false witness against a prophet of God."

She shuddered as if enduring a second bout of the ague. Three syllables, *char-la-tan*, each like a sudden slap on the cheek (and she was not inclined to turn the other). But before she could protest, Eggwort wrenched the glass away from Ralph and, elongating the implement, pointed it at her as if wielding a rapier.

"If you're really the apple of Jehovah's eye, Miss Omega, how's about partin' the waters of Post Office Bay fer us? Why don't you go prancin' atop the waves or changin' 'em into wine? While you're at it, make Mount Pajas erupt in flames and lava."

"That's the stuff, Orrin," said Rebecca. "Show the imposter what fer."

Chloe accorded Eggwort the same piercing stare she'd perfected whilst playing Mr. Coleridge's wraith. "I don't do ostentatious tricks."

"Back in Minor Zion, we don't call 'em tricks," the Emperor retorted. "We call 'em signs and wonders, two exhibitions evidently beyond your powers."

"No, that's not true," said Solange. "Lady Omega is a fount of signs and wonders. She made me walk again."

"The sooner you return to England," said Eggwort to Chloe, "leavin' these Peruvian Hebrews to protect the ark without you crammin' their heads full of theological poppycock—the sooner you do that, the better."

Executing an about-face, the Emperor rested the glass atop the anchor windlass, then marched towards the rope ladder that held the dinghy to the *Covenant*.

"She made me walk!" cried Solange.

Eggwort issued an imperial sneer and, wives in train, climbed down to the dinghy. Whilst Rebecca and Hagar worked the oars, their husband sat in the prow and bellowed a verse from the Book of Mormon. "'And it came to pass that when they were buried in the deep there was no water that could hurt them, their vessels being tight like unto the ark of Noah'!"

Slouching against the starboard gunwale, the English adventurers stared at a flock of red-pouched frigate birds wheeling above the ranting emperor. With their enormous wings, scissor-shaped tails, and beaks suggesting sabers, the creatures seemed to Chloe a kind of hellish weapon—and from a storm petrel's perspective, frigate birds were indeed satanic: in his travel journal Mr. Darwin had described seeing one such predator overtake a petrel in flight and eat it alive on the wing.

"You were right, Solange, and I was wrong," said Chloe. "Eggwort will never be our ally."

"Obviously you should've sought the counsel of your favorite deity before inviting that lunatic to help us," said the courtesan.

"And it came to pass that Chloe Bathurst and Solange Kirsop agreed never again to discuss metaphysical matters," said Ralph, "lest the Western world become embroiled in yet another war of religion."

According to *The Voyage of the Beagle*, getting from one Galápagos island to the next posed severe navigational difficulties. The sudden doldrums and rogue winds were bad enough, but the archipelago also challenged mariners with a patchwork of incompatible currents, including the Humboldt, the Cromwell, the Panama, and the South Equatorial. Prepared for the worst, the company of the *Covenant* was hardly surprised when it took them the rest of the morning to make the fifty-mile run from Charles Isle to the northern shore of Indefatigable.

Upon arriving in the Bahía de Cormoranes, the masquerade troupe agreed that, in light of the Eggwort disaster, the best plan would be for Ralph to pay Jonathan Stopsack a private visit, drawing him into a chummy conversation, Englishman to Englishman. And so, after dropping anchor and reefing the sails, Ralph instructed Ascumiche and Yitogua to row him across the bay and up the inland waterways to the Governor's hacienda.

The party returned at dusk. The news was heartening. Not only did aquatic iguanas thrive up and down the Indefatigable coast, not only did tortoises and terrestrial lizards abound in the swamps, but Stopsack had proved a rational and subtle member of the Anglican Communion, the kind of Christian who might very well be persuaded that Wilberforce's designs on the Encantadas turned on a dubious theology at best.

Early the next morning, Cuniche and Nitopari having brought her by longboat into Black Turtle Cove, a white-robed Chloe stepped onto the sugared sands, and shortly thereafter the rest of the troupe arrived in the cutter. Disembarking, Ralph directed Chloe's attention to Eugenio and Sancho, two swart and limber Mephistropolis prisoners, currently on furlough so they could function as Stopsack's servants. At the moment both Ecuadorians were engaged in harvesting sea snails for the Governor's dinner table.

Seizing the mooring lines, the Huancabambas dragged the longboat and the cutter through the surf to the estuary, whereupon Chloe and her fellow troupers scrambled aboard their respective launches. Anxious though she was to raise the curtain on the masquerade, she savored the upstream journey, which proceeded through a labyrinth of marshy channels bounded by mangrove glades. Dozens of devil-rays glided beneath the shallow waters like organic parasols. Egrets and herons waded along the banks, striking at the hapless fish congregating amidst the prop roots. On all sides green sea turtles lay embedded in the submarine sediments, occasionally poking their heads above the surface to draw a breath or cast a reverential eye on the sun.

In time the troupers reached the hacienda, a rambling affair set on stilts above a stagnant lagoon coated with algae, the rootless scum spreading everywhere like a film of grease on workhouse soup. Lashed to the dock was a double-masted schooner, the *Hippolyta*, flanked by assorted skiffs and *tolda* canoes. Long-billed mockingbirds and slim-beaked finches perched on the wharf railings, prospecting for bugs and grubs.

The first meeting between the Encantadas Salvation Brigade and the administrator of Her Majesty's Galápagos Protectorate occurred in his front parlor, a commodious space suffused with buttery sunlight sifted through mosquito-netted windows, the walls decorated with oil-painted views of rural England: a flowering hedge, a thatched-roof cottage, a mill with a waterwheel—affectionately observed but crudely rendered. According to the signatures on the canvases, the artist was none other than their host, Governor Stopsack, a gorbellied man with a doughy face, his surfeit of flesh constrained by a white linen suit, a watch chain slung in a golden grin between his waistcoat pockets.

Ralph introduced his companions as "Lady Omega and Bianca Quinn, bestower and beneficiary respectively of the most astounding miracle ever to occur in Peru," then identified the Indians milling about on the veranda as "the objects of my anthropological investigations."

The English visitors were treated to raw oysters, crake-liver canapés, and glasses of *pisco*, the succulent repast served by two more furloughed Mephistropolis prisoners, the youthful Pablo and the wizened Virgilio. To Chloe's dismay, the Governor neither welcomed the Huancabambas into the hacienda nor offered them any refreshment. When he invited his guests to spend the night, it went without saying that the proposal did not extend to anyone of an aboriginal cast of mind or skin.

Stopsack snapped his fingers, gaining the attention of both Mephi-stropolis inmates. *"Nuestros invitados tienen calor,"* he said, then turned to his guests. "I've ordered them to cool you off." Throughout the ensuing conversation, the furloughed Ecuadorians operated a pair of palm-leaf fans, Pablo blessing Chloe and Solange with artificial breezes, Virgilio doing the same for Ralph and the Governor. "Tell me, Professor, what do you make of Orrin Eggwort?"

"At first blush, our Latter-Day Saint seems a harmless eccentric," said Ralph. "Yet I can imagine his egotist's utopia expanding to a point where it threatens your own authority. If I had Lord Russell's ear, I would advise him to depose this petty autocrat."

"And if *I* had Lord Russell's ear, I would advise him to hire *you* as my lieutenant," said Stopsack, "for you are obviously an astute judge of men and their vanities."

"I appreciate your flattery, sir, but my present career satisfies me."

From his pained face and enervated posture Chloe surmised that the Governor was not a happy man, a theory corroborated by his next remark.

"The dismal truth is that for me this whole blasted archipelago is a prison—not just Mephistropolis." Elaborating, Stopsack complained that he was expected to heed not only the caprices of Whitehall but also the whims of Quito, the Encantadas being at once a British mandate and an Ecuadorian possession. "President Ascásubi's minions, confound them, are forever mailing me complaints through the Colnett barrel. 'Señor Stopsack, when will you send us fifty pounds of succulent sally-lightfoot crabs?' 'Señor Stopsack, when will you clean out the pirate lairs on the northern isles?' 'You must grow more *orchilla* moss, Señor Stopsack, so that Ecuador will eclipse Peru in vegetable-dye production.' As for the whaling masters who show up every fortnight or so—they're even worse. 'Have you no fresh fruit, Señor?' 'Can you row a wench or two out to my ship?' 'When will you increase the tortoise-meat quotas?'" He gestured towards his paintings of pastoral England. "Lord, what I wouldn't give to see Shropshire again."

"If the tortoises were literate, they would write paeans to Jonathan Stopsack," said Ralph. "You have preserved them from extinction."

"If I'm to believe Bishop Wilberforce's dispatches," said the Governor in measured tones, "those tortoises trace to the Devil and should be exterminated."

"Though an able priest, Wilberforce does not speak for the Almighty," said Ralph. "There is one amongst us, however, for whom the divine will is an open book." He gestured towards Chloe. "Behold the woman whom the Hebrew river-folk regard as a holy messenger. You won't be surprised to hear that Eggwort failed utterly to apprehend her intimacy with our Creator."

At a signal from their prophet, Cuniche and the other Indians filed into the parlor. The masquerade commenced immediately. Slumped in his wicker chair, the Governor greeted each successive fabrication (the seafaring Hebrew clan, the preserved Genesis ark, the ministry of Lady

Omega, the healing of Bianca Quinn, the Almighty's anger over the impending slaughter) with an expression as blank as an unmarked grave, and yet his occasional interjections—"fascinating," "extraordinary," "remarkable"—suggested that he was finding the narrative compelling. Once again the Serugites garbled their speeches, Cuniche declaring, "Lady Omega turned the Tower of Babel into a jolly rod of many colors," Nitopari asserting, "Lot's wife crucified the ram in the thicket," but these infelicities caused Stopsack no obvious distress.

"Like our Galápagos seaweed, your stories are not easily digested." The Governor's gaze traveled from Chloe to Ralph to Solange and back again. "Perhaps Noah's ark has come to Galápagos, bearing an English mystic"—his tone was at once deferential and sardonic—"plus emissaries from an Israelite tribe. It's difficult to say. Perhaps Madam Prophet cured Miss Quinn's paralysis. I have formed no opinion as yet. But I do know this. I shan't allow Hallowborn to harm a single bird nor beast ere he hears this strange chronicle."

"You are a wise man," said Ralph.

"I am a prudent man," said Stopsack. "For it's conceivable that, thanks to Hallowborn, Her Majesty's Galápagos Protectorate is about to witness the worst mischief yet wrought by Her Majesty's One True Church—and if Her Majesty's Encantadas Governor managed to avert said mischief, then Her Majesty's Bountiful Largesse might very well descend on the administrator in question. And now you must excuse me whilst I attend to my gubernatorial duties. Feel free to tour the estate. As my Ecuadorian overlords say, *Mi casa est su casa.*"

It turned out that Jonathan Stopsack's gubernatorial duties consisted largely in getting Pablo and Virgilio to perform his gubernatorial duties for him. He ordered the furloughed Ecuadorians to collect his mail, assess the status of the James Isle *orchilla* crop, repair the Puerto Villamil dock on Albemarle Isle, and remind a whaling master recently arrived on Narborough that he was permitted to catch but ten tortoises.

Whilst Pablo and Virgilio rushed off to accomplish these tasks, the masquerade troupers returned to the wharf and, descending to the lagoon, strolled along the shore. In time they came upon a flock of Floreana flamingos sweeping their bills through the water to catch crustaceans and aquatic insects. With their graceful legs and skirts of pink plumage, the birds struck Chloe as ballerinas by other means—and, like ballerinas, they worked hard for their living: in his journal Mr. Darwin had recorded that a Floreana flamingo might spend twelve hours a day feeding itself.

The English adventurers agreed that, owing to their heartfelt performance, Stopsack should now be counted a provisional (perhaps even a permanent) friend of the Encantadas Salvation Brigade. Against Chloe's expectations, two Indians now joined the discussion, having evidently acquired a smattering of English during their tutorials in Chief Nenkiwi's council lodge.

"I create a mistake—so sorry," moaned Cuniche. "I should have said, 'Lady Omega has forbidden Lot's wife to eat the Tower of Babel.'"

"That's quite all right," said Chloe.

"I, too, make a blunder," added Nitopari. "I should have said, 'The ram in the thicket has forbidden the foreskins of men to be crucified.'"

"How much more times we do this, Miss Bathurst?" asked Cuniche. "We are bored to be Jews. Want to be Huancabambas again."

"One additional performance, and we can all go home."

Chloe was about to reiterate her promise when a *tolda* canoe appeared on the lagoon, paddled by a gasping, groaning Eugenio. In a stentorian voice he announced that a brigantine had blown into the Bahía de Cormoranes. His shouts brought Stopsack dashing onto the veranda.

"*Se llama el H.M.S.* Antares!" cried Eugenio. "*Precisamente la nave qua hemos estado esperando!*"

A great tumult ensued, the flamingos ascending in a flurry of flapping wings as the English adventurers, the Huancabambas, and the Governor scrambled into the launches and cast off. The Indians took charge of the oars. Furiously the longboat and the cutter plowed through the mangrove glades to the beach, where Sancho was still hunting sea snails, oblivious to the recent arrival of an angel of death from Oxford.

The *Antares* lay at anchor, her Union Jack snapping in the wind, not fifty yards from the *Covenant*. As Chloe and Ralph passed Stopsack's spyglass back and forth, the brig discharged a half-dozen longboats crammed with men shackled to one another—a treacherous arrangement that prompted Chloe to imagine a mass of connected convicts falling into the bay and disappearing like chunks of bait strung along a crabbing line. But no such catastrophe occurred, and within twenty minutes the prisoners had reached the shore, accompanied by several officers and most of the *Antares*'s crew.

Leaping over the prow of the lead launch, a large and florid man wearing the dress blues of a British naval captain marched up to Ralph. "Is that your peculiar vessel out there?"

"I am Professor Edward Cabot of King's College, Cambridge," said Ralph. "The craft in question is the great fauna carrier *Covenant*, lately out of Puerto Etén, originally out of Mount Ararat. In recent weeks it has indeed been my privilege to command her."

"Ararat?" said Captain Garrity—for that was surely his identity. "You mean where the ark came to rest?"

"The *Covenant* is well and truly the handiwork of that divinely inspired shipwright, Noah," said Ralph.

"We'll see about that," said Garrity, scowling strenuously.

Four white-jacketed sailors unloaded a pair of mahogany sea chests and set them on the sand, flinging back the lids to reveal a jumble of steel machetes and wire garrotes. Whilst the implements glistened in the equatorial sun, a cleric in a black cassock jumped free of his launch and approached the Governor. What most intrigued Chloe about the Reverend Mr. Hallowborn was the congruity between his physiognomy and the mental image she'd formed many months earlier. She'd pictured her *bête noire* as a cadaverous marionette, and it was precisely such a figure who now presented himself, his fingers curled and sharp like dockers' hooks, his skeleton wrapped in the pallid flesh of an incompetent vampire, his brow marred by an ellipsis of round scars.

"Governor Stopsack?" the rector inquired.

"At your service, Reverend. I expected you rather sooner."

"Doldrums, mercurial winds, the vicissitudes of the Horn." Hallowborn cast a suspicious eye on Chloe and Solange. "Have I the pleasure, Governor, of beholding your wife and sister?"

"Miss Quinn is an aerialist, crippled in a fall but recently restored to health," Stopsack explained. "Lady Omega is a mystic prophet, presently intent on being a thorn in your side."

The rector glowered at Chloe. "You don't *look* like a thorn. More like a blossom."

"I am a thorn and a rose, a prickle and a lily, a briar and a dahlia."

"We seek word of the wayward *Equinox* and her company of free-thinkers," said Captain Garrity.

"According to a broadsheet beside the Colnett barrel, the *Equinox* went down in a hurricane, all hands lost," said Ralph, deftly dissembling—and thereby kindling Chloe's admiration: how clever of him to preclude any speculation that Lady Omega and the Transmutationist Club's leader might be the same person.

"All hands?" said Hallowborn, struggling to purge his voice of glee. "Including Chloe Bathurst?"

"The name is not familiar to me," said Ralph, "but the ship's entire company was reportedly drowned."

The rector grew suddenly somber. "Allow me a moment of silent prayer, for the passenger manifest included Malcolm Chadwick, Vicar of Wroxton. I barely knew the man, but I am always aggrieved to lose a colleague in Christ."

For a brief interval not a syllable was spoken in Black Turtle Cove, the quietude broken only by the cries of the boobies and the coarse whisper of the surf. Chloe took the opportunity to survey the prisoners and the brig's company. To a man, the convicts wore their hard lives on their damaged faces: patched eyes, missing teeth, broken noses, livid scars. Even as they trained their pistols on the convicts, the crewmen glanced furtively at the machetes and garrotes, evidently anxious for the slaughter of the Devil's menagerie to begin. The attendant irony—armed guards eager to equip their prisoners with weapons—did not escape Chloe's notice.

Hallowborn set a bony hand on the Governor's sleeve. "This afternoon, with your permission, our convicts, now ninety in number—we lost two south of the line—our convicts will practice their cleansing skills here on Indefatigable, eradicating several score iguanas and tortoises. Tomorrow we sail to Albemarle and begin the extermination in earnest."

"I understand your desire to move swiftly," the Governor replied, "but it happens that theological conditions on our little segment of the equator have grown complicated of late. There will be no exterminations in Galápagos until Lady Omega, Professor Cabot, and Miss Quinn tell you of their recent adventures. Ergo, I must ask you to send Garrity and the convicts back to the ship."

Hallowborn went suddenly flush. There was blood in his veins after all. "You promised Wilberforce we would enjoy your complete cooperation!"

A truculent thrumming echoed through Stopsack's nasal passages. "Whilst the prisoners return to the *Antares,* my servants will paddle you to my hacienda, where we'll down a glass of *pisco* and give Madame Prophet our rapt attention."

"I cannot believe my ears!" wailed Hallowborn.

"Shall I draw you a picture?" said Stopsack. "Someone get me a stick."

"Your proposition is outrageous! Are you aware that I speak for the Anglican Communion and by extension God Almighty?"

"I, on the other hand, speak for Lord Russell and by extension the Queen of England," said the Governor, "and at the moment I would rather risk God's wrath than Her Majesty's. Be of good cheer, Reverend. You'll probably get your massacre. But before we put any reptiles to the sword, I must impose my hospitality on you."

The third and presumably final performance of the masquerade commenced at sundown. Assembled in Stopsack's front parlor, the troupe reached an unprecedented pitch of conviction (or so it seemed to Chloe) as they sought to bedazzle Simon Hallowborn. Lady Omega told the rector, "Heaven is as dismayed by priests who would scour the Encantadas as by pagans who scorn the Almighty." She declared that every slaughtered bird and beast would be "an offering not to the Lord but to Lucifer."

As usual, her disciples muddled their speeches, so that Lot's wife circumcised the Tower of Babel, and the ram in the thicket crucified Cain. Like Eggwort and Stopsack before him, though, Hallowborn seemed more charmed than perturbed by these aberrations, and after the curtain fell he declared, "The harrowing will be deferred by a day at least, perhaps a week, perhaps two, during which interval I shall pray and fast."

Later that evening, sprawled across her bed in the Governor's guest suite, her stomach churning like the turbulent surf of the Bahía de Cormoranes, Chloe once again opened her heart to Heaven, imploring her sacred entity to extend its aegis from one edge of the archipelago to the other. Having prayed, she slept. The Presence visited her dreams, promising to soften the rector's heart and scrub all demonology from his brain.

She awoke at dawn, in thrall to doubt and engulfed by misgivings. Infinity, she feared, was no longer on her side. Her dreams had partaken less of prophecy than of yearning. Inevitably she recalled an immense fishing net hanging from the spars of a half-sunken brigantine in Pacasmayo Harbor. So cryptic, that grid, more space than substance, more air than essence, good for catching puffers but not for holding prayers.

With a machete in his hand and a rumbling in his gut—he'd been fasting for forty-eight hours—Simon Hallowborn wandered amidst the coastal rocks of Indefatigable Isle, sucking in the salty afternoon breeze as he surveyed the huddled iguanas. Their hides displayed tell-tale demonic hues (the splotches ranged from terra-cotta to bright red), and their claws were as sharp as Lucifer's own. Questions haunted him, ambiguity's obstreperous imps. His gift for recognizing Heaven's enemies was indisputable—but did it testify to an analogous talent for knowing God's allies? If so, what did this rarefied sense tell him about the woman who'd transfixed him in Stopsack's parlor?

By the law of averages, this so-called English mystic was a fraud.

False prophets, after all, were ubiquitous. In the Sermon on the Mount, Christ had addressed this scandal directly, warning of miscreants "which come to you in sheep's clothing, but inwardly they are ravening wolves." Professor Cabot's news that the *Equinox* had foundered, dragging Chloe Bathurst to the bottom of the sea, constituted another reason to judge Lady Omega a fraud. Surely the storm bespoke a divine decision to terminate Miss Bathurst's quest, which meant that the Great Winnowing— conceived not only to thwart the actress but also to discourage her fellow freethinkers from following in her wake—in fact enjoyed Heaven's blessing.

And yet he was not at peace. Like the temptations endured by Saint Anthony, a thousand taloned uncertainties clawed at his breast. Against all reason, a peculiar harmony ruled these shores, belying any notion that Satan had made the archipelago his protectorate. Roaming the wild terrain, Simon had observed not only acts of predation but also gestures of affection: a pair of albatrosses doing a courtship dance, a quick-tongued lizard flicking flies from the eyes of a basking fur seal, a finch removing parasites from a giant tortoise's toes. Even the wretched aquatic iguanas had allies, brilliant scarlet crabs who harvested nettlesome bugs from beneath their scales. Why would the Devil permit such benevolence in his *pied-à-terre*? Why would he trouble himself about the comfort of a fur seal or the prosperity of a tortoise? What possible investment could Hell have in the next generation of albatross?

Then there was the indubitable charisma of Lady Omega herself. With her mesmerizing voice and bizarre utterances she really did seem touched from on high. And her story made sense—a forgotten shoot of Jacob's line crossing the Atlantic in Noah's ark, guarding the vessel generation upon generation, receiving God's reward for their constancy: a female prophet, eager to dissuade them from shrinking human heads, eating human flesh, and otherwise risking their immortal souls. The previous afternoon, at Professor Cabot's invitation, Simon had visited the ark, and he'd immediately known it for a consecrated vessel. Descending into its depths, seeing the stalls and corrals, he'd grown delirious with joy, overwhelmed to be standing where once had dwelt the

Adam and Eve of all the world's giraffes—the Adam and Eve of its elephants, zebras, lions, tigers, and rhinoceroses.

Tightening his grip on the machete, he approached an especially fearsome iguana, a four-foot dragon with a gelid eye and ghastly wrinkled skin. He raised his arm. According to Garrity, the blade was sharp enough to behead the reptile in a single stroke. *Show me a sign, O Lord. Give me a reason not to begin the harrowing here and now.*

For a full minute he maintained an executioner's stance. And then it happened, the requested theophany. A vast, clamorous, bulbous form coasted over a stand of banyan trees, casting a shadow as dark as Beelzebub's, and now the intruder drew closer still—a kind of flying-machine, the *Jean-Baptiste Lamarck,* boiler whistling, engine chugging, propellers grinding. The wind rippled the ovoid hot-air bladder, widening the smile of the decorative Man in the Moon. Slowly the airship descended, until the gondola hovered barely twenty feet above the beach. A rope ladder spilled forth. Waving to Simon, two human figures climbed down.

He lowered the machete.

Recognizing the woman, Simon was taken aback. How strange that a creature so ethereal and otherworldly as Lady Omega would place herself aboard a machine so oily and profane as the *Lamarck.* The male passenger, meanwhile, was amongst the last people Simon had ever expected to meet again. But here came the Reverend Mr. Chadwick, presumed dead, full fathom five and all that, striding across the scattered pumice.

"Top of the morning, Simon!"

"Good heavens, Malcolm, is it really you?"

"Yes, but it almost wasn't," said Chadwick, shaking Simon's hand. "The sinking of the *Equinox* nearly did for me. Sad to say, the storm drowned Captain Runciter, Miss Bathurst, and everyone else, or so I surmise. By God's grace I grabbed a floating spar, which bore me to the mouth of the Rio Amazonas." The vicar pointed towards the *Lamarck.* "I was rescued by the master of this ship, who invited me to accompany him on his travels."

"We may have our theological differences, Malcolm, but I'm pleased to see you," said Simon. "Wilberforce's drawing-room seems six thousand miles away, doesn't it?"

"Wilberforce's drawing-room *is* six thousand miles away."

Resuming his tale, Chadwick explained that Capitaine Léourier had in recent years become fascinated by legends of El Dorado, eventually concluding that the object of his quest lay hidden beneath Albemarle Isle. And so the vicar and the aeronaut had flown the length of the Amazon basin, crossed the mountains, and tracked the Humboldt Current to Galápagos. Soaring over the Bahía de Cormoranes earlier that afternoon, the adventurers had spotted a ship that corresponded to the average Christian's mental image of Noah's ark. Curious, they'd touched down here on Indefatigable, soon meeting the Governor, who introduced them to Lady Omega, messenger to the Serugites.

"Quite the most remarkable woman I've ever met," said Chadwick.

Simon faced Lady Omega, who now stood atop a lava rock, aquatic lizards arrayed at her feet as if waiting to receive the Sermon on the Slag. The setting sun enveloped her in a rosy-gold halo, the coruscations dancing along her brilliant white robe and bountiful chestnut hair. Perhaps she was an imposter. Perhaps he should raise his machete and dispatch the immediate iguana. It was all so perplexing.

"More than remarkable in fact," Chadwick continued. "I believe God has blessed the ark keepers with a divine prophet. If I were you, I should heed her every word."

"For he who liveth by the sword shall perish by the sword," said Lady Omega, pointing to Simon's machete.

"My heart quavers," he said.

"I do not doubt it," said Lady Omega.

"My soul trembles."

"Blessed are the marine iguanas," said the prophet. "Blessed are the land lizards, domeshelled tortoises, saddlebacks, slopebacks, mockingbirds, flycatchers, and finches. For they are all of them, each and every one, children of God and beloved of Christ."

"She's telling you to cancel the massacre," said Chadwick.

"I am aware of that," said Simon. "I shall render my decision within a fortnight."

12

Ralph and Solange Are Charged with the Capital Crime of Blasphemy, a Crisis That Rekindles Our Heroine's Passion for the Tree of Life

The dazzling extravagance of the dinner party through which Governor Stopsack sought to celebrate Mr. Chadwick's safe landing in Galápagos, likewise Capitaine Léourier's arrival, at first puzzled Chloe, but by the middle of the feast her confusion had evaporated. To account for the Governor's prodigality—which extended not only to devil-ray soup and breast of flamingo but also to sally-lightfoot crabs, hammerhead-shark fillets, and vintage claret—one need merely consider that he'd probably never before hosted simultaneously an Anglican priest, a Cambridge professor, a Gallic aeronaut, a Peruvian aerialist, and an English mystic.

"A veritable banquet," said Solange, her sea-witch voice chiming above the heron cries wafting into the dining hall.

"If not a bacchanal," said Ralph.

"Tonight's pleasures will come at a price," said Stopsack. "You must sit and listen whilst I outline a scheme designed to serve my material ambitions—and yours as well, I hope. I shall begin by asking Mr. Chadwick whether he tracked down Mr. Hallowborn yesterday."

"We found him on the point of decapitating an iguana," the vicar replied. "Ultimately he relented."

Forgoing the soup, Chloe speared a shark fillet with her fork and transferred it to her china plate. "I believe he's now in rebellion against Wilberforce's theology."

"Alas, Madam Prophet, I would not wager one peso on Hallowborn sheathing his machete for good," said Stopsack. "There's more to this affair than you imagine."

In lieu of an elaboration, the Governor hurled his linen napkin onto the table and, rising, disappeared into the front parlor. He returned bearing desiccated copies of the *Evening Standard*. "I subscribe to the world's most diverting newspaper, receiving a bundle of issues every month through the barrel." He opened the topmost copy to an article headed SUPREME BEING SURVIVES BIBLICAL CONTRADICTIONS and subheaded DILUVIAN LEAGUE TO RECOVER GENESIS ARK FROM ARARAT. "The journalist Popplewell routinely reports on something called the Great God Contest. Have you heard of it? In this particular piece, he tells how the Percy Shelley Society was convinced to sponsor a search for Noah's ark."

"Not only have I heard of it," said Mr. Chadwick, cracking a crab's fighting claw, "but I once served on the judges' bench."

"Do you mean you're *this* Reverend Chadwick?" gasped Stopsack, pecking Popplewell's article with a rigid forefinger.

"Indeed. Has the prize been awarded yet?"

The Governor devoured a forkful of flamingo and shook his head. "Not according to the most recent issue to reach the barrel." Retrieving the next paper in the stack, he turned to a headline reading ATHEIST JUDGES UNIMPRESSED BY COSMIC COINCIDENCES and subheaded FREE-THINKING FEMALE NATURALIST TO SEEK PROFANE "TREE OF LIFE." "Here we learn how the Society dispatched a band of freethinkers to Galápagos, which supposedly harbors species useful in illustrating a disproof of God. They set sail on the *Equinox*"—Stopsack pointed his fork at Ralph—"the same brig that occasioned Garrity's question to you yesterday. Blasted by a hurricane, right? No survivors?"

"So say the rumors on display in Post Office Bay," said Ralph.

"The rumors, alas, are true," said Mr. Chadwick to the Governor. "On orders from Wilberforce, I was traveling with the very religious skeptics of whom you speak, that I might learn whence the naturalist got her theory. I grew quite fond of the woman."

"Her death must have caused you considerable grief," said Solange.

"Female naturalists, I would imagine, are inherently adorable creatures," said Ralph.

"Considerable grief, yes," said Mr. Chadwick, his voice breaking, a display of sentiment that surprised but did not displease Chloe.

"You can see why I accuse Hallowborn of pursuing the extermination with mixed motives," said Stopsack. "Perhaps he really believes Satan fashioned the ancestors of certain Galápagos fauna, but his *real* goal is to obliterate evidence for the late Miss Bathurst's Tree of Life."

"Which means you're more prepared than ever to defy Hallowborn?" asked Chloe.

"Which means I'm eager to undertake an audacious project," Stopsack replied. "Esteemed guests and fellow Christians, a great opportunity lies before us. We can win the Shelley Prize!" Bending over his *Evening Standard* collection, he pounded his fist on COSMIC COINCIDENCES. "Think about it! The Diluvian League won't find the Genesis vessel on Ararat, for it's sitting under our very noses! I invite you to join me as I sail the ark to Panama, drag it across the isthmus, and display it before the judges!"

"A splendid idea," said Capitaine Léourier. *"Quelle ingéniosité!"*

"A wretched idea," said Mr. Chadwick. *"Quelle stupidité!* Governor, you should know that I desire no further truck with the Oxford sybarites. The Great God Contest is a corrupt institution, and I regret that I once lent it my good name."

"I agree with the vicar," said Ralph (by which he doubtless meant, *As a devotee of Omar Khayyám, I cannot be a party to God's corroboration*).

"It sounds like a silly competition," said Solange (surely meaning, *I love the Great God Contest, but only if it sends the Almighty packing*).

"A silly competition that could place nearly two thousand pounds in the pocket of every person at this table," noted Stopsack.

"With such a sum I could mount the ultimate search for El Dorado," mused Léourier.

"I should like to know Madam Prophet's opinion." The Governor indicated Chloe by pointing with a flamingo bone. "Do you doubt that Heaven would have us go to Oxford? Are you not eager to inform Christendom that, owing to the ark and its Hebrew guardians, modern men and women may now hold the God of Abraham factual?"

Despite her knowledge that the vessel anchored in the Bahía de Cormoranes was not the Genesis ark, Chloe found herself in sympathy with Stopsack's plan. For if the *Covenant* indeed enthralled a majority of Shelley Prize judges, with Popplewell reporting that momentous outcome in the *Evening Standard*, did it not follow that thousands of ambivalent Christians throughout England and the Continent might progress from a manifestly plausible belief in the prophet Noah to a shattering apprehension of the Presence? Might not a man who understood the rainbow covenant to be a real historical event soon come to hear the morning stars sing together?

"I pray you, Governor, restrain your excitement for the nonce," she said, eating a morsel of shark. "First we must hear Mr. Hallowborn's decision. Only then might we speak of winning the gold."

"It's not *worth* winning," Mr. Chadwick insisted.

"Whenever there's a ten-thousand-pound purse at stake," said Stopsack to Chloe, "you will find me the paragon of patient men"—he took a sip of *pisco*—"and the very soul of forbearance."

A wakening in the Governor's guest suite shortly after sunrise, Chloe put on her white robe and, as she'd done every morning for the previous ten days, repaired stealthily to the kitchen. Finding Pablo about, she requested that he serve her coffee on the veranda. By nine o'clock she was relaxing in the open air, munching on cassava bread and using Pablo's brew to dilute the previous evening's indulgence in *pisco* and *caxirí* beer, her face shaded by a pink parasol planted on the deck like a conquistador's flag.

A *tolda* canoe appeared, Eugenio working the paddle, the Reverend Mr. Hallowborn seated stiffly beneath the canopy like one of Charon's fares crossing the Styx. He cried out to Chloe, saying, "I would have a moment of Lady Omega's time!" She called back, proposing that they share her carafe of coffee (though warning him it was strong to the point of proximate sin), an invitation he accepted without hesitation.

As Chloe revisited the kitchen and procured an empty coffee cup for the rector, a question wrapped itself, serpent-like, about her mind. If Hallowborn joined with Eggwort in pronouncing Lady Omega a fraud, would she feel deserted by the God of her epiphany?

The question continued to haunt her after she returned to the veranda.

"You have transformed my dark night of the soul into a bright noon of the spirit," said the rector, pulling up a chair and joining her beneath the parasol. "Had Lady Omega not come to Galápagos with her Indian disciples and their ark, I would have stained my hands with the blood of blameless beasts."

For a glorious instant Chloe's heart occupied every part of her body. Her veins all pulsed with joy. Hands trembling, she directed a stream of coffee into Hallowborn's cup. "How pleased I am that the morning stars have sung to you."

"One day you will be designated the Church of England's first mystic."

It would be unfitting, she decided, for a divine messenger to dance about the wharf like a gypsy. Instead she took a bite of cassava bread and said, "In Heaven you will be honored largely for sparing the animals, though your appreciation of Lady Omega will also draw praise."

Hallowborn took his coffee in hand, fluted his lips, and sipped. Setting down the cup, he stretched out his arms in a benediction embracing the wharf's *habitués*, twenty birds at least, the majority engaged in extracting invertebrates from the railing. "I hereby ask absolution of these finches and thrushes."

"They are gracious creatures, certain to forgive you. What will you tell Bishop Wilberforce?"

"That Chloe Bathurst is dead. That a wayward Israelite tribe is flourishing in Peru. That God gave them a prophet. That the Devil authored not a single Encantadas species."

For a wordless interval Chloe and the rector savored their coffee, until at last she squeezed his hand and said, "Reverend, might I solicit your counsel in a theological matter? No, not just theological—political as well. Before the month is out, Governor Stopsack and I hope to transport Noah's ark to England and display it before the citizenry in corroboration of Hebrew Scripture. What do you think of our project?"

Hallowborn interlaced his long fingers. "Though my own faith has never required tangible testaments, I suspect such an exhibition might benefit the great mass of men. But I must advise you to stay clear of Oxford, where the local rakehells have turned the God question into a ridiculous sport played for a large cash prize."

"You may be sure that Lady Omega eschews all such profane competitions," said Chloe, thinking that an apostle of the Presence might take a more nuanced view of the matter.

The rector untangled his fingers and said, "I would never have imagined otherwise."

Upon finishing his coffee, Mr. Hallowborn took leave of Chloe, citing an obligation to return to the *Antares* and offer the ninety convicts one last sermon before their incarceration. She spent the morning spreading the good news throughout the hacienda, so that breakfast became a *carnaval de la victoria* in which even the Governor participated. Throughout the meal, Ralph, Solange, and Mr. Chadwick heaped accolades on the English mystic, being careful not to accidentally call her "Chloe" or "Miss Bathurst." Perhaps Stopsack had already deduced that the whole Lost Thirteenth Tribe business was a hoax, but in any event he kept his own counsel, speaking only to laud Madam Prophet's compassion for the Encantadas fauna.

In the days that followed, Chloe realized that the ghost of Doubting Thomas had laid claim to her imagination. Peace of mind would elude her until she'd witnessed in person not only the relocation of the ninety prisoners to Mephistropolis but also Simon Hallowborn's subsequent departure for England. She shared her forebodings with the Governor, who explained (to her immense relief) that he was about to take up the pen of his authority and write the final chapter in the short, shabby history of the Great Winnowing.

"Tomorrow is the Hebrew Sabbath," he said, "and then comes the Christian Sabbath, and the very next day, Madam Prophet, we shall bring this distasteful matter to a conclusion, whereupon you and I can set about claiming the Byssheans' treasure."

The Monday in question dawned ominously, a thick and treacherous fog swaddling Indefatigable, but Stopsack decided to attempt the crossing anyway. Shortly after eight o'clock the *Hippolyta* sailed out of the cove, crewed by all four furloughed Ecuadorians and carrying the European adventurers (minus Léourier, who'd elected to spend the morning browsing through the Governor's library). The mood aboard the schooner was at once festive and tense. Although the masquerade troupe still took satisfaction in their recent feat, they could not ignore the shadow cast by Stopsack's intention to win the prize. Whereas Ralph, Solange, and Mr. Chadwick made no effort to disguise their distaste for the scheme, Chloe, braving a trio of sneers, speculated aloud that a finding in God's favor at Alastor Hall might bring solace to countless Christians presently enduring crises of faith.

Soon after the *Hippolyta* rounded Pelican Point, the fog lifted, and the balance of the voyage occurred without mishap, the company reaching Post Office Bay in time to see the *Antares*'s crew pilot her along the wharf towards a berth adjacent to Eggwort's shallop. The furloughed Ecuadorians guided the *Hippolyta* into the outermost slip. Disembarking, the Governor headed for the prison ship, whilst Chloe and her friends ascended to a natural balcony of frozen lava near the summit of Mount Pajas, so they might observe the maneuver from a safe distance (an eleventh-hour revolt by the convicts being all too easy to imagine). The balcony offered an unobstructed view of Mephistropolis with its grim watchtower and stout brick wall, a panorama that the adventurers enlarged by means of Léourier's glass.

Although Stopsack had probably never before directed such an undertaking, he performed his duties with brio, skillfully heaping verbal abuse on the manacled inmates ("Step lively, you dunderheads!" "Keep moving, you walleyed toads!" "Stay in line, you hairy apes!"), whilst Captain Garrity's sailors, fowling pieces in hand, poked and prodded the ninety down the *Antares*'s gangplank, along the wharf, across the tuff-strewn

basin, and through the thorny perimeter fence. All during this fitful
march, the elderly Kommandant Hengstenberg, whose Prussian affecta-
tions included a monocle, a waxed mustache, and a riding crop, likewise
sought to intimidate the convicts. In a voice so loud it easily rode the
torpid air to Chloe's ears, he told the prisoners they must not imagine
swimming to freedom, the waters off Duntopia being "inhabited by
hammerhead sharks with an appetite for English flesh." Mr. Hallowborn, meanwhile, assumed a consoling role, assuring the convicts that
once they'd atoned for their crimes through hard bondage, God would
look favorably on their petitions to enter Heaven.

After the ninety had passed through the main gate and assembled in
the exercise yard, an ursine capitán strode out of the stone keep leading
a dozen guards brandishing carbines. With so many men waving firearms in their faces, the convicts grew visibly alarmed, but then Stopsack
made a momentous announcement (far more heartening than Hallowborn's soggy promises of salvation). Every man who toed the line, causing no trouble whilst residing in Mephistropolis, would have his sentence
reduced by one-quarter, just as if he'd butchered his share of reptiles.

Despite their shackles, the inmates crossed the yard with a buoyant
gait, disappearing into the keep.

His mission accomplished, Stopsack took leave of Hengstenberg and,
transcending his bulk, climbed Mount Pajas to converse with Chloe and
her friends. Wheezing and sweating, he explained that for the next two
hours he must ensconce himself in Hengstenberg's office, signing papers
legalizing the convicts' deracination from Dartmoor Prison to Her Majesty's Galápagos Penal Colony, the better to establish that Charles Isle
was now of a piece with the British Empire.

The troupe and the Governor descended in tandem. As Stopsack
returned to Mephistropolis, Chloe and her friends strode towards
Post Office Bay, taking satisfaction in the lush fecundity they observed
along the way. Here on the lava field: a bright yellow short-spined lizard
they'd delivered from the wrath of Wilberforce. There, near a fresh-water
spring: a clan of saddleback tortoises who would never suffer the garrote.
Beyond, in a thicket: a scattering of ground finches, forever spared the

fowling pieces of Garrity's sailors. In time the adventurers reached the wharf, where Chloe basked in the imagined gratitude of the very iguana colony she'd observed upon landing in the Encantadas.

For several silent minutes she stood and watched topsails and head-sails blossoming on the spars of the *Antares*. The crewmen raveled up the mooring lines, and the brig blew free of her berth, then headed south across the bay towards the open sea. There, it was finished: she'd beheld Simon Hallowborn exit her life and the prisoners enter a place where they could work no mischief. Having fulfilled her sacred obligation to the Galápagos fauna, she could now turn to the formidable—perhaps impossible—task of getting the ark to Oxford.

During the week that followed the *Antares*'s departure for England, Malcolm enlisted all his powers of persuasion in attempting to discourage Stopsack from becoming a Shelley Prize contestant, an endeavor in which he found ready allies in Dartworthy and Miss Kirsop but a stubborn antagonist in Miss Bathurst, who continued to argue (despite her knowledge of its origins) that the ark, astutely deployed, might bring spiritual blessings to the multitudes. Whilst Dartworthy tried to convince Stopsack that hauling the *Covenant* across the isthmus would prove an endeavor only slightly less insane than trying to sail her around the Horn, Miss Kirsop told the Governor that, in the event the ark failed to win the competition, the Roman Church might sponsor its own version of the Great Winnowing, thereby causing no end of headaches for his administration. But it was Malcolm who (in his own estimation at least) offered the most persuasive case. The Shelley Prize was a moral miasma. No genuine Christian would imagine acquiring so sordid a reward.

Despite Malcolm's exhortations, or perhaps because of them, the seventh evening in September found the Governor leading Eugenio, Sancho, Pablo, and Virgilio in a raid on the *Covenant*. Armed with truncheons, Stopsack and the furloughed Ecuadorians sailed the *Hippolyta* out to the ark, dragged the sleeping Indians from their hammocks, and ferried them to shore, leaving all six to fend for themselves in the mangrove glades. In his subsequent gubernatorial proclamation, Stopsack explained that his devotion to the Anglican Communion had compelled him to appropriate "one of Christendom's most sacred relics, lest it devolve to those who would use it for personal gain," by which of course he meant that, bent on using one of Christendom's most sacred relics for personal gain, he'd sought to prevent its devolving to anyone else.

From his most recent conversations with Dartworthy and Miss Kirsop, Malcolm had concluded that the Governor's hunger for the prize no longer distressed them, for they seemed exclusively focused on their scheme to visit every whaling ship, sealing brig, and survey vessel stopping in the Encantadas until they finally found a captain who liked the idea of taking on four English explorers pledged to serving him faithfully in exchange for their eventual passage home. It thus came as a shock to Malcolm when Dartworthy and Miss Kirsop appeared at his bedside late one night, kerosene lanterns in hand, and announced that they'd discovered how to prevent Stopsack from entering the contest. Annoyed and confused, Malcolm nevertheless agreed to board the longboat and accompany them as they rowed through the inland waterways and beyond. And so it happened that, after a half-hour's journey (during which his companions refused to specify whatever game was afoot), he found himself in the Bahía de Cormoranes, heading towards the ark.

"We hope you will sanction tonight's escapade," said Dartworthy, "though we mean to carry it out in any case."

"We thought it would be wrong to burn the *Covenant* without telling you first," added Miss Kirsop.

"Burn it?" gasped Malcolm, appalled.

"Given the success of the masquerade, Solange and I now deem Miss Chloe Bathurst capable of whatever ridiculous feat might catch her fancy," Dartworthy explained. "With Stopsack cheering her on, she'll drag the ark over the isthmus, sail it across the Atlantic, pilot it up the Thames, adopt the persona of a conventional Christian, and convince all six Oxford judges that a proof of God lies to hand."

"This is madness," said Malcolm.

"What choice do we have?" asked Miss Kirsop.

"The choice not to burn the ark," said Malcolm.

"I thought you were now a freethinker, Reverend," said Miss Kirsop. "Evidently I was mistaken."

Throughout the remainder of the crossing, Malcolm simply sat and brooded, mutely formulating arguments against the intended crime and imagining the arsonists' rebuttals. Miss Kirsop countered his silence by chattering about the imminent adventure, explaining how every night for the past week she and Ralph had collected kindling from the arid inland thickets, furtively borne the sticks to the vessel, and distributed them throughout the cargo hold. The *Covenant* was a floating tinderbox, awaiting a fateful spark.

No sooner had they all climbed the rope ladder to the weather deck than Dartworthy disappeared into the forecastle. He returned carrying a bundle of dried reeds, which he proceeded to ignite with the flame of his lantern. When Malcolm made a final plea for canceling the plan, asserting that no person had the right to obliterate an artifact so central to the Huancabamba religion, Dartworthy reminded him that for the past century the Indians had been happy to let the ark rot in a salt marsh.

As she dragged the door free of the hatch, Miss Kirsop quoted Macbeth. "If it were done when 'tis done, then 'twere well it were done quickly."

Burning faggot in one hand, lantern in the other, Dartworthy descended into the hold, bound for the secret pyre.

"Do you remember my constellations?" Miss Kirsop asked Malcolm. Stretching an arm towards the Milky Way, she sifted the stars through her splayed fingers. "When we met on St. Paul's Rocks, I told you I'd sown the sky with constellations made of my personal demons."

"Miss Kirsop, I am not now, nor shall I ever be, interested in your mental disease."

Despite this protestation, she insisted on telling him of a starry succubus fond of poisoning village wells, and she was about to relate the story of "my most demonic alter ego, a streetwalker adept at castrating her clients with her father's shaving razor," when Dartworthy emerged from the hold, followed by a helix of thick gray smoke.

"It would be in our collective interest to abandon ship," he said.

A half-hour later, Malcolm, seated on a lava rock, observed the burning *Covenant*—as did Dartworthy and Miss Kirsop, standing together on the beach. Already the flames had broken free of the hull and begun stabbing through the weather deck. The Bahía de Cormoranes mirrored the blaze, the glimmering orange tongues flashing across the waters like colonies of phosphorescent algae. Now the flames were climbing the masts, turning the spars into torches, the sails into billowing scarlet clouds. Like some hellish tree dropping overripe fruits, the ark shed great chunks of burning canvas, the embers hitting the bay and expiring in reptilian hisses.

"'Tis done—and quickly," said Miss Kirsop.

"And well," added Dartworthy.

"Nothing good will come of this," said Malcolm.

"Stay where you are!" a male voice bellowed from out of the swamp.

Armed with a pistol, Governor Stopsack quit the shadows, accompanied by Eugenio and Sancho. Shackles jangled on the servants' belts. When Stopsack, raising his kerosene lantern high, shouted the inevitable command—"Arms out! Wrists together!"—Malcolm was the first to comply, though the arsonists (having every reason to suppose the pistol loaded) also assented in a timely manner.

"Your crime played out more conspicuously than you would have wished," the Governor explained whilst Eugenio manacled Dartworthy's wrists and ankles. "I saw the flames from my veranda." He turned to Malcolm, offering him a dispensational smile. "As a mere bystander to this incident—or so I assume—you may leave whenever you wish. Professor Cabot and Miss Quinn, however, are going to Mephistropolis, there to remain till Eggwort puts them on trial or the Devil sponsors a frost fair, whichever happens first."

As Sancho shackled Miss Kirsop, she told Stopsack, "You are correct to hold Mr. Chadwick blameless—and mistaken to imagine God ever wanted you to enter the contest."

"Your frustration is understandable, Governor," said Malcolm. "But in binding two stalwart British subjects over to Hengstenberg you'll be simultaneously committing a cardinal sin and making a grave political miscalculation."

"You can't detain us without bringing formal charges," noted Dartworthy.

"Then I formally charge you with gross sacrilege, radical impiety, and arrant blasphemy," replied Stopsack.

"Let's be honest, Governor," said Miss Kirsop. "Your sensitivity to sacrilege is such that you wouldn't care if we made a chicken coop of the True Cross or a spitoon of the Holy Grail. The problem is that you think we cheated you out of ten thousand pounds."

"Five thousand," said Stopsack. "I was prepared to split the prize with Madam Prophet."

"Here's a detail for you to ponder—the *Covenant* is a fraud," said Malcolm. "It was built by a Huancabamba religious sect a mere hundred years ago."

"Mr. Hallowborn has judged the ark authentic," Stopsack replied. "Eggwort believes in it, too, for that matter. Those endorsements are good enough for me."

Silence descended on the cove, the various factions having turned their attention to the dying *Covenant*. As seawater flooded the gutted hull, the ark begin its vertical voyage, plank by plank, yardarm by yardarm. Soon only the mainmast was visible, piercing the waves like a sword—and then even that flaming Excalibur was gone.

"Miss Quinn and I eagerly await our day in court," Dartworthy insisted.

"We are keen to advertise our low opinion of piety," added Miss Kirsop.

"Allow me to remind you that Eggwort will be conducting the trial," said Stopsack. "If I were you, I'd be dreading my day in court with every fiber of my being."

Only through the application of hindsight did Granville Heathway understand that any painting titled *No Transmutation Without Plenary Copulation*, much less one featuring a man and woman engaged in the marital act, would distress his custodians. At the time, however, Dr. Earwicker's anger surprised him, as did Dr. Quelp's conclusion that poor old Heathway must be madder than previously supposed, for who but a victim of satyriasis would create so scandalous a tableau? Happily for Granville, nobody had made an initial accounting of his art supplies, and so when Tobias the orderly sought to repossess them, barging into his cell and bearing away four camel's-hair brushes and seven tubes of paint (plus every one of his pictures), two brushes and four pigment capsules went unclaimed, Granville having secluded them in the dovecote, where the fastidious Tobias had not cared to search.

There remained the challenge of finding an object upon which to apply the paint, a problem whose solution, he now realized, was staring him in the face. He would produce his next work on the north wall of his cell: a barren whitewashed plane, surely as suitable for his visions as was the Sistine Chapel ceiling for Michelangelo's. Pondering potential subjects, he decided to adorn the wall with a representation of itself. Through this clever choice of theme, he would avoid consuming any actual pigment, for he could achieve a convincing effect simply by running his brush, its bristles moistened with drinking water, along the naked surface.

Before Granville could begin creating *Wall on Wall,* Achilles wafted into the cell and landed on the dovecote. Granville set his brush aside, for every message from Constantinople deserved the same immediate attention he would accord an angelic annunciation or a *mene mene tekel upharsin.*

> *Dearest Father,*
>
> *Is it possible that, concerning Noah and the Flood, the Mussulmans' Koran is more accurate than the Hebrews' Bible? In any event, two days ago the Grand Vizier received a semaphore message from Mr. Dalrymple. NO ARK ON ARARAT. DISMAYED BUT UNDAUNTED. ON TO AL-JUDI.*
>
> *Naturally this news put me in a melancholy frame of mind. Were it not for yesterday's encounter in the hookah-den, I would now be awash*

in self-pity. The longer I talked with Dr. Rosalind Franklin, however, the more trifling my own troubles seemed, and in time I forgot Mr. Dalrymple's communiqué.

No sooner had I entered the grotto than Yusuf Effendi urged me to present myself to the disconsolate woman sitting beside the samovar. Dr. Franklin, he explained, had traveled here from London, seeking an educated person with whom she might discuss her illness whilst inhaling the hookah-den's famously potent hashish—for Cannabis *reportedly mitigates the collateral effects of "cobalt radiotherapy," a treatment that the physicians at the Royal Marsden Hospital had recently inflicted upon her.*

A petite woman with pleasant features and lustrous black hair, Dr. Franklin at first seemed wary of me, she being a Jew, a scientist, and a resident of the year 1958, I being a Gentile, a schoolmaster, and a denizen of 1850. Undaunted, I told her I had recently conversed with two great natural philosophers. Although a Francophile, Dr. Franklin could recall no Teilhard de Chardin, even after I cited his discovery of Peking Man. My acquaintanceship with Abbot Mendel, by contrast, impressed her, his triple-cross pea plant experiments being (as she phrased it) "amongst the most elegant in the history of science." Before I knew it, she was sharing her hashish, her confidences, and that je ne sais quoi *a charming woman exudes wherever she goes.*

"I was always such an athletic girl, scrambling up and down the Alps like a goat, and now, suddenly—" She passed her splayed hands up and down her slender torso. "Right now I can't tell if it's the cancer itself or the treatment that has me feeling so bloody wretched. Intravenous radiotherapy entails many unintended consequences. Nausea, fatigue, dry mouth. At least I've kept my hair."

Yes, Father, she did say "cancer." I'd never heard anyone speak that word before.

"You indeed have splendid hair," I told her.

"The rest of me's all chopped apart."

"I'm sorry."

"Left ovary gone, right ovary, uterus."

"My poor Dr. Franklin."

She filled her lungs with smoke and held her breath, sending the hashish on an errand of mercy. "A double paradox presents itself. X-ray crystallography is the love of my life, and yet all those high-frequency emissions probably caused my tumors, and to top it off I'm now pumping myself full of radioactive elements, hoping to arrest a disease attributable to radioactive elements."

"Tonight I shall pray that your illness remains in abeyance until a cure is found."

"Don't be a schmuck.*"*

"You mustn't talk that way, Miss Franklin."

"Call me Rosalind."

"Is that truly acceptable to you?"

"Anything but Rosy."

"Call me Bertram."

My companion consumed another billow of hashish. "I hope I'm not remembered as a martyr. I detest martyrdom. Jews have enough problems. I can just imagine my obituary in the Times. *'Heedless of the hazards posed by her X-ray diffraction machine, Dr. Franklin sacrificed herself to the cause of English scientific supremacy. For it happens that without her unprecedented images the Cambridge team of Watson and Crick would probably not have been the first to reveal the secret of life, as the American Linus Pauling was also bent on divining the structure of DNA.'"*

"DNA?"

"Deoxyribonucleic acid," Dr. Franklin explained.

"The secret of life?"

"A tedious molecule, to be sure, only four nucleotides, but it contains all the information needed to make a carrot or a cricket or the Archbishop of Canterbury."

"So this DNA is the stuff through which God brought forth living things?"

"Frankly, Bertram, I don't think God had much to do with it. Back at my Birkbeck College laboratory, we sometimes joke that DNA stands

for Deities Needn't Apply." Again she inhaled a quantity of Cannabis. *"Tell me about Mendel."*

"A frustrated man," I said. "He knew he would never gain proper recognition in his lifetime."

Dr. Franklin flinched. "At least he had a lifetime. No, forgive me— I'm feeling sorry for myself. I've had a career. Not only my DNA pictures and my virus work but also my early days in Paris. I discovered precisely how heated carbons that turn to graphite differ chemically from those that don't. I'm curious, Bertram, what did Mendel call his hereditary units?"

"Hereditary units. What do you call them?"

"Genes. G-e-n-e-s." The hash began to work its magic, eliciting a melodious "Hmmaaahhh" from Dr. Franklin. "Every human cell is crammed with genes, clustered in forty-six paired packets—chromosomes—except for our reproductive cells, of course, which contain twenty-three per egg and twenty-three per sperm. Hmmaaahhh. For many years smart money said genes were composed of protein, but then somebody figured out that DNA carries the code in toto. *I'll give credit to Crick, and even Jim Watson,* schnorrer *though he could be. They believed that if you built an accurate DNA model, you'd expose the molecule's method of self-replication, which means you'd understand exactly how encoded characteristics and blueprinted traits are passed from cell to cell and ultimately generation to generation."*

"Schnorrer?"

"It's what it sounds like. Hmmaaahhh. Francis and Jim chased after that structure like beagles on a bunny, and by God they caught it, whereas I was always more interested in how nucleic acids fit into the general scheme of things."

"'Characteristics' and 'traits'—the very terms Mendel used!"

"You actually got to blow hash with the man. I must say I'm jealous. Imagine how you'd feel if I'd gone pub crawling with Jesus."

"I can't tell if you're being reverent or facetious."

"Me neither. Hmmaaahhh. My sickness is a double paradox, and DNA is a double helix: two sugar-phosphate chains, intertwined like

bootlaces, forming the backbone of the base pairs, adenine always joined to thymine, guanine to cytosine, the bonded chemicals spanning the spirals to create the most momentous ladder since Jacob dreamed of climbing to Heaven. How's that for a bit of Torah from a secular Jew? During cell division, the thing unzips along its length, each helix becoming the template for a new one. Francis and Jim published right away. 'It has not escaped our notice,' they concluded, 'that the specific pairing we have postulated immediately suggests a possible copying mechanism for the genetic material.' I love that. 'Not escaped our notice.' Reverse chutzpah. *Someday those boys will get a bloody Nobel Prize, though I doubt they could've done it without those nice crisp DNA photographs I was snapping down at King's College. My best shots revealed that the molecule has a dry crystalline A-form and a wet paracrystalline B-form. I'm convinced that my boss appropriated my sharpest wet-form image, number fifty-one, and gave it to Jim."*

"*Then your boss is a* schnorrer, *too.*"

"*Hmmaaahhh. Look at number fifty-one with a scientist's squint, and you'll see that DNA is a bloody double helix. I'm pretty sure my data also fell into Jim's hands, notably my deduction that the chains are anti-parallel, like escalators moving in opposite directions.*"

"*I think you should get a Nobel Prize, too, Rosalind, not just Watson and Crick.*"

"*Think again,*" she said. "*You see, they don't give that award to—*"

"*To Jews?*"

She shook her head.

"*To women?*" I asked.

"*To the dead,*" she replied with a brittle laugh. "*Guess what, Bertram? I'm feeling better. The queasiness is gone. I can bear the abdominal pains. Cannabis is the best idea Nature ever had. Cannabis and companionship.*" My crystallographer looked me in the eye, and I realized she possessed not only the sensual beauty that will emanate from a female face but the ineffable beauty that will arise from a female brain. "*I wish we could get to know each other,*" she continued. "*Given sufficient time, I'm sure I would find you fascinating.*"

"The mystery of it all," I said.

"The mystery of it all," she echoed, then set down her hookah hose and, gaining her feet, smoothed her skirt with her palms. "Here's my pledge, Bertram—to you and to biophysics and to the God of my fathers. This won't be the last time you see me. Tu comprends, mon cher? I'll go home to London, and I'll keep picking viruses apart—polio, tobacco mosaic, turnip mosaic—and I'll take my bloody radiotherapy at Marsden, and then I'll come here for more Cannabis."

"Père Teilhard also spoke of viruses."

"Cause of la grippe, amongst other things." Dr. Franklin sidled away from the table. "First they shot me full of radioactive cobalt, then came radioactive gold. There are lots of elements left. Iodine, zinc, lead, lithium, titanium."

"I'll be waiting for you, Rosalind. I'll keep the pipe loaded."

"Yes. Do that."

"Once you're back in 1958, please perform a boon for me. I would know Père Teilhard's present situation. Is he alive? Did Rome permit him to publish?"

"Your Rosalind is on the case." She sidled into the hookah-den's impacted gloom. "Au revoir, Bertram." The darkness consumed her. "Je crois que je t'aime."

My French is feeble, Father, but I know what she said. My emotions are a dizzying mixture of exhilaration over her affection for me and bitterness concerning her plight. Will you pray for her?

Your devoted son,
Bertram

After securing Achilles's message in the nightstand, Granville pondered his son's attitude to Miss Franklin. At one time the thought of Bertram developing a passionate friendship with a woman of the Abrahamic religion would have troubled him, but as a madhouse resident he saw no reason to favor the Gentile persuasion over the Hebrew. Of course, there was little point in imagining Bertram and Miss Franklin spending their lives together. They might marry outside their respective faiths but not their respective centuries. And beyond the metaphysical difficulties loomed the tragedy of Miss Franklin's ruined health. If Granville was correctly interpreting her words, such future cancer-fighting miracles as cobalt infusions and titanium injections suffered from the drawback of not working very well.

Solemnly he returned Achilles to the dovecote, then bowed his head, clasped his hands, and entered into negotiations with Heaven. He prayed that a Dr. Rosalind Franklin not yet born might be cured of tumors not yet grown, for her destiny was to apprehend crystals and *la grippe* as had no person before her. Surely that wasn't asking too much.

When Chloe learned that Ralph and Solange had burned the *Covenant* and that Stopsack had in consequence imprisoned them in Mephistropolis, she underwent a kind of sea change. For three tumultu-ous days she ceased to be an apostle of the Presence and became instead a force of Nature. Sparks streaked through her veins. Bitter winds churned the marrow of her bones. Even Françoise Gauvin, excoriating her fellow *Raft of the Medusa* castaways for descending into barbarism, had never attained such an apex of rage.

Although Chloe focused her anger primarily on the Governor, whose vindictive behavior merited its own chapter in the annals of spite, she was no less furious with Ralph and Solange, who'd so recklessly shut the portal through which thousands of wretches might have glimpsed the light of eternity. "They had no right to destroy the thing!" she fumed at Mr. Chadwick. "Why did you let them do it?"

"I protested their escapade in the strongest possible language."

"Come clean, Reverend. You protested, but you were just as happy to see the *Covenant* sink, lest I bring the Presence to Christendom."

"I shall attribute that false accusation to your agitated state of mind."

It went without saying that she would not remain a guest at the Governor's hacienda, but she said so anyway, to his face, using the occa-sion to call him "the prince of piranhas." Mr. Chadwick was also eager to leave Indefatigable, likewise Léourier, whose high opinion of Stopsack (based on nothing beyond the Governor's clever plan for winning the contest) had dissolved the instant he learned of Ralph and Solange's incarceration. The Huancabambas were equally impatient to depart, having spent the past two weeks coping with rain and hunger in the mangrove glades.

After studying Léourier's chart, Chloe decided to transplant everyone to Hood's Isle, a flat and featureless zone renowned for its colonies of sea lions. As the southernmost Galápagos formation, Hood presented few navigational difficulties, and it lay sufficiently close to the penal colony to facilitate visitations with her friends.

Whilst Mr. Chadwick and Léourier made the crossing in the *Lamarck*, Chloe and her disciples traveled to their new home aboard the *Hippolyta*, crewed by the furloughed Ecuadorians on orders from the Governor (who now wanted this dubious English mystic out of his life as soon as possible). Hood proved eminently habitable, having once been a destination of religious ascetics, runaway slaves, and social outcasts. In the previous century these fugitives had built a row of hovels and shacks along the central ridge, and it took Chloe and her company but five days to refurbish the deserted town.

Throughout their subsequent sojourn, an interval that the settlers measured first in weeks and then in months, Chloe moped about the island observing the sea lions and dreaming up unlikely schemes for rescuing Ralph and Solange, the most untenable of which had her abducting Orrin Eggwort with the aid of her disciples. As for the Indians, they found considerable amusement in constructing three outrigger canoes using timber harvested from verdant Indefatigable. At first Cuniche, Nitopari, Pirohua, Ascumiche, Yitogua, and Rapra were content to employ these craft as a fishing fleet (so that the community's larders were always bursting with seafood), but then they became more adventurous. Upon organizing their fellowship into three two-man teams, they staged an arduous month-long regatta that required them to thrice circumnavigate the entire archipelago, including distant Wenman and remote Culpepper.

Mr. Chadwick, meanwhile, essayed the role of diplomat. As Hood's ambassador to both Her Majesty's Galápagos Protectorate and the Empire of Duntopia, he employed the *Lamarck,* Léourier at the helm, to visit Stopsack every Tuesday and Eggwort every Thursday. Come evening, Chloe would stand on the lee shore and watch the clattering airship touch down, sending a dozen annoyed sea lions retreating into the surf, and then Mr. Chadwick, disembarking, would deliver yet another dispatch she did not want to hear.

By the vicar's account, Stopsack had washed his hands and cleansed his conscience of the whole *Covenant* affair, refusing to allow that in condemning two British subjects to the whims of a monomaniacal American expatriate he had woefully exceeded his authority—refusing, even, to acknowledge that Cabot and Quinn were in prison. As for Eggwort, although he insisted that the arsonists would be "dragged before the bar to answer for their impiety," he declined to specify a date for their trial, nor would he explain how such a proceeding might occur on an island devoid of courts, barristers, and judges. Naturally Mr. Chadwick kept asserting that the arsonists were innocent of blasphemy, the incinerated vessel being naught but an aboriginal totem. Eggwort invariably replied that, having trod its boards and touched its sails, he knew the lost *Covenant* was the original Genesis ark. Mr. Chadwick's requests to visit the prisoners were met with Eggwortian rigidity, the Emperor claiming that Kommandant Hengstenberg never permitted outsiders to enter Mephistropolis, for such intrusions always led to riots.

Upon returning from his fourteenth audience with Eggwort, Mr. Chadwick approached Chloe and said, "I bear two pieces of news, one felicitous, the other not," his ashen complexion and quavering voice attesting to the dreadfulness of the second development. "Brace yourself, Miss Bathurst. Eggwort has issued an edict proclaiming that throughout Duntopia the crime of blasphemy is henceforth punishable by death."

Suddenly she was back in the sky above the Peruvian savannah, plummeting towards the Jequetepeque valley as the condors slashed the balloon. Punishable by death? Subject to the gallows, like Pirate Anne? The chopping block, like John the Baptist?

"Oh, what a foul piece of work is that man!" she seethed.

"Utterly abominable," said the vicar.

"Now tell me the good news."

There was indeed a pearl of great price in the offal that Mr. Chadwick had dumped at her feet. Come Saturday morning, Eggwort would be willing to meet with "the false prophet Miss Omega" on Barrington Isle, a formation that (being equidistant from Hood and Charles) he regarded as neutral ground. If the parlay proved productive, he would arrange for the trial to occur posthaste.

"Which means that, if the jury acquits them, Dartworthy and Miss Kirsop will walk free of Mephistropolis," Mr. Chadwick explained.

"Does Eggwort really believe he has the right to hang our friends?" she rasped.

"No less than he believes the *Covenant* was Noah's ark," said Mr. Chadwick.

Heavy of heart, unquiet of mind, Chloe retreated to her shack. In recent days she'd contrived to offset the dreariness of the place, adorning the walls with the scarlet shells of sally-lightfoot crabs, the windows with passionflower garlands, and the table with a bouquet of cactus flowers set in an empty Madeira bottle. She'd never been so appreciative of these appointments, for each now had its part to play. Slowly, methodically, she tore the crab shells from their pegs and ground them to powder beneath her boot heel. *Sic semper tyrannis.* She pulled the garlands from the windows and ripped them to shreds. Thus to all emperors.

Lifting the bouquet of cactus flowers from its vase, she seized the stems directly below the petals and with her free hand rotated the blossoms. Satisfied that she'd choked the flowers to death, she let them slip from her hand, musing on the curious fact that there was no word in the English language, or any other tongue as far as she knew, for the corpse of a plant.

When the designated hour arrived and the *Lamarck's* company touched down on Barrington Isle, not far from a population of high-spined land iguanas, Orrin Eggwort was waiting for them, having traveled from Charles in the *Cumorah*. He'd brought along four wives, each armed with a holstered pistol riding on her hip. Throughout the crossing, this contingent of his harem had doubtless hoisted the canvas and worked the helm, though for the remainder of the afternoon they would evidently function as his bodyguard.

The Emperor guided Chloe, Mr. Chadwick, and Léourier to a dry lake bed perhaps a furlong beyond the tide line, explaining that in days of yore rival pirate bands had periodically assembled here to negotiate pillage and rapine rights. To enhance the congeniality of these gatherings, the pirates had hewn furniture from the freestanding rocks, transforming the lake bed into a kind of outdoor moot hall—the perfect venue for deciding which gangs would get to plunder the Ecuadorian coastal villages, which would provide the Peruvian tin mines with Indian slaves, and which would attack the royal treasure galleons plying between Manila and Acapulco.

"Though the pirates certainly never envisioned its becomin' the site of the pretrial colloquy in *The People of Duntopia versus Edward Cabot and Bianca Quinn*," Eggwort added, lolling on his stone settee.

"You may use such exalted terms as 'pretrial colloquy' if you wish," said Mr. Chadwick, perched on his lava chair, "but you know this proceeding enjoys not a shred of legitimacy. Nowhere else in Christendom might a man be executed for blasphemy."

"The same holds true for pagandom," said Léourier, shifting on his pumice sofa. "Only in the Mussulman countries will sacrilege send a person to his death."

"Then the Mussulman countries got a thing or two to teach us," said Eggwort.

"Consider this, Your Excellency," said Mr. Chadwick. "Having populated Mephistropolis with ninety British subjects, Her Majesty is poised to assert jurisdiction over Charles Isle. Continue persecuting the illustrious Edward Cabot, and the Crown will have no choice but to shut down Duntopia, your Ecuadorian deed notwithstanding."

"Given the British Empire's proclivity fer gettin' its way most ever'where on the planet, I reckon my deed will end up wrappin' mackerel no matter what. But first I'm gonna fight the good fight fer God's honor."

"Your good fight is a travesty of justice," said Mr. Chadwick.

"'A travesty of justice,' I like that. An ideal worth strivin' fer—wouldn't you say?—so very Duntopian." Rising from his settee, Eggwort poked his sternum with a rigid thumb. "In keepin' with our goal of maximum travesticity, I hereby appoint myself chief magistrate. The job of chief prosecutor, meanwhile, will go to Jethro Tappert, our Associate Emperor. Fer the jury we'll be recruitin' twelve prisoners from Mephistropolis."

"And who's to function as chief counsel?" Chloe asked Eggwort.

"You applyin' fer the post, Miss Omega?"

In a shadowy sector of her brain the seed of an audacious idea coalesced. "I intend to join the defense team, yes, but in the role of expert witness. Meanwhile, Mr. Chadwick and Capitaine Léourier"—she bestowed furtive smiles on the vicar and the aeronaut—"will become the advocates for our anthropologist and our aerialist."

"Very well," said Mr. Chadwick, without conviction.

"*Bonne idée*," said Léourier, scowling.

"I'll fill the vacancies as you wish, with one provision," Eggwort told Chloe. "Your expert testimony must be outlandish enough—I'm talkin' unadulterated Book of Mormon flummery—to keep Mr. Tappert and myself amused. Fer example, you could insist that the *Covenant* was burned by the brownies, with Cabot and Quinn appearin' on the scene only because they hoped to put out the fire."

The audacious idea germinated, sending forth roots and branches. "Or perhaps I could demonstrate that—" Rushing from her brain to her larynx, the sounds she wished to utter became lodged in her throat like a bone. She closed her eyes and coughed the syllables free. "That God does not exist."

Gales of laughter coursed through the Emperor. "Perfect! He don't exist! As outlandish a notion as a Latter-Day Saint could wish! Naturally Psalm Fourteen, verse fourteen, comes to mind, don't it, Rebecca?"

"'The fool hath said in his heart, *There is no God*,'" the sultana recited.

"Because if there is no God," added Chloe, "then He couldn't have ordered Noah to build an ark, which means the sunken vessel wasn't remotely sacred."

"Astonishin'!" trilled Eggwort. "Travesticity on stilts! Miss Omega, I insist you make such ratiocinatin' the be-all and end-all of the blasphemers' case!"

"Naturally Capitaine Léourier and I must meet straightaway with Professor Cabot and Miss Quinn," said Mr. Chadwick.

"'Fraid that's out of the question," said Eggwort. "Visitations spark riots—ask the Kommandant."

"In every civilized nation on earth, a lawyer is permitted to consult with his clients," said Mr. Chadwick.

"I'm sure you're right, Padre," said Eggwort, "exceptin' you ain't no lawyer, and only an idiot would confuse Duntopia with a civilized nation." He fixed on Chloe, his lips parting to display two decks of gleeful teeth. "'No God'—your heart won't be in it, am I right, Miss Omega? Even a false prophet must have her pride."

"I may be a false prophet, but I am faithful to the light of eternity," said Chloe.

Yes, my heart won't be in it, she thought.

Eggwort faced his eldest spouse and said, "It's all too delicious, don't you think?"

"Delicious, yes," said Rebecca evenly.

"Certainly not distasteful," said Sarah.

Chloe's stare drifted towards the beach, where the male frigate birds paid court to prospective mates. Their hearts were in it. In fact, their method of commending themselves to the opposite sex—large red breastpouches that rhythmically inflated and deflated—suggested nothing so much as joyous, throbbing, externalized hearts.

Eggwort said, "Forty days hence—a good, round, Noahistic sort of number—forty days hence, the good Lord willin' and the crick don't rise, we'll all gather at the tabernacle, there to cross swords in *Duntopia versus Cabot and Quinn*."

Chloe closed her eyes and pressed a fist against her stomach. Was she truly prepared to malign the Presence in a futile effort to deliver her friends from the gallows? Of course she was—though the situation was causing her a magnitude of remorse such as she'd often feigned (as when Pirate Anne had left her baby at the orphanage) but never before felt.

"And now I must return to Minor Zion and reassume my horizontal throne," said Eggwort.

"Rank hath its privileges—and privilege its rankness," said Mr. Chadwick. "See you in court, Your Excellency."

Having appeared sixty-eight times as Pansy Winslow in *Lanterns on the Levee,* Chloe retained vivid memories of the scene in which the Southern belle's lover, a gambler named Travis McQuaid, was dragged into the woods one night by a half-dozen fellow cardsharpers for allegedly using a marked deck. The gambler vilified the subsequent hearing, calling it "this monstrous kangaroo court, this unholy drumhead tribunal," but his denunciations were unavailing. As the sun rose over Mississippi, the mob slipped a noose about his neck and hung him from an ironwood tree.

Once again a kangaroo court had entered Chloe's life, and yet she could imagine no other means by which Ralph and Solange might be spared the fate of Travis McQuaid. "The universe holds but one entity that cherishes me," she told Mr. Chadwick, "and now I am forced to betray it."

"I cannot speak for the universe, but know you are cherished by the former Vicar of Wroxton."

"I appreciate your sentiments, Reverend. Alas, I've come to believe that human affection, like human flesh, is grass. Only divine love endures."

"If you're alluding to Ecclesiastes, it's the *Earth* that endures. Divine love, in my experience, is a far less reliable commodity."

"Bring me the sandalwood box."

Upon receiving "An Essay Concerning Descent with Modification" from Mr. Chadwick, Chloe retreated to her shack. Hour after hour, she perused the thirty-five pages by every imaginable sort of light—the blaze of noon, the glimmer of a candle, the beam of a kerosene lantern, the glow of the moon—all the while availing herself of Léourier's *epená,* though the resin failed to ameliorate her misery. Whatever its outcome, this trial would send her in search of forgiveness. She must ask absolution not only of the God of her epiphany but also of the Galápagos fauna—for dismantling the Jehovah hypothesis would mean framing all the world's birds and beasts not as benefactions from the Presence but as the accidental efflux of an indifferent machine.

When not pondering the essay, she prepared a catalog of the essential illustrative specimens, one page per creature—a bestiary she came to regard as the *dramatis personae* of her testimony. Two exhibits posed transportation difficulties. Carefully she explained to Cuniche that she needed to ferry a pair of tortoises to Charles Isle, lest Señor Dartworthy and Señorita Kirsop go to the gallows. Although her logic eluded him, Cuniche translated Chloe's desires for the other Huancabambas, whereupon Ascumiche, Yitogua, and Rapra volunteered their services. Later that afternoon, Léourier flew Chloe and the tortoise team to James Isle, where the Indians took hold of a domeshelled female and deposited her in the gondola. Burdened with five human beings and a tortoise that weighed more than an anvil, the *Lamarck* would not budge until Léourier inflated the silk balloon to full capacity, and even then the ship performed poorly, gliding barely ten feet above the waves throughout the crossing to Charles Isle.

Shortly after the Indians unloaded the prodigious creature, releasing her in the same Mount Pajas lava field where the saddlebacks roamed, three of Eggwort's wives appeared before Chloe and Léourier.

"Lady Omega, we're hankerin' to have a talk with you," said Rebecca. "You should know where us sultanas stand in the matter of the forthcomin' trial. Even if you're a false prophet like Orrin believes—"

"Somethin' we got no way of knowin'," said the pregnant Naomi.

Rebecca continued, "And even if the sunken ark was the genuine and boney fide article—"

"Somethin' else we got no way of knowin'," said Sarah.

"Well, despite all that, we don't think your friends deserve to hang," said Rebecca. "The upshot is that we're placin' ourselves at your disposal."

Though perplexed by the sultanas' offering, Chloe could sense no ulterior motives therein, and so she shook the hands of her new factotums and said, "Lady Omega gratefully accepts your assistance, Mrs. Eggwort—and Mrs. Eggwort and Mrs. Eggwort."

"Just tell us what needs doin'," said Rebecca.

"Beyond tortoises, my expert testimony will incorporate several varieties of lizard and bird," said Chloe. "May I depend on you to mind them? Zookeeping is an honorable trade—I once practiced it myself."

"We'll tend your exhibits as faithfully as a sheepdog guardin' the fold," said Sarah.

"I can't imagine Monsieur Eggwort sanctioning this turn of events," said Léourier.

"We'll tell him Miss Omega's testimony can never reach a pinnacle of outlandishness without she's got a passel of live critters at her fingertips," said Rebecca.

"And if he don't buy that argument," said Naomi, "we'll tell him his remainin' days as a priapically happy emperor are fewer than he imagines."

The following afternoon the tortoise team loaded a slopeback male from Indefatigable into the airship's gondola. Being lighter than his dome-shelled cousin, the creature proved easier to convey across the channel, but Chloe still felt a sense of accomplishment when the *Lamarck* landed on Charles.

Having struck the tortoises off her list, she turned her attention to the lizards. It took her and Léourier a full day to supplement Duntopia's indigenous red marine iguanas with two small blacks from Tower Isle and two multicoloreds from Narborough. Collecting the terrestrials—a short-spined specimen from Hood and a high-spined specimen from Barrington—also consumed Chloe's energies from dawn to dusk. Rebecca ingeniously provided each creature with a calico neckband on which she'd embroidered the name of its native isle. The collars gave the lizards a clerical appearance, as if they'd been called by their Creator to save the souls of fellow reptiles.

"Orrin now knows we're in your employ," Rebecca informed Chloe.

"I assume he wasn't overjoyed."

"Never seen him so riled," said Naomi with a tilted smile.

"But when he realized the nine of us was fixin' to make him a monk," said Sarah, "he threw up his hands and shouted, 'Let it be known I gave Miss Omega every consideration under the sun!'"

"At your earliest convenience, I should like you to hunt up two exhibits," Chloe told the sultanas. "A live puffer-fish and a human skeleton."

Rebecca announced that she knew where to find the second commodity: decades earlier a man had been hanged from a catclaw tree in Storm-Petrel Cove—most likely a pirate who'd fallen out of favor with his colleagues. "The birds and worms made short work of him. But how do them bones figure in your scheme fer enchantin' the jury?"

"My testimony turns on transmutationism," said Chloe. "This theory invites us to ask, 'Why does God go to all the bother of existing?'"

"I don't know what you're talkin' about," said Naomi, "but if you succeed in vexatin' Orrin, that's good enough fer us."

Before leaving Duntopia, Chloe visited the Colnett barrel. By her calculation sufficient time had elapsed for Algernon to have reached England, rescued Papa, and entrusted the news to a whaling master bound for the Horn and points north. Sorting through the heap of printed matter, she indeed encountered a version of her name, though the message couldn't have originated with Algernon, who would never have addressed a letter to KLOWEE BATHIRST ON THE GUVNOR'S EYELAND.

Evidently the Jesuit missionaries had established a tradition of literacy amongst the Huancabamba *pagés*, for Princess Akawo began her letter by explaining that she'd dictated it to the village shaman. Despite its orthographic irregularities, Chloe easily apprehended Akawo's heartening message. Not only had Princess Ibanua and the liberated *seringueiros* arrived safely in the Jequetepeque valley, but Prince Gitika had appeared shortly thereafter with the remaining Indians, the Marañón valley campaign having played out exactly as planned.

After securing the letter in her rucksack, she continued excavating the barrel. Alas, no word from Algernon. Inevitably an unnerving question popped into her brain. If the scheme to free her father had gone awry, and if by some quirk of circumstance *Duntopia versus Cabot and*

Quinn persuaded the jurors to disavow their Creator, would she then be obligated to visit Alastor Hall, recapitulate her disproof, and win the £10,000 on Papa's behalf? This imagined *scenario* was surely amongst the most disturbing ever visited upon an apostle of the Presence, and she spent the remainder of the day attempting, though without success, to evade its contemplation.

It was on the vast and sumptuous Galápagos isle of Albemarle that Chloe Bathurst, galvanized by her previous night's study of Charles Darwin's essay and her inability to imagine an event more calamitous than the public execution of her friends, at long last found her Tree of Life.

Her revelation occurred at noon, heralded by perfume, the *Lamarck* having touched down in a flowery depression between the dormant Sierra Negra and Mount Azul volcanoes. Spun from some trade wind or other, a vagrant breeze wafted through the larboard window, cooling her brow and filling the carriage with the scent of orchids and hibiscus.

Bamboo birdcages fashioned by Orrin Eggwort's harem jammed the gondola floor to ceiling. Chloe selected four cages, wrapped her arms about them, and, taking leave of Capitaine Léourier, strode towards the valley in search of ornithological ripostes to the Jehovah hypothesis. According to her bestiary, the defense exhibits must ultimately include the three Galápagos varieties of flycatcher, the four distinct kinds of mockingbird, and at least six species of finch. Presumably the task would prove simple, Encantadas birds being so famously tame.

And suddenly there it was, rising from the island's heart, a towering plant with glowing ivory limbs and fragrant white blossoms. In his travel journal Mr. Darwin had identified this species as the *palo santo*, the "holy wood" tree. The name was at once pagan and Christian, tracing not only to an alleged efficacy against *mala energía*, "bad energy," but also to a familial relationship with frankincense and myrrh.

She knew her Tree of Life not by its fruits but by its tenants. At that moment the *palo santo* hosted three sorts of bird. Sprightly descendant of the South American grassquit (or so the transmutation sketch averred), a male woodpecker finch exhibited a characteristic behavior, using a prickly-pear cactus spine to pry an insect larva from a branch. Evolutionary offspring of a long-tailed songster still thriving on the South American continent, a male short-billed mockingbird, wreathed in gray feathers, gave voice to a serenade. Creamy of breast, brown of wing, and boasting (like her fellow *palo santo* occupants) a genealogy tracing to the mainland, a female broad-billed flycatcher stared directly at Chloe. For anyone who'd read *The Voyage of the Beagle* the bird's intentions were readily discerned. The creature meant to abandon the tree and plunder Chloe's scalp, human hair being amongst those materials with which flycatchers were pleased to build their nests.

She set down the bamboo cages. Woodpecker finch, short-billed mockingbird, broad-billed flycatcher: three distinct species descended with modification from a common ancestor that had in turn descended with modification from a creature that had likewise descended, so that if you applied your imagination fully to this Tree of Life, making a fanciful pilgrimage downwards along its twigs and branches, you would find that the avian families represented here were connected not only to all the world's other birds but also (in some astonishingly long-ago era) to the domeshelled tortoises now shambling through the dale, to the terrestrial iguanas sunning themselves on the rocks, to the prickly-pear cactus (here the wayfarer needed to visit a time before Professor Owen's dinosaurs) from which the woodpecker finch had taken his tool, and even to the very *palo santo* where the birds were presently perched. Eyes welling with tears, she apprehended the whole tapestry, an immense and magisterial network binding together everything that now lived, had ever lived, and ever would live—and so it was that she became once again a devotee of the theory of natural selection: a loyalty that would long endure, she suspected, woodpecker finches, short-billed mockingbirds, and broad-billed flycatchers being such incontrovertible conjunctions of beaks and claws and feathers, such irrefutable incarnations of flight and song and reproductive success.

"When the defense makes its case next week," she told the uncomprehending birds, "the Covent Garden Transmutationist will testify."

Having found the object of his quest, the woodpecker finch took wing, bearing away the delicious insect larva and the God of Chloe's epiphany. Next the mockingbird flew off, leaving behind a bracingly profane absence. Finally the flycatcher quit the *palo santo* and soared straight for her. Landing atop Chloe's head, the bird snapped at her scalp, then delivered the hair to an emergent nest in a nearby catclaw tree. An instant later the flycatcher, returning, stole a second hair, adding it to her nest, and then she claimed a third such strand.

"I saw the bird attack you," said Léourier, arriving on the scene. "By your tears I know she caused you pain."

"I felt no discomfort," said Chloe, retrieving the topmost cage. "*Attendez, mon ami.* The angels have molted and died. There is no God."

"Mademoiselle, *je suis désolé.*" Léourier placed a sympathetic hand on her shoulder. "I remember when I first understood that life lacks a supernatural meaning, a traumatic event for me, *très triste.* The loss of faith is always an occasion for weeping."

"But these are tears of joy."

"*Larmes de joie?*"

"Because today it was my privilege to befriend a broad-billed flycatcher," she explained. "No, not simply to befriend her, but to secure her family's prosperity. At this particular moment I ask nothing more of the world."

13

The Tortoises of the Encantadas at Long Last Have Their Day in Court, as Do the Land Lizards, Marine Iguanas, Mockingbirds, and Finches

W hat most pleased Malcolm Chadwick about Miss Bathurst's latest change of worldview was that, this time around, she'd embraced Charles Darwin's theory not for monetary gain or personal aggrandizement but because she believed it to be true. On first hearing of her return to the transmutationist fold, Malcolm enacted within his heart a private *carnaval de la victoria*, as well as a scene of Miss Bathurst and himself connecting with a kiss. Until that startling moment he'd certainly regarded her as a worthy person, but now it seemed his attitude also partook of Aphrodite's domain. He decided to tell Miss Bathurst nothing of this development, as any romantic protestation on his part would surely distract her from the daunting task at hand.

"I hope your inverse Road to Damascus has not pained you intolerably," he said.

In an absent tone Miss Bathurst replied, "My emotions are not unlike those that attended my long-ago miscarriage—exhilaration mingled with bereavement."

"I see," said Malcolm, though in fact he did not.

"And now, Reverend, having made that paradoxical observation, I would ask that we speak no more of the matter."

He nodded and said, "The world is already too full of words."

Whilst preparing the case for the defense, Malcolm soon realized that Capitaine Léourier's perspective on the Tree of Life would prove indispensable. Though a man of scientific sensibility, the aeronaut found the idea of non-Lamarckian evolution far from self-evident, which made him the ideal critic of the team's intended strategy.

After listening to Léourier's analysis of their rehearsals, Malcolm and Miss Bathurst concluded that, during the phase of her testimony concerning birds, she should refrain from naming any living South American species that might have given rise to a Galápagos variant, lest Eggwort demand that exemplars be brought before the jurors. (Instead she must aver that the continental forebears of all Encantadas birds were extinct, their fossilized bones still awaiting discovery in Ecuador, Peru, or Chile.) Equally vital was Léourier's anticipation of an argument with which the chief prosecutor would surely attempt to rattle Mademoiselle Bathurst. Why should a scientifically inclined Christian not insist that the principle of natural selection had originated in the mind of God?

"One need merely assert that the Almighty put this process in place on the eighth day of Creation," said the aeronaut, "so that his newly formed animals and their descendants could adapt to future changes in their environments, and—*voilà*—the atheist position crumbles."

Malcolm recalled how, back in Manáos, the naturalist Alfred Wallace had proclaimed that God was the author of evolution. At the time Malcolm had found the young man's stance untenable. ("Mr. Wallace is merely saying that the universe exists, something I already knew.") Today, however, as articulated by Léourier, this alternative to a wholly materialist view of evolution seemed formidable indeed.

"You are advancing an argument that might be called . . . well, I'm not sure what to call it," Malcolm told Léourier.

"Evangelical Deism?" suggested Miss Bathurst.

"Very good," said Malcolm. "When in doubt, devise an oxymoron. In the beginning God the Father created the laws of Nature and proceeded to dwell within them, whilst Christ the Son and his associate the Holy Ghost set about securing eternal life for the more pious members of their favorite species. Should Darwin's theory ever become ascendant, we may be confident that some form of evangelical Deism will rise along with it."

"Then let us toast the theologians of the future," said Léourier in a sardonic tone, "who will appropriate the bread of science even as they devour the wafers of salvation. Such clever apologists. They will have their Host and eat it, too. But how do we dismantle their argument?"

"I haven't the foggiest idea," said Malcolm.

"At the eleventh hour we shall formulate a riposte," said Miss Bathurst. "We may never overpower Mr. Darwin's antagonists, but we can certainly out-think them."

On the morning that the trial was to commence, Malcolm and Léourier escorted their expert witness from her Hood's Isle shack to the moored *Lamarck*. Dressed in her pirate regalia and Panama hat, she clutched the boxed transmutation essay and an equally crucial document, the bestiary, its pages now arranged to indicate the order in which Eggwort's concubines must bring each exhibit on stage. Under clear skies the defense team flew to Charles Isle, landing in Post Office Bay. Sorting through the contents of the Colnett barrel, Malcolm determined that no letter had arrived from Algernon Bathurst, nor had Bishop Wilberforce sent a message concerning the disposition of the Shelley Prize. How weirdly poetic it would be if the recently resurrected Albion Transmutationist Club brought atheism to Duntopia on the very day the Mayfair Diluvian League sailed a gopher-wood proof of God up the Thames.

After negotiating the foothills of Mount Pajas, the defense team entered Minor Zion, whereupon Miss Bathurst presented the eldest of Eggwort's concubines with the bestiary. "Yesterday our high-spined lizard went a-missin', but I'm happy to report he showed up this mornin'," said Rebecca Eggwort, leafing through the *dramatis personae*. "'Fraid we lost track of them two little black iguanas from Tower, but we got everythin' else you need, includin' the puffer-fish and the pirate skeleton."

"You must find those lizards posthaste," Miss Bathurst insisted.

"Might a couple extra Duntopian reds suffice?" asked Mrs. Eggwort. "Or maybe we could sail across the bay and catch us some Indefatigable multicoloreds."

"Thank you, Rebecca, but I require *varieties,* the more the better."

The defense team proceeded to the plaza, where scores of shackled men, quite likely the penal colony's entire English-speaking population, occupied themselves with scratching their armpits and spitting into the dust. Dressed in burlap tunics so tattered they would have embarrassed a scarecrow, their heads covered with burlap skullcaps, the inmates fidgeted beneath the stern gazes of a dozen armed guards commanded by the same strapping officer who'd taken the convicts in hand five months earlier. A lanky Duntopian with watery eyes and an Old Testament beard approached Malcolm, introducing the commander as Capitán Machado and himself as "Associate Emperor Jethro Tappert, the Latter-Day Saint who'll be representin' the Divine Plaintiff in this here case."

"I must say, you look the part of God's attorney," Malcolm observed.

"I think of myself more as Satan's bane," said Mr. Tappert, wiping his brow with a red kerchief. He wore pristine dungarees and a green-and-black checked cotton shirt. "So tell me, Mr. Chadwick, why does so distinguished a gentleman as yourself decide to defend the slimy likes of Cabot and Quinn? In my view the gallows is too good fer such varmints. I would sooner see 'em boiled in oil or quartered by giant tortoises, but our charter don't allow it."

"Good sir, have you forgotten the most sacred principle upon which Anglo-American jurisprudence is founded?" asked Malcolm. "I refer to the presumption of innocence."

"Presumption of innocence, hah—I *knew* you'd try some sleazy lawyer trick! Maybe it works with the hoity-toities, but here in Duntopia we don't coddle blasphemers. Right now Orrin wants us to pick the jurors, a task fer which we'll be needin' the wisdom of Solomon and the forbearance of the martyrs."

"I have neither," said Malcolm.

"Truth to tell, I don't see how we're gonna manage it." Tappert guided the defense team towards the White Horse Prophecy Tabernacle. "*I'll* be hopin' to plant twelve God-fearin' believers in the jury box, and *you'll* settle fer nothin' less than a dozen libertine atheists."

Now Miss Bathurst spoke up, explaining that her team would be satisfied to put but a single question to each prospective juror. "It's a mere ten words long," she told Tappert. "Quote, 'Do you think it possible dogs were bred from wolves?' Unquote."

"Wolves?" said the chief prosecutor. "There ain't no wolves in Galápagos."

"Attend my testimony carefully, Mr. Tappert," said Miss Bathurst. "Thou shalt learn whence thou came and whither thou goest."

As Malcolm entered the building, pieces of his past came flooding back—his oft-repeated experience of walking into a rustic church and finding himself deeply moved by its holy simplicity. With its bronze candlesticks instead of gold and its windowsills supporting not stained-glass mosaics but vases of modest yellow cactus flowers, the Mormon tabernacle was precisely the sort of place God would have been pleased to visit back in the days when He existed. Someone had rearranged the furnishings, pushing aside the pulpit, piano, and baptismal tub, giving preeminence to a mahogany altar. On Sunday this appointment would again perform a sacred function, but for now it was a judge's bench. Balanced on an adjacent stool, wearing a solemn black suit that would have served him equally well for conducting a funeral, Orrin Eggwort scanned the Book of Mormon. A few yards away, seated at a table bearing a sign reading PROSECUTION TEAM, a corpulent Latter-Day Saint dressed in striped blue overalls pored over the same consecrated text.

"Meet my deputy, Assistant Emperor Linus Hatch," Tappert told Malcolm. "Linus, this here's the chief counsel."

"Tell me, Mr. Hatch," asked Malcolm, "what is your opinion of the presumption of innocence?"

"As a fallen man," the deputy prosecutor replied in a gravelly voice, "stained by Adam's sin though redeemed by Christ's blood, I would never go around presumin' anyone's innocence, includin' my own, and certainly not the innocence of guilty folk like Cabot and Quinn."

Malcolm rolled his eyes and faced the bench. "Emperor Eggwort, do you concur with these peculiar views?"

"It's *Judge* Eggwort today." The chief magistrate snapped his Book of Mormon shut. "Like my fellow Duntopians, I'm disinclined to hold any person blameless. Noah was blameless. Job was blameless. It's a short list."

"Permit me a second question," said Malcolm. "It concerns arithmetic. Because my clients are accused of a capital crime, the jury must reach a unanimous verdict, correct?"

"Unanimous, yep," said Eggwort. "Convince all twelve that God don't exist, and I'll cancel your clients' appointments with the hangman."

Malcolm suddenly found himself back on the pitching deck of the *Equinox,* the gale howling all about him. "By the norms of English justice, we need to convince but *one* juror!"

"If you've got an itch fer English justice, Padre, I suggest you take a trip to England. That said, I'm not averse to compromisin'. If eight jurors cast 'not guilty' votes, both defendants will walk free."

"Make it four."

"No," said Eggwort.

"I implore you, sir, four. Or else five."

"Six."

"Very well, six," growled Malcolm. He exchanged dismayed glances with Miss Bathurst and Léourier, then approached a table on which a sheet of foolscap displayed the words DEFENSE TEAM. "Judge Eggwort, I suspect you're about to be hoist by your own petard. Once word of this trial gets out, the world at large will call for your abdication."

"We ain't keen on the world at large around here, and the same goes fer petards," Eggwort replied. "Mr. Hatch, go fetch us the first candidate."

Thanks to the elegance of Miss Bathurst's membership criterion, whereby a man might join the jury merely by allowing that dogs may have descended from wolves, the selection process proceeded apace. Of the twenty prisoners interviewed that morning, Tappert rejected one on grounds of professed atheism, two in consequence of imbecility, and a fourth for being as deaf as a clam. Malcolm, meanwhile, eliminated two who claimed that dogs were designed by God, plus one who thought the defendants Satanists who'd accidently burned the *Covenant* in a human sacrifice gone awry. Thus it happened (in an irony of the sort Miss Bathurst savored) that a panel of twelve accomplished lawbreakers were empowered to bring justice to Duntopia. The arsonists' destiny lay in the dubious hands of Joe the poacher, Ben the horse thief, Jake the fornicator, Harry the panderer, Tim the anarchist, Pete the highwayman, George the train robber, Dick the swindler, Walter the forger, Nathan the pickpocket, Amos the sodomite, and Clarence the usurer.

"Not the ideal *fraternité* for our purposes," said Léourier. "I fear Monsieur Darwin's argument will elude them."

"Let us remember that Christ's disciples were likewise an inauspicious lot," said Malcolm. "Just as the Galilean turned twelve unpromising Judeans into Christians, so shall we turn twelve unpromising Christians into transmutationists."

"In fact, the odds are better in our case," said Miss Bathurst. "We've got our tortoises and our iguanas, our mockingbirds and our finches, and all Jesus had were some gaudy miracles and his supposed descent from on high."

Without saying a word, Malcolm sidled towards his expert witness and, forming his arms in a loop as wide as the Colnett barrel, embraced her. What he most admired about Miss Bathurst was that she never stopped being a little bit mad.

Although Galápagos was cooler than the majority of tropical archipelagos, or so Mr. Darwin's travel journal asserted, the noon hour brought waves of blazing heat to the White Horse Prophecy Tabernacle. Seated at the defense table, talking amongst themselves, a perspiring Chloe and her equally damp colleagues considered how they might counter evangelical Deism, that formidable argument whereby, far from being displaced by the Tree of Life, God lay immanent in its every leaf.

Suddenly Mr. Chadwick clucked his tongue and, fanning himself with his straw hat, informed Chloe and Capitaine Léourier that he might, just might, have the answer.

"I recall a gathering of the Oxford rakehells at which somebody read from Lucretius's *On the Nature of Things*, a long first-century poem celebrating Epicureanism—Shelley's preferred philosophical system. The passage concerned the outrageous death of Iphigenia."

"Sacrificed by her own father for a fair wind," said Léourier. "Trojan War stories have always held a particular fascination for me."

"Arguably our species once stood at a crossroads," said Mr. Chadwick, "a moment when, owing to Lucretius, *Homo sapiens* might have acquired a modest cast of mind, refusing to fancy itself a phenomenon of abiding interest to the gods. We know what came to pass. The Roman poet lost. The Roman Church won. But events might have unfolded otherwise. In my reimagining of human history, our species has adopted Epicurus's humble materialism, which Democritus so memorably anticipated. 'By convention bitter—'"

"'By convention bitter, by convention sweet,'" quoted Léourier. "'By convention hot, by convention cold. But in reality: atoms and void.'"

"Exactly," said Mr. Chadwick. "Now suppose that one fateful day a bearded prophet stumbles out of the wilderness, claiming that a supernatural entity, at once immaterial and very human-like, inhabits the laws of Nature and makes them happen. Do our atomists face a philosophical crisis? Well, no. Do they worry about harmonizing the prophet's worldview with their own? Certainly not. Bound by their ideals of humility and reason, they listen carefully to the hairy visionary, then politely inform him that his argument would be impressive were it not absurd."

"Though it remains to be seen whether our jurymen are likewise bound by ideals of humility and reason," said Chloe, "I believe your Epicurus may have saved the day."

Brow gleaming with a tiara of sweat, Rebecca Eggwort burst into the room and announced, to Chloe's great relief, that the wayward Tower Isle iguanas had been found, after which Miriam, Sarah, and pregnant Naomi entered carrying ceramic pitchers and tin cups. Bustling about the tabernacle, the sultanas supplied the court personnel with fresh water, not excluding the jury foreman—Joe the poacher—and his colleagues, chained together in three ranks and seated uncomfortably in a gallery constructed of cheese casks. Next to appear were Eggwort's five remaining wives, bearing copper tureens filled with crab chowder, which they served in wooden bowls to the jurymen. With noisy passion the twelve devoured their lunches. Obviously they'd not had a proper meal since leaving England.

No sooner did the jurors finish eating than dozens of Minor Zionists, children as well as adults, swarmed into the tabernacle, eager to be entertained by *Duntopia versus Cabot and Quinn*. Taking their places in the spectators' pews, they set about improvising fans from hats, bonnets, palm fronds, and catclaw leaves. Now Jethro Tappert and Linus Hatch arrived, gaggles of progeny in tow, including the thirty-six Eggwort offspring. Collectively these boys and girls impressed Chloe as more sedate and domesticated than the Down House children, though perhaps rather less at home in the world.

Judge Eggwort struck the bench with a roofing mallet, calling the Court to order. The doors swung back, and Capitán Machado led the two defendants, dressed in burlap tunics and matching skullcaps, towards the defense table. Ralph looked as though he'd just crawled away from a second wreck of the *Lamarck*. Solange appeared not so much injured as sickly, as if she'd contracted some insidious equatorial disease.

"One hundred and fifty days in Perdition," said Ralph, fingering his tangled beard.

"Five months that lasted forever," rasped Solange, blinking her bloodshot eyes. "They stole my ruby pendant and what remained of my dignity."

"My dear and noble Ralph," whispered Chloe. "My poor suffering Solange."

The instant the defendants assumed their chairs, Mr. Chadwick told them, *sotto voce*, "I've been appointed your barrister. Léourier is my assistant. Miss Bathurst is our expert witness. I suggest you accept our services."

"How can *you* be a witness?" said Solange to Chloe. "You weren't even *there*."

"We have a strategy," said Chloe.

"Doubtless involving all your most precious hallucinations," said Solange.

"Is it true they're determined to send us to the gallows?" muttered Ralph.

"Yes, but I am equally determined to set you free," said Mr. Chadwick.

Judge Eggwort sneezed, sipped water, and said, "We shall begin with a reading from the Book of Mormon. Mr. Tappert, please favor us with Third Nephi, chapter two, verses thirteen through sixteen."

The chief prosecutor opened the holy book, then declaimed in a thundering voice, "'And it came to pass that before this thirteenth year had passed away the Nephites were threatened with utter destruction because of this war, which had become exceedingly sore. And it came to pass that those Lamanites who had united with the Nephites were numbered amongst the Nephites. And their curse was taken from them, and their skin became white like unto the Nephites. And their young men and their daughters became exceedingly fair, and they were numbered amongst the Nephites, and were called Nephites.'"

"And it came to pass that Miss Kirsop vomited forth her breakfast," Solange muttered.

"Mr. Hatch, you will read the indictment," said Eggwort.

The deputy prosecutor rose, smoothing a sheet of crumpled paper against his Book of Mormon. "'On the evenin' of September the twenty-first, 1850, shortly before midnight, Professor Edward Cabot and Miss Bianca Quinn boarded a three-masted vessel called the *Covenant,* then anchored off Indefatigable Isle. The accused proceeded to set said vessel aflame. Because the object of their arson was built to specifications laid down millennia ago by God Almighty, maker of Heaven and Earth, this behavior must be reckoned an egregious act of blasphemy.'"

"Good jurymen, allow me to embellish the charges by addin' that the torched vessel was well and truly the original Genesis ark," Eggwort told the twelve. "Earlier this year I walked its decks, and I knew straightaway that every plank had been nailed in place by Noah hisself under Jehovah's supervision. The Court will admit no testimony aimed at impugnin' the vessel's authenticity."

"Impugning the vessel's authenticity—isn't that the essence of our case?" asked Ralph in a low voice.

"We've got something bigger up our sleeves," Mr. Chadwick replied.

"We're going to prove God doesn't exist," added Chloe.

"I don't like it," said Solange.

"This isn't a bloody meeting of the Shelley Society," said Ralph.

"Eggwort will allow no other strategy," Chloe explained.

"You should've left me on St. Paul's confounded rocks," said Solange.

"Here's a fact to soothe you," said Chloe. "I'm now one of those free-thinking materialist atheists we hear so much about these days."

"And I'm Josephine Bonaparte," said Solange.

"No, really," said Chloe. "I've parted company with eternity."

"If we turn but six jurymen into transmutationists," the vicar informed Ralph and Solange, "you won't be meeting the hangman."

Judge Eggwort cast a fiery eye on the chief counselor. "Mr. Chadwick, the Court wishes to know how your clients plead."

"Not guilty!" shouted Ralph.

"Innocent, in fact!" cried Solange.

"Mr. Tappert, you will now explain to the jurors why the defendants must go to the gallows," said Eggwort

The chief prosecutor rose and, clearing his throat, announced that he had in hand an affidavit from the Governor, "a document that he dictated with one palm set squarely on Scripture and the other on the Book of Mormon." Tappert proceeded to read the deposition aloud. On the night in question, Stopsack had "arrested and shackled Edward Cabot and Bianca Quinn" as they stood on the beach of Black Turtle Cove "hurling curses at their Creator and watching the *Covenant*, which they knew to be the Genesis ark, sink beneath the waves." Stopsack had added that he hoped a full measure of Duntopian justice would be visited upon the defendants, their guilt being unequivocal.

"There you have it, gentlemen, the grit and gristle of the prosecution's case," said Tappert, facing the jury box.

"I say we hang 'em!" cried Nathan the pickpocket, rising.

"So do I!" declared Walter the forger.

"Jurymen, I appreciate your zeal," said Eggwort, "but the trial's not over."

"I have yet to examine the arsonists," added Tappert.

"And the defense hasn't made its case," noted Mr. Chadwick.

"But I'm bored *already*," grumbled Nathan, resuming his seat.

"The prosecution calls Edward Cabot," said Tappert.

Despite his infirmities, Ralph hobbled briskly towards the witness chair and assumed it with considerable panache. Linus Hatch pressed the Book of Mormon into his grasp and said, "Do you swear that the testimony you're about to give will be the truth, the whole truth, and nothin' but the truth, so help you God?"

"That depends on what you mean by 'God,'" Ralph replied.

"No, it don't," said Hatch.

"The Court is satisfied that the defendant has promised to speak truthfully," said Eggwort.

"Listen carefully to my first question, Perfessor, as your life will be teeterin' in the balance," said Tappert. "What possible motive could a sane man have fer destroyin' one of the holiest objects in Christendom?"

"It *wasn't* one of the holiest objects in Christendom," Ralph insisted. "Ask our Peruvian Indians. Their ancestors built it a century ago."

"The jury will disregard Perfessor Cabot's mendacious history lesson," said Eggwort.

"I shall be happy to explain why we sank the thing," said Ralph. "I wanted to keep Governor Stopsack from taking it to England and using it to claim the Shelley Prize."

"And what, pray tell, is the Shelley Prize?" asked Tappert.

"Ten thousand pounds to the first contestant who can verify or refute the existence of a Supreme Being."

"In other words, you thought it would be a terrible thing if somebody proved that God exists?" said Tappert.

"If that verification turned on fraudulent evidence—yes," said Ralph.

Chloe bit her lip and waxed pensive, pondering the uncomfortable fact that not long ago she'd pictured Jonathan Stopsack and herself hauling the Huancabamba ark to England.

"The jury will disregard the characterization 'fraudulent evidence,'" said Eggwort.

"Be honest, Perfessor," said Tappert. "The reason you didn't want Stopsack to collect this so-called Shelley Prize is that you believe God is an illusion—am I right?"

"I'm on trial for blasphemy, not atheism."

"Ah, so you *do* believe God is an illusion."

"I wouldn't put it that way."

"How would you put it?"

"The *Covenant* was no more Noah's ark than a woodcutter's privy is Her Majesty's throne."

Eggwort said, "The jury will—"

"Disregard the defendant's last statement," said Mr. Chadwick drily. "We're miles ahead of you, Judge."

"No further questions," said Tappert.

"Mr. Chadwick, you may cross-examine the defendant," said the chief magistrate.

"Because you won't allow the jury to hear opinions concerning the sunken vessel's provenance," the vicar replied, "I have no questions for the professor."

Next Jethro Tappert put "Edward Cabot's notorious co-conspirator" in the witness chair. For the remainder of the afternoon he questioned Solange's *alter ego*, Bianca Quinn, in a spirit that for Chloe evoked the Inquisition scene in Bulwer-Lytton's worst melodrama, *The Curse of Torquemada*. Why did Miss Quinn hate God? (She didn't, Solange insisted.) Why did she burn Noah's ark? (It wasn't Noah's ark, she averred.) Why did she burn the vessel specified in the indictment? (So that the Shelley Prize wouldn't be awarded on fraudulent grounds, she explained.) In other words, you're an atheist—am I right, Miss Quinn?

"Well, *everybody's* an atheist of one sort or another," she replied.

"You're an atheist when it comes to Apollo. Judge Eggwort's an atheist in the case of Isis. I just happen to believe in one god fewer than the Latter-Day Saints in this courtroom."

"As you just heard, the defendant has takin' to convictin' herself out of her own mouth," said Tappert to the jurymen. "No further questions. Your witness, Mr. Chadwick."

"I waive the privilege of cross-examination," said the vicar.

"Then the prosecution humbly and respectfully rests its case," Tappert asserted.

"I say they're guilty!" shouted Nathan the pickpocket.

"Guilty in spades!" added Walter the forger.

"Hold your horses, jurymen!" cried Judge Eggwort, whacking the bench with his roofing mallet. "The Court is adjourned until nine o'clock tomorrow morning!"

Shortly after completing *Wall on Wall*, which he'd wrought as planned by dipping his brush in drinking water and covering his cell's northern surface with a transparent wash, Granville Heathway concluded that painting no longer satisfied his creative urges. He needed a new pastime. The answer, he soon realized, lay in the happy fact that his dovecote, once as barren as Christ's crypt on Easter morning, now contained a half-dozen winged messengers.

Six—a veritable circus troupe, waiting to astonish audiences from Edinburgh to Brighton with acrobatic feats. In his mind's eye he beheld the whole spectacle: pigeons swinging on trapezes, balancing hazelnuts on their beaks, and climbing atop one another to form a wondrous feathered pyramid. If Heathway's Columbine Carnival proved half as magnificent as he imagined, Dr. Earwicker and Dr. Quelp might even declare him cured.

He began by creating a tightrope act, teaching his most agile birds to walk along a string stretched above his head, one end tied to the transom, the other to his escritoire. No sooner had Achilles and Guinevere mastered this trick than a seventh pigeon swooped through the barred window, the stately Calpurnia. Granville seized his quizzing-glass, unstrapped the capsule, and removed the scroll. Glancing at his son's handwriting, he immediately saw that Bertram was in low spirits, for how else to explain the jagged crosses on his *t*'s and the jittery swerve of his commas?

Dearest Father,

I shall make no effort to conceal my spiritual condition. From my spidery scrawl you will infer that your son has grown melancholic. I cannot say which news caused me greater woe—the failure of the Ararat expedition or the fate of Dr. Rosalind Franklin—but I shall begin with the former disaster.

Mr. Dalrymple's semaphore message to the Grand Vizier was as terse as it was discouraging. NO ARK ON AL-JUDI EITHER. PERPLEXED AND DESPONDENT. RETURNING IMMEDIATELY. I am truly sorry, Father. I know how fervently you wanted us to recover the sacred vessel.

Upon her arrival in Constantinople, Dr. Franklin sent word to the palace. As I confessed earlier, she has aroused in me feelings of an affectionate nature, so you can imagine my dismay when I walked into the hookah-den and beheld the shriveled sack of bones wherein now dwelt my once vibrant water-pipe companion. Her smile has lost its light, her hair its luster, her eyes their fire. She sucked up the Cannabis *with the avidity of a person in great physical distress.*

"I suppose I should wax poetic now," she said, "and insist that my real anguish is intellectual—all those experiments I'll never be able to finish—but what's the point of lying? All I want is for the pain to go away."

"I understand," I said.

At this juncture I noticed three young men hovering in the shadows, exuding an aura of protectiveness towards Dr. Franklin. She identified them as her research team, presently investigating helical and spherical viruses at her Birkbeck College laboratory. "I hope to attend the Brussels World's Fair next week," she said, gesturing towards her guardians. "Ken Holmes here, also John Finch and Sam Scheiner—the whole

Birkbeck group, in fact—they'll be presenting our findings in the Sci-
ence Pavilion. I built the exhibit myself, a five-foot-high model of the
tobacco mosaic virus. Why does God hate me so?"

"God loves you," *I assured her.* "Your team loves you. I love you."

"God hates me," *Dr. Franklin reiterated. Softening, she ran her fin-*
gers along my bare wrist like a flautist working her instrument, using
her free hand to inhale a draught of hashish. "What I've been missing
all these years is an empathetic partner, and finally I've found one,
except—damn—it doesn't matter."

"My dear Rosalind," *I said, immeasurably touched to infer she*
imagined joining her life to mine.

"Watson had Crick," *she continued, coughing,* "and Crick had Wat-
son, and at long last I've found Aaron Klug. Ours is an extraordinary
collaboration. We keep each other honest. Ah, what heights we might
have scaled together."

"By my reckoning," *I said, struggling to conceal my disappointment,*
"you've accomplished more in thirty-seven years than most people do in
seventy."

"You think so?"

"Absolutely. Your story will become a hallowed chapter in the chron-
icles of biology." I salved my psychic wound with a puff of hemp. "I can-
not but think of Père Teilhard. He, too, found the perfect partner, a
sculptress named Lucile."

"I looked into Teilhard as you asked. I'm afraid that three years ago
your friend suffered a fatal cerebral hemorrhage—though at least this
meant his eccentric views on evolution could finally see print. The Vati-
can loves dead visionaries. I read Le Phénomène Humain *as my*
young men were carrying me to Constantinople."

"A beautiful book, is it not?"

"I wouldn't know. Your Gallic biomystic is rather too deep for me. No,
let me be candid, Bertram. I didn't care for Le Phénomène Humain. *In*
my view orthogenesis, like all teleology, is an insult to a God whose non-
existence is one of His few admirable attributes. How could Teilhard have
possibly seen a benign hand at work in the spectacle of Australopithecus

africanus *involuntarily ceding the planet to* Pithecanthropus erectus, *who then must yield to* Homo neanderthalensis, *who in turn gets shoved aside by the Cro-Magnons? Is such epic disorder really the only way the Supreme Being could have gotten His darling* Homo sapiens *on stage? If the ugly, wasteful, brutal mechanisms of evolution strike your priest as sacred, I shudder to imagine what he finds profane."*

"I'm sure Teilhard could address your bewilderment."

"No doubt." A diminutive woman under the best of circumstances, Dr. Franklin suddenly seemed to shrink in upon herself. "So much work ahead. Aaron will do me proud, I know it." She coughed convulsively. "Heed the words of Rosalind the Jewish prophet. Throughout the first half of the dreadful twentieth century humanity made war on itself, but in the second half microbes will make war on humanity."

"Microbes?"

"Tiny lives devoted entirely to their own self-interest," she rasped. "Darwin himself was probably a victim of the protozoan that causes Chagas disease. In Patagonia he was attacked by the benchuca, the great black bug of the Pampas, known to carry Trypanosoma cruzi." *A spasm racked her frame, and then another, and another, each episode accompanied by a cry of pain, and yet she managed to continue. "Insidious as protozoans and bacteria can be, viruses are even worse. Opportunists, one and all, exploiting whatever works: exotic mutation, promiscuous variation, indiscriminate reproduction. Unless we cause polio and smallpox and their ilk to go extinct, gone with the trilobites, they'll gain the upper hand. It's all about mindless evolutionary strategies, not imaginary Omega Points. One day the unthinkable will happen. Courtesy of some malign enzyme or other, a family of single-strand RNA viruses will learn how to transcribe themselves into DNA, the better to appropriate our cells. But we'll fight back. We always do. I want to be there on the front lines. I don't want to see Brussels and die."*

I must finish this message ere my tears strike the ink and smear my words. Alas, Father, in truth even Brussels was denied to Dr. Franklin. Shortly after making her point about malign enzymes, she fell across my lap. I felt for her pulse. She had none.

*Immediately her young men took charge, explaining that they must
get her back to the Royal Marsden Hospital ere she was missed. At a
funereal pace they bore their mentor out of the smoky grotto, feet first, as
if preparing to bury her at sea, so that my final glimpse of Dr. Franklin
included her silent lips, lifeless eyes, and lovely brow. Against the odds,
she'd never lost her hair.*

Your sorrowful son,
Bertram

In light of the lachrymose contents of this latest message, Granville
canceled the rehearsal of Heathway's Columbine Carnival. To pursue so
frivolous a business would constitute an affront not only to Mr. Dalrymple (who had so devoutly desired to shore up Christendom with a three-
hundred-cubit corroboration of the Deluge), not only to Miss Franklin
(who would never see her virus exhibit displayed in Brussels), but also to
his grieving son. Instead Granville decided to honor the late crystallographer. Taking up his brush, he began to impose a second image atop *Wall
on Wall*, rendering his vision through bold strokes and vivid colors.

Within the hour the tribute was complete: a still life comprising
a dozen DNA double helices, each boasting two sugar-phosphate spirals
rendered in magenta, as opposed to the cyan and yellow Granville had selected for the adenine-thymine rungs, and the orange and green he'd employed (being skilled in concocting secondary colors from primaries) for the
guanine-cytosine pairs. The molecules all pointed in different directions,
like compass needles that knew nothing of north. Dr. Franklin, he decided,
would have wanted it that way: no ultimate purpose, no teleology—just
logical, coherent, and beautiful forms, signifying everything.

That night the defense team bedded down in the gondola of the airship, but only Léourier, aided by Peruvian snuff, actually slept.
Chloe and Mr. Chadwick huddled in the darkness, drinking *pisco* and
talking of God-driven evolution. The argument that natural selection
could be construed as "a kind of divine musical instrument," in the vicar's

words, "always needing the Almighty's breath to make the notes come forth," was not easily countered—and yet the worldview of the worthy Epicurus seemed equal to the task. Shortly before dawn, Chloe and Mr. Chadwick closed their eyes, soothed by their belief that if they lost *Duntopia versus Cabot and Quinn* it would not be for want of a retort to evangelical Deism.

The next morning Chloe arrayed herself in her Lady Omega gown and Panama hat, strapped on her grandfather's bayonet, seized the sandalwood box, and led the defense team to the tabernacle. Judge Eggwort's seraglio was waiting outside, surrounded by a menagerie of tethered lizards, free-roaming tortoises, and caged birds. Chirps and twitters filled the muggy air. Whilst Rebecca and Hagar held up a glass punch bowl wherein swam the requested puffer-fish (just then the creature was deflated, its bristles invisible), the pregnant Naomi pointed to a wicker basket and announced that it contained the promised human skeleton. Chloe instructed the cleavewives to have both the skull and the lower spine at the ready.

The defense team entered the steamy courtroom. Fans fluttering wildly, the spectators suggested a flock of Floreana flamingos beating their wings whilst ascending *en masse* from Stopsack's lagoon. Ralph and Solange had already taken their seats, each wearing the despondent expression of a person playing piquet with the Devil. Judge Eggwort lost no time hammering the Court to order.

"Mr. Chadwick, you may examine your first witness."

"My first and only witness," said the vicar. "The defense calls Lady Omega."

Snatching up the sandalwood box, Chloe approached the witness chair. Inevitably she imagined that she was crossing a London stage, swathed in limelight, the curtain having just risen on *The Ashes of Eden*, an edifying spectacle written by Miss Bathurst of Covent Garden. Linus Hatch came forward and bid her swear to speak nothing but the truth, so help her God. She raised no theological objections. The goal, after all, was not to hoard every pawn but to put her opponent's king in irremediable check.

Squeezing the Book of Mormon with one hand, the grip of the bayonet with the other, she said, loudly and clearly, "I so swear."

"Lady Omega, please tell the Court how you came to be in Galápagos," said Mr. Chadwick.

She began by praising Judge Eggwort for his discernment. Of all their Encantadas acquaintances, she declared, he alone had apprehended that, although it had once amused her to play a divine messenger, she in fact held no such heavenly commission.

"If you're not a prophet, then who are you?" asked Mr. Chadwick.

"Simply another English explorer with a passion for the tropics," Chloe replied. "Unlike my colleagues, however, I am moved to acquire specimens that tell against the existence of God." It took the jurymen and the spectators a moment to assimilate this startling sentence, whereupon they gasped in unison. "I fell upon this theory whilst working at a private zoological garden built by a Derbyshire naturalist whom I shall call Derrick Caedmon."

"During your employment by Mr. Caedmon, did you go by the name of Lady Omega?" asked Mr. Chadwick.

"I was merely Miss Chloe Bathurst."

"English naturalists don't normally build private zoos."

"It was a combination aviary, arboretum, and herpetorium, ideal for Mr. Caedmon's scientific investigations. When he began his work, discovering a disproof of God was the last thing on his mind, but that is nevertheless what occurred." Chloe unboxed the transmutation sketch. "He summarized his findings in this treatise, which frames the natural world as an unimaginably dense tree or bush, each branch and twig reserved to a particular species, some living, others extinct. Allow me to quote the final paragraph. 'There is grandeur in this view of life, with its powers of growth, assimilation, and reproduction having been originally breathed into one or a few kinds, and that whilst this our planet has gone circling according to fixed laws, and whilst land and water, in a cycle of change, have gone on replacing each other, that from so simple an origin, through processes of gradual selection and infinitesimal modifications, endless forms most beautiful and most wonderful have been evolved.'"

"As I understand this theory," said the vicar, "the primal creatures in question were animalcules capable of sexual reproduction."

Chloe nodded sagely. "But because they died out long ago, leaving no trace, we must begin with something more complex." She clapped her hands. "Fish!"

Rebecca and Hagar strode into the courtroom jointly carrying the puffer in its punch bowl. Léourier relieved them of the glass receptacle and, approaching the jury box, displayed its deflated occupant.

"Let's pretend that this puffer isn't a modern fish but a very ancient species, long since vanished," said Chloe as Léourier set the punch bowl on the defense table. "In other words, a proto-puffer, lacking the barbs that will characterize its descendants. Mr. Caedmon asks us to imagine that, millions of years ago, several populations of proto-puffers became isolated from one another—perhaps owing to falling sea levels or to coral-reef formation or volcanic activity. Inevitably the offspring of the offspring of these cloistered fish would have diverged from the ancestral type in form and custom, for such is the way of all fins, scales, plumage, fur, and flesh."

"A natural law understood by every animal breeder," noted Mr. Chadwick.

Chloe fanned herself with the essay. "When we consider the external stresses continually visited upon animal populations—I speak of famines, predators, contagions, floods, and frosts—when we consider these pressures in all their frequency and intensity, we may safely assume that *most* of the spontaneously occurring variations in an individual's fins, scales, plumage, fur, or flesh cannot possibly secure its prosperity. *Most* such variations, yes—but not *all*. Some of these accidental novelties may bless the creature with an advantage in the struggle for existence. Perhaps Nature favored a few proto-puffers with uncommonly strong tails, or keener eyes, or camouflaging scales."

"Or protective needles," Mr. Chadwick suggested.

Chloe rapped on the punch bowl, and the fish inflated itself like Léourier's balloon, becoming a sphere of fearsome spicules. "Protective needles, indeed, an endowment so discouraging to predators that many of these lucky fish reached sexual maturity and reproduced, thus passing on the desirable trait, which in time spread through the entire population. Please note that this transmutation, proto-puffer to modern puffer, has occurred without the intervention of any outside agency."

"Such as, for instance, God?" asked Mr. Chadwick.

Chloe smiled obliquely and said, "Now imagine that over the ages Nature bestowed primitive lungs and rudimentary limbs on some puffer populations, with the result that their descendants' descendants' descendants could survive on land as well as in water, an innovation so advantageous that those lungs and limbs proliferated. Obviously the creatures in question have long since ceased being puffers, or even fish, but must instead be classified as amphibians." Again she clapped her hands. "Land iguanas!"

Sarah entered the tabernacle, the flat-spined terrestrial iguana draped over her outstretched arms like a coiled rug. Behind her walked Miriam, cradling the high-spined specimen to her bosom.

"What disgustin' monsters," gasped Jake the fornicator.

"Newly escaped from Lucifer's zoo," declared Clarence the usurer.

"The epochs roll by," intoned Chloe as the cleavewives displayed the iguanas to the jurymen. "In time the animals we now call reptiles emerge from some amphibian stock or other. More epochs roll by. On the Galápagos archipelago, two distinct sorts of terrestrial iguana appear. A question springs to mind. What manner of capricious and possibly unhinged God would make a bright yellow, flat-spined iguana for most of these islands and a sallow gray, high-spined kind for Barrington alone? Rather than appealing to a fanciful deity, I believe we should instead trace *both* varieties back to a common ancestor. Allow me to posit a colony of Ecuadorian or Peruvian lizards who, millions of years ago, were blown into the sea by a storm, subsequently traveling to the Encantadas on uprooted trees or mats of floating vegetation."

"I'm told such natural barges have been observed riding the Humboldt Current," said Mr. Chadwick.

"Although most of the immigrant lizards transmuted into the pervasive flat-spined type," said Chloe, "their isolated cousins on Barrington became a species unto themselves." Once more she clapped. "Marine iguanas!"

Three pairs of aquatic lizards came creeping into the tabernacle, connected by leather leashes to Constance, Charity, and the pregnant Ruth. The cleavewives perambulated the creatures before the jury box as a servant might walk his master's dogs through Kensington Gardens. The multicoloreds, the blacks, and the local reds all looked equally miserable, a symptom no doubt of their being so far from their beloved surf.

"Why would the Almighty place a gaudy species of marine iguana on Narborough Isle"—Chloe pointed to the exemplar in question—"a dark species on Tower"—again she pointed—"and crimson ones here on Charles, even as He whimsically decided against installing aquatic iguanas anywhere else on planet Earth? The answer is that God had no hand in the matter. Go fossil hunting in South America, and you'll find evidence of a land-bound reptile whose evolutionary descendants would ultimately include *every* type of Encantadas iguana, aquatic as well as terrestrial."

Suddenly all eight lizards grew obstreperous, hissing and snorting with reptilian discontent. The jurors engaged in a synchronous cringe. The iguanas' respective keepers hustled them out of the tabernacle. Rebecca and Hagar retrieved the puffer-fish and likewise exited.

"Miss Bathurst—since that is apparently your real name—Miss Bathurst, I gotta put a question to you," said Eggwort. "How in the world could so many sorts of bird and beast spring from a process of such blind and arbitrary randomness?"

"I was coming to that."

"You're not an easy gal to stump, but I'm a-tryin'," said Eggwort.

"I bid Your Honor consider how our forefathers turned a single species, the wolf, into dozens of dog breeds," said Chloe. "Or consider the many sorts of modified pigeon thriving everywhere in Christendom. Or consider the livestock your subjects brought with them here to Charles Isle. Through the application of selective breeding principles, a Duntopian could in time create a woollier sheep or a more fecund goat or a fatter pig. Of course, unlike dog breeders, pigeon fanciers, and pig farmers,

Nature does not traffic in intention—and there's the rub, Your Honor: she doesn't need to."

"If Nature was here in this courtroom," said Eggwort, "she wouldn't like the way you're presumin' to speak fer her."

Rolling the essay into a tube, Chloe thrust it towards the jury box. "Instead of a conscious will, Nature boasts a workshop filled with the tools of transmutation—not only the erotic urges exploited by breeders but also incalculable quantities of death, countless episodes of extinction, myriad modes of isolation, and vast tracts of time. By incessantly wielding these five implements, Nature has unwittingly sculpted what Mr. Caedmon calls 'endless forms most beautiful.'" She whistled sharply. "Tortoises!"

For the first time since it was built, or so Chloe assumed, three giant tortoises entered the tabernacle. Eyes fixed on the jury box, Rebecca, Constance, and Sarah shuffled across the room carrying the saddleback male. Per the instructions on his bestiary page, the tortoise bore a prickly-pear cactus, the earthenware pot balanced atop his carapace like Miss Annie riding about the Down House vivarium. To Miriam, Hagar, and Charity had fallen the task of transporting the massive domeshelled female, the women gasping and groaning as they set the creature before the twelve. Finally, the Huancabamba tortoise team—Ascumiche, Yitogua, Rapra—appeared hauling the slopeback male, having evidently crossed to Charles in one of their outrigger canoes so they could spare Naomi and the other two pregnant cleavewives the effort of moving the beast.

Invited by Mr. Chadwick to talk about the tortoises, Chloe argued that they were descended from a small, vanished, domeshelled species that had long ago arrived from the mainland on seaweed rafts. Thus far, the crude carapace of the James Isle specimen had not hindered her, food being plentiful on her native formation. Here on Charles, however, her igloo-shaped shell would prove maladaptive.

"Hundreds of thousands of years ago, the island on which we stand was lush," she elaborated. "But then, like all environments, it began to change, nutritious vegetation becoming increasingly rare. Even as many of the domeshelled tortoises on Charles starved and went extinct, the descendants of the surviving descendants of *their* surviving descendants evolved the type of flared carapace you see before you."

Extending her right hand, Chloe snapped her fingers and pointed to the saddleback exhibit. Léourier removed the potted cactus from atop the tortoise and set it on the floor. As if responding to a theatre director's cue, the animal stretched out his serpentine neck and began feasting on the higher pads. Sodden clots of green mash dribbled from his jaws.

"Thanks to the arch in his shell, our saddleback friend can elevate his head and reach the upper fruits," said Chloe.

"And what of the third type of tortoise?" asked Mr. Chadwick.

"If his homeland loses its flora," said Chloe, "this Indefatigable slope-back and his immediate kin will probably disappear, though perhaps his descendants' descendants' descendants will transmute into saddlebacks." Again she whistled. "Birds!"

Leaving the tortoises in place, the Indians exited the courtroom, as did Rebecca and the other cleavewives. Eggwort's entire harem appeared in a trice with a dozen bamboo birdcages, stacking them before the jury box in a chirping, tweeting, trilling pyramid. Chloe proceeded to discourse on the feathered exhibits, making the same points she'd overheard during the momentous Down House luncheon. How the four distinct species found within the mockingbird group bespoke a common ancestor, a principle that also applied to the three species of flycatcher and the half-dozen species of finch. How individual birds accidentally gifted with advantageous tails and wings enjoyed procreative success, likewise those favored with felicitous bills (certain forms being well suited to penetrating cactus fruit, others to cracking seeds, still others to tweezing insects), whilst the poorly endowed went extinct. How the progenitor of *all* the world's birds had not arrived full-blown upon the face of the Earth but had itself descended from a beaked, egg-laying, featherless, wingless creature of reptilian pedigree.

"The jury is eager to learn whether the theory of natural selection applies to our own species," said Mr. Chadwick.

"No, we're not," said Nathan the pickpocket.

"Mr. Caedmon is hardly the first scientist to remark on a physical resemblance between apes and humans," said Chloe. "Squint, and a marmoset looks remarkably like a marquis. According to evolutionary theory, if we follow certain particular limbs on the Tree of Life back far enough in time we'll encounter an extinct, hairy, four-legged, forest-dwelling, tail-sporting beast whose offspring's offspring's offspring will one day find themselves walking the Earth not only as apes and monkeys but also as the animal called *Homo sapiens*." Once more she whistled. "Bones!"

Pregnant Naomi marched into the tabernacle bearing Chloe's requested skull and the collateral spinal-column segment. Like a relic monger exhibiting bits of saints to prospective customers, Naomi paraded the bones before the jurymen, then deposited them on the defense table.

"Mr. Caedmon contends that our skeletons reveal signs of an extinct ancestor held in common by today's apes and men." Brandishing the spinal-column segment like Pirate Anne wielding a cutlass, Chloe indicated the nethermost vertebra: a narrow, tapered, dagger-like vestige. "Behold the human coccyx, a small but graphic reminder of our descent from creatures that had tails."

"I never had a tail," protested Clarence the usurer.

"My uncle did," said George the train robber.

"Now consider those implements with which we chew our food." Chloe slipped her index finger beneath her upper lip, sliding it back and forth. "Run a finger along your top gum, and you'll encounter two enormous canine roots. Go ahead, gentlemen. Try it yourselves."

The jurors probed their gums, as did everyone else in the tabernacle.

"Why are these teeth so elaborately anchored?" With the aid of the bayonet Chloe prised both upper canines free of the skull, fat roots included. She passed them to Léourier, who straightaway presented the evidence to the jury. "As you can see, the usable parts of a modern man's cuspids are not a whit more impressive than his incisors or molars. Ah, but the canine teeth of our simian ancestors were in fact *weapons*, long and sharp like those of a baboon."

As the aeronaut returned the teeth to Chloe, she found herself recalling *The Murders in the Rue Morgue*. In both the play and Mr. Poe's original tale, the killer had proved to be an escaped orang-utang. The ape did it. *Duntopia versus Cabot and Quinn* had the same plot, she realized. On this sweltering tropical morn, here in the White Horse Prophecy Tabernacle, a deicide had occurred, for when a simian shambles free of the jungle and enters the savannah, where her posterity will over the course of innumerable generations discover fire, make tools, plant gardens, build bridges, write poetry, and name the stars, then God has in effect been murdered. The ape did it.

"Miss Bathurst, will you please summarize your case against the Almighty's alleged factuality?" asked Mr. Chadwick.

Rising in as regal a fashion as she could contrive, Chloe glided away from the witness chair and approached the jury box, locking eyes with each of the twelve in turn. "If our essential written testament to God's *modus operandi* is naught but a myth, then that is a reason to doubt His reality. If there was no first man called Adam, merely tribes of apes being buffeted about by time and chance, then no divine Galilean rabbi was needed to redeem that nonexistent first man's fall, the lapse having never occurred. If the pageant of life on this planet, from worms to wolves to we ourselves, has drawn its energy solely from the Earth, then Heaven and its denizens may very well be fictitious."

She returned to the witness chair at a stately pace, pausing in a shaft of sunlight (so that she briefly became an English mystic again), then stepping abruptly away as the curtain descended on *The Ashes of Eden*.

"No further questions," said Mr. Chadwick.

"Miss Bathurst, you have exceeded my expectations," said Eggwort. "Mr. Tappert, when you cross-examine the witness, please try to elicit more such outlandish bellywash."

"I'll do my best, Your Honor," said the chief prosecutor.

Taking up his mallet, Eggwort struck the bench and declared a midday recess. Straightaway his harem appeared with wooden bowls and steaming copper tureens filled with the day's chowder. The noises that subsequently resounded through the tabernacle recalled for Chloe her first day on Galápagos: the Charles Isle saddlebacks slurping mossy water from their pool.

As Chloe and Mr. Chadwick returned to the defense table, the vicar told her, "You were brilliant."

"*Magnifique!*" Léourier declared.

"My fair philosopher," said Ralph, "you were born to play the part of Derrick Caedmon's zookeeper."

"The part of his fellow transmutationist," Chloe corrected him.

"Mr. Caedmon sounds like a remarkable man."

"The most remarkable I've ever known," said Chloe.

"I'm grateful to have my she-devil back, but they're going to hang me anyway," said Solange.

"I won't let them do that," said Chloe.

"We need more marmosets in this courtroom," said Ralph, "and fewer kangaroos."

Despite the turbulence in her guts, Chloe forced herself to consume her entire portion of chowder, lest she grow weak during her battle with the chief prosecutor. It was thus with a full stomach, though not a settled mind, that she returned to the witness chair, sandalwood box in hand, and made ready to endure Jethro Tappert's assault. He approached her with the confident swagger of a royal headsman applying for the job of village butcher.

At first the chief prosecutor offered only the most conventional objections to Derrick Caedmon's theory. The Earth was too young, the fossil record too spotty, for a rational man to favor a secular Tree of Life over a divinely seeded Garden of Eden. Although advantageous novelties might appear from time to time, each such trait would be diluted long before it could guarantee its beneficiaries' evolutionary success.

Flourishing the transmutation sketch, Chloe articulated the ripostes that lay therein. No, the Earth was *not* too young. Read Charles Lyell or any other competent geologist. Of *course* the fossil record was spotty. The search for such evidence had barely begun. As for the alleged dilution problem, the persistence of hemophilia from generation to generation ruled out blending as the primary mechanism of heredity.

"Even if we allow that natural solicitation has occurred on our planet," said Tappert, "what's to prevent a pious scientist from sayin' it's nothin' but the method God uses to make new species and fit 'em into convivial habitations? All your Mr. Caedmon did, it seems to me, was put some names to them 'fixed laws' our Creator laid down at the beginnin' of time, which means there ain't no need to choose between believin' in God and trustin' in transmutation."

So now it was upon her, that dreaded paragon of oxymorons: evangelical Deism. Hear me, O Epicurus. Help me, mighty Lucretius. Come forth like Lazarus and save my friends from the noose.

"Judge Eggwort, Mr. Tappert, good jurymen, I invite you to picture a world in which the gods are regarded as irrelevant to human affairs," said Chloe. "Instead of inventing Judaism, Christianity, Mohammedanism, Hindooism, Buddhism, and the rest, people have elected to account for reality in largely materialist terms. Such a philosophy, in fact, once flourished. I refer to the ideas of the ancient sage Epicurus, as immortalized in the first century B.C. by the poet Lucretius in *De Rerum Natura*. Along with an earlier sage called Democritus, Epicurus taught that ultimately nothing exists save for atoms and void." She removed her Panama hat and fanned herself with the brim. "Can we be confident that a world keyed to Greek atomism would adopt a non-supernatural theory of evolution? I think so. And would this world eventually come to include steam trains, clipper ships, spinning jennies, landscape paintings, love ballads, piano concertos, theatrical melodramas, vintage wines, and other such secular amenities? I don't doubt it."

"It's a far better place than Mephistropolis," noted Harry the panderer.

"Now imagine that, after our hypothetical atomist civilization has been thriving for several thousand years, a bearded patriarch comes traipsing out of the desert. 'Harken!' he cries. 'An invisible but very talkative and person-like entity has manifested Himself to me! Harken! This entity is the very Architect of the Cosmos, dwelling everywhere and causing everything! You must outgrow your childish affection for the given world and fall down in awe before the One True God!'"

Slipping free of the witness chair, Chloe marched towards the jury box, where she favored each inmate with the same beguiling smile she'd cultivated whilst playing Queen Cleopatra.

"Very well, I suppose it's *conceivable* that our atomists would leap for joy, turn to the patriarch, and say, 'My goodness, sir, you certainly got *that* right—your One True God theory harmonizes *perfectly* with our materialist understanding of the world. Your revelation accords *completely* with our reason. Thank you for bringing us this marvelous gift.'"

"Miss Bathurst, sit down!" cried Eggwort. "You're attemptin' to mesmerize the jury!"

"Conceivable, good sirs, but implausible! So implausible in fact that I shall abstain from elaboration, lest I insult the shade of Epicurus by taking his foes seriously!"

As Chloe strode back to the witness chair, an exasperated Tappert flicked his wrists as if to shake water from his fingertips. "I'm no longer angry with you, Miss Bathurst. Your derangement evokes only my pity—everythin' else has dropped away. I got no further questions."

Surveying the saddleback tortoise, who seemed to meet her gaze with sympathetic eyes, Chloe reassumed her place at the defense table.

"Epicurus served us even better than I'd hoped," declared Mr. Chadwick.

"On returning to France, I shall read my Lucretius again," said Léourier.

"On arriving in Hell, I shall tell both sages they almost saved my life," said Solange.

"The jury will retire to their prison cells and begin deliberatin'," Eggwort announced.

"Your Honor," said Ben the horse thief, rising from his egg crate, "I would ask a boon of the expert witness." Doffing his burlap skullcap, he turned to Chloe. "Miss Bathurst, might I borrow that treatise of Mr. Caedmon's? His ideas are probably too dense for us, but we ought to give it a try."

Although she had never imagined that Mephistropolis might be amongst the way stations where "An Essay Concerning Descent with Modification" stopped during its South American odyssey, she did not doubt the juror's sincerity. She handed the sandalwood box to Léourier, who in turn delivered it to the horse thief.

"Tomorrow at nine o'clock we'll convene to hear the verdict, after which I shall pass sentence on the defendants," said Eggwort.

"Unless we're found innocent," noted Ralph.

"Perfessor, you seem to ferget where your sinful flesh and sorry bones reside at present," said Judge Eggwort. "In Duntopia, we navigate by the Tablets of the Law, not the lodestone of your predilections." He hammered the bench with the enthusiasm of a latter-day Samson crushing the skulls of the Philistine army. "This court is adjourned!"

There was nothing like a blast of Peruvian snuff for scraping detritus from the walls of a person's skull, all that encrusted dread, those barnacles of remorse, and so Chloe imagined that the *epená* would shield her from the imminent verdict in *Duntopia versus Cabot and Quinn*. Sprawled across the gondola floor, she groped about in the murk of dawn, eventually finding the rubber syringe. She filled it with resin, slipped the nipple into her nostril, and squeezed the bulb. Her brain soon found itself in El Dorado, afloat in the city's most peaceful fountain, the limpid blue waters washing over her cerebral convolutions even as the rest of her remained in Galápagos.

Cradling the syringe and a phial of snuff, she followed Mr. Chadwick and Capitaine Léourier as they exited the airship, crossed the glittering beach, and hiked over the cinder cones towards Minor Zion. Starting along the frozen-lava path that led to the courthouse, Chloe and her companions encountered Rebecca Eggwort, who reported that the Huancabamba tortoise team had just embarked for Hood's Isle in an outrigger canoe.

"I figured we was done showin' the jury the domeshelled female, so I told the Indians they could leave," said Rebecca. "But if worse comes to worst, the half-dozen of us not with child at the moment—well,

Constance ain't so sure of her situation—we six could probably parade her up and down in front of the jury box."

"Our domeshell illustration has played her part, likewise the other creatures in the bestiary," said Chloe. "After we hear the verdict, you might as well set all our local exhibits free—the saddleback male, the red iguanas, the Charles Isle finches."

"I shall never look at a finch's beak in quite the same way again," said Rebecca.

"May I tell you something, Mrs. Eggwort?" said Chloe. "I spoke that very same sentence two years ago in Mr. Caedmon's zoo, right after I'd first heard him explain his species theory."

"I'll bet you understood it right away, Miss Bathurst, you bein' such a bright lady," said Rebecca.

"Truth to tell, Mrs. Eggwort, I couldn't make heads or tails of it."

The defense team proceeded to the tabernacle, pausing before the illustrative specimens: birds fluttering in their cages, tethered aquatic lizards breaking their fast with algae, penned terrestrial lizards munching cactus-plant fruits, tortoises gawking at passing Latter-Day Saints—a tableau suggesting Noah's menagerie queuing up to board the ark. Owing to the *epená,* Chloe entered into conversation with the saddleback male.

"Were you satisfied with my performance?" asked the tortoise. "Did I demonstrate the evolutionary advantages of an unencumbered neck?"

"Should the jury find against my friends, you'll share not a particle of blame," she replied.

"What are we doing here, Miss Bathurst? In the universe, I mean."

The *epená* summoned a meandering smile to her lips. "You're asking the wrong woman. I'm merely a transmutationist. The universe is not my line of country."

The tabernacle was already packed, spectators thronging the pews, jurors poised on their cheese casks, Judge Eggwort tenderizing his palm with the roofing mallet, Tappert and Hatch perusing the Book of Mormon. Speaking not a word, Chloe assumed her seat and passed the resin syringe to Solange, who availed herself of its magic.

"I know what I'm requesting for my last meal," said Solange, handing the latex bulb to her co-defendant. "A bottle of *pisco* and a pound of Peruvian snuff."

"Two bottles for me," said Ralph, "and enough *epená* to fly me to the brothels of Baghdad."

Judge Eggwort called the proceeding to order. Silence descended, a quietude so intense as to make the rude building seem like what it really was, a house of prayer.

"The jury foreman will deliver the verdict," said the chief magistrate.

Joe the poacher stood fully erect. "'May it please the Court,'" he read in a halting voice, eyes fixed on a scrap of paper fluttering in his hand. "'As it 'appens, we all 'ad different reactions to the testimonies, the upshot being that each man will speak 'is mind in turn.'"

"Six votes for acquittal, and you walk free," Mr. Chadwick reminded his clients.

"I vote we send 'em to the scaffold," said Nathan the pickpocket, rising. "Nobody has the right to destroy God's private property, and that's the long 'n' short of it!"

"Bloody hell," said Ralph.

Much to Chloe's dismay, the *epená* was failing to do its job. She remained mired in Galápagos, a place where six not-guilty votes were a statistical impossibility and Her Majesty's governors never issued pardons.

"I agree with Clarence," said Walter the forger, gaining his feet. "I appreciate Miss Bathurst's fervor, but this transmigration business is a cartload of flapdoodle. The defendants must 'ang!"

"*Merde*," said Capitaine Léourier.

"It's not flapdoodle, but it's not a disproof of God either," asserted Pete the highwayman. "That said, Miss Bathurst has set me to thinkin' that the folk who wrote the Bible didn't hold themselves to the highest standards of truthfulness, especially concernin' Noah and the Flood, which means I vote for acquittal!"

"That wight can rob me blind whenever he wants," muttered Solange.

Chloe simultaneously squeezed Ralph's sinewy forearm and the seawitch's slender knee. They had just won a victory. Was it too much to hope for five more?

"I say Pete's talkin' sense," declared Amos the sodomite. "The Tree of Life is a feisty idea, but it ain't about to give God a bad night's sleep. It seems to me the big loser in this trial is the prophet Noah, who I'm startin' to suspect was no more 'istorical than Old King Cole. Yes, the defendants burned a boat that night, but it wasn't the Genesis ark. Seein' as 'ow you can't commit sacrilege against a thing what ain't sacred, I 'ereby vote for mercy!"

"Buy that man a beardless youth," whispered Solange.

"I'll probably roast eternally for sayin' this, but Miss Bathurst has convinced me that God's not a deity to be taken seriously," said Tim the anarchist. "Judge Eggwort, you must set the defendants free!"

"All hail our prince of disorder," said Solange.

"I'll tell you what I think," said Ben the horse thief, clutching the sandalwood box to his chest. "I think Mr. Caedmon has done nothin' more and nothin' less than to describe the methods our Creator employed for makin' all the world's plants and animals. Given that He's the spirit of transmutation, He's got no interest in becomin' the plaintiff in a blasphemy trial. Ship the defendants back to England, Your Honor. I wish I could go with 'em!"

"I owe that man a romp in the rye," said Solange.

"Forgive my presumption, Ben, but your logic's leaky as a sieve," declared George the train robber. "Yes, a transmutation or two might have occurred here in Galápagos and elsewhere, but that don't give a person license to burn Noah's ark. The arsonists must pay for their crime!"

"Faugh," grunted Chloe.

"George said it better than I ever could," averred Dick the swindler. "There may be some truth to Mr. Caedmon's notions, but God is the greatest truth of all. Judge Eggwort, it's your sacred duty to chastise the ark burners!"

"Four nods towards the noose, four towards Mother England," whispered Mr. Chadwick.

"When I first came into this courtroom, I believed each and every word in the Bible," said Jake the fornicator. "Well, Your Honor, that's still true—which means you must schedule a visit to the scaffold for both these criminals!"

"My opinion of fornication has just been lowered considerably," said Ralph.

"Unlike some of my fellow freethinkers, I'm not afraid to shout the good news from the 'ousetops!" proclaimed Harry the panderer. "There is no God! There never was a God! There never will be a God! Let these people go!"

"Such a splendid flesh merchant," said Solange.

"We need but one more friend in the jury box," noted Mr. Chadwick.

"Now *I'm* gonna do some shoutin'," proclaimed Clarence the usurer. "God is alive! Jesus is Lord! Dispatch the blackguards to the Devil's scullery!"

"He's not the one," observed Ralph.

All eyes fell on the remaining juror. Gaining his feet, Joe the poacher spat into his palms and rubbed his hands together. "Durin' the course of my chosen vocation as an appropriator of superfluous game, I became a votary of the natural world. When Miss Bathurst tells as 'ow all the plants and animals are knitted together in a kind of crazy quilt, I must say I'm impressed, and if God 'ad nothin' to do with it, then let's not give credit where credit ain't due. To wit, I cast my vote with the freethinkers!"

In a spontaneous yet synchronized spasm, the defense team and the accused blasphemers leaped to their collective feet.

"Hoorah!" cried Chloe.

"We did it!" shouted Mr. Chadwick.

"*Merveilleux!*" declared Léourier.

"God bless the poacher!" exclaimed Ralph.

"Praised be all highwaymen, sodomites, anarchists, horse thieves, and panderers!" trilled Solange.

Judge Eggwort banged on the bench with the frenzy of an unscrupulous undertaker attempting to secure a coffin whose occupant had just stirred. "Silence! There's entirely too much jubilatin' in this courtroom! Silence! It appears that the jury has gotten itself stuck midway between an acquittal and the gallows, so now it's up to me to break the tie. I hereby declare Edward Cabot and Bianca Quinn guilty as charged, and I condemn 'em both to be hanged by their necks until dead. Executioner Ordoñez will carry out the sentence seven days hence."

"No!" Chloe shouted.

"Outrageous!" screamed Mr. Chadwick.

"*Incroyable!*" cried Léourier.

The spectators' pews erupted in an impassioned cacophony. Whilst the three emperors cheered and whistled, along with a scattering of their sons and daughters, the twenty-one wives and a majority of the children filled the courtroom with hoots, hisses, groans, and catcalls.

"Six not-guilty votes to set them free—you said that on Thursday!" a sputtering and livid Mr. Chadwick reminded the bench.

"Innovation is ever on the march here in Duntopia!" retorted Egg-wort. "The punishment will be administered Saturday a week at ten o'clock in the mornin', with all Mephistropolis inmates assembled in the yard to watch!"

Four of Capitán Machado's guards tromped across the courtroom and, seizing hold of Ralph and Solange, began hauling them out of the tabernacle by main strength.

"My ghost will haunt you till the end of your days!" a livid Ralph told Eggwort.

"My demons will unsex you in your sleep!" cried Solange, weeping.

"The Court is adjourned!" yelled the chief magistrate.

"It's not over!" insisted Chloe, calling after her friends. "Don't despair! It's not over!"

Gradually the commotion passed, and a punctuated hush settled over the tabernacle, the cleavewives exchanging staccato sighs, the children speaking in choked whispers.

Chloe imagined she might salve her despair with a fresh infusion of Peruvian snuff, but she took up the syringe only to set it aside. She folded her arms on the defense table and lowered her head into the sleeves of her white gown. Her tears flowed freely, like meltwater rushing from the Andes into Amazonia.

Somewhere in her vicinity a man cleared his throat and snorted. She lifted her gaze. Ben the horse thief stood over her, chained as always to George the train robber, Dick the swindler, and Amos the sodomite. "Almost forgot to return this," Ben muttered, pressing the sandalwood box into Chloe's grasp, then added, more softly still, "When you get the chance, look at the back of page twenty-three."

And with that cryptic remark he permitted his fellow prisoners to drag him away, their manacles and chains clanking discordantly. To distract herself from the infinite awfulness of the moment, Chloe imagined that the convicts were a gang of mercenary flagellants—sinners for hire, employed by recently deceased Christians to perform penitential acts on their behalf. If that was how the afterlife worked, then Orrin Eggwort would be well advised to sell his island for gold and pour the doubloons into his coffin, because otherwise, arriving penniless in Purgatory, he would be sentenced to breaking rocks and picking oakum for the greater part of eternity.

14

Although Untutored in Geology and Lacking in Divinity, Our Heroine Presumes to Practice Vulcanogenesis

True enough, Chloe had failed to save her friends—but she could at least do right by the nonhuman players in *Duntopia versus Cabot and Quinn*: so ran the tangled thread of her disordered thoughts following the catastrophic verdict in Orrin Eggwort's courtroom. As the perpetual champion of all Encantadas creatures, she resolved to restore the illustrative specimens promptly to their native habitats. Before leaving Charles Isle, she directed the sultanas to fill the *Lamarck* with all the imported birds and iguanas. By the time Léourier had weighed anchor, the flying-machine's company included not only the defense team but also three dozen twittering, cheeping, hissing, sibilating exemplars of Derrick Caedmon's species theory.

"You put up a brave fight, Miss Bathurst!" cried Rebecca Eggwort as the balloon lofted towards the clouds.

"I'm namin' my next daughter Chloe!" shouted Naomi, laying a palm on her protuberant belly.

"If Orrin tells us to bring the children to the executions, we're gonna spit in both his eyes!" declared Hagar.

"I'll be back!" Chloe called down from the wicker carriage.

"Fer the domeshell?" asked Rebecca. "Fer the slopeback?"

"For the domeshell and the slopeback!" Chloe replied. She considered adding, *and also for Professor Cabot and Miss Quinn*, then thought better of the idea. In the absence of a plan for her friends' deliverance, it behooved her to refrain from bravado.

The crestfallen defense team spent the day making a circuit of the Encantadas in the *Lamarck*, dropping off the specimens, then landed on Hood's Isle shortly after, by the reckoning of the vicar's pocket watch, 9:00 p.m. Although the Huancabambas had a meal waiting (a pelican stew cooked by Cuniche, a seaweed salad assembled by Nitopari), when the defense team sat down to eat they realized that Eggwort's verdict had robbed them of all appetite. Instead they drank *pisco*.

Only after finishing her third glass did Chloe recall the remark Ben the horse thief had made when returning the essay. At some point during the jury's deliberations, he'd apparently scrawled a note on the back of page 23. She fetched the sandalwood box, imagining she was about to read a love letter. Over the years she'd received many such epistles, some touching, others pathetic, a few impossibly vulgar. Crudely lettered with a stick of charcoal, the horse thief's words could hardly be described as romantic, but they were not wanting in audacity.

Dear Miss B,

I write this knowin the virdict will probubly go against Perfesser C and Miss Q. From the very 1st, Judge E wanted em to hang. I ment what I sed when explainin my vote. God has no need to chastize blasphemurs. In my view this makes Him a greater, not a lesser, Supreem Bein. Cud it be that you, too, have powers, Miss B? I remember what Guvnor S told Reverend H on the beech. You are a mystik profett.

Heres what you shud do. When the hangins ar about to happin, you and yur friends shud create a stupendis diverzion. I have three suggestshuns: tell the lizurds to attack Capten B's men, or hipnotize the guards into thinkin their guns have becum snakes, or make the volcayno seem to spit fire.

I say the volcayno illuzion wud be best. During the eruptshin, yur allies here in Mefistropolis will add to the kaos, that is, myself plus the

othurs simpathetic to transmutayshun. (I meen Joe, Harry, Pete, Tim,
and Amos.) This will distract Execueshuner O and allow you to carry
off Perfesser C and Miss Q so that justis can preevale.

Your friend,
Ben Colby

She showed the message to Mr. Chadwick, who read it wearing a frozen face, then passed the page to Léourier. Although an iguana attack was out of the question, likewise mesmerism, the diversionary volcano appealed to Chloe. Such a feat could hardly be more difficult than traveling from Belém to Manáos in a decrepit side-wheeler, crossing the Andes in a rickety flying-machine, or canceling the Great Winnowing.

"I'm intrigued by our horse thief's notion of staging an eruption," she said.

"This is Galápagos, Miss Bathurst, not the West End," said Mr. Chadwick.

"At first blush I would agree with our *curé*," said the aeronaut. "At second blush, I see how we might make Mount Pajas explode."

Léourier proceeded to explain that, although the *Lamarck* was a hot-air device, he'd occasionally flown ships whose bladders were filled with hydrogen. In learning how to generate that gas in far-flung locations, he'd become fluent in the science of chemistry. "A scheme such as our horse thief proposes, *mes amis*, would depend on our collecting a quantity of bat excrement, 'guano' in the Quechua language. The active ingredient is saltpeter, a nitrate used in making bullets, petards, artillery shells, and—*nota bene*—fireworks. Were we to launch dozens of guano-fueled skyrockets from the summit of Mount Pajas, plus as many boulders propelled by guano bombs, the effect might be indistinguishable from an eruption."

It occurred to Chloe that her life was being measured out in volcanoes. During the long run of *The Last Days of Pompeii* she'd fled Vesuvius over a hundred times. Back at Down House she'd frequently reread Mr. Darwin's account of the Chilean volcano Osorno. And now she was hoping to bring a moribund Mount Pajas back to life.

"In his travel journal Mr. Darwin tells of bat caverns under Chatham Isle," she said. "How much guano might we need?"

"By adding the fuel requirements of our rockets to their payloads," Léourier replied, "then factoring in the bombs and fuses, I would estimate ten pounds. Assuming the Chatham caverns contain significant deposits, we might gather that amount in two or three days."

"When describing Mount Osorno," said Chloe, "Mr. Darwin wrote that the spewing lava at first suggested an exploding star, then a luminous tree, its silvery branches reflected in San Carlos Bay."

"Ah, so the eruption was an omen," said Mr. Chadwick.

"Mr. Darwin doesn't believe in omens," said Chloe.

"An allegory, then," the vicar persisted. "Today the Star of Bethlehem has been superseded by the Tree of Life."

"You do Mr. Darwin a disservice," said Chloe, "for he saw in Mount Osorno what he sees everywhere else in Nature, no allegories or lessons, merely intimations of an impersonal universe, animated only by itself." Numb with fatigue, she rose from her clinker stool, her imagination fixed on her soft seaweed mattress. "Of course, there are times when a woman thrown into such a world must make her own volcano"—she staggered towards her shack—"rather than waiting for God or geology to do the job. Sleep well, gentlemen, for tomorrow we become connoisseurs of shite."

Taking off from Hood's Isle aboard a cramped and distressed *Lamarck*, its engine protesting the ponderous load with metallic shrieks and steam-powered groans, Chloe and her friends and disciples flew to Chatham Isle (which from the air resembled an enormous kidney bean). The party landed on the northern shore, near a slopeback graveyard mentioned by Mr. Darwin in his journal, where they seized hold of an empty tortoise shell to use as a guano cistern. After equipping themselves with soup-spoons from the airship's galley, they hiked over petrified waves of lava to the bat-cavern entrance, whereupon, like Orpheus before them—like Aeneas, Persephone, and by some accounts Jesus of Nazareth—they descended into the Earth.

Shite mining quickly proved as grueling as it was tedious. Hour after hour, the Europeans and the Indians toiled within the stinking, stifling, lantern-lit reaches of the labyrinth, their eyes straining to spot the veins of excrement rippling along the formerly molten walls and twisting across the frozen floor. The Huancabambas took to grumbling, their discontent persisting even after Chloe explained to the two English speakers that the task was vital to the welfare of Señor Dartworthy and Señorita Kirsop.

"This work not so bad as what my cousins do on the rubber plantation but still make us feel sick," complained Cuniche.

"First you say to carry heavy tortoises around will save Señor Dartworthy and Señorita Kirsop," protested Nitopari. "Now you say to collect guano does the same. What next? We catch a hundred hammerhead sharks and dye them purple with *orchilla* moss, and *then* your friends be safe?"

"I simply must ask you to trust me," said Chloe.

"Long ago we learn not to trust people who wear shoes," said Cuniche. "This the last task we perform for you, Señorita Bathurst."

"Fair enough," said Chloe.

"With God's guidance, we built a volcano for our prophet," added Nitopari with an acerbic smile, "and then we did her no more favors."

Like Job scraping himself with a potshard, each shite miner employed his soupspoon to peel the vital substance from the cavern walls, depositing the gleanings in the tortoise-shell receptacle. Usually the stuff came away in fat and satisfactorily dollops, but sometimes it disintegrated into tiny chips, like flecks of theatrical paint, which the miners had to roll into pellets with their fingertips. The resident bats filled the grotto with demonic screeches, even as the most ornery of them attacked the intruders, clawing at their scalps, so that the miners' brows became studies in blood, sweat, ashes, dust, and guano.

By late afternoon both cisterns were filled to capacity, a harvest so impressive that Chloe bid everyone relax for the rest of the day. But before they left Chatham, she insisted that the miners launch a trial skyrocket—a test that must be conducted whilst the sun still shone, lest it attract the notice of the prison guards on nearby Charles Isle. After obtaining a hollow strut from the *Lamarck*'s trove of spare parts, Léourier stuffed the wooden tube with guano, then prepared the nose cone by wrapping a wad in a fragment torn from his map of Patagonia. He placed the finished device upright against a rock and, striking a lucifer match, touched the flame to the saltpeter fuse.

The rocket whooshed skyward, attaining an altitude of at least a hundred feet. Within five seconds the fire consumed the propellant, then ignited the map fragment, so that the nose cone exploded in a brilliant shower of sparks. A spontaneous cheer went up from all nine miners.

"Not the Star of Bethlehem," said Mr. Chadwick, "nor even Halley's Comet, but 'tis enough, 'twill serve."

"*Mon Capitaine,* I congratulate you," said Chloe to Léourier. "Between your airship and your rocket, I have never known a man so adept at defying gravity."

The instant Léourier got them back home to Hood's Isle, landing the *Lamarck* on the southern shore, the miners burst out of the carriage and plunged into the surf, washing away the encrusted filth of the day's labors. Not since her immersion in the copper washtub at the Hotel da Borboleta Azul in Manáos (the three Arauaki women dissolving the residue of her voyage up the Rio Amazonas) had Chloe taken such pleasure in the act of bathing. Although the sea lions did not appreciate this invasion of their private beach by human beings, they made no attempt to shoulder the intruders aside but instead confined their hostility to irate stares and roars of annoyance.

The following morning the miners returned to Chatham Isle and resumed their troglodytic agenda. Despite the sweltering heat and the sporadic bat attacks, they extracted from the cavern enough guano to fill a second slopeback shell. As evening came to the Encantadas, Léourier declared that by his calculation they'd reaped the necessary ten pounds.

Back on Hood, Chloe realized that the forthcoming spectacle required a carefully wrought *scenario.* Given the success of her Lost Thirteenth Tribe masquerade, the task of structuring the eruption must obviously fall to her—and so that night she drifted off to sleep imagining an ineluctable progression from act one, "The Smoldering Summit," to act two, "The Exploding Pumice," to act three, "The Flying Stones."

Wednesday found the vulcaneers boarding the *Lamarck* and flying to Indefatigable Isle on a threefold mission. Whilst Chloe wandered through the lowlands, harvesting bamboo shoots with the help of Cuniche, Nitopari, and Pirohua, the other Indians searched for supplementary guano in the cliff-side caves, even as Mr. Chadwick and Léourier attempted to persuade the Governor of his Christian obligation to reprieve the convicted defendants. Each initiative played out as Chloe had anticipated, her own team leaving Indefatigable toting a sack of rocket bodies, the guano party carrying off a full bucket of explosive material, and the vicar and the aeronaut bearing away distasteful memories of their encounter with Stopsack.

"He insists that clemency is out of the question," Mr. Chadwick told Chloe as the flying-machine carried them home.

"I wonder if he'll dare show his face at the executions."

"Not only does he plan to attend, he claims he'll do so with a clear conscience," said the vicar. "As he puts it, 'If Christians forbear to excise the cancer of blasphemy here in Galápagos, the tumor will spread throughout the Empire.'"

The vulcaneers devoted Thursday to assembling their ordnance. Owing to the Huancabambas' skillful hands, a pyrotechnic cottage industry soon emerged on Hood's Isle. To produce each bomb, Léourier required the Indians to stuff a prickly-pear cactus pad with a presumably optimum quantity of guano—enough to heave a boulder towards Mephistropolis, though not so much as to endanger anyone in the exercise yard—and by the noon hour thirty such devices filled a vacant shack.

Skyrocket production proceeded less efficiently. At one point the vulcaneers ran short of nose-cone material, the *Lamarck* having but a half-dozen maps on board and the leaves from Chloe's Bible being too flimsy to hold scoops of guano. But then Mr. Chadwick observed that the thick and creamy pages of "An Essay Concerning Descent with Modification" might accomplish the job.

Although there was no question that the treatise must be sacrificed, Chloe regarded this prospect with bittersweet emotions. Watching the Huancabambas smothering shite in evolutionary theory, she recalled the anxious night she'd copied the sketch by candlelight at Down House, back when Miss Annie was a healthy child and the Albion Transmutationist Club not yet born.

Friday was given to strategizing. The team agreed that Mr. Chadwick should station himself atop Mount Pajas, the perfect vantage from which to orchestrate the illusion. As the volcano erupted, Chloe and Léourier would exploit the pandemonium, piloting the *Lamarck* towards the scaffold and spiriting away Ralph and Solange.

There remained the task of rigging the mountain in accordance with the *scenario*. Under cover of twilight Chloe and her friends took off for Charles Isle in the *Lamarck,* accompanied by Cuniche, Nitopari, Pirohua, and Ascumiche, the gondola jammed with thirty bamboo skyrockets, as many cactus-pad bombs, and two pots of guano for the fuses. Léourier skillfully guided the overburdened flying-machine across Villamil Quay, touching down in a wooded area, its soaring palms and *palo santo* trees presumably shielding the balloon from the scrutiny of prison guards and Minor Zionists.

After gathering together bundles of dry sticks and mounds of wet seaweed, the vulcaneers made a series of moonlit ascents, bearing the ordnance up the north face of Mount Pajas. Once the rockets and bombs were deposited at the peak, Léourier and the four Huancabambas set the stage for act one, "The Smoldering Summit," ringing the crater with twenty stacks of kindling, each topped with enough sodden kelp to guarantee an ominous quantity of smoke. Léourier next turned his attention to act three, "The Flying Stones." Descending a dozen paces to a broad outcropping of hardened lava, he decorated the ropy terrain with guano fuses, the white lines traversing the shelf like frosting on a hot-cross bun. At each intersection he and the Indians placed a cactus bomb surmounted by a boulder, so that when the axial fuse was lit the mountain would seem to disintegrate, hurtling pieces of itself towards the penal colony.

Whilst the aeronaut and the Huancabambas labored on the slopes, Chloe and Mr. Chadwick took up turtle-oil lanterns and climbed into the crater. The stench of sulphur suffused the cavity: the Devil's anteroom, mused Chloe—the foyer of the Inferno. Gingerly they moved along the jutting ledges of frozen lava, securing the bamboo projectiles with tuff and cinders, the nose cones all pointed towards the mouth of the volcano and the starry sky beyond. The vicar ran a stripe of guano from each rocket engine to the master fuse, which the *scenario* required him to ignite at the beginning of act two, "The Exploding Pumice."

Considering the bleakness of their surroundings, this pit of ashen air and black rock, the last thing Chloe expected just then was an evocation of a sun-drenched and amorous moment from *Siren of the Nile*—Antony sauntering through an outdoor market in Alexandria, composing a love poem aloud. But soon it became clear that Mr. Chadwick would not leave the crater ere its walls resounded with his heart's deepest longings. "Might we return to the night you endorsed Stopsack's scheme for winning the Byssheans' gold?" he asked. "Responding to your question about Miss Bathurst's fate, I averred that her death had caused me considerable grief. That sentiment was utterly sincere. The simple fact, dear lady, is that I am smitten with you."

"There was indeed a time when I believed that taking the ark to Oxford would serve humankind's best interests," said Chloe, sidestepping the vicar's protestation.

"Once we are back in England, I hope you will become my lifelong companion," Mr. Chadwick persisted. "True, my future is hardly auspicious. No income, no property, no prospects. And yet, were you to marry me, my dear Chloe—may I call you 'my dear Chloe'?—I should count myself the happiest of men, sworn to making you the happiest of women."

Her tongue grew palsied. No word of reply gained access to her lips. She found Mr. Chadwick's proposal at once poignant and ridiculous, touching and bumptious, but to share any of those adjectives with him just then would be to start a conversation she did not wish to have. She merely said, "You may call me 'Chloe' but not 'my dear Chloe.'"

"Am I to infer you are spurning my proposal? You will not become my bride?"

"I am gratified by your attentions, Reverend," she replied, scanning the web of guano fuses for fractures, "but at present I can think only of my friends' predicament."

"Should tomorrow's escapade cause you harm, I shall take solace in knowing that tonight I spoke my mind."

"What is your meaning, Mr. Chadwick?" she snapped. "If you find yourself attending my funeral service ere long, you'll imagine it's really our wedding? That's not a very romantic thought."

"Obviously I picked the wrong time and place to raise this subject. You are preoccupied."

At last he'd made a sensible remark. She was preoccupied—and she remained so when, shortly after two o'clock in the morning, the mountain being primed and ready, the vulcaneers descended to sea level.

Upon her return to Villamil Quay, Chloe considered inhaling *epená* to hasten her passage to Morpheus's domain, then decided against it, having consumed such extravagant quantities during the final hours of *Duntopia versus Cabot and Quinn.* Instead she harvested a dozen palm fronds and spread them across the gondola floor to create a luxurious mattress. Stretching out along her new bed, she soon found herself astride a winged dragon as it wheeled above Léourier's lost city, melting the golden spires with its volcanic breath, a dream that needed no interpretation.

The Reverend Granville Heathway was a pigeon priest in both senses of the term. He was a priest who happened to raise pigeons—and he was gifted in ministering to a rock dove's deepest spiritual needs. The soul of a pigeon was for Granville as accessible as its feet. Thus it happened that Heathway's Columbine Carnival proved a great success, an awesome spectacle of birds walking on tightropes, diving into pails of water, pirouetting in pairs as their teacher whistled a waltz, and playing cricket using a grape for the ball and a paintbrush for the bat.

Amongst the carnival's patrons was Dr. Earwicker, who afterwards asked Granville to conduct bird-training classes for the other inmates. Though flattered by this invitation, he declined, being loath to abandon the security of his immediate accommodations. For it happened that the scarecrows were on the march again, sweeping westward from Wellingborough and Ecton, and there was no safe haven in Warwickshire except the cell he called home.

Against the odds, Charlemagne returned. Somehow the indomitable courier had slipped past enemy lines and found his way to the dovecote. In light of Bertram's previous missive, with its woeful account of the Diluvian League's loss and Miss Franklin's death, Granville steeled himself for sorrowful tidings—and yet Charlemagne had brought an uplifting message.

Dearest Father,

I am writing to you from Paestum on the southern coast of Italy. Shortly after we departed Constantinople, the Reverend Mr. Dalrymple decided that, rather than sailing directly for England, we should spend a day rambling about the ruins of this Greco–Roman city, famous for its archeological treasures. Such a respite would do us a world of good, he insisted, salving the pain of our failure to procure the ark.

"In recent weeks," Mr. Dalrymple told the Paragon's *assembled company, "I have searched my soul as extensively as we scoured the slopes of Ararat, asking myself, 'Why did we not find the Relic of Relics?' Now I see the answer. Over the years God has favored Mankind with three incomparable gifts: the Old Testament, the New Testament, and a disposition to believe that both are true. For Him to have proved His existence through the ark would be tantamount to His taking away that third great blessing, faith. Our recent disappointment is in fact a species of gospel, good news. It merely* seemed *to be malspel, bad news—or, rather, it was malspel only for those unworthy of following our Savior in the first place."*

We began our explorations with the Temple of Neptune, a remarkably well-preserved structure in the Doric style, the architraves and pediments still in situ. *Our group then strolled to the adjacent Basilica, another Doric* tour de force—*though I cannot fathom how a name indicating a Roman secular building became attached to a Greek temple.*

I now abandoned our party and hiked on my own to the isolated Temple of Ceres, the city's third Doric masterpiece, where I enjoyed an extraordinary encounter with a German philosopher. As a young man, Herr Doktor Schopenhauer had traveled throughout Italy, and now at age sixty-three he was pleased to find himself in Paestum again.

Upon inquiring about my own journey, Schopenhauer became greatly excited to hear that my Paragon *companions were Shelley Prize contestants who'd hoped to find and exhibit Noah's ark. Pulling a manuscript from his valise, he explained that, having read of the Great God Contest in a German-language newspaper, he'd recently composed a short essay for Lord Woolfenden's eyes.*

"As the world's greatest living philosopher, I felt obligated to inform the Byssheans that their competition is misguided," Schopenhauer explained. "Personally, I've never had much use for the God hypothesis, unless by 'God' we mean Aristotle's Unmoved Mover or Spinoza's inscrutable pantheist entity, which is hardly the quarry your Oxford flâneurs *are after. Sift through my writings, and you'll find definitive rejoinders to the Ontological Proof and the Cosmological Proof. Evidently your Mr. Dalrymple was pinning his hopes on the Argument from Relics, but of course he failed to find the necessary artifact, the Deluge story being utterly fanciful."*

"Now see here, sir—"

"Which is not to say the atheists will win the day. Both sides in this wearisome debate make the same logical error."

Schopenhauer proceeded to teach me about Modus ponens, *the rule of inference that underlies so many philosophical proofs and disproofs. It takes the following form, with* P *the antecedent and* Q *the consequent:*

If P, then Q.
P.
Therefore, Q.

When it comes to verifying the Almighty, with Q standing for "God exists," the religious man has hundreds of P's at his disposal, such as "There must be a First Cause" and "Nature has obviously been intelligently designed" and "Morality does not admit of a secular explanation." The problem is that atheists will grant believers none of these antecedents, and so we never get to the consequent.

When disbelievers take the field, Q now stands for "God does not exist," with P ranging from "Innocent people suffer" to "Scripture contains internal contradictions" to "Science provides reliable information about the physical universe." But of course no sane believer would grant veto power to such assertions, and so the disproof works only for those who are already atheists.

Leaning on his walking-stick, Schopenhauer gestured towards the medieval burial vaults embedded in the temple floor. "I have always disdained the Christian mania for imposing churches on pagan places of worship. Your Byssheans may be idiots, but I understand their desire for classical conviviality: drinking wine, reciting verse, playing with ideas—what could be more sublime? Let me ask a favor, Herr Heathway. The Italian postal system being what it is, might I prevail upon you to bear my message to Lord Woolfenden in person?"

"I should be pleased to do so."

"I am grateful beyond words," said the philosopher, placing the manuscript in my hands. "When you get to Oxford, tell them that in Doktor Schopenhauer's view our brutal and irrational world has no need of Western religion's brutal and irrational Deity. Give me rather our aesthetic accomplishments and ethical attainments. Give me art and pity. Your Mr. Dalrymple has every right to keep chasing after his nonexistent ark, though for me there is but one worthy quest, its objects being beauty, truth, and love."

And with that rousing speech (so reminiscent, Father, of your better sermons) Schopenhauer took leave of me, being much in need of sleep.

Your loving son,
Bertram

Smiling broadly, Granville secreted the message in his nightstand. As he returned Charlemagne to the dovecote, another sort of bird, the lark of joy, built a nest in his heart. Paestum to Sardinia to Gibraltar to Plymouth: a voyage of perhaps two thousand miles, easily completed within twenty days by a sailor of Captain Deardon's experience. Before the month was out, Bertram would be standing in this very cell, entertaining Granville with Oriental adventures.

Whistling a festive air, he sauntered to the barred window and surveyed the pasture, bathed in muted lunar light. The legions of stuffed men had arrived in force, pouring across the hills and swarming towards Coventry. He considered summoning Dr. Earwicker and insisting that he alert the County Council—but what would be the point? If the world regards you as sane and pious, you can torture foxes (as did Samson) or arrange the death of your mistress's husband (as had David), and no one will think the worse of you. But if you've been pronounced a lunatic, you can testify to an imminent scarecrow invasion from now until Michaelmas, and all you'll get for your trouble is a room in a madhouse.

Sweat assailing his eyes, pumice scratching his hands, Malcolm Chadwick led his Indian vulcaneers—Cuniche, Nitopari, Pirohua, Ascumiche—up the north face of Mount Pajas. Slowly but inexorably, the darkness lost its substance, like a bottle of ink poured into a lake. Reaching the array of boulders sitting atop cactus bombs, he paused to catch his breath. Briefly he imagined himself as a vulture lying in wait above a killing field, though his intention this morning was not to consume carrion but to prevent its creation.

From his rucksack he removed the *Lamarck*'s spyglass and three boxes of lucifer matches. He checked his pocket watch. Eight o'clock. In a mere sixty minutes the hangman was due to practice his profession on Dartworthy and Miss Kirsop.

Lifting the glass to his eye, he peered towards Mephistropolis. In the center of the exercise yard rose the scaffold, a ramshackle affair suggesting a decrepit footbridge leading to an impoverished village. A brawny guard ripped a worm-eaten board from the platform and nailed a fresh one in its place. Oscillating in the sea breeze, two nooses hung from the cross-beam, empty and ominous, like eye sockets in a skull, each swaying above its own trapdoor.

The portal of the keep flew open, disgorging a mass of convicts clad in burlap, attended by a corps of twenty guards. Goaded by the rifle butts of Capitán Machado's men, the ninety English prisoners and their Ecuadorian counterparts marched across the yard towards the gallows, blinking and wincing in the morning light. Though lacking their customary fetters, the prisoners could hardly be entertaining thoughts of escape—especially when they considered the pair of sentries manning the watchtower and the other two guards patrolling the wall. Ordered to attention by Machado, the convicts stiffened into the required pose. Malcolm directed his enhanced gaze across the assembled wretches, noting to his relief that their ranks included Ben the horse thief and his five fellow conspirators.

Whilst the prisoners sweated and thirsted, a solemn throng of Duntopians flowed into the yard, including Orrin Eggwort, Jethro Tappert, and Linus Hatch, dressed in their Sunday finest and supervising their respective concubines. No sons or daughters accompanied the cleave-wives. Evidently all three harems had dissuaded their masters from allowing the children to see two English citizens hanged for no particularly good reason. The emperors installed their rumps in high-backed throne chairs, even as the concubines and the other spectators occupied a grid of stools. Now Governor Stopsack made his entrance, smartly attired in his white linen suit. Strolling past the Duntopian royalty, he appropriated the remaining throne chair, then pulled a fat cigar from his vest pocket and bit off the end.

Riding crop tucked under his arm, Kommandant Hengstenberg emerged from the keep leading a blindfolded and trembling Miss Kirsop by her manacles. An instant later a red-bearded guard appeared, dragging Dartworthy, likewise shackled and blindfolded, followed by a dusky boy of perhaps eleven, banging out a funereal cadence on a snare drum.

Bringing up the rear of the parade was Executioner Ordoñez, a hulking man with shaggy arms, his features obscured by a black cloth hood.

As Stopsack lit his cigar, Malcolm set the seismic chicanery in motion, distributing the matchboxes amongst the Indians and ordering them to set the tinder aflame. Cuniche, Nitopari, Pirohua, and Ascumiche crept along the lip of the crater, igniting the twenty stacks of kelp-topped kindling. Flecked with sparks, a billowing mass of smoke soon filled the skies above Minor Zion, giving Ben the horse thief a credible reason to point towards the mountain and scream, with feigned dismay, "Look! The volcano! Look! Look!"

Shocked by Ben's discovery, the inmates chattered excitedly amongst themselves, as did the guards, emperors, concubines, and ordinary Duntopians. Act one, "The Smoldering Summit," had begun.

"It's alive!" cried Joe the poacher, clearly relishing his part in the diversionary strategy. "Alive! Alive!"

The crater released more deceptive vapors. Lurching free of his throne chair, Stopsack strode up to Eggwort and issued a gubernatorial decree, his words echoing across the yard and up the face of Mount Pajas—"Tell Hengstenberg to postpone the execution!"—to which the Supreme Emperor replied, "I'll give that order at the good Lord's urgin' but not yours!"

"The volcano will kill us!" yelled Pete the highwayman, impersonating panic.

"As when God squashed Gomorrah!" added Harry the panderer.

The time had come to raise the curtain on act two, "The Exploding Pumice." After collecting the matchboxes from the Indians, Malcolm climbed to the summit, passed through the ring of smoldering kelp, and, descending into the crater, ignited the master fuse. He returned to daylight, then made his way back to the field of boulders and hunkered down, commanding Cuniche, Nitopari, Pirohua, and Ascumiche to do likewise.

With a monstrous roar, like the cough of a consumptive troll, a sky-rocket shot out of the crater, arced towards the penal colony, and exploded, releasing a blossom of embers above the exercise yard.

"These are the last days of Duntopia!" declared Amos the sodomite.

A second rocket took flight and exploded.

"The last days of Galápagos!" yelled Tim the anarchist.

Three more rockets flew heavenward and detonated.

"Proceed with the execution!" shouted Eggwort, addressing Ordoñez.

"Halt the execution!" cried Stopsack, not so much speaking the syllables as hurling them in Eggwort's face like birdshot.

"Governor, your jurisdiction ends on these shores!" the Supreme Emperor asserted.

To the anxious cadence of the miserable drummer boy, Kommandant Hengstenberg began shoving the sightless Miss Kirsop up the warped steps of the gallows. She tripped on the last riser, sprawling across the planks. The Kommandant forced his prisoner to stand, then positioned her atop the nearer trapdoor, the noose caressing her shoulder. He returned to the ground. The red-bearded guard hauled Dartworthy onto the gallows, propelled him past Miss Kirsop, and aligned him with the second noose.

The guard abandoned the scaffold. A sixth rocket transmuted into a fiery bouquet. The boy stopped drumming.

"Don't leave my men here to die!" the capitán implored Hengstenberg.

"Your Excellency, you must cancel the execution!" the Kommandant in turn beseeched Eggwort.

A seventh explosion, a seventh celestial blossom.

Ordoñez mounted the gallows and, as if awarding her a medal on a neckband, dropped Miss Kirsop's noose over her head, then provided Dartworthy with his own mortal cravat.

"I beg you—spare me!" screamed Miss Kirsop as the masked hangman took hold of the lever beside her trapdoor.

"A pox on Duntopia and all its dictators!" cried Dartworthy.

"Perfessor Cabot, Miss Quinn, you will now confess your sins before our Savior!" shouted the Supreme Emperor, leaping up from his throne chair. "You must beg Christ's fergiveness fer torchin' the holy ark!"

"No, *you* must beg Christ's forgiveness for murdering innocent people!" yelled Dartworthy.

An eighth explosion.

"Gotta save the children!" shouted Rebecca Eggwort, rolling off her stool. "We'll take 'em to Albemarle on the *Cumorah*!"

"Thou shalt not abduct my sons!" cried the Supreme Emperor.

"Go kiss a squid!" retorted his eldest wife.

Mrs. Eggwort's declaration inspired her sorority of concubines to rise in a body and collect about her considerable frame. Hips swaying, elbows swinging, the nine rushed across the exercise yard, headed for the main gate.

"Wives, come ye back!" insisted Eggwort, dancing in irate circles about his throne chair.

"Husband, go to Hell!" replied Hagar.

Inflating like a puffer-fish, the Governor rushed towards the gallows, screaming, "No executions during eruptions! It isn't done! Hangman, remove the nooses!"

Ordoñez obeyed, detaching the ropes from Dartworthy and Miss Kirsop.

"Hangman, do your duty!" demanded Eggwort. "Stopsack's got no authority here! Ferget the volcano!"

Ordoñez restored the nooses to the prisoners' necks and then, seized by a fit of insubordination, jammed both hands in his pockets.

"Open the traps!" yelled Eggwort.

"Keep 'em closed!" shouted Stopsack.

"God sent this cataclysm to test our faith!" averred Eggwort.

"God sent this cataclysm to test *your* faith!" retorted Ordoñez, his words muffled only slightly by the cloth hood. "You heard the Governor! No executions during eruptions!"

Now Mr. Tappert's harem joined the exodus, followed shortly thereafter by Mr. Hatch's six concubines.

"Halt!" cried the Associate Emperor.

"Not another step!" screamed the Assistant Emperor.

The ninth rocket exploded. The revolt of the concubines continued.

"Pull the lady arsonist's lever!" shrieked Eggwort, hopping up and down to gain Ordoñez's attention. "Render her unto Satan! Obey me now! I'm the Supreme Emperor!"

"Not anymore you aren't!" declared Stopsack. "This prison complex belongs to the Crown, which makes Charles Isle a British possession as well!"

"We're all gonna die!" shouted Clarence the usurer.

"I don't wanna die!" yelled Jake the fornicator.

"Your Excellency, allow us to flee!" pleaded Hengstenberg.

"Open the woman's trap!" ordered Eggwort. "Punish her blaspheming flesh!"

The hangman tore off his hood and cried, "*Es imposible*, Your Excellency!"

Were it not for the ropes about the necks of Dartworthy and Miss Kirsop, Malcolm would have regarded the diversionary strategy as an unequivocal success. But the nooses could not be denied. Fixing on the array of cactus bombs, he struck a match and ignited the axis of the interconnected fuses, thereby inaugurating act three, "The Flying Stones." The combustible cords sizzled and hissed as a dozen flames ate their way towards the explosive fruits. He faced east, scanning the skies for Chloe and the Frenchman, but he saw only the rising sun, a herd of cumulus clouds, and a flock of vicious frigate birds, searching for prey.

Boiler roaring, propellers swirling, the *Jean-Baptiste Lamarck* pursued a steady course towards Mephistropolis. Whilst Capitaine Léourier manned the helm, Chloe, dressed in her buccaneer regalia, pushed back the starboard hatch and fixed it open by wedging a maul between the door and the jamb. In a gesture not unlike the dropping of a death-egg, she unfurled the rope ladder into the turbulent air, so that the threaded rungs dangled from the gondola like the tail of a stupendous kite.

Oddly enough, the aeronaut was exhibiting greater anxiety now than he had when attacking Castillo Bracamoros, even though the impending escapade would involve far fewer armed adversaries. As the *Lamarck* traversed the range of cinder cones, Léourier revealed the source of his distress, a madness of the very strain that had affected Mr. Chadwick.

"*Chère mademoiselle*, I realize I have not selected *le moment parfait* for you to consider a proposal of marriage."

"Marriage?" said Chloe. "What are you talking about?"

"*C'est-à-dire*, these are hardly ideal circumstances under which we might pledge our troth. Nevertheless, I'm hoping—"

"Hoping? Hoping? *I'm* hoping to save my friends, *mon Capitaine*! Troth—bosh! Bosh and double bosh! Have you taken leave of your senses?"

"I have not lost my mind but rather my heart. *Je vous aime, mademoiselle*. For you I would walk on burning coals, tie a knot in the Devil's tail, insult a Bonaparte to his face. Oh, such glorious adventures we shall have as we sail the skies of Amazonia in search of El Dorado—and after we find our golden utopia, we shall seek out other treasure cities: Quivira, La Canela, Cibola!"

"Do me a favor, *s'il vous plaît*."

"Anything."

"Say not one word more of burning coals or golden cities until Ralph and Solange are safely on board."

"*D'accord*."

Placing the glass to her eye and leaning out the larboard window, Chloe observed the harems of Eggwort, Tappert, and Hatch racing through the main gate towards Minor Zion, doubtless intending to collect their children and bear them away from the angry mountain. Act two was now in progress, a skyrocket taking flight every thirty seconds. Throttle wide open, the *Lamarck* cruised over the brick wall, its shadow slithering across the ground like a devil-ray gliding through a mangrove glade.

An instant later the airship arrived in the exercise yard, site of an unnerving tableau: Ralph and Solange, poised on the gallows, bound and blindfolded, necks encircled by nooses. Gripping his black hood, a bareheaded Executioner Ordoñez leaned over the scaffold rail, alternating his gaze between Kommandant Hengstenberg and Orrin Eggwort, the former using his monocled eye to scan a tattered tract printed on yellow paper, the latter standing on his throne chair as if seeking to evade Amazonian fire ants. Stopsack, meanwhile, charged back and forth between the scaffold and the Supreme Emperor like a cricket batsman scoring runs.

"For the last time, Señor Ordoñez, pull the woman's lever!" cried Eggwort.

"For the last time, Your Excellency, I shall not!"

Abruptly the curtain rose on act three. A tremendous *ka-boom* echoed off the mountain slopes, followed by the abrupt arrival of a boulder in the exercise yard. The projectile landed with a reverberant *thud* not twenty feet from the ranks of inmates, sending up a plume of dust. In a single clockwork motion scores of human heads, some belonging to frightened convicts, others to stupefied guards, still others to bewildered Duntopians, turned towards the fallen rock.

"Every man for himself!" screamed Ben the horse thief.

"*Merde!*" cried Léourier. "We put too much guano in the bombs!"

A second *ka-boom* rattled the vale. Another boulder crashed into the yard. Stationed at the base of the scaffold, a petrified drummer boy began to cry.

"The mountain's coming apart!" yelled Joe the poacher.

"The whole world's coming apart!" shrieked Tim the anarchist.

"I shall never underestimate excrement again!" declared Léourier.

Eggwort jumped off his throne chair and scuttled towards the corps of guards. "Shoot any man who attempts to flee!" he instructed Capitán Machado.

"Spoken like the depraved bourgeois pig you are!" shouted Kommandant Hengstenberg.

"Pig?" said Eggwort, perplexed. "What?"

"*Schwein! Porco! Cerdo! Cochon!*" Holding his tract aloft like a centurion brandishing a sword, Hengstenberg faced the capitán and yelled, "Hear me, Comrade Machado!" Enlarged by the glass, the pamphlet proved to be the ubiquitous *Manifest der Kommunistischen Partei*. "All men are brothers!" Hengstenberg's intended audience, Chloe realized, included not only Machado but also his soldiers, the disgruntled executioner, and the weeping drummer boy. "We must acknowledge our universal humanity, make common cause with our prisoners, and together escape the volcano!"

"Let's start with the escape!" suggested Machado.

"*Una idea excelente!*" added Ordoñez.

Now Hengstenberg addressed the assembled convicts. "I offer you

complete and total amnesty, as do Comrade Machado and Comrade Ordoñez! With the help of Comrade Jesus, we shall flee this doomed island! Unite with your former oppressors! You have nothing to lose but
your chains!"

"If we're losin' our chains," cried Ben the horse thief, "let's have
Machado's men lose their guns!"

"The guards must remain armed!" insisted Hengstenberg. "What say
you, prisoners? Are you with us?"

"We're with you!" shouted Pete the highwayman.

"All for one and one for all!" cried Tim the anarchist.

"*Kommandant,* this is an outrage!" exclaimed Eggwort.

"No, it's a revolution!" retorted Hengstenberg. "Under the tyranny of
the bourgeoisie, all that is solid melts into air! All that is holy is pro-
faned!" He thrust his riding crop in the direction of Post Office Bay. "To
the wharf, comrades!"

A third rock came screaming into the yard, landing at the base of the
watchtower.

"The *Hippolyta* is ours!" shouted Harry the panderer.

Before Chloe's astonished eyes the guards and their charges fused
into a collective entity, Hengstenberg in command. The sentries in the
watchtower, their compatriots on the wall, and the trembling drummer
boy abandoned their posts and joined the insurrection, even as Ordoñez
fled the gallows and merged with the revolutionaries. Although Machado's
men retained their weapons, they truly seemed to regard the convicts—
Englishmen and Ecuadorians alike—in a fraternal light, just as Marx
and Engels would have wished. It was a remarkably harmonious mob
that now streamed through the gate, trampled down the perimeter fence,
and surged towards the bay, taking care to avoid the falling chunks of
Mount Pajas. For an instant Chloe imagined the late Padre Valverde
peering down from Heaven and smiling to behold the inexorable Wheel
of History turn once again.

"Come back here!" screamed a livid Eggwort at the Marxians in general and Ordoñez in particular.

Whilst the guards were busily forging bonds of brotherhood with their former prisoners, Léourier had deftly maneuvered the *Lamarck* so that it now hovered above the scaffold like a hummingbird poised to siphon nectar from an orchid. Léourier dropped his anchor, catching one prong on the rail. Drawing forth her bayonet, Chloe exited the gondola and descended the rope ladder rung by rung even as Eggwort turned his attentions to the stalled executions.

"Reckon I'll have to do it myself!" he declared, charging up the scaffold steps, Stopsack at his heels.

As Chloe jumped from the ladder to the platform, she recalled her final appearance at the Adelphi Theatre. Evidently her tropical adventure would end as it had begun: the headstrong Miss Bathurst, standing on a scaffold, determined to strike a blow against the status quo—only this time she needn't make a speech denouncing the prevailing economic order, Hengstenberg having already done that for her. Instead she yanked off Solange's blindfold and lifted the noose over her head.

"My darling she-devil!" cried Solange.

A boulder landed squarely atop the brick wall, gouging a breach worthy of a cannonball.

Arriving on the platform and noting to his dismay that Solange was no longer tethered to the crossbeam, Eggwort undertook to facilitate Ralph's execution. The Supreme Emperor grabbed the far lever, pulling it with murderous intent, abandoning the endeavor when Stopsack kicked him soundly in the shins.

Chloe plucked off Ralph's blindfold and, extending her bayonet arm, brought the blade to rest midway between his noose and the crossbeam.

"'O little, fragile, laughing soul that sings'!" he cried, giddy with his deliverance.

Frantically Chloe sawed, the hemp fibers parting like flesh under a surgeon's knife, even as Eggwort retaliated against Stopsack, punching him repeatedly in the face. The Governor was soon supine on the planks, stunned and spread-eagled. Eggwort finished pulling the lever. The trapdoor opened, hurtling Ralph into the void. From the thumps and coughs that followed, Chloe surmised that the shredded rope had snapped beneath his weight, depositing him, abused but alive, under the platform.

"My precious sea-witch!" she cried, slicing the thongs from Solange's wrists.

"Hear me now, Orrin Eggwort!" Regaining his feet, Stopsack used his white linen cuff to absorb the blood leaking from his ruptured lip. "Perhaps we're about to sink beneath the sea like Atlantis of old—perhaps not—but in any event this island isn't yours! Every stone, tree, beach, bird, and beast lies within Her Majesty's realm!"

But Eggwort was not to be so easily disenfranchised. He wrested the bayonet from Chloe's grasp and, hugging Stopsack, thrust the blade into his stomach. Blood splattered forth, painting the planks. The Governor broke the embrace, the bayonet protruding from his solar plexus like a croquet peg, and collapsed in a hemorrhaging but otherwise inert heap.

"This is *my* island!" screamed Eggwort, addressing the corpse. "I have a deed from Ecuador!"

Climbing onto the platform, Jethro Tappert dashed towards the Supreme Emperor and said, "The Assistant Emperor and me got a bone to pick with you."

"More than a bone," said Linus Hatch, likewise gaining the platform. "A whole skeleton, really, coccyx and all. This seems a purty good time fer discussin' the matter."

"I just killed a man!" cried Eggwort. "It ain't a purty good time fer discussin' *anythin'*!"

"It concerns our women," explained Tappert. "I happen to know you been conjugatin' with my Mildred and my Patricia."

"You also been seen gavottin' with my Kitty and my Meg," added Hatch. "As if you ain't got wives enough already!"

"Joseph Smith is angry with you, and Jesus is mighty displeased as well, not to mention Linus and myself!" Tappert pointed to the noose that had almost broken Solange's neck. "In accordance with God's will, this rope won't go to waste!"

"No!" protested Eggwort. "I'm the Supreme Emperor!"

A boulder crashed through the wall and rolled into the yard, leaving behind a trail of shattered bricks.

Dazed but buoyant, Ralph staggered onto the crowded platform.

Solange plucked the bayonet from the corpse and applied the blade to the thongs binding the mariner's wrists. After instructing her friends to climb the rope ladder—an order they obeyed without hesitation—Chloe unhooked the anchor, ascended rung by rung, and hoisted herself into the gondola. As Léourier opened the throttle, she scrolled up the ladder, and the *Lamarck* flew free of the gallows.

"Evidently Lady Omega has been touched from on high after all," said Solange, setting the dripping bayonet on the empty chart table.

Wheezing and sweating, Chloe closed the starboard hatch. She slumped against the compass binnacle, caught her breath, and, grasping her bayonet, used her pirate kerchief to wipe Stopsack's blood from the blade. Another cactus bomb detonated, followed by the thunder of a boulder smashing through an upper window of the keep.

"*Excusez-moi, mon Capitaine,* but we seem to be headed for the volcano," noted Ralph. "Surely that's a bad idea."

"The eruption isn't real," Léourier explained. "We made it from bamboo and bat shite."

"Where's our favorite vicar?" asked Solange.

"On the summit, geologizing," Léourier replied.

Chloe glanced through the aft window. As the airship soared away from the penal colony, a gruesome dumb show unfolded on the gallows. Acting in complete and wordless harmony, Tappert and Hatch employed the discarded bindings to tie Eggwort's hands behind his back. The Associate Emperor inserted Eggwort's head into the noose once intended for the blaspheming Bianca Quinn. The Assistant Emperor pulled the lever. The trapdoor opened. The Supreme Emperor vanished from view, plunging towards oblivion, or perhaps the maw of Hell, or conceivably the gates of Heaven, though from Chloe's present vantage in time and space the latter two fates were obviously synonymous with the first.

As the *Lamarck* cruised along the silicate-coated shores of Post Office Bay, the noonday sun caught the notice board beside the Colnett barrel, causing the broadsheets and bulletins to glow like the gold plates of

Cumorah. The carriage, Chloe noted, had not been this crowded since the guano expedition to Chatham, jammed with not only herself, Léourier, and the defendants in *Duntopia versus Cabot and Quinn* but also Mr. Chadwick and his four Huancabamba vulcaneers. The engine issued corresponding objections. Throughout the flight across the cinder field, Ralph and Solange lavished praise on their saviors, complimenting Chloe on her ingenious *scenario*, the capitaine on his knowledge of chemistry, the Peruvian aborigines on their industry, and the vicar on his management of the eruption.

Piloting the flying-machine along a course that veered into the bay and back to the beach, Léourier dropped anchor in a black dune, then moored the gondola a mere three feet above the ground. Chloe jumped onto a tract of tuff, raced to the barrel, and glanced at the notice board. A third Kaffir War had broken out in Southern Africa. The United States Congress had passed a Fugitive Slave Law. Alfred Tennyson was now the British Poet Laureate.

Like Joe the poacher gutting an ill-gotten deer, she plunged both hands into the barrel's papery depths. She sifted through scores of packets, inspected dozens of envelopes, but found nothing bearing her name. Melancholy swelled within her, a lump of indigestible disappointment. Whither Algernon? Had he gambled away his three hundred *contos de réis* on the stern-wheeler back to Belém? Was Papa still alive? Had his Holborn Workhouse masters tasked him to death?

Throughout Post Office Bay several species of chaos reigned. In keeping with Kommandant Hengstenberg's directive, the prison guards and their former charges had climbed aboard the *Hippolyta*, cast off the mooring lines, and set her adrift. Alas, none of the embryonic Marxians knew how to skipper a two-masted schooner, and so everyone began screaming imprecations at his comrades. Hengstenberg held the helm, doing his best to steer the vessel towards Albemarle, though until somebody figured out how to hoist the sails his efforts would clearly be in vain. The *Cumorah*, meanwhile, was on the point of putting to sea, Rebecca Eggwort having piloted the shallop out of its berth whilst the other sultanas coiled the lines and spread the canvas. But the *Cumorah*'s departure would not be free of complication, for Tappert and Hatch had just arrived on the shore. Charging down the wharf, the unhappy Latter-Day Saints addressed the renegade women in tones of urgent indignation.

"Mildred, bring that boat back here!" shouted Tappert.

"Not in a million years, you salamander!" Mildred replied.

A boulder came hurtling over the cinder cones and crashed into the bay, throwing up a funnel of spray.

"Kitty, you got no right leavin' us to the volcano's wrath!" cried Hatch.

"We're leavin' you to God's mercy!" explained Kitty.

"You got no right doin' that, either!"

"Cleavewife Patricia, you can't take my sons from me!" wailed Tappert.

"You don't even know their names!" retorted Patricia. "In fact, you don't even know they're your sons!"

"Where's my husband?" inquired Rebecca Eggwort.

"We hanged him!" answered Hatch.

"Successfully?"

"Yes!"

"You still can't come with us!" shouted Rebecca.

Chloe hurried back to the airship and climbed the rope ladder to the larboard hatch, thus prompting Léourier to raise the anchor, ignite the boiler, and take flight.

Eventually the bewildered Marxians on the *Hippolyta* concluded that, since the *Cumorah* was likewise headed for Albemarle, they should exploit the nautical expertise of Eggwort's harem. When at last the schooner came within shouting distance of the shallop, Hengstenberg pleaded with Rebecca to send over her best sailors. Shortly before the *Lamarck* blew free of the harbor, Chloe slid the glass through the larboard window and beheld four erstwhile Mormon wives row themselves to the *Hippolyta*, scramble aboard, and set the schooner on a westerly course, Hagar in command, Miriam at the helm.

One hour later the flying-machine alighted on Hood's Isle. Chloe surveyed her fellow adventurers, all of them faint from hunger and exhaustion following a morning filled with a raging volcano, a seraglio rebellion, a Socialist revolution, an aerial rescue, Stopsack's assassination, and Eggwort's fateful encounter with the noose. Yitogua and Rapra, the

Huancabambas who'd stayed behind, had cooked up a large quantity of crab chowder, and the vulcaneers gratefully availed themselves of the feast, as did Ralph and Solange.

"We played our parts admirably, don't you think, Chloe?" said Mr. Chadwick. "Our aeronaut, the Indians, the ex–vicar of Wroxton—and, of course, you yourself. I daresay, I found the whole *scenario* exhilarating."

"I did not share your amusement," said Chloe. "I shan't soon forget the image of Ralph with a rope about his neck."

"Nor shall I," said Solange.

"To say nothing of our sea-witch's noose," said Chloe.

"An artifact arguably even less amusing than Ralph's noose," said Solange.

Everyone agreed that siestas were in order. The plan presented no logistical difficulties, Yitogua and Rapra having readied a lean-to for Ralph and a hovel for Solange. Yawning extravagantly, Chloe stumbled to her shack, collapsed on the seaweed mattress, and attempted to quiet her brain.

But the organ declined to cooperate, being obsessed with the shattering effect her testimony had exerted on Tim the anarchist, Harry the panderer, and Joe the poacher. Having successfully subtracted God from the worldviews of three penal-colony inmates, was she not now obligated—for her father's sake and perhaps the human race's as well—to head home bearing a panoply of Galápagos fauna? Was she not duty-bound to make unbelievers of as many Anglican judges as possible? For an hour the problem tormented her, and then by the grace of Morpheus she drifted off to sleep.

Awakening in darkness, she left her shack and wandered towards the inlet, drawn by the pulsing of the surf and the guttural discourse of the sea lions. A wash of stars spilled across the equatorial sky. The moonlit breakers wore coronas of foam. Anchored to the beach, the *Lamarck* rocked on its tether. Dressed in silk shifts improvised from the airship's stores of balloon material, Ralph and Solange sat together on a lava boulder, limned by the glow of the cooking fires and speaking softly to each other. As Chloe drew near, her friends stiffened and their voices dropped away. The topic of their conversation, evidently, had been she herself.

Rumbling like shook canvas, the tide rolled in. The sea lions growled sotto voce. After an awkward interval, Ralph spoke to Chloe: "We've decided that, rather than brooding any further on the question, we shall put it to you."

"The question being, in a word, matrimony," said Solange.

An eddy of jealousy swirled through Chloe—a reasonable reaction, she decided, given her dalliances with Ralph and her residual yearning for his prowess—but it quickly passed, her feelings towards the mariner being no longer amorous, and how wonderful that two people she held in such high regard had become for each other a source of joy.

"Let me be first to congratulate you," she said.

"You don't understand," said Ralph. "I desire to marry *you*, the woman who saved my life."

"I, too, wish to spend my remaining years basking in my deliverer's smile," said Solange. "Occasionally I've bitten the Sapphic apple, and I'll wager that any she-devil worthy of the name would find such fruit to her liking."

As if responding to this peculiar conversation, the sea lions emitted a strange laughing noise: perhaps they were guffawing at her friends' operatic emotions, or perhaps they were amused by the human preoccupation with matrimony—Chloe couldn't tell.

"You should know that, owing to the pleasure I took in playing Edward Cabot, I mean to retire from the sea and become an actor," Ralph persisted. "My fair philosopher, you will have in me both a loving husband and a sympathetic colleague."

"My own ambitions are no less lofty," said Solange. "One day I shall be mistress of my own house, a brothel as elegant as the cathedral in Belém."

"In making your decision take all the time you need," said Ralph.

"Though sooner would be preferable to later," said Solange.

"Perhaps I'll pick neither of you," Chloe declared. "For it seems I've also sparked romantic sentiments in Mr. Chadwick and Capitaine Léourier."

"The vicar?" said Ralph, indignant. "I think not."

"The Frenchman?" said Solange, incredulous. "How risible."

"Dear friends, I am flattered by your proposals," said Chloe. "I can imagine many reasons to become your wife, Ralph. And though my inclinations don't correspond to yours, Solange, I shan't deny your witchy charms. As for seeking lost civilizations with Léourier, I confess to finding glamour in the idea. And Mr. Chadwick? Surely he would prove a fond and devoted helpmate. But betrothal is the last thing on my mind, *mes amis,* for I fear my father yet languishes in the workhouse, and so I must decide whether our fellowship should still attempt to win the ten thousand pounds."

"I have an opinion on the matter," said Solange.

"So do I," said Ralph.

"Permit me to suggest that we three now walk together along the beach of this fair isle," said Chloe, "speaking not a word of matrimony or Shelley Prizes but instead reviewing our adventures." Her friends dipped their heads in assent. "The murmur of the surf will soothe us, likewise the lowing of the sea lions, and is there any sight so enchanting as moonbeams dancing on spindrift?"

15

A Book is Born, a Bishop Is Bested, and a Scientist Receives Solace on His Deathbed

Throughout the week that followed the noisy and extravagant rescue of her friends, Chloe pondered the quartet of marriage proposals she'd received on that tumultuous day. Although she could no longer read the transmutation sketch, its pages having been converted into skyrocket nose cones, her mind kept circling back to the author's argument concerning sexual selection. According to Mr. Darwin, the female gender, vertebrates and invertebrates alike, had played as decisive a role in evolutionary events on planet Earth as had their male counterparts—a notion she found so congenial as to be exhilarating.

As decisive a role? Quite so. For the choice of who might one day confer a child on Miss Chloe Bathurst—whether the mariner, the aeronaut, the vicar, or, against the odds, the sea-witch—ultimately lay with her. That said, Chloe felt no special desire to bring forth a baby (a category of mammal that had rarely stirred in her any emotion loftier than indifference), and she would always count her miscarriage during the premiere of *The Haunted Priory* amongst her life's more fortunate turns.

Although she had no idea what sort of husband and father Ralph might make, everyone believed he was the best person to fill the late

Jonathan Stopsack's post. Despite this vote of confidence, Ralph assumed the mantle of Interim Governor only after his fellow adventurers promised to provide him with daily counsel. The first order of business, the new junto agreed, must be getting the half-dozen Indians safely home to the Jequetepeque valley. Léourier soon decided that the *Lamarck* would be equal to the task, having borne himself and five others over the Andes with only a minor disaster involving condors.

The ceremony of farewell occurred in Black Turtle Cove, the flying-machine bobbing about on its tether, envelope fully inflated, anchor embedded in the sand. At long last the European explorers and the Peruvian aborigines had discharged their duties to one another. The scales of obligation stood in equipoise. Hands were shaken, tears shed, embraces solicited and accepted, jokes traded in fractured Quechua and pidgin English.

Slowly and solemnly, Lady Omega's former disciples climbed aboard the *Lamarck,* Cuniche pausing long enough to inform Chloe that, although he and the other Huancabambas had taken little satisfaction in learning about Jehovah-Jesus, portraying transplanted Hebrews, living like savages in the Indefatigable mangrove glades, or filling tortoise shells with guano, the eruption had greatly amused them, and they would be "pleased to build another volcano for Señorita Bathurst one day." No sooner had Chloe thanked the Indian for his sly sentiments than a favoring wind swept across the shore. Léourier ordered the anchor raised, then fired up the boiler, manned the helm, and set about bearing the Indians back across the Humboldt Current to the mainland.

It was apparent to neither Chloe nor Léourier when they would see each other again. Before his departure from Peru for Galápagos, the aeronaut had burdened the *Lamarck* with, as he put it, "every last drop of distilled petroleum in Puerto Etén." Although he had sufficient fuel to reach the Jequetepeque valley, he would have to postpone his return until he located more kerosene, "and God alone can reckon where I'll find it—and even He, being nonexistent, will have difficulty making the calculation." That said, Léourier declared that he was determined to "cast an eye on my fellow explorers once again, and perhaps even talk some of you into joining the search for El Dorado."

As far as Chloe could tell, her silence concerning Ralph's marriage proposal had caused no rift between them, and so she eagerly played her new part as his grand vizier. She and her friends had recently moved to the hacienda, where they enjoyed the services of the four furloughed Ecuadorians (who now received a weekly stipend of sixpence from the treasury of Her Majesty's Galápagos Protectorate). Much to Chloe's satisfaction, Ralph proved happy to indulge her obsession with shielding the tortoises from the predations of visiting brigs. Perhaps this was his way of wooing her, but in any event she was pleased to draft a gubernatorial decree to the effect that all vessels landing in the Encantadas must assent to a thirty percent reduction in the traditional hunting quotas or face imprisonment in Mephistropolis for poaching.

Beyond advising Ralph, Chloe took it upon herself to read the late Governor's mail, for packets addressed to that unfortunate official routinely appeared in the Colnett barrel, word of his death having not yet reached England. Thus did she learn that, owing to the complaints of the archipelago's Ecuadorian proprietors, Prime Minister Russell no longer regarded Jonathan Stopsack as the right man for the job. Rare was the week in which Whitehall had not received from Quito a denunciation of Stopsack's failure to increase *orchilla*-dye production, clean out the pirate havens on Abingdon Isle, impose a tortoise-catching fee on the whaling masters, or solve the Eggwort problem. The ax, in fact, had fallen. As of Lord Russell's most recent letter, a replacement governor, one Richard Hilliker, would soon be dispatched to Indefatigable aboard H.M.S *Apogee*, under the command of Captain Hugh Pritchard.

Chloe nearly swooned. Hugh Pritchard, Solange's former swain and the *Equinox's* second officer, a man she'd last seen boarding the stern-wheeler *Sereia* in Manáos—accompanied by her brother. She could not say whether the Lords of the Admiralty had made a wise decision in giving Mr. Pritchard a ship of his own. What mattered was his imminent landing on Galápagos, an event that promised to provide her with news of Algernon and Papa.

When not running Ralph's administration or scanning the horizon in search of the *Apogee*, Chloe cruised about the islands in the *Hippolyta*, recently returned by the Marxians to her customary berth in the hacienda lagoon, the furloughed Ecuadorians manning the helm and working the sails. These daily voyages enabled her not only to restore the slopeback tortoise to Indefatigable and the domeshell to James Isle but also to study the peculiar utopia that Kommandant Hengstenberg, Capitán Machado, Rebecca Eggwort, and the other fugitives had created on Albemarle. Ideologically this brave new world represented an amalgam of *The Communist Manifesto* and the biblical Book of First Kings, notably its account of Solomon and his many concubines. In the case of the People's Republic of Albemarle, however, the practicing polygamists were all women. The arithmetic would have it no other way. Whereas Eggwort, Tappert, and Hatch had once boasted amongst them twenty-one wives, the adult male population of Albemarle, including ex-prisoners and former guards, numbered one hundred and twenty-six. For the sake of matrimonial equity, each adult female had received a seraglio of six. Apart from inevitable squalls of jealousy and clashes of temperament, this heterodox arrangement had proven satisfactory to all concerned. During a particularly bracing visit to Albemarle, Chloe briefly imagined resolving her own matrimonial dilemma by recruiting Ralph, Léourier, Mr. Chadwick, and Solange into a harem of her own, but she doubted there was enough *epená* in Peru to make that solution acceptable to herself or anyone else.

Ten weeks after Ralph became Interim Governor, the officially appointed administrator of Her Majesty's Galápagos Protectorate appeared in the Bahía de Cormoranes, borne by the eagerly anticipated *Apogee*. Ralph dispatched Eugenio and Sancho with a message inviting Captain Pritchard and his illustrious passenger to a dinner that evening. At sundown Governor Hilliker entered the hacienda clutching a bottle of port from his private store and bearing news that was for Chloe most unwelcome: Hugh Pritchard would be indefinitely delayed, having become embroiled in an altercation with his first officer, and he'd requested that the feast proceed without him.

As staged by Eugenio and Sancho, the meal proved as lavish as the banquet at which Stopsack had presented his case for dragging the ark to Oxford. The opulence was much appreciated by Hilliker, a pistol-toting cavalier given to gluttony and braggadocio. Taking Pritchard's place at the table was Léourier, who, after bringing the Huancabambas home, had managed to build a private petroleum works on the Peruvian savannah, eventually distilling enough kerosene for a return voyage to Indefatigable.

Upon learning that his predecessor had been fatally bayoneted by the self-appointed Supreme Emperor, who was in turn hanged by his fellow emperors, Hilliker reacted with unconcealed dismay. (Evidently he'd been looking forward to making life miserable for both Stopsack and Eggwort.) Regaining his equilibrium, he asked about the two assassins, whereupon Léourier revealed that during his recent flight over Charles he'd witnessed Tappert and Hatch assembling a raft, doubtless with the aim of fleeing to one of the northern isles.

"Allow me to suggest that, as cold-blooded murders go, Eggwort's death was a felicitous event," said Ralph. "At the risk of appearing derelict in my duties, I declined to hunt down the perpetrators."

"The wisest course of action is often inaction," said Hilliker, nodding. "Now tell me about these anarchists we've got on Albemarle."

"They consider themselves Socialist revolutionaries," noted Ralph. "I must confess to a certain sympathy for their experiment. Assuming they assert no prerogatives at odds with the Empire's interests, I would urge a policy of benign neglect."

Hilliker slammed a corpulent palm on the table. "Done and done."

For the next half-hour, Chloe attempted to alarm their guest with her deduction that, if the plundering of Encantadas giant tortoises continued at its present rate, the species would go extinct by the turn of the century. ("I've learned how to protect our reptiles from misguided theologians," she explained, "but not from hungry sailors.") By the time Hilliker had eaten his fourth hammerhead-shark fillet, she'd extracted his promise to enforce the same draconian quotas that had obtained during Ralph's tenure.

If Hilliker's vow was music to Chloe's ears, then the next sound she heard was a lyric poem—the familiar *chee-chee-chee* of Bartholomew the monkey. An instant later Hugh Pritchard strolled into the dining hall, dressed in the blue, brass-buttoned uniform of a British Merchant Navy commander, his pet capuchin sitting atop his head like a busby. Fortunately, Eugenio and Sancho had anticipated his arrival, and by the time Pritchard reached the far end of the table his chair had been deployed, his place set, and his plate laden with two sally-lightfoot crabs and a flamingo breast.

"How gratifying to find my fellow *Equinox* survivors possessed of such cheery dispositions and—to judge from the barren china—such hearty appetites!" Pritchard exclaimed, then turned to Solange and said, "When we parted company, your fellowship included Merridew Runciter."

"Alas, he succumbed to an anaconda on the Solimões," Solange explained. "Allow me to introduce the newest member of our party. *Je vous présente Capitaine Léourier,* a brilliant balloonist who came to South America in hopes of finding El Dorado."

"A quest I have not abandoned," said Léourier.

"Pray tell, Captain Pritchard, how fares my family?" asked Chloe, unable to contain herself any longer.

"You'll be gratified to hear that your brother and I enjoyed an uneventful voyage down the Amazon," said the master of the *Apogee.* "Well, not *entirely* uneventful. Algernon pocketed another hundred *contos de réis* at the gaming tables."

Continuing his tale, Pritchard related how, on reaching Belém, Algernon had exchanged his winnings for English pounds, and so after landing in Plymouth he had no trouble settling his father's debts and liberating him from Holborn Workhouse. Before the month was out, Algernon had relocated Mr. Bathurst and himself to a manse in, of all places, Oxford, a town he'd evidently held in high regard ever since his visit to the rakehells. "I should be happy to transport you and your companions home," Pritchard concluded, "though I hope Mr. Dartworthy might become the *Apogee*'s new first officer. The man who once held the job, the thieving Mr. Snead, has been relieved of his duties."

"I stand prepared to serve your ship," said Ralph.

As Chloe apprehended this cornucopia of good news, her heart went

on holiday, capering within her frame like some fabulous tropical creature awaiting discovery by Alfred Wallace. Mr. Pritchard now com-
pounded her delight by pressing a letter into her hand. Anxiously she
broke the seal and scanned the page, her joy rising to heights their local
balloonist could only dream of reaching. Algernon's words corroborated
everything she'd heard from Pritchard, though the captain had omitted
one nontrivial detail: her brother had joined the Shelley Society—hardly
a surprise, given his hedonistic inclinations.

*The freethinkers and I play at cards every evening. Until I came
amongst them, they knew nothing of poker (only faro, basset, and
piquet)—can you believe that? I normally leave the table five pounds to
the good. It's like having a job, and so convenient, Alastor Hall being
but a ten-minute walk from the property Father and I purchased at
Three Manor Place.*

"There remains the matter of our original mission," said Solange, facing Hugh Pritchard.

"Do you mean our dalliance in Manáos? I'm a married man now.
When I left Plymouth, Phoebe was four months gone with child."

Solange rolled her eyes and said, "I mean the mission that sent us up
the Amazon. Tell me, Hugh, old friend, does the Shelley Society still
have ten thousand pounds on its hands?"

"Prior to our departure, I routinely checked the *Evening Standard*,"
Pritchard replied. "As of Guy Fawkes Day, no one had proved God fictitious, nor had the ark hunters returned from the Orient. I could easily be
persuaded to carry Miss Bathurst's illustrative specimens to England.
Simply offer me the late Captain Runciter's share."

Chloe sucked in a breath, fixed her face in a philosophic frown, and
in two measured sentences consigned the Albion Transmutationist Club
to a fate that perplexed all interested parties, herself included. "Dear
friends, I must tell you we no longer seek to assassinate God. The Covent
Garden Antichrist will always dream of deicide, as will the She-Devil
from Dis, but Miss Bathurst desires only to join her family in Oxford."

"Chloe, I'm proud of you," said Mr. Chadwick.

"Lord Woolfenden will not appreciate your decision," said Ralph, "especially when he remembers the three hundred pounds with which he seeded your mission."

"I intend to pay back every penny," said Chloe. "My brother is now a man of means."

"Darling, I love you, and I want to wring your neck," said Solange.

"*Au sujet de l'amour,* Mademoiselle Bathurst, please know that I still wish to marry you," said Léourier.

"As do I," said Mr. Chadwick.

"Gentlemen, please," said Chloe.

"Our leader has been enjoying a surfeit of marriage proposals," Solange explained to Hilliker. "Are you smitten with her, too? You'll have to get in the queue."

"*Hélas,* I've failed to fire you with a passion for either El Dorado or myself," said Léourier to Chloe. "*C'est vrai?* You will not become my bride and beacon?"

"Although your offer holds much allure for me, *mon ami,*" said Chloe, "I've had my fill of quests lately, particularly those involving South America."

Léourier smiled plaintively. "I have always tried to live by that profound Italian sentiment, *Quel che sarà sarà.* Whatever will be, will be." Elaborating, he announced that he would soon take to the sky again, retrieving his helmsman and his navigator from the Dominican mission in Peru, and then the three of them would set about tracking down every lost jungle city known to legend, lore, and lie. "Mademoiselle, though we are not fated to enjoy a future together, we do have our boisterous past. I shall evermore cherish my memories of flying you over the Andes, ferrying your tortoises to Duntopia, and making a volcano out of guano." He raised his goblet. "Here's to you, *ma chère.*"

"To Chloe!" said Solange, lifting her wine to the elevation of Léourier's.

"To Chloe!" chorused Ralph, Mr. Chadwick, Captain Pritchard, and Governor Hilliker.

As the goblets sought one another out, making melodic contact in the sticky air, Chloe recalled not only Runciter's dinner guests drinking to God's unmockability but also the *Equinox* castaways toasting their leader's avarice, as well as the Encantadas Salvation Brigade raising their glasses to the Down House tortoises. The present ritual was rather less momentous, but she savored every chime.

No sooner had the goblets settled onto the table than Bartholomew began slapping his paws together. Perhaps he was simply resonating with the cheer of the moment, but Chloe decided he'd been vouchsafed a vision of the future, and he'd seen that it was laudable. Well, not entirely laudable: dreadful in many ways—the usual gallimaufry of war, greed, predation, theology, and rubber barons. And yet there was this happy fact. After Mr. Darwin's treatise received its posthumous publication, people would acquire a newfound appreciation for finch beaks and puffer-fish spicules, for the arched shells of saddleback tortoises and the vestigial tails of newborn babies, knowledge that, lovingly nurtured and thoughtfully propagated, might help the human race to feel more at home in the world, more like citizens of planet Earth and less like tourists, and so the monkey clapped.

By Chloe's calculation an interval of five hundred and sixty days, the better part of two years, had elapsed between their departure from Plymouth and her short trip—on the 3rd of May, 1851—up the gangplank of the ship that would presumably take her back to England. Whilst Hugh Pritchard stood on the weather deck of H.M.S. *Apogee*, arranging for the anchor to ascend and the canvas to drop, Chloe doffed her Panama hat and waved it at the well-wishers assembled on the beach. This party included not only Capitaine Léourier and Governor Hilliker but also a contingent from the local Socialist utopia: Kommandant Hengstenberg, Capitán Machado, Rebecca Eggwort—plus all the other polyandrous ex–Mormon wives. Unfurling the flag of the People's Republic of Albemarle, a patchwork banner featuring a domeshelled tortoise on a green background, the Marxians variously blew kisses, flourished handkerchiefs, and shouted, "Farewell, comrades!"

Thus did the *Apogee* commence the long voyage southward, destination Tierra del Fuego. Although her progress was impeded by unfavorable winds and the imperative to stay far west of the contrary Humboldt Current, nobody minded terribly—for they were finally going home.

Shortly after the brig reached the fifteenth parallel, Chloe opened her heart's book to the chapter called "Crossing the Andes with a Debonair Aeronaut." She soon concluded that in refusing Léourier's marriage petition she'd made a sensible decision. Should she ever find herself yearning to discover a lost jungle city, she would straightaway seek out the Frenchman, knowing that their collaboration might eventually acquire a romantic cast, but it all seemed most improbable.

Throughout the epic battle with the Cape Horn weather, from the 29th of June to the 3rd of July, Chloe repeatedly visited the phantom volume, perusing the chapter titled "Reading the *Rubáiyát* with Ralph," even as she observed his present performance as first officer. There he stood, the dauntless mariner, hurtling imprecations into the wind's teeth whilst pounding orders into the sailors' heads. Thanks to Ralph, the canvas was sufficiently reefed to keep the *Apogee* from foundering, though not so short as to prolong their voyage through the Strait of Magellan. She had loved him once. Their interludes in Manáos had transported her to realms more rapturous than a resin dream. And yet even when she gave fleeting credence to his ambition of becoming an actor, she felt no more prepared to wed this footloose gallant than she did the Gallic balloonist.

Upon escaping the grasping seas off Tierra del Fuego, the *Apogee* tacked north, reaching Trindade Isle (linchpin of the Martin Vaz archipelago) on the 31st of July, which happened to be Solange's birthday. There was, to be sure, a facet of Chloe that wished to make the sea-witch a *bonne anniversaire* present of an amorous declaration—*Dear friend, let us live together as woman and wife*—but whereas Pirate Anne, Queen Cleopatra, or Carmine the vampire might have embraced this *modus vivendi*, Chloe could not align her imagination with such an outcome, and, moreover, what sense did it make to predicate her happiness on a person even more harebrained than her father?

The ides of August began with a gaudy sunrise, as colorful as Capitán Torresblanco's macaw. Later that morning, having assembled the crew and passengers on the weather deck, Ralph announced that the *Apogee* was but two days from the line, and so anyone wishing to mark the crossing with a pageant had better start laying plans. Mr. Chadwick stepped forward and declared that if the ship's company were very lucky their resident actress would organize a spectacle of the sort she'd produced ere the *Equinox* went down.

"Truth to tell, Reverend, I'd forgotten about my equatorial pageant," Chloe informed him as they stood together on the quarterdeck that evening. The heavens were studded with stars, as if some cosmic knight-errant had spread a hauberk of luminous mail across the sky. "I'm pleased that you retain agreeable memories of our effort, but it was still a trifle."

"Though lacking the complexity of your Lost Thirteenth Tribe masquerade, that pageant is by no means the least of your *oeuvre*," said Mr. Chadwick.

"And what *is* the least of my *oeuvre*?"

"May I speak candidly, Chloe? I must express disappointment with the prologue to your Mount Pajas extravaganza, 'An Atheist Vicar Proposes to an Erstwhile Actress and Is Rebuffed.'"

"Then it's time you heard about the epilogue."

And Chloe wondered: if I tell him what he wants to hear, will I be allowing a mere poetic conceit, the Mount Pajas eruption as three-act drama (plus prologue and epilogue), to trump the truth of the matter? No, she decided. No, not at all. For in fact she cherished Malcolm Chadwick, this person who'd ministered to her guilt over Mr. Flaherty's death on the Rio Amazonas, convinced her she wasn't responsible for Captain Runciter's suffocation by an anaconda, and defended her against Ralph's and Solange's aggressive critiques of her Manáos revelation.

"Epilogue?" he asked.

"It's called, 'The Erstwhile Actress Realizes She Would Be a Fool Not to Wed the Atheist Vicar.'"

"Do my ears deceive me?"

"Call me your darling, and credit your ears—those vessels into which I intend to pour my endless admiration for the brave and subtle Malcolm Chadwick."

"Excuse me, my darling, whilst I visit the moon," said the vicar.

"You must take me with you," said Chloe. "Give me a moment to find my hat."

Thus it happened that instead of an equatorial pageant a different sort of ceremony occurred aboard the *Apogee*. Asserting a sea captain's most venerable prerogative, Hugh Pritchard united Chloe and Malcolm in a variety of matrimony not precisely holy but unequivocally legal. Once the vows were exchanged and the bride duly kissed, Solange enfolded both partners in an immoderate embrace, whilst Ralph presented the couple with a wedding gift, his well-traveled manuscript of *The Rubáiyát of Omar Khayyám*.

"'Know your own wonder—worship it with me,'" he recited, addressing Chloe, then turned to Malcolm and said, "A great responsibility lies upon your shoulders, Reverend. You are charged with making your bride know her own wonder."

"I already know it," Chloe protested.

"My darling, you know the marvel of the theatrical arts and the magnificence of the Tree of Life," said Malcolm, "but your own wonder still eludes you."

Solange cupped Chloe's jaw in her hands and administered her most piercing sea-witch gaze. "I hereby require you to have an exceptionally happy life, Mrs. Chadwick, though I suspect you will remain an object of my adoration for many years to come."

Like a ray of pure and perfect possibility streaming forth from Teilhard de Chardin's Omega Point, a glorious realization flowed into Granville Heathway's brain. By his calculation, young Bertram would arrive forty-eight hours hence, on the 5th of September, the very day that the dear boy had come into the world. Moreover, the perfect birthday gift lay to hand: eight gifts actually—the pigeon missives Bertram had sent from Constantinople and Paestum, each destined to become a chapter in an enthralling memoir, irresistible to any serious publisher in London or New York.

On the pretext that he wished to write a treatise preserving the ornithological knowledge he'd acquired whilst turning his pigeons into circus performers, Granville cajoled a stack of foolscap from Dr. Earwicker, then sat down at his escritoire and got to work. Hour by laborious hour, he transmogrified the dispatches, converting them from his son's infinitesimal scrawl into his own neat hand, sustaining himself throughout the arduous task by eating the Book of Genesis.

Shortly after ten o'clock on the morning of the fifth, he copied out the final sentence, "Schopenhauer took leave of me, being much in need of sleep." According to Bertram's last *communiqué*, he would be in Warwickshire by five o'clock, which meant that the boy would indeed receive the gift on his twenty-sixth birthday. In considering what to call the book, Granville rejected Mustafa Reshid's playful confection, *Hookahlucinations* (too pleased with itself) and also Teilhard's poetic phrase, *The Axis of Eternity* (hopelessly obscure). Eventually he settled on *Decrypting the Descent of Man*.

"Happy birthday, son!" declared Granville as a youthful figure (more weathered than when he'd left for Constantinople but still unmistakably Bertram) strode into the cell. "On the morning you came into the world, I felt blessed by every angel in Heaven."

"Dearest Father, how gratifying to see you looking so well!"

Granville and Bertram indulged in a prolonged embrace.

"I must credit my vigor to Scripture," said Granville. "Two days ago I started at the beginning, eating my way from Eden to Jehovah's curse on Ham—Ham the son of Noah, I mean, not the pig meat, though evidently our Creator is equally contemptuous of swine flesh and Ham's descendants. This morning I consumed Leviticus."

"If you want me to have a happy birthday, Father, you must promise to drop God from your diet." Bertram gestured towards the dovecote. "Eight birds, splendid—all my messages got through. At the end of the week I shall travel to Oxford, there to present Lord Woolfenden with Doktor Schopenhauer's letter."

"Tell me, Bertram," asked Granville, "when on Crete did you perchance encounter the Minotaur?" Apprehending his son's woebegone face, he added, "They're everywhere, you know, Minotaurs. We've got one in the cellar."

"Please, sir. Mother will stop visiting if you persist in saying things like that."

Granville frowned, inflating his lower lip into a pout. "I have a gift for you!" Retrieving the manuscript from its hiding place behind the dovecote, he deposited all seventy-two pages, plus the title sheet, in his son's hands. *"Voilà!"*

"Well, well, what have we *here?*" said Bertram with affected delight. "It seems to be a book. *Decrypting the Descent of Man.* My, my."

"It's *your* book, son. I transcribed all eight messages, so they might be read without a quizzing-glass. I daresay, you'll find a publisher in a trice."

Perplexity shadowed Bertram's face. "I sent you no more than two hundred words altogether. This stack contains dozens of pages."

"You wrote in the tiniest hand imaginable."

"How could my brief messages undergo so spectacular a transformation?"

"Don't you like your gift, son?"

"I like it, Father, but I don't *understand* it," said Bertram, leafing through the manuscript. "What's this business about a monk named Mendel?"

"You don't remember Gregor Mendel? He traveled to the Hookah-Den of Yusuf ibn Ziayüddin from the year 1864."

"During my sojourn I occasionally visited Yusuf Effendi's establishment, but I met no monks there, certainly none from the—uh—future."

"What about a twentieth-century scientific mystic called Teilhard de Chardin?"

"The name is not familiar to me."

"The British crystallographer Dr. Franklin? She made daguerreotypes of God's ideas, hence the helices on my wall. She was dying of a malignancy. You grew fond of her."

"Your helices are beautiful. I had no such encounter."

Granville sucked the insides of his cheeks, drawing the spongy tissues into the void above his tongue. Slowly he paced his cell, following an ellipse marked by Bertram at one focus and the dovecote at the other. "I shall never get well," he moaned, tears coursing down his face. "I shall never be more than my disease."

"Oh, my poor distracted father." Now Bertram, too, was weeping. "Know that in your time you brightened the lives of countless parishioners. You visited them when they were sick, clothed them when they were naked, fed them when hungry, cheered them when despondent."

"Someone should start a religion based on such principles."

"Tell me more about your Minotaur."

"He's really not so terrible a creature," said Granville, daubing his tears with his sleeve. "He's merely lonely. My fellow madmen are loath to befriend a pagan chimera."

"Then *we* shall become the Minotaur's friend."

"Do you mean that?"

Bertram said, "Quite so. I'll ask Dr. Quelp to let us visit the cellar—unless you fear we'd get lost in the labyrinth."

"That maze is devilishly complex," sighed Granville, nodding. "We'd best avoid it. The Minotaur will understand. Happy birthday, son. Or did I say that already?"

What most astonished Chloe about Algernon's choice of Oxford abode was its general want of luridness and its marked deficiency in the grotesque. Given her twin's affection for decadence, she thought perhaps he'd purchased an abandoned brothel on the outskirts of the city or a shuttered abbey frequented by itinerant vampires. Instead Three Manor Place proved to be a staid and respectable town house situated on the banks of the Holywell Mill Stream. Were it not for Algernon's membership in the Shelley Society, just around the corner, she might have worried that his environment had become so wholesome that his health would deteriorate, shocked by this assault on his customary dissolution.

Stomach a-flutter, she strolled through the garden gate, Malcolm at her side, and rapped on the front door. When this gesture met with neither footfalls, voices, nor barking, she proceeded to the back lawn, a grassy tract hedged with boxwood and bathed in the beams of a surprisingly warm September sun. Algernon and Papa were engaged in a croquet match, along with two Oxonians already known to Chloe—Lord Woolfenden and his mistress, Lady Isadora—plus a sunburnt young man and a plump cleric, the latter being, of all people (or so Malcolm asserted), Bishop Samuel Wilberforce.

The instant Chloe saw her father's aged but agile form staring in bewilderment at his recently roqueted ball, she knew that the Transmutationist Club's odyssey from the docks of Plymouth to the gaming tables of Manáos—that farrago of angry protestors, tropical hurricanes, rickety boats, suffocating heat, nasty sand flies, and voracious mosquitoes—had been worth every attendant hardship. As she and Phineas embraced beside the mill stream, tears rolling down their cheeks like raindrops healing a parched farm, it seemed to her that (per Mr. Browning) the lark was on the wing, the snail on the thorn, the hillside dew-pearled—and a great deal was right with the world. Should Phineas ever again find himself incarcerated in a workhouse whilst facing debtors' prison, redeemable only at a cost of £2,000, she would immediately look about for a band of rakehells offering a large cash prize to anyone who could prove the Earth flat, the moon inhabited by Epicureans, or everyone in Lord Russell's cabinet a werewolf.

"Praise Heaven for my daughter's love of adventure and my son's luck at cards," said Phineas, addressing Chloe in a hoarse but cheery voice. His hands, though callused, were free of workhouse blisters, and he'd gained at least a stone in weight. "My dear children have snatched me from the depths of Perdition and deposited me on the shores of Elysium."

"From which place, Papa, you must promise to go a-wandering no more."

Brother and sister were equally forthcoming in their sentiments,

Algernon extolling Chloe for her choice of spouse and also her decision to withdraw from the contest. They broke their embrace, then drifted towards a freshly painted wooden pavilion, where Papa was taking tea with Bishop Wilberforce, Lord Woolfenden, Lady Isadora, and the sunburnt young man. Drawing within earshot of a conversation between her husband and her father, Chloe overheard Malcolm apologize for not obtaining Phineas's permission ere marrying his daughter.

"But with the *Apogee*'s company in so festive a mood," said Malcolm, "and Captain Pritchard eager to perform the ceremony, I decided that the apple of opportunity was too ripe to leave unplucked."

"Although I never imagined Chloe being plucked by a vicar, you seem a decent enough chap to me," said Phineas. "Welcome to that consortium of dreamers and zounderkites called the Bathurst family."

"Actually, I'm an ex-vicar," said Malcolm. "The horrors of Amazonia took half my faith away, and the other half succumbed to a treatise concerning descent with modification." He turned to the bishop and said, "I knew that my gamester brother-in-law had joined the Shelley Society, but I never imagined *you* becoming a rakehell, Sam."

"Don't be ridiculous," said Wilberforce. "But now that the contest is over, I see no reason we Oxonians can't all be friends."

"It's over?" said an astonished Chloe.

"Hello there, Mrs. Chadwick," said Wilberforce. "We meet at last. By Hallowborn's account, you went down with the *Equinox*. I'm pleased to infer he was misinformed."

"It's over?" persisted Chloe, touching Wilberforce's sleeve.

"Hallowborn returned from the Encantadas bearing a startling theological insight," the bishop continued, ignoring her question. "Contrary to the General Synod's original speculations, the archipelago boasts a peculiar harmony. It's not the Garden of Eden, but neither is it Satan's *pied-à-terre*."

"Over?" wailed Chloe. "As of when? Who won?"

"During the past three months my friends and I could not but notice that the competition no longer enthralled us," Lord Woolfenden explained. "Then Mr. Dalrymple told us he'd failed to find the ark, which further dampened our spirits. Finally, three days ago"—he indicated the young man—"this splendid fellow arrived bearing a message from the world's greatest philosopher. Thanks to Doktor Schopenhauer's arguments, we now understand that the God question cannot be resolved rationally, and so we ended the game."

"What about the ten thousand pounds?" asked Chloe.

"We'll spend it on ourselves," said Woolfenden. "With each passing year, depravity grows more costly to sustain. Later this month I'll summon that Popplewell fellow from the *Evening Standard* and tell him God's been reprieved. I'm sure he'll want to talk to you."

"And I'm sure I *won't* want to talk to him," said Chloe.

"Did you return with any animals in tow?" asked Lady Isadora. "I'm afraid they won't do you much good. Bobo and I apologize for whatever inconvenience we may have caused you."

"The *Apogee* arrived in Plymouth *sans* reptiles and birds," said Chloe, "but I did bring back a superb specimen of husband."

"So you found no creatures illustrative of your theory?" asked Woolfenden.

"*Au contraire*, Your Lordship, Galápagos offers an embarrassment of such riches. But after deploying the Tree of Life by way of preventing a mad American expatriate from hanging two of my friends, I realized I'd grown sick of the whole wearisome business of killing God."

"That is not a sentence one hears every day," noted the mysterious young man, bestowing an elfin smile on Chloe. "Will someone accord me the pleasure of an introduction?"

"Bertram, meet Mrs. Chadwick, formerly of the Albion Transmutationist Club," said Algernon. "Chloe, meet Mr. Heathway, late of the Mayfair Diluvian League."

"Delighted to make your acquaintance," said Chloe as she and Mr. Heathway shook hands. "Do I correctly surmise that last spring found you scrambling up Mount Ararat?"

"I was obliged to remain in Constantinople," Mr. Heathway replied, "smoking hashish whilst dispatching homing pigeons to my poor lunatic father—formerly a Down Village parson, presently a resident of Wormleighton Sanitarium."

"That, too, is not a sentence one hears every day," noted Chloe. "Are you now an Oxonian?"

"At some point during my absence, my employers at St. Giles Grammar School began to despair of my return, so they gave the post to another," said Mr. Heathway. "On the bright side, the Shelley Society was so grateful to have their disenchantment vindicated by Doktor Schopenhauer's essay, they have granted me rooms at Alastor Hall until I find employment."

"My generosity has its limits," said Woolfenden to Chloe. "Having abandoned your quest *in medias res*, you owe the Shelley Society three hundred pounds."

"The very sum you owe *me* from last night's game," said Algernon, pitching Woolfenden a grin.

"Then we shall consider your sister's debt settled," said Woolfenden.

"Tell me, Mr. Heathway, do you expect your father will ever be released from the madhouse?" asked Chloe.

"Alas, I see no cure on the horizon," said Bertram.

"A Down Village parson, was he?" said Chloe. "It happens that I once worked as zookeeper to a County Kent landholder. My employer's wife was in your father's congregation."

"You speak of Mrs. Darwin," said Mr. Heathway. "She was forever trying to get her husband to attend Sunday services at St. Mary's."

"No, her name was Mrs. Caedmon," said Chloe, offering the young man a furtive wink.

"Finished!" cried Phineas, indicating the spire he'd just constructed from a dozen lumps of sugar. "And lo, the ants of Albion built a great altar to their candied god, higher even than the Tower of Babel."

"Most amusing," said Wilberforce, unamused, before turning to Chloe. "There's a question I've always meant to ask a transmutationist. Do the apes generally appear on the *grandfather's* side of a person's family or on the *grandmother's* side?"

"I'm bored, Bobo," said Lady Isadora to Woolfenden. "Everyone here is so tediously droll."

"You're always bored."

"To begin with, Your Grace," said Chloe to Wilberforce, "as with every other creature on planet Earth, my descent involved *four* grandparents, not two. When I look back further, I find eight ancestors, then sixteen, then thirty-two, then sixty-four. It all gets very complicated very quickly, until we're knee-deep in that stew of relentless pressures, incessant couplings, and incalculable quantities of death that makes evolution by natural selection so plausible a hypothesis."

"So you say," grumbled Wilberforce.

"For what it's worth, Your Lordship," said Malcolm to Woolfenden, "I disagree with Schopenhauer that the God question cannot be resolved rationally. Now and forever, Mrs. Chadwick's theory remains the *bête noire* of theism."

"Oh, so it's still *Mrs. Chadwick's* theory, is it?" said Wilberforce. "As you may recall, Malcolm, I've always been a skeptic on that point."

"I shan't pretend the Tree of Life sprang full-blown from my brow," Chloe told the bishop, "but I'm not at liberty to divulge my collaborator's identity."

"With the contest now defunct, the point is moot," said Wilberforce, lathering his hands with phantom soap. "Malcolm, I assume that, given your present godless state, you have no desire to mount the pulpit again. Please know that, should your faith ever return, I shall help you find a new parish."

"If that offer is your way of suborning me from telling all I know about the Great Winnowing, I shan't swallow the bait," Malcolm informed the bishop. "That said, I'm willing to ascribe your plot against Galápagos to a momentary lapse in judgment."

"Thank you," said Wilberforce with appreciable chagrin. "You are a gracious atheist indeed."

"I know little of graciousness, but I fear my atheism is a permanent condition."

"Since you're evidently leaving the clergy for good," said Phineas to Malcolm, "it behooves me to ask how you intend to support my daughter."

"In fact, I have a scheme," said Malcolm. "It involves not only myself but also my dear wife and, if he's amenable, Mr. Heathway here. My education equipped me with a grasp of Latin and Aristotelian logic. Mrs. Chadwick, meanwhile, speaks a passable French and knows a thing or two about zoology. As for young Bertram"—he fixed his gaze on the former ark hunter—"evidently he's no stranger to the classroom. You can all imagine what I'm about to propose."

"That we start a school?" said Bertram.

Malcolm nodded and said, "A sanctum for young minds, right here on the banks of the Holywell Mill Stream."

"That's an ace of an idea," said Bertram.

"Smashing," said Phineas.

"Every forward-thinking Oxonian will want to entrust his children to our Rousseauian expertise," said Chloe.

"Count me out," said Algernon.

"I already have, dear brother-in-law," said Malcolm. "We're not about to corrupt our charges with games of chance."

"You'll be too busy corrupting them with transmutationism," said Wilberforce.

"It's time we resumed our tournament," announced Lady Isadora, rising. "You may play, too, Mr. Chadwick—and you as well, Mrs. Chadwick."

"I'll trounce the lot of you!" proclaimed Algernon.

"To the wickets!" declared Wilberforce.

"Please recall, Mr. Bathurst, that you've just been roqueted by me," said Woolfenden to Chloe's father.

"I shall accept my fate stoically," said Phineas. "I cannot answer for the ball."

"I insist that the game be free of banter," declared Lady Isadora. "The instant anybody says something clever, I'll lay into him with my mallet."

At the risk of inconveniencing her brother and father, Chloe accepted Algernon's offer of temporary accommodations at Three Manor Place, an arrangement whereby the second-floor suite would be reserved to Mr. and Mrs. Malcolm Chadwick to do with as they pleased for as long as they pleased. Being newly wedded, Chloe and Malcolm in fact had much doing and pleasing to accomplish. Though not as poetic a paramour as Ralph, the ex-vicar acquitted himself well in the conjugal domain, and thanks to a supply of Colonel Quondam's devices from the Shelley Society's stores, they had little fear of inadvertent procreation.

When Mr. Popplewell responded affirmatively to Lord Woolfenden's invitation to visit Oxford and learn about the final days of the Great God Contest, Chloe changed her mind and consented to an interview. After all, she knew more about the Tree of Life than any other member of the Albion Transmutationist Club. Neither Ralph, Algernon, Solange, nor even Malcolm could explain as well as she the implications of iguanas for theology.

In a departure from Fleet Street protocol, Popplewell questioned Chloe and Bertram Heathway in tandem, believing that the juxtaposition of their respective stories—the Tree of Life quest versus the Ark of Noah hunt—would make for "a verbal concerto of comparisons and contrasts." As it turned out, Bertram's insipid experiences (moping around in a Constantinople hookah den, receiving depressing messages from Mr. Dalrymple in Anatolia, sending equally depressing messages to his father in the sanitarium) provided no compellingly counterpoint whatsoever to Chloe's sweeping chronicle of the equatorial Atlantic hurricane, the perils of the Amazon basin, Léourier's flying-machine, the fall of Castillo Bracamoros, Eggwort's kangaroo court, the artificial volcano, and Hengstenberg's Socialist utopia. In relating the convicts' intention to lay waste to Galápagos, she assented to Malcolm's wishes and declined to mention that the scheme's architects were Wilberforce and Hallowborn, though she noted that the massacre was thwarted largely in consequence of her own initiatives.

On the thirteenth day in October, Popplewell's final article about the Shelley Prize appeared in the *Evening Standard,* headed NO WINNERS IN GREAT GOD CONTEST and subheaded AN ENTHRALLING ACCOUNT OF A TREE OF LIFE, QUESTED BUT NOT ACQUIRED, AND A SACRED VESSEL, SOUGHT YET STILL SECLUDED. Chloe readily admitted that the journalist had accurately summarized her adventures (though he spelled "Schopenhauer" four different ways, all incorrect). Two days later she received

an envelope addressed to MRS. MALCOLM CHADWICK, C/O MR. ALGER-
NON BATHURST, THREE MANOR PLACE, OXFORD (Popplewell's article had
en passant revealed her location and marital status), the return label indicating that the letter was from Down House.

So brief it might have been a telegram, Mr. Darwin's message omitted any mention of Annie's fate, information he presumably preferred to
convey in person.

14 October 1851

Dear Mrs. Chadwick,
    Just finished reading Popplewell's Evening Standard *piece. Im-
perative we talk. Come at earliest convenience. Bring overnight valise.*
                                                     Yrs., C. Darwin

The following day Chloe rode the train from Oxford to London, took
a second train to Bromley, then hired a fly to Down Village. She alighted
within view of St. Mary's Church. How remarkable, she mused, that the
adjacent parsonage was once inhabited by Bertram Heathway's father.
Quite likely she and Granville Heathway had passed each other on the
street ere the priest lost his reason and required incarceration in Wormleighton.

She resolved to visit the churchyard. Fearfully scanning the jumble
of moss-cloaked stones, she was gratified to find only one reading
Darwin—the resting place of Mary Eleanor, Charles and Emma's third
child, who'd died within weeks of her birth. Was it possible that Miss
Annie had grown stronger than her disease?

After a ten-minute hike Chloe reached the estate, then started towards the zoological dome, where she hoped to discover children at play.
Annie would be ten now, still young enough to enjoy a tortoise ride. The
walk across the meadow proved bracing, a membrane of October frost
crunching beneath her boots. Cautiously she pulled back the bronze
door. No children met her gaze, yet the place was as fecund as ever, land
lizards sunning themselves on the rocks, birds soaring beneath the crystalline roof. The tortoises regarded her with their usual reserved de-

meanors and sage faces, even as the aquatic iguanas slithered off their sandstone pylons and crashed into the pond. But the creature that most attracted Chloe's notice was of the species *Homo sapiens*: her former rooming-companion, dressed in twill breeches and mucking boots, busily distributing bird food.

"Do my eyes deceive me? Can this be Fanny Mendrick?"

"Chloe!" cried Fanny, throwing down a handful of sunflower seeds.

"Do you no longer tread the boards at the Adelphi?"

"Alas, the company fell on hard times, and I was let go." Fanny rubbed her oily palms on her trousers. "But, happily, it is a truth universally acknowledged—to paraphrase your paraphrase—that a naturalist who has lost his zookeeper must be in want of a replacement. So I wrote Mr. Darwin, reminding him that he'd enjoyed my performance in *Via Dolorosa*, and he summoned me."

"Today I am likewise summoned, though I know not why."

"I read of your adventures in the *Evening Standard*. Up to a point, I'm glad you found your Tree of Life."

"Had I not found it, my friends might have died on the gallows," said Chloe. "Their salvation was abetted by six newly minted transmutationists."

"I sometimes imagine Mr. Darwin hired me so his wife would have an ally in her efforts to bring him to Christ, which I'd say speaks well of the man." Fanny pointed east, then scratched her brow with the same muddy finger. "When last I saw him, he was in our new potting shed, adjacent to the vegetable patch. Oh, Chloe Bathurst, 'tis so *marvelous* to clap eyes on you again. I should like nothing better than to reforge our former bond."

"It would be petty of us to allow the origin and purpose of the universe to stand in the way of our friendship. But before we part, I must ask—"

"About Annie?"

"Yes."

"Her soul is now in Heaven."

"Her soul, yes." Chloe's throat congealed as if invaded by a tumor. "And where is the rest of her?"

"Mr. Darwin buried his child in Malvern. He'd taken her there last spring for Dr. Gully's cold-water treatment. Mrs. Darwin had to stay home—she was carrying Horace, and the other children needed her as well. It was all entirely awful."

"Cold-water treatment—faugh," said Chloe as a different sort of water, warm and briny, trickled down her cheeks. "Poor Mr. Darwin," she sobbed. "Poor Mrs. Darwin."

"Poor Annie."

Drawing forth her handkerchief, Chloe daubed her tears and blew her nose, then kissed Fanny good-bye and made her way back across the meadow.

The new botanic facility was no mere potting shed but an elaborate greenhouse, complete with a sloping glass roof and a network of boiler pipes that, being patterned after the vivarium's heating system, endowed the air with an agreeable tropical warmth. She found Mr. Darwin, outfitted with canvas gloves and a straw hat, in a compartment devoted to orchids. He was securing a large species labeled ANGRAECUM SESQUIPE-DALE in a terra-cotta pot, its long white petals radiating outward like the propeller vanes on Léourier's airship. Glancing up from his labors, he offered a wistful smile, thanked her for coming, then asked, doubtless in response to her reddened eyes, "Who told you?"

"Miss Mendrick."

"Did she mention that I had to bury her—"

"In Malvern, yes."

"Shortly after Easter." Mr. Darwin clenched his jaw and winced. "I lowered the coffin into the ground myself. She still had that *Petit Chaperon Rouge* doll you gave her. The stone in the churchyard reads, rather blandly, 'A dear and good child.'"

"'Dear and good'—that she was, sir."

"I didn't know what else to say," he rasped, weeping.

"Simple is always best."

"'Dear and good—'" Mr. Darwin blotted his tears with his sleeve. "Up to a point my work sustains me. My pigeons and my barnacles and—"

"And these orchids, too, I'll wager."

"My orchids, yes." He swallowed audibly. "I believe I've demonstrated that, for most plant species, attracting a unique pollinator is an evolutionary priority. The nectar of this comet orchid resides within so deep a cavity that only an insect endowed with a thirty-centimeter tongue might hope to feast upon it. And yet so highly does Nature prize cross-fertilization over self-fertilization, I'm confident that such a moth or butterfly will be found."

"We should sponsor a competition. Two hundred pounds to whoever nets the pollinator in question. With an entry fee of sixpence, we're certain to turn a profit."

Mr. Darwin laughed gaily and said, "Dear Mrs. Chadwick, how delightful to have you about the place again. Did you truly experience all the adventures Popplewell described?"

"Plus several I never told him about."

"I was surprised to learn you married a man who'd spent a year dismantling atheist arguments at Alastor Hall."

"It was one of those Newtonian romances," said Chloe breezily. "Mr. Chadwick and I found ourselves on the same swirling planet, and one day we said to each other, 'As long as we're here, let's make the best of it.'"

Having finished potting the *Angraecum*, Mr. Darwin inhaled with Epicurean appreciation, savoring the ambrosial aroma of the greenhouse. "I was particularly intrigued by your friends' trial. Of the twelve jurymen in *Duntopia versus Cabot and Quinn*, half proved sympathetic to the evolutionary view—did Popplewell get that right?"

"Upon my soul, I believe I gave the performance of a lifetime," said Chloe, nodding. "Of course, only three of my six converts decided that evolution calls God into question. The others found no enmity whatsoever between monotheism and mockingbirds."

"Mrs. Chadwick, by now you should know I simply don't *care* whether my idea calls God into question." Absorbing her chiding smile, Mr. Darwin added, "Very well, I *do* care, but my *point* is that, back in Galápagos, an entire courtroom—"

"A tabernacle, actually."

"So much the better. An entire tabernacle sat still whilst you mounted a defense of transmutation. People listened. They learned. Mrs. Chadwick, you have demonstrated that, despite my promise to Mrs. Darwin, I mustn't wait till I'm dead before publishing my species theory. Tomorrow I'll hunt up the scrivener's copy of my old manuscript, dust it off, and start turning it into a book."

"How pleased I am to have made my small contribution to God's demise."

"Stop it."

"Yes, sir."

"I picture a mammoth tome, bursting with evidence drawn from every sphere of science." Mr. Darwin took Chloe's arm and guided her towards a door marked CLIMBING PLANTS. "The title, of course, will be *Natural Selection*." As they entered this second compartment, he directed her attention to a row of unassuming potted specimens, each snaking up its own trellis. "I'll devote a whole chapter to my wild cucumbers. *Echinocystis lobata* exhibits an adaptation I call circumnutation, gyrating about an axis as its tendrils ascend. Even stronger than that urge is heliotropism, whereby a sunbeam will halt a plant's upward aspirations and cause *horizontal* motion instead. My research has persuaded me that virtually all members of the vegetable kingdom key their lives to the sun. When night comes, some of them even sleep."

"If orchids and creepers sleep, does that mean they dream?"

"I have no opinion, but you've asked a splendid question." With his dirt-smudged fingertips Mr. Darwin caressed the nearest *Echinocystis*. "By the by, it was Wilberforce, wasn't it? The schemer behind the planned massacre was Soapy Sam—am I right?"

"Per my husband's wishes, I must decline to reveal his identity," said Chloe, nodding.

"I pray you, madam, continue that policy. I make my request in deference to Sam's father, a tireless crusader for the abolitionist cause. A mile from here stands the oak where the Reverend William Wilberforce was called from on high to fight the slave trade."

She promised Mr. Darwin that her lips were sealed. Satisfied, he began to hum, then led her into a third compartment, labeled INSECTIVO-

ROUS PLANTS. A dozen exemplars of the sundew, *Drosera rotundifolia*, a bulbous creature spouting dozens of sticky tentacles, rested on the benches in terra-cotta pots.

"Now that I think on it, sir, there's a *second* reason you may wish to publish sooner rather than later," said Chloe. "Whilst in Manáos I had lunch with a naturalist, one Alfred Wallace of Hertfordshire, who makes his living feeding the English appetite for stuffed specimens. He was keen to find a law explaining why different marmoset types inhabit opposite banks of the Rio Negro."

An expression of alarm flashed across Mr. Darwin's face. "I assume you told him nothing of my own species theory?"

"Not a peep—though I confess I was less interested in protecting your future reputation than in learning whether Mr. Wallace planned to enter the Great God Contest. In retrospect I realize that, being en route to the East Indies, he posed no threat."

"Having friends in both the Geological Society and the Linnean Society, I am well situated to become the *paterfamilias* of natural selection—certainly better positioned than an itinerant taxidermist from Hertfordshire. I'll tell my colleagues to be on the lookout for a packet from the Spice Islands bearing a scientific paper by an *arriviste* called Wallace."

"So that they might suppress it? Isn't that rather predatory of you?"

"Competition is the way of the world, Mrs. Chadwick, a point you doubtless made during the blasphemy trial. That said, please understand I have no wish to disrupt the man's career. But I cannot allow him to gain preeminence over me." Mr. Darwin gestured towards the tentacled plant. "Now here's a *real* predator. My sundew can wrap her arms about unsuspecting flies and gnats—an essential adaptation, her aboriginal soil being poor in nitrogen. I've taken to feeding her egg white, bits of raw beef, even fingernail clippings. Mrs. Darwin says I won't be satisfied till I've proved that *rotundifolia* is not a plant but an animal."

"A hideous creature, by my lights," said Chloe, adding, with a wry grin, "and yet there is grandeur in this view of life—is there not, Mr. Darwin?—with its powers of growth, assimilation, and reproduction having been originally breathed into one or a few kinds—"

"Good heavens, Mrs. Chadwick, you stole and transcribed my essay after all, didn't you?"

"That I did, sir."

He smiled softly and said, "And that whilst this our planet has gone circling according to fixed laws . . ."

"That from so simple an origin . . ."

"Endless forms most beautiful and most wonderful have been, and are being—"

She said, "'Are being'?"

"I added that flourish recently. Also, I now prefer 'beginning' to 'origin.'"

"So do I," said Chloe, and together they recited, "That from so simple a beginning, endless forms most beautiful and most wonderful have been, and are being, evolved."

"I miss her so much," said Mr. Darwin.

"Of course."

"She defied the world with her joyousness."

"Truly."

"To bring her back I would give up my work, my sanity, my breath. But the universe doesn't work that way."

"No, sir, it doesn't. Allow me to suggest that you defy the universe with your book."

Of all the rejoinders to Genesis that Chloe had encountered in her career as a Shelley Prize contestant, the one that had most captured her fancy was the Chelmsford apothecary's inversion of Saint Anselm's Ontological Proof. The only thing more awe-inspiring than a universe created by a *bona fide* supernatural being would be one created by a nonexistent supernatural being. The longer she thought about this absurd argument, this Nontological Proof, the more it enchanted her. By the time she'd settled into her new life in Oxford, she imagined that her fortunes were being supervised by the Nontological God, the Nog, of the apothecary's whim.

During the eight years that elapsed between her reunion with Mr. Darwin and the publication of his book, Chloe and her colleagues created and sustained Holywell Academy. What had begun as a modest school housed at Three Manor Place, catering to boys ages nine through eleven, evolved into a plenary institution embracing ages seven through fifteen, both genders accepted, so that its founders became obliged to employ more instructors (including the irreproachable Fanny Mendrick, hired to teach penmanship and ethics) and take over the premises of the recently failed St. Philomena's Ladies College in Cowley Place. Whilst Chloe and her family moved into a town house across the street, Bertram made his home on the top floor of the school, where he passed his evenings devising lessons, caring for his aged mother, and—during most of the year 1858—grieving for his late father, the Reverend Granville Heathway, who'd died of an apoplectic seizure at Wormleighton Sanitarium on St. Valentine's Day.

Of the many felicitous events overseen by the Nog with characteristic detachment was Phineas Bathurst's decision to start taking himself seriously as a puppeteer, enriching the Holywell Academy curriculum with his talents. The old man's British history lessons were particularly memorable. Although the Holywell students were generally a rowdy breed (and had therefore been denied admission to more venerable Oxford educational establishments), even the most fractious young scholar found himself caring about the Long Parliament when its vagaries were explained by a puppet representing Oliver Cromwell. As for the fortunes of Charles I, his execution proved singularly absorbing when the presentation included the puppet's head falling off its shoulders and rolling across the classroom floor.

Of the other happy occurrences surveyed by the Nog with its usual indifference, three brought Chloe particular satisfaction—the first being Malcolm's resolution to finally forgive himself for killing two mercenaries during the attack on Castillo Bracamoros, the second being the marriage of Ralph Dartworthy, master of H.M.S. *Inalienable* (survey ship *extraordinaire*) to Solange Kirsop, mistress of Cornucopia House (brothel *non pareil*), and the third being the birth of a rambunctious but winsome primate named Sophie Anne Chadwick. Malcolm proved a loving father, Phineas an indulgent grandfather, Algernon a solicitous uncle, and Chloe an attentive mother. Owing to her hours spent in Sophie's exuberant presence, she soon came to understand what Mr. Darwin meant by Annie defying the world with her joyousness, though each time she considered the sentiment her eyes welled up with tears.

For some reason Mr. Darwin had decided to call his book not *Natural Selection* but rather *On the Origin of Species*. Perhaps this more provocative title contributed to its triumph. On the first day following publication, the book sold out an initial printing of 1,250 copies, then went on to become at once a *cause célèbre* and a *succès de scandale*. As for the change of title, this mystery was solved when a stocky, bearded, pasty-faced gentleman showed up at Chloe's door, portmanteau in hand, and presented her with a letter of introduction from Down House.

25 June 1860

My Dear Mrs. Chadwick,

The bearer of this letter, Mr. Thomas Huxley, biologist, has recently emerged as a tireless champion of my evolution theory (whose publication last year under the title On the Origin of Species *perhaps drew your attention).*

Before I forget, let me thank you for alerting me to the conjectures of the peripatetic specimen monger Alfred Russel Wallace. Because of your warning, I attended immediately to the manuscript that arrived in June of 1858 from the Malay Archipelago. Mrs. Chadwick, it was just as you predicted: your acquaintance had articulated an argument so close to my own in spirit and specificity that I might have written it myself.

In a political masterstroke, Mr. Lyell and Mr. Hooker (you will recall those gentlemen from your Down House days) arranged for Mr. Wallace's "On the Tendency of Varieties to Depart Indefinitely from the Original Type" to be read at the Linnean Society in tandem with "An Essay Concerning Descent with Modification" (a sketch with which you are promiscuously familiar), so that the specimen monger and I would receive equal credit for the germ of the idea. Owing to this strategy, I have shed any obligation to collaborate with Mr. Wallace in future. Seeking further to establish my claim, I abandoned Natural Selection and began furiously to compose a shorter and more intelligible work.

So why is Mr. Huxley at your gate? Later this week, the British Association for the Advancement of Science will convene in Oxford's newly built museum of natural history. Amongst the papers to be read are several that touch upon my Origin of Species. Fleet Street is framing the event as an epoch-making battle between Religion and Science. Looking after God's interests will be Richard Owen, one-time Shelley Prize judge, as well as the ubiquitous Samuel Wilberforce. Mr. Huxley, meanwhile, will undertake to defend evolution against the slings and arrows of the Church of England.

It seems to me that, having made a case for descent with modification before a jury in the Encantadas, you are uniquely qualified to help Mr. Huxley rehearse his performance. Should you decide to offer him lodgings and, more importantly, to tutor him, you will earn my undying gratitude.

Yours, etc.,
C. Darwin

P.S. In his cover note Mr. Wallace mentioned his chance encounter in Manáos with a female naturalist called Chloe Bathurst, adding, "If this extraordinary woman has returned to England, you may wish to look her up. When I told her about the curious distribution of marmoset types along the Rio Negro, she apprehended why the mystery matters."

Briefly Chloe considered attending the British Association gathering, but the thought of hearing Wilberforce and Owen pontificate about a theory they did not understand dismayed her. Better to send Huxley into the fray. After according her visitor a cheery welcome, she escorted him into the drawing-room and introduced him to her family. Malcolm was busy planning a lecture about the Norman Conquest. Sophie was busy preventing her father from planning a lecture about the Norman Conquest, an undertaking that required her to gallop about the room on a hobbyhorse whilst reciting nursery rhymes at the top of her lungs.

Upon learning of the imminent clash at the university museum, Malcolm announced that he wished to be amongst the observers. "I hope you won't mind if I remain at home," Chloe told her husband. "Simply being in Wilberforce's presence gives me the fantods."

For the balance of the evening Chloe and Malcolm attempted to recapitulate for Mr. Huxley the arguments they'd advanced during *Duntopia versus Cabot and Quinn*. Scribbling in his notebook, the biologist ornamented their narratives with smiles of approbation. The three of them speculated that, judging from the withering notice he'd accorded *On the Origin of Species* in the *Edinburgh Review*, Professor Owen would attempt a neurological line of attack. As the world's most respected anatomist, he would testify that a gorilla's brain mapped far more completely onto that of even the lowest lemur than onto Man's exalted cerebrum.

"If that's his game, I'll happily take the field against him," said Mr. Huxley. "When it comes to comparative neurology, the views of the world's most respected anatomist suffer from the defect of being untrue."

"As for Wilberforce, he'll probably ask whether your simian relatives occur in greater abundance on your grandfather's side of the family or your grandmother's," said Chloe. "If I were you, I would invite him to consider that, lost in the dark wood of his wit, he has missed the very Tree of Life flourishing at the heart of the argument. Yes, the theory of natural selection has a thing or two to say about apes and Englishmen, but Mr. Darwin somehow wrapped his mind about the whole of Creation—*that's* the glory of *On the Origin of Species*."

"Or you might simply say you would rather have an ape for a grandfather than a bishop," Malcolm suggested.

Instead of allowing Wilberforce and Owen to spoil her day and her digestion, Chloe spent the 30th of June deploying bird feeders about the grounds of Holywell Academy, assisted by Sophie. Shortly after nine o'clock in the evening Malcolm and Mr. Huxley returned from their adventure, both in high spirits. Eavesdropping on the ebullient chatter at the reception marking the end of the British Association sessions, they'd quickly concluded that Darwin had carried the day. For all Samuel Wilberforce's formidable rhetorical gifts, the bishop had been bested.

"This morning, it was Owen who commanded the dais," said Mr. Huxley, "serving up his anticipated drivel about gorilla brains."

"Thomas smote him hip and thigh," said Malcolm. "I made a few contributions as well, sharing certain insights concerning tortoise shells and human cuspids."

"We ate lunch at the Lamb and Flag," said Mr. Huxley, "then sallied forth to tilt with Wilberforce, only to find mobs of students queuing up outside the museum, along with clergymen, dons, and ladies in crinolines. The building had no single space that might accommodate such a crowd—none save the reading room, which is still under construction."

"Lord Woolfenden and Lady Isadora came to the rescue, suggesting that everyone adjourn to their manor house down the street," said Malcolm. "How strange it was to be back in the Alastor Hall library, preparing once again to participate in a debate about God."

"Wilberforce lost no time assuming the dais," said Huxley. "I've never seen him in better form. There's nary a cake of soap to be had in Oxford. And you were right, Mrs. Chadwick. He asked me about my grandparents."

Malcolm said, "Whereupon Thomas turned to me and whispered, 'The Lord hath delivered him into my hands.'"

Mr. Huxley said, "I told Wilberforce, quote, 'If the question were put to me, would I rather have an ape for a grandfather, or a man highly endowed by Nature and possessed of great means of influence, and yet who employs those faculties and that influence for the mere purpose of introducing ridicule into a serious scientific discussion—then I unhesitatingly affirm my preference for the ape!'"

"Well done, sir!" said Chloe.

Malcolm offered Mr. Huxley a puckish grin. "I still believe you should've said you'd rather have an ape for a grandfather than a bishop."

"In any event, gentlemen, you won," said Chloe. "I'm proud of you both."

"It's *yourself* you should be proud of, Mrs. Chadwick," said Mr. Huxley. "Malcolm has been apprising me of your achievements: getting the rakehells to fund your adventure, saving the Galápagos fauna, rescuing your friends—to say nothing of your brilliant performance during the blasphemy trial. Mr. Darwin told me that your account of that proceeding inspired him to publish his book."

"It would appear that, just as Charles Darwin has acquired a bulldog in Thomas Huxley," said Chloe to her husband, "so have I found a cavalier in Malcolm Chadwick."

"I owe you nothing less, my darling," said Malcolm.

And from that moment on, it could truly be said that Chloe of the Encantadas knew her own wonder.

Insofar as it shaped our heroine's fortunes and family, this chronicle of the Great God Contest is now ended—though one additional episode merits a full measure of printer's ink. For it happened that Chloe was present when oblivion's pale priest put on his threadbare cassock, donned his ratty cap, and came in quest of Charles Darwin. Moreover, the scientist passed away in proximity to a metaphysical mystery, a riddle that Chloe and Malcolm would ponder for the rest of their days.

16 April 1882

Dear Mrs. Chadwick,

I regret to inform you that Mr. Darwin is gravely ill. Seizures, chest pains, erratic pulse. Please remember him in your prayers, and call on us if you wish.

Sincerely,
Emma Darwin

At first Chloe rejected the idea of returning to Down House. Fond though she was of her former employer, it would be inappropriate for anyone save his immediate relations to witness his final hours. But then a nocturnal visit from Bertram prompted a change of heart.

"In my leisure time I've been sorting through my parents' effects," he said, following Chloe into the drawing-room, a rectangular package snugged under his arm. "Amongst my discoveries—rediscoveries, I should say—was this emanation from my father's disordered mind." He set the bundle on the tea table, pulling away the linen wrapping to reveal a stack of foolscap. "When I glanced at *Decrypting the Descent of Man* thirty years ago, I dismissed it as the ramblings of an intellect lost to lunacy. But yesterday I read every word, and I realized I'd done my father a disservice. I should greatly value your opinion of this manuscript, for it's replete with scientific matters of the sort you and Malcolm are forever discussing. It even mentions the Charles Darwin who once employed you as his zookeeper."

"I shall read it ere I douse the lights," said Chloe.

That night she perused all seventy-two pages of *Decrypting the Descent of Man*. Allegedly penned by Bertram but evidently authored by his father, it was amongst the most engaging documents she'd ever encountered, as thrilling in its way as *The Voyage of the Beagle*. The following morning she gave the manuscript to her husband and insisted that he read it. Upon turning the last page, Malcolm declared that they must reach Mr. Darwin's side without delay.

Arriving in Down Village early the next day, they secured a room at the Queens Head Inn, then proceeded to the estate on foot. The back lawn featured a scene of benign pandemonium, with Mr. Darwin's adult children milling about the orchard and the walled vegetable garden whilst a tribe of grandchildren ran in all directions, some playing blindman's bluff, others improvising a boisterous rendition of cricket. A more festive death watch could scarcely be imagined.

They found Mr. Darwin slouched in a wheelchair beside the Spanish chestnut, attended by his wife and a sturdy fellow who was surely Master

William grown to manhood. With his long white beard and benevolent gaze, Mr. Darwin rather suggested the God whose alleged factuality he'd permanently problematized, but the analogy did not withstand scrutiny, for the person Chloe beheld was not a Supreme Being but a frail country gentleman, wheezing, febrile, hunched in pain. Mrs. Darwin plied her husband with a draught of quinine—a worthy drug, mused Chloe, though surely more effective in combating malaria than in curing mortality.

"I doubt that you remember me, William," said Chloe, catching the gaze of the eldest Darwin son.

"I could never forget Miss Bathurst, who once played Pirate Anne Bonney and gave me a Satan snow globe. That treasure is still in my possession, sitting atop my wardrobe."

As Chloe and Malcolm approached the wheelchair, Mrs. Darwin stepped discreetly aside, evidently sensing she would not take comfort in what the Oxonians were about to say. Her fears were well founded, for after Chloe made the introductions Malcolm confided to Mr. Darwin that his faith in God had evaporated partially in consequence of transmutationism.

"Is that good news or bad?" asked Mr. Darwin.

"Good, I think," said Malcolm.

"As for my own religious speculations—in recent years I've put both God and Man to one side and rediscovered my passion for lowlier entities." Mr. Darwin directed a trembling finger towards a circular slab set into the lawn like a horizontal millstone. "Behold my latest experiment." Two vertical metal rods etched with calibrations protruded through a hole at the core of the plinth. "My youngest son, Horace, calls it the wormograph. Our observations suggest that, owing to soil displacement caused by earthworms, the stone sinks a full two millimeters each year."

"They're probably deaf, you know—earthworms," Chloe told Malcolm. "When I first met Mr. Darwin, he demonstrated that hypothesis using Mrs. Darwin's piano."

"You must get Emma to play for you," said Mr. Darwin. "She's remarkably gifted."

"Here's something you'll find equally remarkable." Chloe deposited *Decrypting the Descent of Man* in his lap, then told him what she knew of its provenance.

"To employ a locution I first heard from your lips, it sounds like 'a ripping good yarn,'" said Mr. Darwin, stroking the manuscript. "Now allow me to convey some news I hope won't distress you. Our zoo no longer exists. Five years ago I decided that the Galápagos specimens and their progeny had played their parts in my life. I gave the newest generation of birds to the Marquis of Sudbury for his aviary. You'll find the descendants of our original lizards in Her Majesty's Zoo."

"And the tortoises?" asked Chloe.

"Perseus of Indefatigable, Boswell of James, Isolde of Charles—all the rest: they're in the Jardin des Animaux."

"I shall make a point of visiting them."

"Mr. Darwin must rest now," said Mrs. Darwin, inserting herself into the tableau that had formed around the wheelchair. "If you wish to see him again, come back tomorrow morning."

"The quinine is an excellent idea," Chloe told Mrs. Darwin. "I would also recommend the occasional sip of whisky."

"Mr. Darwin has already thought of that," said Mrs. Darwin with an evanescent smile.

Partly to pass the time but mostly because she wanted him to see whence came the seeds of their South American adventure, Chloe took Malcolm on a tour. She showed him the vivarium, now as barren of reptiles and birds as Wilberforce and Hallowborn had intended to make Galápagos. She guided him to the greenhouse, where he took a naïve delight in feeding his fingernail clipping to a carnivorous sundew. The solitary comet orchid (perhaps the original specimen, perhaps a descendant) also fascinated Malcolm, and he decided that Mr. Darwin was well within his rights to predict the eventual discovery of the necessary pollinator, complete with thirty-centimeter tongue.

As dusk drew nigh, they perambulated along the famous sandwalk, four full revolutions, talking of many things. Chloe took note of the irony. On this saddest of days she and her husband were discussing unequivocally pleasant subjects—the unexpected ascent of Algernon Bathurst to the post of Oxford Gaming Commissioner; the bizarre puppet shows that the late Phineas Bathurst had staged for his three granddaughters; the generally successful theatrical career of their firstborn (though the Drury Lane Company's revival of *The Last Days of Pompeii,* with Sophie as Nydia the blind flower seller, had closed after only fourteen performances); the new telescope that daughter Celia had acquired for her celestial explorations; the English translation of Novalis that Tess had recently completed for John Murray, publisher of Mr. Darwin's *The Expression of the Emotions in Man and Animals;* the letter from Philippe Léourier revealing that he'd found, deep in the Peruvian jungle, "the ruins of a city that was surely El Dorado"; the admirable efforts of Ralph and Solange Dartworthy to transform Cornucopia House from an elegant brothel into a haven not only for harlots seeking to escape the trade but also for sailors in need of a final port.

As darkness fell, Chloe and Malcolm ambled to the Queens Head Inn, where they enjoyed a good meal and a quiet night's rest. The following morning found them back at Down House, climbing the staircase to Mr. Darwin's chamber. He lay on a canopy bed surrounded by fat pillows, the bay window giving him a panoramic view of the pasture and the woods beyond. Whilst William applied cold compresses to his father's brow, the other sons took up posts in the corners. Hugging their sobbing mother, the two surviving daughters stood beside a full-length mirror, the glass so pristine it seemed as if three additional women were in the room.

The instant he caught sight of Chloe, Mr. Darwin roused himself and pointed towards the dresser, on which lay the jumbled pages of *Decrypting the Descent of Man.*

"Oh, my dear Mrs. Chadwick, you have brought me such a marvelous gift. That friar Mendel is an authentic genius—how brilliantly he demonstrates that germ cells pursue their lives independently of somatic cells. Why didn't I think of that?"

"You've had many a felicitous thought in your day," said Chloe.

"To blazes with my gemmules," said Mr. Darwin. "To blazes with pangenesis and bloodlines. It's all about our monk's discrete hereditary units. Now we can say with confidence why traits don't disappear through blending."

"So it seems," said Chloe.

"And then we have Teilhard de Chardin and his lovely skulls from Asia, Europe, Africa—Africa, Mrs. Chadwick, the cradle of our species! How *dare* Owen assert that the fossil record tells against human evolution?!"

"He's an even more shameless bluffer than my brother-in-law," noted Malcolm.

"Evidently Teilhard has been sucking on hookahs all his life," said Mr. Darwin. "What a silly mystic goose, and his orthogenesis is a dead end—the universe isn't going anywhere. If we must have an Omega Point, let's not seek it in some fanciful dominion beyond the stars. It's right here. It's in my greenhouse. It's under my wormograph."

"The kingdom of sod is within you," said Malcolm.

"Then we come to Dr. Rosalind Franklin and her deoxyribonucleic acid." Like Madeira leaking from an antique wineskin, tears spilled from Mr. Darwin's eyes. "Every organism contains in each cell the same self-replicating substance. You and I, Chloe, and your husband here, and Mrs. Darwin, and my sons and daughters, and the rest of us, all the plants and animals, we're now and forever bound to one another in the most materialist way imaginable—and hence the most transcendent!"

"Metaphysics without end," said Malcolm.

"And yet it was Miss Franklin's observations about *Trypanosoma cruzi* and Chagas disease that brought me the greatest satisfaction."

"I would not have predicted that," said Chloe.

"*Mirabile dictu*, I didn't curse little Annie after all. I didn't damn her with a weak constitution. My sickness came from the outside, from those ghastly black bugs of the Pampas." Slowly Mr. Darwin's eyelids enshrouded his gaze. "God bless the benchuca." With each successive syllable, his voice grew more feeble. "Devil take the benchuca. Hooray for Mendel. Praised be Teilhard. A toast to Rosalind Franklin."

He slept. Chloe kissed the old man's brow. "Good night, sweet prince," she said, then gathered up the pages of *Decrypting the Descent of Man*, nodded to the assembled family, and—her husband at her side—made a circumspect exit.

I daresay, he won't make it past sunset," Malcolm remarked as they started across the meadow.

Chloe sighed in assent, then paused before the wormograph, which her imagination now framed, for better or worse, as Mr. Darwin's headstone. "I think I see how this thing works." She indicated the plinth with the tip of her shoe. "It's very clever."

"Before we leave, I should like to visit the greenhouse again."

"Hundreds of worms, thousands of worms, working the soil according to their instincts—and moving a mountain in the bargain, two millimeters each year. Yes, my darling, we shall visit the greenhouse."

"Those climbing plants are beguiling," said Malcolm.

"When I called on Mr. Darwin following our return from Galápagos, I asked him a question he thought rather astute. Do orchids and creepers dream?"

"And his answer?"

"He did not venture one."

"I wish to feed a fingernail clipping to a sundew again," said Malcolm.

"Easily arranged, my love."

Dropping to her knees, Chloe pressed her lips against the sunbaked stone. It was warm as fresh bread. Did orchids dream? Did moths grieve? Did bees have regrets? Were worms easily amused? She had no information on these matters, but just then she fancied she could hear the laughter of the subterranean creatures. And this was no soft vermian titter, either, but a roar of elation, as if the worms understood what magnificent chips they were in the mosaic of Creation, as if from their grubby vantage they'd apprehended the whole transmutational scheme of things—as if they knew their own wonder.

She rose and, taking her husband's hand, led him across the meadow toward the greenhouse. Toward resolute cucumbers, hungry sundews, and drowsing orchids. Toward forms most ravishing and rapturous, toward varieties ever evolving—toward life.

AUTHOR'S NOTE

Although the fine print on my poetic license permits me, for the sake of producing a viable work of fiction, to reheat certain established facts to the point of plasticity, I resorted to this privilege only occasionally during the composition of *Galápagos Regained*. With a few obvious exceptions—notably the Great God Contest itself—most of the institutions depicted in this novel map onto the historical record.

Seventeenth years before publishing *On the Origin of Species*, Charles Darwin indeed set down his theory in the form of a thirty-five-page manuscript. I have titled this piece "An Essay Concerning Descent with Modification." As in *Galápagos Regained*, Darwin's 1842 sketch concludes with a longer version of the paragraph later made famous by his book, the soaring thought that begins, "There is grandeur in this view of life . . ." I must note, however, that some of the quotations and concepts Chloe Bathurst culls from the sketch are not in the actual document.

Owing to the transformation of Darwin's estate into an English Heritage site, I was able to walk in my heroine's footsteps as she negotiated Down House and its environs in the early chapters. The zoological dome is, of course, my own invention.

While *Galápagos Regained* may seem to suggest that South American rubber barons had brought their enterprise to a fever pitch by 1850, the industry did not reach its apex for several more years. Sad to day, the sorts of outrages perpetrated against the *seringueiros* in these pages match historians' accounts. My Great Rubber War roughly corresponds to violent events that ultimately occurred in Colombia on the Rio Putumayo and the Rio Cara Paraná.

Throughout the evolution of this novel I consulted many books, Web sites, and scholarly articles, a bibliography too extensive to reprint here. I must make special mention, however, of *The Reluctant Mr. Darwin* by David Quammen, *Darwin: Discovering the Tree of Life* by Niles Eldredge, *Galápagos: Discovery on Darwin's Islands* by David W. Steadman and Steven Zousmer, *Darwin, His Daughter, and Human Evolution* by Randal Keynes, *The Encantadas* by Herman Melville, *Tree of Rivers: The Story of the Amazon* by John Hemming, *A Narrative of Travels on the Amazon and Rio Negro* by Alfred Russel Wallace, *The Jesuit and the Skull* by Amir D. Aczel, *Rosalind Franklin: The Dark Lady of DNA* by Brenda Maddox, the Book of Mormon by Joseph Smith, *On the Nature of Things* by Lucretius, and, of course, four books by Charles Darwin: *The Voyage of the Beagle, On the Origin of Species, The Descent of Man,* and *The Expression of the Emotions in Man and Animals.*

Just as our planet is blessed with a biosphere unlike any other in the solar system, and perhaps the Milky Way, so I am blessed with friends, colleagues, and family members who take satisfaction in commenting on my books in utero. My immense gratitude goes to the witty Joe Adamson, the wise Shira Daemon, the munificent Margaret Duda, the perspicacious Justin Fielding, the insightful Frank Kirkpatrick, the multifarious Elisabeth Lanser-Rose, the erudite Christopher Morrow, the polymathic Glenn Morrow, the thoughtful Tony Palermo, the sagacious Sam Scheiner, the astute James Stevens-Arce, the meticulous Don Thompson, and the passionate Michael Vicario. Let me also thank Michael Homler for his editorial acuity, Arthur Motta for his English-to-Portuguese translations, and two wonderful literary agents, Emma Patterson and the late Wendy Weil, for uplifting assessments of this project when I most needed them.

Finally, I must acknowledge the contributions of my dear wife, Kathryn Morrow, whose felicitous remark—"Isn't about time you wrote your novel about Charles Darwin?"—got the project started, whose editorial comments proved invaluable, and whose love for the natural world inspired me throughout nearly six years of composition.